Window seat
Press

April 4, 2018

Adam, Evelyn, and Enrique,

Thank you so much
for your support and
friendship !

Jane Is
Everywhere

all my
gratitude,

Crystal
Jo
Reiss

Crystal Jo Reiss

Window seat Press

Las Vegas, Nevada

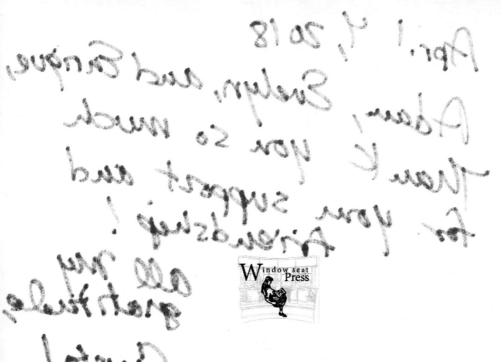

FIRST WINDOW SEAT PRESS EDITION, JANUARY 2018

Copyright © 2018 Crystal Jo Reiss

This is a work of fiction. Names, characters, places, and incidents either are the product of the author's imagination or are used fictitiously.

ISBN 978-0692964453
Library of Congress Cataloging-in-Publication Data
Names: Reiss, Crystal Jo, author.
Title: Jane Is Everywhere: a novel / by Crystal Jo Reiss.
Description: Las Vegas: Window Seat Press, [2018]
Library of Congress Control Number: 2017915863
Classification: LCC PN6120.15-6120.95, PN3311-3503 | DDC 800, 810, 813

Window Seat Press books available for special promotions and premiums.
For details, contact the publisher at www.windowseatpress.com.

Printed in the United States of America on alkaline paper.

This book is dedicated to my father, James Reiss,

∞

and to everyone everywhere.

"...I never liked long walks, especially on chilly afternoons: dreadful to me was the coming home in the raw twilight, with nipped fingers and toes, and a heart saddened..."

—Jane Eyre

"Everywhere, everywhere is my country."

—From a song of the Tiv People,
The Cantor Arts Center, Stanford University,
June 13-17, 2012

Everywhere

Many decades ago there lived a very wise yogi named Bhagavan Namananda known to thousands of followers as the supreme Guru. The story goes like this: One morning an astute devotee spotted Namananda leaning over a lotus in a pond not far from the Ashram. At that same instant, in the Shiva Shankar Temple, the devotee's wife was sure that she saw Namananda aswirl in incense and candlelight, meditating with half-shut eyes while she poured sacred milk and rosewater over the Shiva Lingam.

After that, the Guru of all Gurus— Bhagavan Namananda— was discovered to be everywhere at once. The whole Ashram swore that Namananda could be seen wandering through the garden, seated cross-legged under a banyan tree near the Shiva Shankar temple, curled in a yogic ball in the meditation room, lounging on the oblong bench near the cowshed, praising the sky and the earth near the sulphuric hot spring—all at the same instant every afternoon. Namananda became known as the Everywhere Man, and soon all of Southern India revered him.

"A Phenomenon That Surpasses All Other Phenomena" blazed newspaper headlines. "Man of the Sun, Man of the Moon, Man of Everywhere!" And news of the great Guru shuttled overseas by tanker, luxury liner, airplane, train, automobile, and the great Guru became a curiosity of conversation among binocular, sunhat and camera-wielding travelers. Over the months that extended into years travelers returned home, bronzed and brazen, passing on the information, now spectacular as fireworks against the blackest sky, to people at cocktail parties, seated around dining room tables and at bars, until the news spread to larger and larger audiences.

One audience, gathered in the acoustic hush of Carnegie Hall became captivated by the eloquent storytelling of a platinum blond man whose smooth skin and white teeth represented an ideal state of relaxation. The audience sat in the whisper quiet of the auditorium. Among the astounded was Jane's mother, listening to descriptions of multiple appearances, visions of the planet produced in midair, indigo flames around the head of this Guru of all Gurus.

When Jane was eight years old, she asked her mother how it was possible for a person to be in so many places at once. Her mother explained that all life was like the forking branches of a single tree: "Everyone is everywhere all the time. We are all part of the same tree. There is no separation between the 'I' and the 'you.' When Namananda appears in two places at once, he is showing us this principle."

Thereafter Jane, misunderstanding the concept of oneness, tried to slice her awareness into parts. For Jane there could never be a single point of view. Instead, there was always a multiplicity of viewpoints, the idea that everything was singular and plural at once. This left her in limbo, that quasi-liquid country of "is this what I am or is that what I am? Is this what I want or is that what I want?" Firmness of mind had become impossible. It seemed to Jane that all decisions and opinions were swirling about simultaneously like a fabulous nebula of multicolored stellar gas.

Many years later, Jane tried to explain this notion to her boyfriend Ben. He'd been angry at her habit of evading issues, annoyed at her lack of strong opinion, the slip sliding of her viewpoint. If they needed to choose between dinner at a Chinese restaurant or a French bistro, Jane flipped from bistro to Chinese, shaking her head at this and then the other and finally nodding at both, convinced that each cuisine had a place in their evening plans, convinced that she was incapable of making a decision. Ben's frustration increased with the months, and at last he broke out and asked her to please be decisive. He said she must decide or he could never be sure of her love and commitment to him. In fact, it was a small incident that set everything off.

They were in a movie theater and he'd asked if she wanted popcorn. She nodded, but thought better, and sitting back in the movie seat, told him to get licorice instead. He was halfway up the aisle when she called him back to ask for Bonbons in place of the licorice. When he sat down with the snacks, she took her chilled package of candy quietly without opening it, laced her fingers in her lap and before the movie lights went out, turned to Ben to ask if they could share his popcorn and forego the Bonbons. His frustration surfaced when he decided not to share with her (he hated Bonbons) and she called him on it with, "hey, come on—give me just a handful!"

"I'm sorry, but get your own popcorn," he said, moving the bag of popcorn away from her. She refused to buy her own. Then he said, "You're always changing your mind." And she said, "Why not, I have a right to change any which way I want." And their whispers grew louder in the darkening theater as the trailers finished and the film began. Their argument became so anguished that someone yelled out, "Shut the fuck up!" Ben rose, insisted they leave the theater and marched up the aisle with Jane following, stunned.

They found themselves speaking harshly to one another on the curbside, his hands on hips, her face to one side, eyes watering. He was accusing her, and she was stifling her desire to roar that it wasn't fair, that he should try to see her point of view. That she'd merely changed her perspective on the Bonbons. That for God's sakes, one could be everywhere at once, and what a beauty and a blessing it was to be so. He said that didn't make sense, raised his arm and hailed a taxi. She scooted across the seat and tried to explain the Guru of all Gurus, and he shook his head. He said the only thing that mattered was decisiveness.

"When you see yourself as so-called 'everywhere,'" he said, "you never see the point that matters. Your head's in the clouds." Jane told him to fuck himself. He told the taxi to stop. The driver pulled up in front of a newsstand. "Go on," Ben said, "Get out! This is my taxi—if you have a problem, try understanding this!" and he leaned across her, flung the car door open. It was the first time Jane had heard him shout. The driver cleared his throat. The meter kept ticking. Jane remained in the taxi. She had her arms crossed over her breasts, stared straight ahead. "I said," Ben's voice steady, "get out." She didn't move.

At last he opened the taxi door on his side, calmly got out and without shutting the door and walked away. Jane thought he was going to buy a paper at the newsstand, and would soon slide back into the taxi with an apology. It was his habit to buy newspapers at night. And it was his habit to apologize after disagreements, after he'd had some space and had calmed down. But when the meter in the taxi registered ten dollars more, Jane realized he wasn't coming back.

"I'm sorry," she told the driver, searching her wallet and the little backpack pocket where she kept stray change. "I'm sorry, but I don't have enough—" She scooted out of the taxi, and the driver flared up, punching the palm of his hand, yelling with an accent that she was a whore, a Pandora, a bitch without breasts. Ben still didn't come out of the news shop. Jane bowed her head, feeling the driver justified in his red-faced harangue and gave all the cash in her wallet, keeping a token's worth for a bus ride home. She started walking, had gone a half block when she felt a hand on her shoulder. It startled her and she spun around. His eyes were heavy.

"It's just that you're trying too hard. You don't have to be so giving," Ben murmured, looking at her shoes. "You think you're incapable of making a single decision but you do, and often it's a decision left unsaid. You do it all the time, like in the theater. You wanted popcorn all along but wouldn't admit it—" Jane opened her mouth to protest, to say he didn't make sense, but he continued. "You pretend not to have the ability to make a decision because you think it'll go against some kind of silly idea about everything being valid, whatever that means. It's one thing to be accepting of other ideas and people—to have integrity. It's another thing to be gullible and—I know you don't want to hear this—a dim wit. And you are!" She stood before him, but stared behind him at the streetlights running down the avenue.

"Leave me alone," she said, beginning to walk again. But he kept pace with her and even when she sped up, he was beside her. Soon she paced a fast walk, and then a jog and finally she was running with him panting beside her. She raced him and finally dodged down another block with him falling behind.

"Jane!" he yelled, "Come on!" She heard his voice grow farther away as she kept going, her breath coming fast. Car exhaust billowed, registering itself in the troposphere, stratosphere, ionosphere and she was with each particle of exhaust, filling out, spreading with amoebic elegance everywhere. It was plain to her now. Like her mother, she was the woman of all places, her eyes overflowing, just as statues of The Madonna showed tears of blood at various times in certain South American churches. They should have stabbed Jane's eyes when she was born. She had too much sight, and there was no way around it.

The following week in the middle of the night, she answered the phone. Her housemate was out. A voice she'd never heard before said that something had happened; that the highway had been ripped out from beneath the wheels of a car; that it had happened just that evening when the driver had been on his way back to his father's home in New Jersey; that he'd driven through several lanes, a guardrail and down a hillside. The car had tumbled, crunched, bunched, glass shattering, plastic and metal warping, into a tree in a field. Other vehicles braked. A few people ran down the hillside, peered into the upside down car, saw blood, ran back up to the highway and phoned for help. As Ben's father told her the news, his voice cracked and there were dull pauses and flat notes. It was a voice that had too much to say, but didn't know how to say it. It was a voice without a fixed position. It was a voice without a singular perspective or angle. It was the voice of everywhere.

Jane

Rude Awakenings

"What's done is done."

<u>The Damned</u>

Open your eyes to Hoover Dam as it appears in the movie *Superman*, the 1978 version with Christopher Reeve shot years before he flew from the thoroughbred Eastern Express and shattered his spine in a last act that ultimately killed him. Watch a trillion hot particles ripping through the San Andreas Fault as a nuclear blast triggers the earthquake that produces the hairline fissure along the dam's curving wall, which fractures into the tree of life and then falls into ruin. Run as the chain reaction—electrons smashing into electrons—becomes a party of particles that can't be stopped. Gape at the entire planet as it tumbles into the deluge that becomes the goddess Ganga gushing from Shiva's crown—what my mother's guru has always called "the liberation of Las Vegas."

But no guru will ever know what happened to me that night long ago, when I lay groggy in the dark, phone pressed to my ear. This was before email, before texts and pings, before everything became wireless, when a ring could still startle you awake, when a bad connection didn't exist, when there was no avoiding my ex-boyfriend's father, Rudy, who began directing me to abandon my futon in favor of the first cab to Jersey—land of SUVs, clapboards, and endless boardwalks.

Before I could breathe *hello*, Rudy had maxed out on wheezing, his West Caldwell accent something I'd come to hate, the nasal "r"s, like a dog's tongue slathering my ear.

"NO ONE," he cried. "No one's gonna believe this…LEAST of all YOU! HIS GIRLFRIEND!" Did I know this man? Did he understand that it was past 3:00 AM on a Sunday night? Did he know I couldn't pay rent without a good night's sleep? "This is what it comes down to!" he whined. "Terror! Horror! Always! This is how it's always been, was, and will be!" Somehow, between wheezes, he'd found the breath to yell, while I moronically hadn't found the courage to slam down the phone.

"My son's spitting up blood," he continued. "And all I can think of is what he couldn't stop saying all yesterday. *Jane. Jane. Jane.*" It had to be a joke. "It was him telling me, *Call her dad. Call her. TELL HER*—So, here I am asking you to get in a cab. NOW—"

He could have offered a million dollars in cash and I still wouldn't have moved from my bed. And when I tried to ask questions, I didn't get very far, because he was right. Time didn't give two heartbeats; it just kept going. And so did he—

"There's a problem here," he said, coughing between words. "A very, VERY big problem. So, tell your cabbie to get you here. I'll pay."

None of it made sense because only days ago I'd told Ben to quit my life because of the bonbon episode in the movie theater, and the fact that he'd slept with a mutual acquaintance, a wannabe singer/dancer who practiced yoga but ate Doritos and reeked of garlic. It didn't matter that in return I'd slept with his best friend—a guy named Sam—who sold pot, stank of skunk, and wore his boxer-less jeans so low his butt crack showed. But Sam, unlike Ben, fed me midnight lo mein from the greasy spoon across the street, using the black lacquered chopsticks my roommate stored in the old Bustelo can by the sink. Alas, my new single status didn't stop Rudy from urging me to wave my hand on the corner of 13th and 2nd, where, in those days, few taxis dared to idle.

I refused to budge from my bed as cold air folded over me like a bad mood. It hurt to blink with sandpaper eyelids. Rubbing eyes, I rearranged my legs beneath the covers, my pajamas no better than a sweat-sodden sock. "Okay, okay," I groaned to get him off the phone. "So goodbye." But this only encouraged another wave of hysteria.

"Oh no! OH GOD! What in hell is this?!" His voice swerved into my ear, not unlike a bus through a glass storefront. "NO NO NO! God damn it!!!" I was now beginning to worry the man's ticker would give out—though a minute later, it was all— "Do you have any idea what kind of BS they call coffee? For Christ's sakes!!" Yes, I was now living in a grade B movie about a bipolar noodle-brain who sprayed the night with dog food pellets through a sawed off shotgun. It was all, "I can't breathe. I can't! Oh NO!" If Rudy had been suspended from a fiberglass wire a thousand feet above Fifth Avenue, he couldn't have sounded more panicked. A lot of, "What is this? Glue in my throat? No! Oh no! God damn swill they call coffee!"

In fact, for most of a year Rudy had been as good as lost in space. He refused to be real. In fact, I hadn't met the man during my short-lived relationship with his son. I'd only heard a few pathetic stories that portrayed him as fragile. Ben had gone on about the incessant bedtime drinking of hot milk, the crying through Kleenex boxes over TV commercials, and the brown slippers purchased ten-times-over throughout the last twenty-five years. And, more importantly, I had no memory—*nada*—of Rudy during my kindergarten days. No parental haze surrounded Ben, no birthday party or an early pick-up or a late drop-off. All I knew during the three years between kindergarten and second grade when I ran after Ben in the schoolyard was that Rudy never once showed his face. But that didn't stop him from showing up now, with his, "Get a pen. Here's the address—"

I rested against the phone, now my pillow, knowing that under no circumstance would I rustle up a pen from my coked-up roommate's stash of office supplies. Not a chance. The last time I tried that, she swooped in like an eagle, clawing me with, "Nothing is free. If you use, you better replenish!" After that, we avoided each other for most of a week until I brought home a pad of Post-it Notes from my temp job at the insurance company. The mere memory caused PTSD.

Despite the roommate, I had ears and could hear the hospital staff prodding Rudy with, *"Sir, sir, are you okay sir?"*

"What's wrong?" I said, still dodging the half-dream of Christopher Reeve riding his horse over the dam.

"What?" Rudy said. "What's wrong?"

Only now do I wonder how Rudy had gotten my phone number, or why he'd chosen to call me instead of a relative. But back then, I only knew one thing: the more he rambled the less likely it was I'd leave my bedroom of melted wax and rancid grease where I could watch the moonlight break against the silver paint of the rooftop outside my window, turning the view into an ice field.

●●●

Here's some wisdom I've collected during my few years walking the earth: We humans are born from insomnia. Women in labor pour pain and panic into rooms of incomprehension, panting and groaning through wakefulness as the ropes of fate tighten around their ribcages. But no mother will ever admit to panic, because unfortunately motherhood is too "precious" for the truth. Because who wants to hear the truth when panic infects the newborn, when quick as a blast, truth flashes across its face with a cry. After that first roar, the panic never goes away as hope is startled from every cell in the body, leaving the young to contend with premature old age.

That's how I felt when Rudy blurted his version of the story: crazed. Only hours after Ben drove to the mall to appraise a nest of diamonds plugged into a band of gold at a jewelry shop, he lost control. According to Rudy, the ring cost $1,500, and it fit snuggly into a black box, which the paramedics found in Ben's pocket. "I've got it here for you!" But blood tests showed signs of opiates in Ben's system, and it wasn't clear how he'd paid for the ring.

Rudy refused to believe any of it. "It's a mistake. He never took none of that heroin BS—" But it was clear, Ben had been "driving like a maniac." How else could the vehicle become a knot of metal and plastic? "He was excited," Rudy insisted. "He wanted to give you that ring—"

Barely five hours had passed since the first call at 3:00 AM, but minutes after I stumbled out of bed and into the wall, the phone rang. He sounded less panicked but more hyped on coffee. "Where are you?" he prodded.

"I'm sorry—" I'd knocked my forehead and was sitting on the edge of my futon. But he kept talking, until I said, "I can't come. I have to get into work early. Sorry. I could lose my job." Never mind that I was already behind schedule.

"Call them," he said. "Tell them what happened. You have a boyfriend in the hospital!"

That's when I told him about the break up.

"I don't believe it!! He bought you a ring!!" I shut my eyes. I was already dropping into a migraine.

"Well, sorry. It's true, Rudy. Believe me—"

"But he talked about you all the time! And by the way, I bet he talked about me too! So there. Now we're even."

True, Ben privately called his father, "the Wuss," because, apparently the old man didn't know his ass from his armpit. The butt of a thousand jokes, Rudy became mythic in Ben's circles. For instance, there was the story about the toupee that blew off in the middle of Ben's graduation ceremony.

"Okay, here's one," Ben said over a dinner of cold oatmeal and Guinness. "College graduation. My hero, William Safire, finishes his speech. My buddies are ready to throw up their hats. Some girl I want is an aisle over. Out of the blue, my dad's flying towards me with a fucking bouquet, slamming into every tit in sight, his toupee flapping—I kid you not—like a piece of shit. When he reaches me, it sails off." Rather than laughing, Ben turned bitter, all sun-starved coal miner, still riled up. "He's a pathological idiot. What kind of blowhard doesn't glue down a hairpiece when he's outside on a windy quad with thousands of people?"

I tried to placate Ben, laugh it off, but this only enraged him. He threw down his spoon and got up from the table.

"What the hell," he said, his back to me. "Fuck him!" His hand sliced the air. "Fucking toupee flies into the girl's face! My freak show dad!" I couldn't help laughing as Ben smacked his fist into the table, sloshing our beers and frightening our oatmeal. "Fucking Wuss!"

After that, I avoided the subject of Rudy, but found it difficult. During another meal, this time over lukewarm Eggos, Ben described his father as, "the wannabe lawyer who couldn't get through his first year at community college. No wonder his sole purpose in life was to reorganize cubicles!"

Ben's disgust at his dad, his outrage, seemed reason enough to break it off with the only guy who'd ever given me an orgasm. Back then I liked sex more than grand finales, and betrayals more than truths. So, I never properly met Rudy and never entirely got over Ben.

"You have no idea how much I love him!" Rudy moaned into what had to be a payphone as my roommate's alarm clock rang next door—the signal that it was already 8:30, an hour too late. Sun blazed outside, but only a few rays sleuthed into the dark corners of my room as if sorry that Rudy wasn't aware of Ben's opinion of him—

I had to get to work, but my roommate had taken over the bathroom, the shower spraying white noise over my bed. If I didn't get my sorry ass into the office, I'd be fired. Meanwhile, Rudy kept talking: "Last night, a nurse gave me a pill. And get this. This morning one got me a cup of coffee and a donut."

"Rudy" I said. "I have to go." But he wouldn't hear me.

"And the thing is, I'm having breakfast knowing his teeth broke through his face, everything coming out his nose. Blood spraying from his chest. You know what that looks like? No. Nobody does. You can't believe it till it's right there. May you never know! Never!" In addition to being a Wuss, the man had a gift for describing gore: "His ear was hanging by a thread. His hand too! Completely turned over on itself like a pretzel!" And, sounding like Ben, but not Ben: "There's a hole the size of a moon crater in his chest!" As panic washed over Rudy, his breathing got heavy and fast. The way he was going, he had to be sweating, stumbling around, light-headed. "Right there in his chest! Right beneath his right rib!" It was too late: I began breathing fast too.

Clock ticking, my pajamas rumpled, a vision of my boss waiting at the reception desk, I hyperventilated on my futon, stricken, succumbing to disgust, exhaustion, and a deep freeze. "God help me there was a dark, shiny bulge," Rudy cried. "His liver!!! His liver!!!!" Before I could stop myself, I vomited into my hands, several splotches marking the rug, the smell of wet dog and garbage trucks overwhelming my room.

Rudy kept going as I dropped the phone. I could hear him blathering, panic screaming into my bedroom, a whirlwind of overturned lives.

•••

When I placed the phone back in its cradle that morning long ago—towards the end of my most beautiful year, 1995—I didn't realize how pivotal those moments would turn out to be. Everything in my 10 by 12 foot ledge-of-a-room described normal: wood shelving piled with pearling sweaters and mildewed books I'd picked up at church sales, a black and silver Panasonic radio/CD player layered with dust and prominently displayed as a luxury good, the aluminum-frame window that opened to silver rooftops of neighboring tenements, and the pathetic hand-me-down futon flattened by the sexual tumblings of previous bed-revelers.

For weeks afterwards, the bad news congealed in my bedroom, which was less sanctuary than ventilation trap for the rancid cooking odors wafting up from an apartment below. Barely holding onto my job, I called in sick for a week, taking that first morning to sprawl on the futon and watch a roach scurry over the gray carpet smeared with gutter mud from a thousand shoe soles. No wonder roaches loved my room: Every surface, including my bed sheets, retained the stench of Chinese restaurant kitchen grease, which blended beautifully with my roommate's midnight tokes.

It didn't take long for the word "VACANCY" to enter my room like a flickering neon sign announcing not beer or an X-rated video or a Motel 6 but an emotion gone missing. My bed had been left behind like Chernobyl, a landscape where memories fell like flakes of ash.

Did I love Ben? It was hard to say; he was so self-absorbed— But I couldn't forget certain moments, like when he looked like a baby, lips parted, as he slept. Or when he laughed while spooning oatmeal into a bowl. Oddly, reflected light in my room mimicked the pattern on his tweed jacket—the one he spread in a field for an impromptu picnic of brown rice salad, avocadoes, and black-eyed peas—the single meal he prepared in honor of our second-month anniversary, just a week before we took off for the Southwest.

For days after Rudy's calls, I couldn't figure out what to do, because I couldn't do anything. I was as good as a projectile tossed above the earth. Christopher Reeve didn't fly counter-clockwise around the earth. Instead, he flew down a hillside, landing in a wheelchair, his body split in two like the end of a hair.

It didn't help that most days my downstairs neighbors replaced the non-stop salsa with "Fuck off motha fucka!" As always, the drill ended with a sledgehammer to the ceiling, the kind that took bites out of the plaster, like the hole that hovered over my own bed—some remnant of violence left by a previous tenant. That's how it was in a mildewing tenement on East 13th Street before East 13th gentrified.

The only way to avoid the apocalypse was to own a white noise machine or leave. Since moving in, I wanted nothing more than to escape those Jacob Riis environs. From day one I mapped out a plan. The best-case scenario involved rising above 1st Avenue into the 6th, 7th and 8th Avenues of the West Village, while the unattainable double-digit streets above Times Square—doorman country—amounted to a trip to Mars. Such locations required the cash power of a trust fund or a job on Wall Street, but I had neither.

I did, however, have an old friend, Miranda (a.k.a. Mimi). And through her, I'd snagged another room—this time on the Upper East Side off 2nd, for a miraculous $450. This good news had developed just days before Rudy's call. I was so excited that week before Ben's accident that I'd given notice a month before my move-out date and had already begun collecting boxes from the Duane Reade on 14th. But suddenly, with Ben in the hospital and my job threatened, the new room felt like a nonsensical dream.

I told myself that things weren't so bad. I wasn't being evicted. No one stalked me. I'd never been knifed, had never committed a crime, and my bank account still existed. Yet, I still wore the gifts Ben had left on my futon months earlier—pajamas and three thongs carefully folded in its pink and black striped Victoria's Secret box.

Car accidents happened all the time. Why get upset over a man I'd slept with for less than a year? But as the earth kept turning, I gripped the red-neck-ribbon of a cinnamon-scented teddy bear my mother had won playing penny games at an Atlantic City casino she'd visited with her guru, The Avatar—a man whose name meant the incarnation of Vishnu on earth, and whose interest in black jack, expensive real estate, and young women immediately made him suspect. Hadn't Ben said it first? "I can't believe your mom's into that con-man!" not realizing that I'd also been hooked on The Avatar after a classic Kundalini awakening.

But why should anyone be surprised? Yes, I believed in gurus. My interest in spirituality began with the view that life should be lived as an adventure. Considering this, you can understand how I overlooked The Avatar's slip of tongue when he said: "he's a lie" instead of "he's alive" or "you are mine" instead of "you are mind."

But my mother, Nora Lovins, believed in that which led nowhere—and anyone would be able to sense this in the gifts she presented in uncomfortable places, as when she handed me the stuffed cinna-bear at a café where we celebrated my twenty-third birthday over a pot of tea that might have led to better conversation if I'd chosen the Hibiscus instead of the Moroccan Mint—which had nauseated me. Years later, I finally understood how easily she gave away her life. Though even now, in this era of headless men in orange suits and orange men in headlines, with my mother dissolving like a salt crystal in the ocean of time, the bear she handed me all those years ago still carries a faint whiff of cinnamon.

•••

Is it crazy to think I should have run instead of follow? No, I knew what I was doing. I liked being treated poorly. After all, I'd been barred from Nora's pre-war apartment since college. It was unforgiveable—my own mother shutting me out of my childhood home. And why? Because she had to "protect herself" from "false friends" who "bettered themselves" at her expense. And what did that mean?

Sometimes, painful experiences lead to drug trips. Sometimes they lead to fanaticism. But how do you explain my mother's mission? It began with her storing toxic toner cartridges in her dining room, to be recycled for pennies— (Didn't she realize it was illegal to convert an apartment into a warehouse?) She preferred innocence to knowledge, and the landlord, Mustafa, preferred money to doing good deeds. Toner cartridges gave the guy an excellent shot at kicking her out of a three-bedroom, rent-stabilized, pre-war haven located on the Upper East Side, which meant I might never again use my childhood toilet.

That aside, my mother had another reason for disowning me: It was her dharma to serve humanity. Despite the Mustafa's fury, the three-bedroom became The Avatar's entertainment venue. Somehow Nora pulled it off. Instead of focusing on toner, sloping floorboards, and ripped batik in the hallways, The Avatar's millionaire students marveled at the high ceilings and Lexington Avenue location.

The address reeked of status. And what could be more spiritual than a circle of lawyers mixed with Fortune 500 CEOs? Wealth sat on the floor and binged on curry. Instead of family meals during Thanksgiving or Christmas, my mother hosted The Avatar's pun-riddled intensives called, "Knights of Gratitude" and "Mourning into Delight," where followers spent hours humming and swaying until one devotee after another disappeared into the primordial "OM"—which had dropped it's first M, cutting the umbilical cord between the word MOM and the unknown.

But why dwell on mothers or Ben's car crash? As so many have said, "everything eventually crumbles." Bank accounts, Hoover Dam, the Ramayana, and even as I now know, the God Particle.

Super Ruins

Because sunlight will force a person to blink, I eventually left my futon for the tiny bathroom recently vacated by my roommate. I peered into the mirror and found a scattering of red beads on my cheeks. They stopped only at the dark circles under my eyes.

Since leaving home, I'd battled rosecea and regular headaches, leaving me no option but to rummage through my housemate's shelf for Ibuprofen. Cupping hands beneath the faucet, I gulped down the pill. The day before the hot water heater blinked out yet again, leaving my fingertips icy. Winter, and therefore hypothermia, was nearly upon us. Without central heating, the only warmth in the apartment would escape from an over-priced space heater my housemate scored after an eight-store search two years earlier. Last winter, icicles developed on our teacups, forcing me to cocoon in bed with squares of temporary heating pads thrust down my underpants.

Under the circumstances, it was easy to hyperventilate. No paper bag in sight, I fell to the toilet seat and forced my head between my legs. Nausea swarmed like bees up my mid-section to my ears.

It's hard to know when my housemate returned, but the first indication of her presence was off-key singing. She was probably flying high on dope and Glenlivet, a combo enjoyed by her ex-convict boyfriend who made a living teaching CEOs how to box at a gym in Brooklyn.

All I know is that she found me crumpled on the linoleum with an inch-long cut to my hip. After pressing a towel to the gash, she pulled my arm around her shoulder and helped me to my futon, rasping weed breath and mumbling, "just inhale, you know, hold one in for three seconds, let out for five and do it again. This happens to me all the time."

Scratching a match against sandpaper, she lit a joint and left me to wilt in my room. Later, she padded to the doorway wearing her tiger-print silk robe, her boobs shimmying beneath. A cloud of lavender oil, pheromones, and garlic floated into my room as she asked if I needed anything: a glass of water, some raw sugar, Echinacea, cayenne pepper. It was a rare show of kindness from someone who'd been a virtual stranger—our schedules rigged to provide us with optimal lone-time. I was fine, I told her. "Really, I'm fine," I said. But no, how could I be anything but miserable as the four corner states flooded in?

•••

Before I flew to Arizona, my parents finalized their divorce. "It's done," Nora said. She'd called to wish me a nice trip. "When you're back, we'll get tea and celebrate—"

In the desert that first night, Ben bunched newspaper on a bed of coals and started a fire while I stared at layers and contours. Anyone else would've understood that *there would never be anything like that moment ever again.* But I felt separate, a thick film between me, the fire, the air. No smells of mesquite or charcoal or the nylon flaps of our tent because time sped by so fast that I couldn't grab its fender, even as we drove north until we smashed into the San Juans.

We set up tent as a hailstorm blew ice the size of walnuts into the campsite. We hugged each other, refusing to take refuge in the car, afraid of windshields. I sniffed Ben's knees, the hair on his arms tickling my nose, our foreheads and hair one. Shivering with damp, we pressed closer. The thud of ice smacked the tent. We were hiding from dinosaurs, and we knew what it felt like to be ice pellets dispelled from a falling sky in a universe of skies falling as they do in children's books about falling skies.

We were in our twenties, which meant that differences felt like betrayals, as when he wanted to hike Zion while I wanted Bryce. For him: melon. For me: toast. There was the time I refused to take the train to West Milford to meet Ben's buddies. "It's only an hour away!" But I made excuses and Ben didn't see me for a week.

Later, I had a friend in town, "Take the train," I said.

"Can't," he said. "Too much to do—" like fixing his car. Tit for tat—each "no" and "can't" piled up to form a mound of resentment, hurt, and refusal. During the trip, I didn't give him sex for three nights. Through thunder and lightening we lay in our sleeping bags, stiff, awake, cold. He wouldn't build a fire. We ate peanut butter and jelly and pretended we didn't care. In the end, he poured me wine and smoothed cream over my legs.

He still sits on a rock in my mind, wearing jeans, flannel shirt, and hiking boots, the red backpack at his side—the one he hefted as we crested a ridge. His chest smelled like grief, a piney scent that has remained with me the way the ruins at Wupatki—village of the Anasazi, the lost people—have remained despite weather.

Yes, I've romanticized the trip, but for good reason. The only photo I own of him shows Ben with arms raised: Ben as Superman, fresh from a flight around the world after turning back time. He stares at Wupatki's stones, saluting like a Nazi though he's Jewish through and through.

Perched on a slab of Anasazi stone fifty feet away, I zoomed in, watching what the light did, the way it loosened his face and dragged it down. He raised a palm to his forehead. "Smile," I yelled, but he didn't hear me.

•••

Of course the Anasazi were related to the Aztecs who were related to the Mongolians who were related to the Pashtuns and Hindus who were related to the Greeks and therefore the Egyptians who migrated at some point to the Pyrenees and therefore, Ben, with his Basque bones and Gypsy eyes and twisted nose had Anasazi blood in him.

Of course we laughed at these new-agey associations while our skin fried, the two of us twisted in each other's arms on the radioactive sand. Of course a completely dead seafloor could draw tourists—many of them hefty folk who took annual tours in R.V.s and S.U.V.s, guzzling colas and gas to staunch hunger. Of course I even bounded up a pile of stones and lectured to a parked SUV about the origins of humankind. Pointing at a pebble, I said, "We are a species that has evolved towards girth and stupidity rather than the wisdom and kindness of Satya-Yuga and Nirvana!"

Of course my snobbery can be attributed to an IUD Ben encouraged because we fucked and we bled sarcasm—condescending in our insecurity—because we had what everyone else wanted: youth, possibility, the intellectual prowess of urban-centrics. Feeling eternal, Ben and I began talking of a move to some small western town like Durango. We'd live off the land, become New Age post-hippy sex fiends, and devise absurd plans—absurd as the idea that Ben was a direct descendent of the Anasazi.

• • •

After the first visit to the hospital I tried everything Nora taught me. I meditated over a candle. I drank very hot water every four hours. I practiced yoga and Feldenkrais. I clicked mala beads and stood naked before a mirror, staring into the space between my eyes. Nothing worked— I couldn't get Ben's amputated hand and ear out of my mind, the smell of pus lingering like a dream as I drank morning tea. I breathed in the sterile odor of the white wraps that taped his chest, nose, and eyes into place, and I stumbled up against the formations of his sliced-open cheekbones, floundering against their awfulness.

Virtually ripped down the middle, he'd been carelessly stitched back together like a feather pillow. When I slept, I saw blood spilling through his lips. In fact, when his car collided with the guardrail, and then a tree, he clenched down so hard the enamel on his teeth had been "blown off." Strange, because somehow his poorly maintained car—which had always appeared toothless due to several missing grates beneath the hood—seemed to preordain the tragedy. More weirdly, years later I'd get sucked into hospitals as a paid research subject and then as an employee confined to windowless rooms, where I tapped out medical records for incoming patients.

But in the days, after the accident, I only wanted to escape Rudy. I soon learned that he needed only the slightest excuse to phone me. Talking double-time, he left out few details, seemingly enjoying it as he flung gory facts at my ears. There was the description of rib bones puncturing Ben's left lung—what he described as a grayish-white washcloth riddled with torn blood vessels soaked in red syrup. He compared the destruction of Ben's left pectoral to that of a Siberian Tiger's mauling. Because of it, Rudy would never again eat spaghetti in marinara sauce. Nor would he go near a steak. (My boy's thigh, cut up like London broil.) More upsetting were the partially severed leg, arm, thumb, and Van Gogh ear "hanging by threads." Thus certain amputations. The only saving grace: Blood loss had forced doctors to place Ben in a coma.

To this day, I still can't forgive myself. I avoided the hospital, and Rudy, because it wasn't convenient—too difficult to reach. I didn't own wheels—and if I had, I wouldn't have had the confidence to drive. It freaked me out to be a passenger, let alone a driver—the idea of sitting in a potential death-box. Worse, I didn't have the money.

Located several miles from rail lines in a bucolic section of Jersey—think lakes, forests, fields, farmhouses, dirt roads—a trip to the hospital wasn't cheap. With luck, a car service cost $150. And remember, I had a couple thousand in debt, thanks to that trip to Anasazi-land.

But Rudy kept insisting on paying. "Put it on your card and I'll send you a check." But I didn't trust him. So, I waited one day, then two, before making a plan—if that's what you call it.

It took a week, but I finally got to the hospital whose forgettable name began with "Saint." Exhausted, dehydrated from Port Authority and bus fumes, I stumbled upon the only human who could possibly be Rudy. At first glance, he appeared vulnerable—or was it pitiful? He'd described himself well: short, mid-sixties-ish guy with dark brown hair that appeared suspiciously monochromatic—verifying the wig. And though it was well below freezing outside, he sported a short-sleeve engineer's shirt tucked into dark brown polyester pants that guided the eye to hip handles and other protruding areas. He shifted from foot to foot in a pair of brown vinyl walking shoes—the kind purchased in Chinatown basements or in chain store pharmacies or discount outlets like Walmart or Big Lots, stores located too far from the urban core to have curb appeal. Under the bright hospital bulbs, his face appeared pasty and drawn as if Xeroxed to highest contrast.

In family photos Ben showed me, Rudy didn't smile. On a sofa, he slumped—a blur—against an elbow in his brown living room—brown clearly his favorite color—as if too weighed down or zoned-out to hold up his head. Apparently, he was an addict of game shows and the evening news, but something more was responsible for the heaviness. According to Ben, Rudy had stopped standing up for himself (if he ever had) once Ben's mom Lillian died and the housekeeper—an elderly Puerto Rican lady with a high-pitched voice, bright red lipstick and a penchant for heavy hair ointments, panty hose and floral muumuus—took over domestic duties.

"He cried for a month," Ben had told me, "and settled into this weird little routine that begins and ends with T.V. He hasn't changed the routine or the channel in ten years. Literally. He has no friends, and if he does, they don't know what's happened to him. I don't think he's taken a vacation since I was twelve or thirteen."

Though Rudy and I had talked over the phone, we stood ill at ease with each other in the hospital lobby. His bloodshot eyes wandered the ocean-colored interior as if in search of someone else, as if he knew something embarrassing about me. At first, he said little. Clearly, he hadn't slept in days. With a balled tissue, he wiped his thick nose, sniffling and shaking his head.

Phones rang, a loudspeaker blared: "Ira Schultz, report to Maternity. Ira Schultz report to Maternity." This announcement caused Rudy to waken to something on his mind, which he murmured to himself.

"What's that?" I asked. But Rudy was absorbed in his own scientific analysis of the steady swish of air as people passed by: a new mother lifting a breeze as she strolled towards the exit with her husband and a nurse, who carried a car seat with an unbelievably tiny being strapped inside.

In the weeks that followed, I didn't do much but move my few possessions—thrown into boxes at the last minute—to the uptown room. I sometimes took the bus to Jersey for brief hospital visits where Rudy shook his head and held my hand, disclosing medical updates. I probably took walks in Central Park, and I probably picked up bags of string beans, carrots and sweet potatoes at the corner market, but I don't have specific memories to confirm these facts.

By December, I'd lost my job and begun accruing more debt. A job waiting tables would've been a blessing, but I didn't have the experience or the contacts. So, I frittered away money my grandparents had sweated to save for my education, a future wedding, or down payment on a house, steering clear of friends who oddly never bothered to call because they were too strung out on supper clubs and nightcaps to leave me a message.

Once or twice, I couldn't help myself. I left dramatic descriptions of Ben's accident ("His car's an accordion," "His face looks like its been chewed by a lion." "He's lost an ear like Van Gogh!"). Worse, I made the mistake of remembering the way he massaged my breasts and inner thighs with citrus massage oil "borrowed" from my roommate's assortment—the recollection a ghost between my legs.

•••

As he became more comfortable with me, Rudy routinely called at 6:00 PM, providing updates about Petri dishes of grown tissue, of skin adhering to open wounds, of medications—always talking of nurses.

"Today was awful. That doctor—what's his name." Rudy regularly forgot names. "You know who—anyway, it wasn't him. It was his nurse. Rubin—that's his name—So, he sewed Ben's ear with that blond, what's-her-name. You know, J-somebody, I don't know. Who cares! So the fatty, the brunette who can't speak English, from someplace whose name I can't remember—she said it wouldn't heal right, the ear, and guess what, she was right! It's crooked! I'm telling you—it's the blond's fault, cause I heard she helped other doctors and every single surgery ends up screwy. You ask me, it's better he doesn't have an ear!"

Rarely did these calls involve input from me, even when he claimed ignorance over how to issue a complaint to the proper department. When

I suggested he contact a patient advocate, he shut me down with: "No, no, no— That would upset the doctor. I can't upset a doctor looking after Ben. No— The doctor's got to like us or it'll get worse!"

In the end, I simply chanted what was required of me: "It'll be okay. Ben is strong. He'll make it through—" while Rudy fired off rhetorical questions concerning what the universe meant for us. Eventually, Rudy took a deep breath that signaled release, finally calm enough to demand: "Promise to stay with Ben through thick and thin? He needs you."

I usually responded with a white lie like, "I'll do what I can to help! Don't worry! I'm strong." Which really meant: "I'm full of shit. Cardboard is stronger than me. Don't believe a word I'm saying!"

•••

Ben in a coma, I settled into my new cell overlooking a square of concrete surrounded by red brick walls. My days began and ended with the cigarette smoke that emanated from the bedroom of the apartment's lease-keeper, a mom named Dina—whose kids had left seven years earlier—who'd VW-bused it with an acting troupe from San Francisco in the 1960s. True to her track record of reversing the generational Diaspora, Dina stuck it out when it came to smoking, despite trends opposing the habit. Her salt and pepper hair reminded me a little of "Bewitched," a little of Mrs. Robinson and, for some reason, a little of the old Tang commercials—maybe for the smell of her hair treatments—making her the perfect counterpart to Rudy, had they met.

That she smoked endless packs of Salem's into the wee-hours of the night doing who-knew-what didn't bother me much until the industrial-strength fan that barred fumes from my room broke. After that, the steady hum of an inferior circulating fan—which failed to blow smoke from my bedroom—infuriated me as I tossed against traffic noise and the light pollution of 2nd Avenue. When daylight arrived like a rope yanking my neck, I forced myself up for a jog that saved me from spending the day covering my head with my pillow.

All this led to the afternoon when I returned to Rudy with resolve. I finally knew what to do. I wasn't willing to pretend anymore. Rudy, who planned on meeting me in the now familiar hospital, was late.

In the lobby, intercoms crackled over an array of decorative wall quilts. Nearby, an exhibit called "Thrash Dance" showcased ceramic trolls encased in glass under beam-me-up-Scotty lights. As I waited for Rudy, I examined one of the trolls. It appeared startled, its deformed body leaving me to wonder if this were a medical device company's idea of a sick joke. The troll leered at me in its hot pink tutu, as if overjoyed by my sorry situation, Schadenfreude gleaming in its painted eyes. A molded leg was raised as if to piss while its forehead shimmered with yellow sequin strands that were meant to serve as hair but reminded me of urine, the golden flow trickling down to its purple bodice. Next to the hospital's wheelchairs and crutches and hollow-eyed visitors, there couldn't have been a more sadistic exhibit except for Rudy, coming loud and clear from left field.

By now his entrances felt like ice water in the face. "Half an hour they told me—those nurses. The blond and the brunette. Half an hour!" Never one for pleasantries, Rudy won all whining contests. Newspaper rolled beneath his arm like a megaphone, he looked ready for head smacking.

On this occasion, he wore navy blue polyester pants, disturbingly taut over his groin, with a light blue engineer's shirt endorsed by a metal pen. Chained reading glasses swung around his neck and bobbed against his chest. Loose folds of skin puffed into pale geologic features, overpowering his small, brown eyes. His cheeks drooped, sallow and heavy jowls like congealed candle wax. He scratched his temple and said, "Half an hour—I don't know why we can't see him now. They've got him on some kind of new cockamamie drug they have to monitor—" He rapped his newspaper against a palm.

At a loss, I deflected the mood, moving towards a blue bench. "How are you, Rudy? Want some coffee?" He shook his head slowly so as not to upset his wig while his reading glasses wobbled against his sagging pectorals. He latched onto my questions, as if he'd been given permission to engage in something illicit.

"Who wants coffee?" he began. "When Ben's still all bandages?" He bowed his head and squeezed the bridge of his nose between two swollen fingers whose nails were perfectly snipped, though thicker and more yellow than was healthy—a sign of fungus or a missing nutrient. Needing speech, I settled on a platitude, that beautiful verbal crutch. Quick, easy, lacking specificity, platitudes placated more than original statements. And though my own father loathed tired language ("It's for the living dead!") I could say nothing but, "I feel for your loss," when I might have said, "You need help. But not from me!" So, out flowed vanilla phrases.

On that occasion, I chose, "This too shall pass—" while Rudy rubbed a palm over his cheek, where it stayed for a moment until I cleared my throat.

"What the hell. Come on—" Rudy muttered.

We took the elevator down to the blanched cafeteria, where the odors of steamed cauliflower and canned corn wafted about and left me feeling sick. Rudy purchased a "cuppa joe" and two donuts. We found a table, where he dabbed his eyes—a common activity during my visits—and still I hadn't found the strength to steer the conversation.

And then, his Styrofoam cup became the first casualty, knocked by his elbow, hot liquid spilling like freshly mined oil over the white table. Before I could grab napkins, the black waterfall wet his pants. But Rudy barely noticed as I piled napkins over the fluid.

"If there's one thing," he moaned. "Just one thing I want," He pressed the bridge of his nose, shutting his eyes, "it's to see Ben crack an eye and walk again. Believe me, Janey." He had taken to calling me Janey, and because I hadn't corrected him the first time—not wanting to hurt his feelings—he continued to use this grating endearment. "When he's better, I'm selling the house. I don't care if Lillian said she wanted to keep the house in the family—for grandchildren and all that bull. Forty years in that house. But I can't. She has to understand."

I nodded, wishing I'd rehearsed a speech on the bus ride over. Rudy rambled on about the house: How they'd bought it for only $17,000 back in the 50's, before the birth of their first daughter—now a geologist in Anchorage. They'd had dreams about building a second story so the kids wouldn't have to share a room. All those winters filled with snowmen, games of Monopoly, sled rides—all those John Cheever summers sitting outside on the front lawn while the kids played softball. How Lillian baked her first homemade loaf in that kitchen, the smells of broiled chicken, grilled vegetables and flavored rice flooding the entry when Rudy walked in the door after spending a day of selling office space cum cubicles. How losing Lillian had been the beginning of the end, and now possibly losing Ben— how would Rudy ever recover? All this while ripping the cellophane from his glazed donuts.

"Rudy," I pressed his shoulder. His weathered fingers clutched the putty-like donut. "There's something I need to say." My voice sounded stiff, but he seemed unaware. "First, let me say, Ben has meant a lot to me."

Rudy nodded, took a bite, chewed, swallowed said he knew all this, so why say it? Leaning my head to one side, I continued, trying not to notice the donut-slurry nestling in the creases of his mouth. Looking down at my lap to study my small, useless hands, I lowered my voice, suggesting I was about to disclose a secret. "I've never known anyone like him in my life." I murmured. "He's completely unique—I know that as your only son—and, especially because your daughter—"

"What's she got to do with this?" Anger catching his forehead—

"What I mean is," I continued, my voice and hands a collection of sharp stones. I looked up, understanding that I uttered nonsense.

Rudy squinted at a far corner of the cafeteria, trying to understand, shaking his head and mouthing my words as he heard me speak them. I filled the air with token statements. Out came the rotting language of dollar-store greeting cards. "You know," I burbled. "Life pulls you—" Rudy winced as if his cheek had been struck with a wire hairbrush. "Life's so," I paused, distracted by a tidy woman wearing an embroidered sweater, her hands trembling as she stooped over her walker, struggling with a wallet by the cashier. I saw it coming, just as I saw what was coming to Rudy.

The woman's wallet slipped, jostling her tray, causing a bowl of brown sludge to become airborne as if it always knew its destiny. It tumbled like so many platitudes before it landed in the lap of the obese employee handling the register.

The cashier slipped off her stool and bellowed, "Lady! What you doing!"—as if she'd been hit by a paintball. Confusion rearranged the center of the cafeteria. Grabbing a finger sponge next to the cash drawer, the cashier vigorously wiped her black leggings, brown pudding loping down to her ankle like something excreted, while the elderly woman in her delicate embroidery stared with disbelief, confusion, and finally horror at the scatological mess of her dessert—confirming that every dessert eventually became scat. It was clear: Every sweet moment and every sweet person, including me, could become, in a flash, as low and baseless as shit.

If only I felt something—if only I could become a thoughtful human being rather than a hollowed out, hearse of a creature. But Rudy already understood. I couldn't take any of it back. There was no dodging the bullet now. The man would peg me to the wall and reach down into my gut to pull out the intestinal worst of me.

I spoke, and then, dropping his donut onto a napkin, he dug into me. "Don't!" Rudy shook his head, first slowly then faster and faster as the alarm clock of understanding woke him up. I hadn't noticed the warning signs: the old lady in the embroidered sweater, the spilled coffee, the half-eaten burger wilted in its foil wrapper at the next table.

"Rudy," I said when I shouldn't have, but I had to escape from that iced-over medical pond. "I need to go."

"What?" Rudy's small eyes—dull and opaque as river stones—fixed on me, his pupils birthing a worm, one that struggled through layers of passivity in search of truth. "What do you mean? Leave. You can't leave!" He began shaking his head again, and his wig slipped tectonically along his pate. We were having a blurry conversation with too much noise at the edges.

"Listen," I breathed. "I shouldn't be here!"

"No, but your boyfriend is struggling to stay alive!"

"Well whatever. I can't be two places at once—"

"What?" By now the cashier had settled her mammoth rump on her spindly stool, ringing up trays with her lips pressed shut and her eyelids at half mast while listening to something on her earphones—zoning out the way I wanted to zone out, with that who gives a fuck attitude because her pants were now ruined and had cost enough. "So it doesn't matter if," Rudy said, "he LOVES you?"

I ignored this craziness, without sharing a shortlist of facts that included how we'd rarely slept at each other's places, that I'd only cooked maybe three meals for him, how he didn't read books while I did, that all his friends took heroine, that I wanted to get a job but couldn't because what else? Oh yes, I was a piece of shit going to hell.

"He loves you—"

"Rudy," I pressed forefingers to temples and stared at the sweating donut on the table. If he didn't stop, I was going to tell him that his son called him a Wuss— "I'm going—" I pulled my messenger bag over a shoulder, but Rudy stayed me with the surprisingly strong grip of a thug. I stared at his sorry wig.

"Janey." Rudy's eyelids flickered, a switch flipping on and off. He cleared his throat, turned his head slightly and moved his folded hands over the table as I yammered about my lack of employment, my family in a shambles, how there was no way I was going to inhabit the hospital like a lost soul, forming puddles of sorrow with Rudy among the ceramic trolls. "You know," I said. "You're too good for Ben—" I shouldn't have said it, but I couldn't help myself.

"What!" Baring his teeth, he thrust a finger in my face. Blood pulsed up his neck to his cheeks. *Road rage. Street fights. Massacres.* "Don't tell ME I'm too good for my SON when he's lying upstairs almost DEAD while I'm down here trying to convince his HEARTLESS, stupid, selfish GIRLFRIEND to stay!" He couldn't stop himself from summoning memories of Ben in roller skates, at the dinner table, at birthday parties, slamming me with, "He's all I got! And now it looks like I'm all he's got—And, that's **love**. You got that? **Love!**" He used the word "love" like a curse, spittle flying from his lips and landing on his defeated donut. And yet, the word sounded like a prayer, the L and the V flung into the ether for only a select few on their way to cloud nine.

I sat, barely breathing, feet sweating icicles in my sneakers, unable to look at him, liquid pearling in my eyes, hands trembling, face a stone, the cafeteria airless as if it had been sucked into a black hole. But Rudy didn't throw his donut or empty coffee cup in my face, as I expected. Nor did he slam me in the jaw. Instead, he readjusted his wig—which had slid lower on his forehead—trembling like a dog emerging from water.

"Sorry," I whispered. And why couldn't I shut up?

"Don't give me that!" He groaned, shaking his head. I thought he'd bang his fist on the table and leave, but then he switched gears. "You'll regret leaving. Not just for a few months but for the rest of your life." Rudy's forehead smoothed. "No perspective—" He leaned forward, Old Spice and sweat surrounding us. Calm as a Vegas card player performing for the sky-camera, he said, "Ben is going to make it. He's got punch." He mock-swung his fist and chuckled. "So, think before you act."

Lights buzzed. Air circulated through vents. My skin cooled and warmed. I inhaled and exhaled, a master meditator, not thinking at all, not considering commitment or sainthood or love, just watching the green digits flickering at the register, until my attention hovered close to the cafeteria exit where a trash bin with its Formica flap awaited a balled napkin in my fist.

And then, without warning, I was up, despite Rudy's protest and the cool hand he settled on my arm to still me yet again, despite the alarmed and sad expression on his face, those parted lips and small eyes filled with worms that knew better than to trust my kind of person. Within minutes I had relieved myself of the lackluster donuts, of the heavy canned peas and corn and the odor of industrial ground beef emanating from the metal serving trays behind Plexiglas, somehow flying like Lois Lane in Christopher Reeve's arms down the clinical halls rich with carcinogens
and the scent of something like bubblegum—no doubt lost-lives swimming in formaldehyde—past the urinating, laughing trolls towards the sliding glass doors that opened to the sweat-scented, coniferous hedge and the endless concrete walkways that bordered the parking lot.

About Time

True, I treated Rudy like scum—but you've got to understand I got mine, because the universe is a boomerang. Every action gets vomited back sevenfold. Tell me I made bad choices. Blame it on flakiness. Insist that the yugas of my life bit into my flesh like an attic full of hungry rats. All of it is true. The proof: Years later I collapsed, exhausted, no better than a pile of dirty laundry.

But every post-Maharishi American child expects an age of enlightenment. I was no different. Nora Lovins confirmed this when she read from a black book with gold embossed type: "Every choice is a wire added to the cage of reality. Every choice launches the chooser into the unknown." Meaning, each decision created the maze that was my life, which was a prison built by the choices made during an infinite number of unknown past-lives.

But most of my earliest decisions were based upon my mother's high-speed train-of-thought. Ideological cars flew off the tracks in her mind and wrecked straight into mine. At age seven, I slipped seven dimes (seven being my lucky number) into the donation boxes scattered around the Ashram in Upstate New York. I gazed like a zombie at the gold-framed prints of Lakshmi's magenta, yellow, and green veils, believing I could win life's jackpot if only I prayed long enough. And how I prayed for that stock market reality. But in the end, all I managed was my own spiritual casino.

There is only one truth: Eternity is a cyclone of ever-increasing rewards and debts, because, as everyone knows, "God helps those who help themselves!" and "What comes around goes around."

Yes, I'm a poorly evolved Homo sapien with memories distorted to suit my best interest. Looking back more than a decade to 1997, I find a lot of junk. But understand what it was like the year Hong Kong rejoined Mainland China—when the Twin Towers still existed and Union Square didn't house a Trader Joe's or $3 million condos. Back then, I turned 26, and Ben's hospital bed was a mosquito in the dust behind me as I ran like Lola in the movie *Run Lola Run*. I jettisoned furniture, crockery, household items, photographs, wads of cash I'd inherited. Instead of building a life, I squandered possibilities on kitsch, barely weighing the pros and cons. I either gave everything away to side-step responsibility or stuffed myself with dollar store trash.

And why did I rent my life instead of own it? Did it have anything to do with the fact that at a moment's notice the widow, Dina, who chain-smoked through the night and took my savings in exchange for a bed had the power to kick me out at month's end?

Did it have something to do with Rudy, who, undeterred after I'd screwed him over, masochistically continued to call? Every night the phone rang, and every night I told him—kindly at first, but more forcefully later— that I'd no longer be harassed. But it wasn't so easy to throw him off my heels like a pair of uncomfortable shoes. He would cut me up, piece by piece. Even when I disconnected the line, I couldn't evade him.

He did everything in his power to get my attention, first mailing a rose bush with few blossoms and many spiked branches for the yard I'd never have, following that with the lowest of ploys. He flooded my mailbox with Hallmark cards that contained photos of Ben as a hot teenager in cleats.

But by then I had no choice—because the universe began rattling my chains even more, yelling, "get out now!" That's right, my chain-smoking landlady gave me one month's notice so that her thirty-something-protein-shake'n-son could move into my 8 x 12 foot jail-cell-of-a room. And if that wasn't enough, my daily grind of entry-level duties (photocopying, fixing coffee, ripping open envelopes, typing spreadsheets in a cubicle whose padded walls reminded me of mid-century loony houses—though on reflection, homes for the mad might have been preferable to the office I later considered "hell for bitter people who drank too much coffee")—dried up. In truth, I didn't want to spend years marketing piggybanks and notebooks with sparkly plastic covers, despite the fact that doing so funneled $2,000 a month into my bank account.

Though I'd never been near a volcano, I had no choice but to go. College friends who'd slept in empty warehouses, listened to Hole, and wore stockings with runs in them, glowed about jettisoning Manhattan for OZ. But I never considered leaving until my best friend from preschool, Miranda—mainly known as Mimi—invited me to dine amid cardboard boxes in her kitchen, where she became my Scarecrow, Tin Man, Cowardly Lion, and Toto, and led me to my first breath of real air.

Best Friend

In preschool, I clobbered her with silver dress-up heals, but she forgave me for trading my inferior pink tulle pompom skirt for her superior sequined tutu. She was tall and amber, but she abhorred her slim legs and perfect cheekbones. No one escaped her party vibe or her aura of indigo with flashes of orange. Men got hard on her jokes and lapped up the sight of her slipped collars, which bared breathtaking shoulders. Ease drifted from her like iridescent feathers floating over dinner tables, her laughter tickling others into submission.

In contrast, I was beige. Adults described me as "withdrawn," "solemn," and, when feeling complimentary, as "dreamy." I adhered to swimming pool steps and was called "poor kid," so doomed that adults forgot my existence. And if anyone remembered, they thought I'd ruin the fun.

Of course I grew up into an awkward college student, barely standing average height with hips so wide they overflowed barstools. I never looked quite right in blue jeans—despite jogs and a regime of Callanetics. My breasts remained pimple-sized, my parsnip complexion only making dirty blondness more dirty—no better than a used rag over my shoulders. It didn't help that my hair dropped to the floor like plucked spider's legs, thousands of strands landing on bath tiles, sweaters, and miscellaneous rugs. My scalp released its own snow and scared away even the frailest boys. If I upheld Mimi as shining perfection, I had good reason.

But fabulous bone structure and puckish haircuts didn't save Mimi from misfortune. Even the beautiful got boomeranged. I'd been there after Mimi's abortion when her mother, Cathy, cried for a day but slipped her some weed. Two years later, I comforted Mimi in the hospital after she'd flown from the back of a boyfriend's motorcycle. Miraculously, there were no scars. Instead, dramas somehow increased her glam.

In kindergarten, I hid with her beneath a grand piano in our classroom after her father had been murdered. We played Barbie and brought the dead back to life.

In high school, my mind went blank when she stared me down and said, "What do you intend to do with yourself anyway, Jane?" She never accepted bullshit. If I hid behind apology or caved-in to be done with an argument, she became more insistent. "Sugar, you really need and I mean **need** to be real!" All wise woman of the South, she rarely hesitated especially because she said, "sugar" so often that she nearly splashed lemonade in my eyes. And when she said something bitter like, "Sugar, the world is going to screw you over if you don't know what you are made of! Because if you don't, you're going to be slammed, and I mean slammed!"

Flamboyant but mercurial—that was Mimi in the bright tops and shimmery skirts that her grandmother had patched together from scraps of chiffon and aerophane. Everything she donned challenged the eye with its patterns—her Isadora Duncan scarves, her paisley jackets.

Yet she was expert organizing her office—something I failed at despite all the black outfits in my wardrobe. Did I envy her that she somehow managed to appear corporate in drapey clothing? That somehow she worked full time, made good money, and still headed out with friends for drinks Thursday nights? That these gifts came from her sensible but ambitious mother? Okay. Yeah.

It hurt that Cathy—black sheep in a long line of Anglo-Saxon landowners—founded an HR firm whose goal was to feed the world while harnessing corporate power. Idealistic but resourceful, the inspired mom dedicated herself to Habitat for Humanity, Unicef, and most importantly, women's rights by way of EST, while with equal resourcefulness Mimi and I generated scratches, bruises, scowls, and banged heads in our midtown preschool near Bloomingdales. It was there that Nora and Cathy began a conversation that would last more than thirty years. They curled up on sofas, bonded over *The Women's Room*, meditated on the "doing energy" of the male versus the "being energy" of the female, hosted Mary Kaye and Shaklee vitamin parties, all of which my father loathed.

Disgusted by aphorisms, mantras, and Mary Kaye's lipsticks, my father shortened his earthly time by indulging in marijuana, single malt scotch, and a little coke thrown in for good measure. As if in defiance of spirituality, he juggled one affair after another, the longest of them leading to an aborted pregnancy that pushed his extra woman to an attempted suicide. But there was no shortage of family degeneration in the 70s, so I considered drugs, suicide, and extra-marital affairs to be normal.

Any distress Nora might have undergone only strengthened her bond with Cathy, which in turn deepened my connection to Mimi. Therefore, like sisters, we convened in Mimi's kitchen to hatch a plan that would burn that stovetop of stir fried zucchini and mushrooms into my memory. After all, ours had always been a daring friendship. After all, we'd been preschool tarts, leading the boys through mazes of flirtation as we sat on blue vinyl benches, pretending to read books, giggling and shimmying out of the underwear beneath our skirts. Mimi, with coy smiles, drew David, Jason, Kevin, Scottie, Justin, and yes, Ben, to us, because she liked that the boys pinched our bottoms like ants nibbling freshly baked muffins.

That same recklessness resurfaced as we doused soy sauce over mushrooms that evening in the late 90s. While I chopped garlic against Mimi's plastic cutting board, I confessed that the sound of the knife smacking the board made me think of Ben's bandages, that when the phone rang, I heard Rudy's complaints, that if I sat too long in one place, I remembered Ben with his eyelids pinched shut as he wildly fucked me in our tent. Mimi listened, twisting linguini around fork tines, steam twirling up from the pot and blighting the kitchen window with condensation.

"Jane," Mimi said. "This is crazy. You have got, and I mean **got**, to start packing. Leave this hellhole. You so must get out of here and forget him!" She wore every color in the world, slapping me with rainbows. "Pack. Tonight! Got it, friend? You are so coming with me and tasting Rainier cherries at Pikes Place Market."

As we ate our garlic concoction from paper plates perched on boxes in an apartment full of dust mites and packing tape, she made promises. "You listen to me, my friend. There's nothing I won't do for you. Nothing! We are so bonded! You so totally have to understand that. This is so like a complete phenomenon that I am headed off on this amazing adventure in the mountains. You have to join me!" She grabbed my hand, pulling and squeezing as I spilled my wine cooler, laughing the kind of unfeeling laugh that kept going till it hurt. "I don't care what anyone says," she was saying, "It's just way too easy and brain dead to get super involved in a job and a relationship right now. Because I am so done with stinky city-boy sheets, sweaty thighs, and tasteless coffee that smells like swill. We are so getting on our own two feet." Tears of hilarity ran down my cheeks. She looked at me for a long moment. "You are so ready! So completely ready!"

The day I left, it was already sweltering in the subways. Everyone looked pasty and my scalp itched. I stumbled like a zombie towards what Mimi had started to call our biggest adventure of all time, adding that I'd most definitely, so very **definitely,** find the serenity that lay over the rainbow, because she'd trained me to see only the colors that she liked best. And how she understood that I burned to move for the sake of moving. I would, she said, leave the rot of New York behind and forget what had happened there. There was no questioning any of it, because when Mimi first told me she was leaving for Seattle in June—" You should come with me. What do you have to lose?"—when I'd been so hesitant and blind, there'd been only one true answer:

"Right, there's nothing. Nothing to lose."

Running Away

"Don't dwell on it."

<u>SeaTac</u>

That June, I exited the plane and walked down the ramp, taking my first breath of emerald air. Even in the airport, the city felt like a town ready for a population explosion. People crowded the gates, where airport personnel avoided eye contact. Women in office gear pulled luggage behind them. Men created a breeze while jogging to their planes.

Of course I looked questionable next to the good people of SeaTac airport. My uniform of scuffed boots and man's undershirt tucked into baggy black jeans—not quite Kurt Cobain enough to be a fashion statement—left me feeling like a vagrant. It didn't help that my blemished complexion gave me the appearance of a cadaver. Worse, under harsh restroom lighting, my lips looked blue, my wrists thin as a child's, the tops of my arms almost skeletal. I had become the victim of air-conditioned frigidity.

What could be more nerve wracking than an airport of passengers recently belched from an array of 747s? My endocrine system kept squirting anxiety into my bloodstream.

Unfortunately, I couldn't stop thinking of Nora as she gave directions after pecking my cheeks outside the Vitamin Shoppe on 2nd Avenue. She'd thrust a bag of B12, Niacin, and Calcium into the my hands, saying, "Take half a Niacin in the morning, half at night." In return, I made a false promise: I'd consume animal protein and dulse at least twice a week. Sending me off with squeezes to my shoulder, she added, "Call when you get in!"

Every payphone had someone leaning into it, so I walked towards the baggage claim, where no one knew who would meet me because "the boyfriend" didn't want to run up parking charges.

As mastermind of everything, Mimi had drafted our plan. 1. We'd find an apartment within walking distance of amenities, as neither one of us drove well enough to own a car. 2. We'd temp until people figured out that we were exceptional and offer us high paying jobs. 3. We'd save enough money to buy property with a view. (So what if the plan hadn't accounted for the very real possibility that no one would meet me at the airport?)

Over the phone the night before, Mimi had finally addressed my arrival. She might or might not pick me up—probably not if Todd's car broke down. "No worries either way—and that means **no** worries! Worse case scenario, you can always hang till someone gets there—" In which case, one of Todd's roommates would come for me in a Mazda pickup. She told me to be on the look out for a guy "built like a homesteader." Not to worry, the homesteader could carry five suitcases on top of his noggin.

Was it any surprise that during those first days in Seattle I felt a constant flutter of panic in my solar plexus?

Falling down the escalator with my cluster of luggage and a bankcard loaded with the last of my grandparents' inheritance—about $10,000, which I considered an irreplaceable sum—I saw no one who fit the "homesteader's" description. Breathless, I stumbled off the moving steps.

I tried to imagine all the pros: If Mimi and Todd or the homesteader had tail spun while navigating the twisting streets of Seattle—or worse, had fatally slammed into a truck on the interstate—I could always rummage up the number Mimi had dictated (the number of a friend of a friend whose name was already lost). Barring that, I could grab the Metro to Westlake Station and take a cab to Todd's place.

But holy mother of mothers, I lucked out. I found Mimi and Todd beaming like two tall advertisements for teeth whitener, antidepressants, and skin care products. I stumbled towards them, haggard against Mimi's perfectly glossed lips.

Head to one side, arm around Todd's waist—which was sheathed in a ventilated sport's shirt with the large yellow numbers 27 rising from his belly to his chest—Mimi looked like a contented wife of ten years. Unbelievably, Todd was almost a head taller, his buzzed blond hair less cool because of his toothy grin. Indeed, he looked like someone who'd made the sorry decision to turn down pro-track, high school basketball—thus rejecting the possibility of a scholarship at a four-year institution—instead choosing to join the sailing club.

Exhausted but glad they'd remembered me, I clutched my carry-on while Mimi squeezed my free hand. Todd rolled along behind us, pulling two suitcases and hefting one duffle bag, which he slung over his shoulder. Like a disembodied brain, I glided out to the curb. All the while, Mimi kept going on about Todd's amazing, "oh so completely palatial," house, with its silver, pine, and navy views of Lake Washington, Mercer Island, and Mt. Rainier, its wrap-around deck and garden of rhododendrons, "So like a retreat for a Samurai."

At last, there'd be real views like those photographed for the travel books I'd perused at Barnes & Nobles, all that Northwest water bubbling out of faucets like pearl essence of white glacier. In the bookstore, I'd imagined nude dips into hot springs that bled out toxins during dawn rituals that left pores as expunged of shit as a fetus's. The idea of frolicking up needle-laden, loamy trails to pluck chanterelles and other edibles for a concoction that tasted of fresh soil, decaying tree bark, and damp pine needles, had been exhilarating, better than a syringe of caffeine. For the first time in two years, I genuinely felt hungry.

But Y oh Y

In those days, you could still see the Olympics without the orange scrim that would eventually surround the metropolis. Unlike me, Mimi found fireside chats, daypacks, and excursions into the mountains, an immune system drain. She would avoid anything that sniffed of a dalliance through the ecosystems of Seattle's Arboretum, let alone those of a mountainside. If it were up to her, she'd growl—an updated Pat Benatar—for an audience at the Showbox. "Who knows," she said while we drove into Seattle, "I might give up Hotel Hospitality for music management—"

Always a crowd pleaser, Mimi avoided anything remotely sub-orbital—which was odd, considering that we'd landed in what everyone called the geek capital of the world. And forget trying to praise the black fingernails of a glass blower, or the saw-dusted scalps and wind-blown skin of lumbermen, or the hazy but contemplative expressions of ex-hippy, commune-lovers who'd been converted to peace-nerds. From the beginning, it was clear that we'd diverged in our interests. So there shouldn't have been anything surprising about what came next. And it all began with that detour to the downtown YMCA.

As soon as he deposited me, my luggage, and Mimi on the doorstep of the YMCA, Todd b-lined his hatchback out of parking, elbow cocked on the windowsill, off to run errands for the boatyard. When we finally unlocked the door to our "new home," I'd already been through a traffic jam of headaches with the overweight woman whose ear-length, chopped hair smelled of coconut oil. Her bifocals had slipped down to the bottom of her miliaed nose. Groaning more than speaking, her breath reeked of decaying pickles, spit flying as she exhaled the word "precious." Instead of using a tissue, she thumbed her nose and added, "Here's the keys," nearly throwing them at our faces. I nearly fainted. And yet, Mimi remained enthusiastic, despite the fact that I warned of the high likelihood that we'd be infected with athlete's foot, if not TB.

Despite its chipped linoleum and depleted furnishings, the YMCA had once been a beauty. Its classic slate façade and elongated windows spoke of a grand history, its high ceilings welcoming late June breezes—likely a bane in the winter. However, these assets collided with hazardous chairs whose foam innards sprang through fabrics haling from the 70s. And fluorescent lighting didn't help to buoy spirits, as it emphasized sleep deprivation and skin afflictions.

Once inside our vacuous but faded room, with its snot-colored carpet and pressboard table, I nearly blurted that I needed to go back to New York. But I caught myself, instead asking Mimi when Todd would return.

"Don't know. He might be coming around dinner, might not. Which brings me to—" she said, turning to my four bags, which slumped on the slime-hued rug like dead men next to her single overnight sack— "a question for you," followed by a pause that was almost a drum roll. "What, and I mean you can be completely honest—and I mean honest. Okay? So but," she lowered her voice as if in collusion with me. "What do you think of him?"

Though I'd spoken to Todd briefly over the phone the night before—which seemed eons ago—I hadn't envisioned him as the overgrown seven-year-old he'd revealed himself to be, with his non-stop smile and cocky but empty chatter, which had a way of catapulting through one's head, especially when we'd sped from SEATAC towards the outlines of downtown.

Of course, I never expected an intellect. After all, Mimi met him at a Club Med. **On Turks and Caicos. Where biceps—not brains—ruled.** All she talked about was the way he opened doors for her, how he paid for everything from that first daiquiri to that last calamari, and how he'd stripped the sarong from her hips that last night on the beach. He even paid for her trip to Seattle a month later. Gentlemanly.

But all I'd seen was a single photo of him in front of a boat, holding a fish line that dangled a finned blur. According to Mimi, she'd devoured the sea creature, which Todd had pan-fried after allowing it to bathe in a bottle of merlot. All of this was alluring, though I'd cautioned her to take it slowly.

"He talks a lot once you get him going," Mimi said, bouncing onto one of the twin beds. "Which I love because you know me. If they don't wag their schlongs, well honey, there ain't **no** reason to be anywhere near a man who isn't a man! Unh-unh!" She shook with laughter, and, when through, eyed me with a sigh. "I so hope you find someone who will make you feel good!" She shoved off her clogs and laced her fingers behind her head, only to sit up, annoyed, and unsuccessfully puff her anorexic pillow. "What is it with the cheapness of this place!" She threw the pillow across the room, where it slammed into the wall.

I leaned against the windowsill, my back to a view of the street, not wanting to say a word because I worried I'd fess up and tell her I was returning home, the first flight out. Hands beneath a cheek, she stared at me as if threading a needle to sew something serious into the conversation. "No really, I'm not one to admit. But I have to say, and I so don't know how I ever! But I have to say, I think he might be special." She propped herself up on an elbow, seeming at once both fidgety and relaxed as she caressed the pearled blanket with an index finger. "And I didn't want to go on about him with you at first because I know you're still dealing with the whole Ben thing," her eyes turned to the tracing of an A on the blanket, "but you know. And I really **really** feel for you about Ben, by the way, but I can't, I just really can't keep anything from you. And you so have to get over the whole *I've been abandoned by life* business. So, sugar, I hope it's okay—" She patted her mattress as if it were Todd's back, meaning for me to sit down next to her.

I nodded in the hollow way that had followed me from kindergarten through high school and college. But if I'd known better, I wouldn't have responded at all.

Crud

By 5:00 PM, when it became obvious that Todd had deserted us to watch UFOs on Orcas Island, Mimi stepped into the hall to use the payphone. In the fading light, I flipped through my Seattle guidebook to search for local restaurants with single $ signs. I had to eat cheap—no more than a $5.00 meal for me. But all I could find downtown were overpriced steak-and-potato joints, take-out Chinese (which meant greasy MSG), non-vegan pizza, and a Benihana. Nothing else was within walking distance. I threw the book aside and gazed out the window to spy an SUV groaning up 4th Avenue. Seattle already marked itself as a town of SUVs, sports cars, and Subarus—taxis-less and devoid of the subway noise I associated with livable cities.

Yes, I'd lived in my fair share of hellholes, but this was another story, with my butt burning from sitting too long on the balsa wood fiasco that was supposed to be a chair but had uneven legs and therefore tipped from side to side. And the prospect of lying down on the twin bed unsettled me. Earlier, while opening a suitcase, I avoided the snarled surface of the blanket tucked around the corners of my bed, worrying about lice, fungus, and bed bugs. That night, after much inspection, I finally pulled back the covers. (Next morning, I'd discover that the translucent sheets were so thin that when I turned over sometime around midnight, my knee poked through its flimsy weave.) By 3 AM, I couldn't get the itch of fungus off my body. I lay tossing but cocooned in a nightmare of fabrics, fearful of staying, fearful of getting up in case a thousand roaches had congregated at my bedside. It didn't help that the 30-year-old carpet—nauseating to the feet, though once a plush gold and chestnut weave—presented sections darkened to the color of sludge, increasing my trepidation. (Why hadn't I packed bed sheets, towels, and flip-flops?)

Woe to the night roamer, who was thoroughly fucked! I had to pee, but the bathroom, lit by a stark fluorescent circle, offered a fan that unleashed an ear-throbbing rattle as it spun dust mites into one's nostrils. If I turned it on, the entire YMCA would have cried murder. So, for the remainder of the night, I blinked at the ceiling while Mimi mumbled in her sleep.

The Hell You're Leaving!

My second evening in Seattle I took a five minute shower and changed into a fresh pair of jeans. All day I'd felt jittery, buzzing from two black cups of Seattle's Best, nearly frothing at the mouth as ultra-oxygenated wind blew down from the mountains. Mimi suggested that if Todd couldn't get his big ass and his miniscule hatchback to the Y, we should grab a bus to Leschi, where we could scrounge up some pasta and tomato sauce with one of Todd's very appealing but already accounted for roommates. Oh, and maybe get a view of "the volcano"—which left me wondering if she meant Mt. Rainier or Todd. Though Todd claimed to enjoy ferrying Mimi around because he hoped she'd accept his engagement ring, settle into a clapboard cottage overlooking his sailboat on Lake Union, and pop out three kids (preferably boys), he listed no less than five excuses for why he couldn't pick us up for dinner.

"And you just know that he's having a little hissy fit right now—" Mimi said, shaking her head and batting her eyelids. "I told you, didn't I—I did—that he wanted me to move in with him? I told you back in New York, right?" In fact, she hadn't, but I set that aside as she continued.

"Well, I am definitely and I mean **definitely** not ready to sign a lease with Mr. Todd—absolutely not! Not with the way he fumigates the bedroom every morning!" She burst into a shoulder-quavering laugh, clapping her legs and showing off her teeth. In New York Mimi had told me she'd been very clear with Todd: She'd rent an apartment with me for at least a year—none of this month-by-month bullshit—and then **maybe** think about moving in with her man. To me she explicitly stated that she'd **never-ever** open an oven (except for the occasional fruit pie) or scrape a frying pan with a wooden spoon—and forget scrubbing toilet bowls or

folding socks. She refused to sponge egg yolk off his plate just because he'd used every other clean dish in the house. Mr. Todd would have to accept her **as is**. Plus, without her, Todd could enjoy beer and football, because she was done with that kind of Sunday fun. No, she would not gorge on vats of chili in the living room and pretend not to be aware of the stench of dirty underwear!

Outside, amid a blur of barely perceptible droplets that pelted the sidewalk, we shambled towards a corner store that sold beer, bananas, Hostess cupcakes and boxes of cold cereal. Mimi, in profile, was a coin constantly flipping between heads and tails. One minute she looked giddy and elated, the next exhausted and dejected.

To keep the hope, I plunged into the past. "Just so you know, I'm so oh! Ver it!" I began, calling up words from our teen years. "I was just thinking—" laughing at myself. "No seriously, do you remember how our mothers used to spend hours talking about the "being" and "doing" energy, and then all those afternoons meditating in the living room and going off to chant at the Ashram. Remember Lakshmi? Remember how I thought you looked like her?" Her profile appeared to be embossed into the gray drizzle that had become the thousand coins falling into Lakshmi's wooden donation box.

Mimi snorted and shook her head. This was her half-laugh, the one that indicated she knew she was supposed to laugh but really didn't think anything was funny. "The Ashram. **Please**! I can't believe you still think of that place. It was so clearly a money laundering operation. I don't care what you think about the Guru. She had something going on with that guy, what's his name? The guy you had a crush on? Krishna?" A flint-like piece of dust grazed my eyeball. I stopped walking, blinking, trying to rub it out. "You know that's not going to help." She said, sounding impatient, all mother-in-a-hurry. "Just let it tear out—"

We were damp through and through by the time we reached the beige market. Mimi threw a five down on the counter of swirled, Formica ice cream, and asked for a pack of Parliaments. "I thought you stopped smoking," I murmured, gripping a box of Shredded Wheat—the only thing vegan and sugarless in the store, other than wilted iceberg lettuce.

"Well, you know. I have my moments." Mimi mumbled, stuffing the cigarette pack and some matches in her knitted shoulder bag. "Must be that I'm a creature who despises fresh air," she said. "Yeah, that's it!" We began walking back. "And you, my god, you and your Shredded Wheat—"
she shook with another wave of laughter as we crossed a pristine street, only to be shaken by the soul-shuddering roar of a swerving SUV with tinted windows. Once the acrid odor of burnt rubber and exhaust lifted, and we discovered we hadn't been hit, the entire city once again swooned
beneath spritzed leaves that felt like a dose of St. John's Wart.

We never made it to Leschi, and I still hadn't mentioned my plan to flee.

Driving

Two days later, I was still snacking on that box of Shredded Wheat. I'd scarfed several meals sitting in the rickety chair at that plywood table, and I was beginning to enjoy the taste of sawdust—which should have filled me up but only lined my stomach with acid. By then, Mimi had smoked several forbidden cigarettes in our snot-colored room, leaving me a nervous wreck:

"Stop that! They'll kick us out!"

When, finally, Todd got over waxing his sailboat, Mimi cried, *Halleluiah!* his tan hatchback panting at the Y's curbside like a wasted canine. Finally, I scooted into the backseat, while Mimi dipped into the front, hugging her knitted shoulder bag, and said with a smile, "So what took you so long!"

Todd, whose massive frame emitted the odors of grilled hamburger and sweat, initiated conversation with what I was fast learning to dislike: a disingenuous, beer-drinking bravado harnessed by Northwestern protocol.

"So Mimi mentioned you've never visited the Northwest," Todd began, as if he hadn't picked me up from the airport days before.

"Oh come on!" Mimi cut in, annoyed to the tenth degree. "Leave it!" He claimed brain-fuzz and switched into suburban father-mode, as if driving his daughter (Mimi) and a friend (me) to a movie, taking pleasure in the sound of his voice.

"Brave of you to fly out without anything or anyone to catch you— no job, no apartment, no family or friends but Mimi—Just picked up and left it all behind. Takes mojo. Heard you'd never been here—just blindly came. Mimi told me all about you. She's all stories and music—am I not right?" His gaze flew off the road and onto Mimi's profile.

"I wouldn't say that, Todd," Mimi murmured. I could tell she wasn't amused because her ears looked uneasy with the windshield as backdrop. But she could change in an instant. That's what made Mimi so mercurial. "The man is one big golden pancake waiting for syrup! No, he's a ridiculous and ludicrous salivating piece of pie!" She snorted a laugh and turned to me. "Didn't I tell you? Didn't I? Ludicrous. What **is** in this Seattle air?! I mean, there's so got to be mind-warping influences, little UFO brain tags floating down, because someone in this car, who likes pretending he's so big and strong is getting carried away—" She fell into a mash-up of giggles and snorts as if the front seat were an orgasmatron.

"Come on, Mimi," his voice turned soft as melted chocolate. "Admit it. You're good at getting people interested in things they wouldn't be interested in if it weren't for you. Look what you did to me." Todd, smiling, slathered on the flattery, bulking up his shoulders like an exotic bird fluffing up its mating feathers. "You crazy little spitfire." He eyed her with a combination of hunger, anger, and amusement. "My little concierge."

This was how we motored the Alaskan Way, the Puget Sound's undulating surface of indigo crosshatched with slate, an occasional boat light slashing it with gold. All that romance shot to hell with, "Jane. Bet you didn't know this is the new Rome. Seven hills." Todd said, nodding as if to music. Maybe he was high. Maybe it was the prospect of sex with Mimi. Or, maybe, just maybe he wanted to dig me out of the picture like an ugly stone in a perfect field.

But what did it matter? Eventually, Todd turned off the overpass and motored while humming, *The Hills Are Alive* from the Sound of Music.

"Oh please," Mimi laughed. "Spare us!"

By the time we were touring Queen Anne, he'd transitioned to college jock, on a rampage as he discussed the pros and cons of improving Lake Union while I leaned my forehead against the window and thought of carrots, peas, and bagels. "Yeah," he continued. "There's not a single place down there with a decent lager. We've got some serious hazing ahead. And that includes Mimi! Right, MEEE?" He glanced at her fingers as she ran them through her hair, his eyebrows going up and down in a 1-2-3 of rapid-fire. We took a sharp turn and my head smacked the glass.

"Shit," Mimi said. "Slow down! Take a breath, will you?"

"Why?" He was laughing. "Everyone gets to see the seven hills, followed by a local brew at the Alibi Room. Or better, I've got a case back at the house." He eyed me in the rearview, and the Shredded Wheat I'd downed that morning burned in my chest. "I highly recommend the Hef, though Mimi says it tastes like piss. But come on. The Hef."

"Okay Todd, you win—I'll have the Hef—" I could tell Mimi was rolling her eyes as she said this. He thumped the wheel with the palm of his hand, causing the horn to burp like a clown.

"Cool! Straight to the deck!" I already felt sick, but Mimi was laughing again.

Other than Rudy, I'd never met anyone who loved the sound of his own voice more than this guy. He nearly munched his way through syllables as if they were honey-coated clusters of northwestern granola. Against that, all I could do was press fingers to my temples.

At a green light, Todd floored the accelerator and we lurched forward.

"Todd! Calm down!!!" Mimi yelled, but he was on a roll.

"Nothing's calm in Seattle! This is my town! WOO HOO!" He cocked his blown-out head towards an invisible stadium. "Go **Seahawks**, Uhun!!!" His fist flew up in solidarity with the team, knuckles hammering the tan padding of the car's ceiling. How had Mimi—who peered out the window with a look of boredom and disgust—gotten herself into this mess? No one needed to ask how long the relationship would last.

Eat Me

As the hatchback squandered fuel and shuddered down to the waterfront, my empty belly shrank into growls. We'd been driving Seattle into sunset and starlight, careening through the I-District and picking up Pike.

Todd pointed out destinations, nodding at Pioneer Square, Elliot Bay Books, Occidental Park, the W Hotel, the Showbox and Paramount marquises already lit for midnight junkies. By then, my eyelids felt like they'd been painted shut, and all I wanted was to bed down and bleed dreams next to a bowl of steamed vegetables.

But everything about Todd's junk heap-of-a-car rattled—the hubcaps, the motor, the springs—which only jangled my nerves, causing my blood sugar to further plummet like the Stock Market after the 1929 crash. Somehow, I rolled down a window where a blast of air that smelled of dead fish spread tears across my cheeks.

As we skimmed Harborview and grazed the base of Capital Hill, Todd tried to sell the hood. "Cheap studios and one bedrooms here. Perfect for single women. Everything's month-to-month! No strings attached!" He added that I'd be close to downtown. And since I didn't own wheels or know anyone who did—other than him—it made sense to be within walking distance of mass transit and shopping. "I can't drive you everywhere. Sorry." He drum-rolled his left palm against the wheel in a way that made me think of cheap cologne. He glanced at Mimi, who sat oddly quiet.

As a shaft of streetlight swept diagonally across her cheekbones and shoulders, she turned to me, her eyes like hot metal balls in dark water. I could tell that he was squeezing her knee, and I stared back as she turned away. "You get it, right?" He murmured, as if we'd all made love. She smiled at him with a tight nod, but then twisted around to look at me again, her eyes swelling with irritation—a look I took to mean that we would stick together, through thick and thin.

At first I had no idea what he meant when he said, "Take what you can get— Forget that apartment in Fremont!" But then I woke up. Had they been looking for places without me? I said, "Fremont? What place in Fremont?"

Mimi glared at Todd, shaking her head. We could have been sitting in an upside down, empty box of Cracker Jacks and still I wouldn't have played nice. I said, "What about Fremont?"

Finally, Mimi spoke, talking like a sitcom girlfriend. "Todd, you need to keep your mouth shut, okay? I mean really, you just need to let this go. Just give it up, okay? We're not renting places tonight—and, actually, I could really use some dinner!"

"Oh come on, MEEE! Tell her." Todd blurted.

"Oh give it up, Todd. I'm not getting the studio, because as anyone can see, you're too busy to help out—" The car gurgled, and Todd kept stinking of hamburger and sweat. My head pounded and the streets blurred. When I shut my eyes, I fell through an endless, thick and foreign atmosphere, all my suitcases sprung open with contents floating away, over the ocean.

"Figure it out, MEEE," Todd's pulsing voice like high blood pressure. "I'm way busy. You don't drive, which means there's no way to Fremont other than a long bus ride." Mimi stared at him, her mouth ajar, eyelids fluttering in shock. "Oh," he kept going. "And do you even have a license? I don't think I even know that. And what about you, Jane?" Through the rearview, he pinned me with the black darts of his pupils as we hung a right turn uphill. "New Yorkers don't drive, right? No drive, no Fremont. If you end up working in Redmond, it's hell catching a bus." I closed my eyes to spiraling arms of fatigue. Was I witnessing their first fight?

Mimi usually didn't take shit, especially from her men. But she didn't say a word. Instead, hostage in his car, she let Todd drone on about commutes and the Metro, which wasn't reliable—especially along the Fremont-Ballard-Madrona corridor.

"So, Jane," he said when we topped Capital Hill. "You haven't mentioned what kind of job you want." He had a stranglehold on the pause that followed, only to unfurl another cause for concern: Had anyone thought about money? Rent might be cheaper than in New York, but a free ride Seattle was not! Especially with the tech boom!

Sucker punched, I winced at the fireworks in my belly—possibly the beginning of an ulcer. "Don't let small town charm fool you," Todd lectured. "There's competition here." Wielding his pickax, Todd completely obliterated his tour-guide surface with, "You're up against Ivies and India. My friend, you know Jack, right MEEE? He's got a Ph.D. from UW? So, he just got an admin job at Microsoft making close to eighty. **And** he's got stock options, which means my man is retiring at thirty!"

At last Mimi took command: "Todd, honey, you know what we're planning to do, so let's just drop it, okay?" Okay, fine, he would, but not before: "I'll drop it. But you told me she came with a job— And now, she says this morning over the phone she doesn't have anything lined up. So. What the hell?"

Fuck Off

It had to be the sex. Why else would she endure his chain talking? And what about the relentless stink of burger grease and ketchup that seemed to collect around and emanate from his groin? Whenever he said something like, "Oh come on Mimi!" the enormous ivory squares of his teeth grazed the saliva glimmering on his lower lip. And as he cycled faster and faster through phrases, his teeth generated a kind of cheese. Anyone sane would blurt, "Enough! Enough already!" But Mimi and I had lost it. We never put our foot down.

It was true: For Mimi sex was currency, endowing her with a "power-wand," which she lorded over other women. She'd started early, manipulating social strings in grade school with the blond girls in designer jeans. Though she tolerated me, by second grade I'd become a shadow next to cooler girls. At lunchtime, I endlessly wandered the playground in my Good Will dungarees, spinning boredom around the flagpole. Eventually, I hung out with the recently relocated from Guatemala whose circle of broken English and hand-sewn clothes one day would be cool but back then ranked me slightly lower on the social scale— As a group, we were invisible.

So, why didn't Mimi have gumption? In Todd's car we were like Charles Lamb's "Superannuated" women. After reading Lamb, I swore never to waste another eight hours shuffling papers and butt licking superiors— But, there I was, licking Todd's butt as he drove me crazy with questions about what I'd do for a living. I fibbed like a first grader, laying out big plans involving an administrative position at the University of Washington, though I had intention of following through.

Years after I'd handed in my undergrad college thesis on the philosophical bridge between Voltaire and Emerson, I still nursed unrealistic ambitions. Frequently, I spent down time revising the thesis, daydreaming about going to grad school. Instead of taking the GREs and sending off an application, I toyed with my toenails and thought of Ben's crooning cock. Under the circumstances, it seemed best to embrace the itinerant life, which meant moving for the sake of moving. It was easier to lie and claim to be job hunting than to wake with nothing to do but walk without destination— which was actually a kind of meditation on the meaninglessness of life. It didn't matter whether I roamed thickets of 500-year-old Douglas fir, or spent whole days flipping through thrice-read Bronte novels. It wouldn't have mattered whether I mowed lawns or dragged garbage bins across the sidewalk, just as it didn't matter whether my toenails split and my hair fell out—because it didn't matter what I did.

True depression had set in.

But "you so completely have opportunity coming to you!" Mimi said before we left New York. "It's completely up to you to create a new perspective." Apparently, I'd be cured by getting over New York, my mother, and Ben—who'd wrecked his body and therefore my future. All I had to do was remove myself from old memories. I could "get a fresh perspective!" on a "Fantasy Island" called "disappearance." So, I took the "get a fresh perspective" jingle to heart, daily chanting the phrase.

What Mimi and Todd didn't know was that I already felt outdated— so **not** able to get perspective. I was an ear of shucked corn, de-kernelled, dried, and left to rot in a field. I was a pair of shoe soles worn to the thinness of a rubber band. I was a chicken bone whose marrow had been sucked out through a straw. I was the cowbell that dangled from the aging neck of a heifer, where I clonged at all the brown brown brown cow pies lying in an autumn field.

The Underwhelming

I maneuvered through my first week in Seattle dumbstruck, mouth ajar, staring in a famished buzz from the backseat of Todd's clunker. Storybook streets blurred by as I clung to Mimi like she was the only branch in the forest called "now." Little did I know that her scarves had already begun to slap back.

Everything started going south with the crickets. They trilled somewhere in the grass as Mimi rummaged through the fridge in search of Todd's beloved Hef. I stood on the deck that extended from the kitchen's sliding glass doors and listened to the insects' choir. Todd leaned on the deck railing, gripping a bottle and squinting at the dark lake that glowed with the reflected bridge and house lights across the way.

"Mimi is fucking crazy and amazing—" he began, gently knocking his bottle against the wood transverse, his shoulders rounded like those of a tired family man. I issued a "mmmm" and mumbled something about how she'd always been a leader. "That's right. Because," he said, squinting at me. "You guys have known each other for how long?" I told him about preschool, wondering why he didn't already know the whole story.

"Know what I like about the big M?" he queried, reminding me of my mother's term for shit: "BM." He tipped back his beer and poured a long amber leg into the tense circle formed by his lips. "I don't just like—" he said, swallowing. I could smell the fermented wheat and yeast trailing his exhalations. Thinning his eyes and nodding, he swigged again, liquid sloshing against the bottle's neck. Shaking his head, he smiled and said, "She carries a tank top like a firing squad." Against this statement, Mimi looked ludicrous through the glass doors where she hunched over the kitchen counter, popping the tops off two beers. And then he was describing the inch or two of brown belly that peeked out between her shirt bottoms and belt buckle. He used hushed tones, as if we were in on a secret. Then he was yammering about the smooth sheen of her skin, how he'd like to lick his way up to her breasts, finally biting his lip when she appeared by our sides. She thrust a bottle into my hand and took a swig from hers, prompting him to step towards her.

"You know what I love about you?" he murmured like a bad commercial, pulling her tallness into his even taller build. His shoulders sloped around hers as if they were spooning in bed; I had to look away. "I love running my fingers through your hair," taking an in-draft of her scalp.

"Smells so good." She laughed, clearly knowing this to be true.

Though Mimi "never, absolutely never," paid full price for designer-brand shampoos, she knew how to cop the freebies. She got away with using the miniscule sample packs because her hair barely grew past her shoulders before wimping out in split ends. Thus, I was floored by Todd's adoration as he extended a single forefinger and brushed a wisp from her forehead as if arranging peacock feathers. All the while, she leaned against him, eyeing me, a smile spreading over her lips.

"You big mischievous puppy—" She simpered. "You're just trying to distract us because you don't want to grill those very expensive steaks your mother carved from that beast. I so know you— But sugar, I'm so and I mean **so** famished! We really need to eat." He leaned into her neck to kiss beneath her ear like the romantic interest in a bad movie, which made me want to leap from the deck and fall hundreds of feet down for a belly flop in the lake.

Mimi shook her head, possibly sensing my disgust, suddenly looking annoyed—even jaded—no sexier than an eighty year old in a gated community of shuffleboard players. "No, no," she said, as if she'd smoked ten thousand cigarettes. She nudged him away with her shoulder. "I'm not letting you change the subject with a lot of smooching. Uh-unh, not on your life!" She moved across the deck towards me.

"But what could be more delicious—" Unbelievably, he plodded after her, his paws combing her wisps. Worse, he flicked his eyes from Mimi's exposed collarbone to my breasts. And then he grabbed her again and began digging his nose into her neck. By now he'd become a cloud of fruit flies swarming around a pile of grapes. If only I could swat him from view.

Beer against chest, I turned to the lights of Mercer Island while Mimi eased herself like a delicate vase from Todd's arms. She settled on a nearby lawn chair, saying, "Okay. Okay. Fine," and lifted her hand to snap fingers at me. "What do you think, Jane?" I stared at her. What did she mean? "So when should Mr. Todd serve dinner? Any ideas?" Before I could answer, she said, "Aren't you hungry? Or are you planning on nibbling a few carrot sticks?" This was the second or third time Mimi had attacked me for being a vegan. I'd always suspected that she found my adoration of animals abhorrent.

"What does that mean?" I asked. "That I'm difficult?" I spoke more to Todd than Mimi, hoping that our common debasement would make us allies. He simply knocked his beer bottle against the railing and whistled. "I see," I said, trying to show nothing but acceptance. "Just give me some lettuce, an apple, anything fruit and vegetable and I'm fine."

"You want an onion—" Todd burped, beginning to crack up. "We've got a bag full—I hear they're good for digestion—" He laughed out loud, jangling over to Mimi where he leaned against her chair. Mimi, too, began laughing, whacking the armrests with her hands. "I think," Todd yelped. "I've got an old rotten tomato in the back of the fridge—"

"Oh my god," Mimi said through hiccups. "It's so true, sugar. I mean, ever since I've known the girl she's been one to eat anything grown in a field. I mean, isn't that just down right saintly! Just give her a potato and she's peachy!" She shook her head with nose squinched up. Eventually, she settled down enough to eye me. And then it was only with a frightening smile.

Get Me Out of Here

"Okay. Right," I said. I had the jitters from the soulless combo of low blood sugar and peer pressure. As far as I knew diabetes didn't run in my family, but who knew. My fingertips had become numb, and I'd heard stories of people with such symptoms collapsing in hypoglycemic fits. It could happen to anyone. But no—I would never fall apart in front of them. No, I'd rather dissolve into a slurry of shit than show Todd that he'd won a match.

I tipped back my bottle and drank the liquid nitrogen—what Todd called Hef— which streamed down my throat and left me buzzing with brain freeze. This would be my dinner, after all, so I'd better drain every last drop.

"Believe it or not," Mimi sang, twirling her watch over her wrist. "The evening is young. It's just 8:30." She twisted around to flirt with her overgrown chump. "Food dude. It's time for food! Gimme some grilled liver!"

It was clear that beyond Todd's ape face Mimi had no reason to gaze at the charred heavens. Rather, her eyes fell to the decking beneath Todd's feet. "Oh my god!" she cried, as if he were standing in a puddle of piss. "Oh my god—Todd! You didn't!" Her face aflame: "Oh my god, you completely crazy old dog!" Laughter, and there was a truckload of it, burst through her beer-engorged lips. "Oh my god—" She pushed the back of her hand against her lips, muffling her words. "Oh shit. What did I say—" She swiveled around to face me. "The little bastard—oh my god—you can always tell—" She whacked the armrests with her palms, her mouth a chasm, her eyes squeezed shut like a newborn freshly squeezed from the womb. I searched the vicinity around Todd, finding nothing except for the expression of tamped down excess washing away the man's bravado. He stood frozen behind her, one hand in the pocket of his shiny trainers.

"What?" Todd blurted. "What did I do now—" But Mimi continued laughing, shaking her head and clutching her belly, unable to catch a breath. It was impossible for anyone but Mimi to know what was so funny.

When she finally calmed down, tears wiped away, we could again hear the crickets chanting Steve Reich's music—the little chanters in the grass. I felt a little like them, humming along and trying to comprehend, destined for one thing: a quick, postcoital death.

Beautiful People

Mimi had always been a tease, but this was ridiculous. She pulled me aside and said, "Jane, you so need to know—I mean, come on…." She had a way of dismissing confusion. "Okay, alright, so never mind. It was just funny. Okay? Let's move on because I am so and I mean **so** ready to eat. Which brings me to, what are we doing here, Mr. Todd? So how about it? Could you figure out which moldy loaf of bread we can grab from your fridge, because there were zilch chips available, and I need to watch myself or I'll eat your kitchen counter and then your roommates. And you know, that'll just get everyone pissed and I mean pissed! So how about some dinner—" Todd, possibly already used to this, brushed a forefinger over his brow. Later in the confines of the YMCA, she would call him her lumbering beast of prey: "The boy's a bison. He needs some serious hormone therapy for his randy pants, if you know what I mean!"

But to Todd, she said, "If you're absolutely sure you're going to keep those steaks for yourself, then maybe we should just get some Madrona take-out." Todd stared at her from his lowly position, having hunkered down to his knees.

"Whatever you want," he murmured, placing his bottle on the deck boards. He was not quite in love; instead he was docile, pliant, and dumbstruck. As if on cue, the crickets vibrated and Coltrane broke from a neighboring house that had been teasing us with the aromas of simmering tomato and onion—a pot roast in wine. Cooking smells wafted over the deck chairs, cornering our stomachs. What was it with the olfactory nerve's ability to supersede the best intentions? I hadn't eaten meat in years, not since my parents' divorce when we'd dined on meat stew during a disastrous last meal that left serving bowls smashed against the floor, gravy spreading across the rug.

"Look at her," Todd murmured. "Great face, expressive eyes, incredible, amazing, kissable lips." True, Mimi, as one of the beautiful people, had some enviable genetic material, but pointing it out at that moment only made her furious.

Arms wrapped around her knees, she turned to me. "Oh my god, Jane. I've had it. Let's go. It's getting cold out here, and I'm famished. I need dinner!" She got up, shaking herself as if done with everything Todd. "We'll walk if we have to. Come on—" She grabbed my arm with her icy hand and stumbled forward.

"Hey. Wait a minute—" Todd half-assed bolted after us. "I'm sorry—What, Mimi?" But she only twined her arms more tightly around mine, while he stopped at the sliding glass doors and we pressed forward, leaving him behind.

Sugar

Two nights later, they'd forgiven each other. Yes, we'd dropped twenty-five bucks on greasy Chinese after a two-mile trek to the nearest restaurant, which was in the process of closing when we offered to pay extra to place a last order.

"I can't believe you didn't drive us—" Mimi was saying.

"You didn't let me. You were out the door so fast I didn't know what was up."

"Right—" She was snuggling up to him again, laughing but not laughing. We'd managed to land in Todd's kitchen—a wasteland of Formica and cabinets devoid of even the most basic ingredients: salt, pepper, sugar, a true blue apple. This lack drove Mimi crazy, because it meant someone— a.k.a. Todd—would have to drive to QFC for some staples. And besides, she wouldn't give up the idea of baking a pie, even after Todd lit the coals for a barbecue, those oft-talked about steaks (small as biscuits) finally sweating on the counter.

"No way," Mimi said, drying her hands on the ratty t-shirt hanging from the oven handle. "Tonight we are so going to have some serious and I mean **serious** pie! Get some paper, sugar, and I'll write up a list. We are going to sup!" Ever faithful, Todd lapped up Mimi's commands, taking the scrap of paper she thrust into his hand before he scuttled out the door. Moments later, Mimi and I stood next to each other, the exhaust belched from Todd's hatchback still floating through the kitchen.

"You are so going to love my apple pie!" She said as if she'd never said it before, wiping her hands against each other. She knew I couldn't sample a single bite. If I so much as bit into an apple, a thousand red helmets would march like infantry over the battlefield of my cheeks. Between acne and anaphylactic fits, I had little desire to indulge in sugar. I'd come to a place of peace regarding my history of lesions. I'd spent years experimenting with witch hazel, Stridex, benzoyl peroxide, Retin A, and antibiotic creams. Nothing worked. Finally, at age twenty, I'd deduced that sugar was the culprit. I knew this because not hours after downing a handful of grapes, I'd sprout three large pustules around the base of my nose. If I nibbled a brownie, five or six nodules would bloom on my forehead. Two brownies and my chin gave way to a mottled patch of red undergrowth. If I succumbed to birthday cake, volcanic eruptions devastated my cheeks. Eating no longer included baked pleasures, because there was no cure but abstinence.

And Mimi hated me for this. She equated pie with medicine. According to her, I ate like a freak. Years prior, when she'd learned of my vegan, sugarless diet, she'd rolled her eyes and told me I should be institutionalized—which I'd taken as an off-handed, "Whatever!"

"You are not, and I mean **not**—" Mimi said, throwing the hand wipe/t-shirt over her shoulder. "Going to miss this!" The kitchen felt as vacuous as the Krubera cave when she pulled a metal rack from the oven and rattled it on the stovetop, prepping for the moment when Todd would walk through the door with a dozen bags of groceries she hadn't paid for. "And you know, Todd is so not going to eat that entire pie, because it'll just make him a gas bag!"

Later, after the groceries had arrived and Todd had b-lined for the bathroom and then the barbecue, the pie sizzling in the oven, she said as if she'd never said it before, "Never **ever** are you going to eat a dessert this good **ever** again—Unless I bake it! Word of warning: I'm not modest. Watch: There won't be a single crumb left in the neighborhood!"

When the steaming apple-stuffed pustule emerged from the oven, Mimi wielded her pie cutter like a butcher. She knifed the guts of the pie, causing a sucking sound as she pulled the sharp edge from the crumbling crust with its smattering of glazed apples. Liquid innards gushed over the metal as Todd stood guard, panting amazement: "Wow! Wow! I need that now!" as if he'd never before witnessed hot pie.

"Go on. Salivate. Look what you've been missing. You fool." Mimi said, eyeing me with a smile. She flipped the first sugar-slick slice onto a plate. "Take a whiff of this." She circulated the plate and fanned the steam in my direction. "You are **so not** going to miss this—" The hell I would. I'd spend another meal-less evening, famished and enraged rather than ply myself with that pimple pusher.

By the time Mimi began yawning, piecrust lay like ripped cardboard on her plate and my stomach had shrunk to the size of an embryo. But I wouldn't touch the steak or apple concoction wallowing on my plate. Somehow, charred meat of apple reminded me of drug dealers in front of a bodega.

"Mmmm!" Mimi exhaled, patting her belly. She sat on a barstool, propped on her elbow next to a counter covered in apple cores that looked like storm waste. "I am so completely done—" She stared at me with revulsion. "You didn't touch a bite."

I knew she hated me for not celebrating her family's pie recipe— pies that had been lauded by a neighborhood-baking guru named Cooper Biedermeier, a Viennese pastry chef transplanted to midtown in the late

1960s. Word had it that Biedermeier personally served pastries to Katherine Hepburn. For decades, UN reps paid homage to the man, downing thousands of his desserts. On one legendary occasion, an Israeli and an Egyptian haggled over a peace treaty at the bakery's counter. If Biedermeier could praise Mimi's family's pies then I had to be a food Nazi not to partake. In fact, unbeknownst to me, by not tasting I'd initiated an act of defiance that would place my friendship with Mimi in jeopardy.

Only now do I fully understand. Mimi's pies were like edible babies. Rejecting them was tantamount to child abuse. Forgoing pie meant forgoing Mimi. But I didn't see it that way at the time. All I saw was my own face, potentially dotted with a thousand zits. I never imagined that she'd simply exhale me from her life like cigarette smoke.

Meanwhile, Todd had devoured three slices, and sat picking his teeth with a fingernail as he grunted with pleasure.

Hideous

Worse than acne were my gargantuan thighs. True, I wanted to be like Twiggy. I wanted to be a skeletal ghost woman who jerked down the runway with jagged hipbones. I wanted her sallow expression—that hint of starvation. I wanted to be rescued.

But no one rescued the kind of woman who looked "Reubenesque—" What 20th century loony wanted a bloated cloud of flesh marred by a blush? My father Stan was the first to dub me zaftig. Right. I can just imagine the Twitter feed today: *Zaftig bottle blond with acne-prone skin takes Lexington Avenue by storm!*

So, freshman year at college I cut out dairy and meat products, bleached my black hair frost-white and went home on vacations to power walk from the Upper East Side to the Battery. Sophomore and junior years I teetered along an anorexic cliffside, fully understanding that I should hide my anxiety somewhere other than the refrigerator (or in my case, the lack thereof). But, fighting off fits of binging and purging was like fighting time— next to impossible.

After a while, I outgrew my Twiggy complex. Anorexia and bulimia became a mission to save the world. As Americans swelled to Michelin Man behemoths, I devised a philosophy of "energy conservation." Rather than solely conserving fossil fuels, I focused on edible plant matter. By subsisting on uncooked cellulose, I could minimize what would later be called my "carbon footprint."

No need to fall for a midnight snack or over-indulge the senses by ingesting methane-generating cattle. America was ill, whole families devastated by food fetishes, whole office buildings embroiled in tornadoes of Crispy Crème feasting that left millions of people diabetic. I vowed never to fall prey to chocolate, butter, or lard. A rebel, a fighter for the right to refuse food, I'd revel in hunger. I'd viscerally imbibe a third world lifestyle despite access to a first world economy. My figure would emulate a series of 1970s idols such as Olivia Newton John, Lynda Carter, and Diana Ross. I'd be like Sandy in *Grease*, warbling refrains in a black spandex body suit that sheathed my matchstick legs. I would live right, and "living right," meant my thighs would never look like they'd been wrapped in bubble wrap. Essentially, by munching cellulose I'd be stripped clean of cellulite.

During a last summer with my parents, I refused the Entenmann's cookies Stan stashed like pure gold in his upper desk drawer, certain that watching Dan Rather didn't mean I had to stuff my face with chips and salsa.

Later, in college, when friends sweated through heat waves wearing khakis or smock-dresses, I took pride in wandering the quad in cut-offs. It didn't matter that fat (now spelled "p-h-a-t") had become stylish, or that by the mid-90s a woman's cleavage ran down to her belly button—her butt a duplicate of her outsized frontal load. I'd never give in to the hip-hop aesthetic. I'd never be described as Buddha-esque. My style would be the style that saved the world.

So, I felt dizzy leaning against Todd's kitchen counter. I hadn't eaten a single crumb since a bowl of dry Shredded Wheat at 8:00 AM. But I'd become used to feeling fuzzy headed. Countless times I'd dodged fainting spells. By then, I'd mastered the inconspicuous head thrust between legs: tip head down, focus on a single point, take slow, deep breaths. "You look wiped." Mimi sang, rubbing her belly. I knew better than to respond.

Later, back at YMCA central, after I'd pushed the last button of Shredded Wheat into my mouth, I told Mimi to stop "worrying" about me. She'd broken out of self-absorption while Todd drove us back, suggesting that I'd turn into a stalk of celery. "You so have to eat!" she'd said, "Or you'll disappear."

Washing up, she wouldn't let the subject go. "Any conversation about anorexia has got to be a conversation about control, sexuality, and fear of death—" She spoke while leaning over the bathroom sink, splashing water on her face.

"I disagree." I said, standing in the doorway in my pajamas and my unlaced sneakers. I watched with fascination as Mimi dabbed a towel against her forehead. She even smiled at herself, presumably to check for food between her teeth.

Unlike me, she'd thought ahead and packed flip-flops. Somehow, to my mind, this made her more adult, as did the blue satin lingerie that swished around her thighs. "There's nothing sexually wrong with me," I asserted. "Sugar and sex don't go together. And what? Are we all going to go out and fuck the first guy we meet?"

"I'm so not saying that, Jane. You so know that—" She stared at me as if I'd cursed her out.

"Well—I'm not sure actually—"

"Oh please." She threw her towel over her shoulder and brushed past me towards her bed. "Just give it up. Everything is about sex and death. It's so clear." Obsessed with Freud, Mimi wouldn't back down from her argument, wrongly asserting that nervosa stemmed from a desire to annihilate that raw slice of animal instinct in every human heart.

"Just think about it," Mimi continued as she climbed into bed, "Teeny tiny hips and thighs and flat-girl-bellies so completely peg a woman at her most vulnerable sexual moment,"—a moment when male animals most desired females, the time of thrusting through a girl's hymen. More importantly, she added, "tweezer-thighs are weak," making the "chamber of love" (how else was she supposed to describe the vagina?) more accessible than the overwhelming vice-like grip of thunder thighs.

Plumping her pillow, Mimi yammered on about how all desirable women had legs that looked weak—even in our grandparents' generation. "Okay, I'll admit," she said, "Ms. Marilyn wasn't Miss Pencil Legs—But what about what's her name? Betty Grable? She was like a **huge** sex symbol back in the day—completely Miss Stick Hips." Though I agreed—sort of—I continued to disagree that my problem began and ended with sexual frustration and a fear of death.

Turning off the light next to her bed, Mimi wouldn't give it up. "You so completely have a problem with sex, girl! You haven't been with anyone since Ben. And that's been like, what? Two years?" This wasn't entirely true—but I didn't intend to give Mimi any more ammo. For now, Nora Lovins's spiritual coterie and their incestuous dealings would remain a secret.

Vulcan, On The Deck

The next morning, my stomach was in an uproar. I'd lain in bed past midnight, restless and frightened, anxious about money, going over a list of future expenses drawn against my dwindling savings. How I eventually drifted off was a mystery. But Mimi had woken me by slipping into my bed and whispering morning breath in my face. "Come on, Sugar, let's go catch the sunrise!" As we stumbled towards a café through the sunless morning, she again brought up the topic. "You're so going to disappear if you don't ingest something other than Shredded Wheat!" I wouldn't disappear; I'd change the subject.

"I want to see the volcano," I said. At noon, I got my wish. Once again, we stood on Todd's deck as Mt. Rainier faded in and out, and a slash of sunlight grew over Lake Washington, the clouds breaking apart. It was so easy, all this shifting sky—easy as a car rolling off a road; easy as Namananda's appearances and disappearances. What appeared and disappeared came without a plan. A fawn could splinter a windshield and crumple in a roadside death. A volcano could shimmer or it could blow. And yet, that day it rose above the clouds as surely as Mimi prepared for a game of "War." She shuffled cards while Todd showed his huge teeth. And then they bickered while I stared out at Rainier, which hovered like a close encounter.

Though the temperature grazed 70, I shivered on a deck chair, wrapping myself in a scratchy wool blanket pulled from Todd's living room sofa, whose stained velour cushions stank of dry vomit and stale popcorn. While Mimi and Todd battled with cards, my blanket absorbed tears of condensation I'd forgotten to wipe from the chair, leaving my thighs and back damp, making me shiver more.

It turned out Todd's rental house rested on a lip of rock, the entire glass and wood structure daring the hillside to quake. Far from comforting, the house felt precarious—a bit like my financial situation. One push and we'd all be out on the street. If I didn't get a job soon, I'd end up wearing a mini skirt and patent leather halter-top, swinging my hips on a street corner.

"You so can't believe," Mimi said when the game of War was finally over and Todd had sprinted to the bathroom. "How absolutely and resolutely magnificent I think this place is!" Hair dangled over her eyes, and she combed it back from her forehead with both hands. Taking a deep breath as if inhaling the entire world, she said, "Ah! I could sit here for like forever—" and stretched her legs, kicking off her clogs. Half smiling, half frowning, she added, "But then, Todd is totally **not** a morning person—"

"I wouldn't say that!" Todd laughed, bounding back onto the deck, which rattled under his weight. "And what the hell are you doing under that blanket?" He'd finally noticed me, his jaw askew. "It's fucking summer—"

"Don't know," I said. He frowned, but let it go, maybe because his housemates still lay in bed, one of them with a bad case of sleep apnea. We could hear every snort.

"Yeah," Todd said, "Pete's a screwball but nicer'n anyone I know."

As if we shared a secret, Mimi smiled at me. Suddenly we were in tutus, playing house under her mother's grand piano. "Come here, Jane!" She patted the chair next to hers. "You just know that boy is never and I mean **never** going to appreciate beauty!" She lapsed into one of her soundless laughs, shaking her head and squeezing her eyes shut. "And how, let me just ask, **how** will he ever get through this thing called life?!" She raised a forefinger to her ear and twirled it around in a loony tune circle. "I so can't get over that fruitcake of a boy!"

Break Out

I didn't really know Mimi after all. As days passed, I seemed to know less and less of her. I felt like tinfoil ripped from a box, wrinkling at the meaninglessness of being unfurled. With every intention of playing the good friend and savoring morning air, all I could think about was eating and not eating, walking and not walking, washing and not washing. Even so, not once did I phone my mother, though many times I wanted to call, to cry, to ask her if I could come back and stay with her. Regression had set in. But I knew she'd only ask, "Have you taken your vitamins?"

In the YMCA's bathroom, I vomited the pizza I'd scraped clean of cheese after Mimi thrust it at me— A day later, up came a basket of French fries I hadn't ordered. Acid broke down the walls of my stomach as I croaked, "Mimi," the morning after we drank a half bottle of tequila and fell asleep at the Leschi house. I swayed in front of Todd's mattress. Todd was hollering in the shower while I floated over Mimi's half-lidded eyes, confused by her misaligned morning hair and her smooth forehead, pearl light slipping through the blinds. "I need to go home—"

Meditative, she pondered my statement, praying hands beneath one ear. I collapsed into a cold plastic chair next to the bed. What I wanted to say amounted to more than I could say to her face. So I thought about it.

This whole experience is way over my head. I want to eat what I want—walk where I want and go to sleep in my own bed. And don't make me sleep on Todd's filthy sofa ever again! But I could only burp up cheap booze, my esophagus filled with crude oil while stinging bees swarmed around my heavy, waterlogged legs. An ache pulsed my temples, eyelids heavy as velvet.

"Maybe I should fly back to New York next week," I murmured, envisioning an oval window, hearing the sound of germ-infested, 727 air gushing over my face like a waterfall. "I could stay with my mom maybe—" Nora would never take me in, but I had to pretend it was possible.

"I so can't believe," Mimi yawned, propping herself on an elbow, nude shoulder blades becoming deep hollows. "What are you saying?" She stared at me, her eyes sharpening with adrenaline—the precursor of a fight. "So, you're actually thinking after all that you've done to get here, you're thinking that you're going to turn around and go back to that cesspool of a city? Oh my god! I can't believe what I'm hearing!" She expelled a breath, half-barking, half-laughing. "I'm stunned!" From the bathroom down the hall, I heard Todd misfiring the notes of "Purple Rain" through a riff of water.

I hunched forward, staring at the crusted carpet and the way my untied sneakers fit on my feckless feet. "You so have to give it at least two months. Okay?" Her voice sounded flat but final. "You're completely freaking out." Throwing back the covers, she sat up in her pink tube top and black panties, her back to me. Sun finally trickled through the blinds. "And appreciate. Just appreciate this amazing place."

I'm So Over This

At 9:30, we again endured Todd's kitchen. This time a nearly naked man emerged from the hallway of exhaled garlic, sweat, and unwashed hair. Mimi barely seemed to notice the way his Speedos bulged around his balls. Scratching armpits, he yawned, "morning ladies," as if we were his nursemaids. His hyper-muscled arms and legs reminded me of twisted pipe cleaners attached to his torso, everything covered by a net of dark curls. He reeked a friends-with-benefits M.O. "Making coffee?" he mumbled. Scratching his scalp with a "who gives a damn" expression, he resembled a short, dark, squinting Clint Eastwood, hung over. Every time he yawned we got a whiff of his caustic breath.

"Pete, you so know I don't do coffee," Mimi smiled, shaking back her wisps. "So please don't go around acting like the evildoer tempting an innocent." Having showered, brushed her teeth, and changed into jeans, Mimi looked frisky enough to play baseball. Like her, I'd endured the scum-enshrouded shower stall in Todd's bathroom—though unlike her, my cheeks felt like they'd been steamrolled with Saran Wrap after an episode with Todd's bar of Dial soap. "But, there's always chai—" she added because chai was Mimi's everything drink, a morning necessity thanks to Feng Shui and Cathy.

"No fucking way—" Pete rasped, "I'm preparing for assault practice—" He weakly fisted the air, oblivious to the lack of introduction, and continued to ignore me in favor of studying a brew-stained mug. Though my hair lay limp with self-abnegation and my chin sprouted two hard boils, I took offense. But of course I slipped quietly onto a stool. "Hot water's all I demand," Pete managed, wagging his mug. "I'm easy—" At this point, I expected him to pull down his Speedos and gas my face.

With a tip of her head, Mimi ran the faucet, filled the kettle, and placed it on a burner while Pete rummaged through the freezer, pulling out a can of French Market New Orleans coffee. "Just brought this baby back last week—" He head-knocked the can.

"Oh hey," Mimi said when the water boiled and the small talk about the French Quarter had dwindled to one-liners. "I almost forgot. This is Jane; Jane this is Pete." Turning to me she added: "Pete works with Todd at the boat yard and pretty much runs the place." She handed me a half washed ceramic bowl of chai, which burned my palms until it landed on the counter.

"Pleasure—" Pete muttered, pulling a small plate from a shelf. He didn't look at me, but slid the plate and his mug along the Formica counter until he found a spot comfortably far away. Dropping two black scoops into his cup, he poured steam and addressed Mimi: "How's the job search?" His Adam's apple stuck out as he slumped on a stool and blew on his brew.

"Hey, whassup, bro!" Todd said, crashing the party. "You left before I could get a hold of you—" He was semi-dressed in fire engine red basketball shorts, hair dripping onto the towel thrown over his shoulders. Like everyone else, he scratched his scalp. Did the sofa breed lice?

Todd elbowed Mimi and kissed the back of her neck, glancing up at me with his lips pressed to her skin. I looked away. "Can I have a sip?" he asked, placing arms around her waist.

"Not so fast, big guy— This isn't what you think it is." Once again, Mimi sounded like a TV show.

"Aw woman!" Todd said, a parody of a Southern Baptist. "Not more chai. No Baby! Where be the *caffey*? Next thing," he said addressing Pete. "Them dumb fucks be drinking hashish." Turning back to Mimi: "Seattle, woman! This is Seattle!"

"Careful man," Pete said, his lips flirting with the black liquid in his cup. "Chai's infectious. I hear the ladies siphon the stuff from teapots and pour whole gallons into dudes' mouths—" Pete tipped back his mug, gulped, and winked like a French guy toasting himself.

"Shit, give me that cup—" Todd yelled, making a faux move to grab Pete's mug. Suddenly it was countertop basketball with Pete bursting into skittish laughter and sashaying, Speedos and coffee alike, across the kitchen. Half the cup spilled onto the countertop; the other half splashed onto the floor and Pete's thigh. "Shit!" he yelped, his leg already red. "Holy fuck! That burns!"

"There you two go!" Mimi said, shaking her head. She turned no-nonsense eyebrows on Pete, her mouth a straight line, ruling the kitchen. "So, once you two get this," eyebrows indicating the kitchen, "and yourselves cleaned up—Mr. Todd, yes, I'm speaking to you—maybe we can talk about heading downtown for a drop off at the good old Y?" All business, pounding Todd with her eyeballs, she grabbed my arm and said, "Come on, Jane. I'm so over this! Let's leave these two to their antics!" And to the boys: "Really, can we just get a move on?"

<u>Whatever, Motherfucker</u>

But no. There wouldn't be another box of Shredded Wheat at the Y. And, no I wouldn't grab the payphone to call my mother—or book that ticket back East. Instead, while Mimi took her shower, Pete sidled up to my kitchen stool to ask what I thought of Seattle.

"Don't know—" I said, unwilling to reveal my desire to flee. In addition to garlic and head lice, he now stank of coffee. Unnerved by all the pungency and proximity—I had a great view of the pores of his nose—I held my breath.

True, next to him everything felt like a warning label revealing shame. True, I hadn't brushed my teeth either. But I had an excuse: There hadn't been a toothbrush. And at least I'd made an attempt to clean up by swishing someone else's mouthwash and by scraping my tongue with my fingernails.

Pores and stink aside, Pete appeared almost decent in ripped khaki shorts and a navy blue t-shirt, a style that gave him a rough, well-muscled allure. "Haven't been in town long," I continued, turning my face to show my better cheek. "It's interesting here—I like the views, though I'm not crazy about the Y." I hoped to appear blasé as I shrugged and yammered and scraped my stool back by a couple of inches. He nodded, snapped his fingers against his palm, and asked if I'd been to the San Juan Islands yet.

When I shook my head, he grew excited. "Go. Now," he said, brightness around his eyes. "Before summer's over—" He'd provide me with all the info I needed, knew of a great little cabin where I could head out to a meadow at night and watch the sky do weird things. "Most of the time it's overcast, but once in a while—I'll get you all the info." Clearly, that was his job. And my job was to be grateful and impressed. "Just go before it gets ugly in October. Most people go in July, August, think they'll never leave. I knew a guy, got there after the 4th, bought a house early August, sold it for half price after the New Year—" He smiled at the toughness of his lower arms, and at the tan ring of coffee on the counter gaping up like a mouth.

"You guys ever clean this place?" I said, eyeing the stain among a hundred other coffee cup stains. "Wipe everything down. You know, you could get Ecoli or Salmonella—" He stared at me as if I'd told him to slice open his neck. He said nothing for a long moment, and then wandered to the sink to douse the lower portion of the t-shirt he'd slipped on after spilling coffee on his leg. Lackadaisically, he began to wipe down the counter, missing several spots but gazing at me as if saying, "Does that please you, Madam?" For a moment I thought he might tear off his shirt, run for me, and fuck me on the counter.

"So, you're here for good?" he said instead when he finished cleaning.

He aired the shirt by wagging it back and forth over his belly. I shrugged, and he slid a bare elbow along the still grimy but now damp Formica. He settled on a barstool, kept his t-shirt on, but with his pointer finger, drew an invisible face on the counter. I liked his fingers, but looked away.

"Aren't you going to change?" I said, nodding at his wet t-shirt. I covered the boils on my chin with a fist and stared through the sliding glass doors where tissue-like layers of humidity surrounded Mt. Rainier. He stood up and watched me.

"Okay—" he said, but didn't move. I could hear befuddlement and anger in his voice.

"Well," I said. From my vantage point, the volcano's massive head had been painted on an unreal piece of ether. It was completely removed from the reality of the traffic traveling across the lake. "You're lucky. It's really beautiful here."

I watched Mimi stretching on the deck, her short hair bound in an orange scarf, Levi's ripped to threads at the knee, one of Todd's oversized brown sweatshirts tied like an afterthought about her shoulders. Todd, in a red hoodie, hunkered on a lounge chair. Mimi settled on his lap and faced him with pouted lips. Morning sun broke through a hole in the cloud cover, making them glow. They whispered and nodded, last night's sex softening their features. Noses grazed cheeks, kisses became smiles. "And the problem is," I said, watching Mimi toy with a cluster of Todd's hair. "You people don't appreciate it—"

"Yeah, right," Pete said after a long pause, "right." I heard him drumming fingers against his palm. "Anyhow. Welcome. Enjoy the view." Out of the corner of my eye I saw him raise his chin at the sliding glass doors, and then head for the hallway. But then he stopped and turned back. "You know, she usually hides. We don't often see her. It's good luck."

And then he drummed his palm again. "So, the Y. You girls want a ride?" The sound of him was beginning to hurt my ears. In fact, everything about him, including his mind, made me hurt.

"Are you sexist?" I asked, no longer caring what I was saying the way I didn't care about my drab hair, my filmed-over teeth, or the boils on my chin. "Because I'm not a *girl*. Girls went out of fashion with *gals* in the 70s." He stared at me with something hard and flat.

"Motherfucker. You're really a piece of work." He said, moving away from me. "I'm out of here—" He wrenched open the sliding glass doors, startling Mimi from Todd's lips, and leaving me to the stench of his testosterone.

Beaten Up

"It could be worse."

Hiding

When not in Todd's kitchen, tossing in the Y's infested bedding, or stuffing my face with Shredded Wheat, I plodded the streets. My legs were encased in jeans so stiff with dirt that I worried I'd be mistaken for the homeless women I saw wandering the waterfront. Still, I tried to tamp down anger and anxiety. It had been impulsive of me to follow Mimi. What had possessed me to so casually throw away a job and a rented room?

All I could do was contemplate my lack of purpose. I had eons of unpaid time while Mimi already had a temp job. I spent hours worrying about my savings. Not counting the cost of the Y, I'd squandered nearly $70 a week—which meant that after a month there'd be $300 less in the kitty. Cash dwindling, I avoided every extra cost. To save, I "borrowed" soap, shampoo, and toothpaste from Mimi's toiletries, and snatched extra napkins from cafes to be used as sanitary pads. In the mornings, I wandered through Pike's Place Market, picking at the free samples but buying nothing.

In the afternoons, I traced neighborhoods with my feet. Sometimes I topped Capitol Hill and dropped down towards Madison Park with its matronly houses, front porches built for families that wore ironed jeans and plaid shirts. Sometimes I walked Belltown, aiming for the Space Needle and City Center, where I stared at the dancing fountain and tried not to smell the popcorn rattling their glass cabinets. I hiked up Queen Anne, winded and fragile and hungry for the forbidden butter rolls emanating from a hidden shop.

In Wallingford, I caught the Burk-Gilman trail, where there was rumored to be a Troll whose flared nostrils and bulbous lips I didn't find until winter. Wanting to be invisible, I took routes far from commercial districts. And if someone walked towards me, I crossed the street feeling fetid.

These were aimless hours of shambling curved streets of clapboard homes painted blue, green, and gray with front yards of hydrangeas, rhododendrons, dahlias and peonies. I couldn't help envying the family rooms decorated with pottery and stained glass, mantles of candles and figurines, everything giving off security. But all I could do was walk until the balls of my feet became bruised, stopping only to pee in public restrooms.

On more than one occasion, I felt myself trailed by an invisible entity. But then, whoever or whatever I sensed either turned at an intersection or pulled car keys from his pocket to point and shoot at an SUV. Stumbling into the end of a sidewalk overlooking the Cascades and Mt. Rainier, I grew detached and light-headed, symptoms of malnutrition, straining to keep balance as blankness re-congealed into the real.

At the end of the day, my feet burned and my stomach fought spasms as I returned to the Y, which had rewarded my long stay with a strange psoriasis-like rash under my jaw—the probable result of fungus nesting in the pilled blanket that grazed the bottom of my chin during sleep. I didn't have a doctor or insurance, so I lived with my new ailment.

On the nights when Mimi stayed at the Y instead of at Todd's, she slept deeply while I tossed until I got out of bed to watch the street lamps flicker. A last ferry horn often blared over the water. No traffic, only the wan streetlamp until morning, when Mimi woke. All her smiles, all her urges to cuddle—she called me to her bed in the absence of Todd. I held back, uncomfortable. Instead, I pulled on jogging pants still damp with sweat and headed for the waterfront, where I breathed the Puget Sound's salt, diesel, and tanker oil, barely noticing Bainbridge Island or the Olympics. I dashed past the Aquarium, the fish markets with their minerals and rancid fish guts. I ran towards Myrtle Edwards Park, pounding the bike trail by the rail lines, only stopping at the grain elevator where ships named "HanJin" and "Cosco" gathered or deposited cargo. I huffed and turned around in a dozen circles, breathing in the grain dust, wanting the arctic air with its billions of decaying pine needles to clear me out and make me forget everything.

Ignoramus

Daily I threw my body against the landscape while Mimi left for work. Occasionally, we went out together—usually to apartment hunt. On those occasions, we stopped at a café for her must-have chai where she lapped up whipped cream while I stared out a window. Because most of her dinners were assembled at Todd's—while mine were devoured in the sparseness of our room—she didn't have to worry about her budget; thus the whipped cream chais.

In fact, I hadn't been back to Todd's for dinner in some time. Since my interaction with Pete, the house in Leschi had virtually vanished. In fact, there'd been few invitations at all—just two, and they had been off-handed invitations to dine with Todd and Mimi at a restaurant. However, the "I know a place that has big bowls of lettuce—" had been a turn off. Who felt comfortable spending $10 on a dinner that could be had for $2?

The first time I declined the invitation, Mimi said, "I so don't buy your excuse about money!" We were in the room at the Y, and she was trying on clothing for the evening. "You either completely detest Todd or are still sulking over Ben—" In those days, I simply sat stunned when I heard the name "Ben," not yet realizing that whenever she mentioned Ben, it was to make me bend to her wishes. If I responded, I probably didn't say, "Just leave it alone," as I should have.

Slowly I began to understand that Mimi thrived on verbal combat. It finally made sense. After all, her mother had raised her for corporate leadership—especially because her father had died in protest. How had I overlooked this one-two-punch in Mimi's background? Why hadn't I foreseen the blows I'd receive once I relied entirely upon her? Now in a superior position, she could squeeze me like a rubber figurine, press me down to a fraction of my size. Had this always been her plan? Perhaps I'd ignored her faults all those years, overlooking her dark side in favor of her "cosmic nature." Thanks to stories about Namananda, I had become a completely malleable pushover.

Just Joking

The morning Mimi sipped her triple foam vanilla caramel mocha chai whatever, she squinted her eyes and wouldn't let anything go. "So, what's bothering you? All week you've been acting like I'm infected." This accusation not only came out of nowhere—as we'd been chatting about her new job at the W Hotel—but it also sounded like something she might say to Todd. I'd been staring out the window, thinking how I'd buy that ticket back to New York.

More confused than annoyed, I told her to relax; I was fine. And what was she talking about, "infected"?

"Oh come on, Jane. You completely know what I'm talking about!" Her voice had turned into a quavering needle—thin and sharp. You couldn't call it all-out fury, but it was pretty close to the precipice. True, by then Mimi's moodiness had become familiar, but familiarity hadn't curbed the problem of reflux. My throat seized, and I began to cough uncontrollably while she slurped at the last drops of Seattle's Best's sugary manifesto. Straining for air, I bee-lined for the gratis water cooler that lay across the cafe, pouring and then dousing my dry throat with cup after cup. Catching my breath, my pulse pounding, I looked around the shot joint with its worn sofas and sticky tabletops, wondering why I had to return to Mimi's side. But a moment later there I was, feeling like a leashed dog as I explained that I truly hadn't meant to act indifferently.

If chai surged through her bloodstream, I couldn't be held responsible. But that didn't mean Mimi had to agree with anything I said or did or believed in. "You'd better spit it out now," she said before throwing back her head for the last drops that couldn't be siphoned through the straw. "Because," she continued, smacking the cup against the table. "I am not and I mean **not** going to sit around and be someone's battling ram, got it?" Her eyes shot darts against Ella Fitzgerald's "you say to-**may**-toe, and I say toe-**mah**-toe." My stomach a mosh pit, I focused on everything but Mimi, including the line of morning desperadoes waiting for bitter cups of blackness that pretended to contain hope.

Wondering what could be an acceptable explanation for something I hadn't done, I searched the transients. I liked the dreadlocks most, because they seemed approachable, while the one's in combat gear shut me down. Most wore their homes on their backs, some toting musical instruments. All, like me, needed a shower.

"Mimi." I whispered through the rising café din. "What do you want me to say?" This was my buddy. We'd spent hours laughing over a hundred pranks like the mug of coffee mixed with orange juice and milk that we once offered her mother. We'd devoured brownies and Saturday Night Live together. Hoping to send a stranger a message, we crafted "fish lines" of string with notes taped to the ends, gleefully casting them out her 10th story window, only to get outed by the doorman below when a pack of McDonald's cookies landed on a pedestrian's head.

Had Mimi been the driver of these crazy schemes? I suspected so as she sprayed me down with her fire hose of accusations. Nothing she said made any sense. As adults, we should have been reasonable citizens. And yet, here she was, this unnerving person, accusing me.

"I haven't been avoiding you." I said.

"Oh please!" she spat, anger narrowing her eyes. She crumpled her cup until it resembled a totaled automobile. I focused on a self-reflecting, young Yule Brynner who wrote in his journal, his slumped shoulders, black coat, shredded jeans, and pierced nose reminiscent of Chiron. "You've so completely been avoiding me!" No matter what I said, my words would be whipped through the blades of her anger until I was pureed into oblivion, because there had never been a warm, cuddly, enthusiastic, pie-making, soul-shaking lover of life. There had only been a girl who flared her nostrils and hoofed the dust.

Keep Going

"You know what—" I said, when we passed by the Pike's Place fish guys hollering over the salmon and white fish. I'd concocted a good lie, ready to take the path of least resistance. "Maybe it's just that I haven't been sleeping well." Mimi shook her head. She understood what I didn't yet understand.

<u>Long Day's Journey</u>

The din of the cafe surged again. It was the next morning. Or maybe I've got all the memories twisted up. But the espresso machine whirred, and someone hammered out the grinds and the cups started moving while morning chatter mounted.

Maybe I should have found a payphone and flown back that very day. It probably would have been better for all of us. But maybe not, considering what eventually came to pass. But in the end, I tried to be strong, stay the course, and fight the panic.

Mimi picked up her crumpled cup, because every morning that I lived with her in Seattle she had a crumpled cup, and she held it like a baseball. For a moment, I thought she might throw it at my face. But she flung it at the table, where it thumped like a body before landing on the floor by my feet. If not for the background noise, the world would have gawked.

"Never mind—" she expelled, staring at me as the distant notes of Mozart's Glass Harmonica hung in the air, knowing that I wanted to paint the sky as a pearl that rolled down the back of the morning. "Let's just let it go—okay?" Mimi finally said of yet another accusation left unexplained by me. "I've had enough stupidity this week to burst every blood vessel in my head. Come on." Her face an inscrutable series of ink blots dropped in the margins, she left me like a fried bird at a picnic: ready to be torn apart by the hungry.

<u>Morbid</u>

Still, I refused to call my mother because I had something to prove. And, for a while, I actually believed I could bury Ben beneath the mud of each day. But when Mimi and I looked at two apartments near Capital Hill—which Todd deemed "a bad idea" after Mimi circled the ads and sold them to me as "way cool"—I pretended I didn't miss Ben.

According to the ads, both apartments were priced at $700, had ample light, spacious closets, and shared laundry facilities—perfect for a young couple beginning a new life together. Only problem: Mimi and I were not a couple. But that hardly mattered because the first "way cool" building reminded me of a structure from Superman's Metropolis—angled and gargoyled, straight out of the 40s. Plus, its 12-story, brick and limestone stature was within walking distance of the Paramount, the whole package a dream after the single-room shitholes people rented in New York for four times the price.

Sweat soaked our shirts and speckled our foreheads and upper lips as we waited for the bus that whirred towards us like a green and yellow, antennaed insect whose electric wires occasionally sparked. When the vehicle's body jerked to a halt, we boarded at the back to avoid paying—part of Mimi's plan to cut costs.

At Boren Avenue, our stop, Mimi stared at a faded warehouse and said nothing. At the sight of the building, Mimi quickened her pace, purse pressed against her black leather jacket. It was hot, but she gazed ahead, avoiding small talk. I kept pace, puzzled by the unnecessary rush. Once again, it was clear: I'd said something that upset her, though no one could have known what. And wasn't it odd to be treating an apartment viewing like a job interview? Was that the problem? Had I dressed wrong even though I wore my best outfit—slacks and a button down shirt—keeping opinions to myself?

Or did it have to do with the night before, when she'd sat at my bedside, smiling at a book I was reading after she and Todd had inhaled their platters of garlic? When I'd glanced up, she breathed, "You so know," already laughing in that noiseless way that signaled her best mood. "You so have to know that that boy, that absolutely **unbelievably** no good boy is up to something. It's just like him to spread a little butter on my bread before dinner and say he has a surprise for me tomorrow night—but I just know he's going to hand over something like a box of dried fish or a lock of his dead grandmother's hair— But if he thinks I'm going to lie around tossing through the night thinking about a box with a ring or wishing I were in his bed— Oh my god! That is so just like him and so not me!" She'd grabbed my hand and caressed my fingers, shuddering through silent laughter.

As usual, I'd thanked the forces of nature that my friend had returned from the land of crumpled coffee cups. So, I ventured something like: "Yeah, he strikes me as a bit clueless and maybe just a tad-bit manipulative at the edges." Not the best choice, but somehow, at the time, Mimi didn't seem to mind.

We chatted for about ten minutes with most of the conversation idling on Todd and his roommates—Pete a brief point of contention— before she sprang to her bed and burrowed beneath covers with, "Ugh! I am sooooo completely wasted. And we have all that work to do tomorrow—" Grateful for the congenial chat, I fell asleep feeling as though I'd been reunited with her better side.

But now, panting before the stately, brick edifice whose doorways were flanked with white columns, Mimi barely seemed conversational. She muttered, "decent exterior," and flicked eyes from my shoulder up to the second floor ledge.

In New York, the building would have catered to bankers, lawyers, and ad executives. Here, however, no fewer than five vacancies and a basement of washing machines were destined to be shared with bike messengers and café baristas.

Mimi dialed a number into the silver intercom perched next to the entrance. Moments later, the apartment manager—a flash of discordant color introducing herself as Flo—arrived with clipped syllables. "Well, hello, hello, welcome. Why don't you two ladies step inside here—" A round woman wearing eyeglasses with that squared-off-circa-1960-design my mother modeled until 1984 when my father convinced her to update her style, Flo emitted a certain matronly trustworthiness that Mimi glommed onto. Ear-length, bottle-blond (because everyone was blond!) hair puffed like meringue around her forehead, easily making her the more glamorous cousin of the woman who ran the front desk at the Y.

"So nice to meet you," Flo continued, extending a large, mannish hand. She wore peach polyester leggings that were too tight around the butt, every flesh roll and pucker revealed. A floral, polyester shirt, circa 1975, terminated at a patent leather belt, while thick rubber-soled shoes completed the project of Flo's retro-but-not-so-cool fashion choices. Overwhelmed by the odor of dried carnations and fish oil emanating from her smile, I shook her hand.

"I know you'll enjoy the view from our 9th floor apartment," Flo said, over-enunciating as if expecting each word to unveil missed meaning. I could tell Mimi found the woman hilarious, because she shook Flo's hand with a crinkled nose and a breathy titter.

"Why don't we go up and take a look?" Flo said, all teeth and good cheer. She guided us to the elevator, pressing the button with her index finger, which lingered on the plastic while she said: "I live on the 10th floor. You just can't find anything this nice at this price anywhere in Seattle!"

Peering around the ruby hallway, at the patterned carmine and cream carpet that devoured my feet, at the wallpaper of roses over whipped cream, I felt lost. Everything stank of peach and rose. And I felt like a faded letter on a page of to many brush strokes—though after the Y anything would do.

Mimi, on the other hand, "ooohed" and "ahhed," clearly enthralled. And at apartment 911—where the stale carpet cleaner met us in an expansive, red living room of windows that overlooked downtown—Mimi stood in what appeared to be awe. She gazed at the view, all tranquility and relief.

After taking it in, she moved around with excitement, sidling up to a built-in bookshelf. "Oh this is so cute! And look at this amazing nook!" She nodded at an indented section of wall. "And how's the neighborhood?" she asked, enthusiasm in her voice as she ran fingers along the bookshelf's wood stained surface. Flo beamed with her hands folded in front of her peach-encased belly.

"We're so close to downtown, it's just a hop, skip, and a jump!" she purred, her eyes crinkling with a crusty-pie kindness. She pulled the apartment keys from her pant pocket and began absent-mindedly jingling them in a free hand. And then she circled to the panoramic window and swept her other hand grandly across the blue. "It really is magnificent, isn't it?" I half-heartedly nodded, feeling vertigo as I stared at the jagged downtown skyline against the Olympics, while Mimi beamed agreement and circumnavigated the living room, stopping to squint and contemplate the panorama from several spots. I remained stationary.

There was something off about the room—perhaps its shape or the way the light slanted over the blood-red carpet. The room reminded me of the set for a murder mystery, or more accurately, the set of a Tim Burton film—one that had something to do with the death of Edward Hopper. And that didn't take into consideration the fact that the entire building lent itself to *The Shining*.

Watching Flo work to sell the place, I had my doubts. "Has there been any crime in the area?" I ventured, finally inserting an opinion in the form of inquiry. I specifically wondered if that very apartment had been the location of a sacrificial ritual. I aimed for a solid but friendly tone so as not to ruffle Mimi. Flo's smile remained a stiff line as she adjusted her floral midriff to the jingle of her keys, and then crossed her arms.

"That's just the kind of question—" She began, releasing a small titter, light glancing off her yellowing teeth. "So many newcomers ask. Well. Let me just say, Seattle is a city. And there is always something going on in a city." Mimi and I momentarily connected eyes—her's erupting fury, mine pouring out concern.

No Way!

Todd, as our Seattle tour guide, had zero background as a crime statistician. But Mimi insisted he knew one street from another. "My boyfriend so loves this area!" she said.

"I agree," Flo said. "There's a lot to love here." You could have burned "bullshit" into the rug and she'd have still smiled. "Sure, you've got your basic robberies, drug dealing, and different sorts of crimes popping up all the time in neighborhoods all over town. Just the other day, in fact, I read about a woman robbed at gunpoint over in Fremont, if you can believe that. And, you know how it is, there's always something going on downtown or over in Queen Anne or even here next to Capital Hill. We get a lot of people coming from all over the country—these young people who hitch hike—" she spoke the word as two— "Here for the drugs. And you know how it is. They bring their pit bulls along too. It's something recent. I don't remember our town being this way when I was growing up." She shook her head and adjusted herself again, her keys jingling like miniature cowbells. "It was a much nicer place, like a small town. It was such a nice place when I was young, where you knew everyone and not just your neighbors. I can tell you that." She turned away and walked over to the kitchen counter, clinking her keys down on the tan countertop. She stopped before a cabinet and opened it to peer inside. "These are lovely big shelves, aren't they?"

"Well," Mimi said, her smile fading into seriousness. "I know I'm interested. We're so glad to know this place is available. Is your price firm?" I looked at her with our agreed upon signal: widening eyes and a slight shake of the head. Flo caught the gesture and picked up her keys from the counter.

"If it were up to me, dear—" Reluctance tugged at the corners of Flo's mouth. "I'd give it to you for $650, but the landlord has been firm about rental rates since I've managed the place. I can't go to him with a special request. He just won't accept it."

Mimi nodded and asked if we could have a moment to look around on our own. Moments later we stood behind the mirrored closet door of the second bedroom and whispered our opinions. Stooping beneath a closet rod, Mimi argued her point.

"Jane, we so absolutely need to take this! I can't believe you're creating an issue. The view is amazing— Think of all the parties we could have here—" I shook my head and insisted that we see the second $700 listing. "Oh come on— You are being so unreasonable." Anger pinched her forehead and claustrophobia dilated my pupils. "This is Seattle. You've lived on the Lower Eastside. *THE LOWER EASTSIDE!*" More bark than whisper. "A few robberies, some drugs. So what! It's nothing. I so can't believe you're dragging your feet. I know this place will go if we don't sign the lease right here, right now." I broke in, mentioning the blood-red carpet, the whole *Shining* reference, but she rolled her eyes and turned everything on its head. "Just imagine what we could do with that living room! We could so have a mystery night! We could so invite people over for ghost stories. Oh my god! How much fun would that be? And how can you not love that amazing view and that wide open kitchen?"

"Mimi—" I whispered in the ugly rose-scented closet that could have starred in *Rosemary's Baby*. "I didn't come across the country to sign a lease on a place where the crime rate rivals Bedford Sty—"

"Oh my god! Where did you get that? Oh my god—You, Jane, are so ridiculous. Look at you! Rivaling Bedford Sty! Nothing in Seattle rivals Bed Sty! We don't even know what the crime rate is— Remember that hole-in-the-wall in Jackson Heights? Oh my god—" Changing tactics, she smiled in her big mama-cheeks way, all down home southern love. "This is so not the same thing. This is such an **amazing** place!"

But I wouldn't budge. I remained opposed to leasing apartment 911 as I bathed in images of blood pouring out of the bathtub and poltergeists hollering down the emergency stairwell. Resentment burning in her voice, Mimi's enthusiasm faded as she said, "You are so completely unbelievable!" Her eyes glazed and her lips tightened. But still, she wouldn't give up. "Okay, fine. I'll pay $100 more if you'll sign." Plus, she'd give me the larger bedroom with the walk-in closet. But none of these concessions swayed me. Finally, sulking and squinting eyes, she would "let it go." But only if we'd absolutely returned if the other place didn't pan out.

Okay, But

Again she stared ahead and crushed her bag against her ribcage—a sign I'd been crossed off her good side nearly forever. When we arrived at the unthinkable intersection of Harvard Avenue East and Republican (we'd been raised by diehard comrades, who never could have afforded Harvard, let alone the Republican party) she muttered, "You are so not going to find me living here. Don't even get your hopes up. This is so over-the-top, suburban," which puzzled me, because Todd's Leschi looked like deep countryside in comparison.

True, we stood on a block of craftsman houses with fenced-in front yards. And true, the rectangular red brick building greened the corner with Japanese box hedging. But Broadway was one block away.

Scowling at the boarded-up windows of the clapboard house two doors down, Mimi sneered at the green awning as we stepped into a small lobby of wood molding, prewar but well-maintained brass mailboxes, and new beige carpeting that didn't smell of roses or blood. It helped that the apartment manager was the crunchy type of inconclusive age who led us to apartment 202 as if we'd joined him on a camping trip, opening the door with, "Yeah, it's real comfy—" and "Never had any problems with the plumbing or heating—"

I immediately felt at home, the arched doorways like those of my childhood home on Lexington Avenue, which Nora was relentlessly fighting to keep. I appreciated the stained redwood molding, the ample entry that led to the living room, the miniscule enamel-colored octagonal tiles in what my father, Stan, would have called "the snort lair" (a.k.a. the bathroom), the crafted wood and glass cupboards in the kitchen—which included a dining nook equipped with built in bookshelves—not to mention the adorable copper sconces in the bedrooms. Something about the layout reminded me of better times, when Nora and Stan whipped up Sunday breakfasts of pancakes, cut fruit, and orange juice and actually laughed at the table. "I could be happy here—" I said to myself as Mimi wandered to a living room window to *humph* reluctantly. I could hear her mumbling as she opened closet doors and rattled the bathroom cabinets. I gazed at the ceiling, wanting all of it. This would be our home.

It didn't take long for her to appear in the kitchen. She'd ceased mumbling and was hugging her handbag with a squint that I couldn't read. She came up to me and took my arm, steering me into the smaller of the two bedrooms.

"So? What do you think?" I asked. She smiled, glanced at the molded ceiling and began nodding. Yes, she admitted, this most definitely and absolutely would be our place. I gawked, excited but still not sure whether she meant what I thought she meant. I'd been certain we'd never see eye-to-eye.

But yes, she laughed, this had real charm while the other place felt like a cranky-at-the-heals retirement high rise. Plus, she "got a kick" from the corporate gray carpet. "And I'm so glad there's a Starbucks and QFC a block away! We can go for snack runs at midnight!" She was actually laughing.

"But we so need to figure out this rent issue," she added, becoming serious. It was impossible to overlook the fact that one of the bedrooms was a measly 8 x 8 while the other was an ample 12 x 15. To discuss this, we again pressed into a closet. Who, Mimi asked, would pay for what? And what did I think about the apartment manager, Jack—who was humming what sounded like Yankee Doodle in the kitchen?

"He's so absolutely the quintessential Seattle man—" Mimi whispered in the closet. "He's so clearly very cool. What do you think?" I didn't know Jack from a jackhammer, but he seemed like a diehard outdoor enthusiast with his hiking boots and parachute pants that unzipped at the knee to become shorts—which made his stocky build and Irish-looking grin endearing. He reminded me of my uncle Morris—Nora's brother—who'd made his living carving and selling totem poles to college students in Eugene, Oregon. And you had to like that when Jack learned we didn't own a car, he'd pushed his hands into his pockets and said, "Need a ride or anything, just knock on my door—apartment 350."

"Yeah," I whispered. "He's okay—but what about the small bedroom? Who's going to get it?"

Ignoring my question, Mimi pursued the subject. "I so like that he's young and getting a Ph.D. in Geology. You two could be really cute together—" She peered around the closet door, trying to peek at Jack as he hummed and wandered into the living room. "He's so generous!" When Mimi mentioned we didn't own furniture, Jack offered the use of his truck for hauling. "I mean that other woman, what's her face in the peach pants, all she could talk about was crime. She so completely didn't want anything to do with us! And wasn't it so nice of Jack to tell you about that macrobiotic cafe down the street." She nudged me with a nod and a serious stare.

As Jack dashed upstairs to get paperwork, Mimi beamed like a matchmaker hitting jackpot, murmuring, "Sugar, I am so glad we're finally getting settled! It was so right of us to check this place out. I just know this is going to be the most amazing year! Awe, it's so good to be with an old friend. After all we've been through, this is just so perfect." She wrapped an arm over my shoulder and shook me against her armpit.

Before our search, Mimi had convinced me there was no choice but to lie about my employment status—something I should have opposed with every ethical bone in my body. But I was so desperate for a home that she barely needed to reason.

"You just know there's no way we'll get out of that skanky Y unless we say we both have jobs," she'd said. Anyone could see we had no choice. This was true; after more than a month of showering in flip-flops, of tossing beneath infested blankets, of negotiating sweaty stairwells blocked by muttering occupants in smocks, I'd become as vulnerable as a sandbar in the Pacific. Plus, I'd always been too cautious, and caution would get me nowhere. As Mimi pointed out, before I could get a job, I needed a home. And before I could get a home, I needed a job. This catch-22 felt like the insane laws of an absolutist regime we'd never overthrow unless we mastered the lying game. Deceit was our only hope.

Thus, Todd would "hire" me as an administrator, and using his title as partial owner of a boat refinishing business—which was really a nothing business—he'd type a confirmation of employment. On paper, it would look like I made an annual salary of $25,000 a year, which would give Mimi and me a combined annual income of $50,000. For this favor, I should have been grateful—yet another reason why I'd signed the lease before addressing the issue of who would camp out in the 8 x 8 bedroom. We slapped down a $500 deposit ($250 each) plus one month's rent (split equally) and pocketed the keys to our new apartment, ending an afternoon that left us in two different places: Mimi in the carefree and guiltless zone of the laughing class, myself carrying the burden of our fib for the weeks and months to come.

Capital Hill

Not two days after Jack folded our $500 check and shoved it in his pocket, a shirtless drunk sat on our kitchen counter and yelled that everyone needed to get naked. Of course Todd—wearing no shoes, basketball shorts and a "wife beater" that showed his underarm hair—lumbered into our living room gripping two Coronas in his pumped hands, thrusting one at Mimi, the other at me.

"Ladies!" He beamed like a winner, bumping his Sierra Nevada against Mimi's lesser bottle. "So you finally have your own pad!" once again the suburban dad. He hunkered down on his knees in front of Mimi—who lounged on the floor—wiggling his belly and singing: "Time to celebrate mamacita!" Meanwhile, he wagged the opening of his bottle at my groin in a grossly sexual overture that belonged in a frat house, not my new living room. "Time for some serious part-ay-ying—"

He slumped into Mimi, placing his head in her lap, and began playing footsie with the carpet while waving his beer. "You big, no good fool!" Mimi murmured, smiling but serious. She pushed his head off her lap and pulled knees to her chest. "You just know this is such an amazing little pad, and that Jane and I are so completely going to make this the best little sanctuary this side of Capitol Hill." Mimi looked ready to hula in her she-warrior manifestation: an orange halter-top and ripped jeans, hair spiked against a royal blue scarf tied at the hairline. I, on the other hand, nested in baggies and a moth-eaten sweater the color of seawater, having picked up the whole ragged mess at a garage sale that morning.

"We need furniture—" I mumbled, noting the unobstructed carpet. Our only decoration was the strand of Christmas lights Todd had installed an hour earlier in anticipation of our "house warming" party.

"Right you are, Sugar. Tomorrow— And, oh my god, I so need a futon! Todd, you absolutely need to drive me out to that store we saw—" She eyed him as he rested on his belly, fists under his chin. He gazed at her with a leer, and then pushed up to crawling position.

Grabbing Mimi's hand, he mashed his lips into her skin, and cried: "Mamacita, your wish is my command! Tell me when and I'll be there!" This was the kind of mockery no one could take seriously. How could Mimi stand him?

But before she could blow him off, we were joined by two unfamiliar characters, who wandered through the open front door. "Way to go!" They said in unison, with one adding, "Nasty location, dude!" Todd rushed at his buddies, all quarterback, slapping their chests and grabbing more beers from the ice-filled kitchen sink.

Soon, the apartment packed more quarterbacks and cheerleaders, chips and salsa flowing over our barren, once pristine living room carpet, which fast became a mash of crumbs, everything reeking of beer and stomach acid. A plastic cooler someone had dragged in from their pick-up landed in our bathtub, not far from the three couples that lounged in the entry and monopolized the plates of Ritz crackers and Cracker Barrel cheese

Mimi had purchased, last minute, at the QFC. The idea of a housewarming party hadn't been mine.

Sleepless (In Seattle)

But we'd already been through our first sleepless night (like that damn movie) on the living room floor, huddling beneath two of Todd's stinky blankets. And Mimi had already downed her first Starbucks chai in the kitchen nook—a mistake. The combo of whipped cream and built-in cabinets had whip-lashed Mimi into hyper-drive. She insisted we christen our bedrooms as if they were the hulls of newborn ships. At first, she suggested smashing Coronas against the doors of each room—but then she settled for a "simple" party.

"We so have to celebrate!!!" She cried, forgetting that we still hadn't figured out who would get the 12 x 15 room. I made a bid for it, explaining that I needed space for my computer—which Nora would soon ship. It was clear that the 8 x 8 room wasn't large enough for a desk.

"So get a twin bed," Mimi suggested, leaning against the kitchen counter. When I told her I didn't like that idea, she added, "You keep saying you're not planning on meeting anyone. You told me yourself that you definitely aren't inviting anyone back here. Not after Ben. Everyone can see that you're still healing. I'm just saying."

Speechless, I stared at her. Once again she'd brought up Ben, taking out the knife when it suited her. Shocked and furious, I hardly knew what to say. But she knew how to stifle a fire.

"I know!" She said. "I know! How about this—just put your desk in the living room! I don't mind— We'll put the TV in my room." We didn't have a TV—only Todd had a TV—but I said nothing. "That way you can have the whole living room to yourself."

I reminded her that I often woke before sunrise, that I preferred to sit at a desk in a bedroom rather than a common living space where just about every visitor would be able to flip through my books and papers.

"Sugar, one thing you just don't get is how small that bedroom is. I mean you definitely see that I can't fit a queen size bed in there, right?" Which led Mimi to argue that only the larger bedroom could hold a larger bed. And anyone could see that Todd's enormous, basketball legs really wouldn't fit in the smaller room. "The man is a giant and definitely cannot and I mean **cannot** fit into a double!" Because, of course Todd would very occasionally spend the night—

Throughout this discussion, we'd kept our voices low, maintaining calm. But when she mentioned that Todd would occasionally spend the night, I grew uncertain and edgy.

"Mimi," I said, taking my time, trying to breathe. "What about you two stay at the place in Leschi. I don't have other options like you—and I need a place where I won't be interrupted if I need to work at my computer." This would be my only argument, the only position I could take. A bag of cookies Mimi had dropped on the kitchen counter the night before suddenly became a temporary distraction. Ravenous but clearly frustrated, she stuffed her hand into the bag and pulled out a cluster of cookies, biting into the brittle ovals and releasing a shower of crumbs.

"I'm not and I mean **not**," she said through bites, "going to spend another night in skanky boy land!" She glared at me, and then headed for the bathroom to pee with the door wide open. "You just know I cannot, **will not**. You get that, right?" I listened as she unraveled toilet paper, crumpled it into her palm, wiped, and allowed the toilet seat to clatter shut without a flush. "Especially with all those guys in underwear floating around the kitchen like its Hugh Hefner's palace. No thank you—" She stumbled out into the living room carrying a pair of sweat pants, which she pulled on over a pair of silk shorts. Braless in a t-shirt that said "sayonara," she didn't bother with anything else.

"And by the way, have you thought about the fact that you don't have a job?" Mimi asked. I refused to answer that.

The next morning, she shook her head over another Starbucks chai, the light blue hair band that she regularly wore pinching her temples in what looked like a brain-dimming grip. "Unh-uh. No thank you. I am so completely done with that house. And you know that guy Pete? He so completely and absolutely will **not** let Todd have a moment to himself. He so unrelentingly gloms on. And his girlfriend—she's such a case!" Rolling her eyes, Mimi reminded me of some lost high school narcissist, leaving me with one question: What was I doing in Seattle?

Meltdown

And so, the inevitable: The tiger growled from its cage in the corner. "You really don't get it—" Mimi said from her spot on the carpet while the party became a frat-fest. The Christmas lights blinked on and off, causing the mob to blink on and off too. Similarly, all evening Mimi had been flip-flopping from glares to smiles. And of course, Todd had been at her elbow, egging her on and angling for the bigger room with the lock on the door—the one with two windows that opened to the clusters of ivy in the back lot. Somehow he'd gotten Mimi to caress his hair as he balanced his Sierra Nevada on his palm, where it wobbled on calluses. "It's a matter of two instead of one!" Mimi continued, straining over the din that came from two-dozen mouths and someone's borrowed boom box. "You so have to see that!!!"

By now, couples were draped over each other, filling the apartment with sweat and bad breath. One guy stumbled and fell to the ground. Another, with a shirtless, protruding belly and raw elbows, walked on his knees and caused the floor to tremble when he collapsed in laughter, his face pierced by what seemed to me the pain of life. I stared at the dark coils of hair riding up his belly as everything jiggled like a poached egg, his arms flapping in what could have been seen as hilarity, but which I saw as horror. This was, amazingly, Pete. And next to him was yet another blond wagging her body parts in front of him like a cartoon. She had tremendous vase-hips, her pink palms pounding each other in ear-splintering claps. And then came her rowdy laugh with the words: "YOU BUM!"

I turned away in time to detect Todd's, "So, you're getting a futon tomorrow, and I'm staying over for our first romantic evening, right?" Mimi smiled down at him, picking at the hairs on his forehead and wagging her head with a few sidelong glances at me. And then Pete grabbed the blond's monster hips and pulled her down, causing an earth-shaking thump that made the entire building tremble—no one but me thinking of the apartment dwellers below.

"You so completely have me—" Mimi warbled. "But Jane keeps getting in the way of me being haved!" She knew I could hear her, but I wouldn't give her the benefit of a response. I cleared my throat and stood up to a head rush, which only encouraged her to raise her voice. "And I so absolutely need and I mean **need** another beer because tomorrow we must and I mean **must** get that queen size futon! I don't care what Jane does. I am so moving into that bedroom, and I am not sleeping another night on this ridiculous and unbearable floor!" Unbearable it was with all the chips floating like dinghies across the carpet.

Laughter surged around me like water bubbles popping in my ears. Pete bellowed, "HOAH!" when the blond toyed with his chest. And someone else yelled, "TODD, DUDE, SO WHEN CAN WE HAVE SPAGHETTI AND CLAM SAUCE?" This possibly was code for a faintly sexual promise made earlier in the evening.

Eyes glazed, I stumbled towards the toilet, in search of peace, somewhere along the way detecting a bundle of vibrating moans like no one I wanted to know in a bad movie, because the perfume of well-greased erogenous zones sickened me.

I backed away, the sexual fact receding like Ben's disfigurement, my mind and body suddenly as alone as an orphan. Had I ever left the New Jersey hospital with its pissing troll sculptures? When had I last wandered into my mother's Upper East Side apartment? Had my father just overturned the dining table and shattered the casserole dish and all the plates? Did he threaten to shoot my mother and me if we didn't accept his terms? Was my father's forehead a knot of blood vessels that connected to Ben's busted body? Did the car swerve or did it speed straight into the tree? There'd been no reason for any of it. Except that he could have shot us, but then he didn't. And instead of burning rubber and righting itself, the car had kept going until it crunched in on itself.

Paranoia

While everyone breathed down each other's necks, someone knocked at the front door, and only I could hear it from my cave, wondering if it was an ax murderer. No one opened the door, so I took my scissors with me and opened up, and then he said:

Quiet

"We have a policy," He stood in a traditional TV get-up, wearing a papa's plaid pajamas, paternal eyeglasses resting on his nose, hair askew at his right temple. It was past midnight, he said. There'd been complaints. He could sleep through anything, but not the others.

He looked uncomfortable, arms crossed over his chest. Yawning into a fist, he blinked at me with red-rimmed eyes, adding, "We don't allow loud parties after 10:00 PM. House rules. I don't want to call the police, but the other tenants will if I don't." I nodded as the room behind me hiccuping mad giggles. "Okay. So have everything quiet in five and we're all good—" More nodding.

The party hadn't been my idea. Nor had the lie. But he'd caught me, the party ending in the pit of my stomach. He smiled as if he knew this.

"Oh, by the way," He added. "Welcome. Hope your first nights have been okay—" I never stopped nodding, worn out and ashamed. Such a nice guy. In bare feet, Jack turned down the hall, probably headed for his boyfriend.

Ridiculous

The next afternoon, after all the chips and dip had been swept into a bin leaving the stench of spoiled salsa, Todd and Mimi wrestled a monstrous, rolled-up futon into the middle of our living room. I stood watch, wondering how I'd ever sleep again as I imagined a thousand and one nights of hugging the carpet in my sleeping bag while Mimi slept in the clouds.

Dropping the rolled bedding like a dead body, they collapsed over it, laughing.

"So where do we put this thing?" Todd asked, breathless, scratching armpits, and leaning over his haunches, looking very much like a Great Dane.

"Don't ask—" Mimi said, glaring at me from her spot against the plastic-encased bedding, which now looked like a giant maggot.

Solutions

The issue of "where" became a nightmare, during which the maggot, as I began to think of it, dominated our lives—an annoying pest. During the day, I collided with it, tripped over it, and nearly broke my nose on it. At night, I cowered away from it, not wanting to disturb its resident sleepers. In the morning, Mimi refused to convert it into a sofa, claiming that a futon needed to breathe to retain its fluffiness. Like any living creature, she said, it needed lots of air. As far as I knew, the thing deserved to be dumped out the window. But eventually, after days of negotiation, argument, and anger we settled the issue.

Everything came down to economics.

One evening, Mimi came to me with a proposition. If I really and truly MUST have the bigger room, then I'd better be able to pay up. Since, she said, I had close to $10,000 in savings (how she'd gotten this info, I'll never know!) while she had a poorly paid job, it made sense that I pay $150 more per month. But if she took the smaller room she'd have to fold the futon in half—which meant the futon wouldn't be able to breathe.

"I propose that you buy me another futon if this one goes flat," she said, adding that when Todd slept over, he'd have to wrestle the futon into the living room so that it could be opened up to full size. "And if his back goes out, you'll have to help me move it back into my room."

As for Mimi's shelving and storage: One corner of the living room—preferably under an Indian tapestry—would be designated for her stuff. For some reason, I was overjoyed and more than willing to meet these terms. By then, I'd do almost anything for a door that locked—which only the larger room had—especially with all the 10:00 PM spaghetti dinners.

True, dinnertime had never been my favorite time of day. Most dinners involved standing at the counter in front of QFC-bagged salad greens, which were occasionally supplemented with frozen peas or corn that I boiled in an aluminum pot—an item I'd purchased at a garage sale with a pair of Faye Dunaway sunglasses that I never wore. I pretended not to notice the pan-fried smells emanating from the cartons of takeout Mimi and Todd sometimes ordered—though I did notice the grease stains on our once-pristine living room rug. Often they ignored me while I read the literature of the Canon in my locked bedroom. It was hard not to be aware of the growing resentment festering in the silences between their whispers. When I heard their murmurs through the door, I couldn't help but place my book face down and listen, wanting their secrets.

Todd's Again

Though they rarely included me—and never invited me to slurp pasta with them—one evening, the sun still pulsing at 6 PM, they surprised me. Mimi rapped on my door and, looking tired but patient, stuck her head into my room. "Hey. Todd's having one of his barbecues." She eyed my sleeping bag and the pile of clothes strewn next to my "grounded" computer, which had arrived a day earlier. "We're driving over in an hour. You can come if you want." The idea of another night of stuffing my face with bagged salad and infusing myself with the mildewed pages of *Great Expectations* felt like prison next to the galactic freedom of guzzling beer in front of Mt. Rainier. I accepted.

Once again Todd yammered, all suburban dad, as he drove us through bucolic neighborhoods. Again, he leaned on the deck railing, beer swinging precariously like a diamond necklace between his fingertips. Again, I stood next to him, though this time I worried over the clueless neighbor below who could too easily be knocked out by a piece of Todd's beer-bottle sky.

"People," Todd bellowed as the deck shrieked against his weight. "It doesn't get better than this!" Spreading his arms towards the lake, his beer about to free-fall, he flung back his head like a character in Flashdance. This had to be his Shiva pose, or barring that, his absolutist-Stalinista pose. Because, every A-frame, colonial, and oversized cottage perched on the hillside beneath him had suddenly become a series of waves over which his voice surfed. "Damn!" he yelled. "I love this City!"

Turning to the rest of us, he leered a mouth of unflossed teeth. His raging smile and close-cropped hair—clearly chopped by someone in a rush—made him look like an overgrown six year old. Mimi, all mamma, glided over and giggled into his neck. She cooed that he was, "such a great host."

"Yeah?" He straightened his back and wrapped an arm around her shoulder. She settled against him. After living in the same town for mere weeks, they'd cultivated the gestures and squeezes of mom and dad in The Brady Bunch. I wanted none of it.

"Have you ever seen anything so beautiful in your whole life?" Mimi sang, eyeing me from her man's armpit. I stood in the shade of a pine, watching as the deck filled with guests who stooped to drop six packs and bottles of wine into yet another plastic tub. My corner felt abandoned, but I tried to smile.

I said, "Pretty great," vulnerability running through my wires, an expression that seemed to satiate Mimi's appetite for power. She expelled a bark that some might call laughter but which I knew to be schadenfreude.

"So, tonight," She said, glaring at me. "Are you going to gnaw on lettuce or really plunge in?" I could have danced in the nude and still she wouldn't have blinked. "Because, I am definitely and I mean **definitely** not going to watch you plow more leaves into your mouth! Uhn uhn! Got it? We are so having a barbecue!"

I stood in a puddle of ice water, goose bumps up the flimsy plastic straws of my arms and legs. I needed a chair, but all were taken. Blood pooled in my ankles, and I sat down on the deck, wordless. Was it true that all safe havens and rest stops were destroyed by war? Would stability forever be wiped away, entombed the way I'd someday be?

No one noticed me, because the deck had become a madhouse of banter and laughter, of flannel, Spandex, crew cuts, tank tops, bandanas, and tattoos moving through the evening. They were fishermen who spent summers crabbing in Alaska. They were ex-Microsoft employees who'd fled Redmond. They were a dozen frustrated musicians who lugged guitars. And they were military spouses whose other halves had been shipped off.

A tattooed guy stepped on my foot, but didn't notice. I shivered and curled up to warm myself, knowing I couldn't get back to the apartment without a ride. I spied on Mimi as she smoked a Parliament and chatted with a couple whose arms, like languid snakes, were draped around breasts and waists.

Had she wanted to see me as a shrunken head? Had she wanted to float through life like a blown-up character at the Macy's Thanksgiving Day parade? Perhaps. But no one knew except me, because she meandered from couple to couple, laughing and sharing fascinating information that she'd never share with me. Clearly, she'd invited me to show me I had no one, that I was nothing, while she knew everyone and was everything.

Ugliness

I found another reason not to be there. Pete sat nearby, turning gold in the last rays of day. He looked annoyed and uncomfortable as his blond girlfriend—whose name I'd finally learned was Jody—bounced on his lap, her ample rump keeping time with her wagging head as lyrics ripped through the general chatter.

When Jody, like an oversized rag doll, listed to the right, Pete caught me staring. He glanced away, his hair shaggy over his eyes. But then, he pushed Jody from his lap, faking laughter and wordlessly squeezing her shoulders before walking towards the sliding glass doors.

"HEY—" Jody roared. A startled moment as everyone went silent. "HEY, DUMBFUCK! What is this?! WHAT! Come on—" She had "fist-fight" all over her, which Pete, small but macho, didn't acknowledge. The back of his head was all "fuck you" as he patted down the wrinkles of his old man shorts. This was why people popped quaaludes, why Ben slammed his car into a tree. There had to be a way to get past this absurd aspect of being almost-young.

"Yo, Todd," Pete called, arms out like a man bothered by lethargy. "Know where those plastic chairs are?" He glanced at me, and Jody, with her monkey eyes and lollipop mouth gaping.

"Back room, my man." Todd yelled from center-deck, confident man's man kneeling on knees, squinting as he fiddled with the barbecue's grease pan. "Hey Pete!" Pete now in the house. "Grab me some matches."

Jody all eyes—first pinned her attention on Todd, then broke to stare me down with what looked like a blast of sulphur coughed from the mantle. Her vase-like body looked shattered, the rims of her eyes red, arms limp at her side. But anger began building when she crossed her arms and I curled into a ball, turning away as the heat of her blasting me with, "You little fuck! You ugly bitch!"

But instead of tearing my hair out, she screamed and pounded her heel into the wood. "SHIT!" she yelled, scampering across the deck and bounding into the house with, "you little deranged turd. You little fuck! Don't ignore me!!"

I finally escaped the barbecue around 2 AM, after the beer turned to piss, and the bullshit talk blew across the lake, when a walking tattoo said she'd deign to drop me at Capitol Hill.

Stalled

My oldest friend was the only debris from my past that bobbed in the metaphoric waters of my days. But why didn't I get on the first flight back to JFK? What stalled me in Seattle? Better question to ask: Could anyone really help me? Maybe all the answers were wrapped in a brick of other questions. Or maybe I thought there was no better place other than Seattle to have a breakdown.

As I've said, I spent many hours alone, subsisting on air and exhaustion, my days a labyrinth of long walks coiled around books, bagged lettuce, and the necessities of hygiene. If I spoke to anyone, it was a fluke—

even when I initiated conversations, as I did two nights after Jody nearly broke a hole in Todd's deck.

Shamefully, I phoned Nora, aching for verbal mom-hugs. I spewed distress at Nora's clueless housemate—Jillian-of-NYU—who'd innocently picked up with, "Yeah?" and then, "Yeah, hey Jane. So I think your mom's spending the week at The Avatar's place. She sometimes calls in. Want me to give her a message?"

By then, everyone knew that The Avatar owned Nora's mind, body, and soul. But I didn't ask Jillian for her feedback. I only mentioned that I hadn't heard from Nora since I'd left the Y, weeks ago. Nora and I had talked maybe six or seven times since my move to Seattle. There'd been the "Hey there! Glad you got in okay. How was the flight?" chat. And then there'd been the "what to do about the 12 x 15 room" discussion, with the "You'll figure it out. That's life" response. And of course, there'd been the temp agency talk when I mentioned the less-than-living wages I'd be paid, which had led to the, "What about your savings? You've got something left, don't you—" moment.

In the aftermath of these skim-the-surface chats—that made me feel less daughter than stranger —I couldn't eat and often found myself on a park bench overlooking Lake Washington, where I'd stare at the far off cars streaming across the floating bridge. Occasionally, I'd be consumed by the spirals of cigarette smoke Mimi exhaled into the living room as Todd—often with one of his frowzy boathouse friends—gestured ideas for the evening at Mimi's breasts. Disconnected from everyone, I knew I couldn't blame my predicament—or my low self-esteem—on Mimi. I'd made every bad decision all by myself. Yet, I wanted very badly to blame her—and my mother, and Stan—even The Avatar, if not every other stand-in for humanity that I'd encountered!

Only one member of the community—our building manager, Jack—seemed to care. He offered his truck and once stopped by with a plate of chocolate chip cookies that I couldn't eat. I liked that he wore plaid and was studying to be a volcanologist. But Jack had a boyfriend and sometimes painted his toenails black like a Goth, which didn't gel with his all-American cookies.

And why had Pete offered me a deck chair, despite his monkey-faced girlfriend? Did he expect to exchange it for a night in my bed? Since the barbecue, he'd been showing up. One afternoon, he phoned, claiming to be looking for Todd. After I told him Todd was long gone, he paused and asked how I'd settled in. For some reason, I told him I had a job.

"Cool. Where abouts?" he asked. "What's your schedule?" I made something up—and he laughed. "Well, hell, let's get a beer. And, hey, don't forget, if you need anything, just buzz." During another call he added, "Come by, hang out, watch a movie." Which meant, "Let's sit in the dark and get naked to the soundtrack of some grade B action flick."

<u>Seeking Anoesis</u>

Pete intimidated me—especially when I landed in the craters of his Martian influence. Certain pocked occasions bothered me—especially when he sprawled on my living room floor and roared like a jetliner while watching basketball games. I hated the way TV light spilled into his unhinged mouth— how he shoveled chips and chugged beer and vocally bombed the apartment with, "Yo!" and "Dude!" and "Ho!" at the score—leaving me to wonder whether "Ho" was another word for "whore" as in "you ho!"?

But at the same time, I envied his lack of inhibition, his no worries way of dangling arms and legs over anyone within two feet of him—not to mention his careless release of pent-up gas. Perhaps that was why I wanted to join Pete and Mimi and Todd's club, to be enfolded in the word "dude," which promised those who repeated it the prospect of steady paychecks and social acceptance.

Further, it didn't seem fair that Mimi and Todd rolled out of bed at 7:30, while I set my alarm for 5:00—just to appear half awake by 8:00. I'd always wanted to be one of them: free-falling through life successfully without the ever-present anxiety that caused me to cling to thin bits of schedule, my wristwatch an emotional salve—a survival device, hassling me up before dawn and creating a ten-minute routine of washing face, brushing teeth and peeing.

It bothered me that most nights I sat alone in my sleeping bag, like a ball of rubber bands ready to snap, chewing a tasteless dinner and listening to NPR. It bothered me that Todd's buddies shoulder-slapped each other and played football with their dirty socks in my kitchen. I hated that they cashed in endless brews, paid for by corporate sponsors.

It didn't seem right that my days ossified around sock-drenching walks that lacked social stimulation, while lesser intellects effortlessly enjoyed hours of elastic experience. How was it that everyone else got paid to enjoy endless periods of laughter and back slapping? While each of their days grew exponentially more rewarding, each of mine grew darker and dirtier. No matter what happened—fired from jobs, made homeless by a kitchen fire, burned by love or war—they still laughed, while I hadn't sputtered a giggle in years.

Had my life become a carnival of 3 AM jitters that left me sweating and hyperventilating? Well, it was 1997, innocent times—when few knew about the Texas-sized accrual of plastic bottles floating in the Pacific. David de Rothchild's Plastiki and the mass extinction of frogs, butterflies, bats, coral reefs were fictions drafted by a jokester. In 1997, pirates hadn't yet taken down tankers off the coast of Somalia. The only "I" was a reference to the self, not the information "I," as in iPhone and iPad. Satellites hadn't fallen from the sky. A billion Youtube viewers hadn't seen a blindfolded man in an orange jumpsuit lose his head. Gitmo wasn't a word. Al Gore hadn't given away the election—nor had he appeared in *An Inconvenient Truth*. No one imagined Princess Di or John F. Kennedy Jr. dead, or that the World Trade Centers would collapse, because few people believed in collapse. Not even "Burl of the desert" would have believed any of it, least of all you, Bill.

Because time doesn't prepare people. There are no clues beforehand, only afterwards. I should have known this, because before leaving New York, I'd seen the middle-aged woman who looked like me: shot hair bleached at the tips, her wax face set with a smile. Was this how people died? And if so, did they know it was the end? And how had they so easily slipped through the arms of others? Perhaps everyone else who saw what I saw wondered these same things. Or maybe they simply believed in a social order, that America would always exist. It's only right to ask.

Therefore, 1997.

Either/Or

Already rain rippled the Puget Sound and slanted into the city with a bite that transformed pedestrians into refugees. Inside cafes, hoodies huddled over steaming mugs as cloudbursts slashed windows—which left me no option but to contemplate Mimi's perpetual absence. By then, we rarely ran into each other, except through a series of notes that speckled our kitchen counter.

Most weeks, she and Todd spent a single night in the apartment, which now advertised a bright red, shroom-induced chair that featured paisley brocade and the sickening stench of patchouli. The chair had materialized one afternoon while I finished a temp gig at UW and bore a note that read: "Please do not eat or drink on this chair. Thank you."

It wasn't easy to avoid eating or drinking on the chair, as it was the only seat in the apartment. But I did occasionally recline on its plush surface to sneeze at Cary Grant and Grace Kelly as they picnicked on chicken—a scene I watched over and over again. And I did ball a wad of dirty tissues into the crack between the chair's cushion and armrest.

The first time the phone rang after I officially began temping, I expected Mimi to ask about her chair—only to be surprised by Pete's voice instead. Again, he asked for Todd, and again he dallied on the line, with a lot of "heys" in between pauses that made him sound oddly out of breath, as if he'd been pedaling uphill. "Hey. I've been wanting to speak to you. Got a moment to stop by the dock tomorrow?" I should have declined the invitation, but after he mentioned there might be a few dollars involved, I told him I'd make like a bolt of lightning.

The next morning, as I rounded Lake Union on foot, drizzle drove away the gulls. Swirls of mist wrapped Pete's yellow and green gear in gray. Like a colorful ghost, he drifted towards me, stopping by the raised but rusting hull of a stripped sailboat.

"Small project," he said, caressing the boat's belly. "A guy in Redmond has a wad of cash." He fisted the metal, coaxing out a hollow sound. "So," he pawed his neck and stared down at his feet. "Actually, this isn't what I had in mind—" He led me into the damp wind rattling the ropes that dangled from the masts.

"This thing you have for me?" I said, faintly aware of movies, books, and business dealings that indicated this might be about sex.

"This a-way—" The view of "this a-way" appeared to be far from the parking lot and the road of cars splashing by. Boats rose and fell, water slopping against hulls. "I'm thinking maybe you won't go for it," he added, "but then beggars can't be choosers—" So temping amounted to begging. But then I had to admit, he was right. What were my choices?

"Okay—" I said. Being open never hurt the yogis— On the other hand, there were the millions who'd been sucked against their will into the sex trade. As I considered what it might be like to strip and open my legs to a thousand strangers, we stalled by a sailing yacht whose stained wood looked as rich as a shot of whiskey, the year 1928 etched into a gold plaque on its side.

"So this one's into humpbacks," Pete said, running his hand along the wood. "Officially known as John Naughten Boyd, but to us, JNB." I laughed, confused, the initials reminding me of an obscure brand of whiskey. I wondered if JNB was a boat or a man—and if a man, whether he'd be my first customer.

"JNB—" I said, the absurdity of this holdover from the 19th-century.

"Yep," Pete smiled, his eyes fixed on mine. "But hey," he stared me into the kind of discomfort that caused less desperate women to look away. "The guy's got heritage, I'm told. Half royalty." So we were talking about a man. "So, the job." He was going to lead me into a cabin, introduce me to Mr. Bourbon, and tell me to peel off my clothes. "They're headed up North." Pete said, stepping towards me. Everything was clearer than the ice I felt chilling my spine. They were going to kidnap me—and no one would know or care. I wouldn't be missed for days, possibly weeks, because who checked up on me? Mimi would simply assume that I'd locked myself in my room to read Dickens and stuff salad in my face. And my mother? She would never call again.

Pete pressed my shoulder, eliciting something between a jolt. "You okay?" he asked my shivering self. "It's not so bad. They're just going to Alaska." His greased palm slid from my shoulder up to the boat's copper railing.

It turned out, JNB needed someone to scrub and sand his beast of a boat— And because Pete already had too many boats, I got offered the privilege. There'd be, "maybe $150 a week," Pete said, still pinning me with that tough-boy gaze that made my legs want to run. "Less than minimum— but more than volunteer. Off the books, of course."

"You think I can do this?" I asked, fists beneath my armpits, frost settling onto me. "And why are you being so nice?" If I looked like a boat scrubber, that was news to me. There'd be hours of rain, bouts of pneumonia, and a trip to the morgue for those without health insurance.

"I'm doing this because—" He bowed his head towards a broken-down cabin several yards behind us bearing a row of hooks that dangled rubber coats. "I'm a nice guy."

The Rub Down

I won't lie. At first he looked nothing like Ben, who was all tall-rabbi-surfer-dude-with-bleached-hair augmented by pre-hipster, old-style jackets. In contrast, JNB turned out as a scruffy prep in Docksiders—so 1979—with those khakis and all that yellow rubber. But he sported the bookishness that Ben cultivated when he wasn't flying on opiates—the kind of guy who lived on sea foam and propane lamps, drank Guinness before sunset, and read too much Schopenhauer. Also, I found it appealing that he smelled like a musty basement.

It didn't take long for the bullet to sink into my skin. An hour after our intro, similarities blurred into complete likeness. Like Ben, JNB wore a ponytail, was tall with broad shoulders, had a serious mouth, and alert eyes. And when he got excited he gestured widely like a man on stage. He even grew embarrassed when admitting to indulging in brown rice salad—a quirk that countered his five years at Princeton, where pizza and all things meat ruled despite his claim of having taught a freshman course on nutrition and biodiversity when he was a mere sophomore. How could I not gape at these surface likenesses as he told me about his summers recording the calls of diving Humpbacks in Chatham Bay?

True, it was disappointing when, like bad radio, he said, "Yeah, she's mean and hungry for a little love and care—That's my Old Christy." But somehow even this slip-up sounded like something Ben might have said. And for the rest of the afternoon I swayed like a dancer on the undulating dock, absorbing his every gesture and comment as if he were Lazarus, back from the dead: "We need everything!" he said, pawing his neck before caressing the old wood railing. "Everything's got to be done before we head out. Loads and loads, and all in front of the pod."

That evening, as I gobbled bagged lettuce in my room, Ben-cum-JNB sallied through an issue of National Geographic all about car crashes and whales. This JNB/Ben National Geographic sandwich slathered me with feelings of hunger and hope. It was as if a thousand French chefs had teased a starving child with whipped cream and Napoleons. I couldn't breathe without feeling twirls of anticipation in my gut. Every breath was a JNB-invasion. The image of him broke into every activity. The idea of him launched me into the morning where time could be regained like wind off the Santa Maria, like a naked rider speeding over the plains on a buffalo's back. This was high-blown romance, and only JNB could make me adjust my hood against the drizzle that seeped through my gear.

The first morning, in drizzle, I adjusted my hood and hunkered on the boat, blew into my hands, and found it difficult to focus on instructions. He pointed out the spots where the Old Christy needed elbow grease, his ponytail dripping into his pushed back yellow hood, the whole thing a reminder of the 50-to-100 nights that I lay next to Ben.

"Right now, top priority is waxing the hull and topside," he said, climbing a rope ladder to the deck. He didn't extend a hand as I climbed after him, but that only made my performance more important. "Every inch," he said as I straddled the railing. "Here, I'll show you." He leaned down, dug into a ragbag lying on the deck, and squeezed fluid from a bottle onto a cloth. Then he daubed the solution over the wood surface, nodding at me to join him. I grabbed a rag, but remained uncertain. "It's like flipping burgers," he said, nodding as his hands made circles over the surface. "Work with the grain and you'll get every spot. And don't skimp on the Carnauba! She may look like a jalopy but she needs her cream." I squatted on the flooring as he got up and stood over me, appraising my work. Another woman would have balked at the apparent superiority as he said, "Right. Yeah, that's it." But I enjoyed it. "Who would motor this thing past Bainbridge?" He said, slouching down on a knee and patting the bench. "Only a madman!" Around us silver water was no longer separate from gray air. "Everyone needs an overhaul."

Not Covered

Lake Union moved up and down, every yacht and houseboat riding the dream, but Pete was yelling somewhere. I turned to see him in the phone booth that lived next to the rain gear several yards from The Old Christy. He sputtered into the mouthpiece, his face red, the steel phone cord stretched to capacity. When he spotted me staring, he lifted an arm and rolled his eyes, as if I knew it was Jody, a force of nature that made every relationship into a FOX news story. I stood, but felt the ground move beneath me. If it hadn't been for JNB—who reached out to grip my arm—I might have stumbled over the railing and cracked my skull.

"Watch it. You're not covered by my plan."

Ore

It took months before I realized what was wrong. The problem began when I stopped eating enriched Shredded Wheat—which was too expensive—so that not long after I started scrubbing The Old Christy, my legs felt heavy as pumpernickel bread. Breathless, the Great Wall of China cordoned me off from the world. A fork resting inches from my hand seemed a thousand feet away. And reading a paragraph became as difficult as wrangling a job.

My mind flitted from one stimulus to another, never quite digesting information or formulating responses. For someone whose mother popped vitamins like raspberries, it never occurred to me that somehow I'd been freed of the magnetic field that grounded everyone else, sapped of the most ubiquitous of elements: the very same molten ore that poured through caverns deep within the earth.

One evening, as depleted blood swished through my ungrounded body, as I stared at the credits of *To Catch A Thief,* the phone rang. In a daze, I hardly contemplated answering it. After all, I needed to watch the end of Ben's favorite movie, which he'd left in the form of a DVD on my TV more than a couple of years ago. And though I'd seen the movie six times in two weeks, it seemed too difficult to put the phone out of its misery. I struggled to remove myself from Mimi's precious red chair, despite wheezing over the thought that JNB—shorn of ponytail and boat—could easily be Cary Grant.

But the phone kept ringing the way it rang in New York before Rudy left his final voicemail—a fifteen-minute manifesto that boiled down to a little worm-of-a-statement stuck to the end of a fishing rod. Ben, Rudy had said, had something to tell me—but it was too important to record. "Tell you what," Rudy had yammered. "Just give me a call."

But I never did. I simply packed up like a woman wiping her hands of dust, the helium of "ditching it all" lifting me off the earth as I threw odds and ends into storage. So, what more was there than Mimi's red chair and the ringing phone, because people said "hello" when what they really meant to say was "hello, goodbye. Leave me alone," as they would in the years to come when they didn't return emails or texts?

Eventually I grabbed the phone, and a voice murmured, "Hi there." It sounded deep and expressive, a man intoning like a woman. "Were you on the other line?" Casual as a close relative, whoever it was exhaled what sounded like cigarette smoke. Oddly, intimately, the invisible smoke seeped from mouthpiece into the earpiece pressed up against the neural network that formed my brain, causing the cooling system in my armpits to spring sweat. I flipped to PBS—the only channel that fuzzed to life besides FOX—where a dancer in red sequins flashed a smile, her arms and legs like wily tendrils of sea corral.

Hypnotized by the montage, I said, "Yes?" instead of hanging up. My wrists hurt and the thought of moving was exhausting.

"So I, you know, I—" said the exhaled smoke.

"I think you have the wrong number—" This hurt my throat, but only half of me knew the call was a prank.

"Yeah? Yeah. I don't know about that." It said, getting agitated. "I don't know. Yaw. I don't, you know, I don't think so." I stared down the barrel of this verbal shotgun. Something about the cadences and the smack-lip quality of the consonants sounded familiar. I heard fake accents and beneath I heard something I knew: laughter.

"Do I know you?" I said, recognizing every little fucked macho-boy who'd ever said, "bitch, I'm gonna lick you—" It had to be one of Mimi's friends—a cruel practical joke sent like a warning to press me up against the wall and make me pliable as putty.

"I want—" These words tumbled into me, a perverse invitation, a stinky belch from a stranger's gut. Another exhalation, and I imagined a gray form sprawled on a bed, naked and writhing, its appendages like the tubes inserted into Ben's body. "Your big fat juicy—"

I hung up.

The First Time

How could a phone call become a time machine that thrust me back to that period of other prank calls when my father blew marijuana smoke into my nostrils and every girl in 5th grade knew I had a futile crush on a boy named Tyler? How could I suddenly find myself walking over the jagged pavement of my childhood, when the worst calls were left like orphans to haunt payphones—those urine-smoted steel phone cabinets that edged garbage strewn lots? In the pre-texting era, stray calls loitered like stray cats—suggesting the commingling of admiration and aggression—a dichotomy that left one's imagination to the wilderness of tween romance.

In the early 80's, prank calls became common, spiking to an all-time high with the ringing in of my tenth birthday. As I chatted with two guests and lapped up a final slice of carrot cake, the phone rang. My mother picked up, had her head sliced open by curses, slammed down the phone, and walked into the dining room to announce that it was, "one of your shameful admirers." When I asked how she knew this, she threatened to pull me from school.

"What kind of kid uses foul language with a grown up?! Who are these people? What kind of school lets their students walk around with socks in their mouths?! I'll call the principal—To ruin the table on your BIRTHDAY! Absolutely unacceptable!"

Five minutes later, the phone shrieked. This time my father picked up, asked who it was, rearranged his lips around two mottled fingers, and blew spittle and a high peel into the mouthpiece. "That'll take care of him!" he said. "Hope that screws up the son of a bitch's eardrums."

There were no more prank calls until 7th grade, when Tyler was long gone and the heavy breathing and the "I want to fuck you" one-liners hardly grazed my skin. It no longer felt exciting or disturbing when the phone rang like a Phillip Glass mistake. Mysterious callers, even with caller ID, could no longer be seen as potential bedroom mates, leaving me with no choice but to fall asleep on the red chair that was meant only for Mimi and her best buddy, Mr. Todd.

The Sound

I don't remember when it occurred to me that I should research jobs on the Internet, but at some point I hooked a modem to my computer, whose screen hovered over my sleeping bag while all kinds of Star Wars sounds zapped the room into another dimension. And once I took my first toke of the search engine, I blasted off, zeroing-in on the classifieds, never to return.

Running on adrenaline, I pounded my keyboard like a cross-country skier chased by a bear, finally emerging hours later with no job leads other than a smattering of waitressing and barista gigs. Concerned that my talent for grinding coffee beans would barely fund warming my room in the winter, I held off on filing applications. I did, however, make a discovery that kept me up all night. How I stumbled onto that treasure trove of information was a fluke not to be repeated. But it left me so manic that as soon as the sun rose I half jogged towards The Old Christy, feeling dangerously indispensable.

Most mornings I found JNB sipping tea from a bullet-like thermos. He often stood next to a spindly, pug-nosed blond named Laura, who wore

REI and J.Crew over suede riding boots that looked like they belonged on Jackie O. rather than to someone slathering Carnauba and shoveling fish slop. Clearly the two Princeton-ites were intimate, though I could never figure out why. Once in a while, I'd catch JNB patting Laura's shrimp-sized butt—especially when he thought only I was looking. Other times, he ignored her, as when she offered a ditzy question while everyone else was covered in sawdust and wax, like when she said, "So what about throwing together some wine and pasta tonight?" No reply. And if she draped an arm over his shoulder, her hair grazing his earlobe, he merely fondled the boat's railing. Soon, I knew, she'd get sick of being second paddle to an aging yacht. But more likely, she'd realize that he found other women, like myself, more interesting.

Anyone could see that she was on her way out when, as I smudged bourbon-colored circles into the wood, JNB's stare poured caramel-like over my shoulders. And it didn't bother me when he found reason to slip past me in such a way that I viewed his groin. On one occasion, while he inspected my work, he folded himself around me as if modeling male cologne, the smell of Old Spice mingling with sweat. "That's okay, but how about—" his breath a mash-up of chai and mint as he grabbed a rag to wax the wood, before slipping a hand over mine.

Confused, I felt like a twelve year old in danger of destroying something delicate if I got too close. His ponytail dripped onto me while he hammered me with orders like, "Put more grit into that rub!" or "Don't skimp on anything; get more wax—" or "Throw me that rag, and I'll show you how to take that corner—" Impossible to please, I learned what it was to serve a perfectionist—the focus on details never waning, which caused him to grow in my mind.

At night, locked in my room as Mimi and Todd's bellies slammed against each other, as I lay listless in my sleeping bag, JNB was reincarnated as a better-than-life, super-Ben because there were no accidents. In the end, someone had to find out, just as, eventually, everyone would discover everything in the Internet age, when digging became a pastime.

And how I dug. I dug deep, through layers of news articles, kicking up information about his family, pulling out the oddest artifacts, knowing that I'd arrive at the Old Christy to find him looking as charmed as Cary Grant playing a thief.

But then, things don't always work out as expected.

<u>Of</u>

I found him beneath a tarp, alone, Laura nowhere in sight. It was a little after 7:00 AM, most of the other volunteers just stumbling out of bed after a busy weekend. Climbing the ladder, I said, "Where is everyone?" He glanced at me from his kneeling position on the gleaming deck, his forehead level with my pubic bone; we seemed to enjoy regaling each other with our erogenous zones. But when he looked at the floorboards, he became an outline in the gray atmosphere that roused his hair, a ghost about to vaporize. He said nothing, but swished wood polish in its can. I watched his grimy hands find the Old Christy's pressure points where he massaged the wood. "A waste—"someone once said about the kind of men who became fanatical about cars. "What a waste. All that passion and sensuality going into an inanimate object."

"Nice weekend?" I asked, wanting so much to share what I'd learned. He flicked his eyes at me, the anger like a red point that hadn't been on my radar. "Okay," I said. "Well—I'll see you later." I climbed down the ladder, disappointed, metal rungs like old beer cans clattering against the side of the boat. This had to mean bad news.

He paid me $7.50 an hour—tax free, as one would expect from a fiscal Republican. Likewise, his socially Democratic leanings allowed me to leave when I wanted, as long as I worked no more or less than 15 hours per week. It meant something that he used his bike to get everywhere. It also meant something that I knew his parents once paid for everything—the expensive education, the easy confidence, the habit of buying chai from a café rather than settling for a pot of steeped leaves at home. The word was "loaded," and anyone could see it in his perfectly scuffed hiking boots, the less scuffed but appropriately worn-in dock shoes, the deliberate shagginess of his flannel, khaki, whatever-happened-to-be in the bottom drawer that he, like a wannabe Kurt Cobain, threw on his body. "Start over there, work the railings—" He said as if he'd always said things like that. I nodded as he pretended not to have money—though everyone knew he could buy 100 Old Christy's if his dad hadn't been the charitable type, because he reeked of wealth every time he stood up, yawned, and gazed from the water to my pant leg. "You're still with us through the spring." This he stated, never truly asking the question, merely pronouncing it.

Music

I no longer shivered on the boat, though my fingers, toes, lips, and the tip of my nose easily grew numb—which made words difficult. I nodded, the only acceptable answer.

"Okay," he said, smiling to express gratitude. "Great."

It wasn't something Cary Grant would say to Grace. But how could I feel anything but disappointment. Instead of an invitation to dinner, JNB continued making love to the deck, twiddling a knob with a rag like it was the nipple of a mermaid.

Later, I walked to the Puget Sound. By the Aquarium painted the same color as Seattle's winter sky, I stood feeling naked, ashamed, and let down, wanting to eat but not knowing what. A toddler stumbled towards me, his milk teeth shining a smile, his black hair curling over frost-blue eyes.

"Hello!" He patted my leg, his fingers gripping my Levi's.

"Ben! No, no. Come here—" His mother's laughter framed his name. "You little mischief," she scooped him up, her bulk apologetic. "You little love—" She tickled his cheek with the tip of her nose and kissed him. Then she gave a fragile smile that showed the exhaustion of falling in love with her son. "I know people are soooo interesting to you," she sang to her baby. "But we stay close to mommy on big streets." She twirled the little boy away as he half-cried, half-giggled, kicking his legs, the two dancing towards a stroller.

It wasn't just a toddler's smile; it was Ben's and JNB's smiles.

Out With the Old, In With the New

"Get on with it!"

Elliot Bay

A cloudburst followed me beneath the Alaskan Viaduct as I walked towards Pioneer Square, where I found a hierarchy of beaked spiritual beings in the form of a totem pole that a placard said spawned from Tlingit village, Alaska. Futile, these placards in community squares that no one had time for, because why have time for a false sense of time and place when anyone could be anywhere, living in any time, and still be alone?

Cobblestones and gas lamps, shuttered pubs, the yawn of restaurants worn down by too many nights, none of it mattered, not even to the homeless pioneers of the square. A smudge-of-a-man with fried eyes mumbled that his body was a wrecked ship against a bundle of cardboard. I couldn't help him. So, I kept walking until shafts of light broke into the caramel wood that regularly released tectonic claps caused by readers who explored tables covered with titles. For the first time in months, I lost myself in slices of lives inked onto paper. I'd fallen into the reader's world called Elliot Bay where I became a casualty.

The weird boy/man didn't mean to slam a metal cart into my shin, causing me to double over. He didn't meant to seem clueless when he mumbled, "Oh," as if waking from a vision quest. "Sorry." Paperbacks had spilled to the floor, my shin red but not bleeding.

"Here—" He kicked a step-stool at me. I collapsed onto it, grabbed my leg, and blinked at the boy/man's pale face of wire-rim glasses. He looked fifteen but had to be thirty, because he knelt on hands and knees in Ben's tweed, the one with patches at the elbows. Re-piling the books, he paused over a tome titled, **The Art and Architecture of the Indian Subcontinent**—the only hardbound casualty of his overturned cart.

A twitch flashed over his cheeks, but he seemed nonchalant as he puttered, hair crowding eyes like a 1960's rocker meets choir boy, all pug nose and discordant features. Everything about him proclaimed Britain the motherland.

A printed Shiva sprawled next to him, and he said, "You are now," pausing for emphasis, "within inches of one of the best editions of Hindu temple art available." He leaned forward to place an index finger on the glossy paper. "The collection is out of Cambridge, and this interpretation is considered the Bhagavad Gita of Indian Art." His lenses refracted light at me. "Any interest in Krishna?"

This seemed odd. Had I been chanting?

Surprised by the question, I simply studied his twitching face, the way his nose perked like Tinker Bell's. Did the man want to find deeper meaning in my bruised shin?

"Actually no—" I said. He stared at me, fingering his tome. I'd hurt his feelings, so I said, "Do you know much about Tamil temple art?"

"That's pretty specific—" he said, blinking. "But, yes. I can actually say I know a smidgen." I hadn't heard the word "smidgen" since my 5th grade art teacher—a *Preppy Handbook* follower—told the class to put a "smidgen of yellow" on the paper plates at our elbows. Never one to follow instructions, I'd squeezed so hard I'd sprayed paint all over her dress.

"Not that it matters," the bookseller said. "But I favor poetry." He absently turned pages. "Anything from Baudelaire to Ashbury to Ferlinghetti, but sometimes I just have to stray—" He cut himself off, thinned his lips to approximate a smile and thrust out a hand. "I'm so rude. Dan, by the way. Manager of Elliot Bay." I was impressed by his title, because he acted less like a manager than that guy who ran the high school literary magazine. He leaned forward like a scholar, extending his hand over the Rotogravure print of Shiva embracing Parvati. His hand felt as dry as a fallen leaf.

"And they call you?" He raised his eyebrows, again thinning his lips in that bizarre smile, nose wrinkling in a parody of a merry old English man at teatime.

"Right. Jane. But, alas, you're not Dick." He huffed a pretend laugh as the floorboards behind him barked. A rotund, panting man gripped the book cart and stared at me as if his life depended upon it, but Dan didn't notice, too distracted by balloons of laughter blowing in from the magazine section. "Are you okay?" I said to the large, gasping man, but he turned away from me and moved into an alcove.

"Yes?" Dan said, giving me an odd look.

A mother's cadences, a child's whimper. The store felt humid. Dan's eyeglasses fogged over. He shook his head to percussive laughter. But the rotund man reappeared from an alcove, again staring at me breathlessly, easing around a corner towards the stairs to the café. Was I seeing things?

"It's unbelievable," Dan said, leaning in. "Who comes to a bookstore to make noise? Okay, maybe it's not a library, but I mean really. Sometimes all I want to says is, 'shhhhut the fuck up.'" I couldn't help myself. I laughed, and his cheek spasmed.

"Bookstores are full of people who don't really read books," he said, leaning closer with this secret. "But you got to love them for wanting to stock bookcases and impress their friends and sip second-rate bottles of sherry in front of third-rate fireplaces. I've met at least a hundred people like that."

"Really? That many?"

"Absolutely. Most in Spokane, but they're here too." Again, that approximation of a smile.

"Guess I better not buy anything."

He fondled a book rescued from the floor, its cover shiny, black with a single matte red dot at its center. "In Adulation of Mindlessness," he read its Zen script. "Hmm. Yeah. Maybe I'll send this one to Walmart's Board of Directors. Or maybe just leave it with those clueless beings over there—" he bowed his head at the magazine rack and actually showed the upper row of his corn-kernel teeth.

Sucked into the sarcasm, but not quite managing, I said, "Hmmm. Yeah."

"Right." He began to glide like a downhill skier towards the laughter. But then, in a spin of cowardess, he returned to me and dissolved into twitching. He had his reasons: "I really have to stop. Remember, I'm the manager."

"Actually," I began, wanting to enjoy more of him but clueless as to what to say next. "Speaking of reading. Do you know anything about reading groups?"

Villanelle

Joining a book club had never appealed, mainly because I'd dragged myself through high school and college reading lists. And then there was the popular but untrue notion that reading groups were guarded by frustrated moms who nit-picked over plot twists rather than deeper issues—which meant admitting I was a book snob—meaning that I had no confidence in my grasp of narrative flow and character traits.

As if hearing my thoughts, Dan breathed, "Ah yes, reading groups." He knew. I could see it in the way he rubbed his hands together. "Yes, well, I can definitely help you with that if you're willing to pick through the curmudgeons of the English literary canon. It's either that or the worst kind of pulp. Pick your path to hell. The upside: Pulp is very addictive. But I gather you're not exactly interested in David Baldacci, or God forbid, Danielle Steele." He rolled his eyes, as if Molly Ringwaldisms made these indictments less grave. "Of course, there's nothing wrong with book sludge, but I gather you're after a little—" he emphasized the word "little" by pinching his nose, "just a little more depth—God forbid you introduce the words **pulp** and **classics** in a single sentence. Better, instead, to consider something entirely different. Like maybe, oh—" His lips thinned, this time causing two trenches to spread around the corners of his mouth in what I realized was an expression of all-out glee. "Poetry?"

"Verse?" I asked, thinking of Ben's interest in the Pinsky translation of *The Inferno*. "I don't know." I looked down at the photo of Shiva and Parvati resting on the cart. "Sounds morbid." I didn't feel like hearing a post-modernist monologue about the circles of hell.

Like a rabbit, Dan squinted at me, his nose sniffing out an interest. "No one," he said, "is ever **done** with poetry."

"Really?"

"Really," he continued, "You'll see. Poetry is better than anything but ice cream. Shall we discuss the history of the villanelle?"

Pig's Blood Kitchen

I soon learned that Dan had a penchant for rolling his own cigarettes—thus his dry fingers. Unhealthy as it was in this town of mainly wholesome, fresh-air folk, I found rolled cigarettes refreshing. Also appealing was his tweedy wardrobe, which reminded me of Ben, of course.

Haling from somewhere inland (I never learned where, but I knew he'd spent a year in Spokane), he hinted at early exposure to the foster care system. His interest in males was understated, though he'd alluded to it during one of our first poetry meetings after someone read, Oscar Wilde's *Young Charmides*. Later he spoke of avoiding the "scene" on Capital Hill, forgoing clubs for quieter pursuits, which led me to think of him as a soul-sibling.

Our poetry group met every Sunday afternoon, in houses or apartments, never in public places. The first gathering took place in a kitchen that smelled like fried fish and looked like the innards of a pig—everything dark red and spattered with grease. Towards the end, Dan peered through his reflective lenses, taking in our circle of five frowzy readers, his thin fingers grasping a teacup, and asked if anyone could offer a larger space as a permanent meeting location for the next week's foray into Rumi.

"We don't need incense, but we do need light!" He joked, knowing that no one—not even the host—liked reading poetry in the pig's blood kitchen. His eyeglasses roved from one person to the next—one guy twirling his neck in yogic apology, another flexing his fingers and cracking his knuckles with that glazed appearance of guilt. While Dan peered around at the silence, I thought of the intersection of Harvard and Republican, of the vacant living room, it's silver carpet vast and uninterrupted as the floor of a prayer hall. I considered Mimi's schedule. Normally she and Todd stayed away Sunday afternoons, preferring to bed down at the house in Leschi.

I pointed my index finger towards the ceiling and said, "I can host."

Pressing his palms together to sanctify my offer, Dan spread his lips, with, "Perfect. So, next week. 3:00 PM." I nodded weakly, scribbling the time down on the inside cover of my collection of Oscar Wilde poems, giving the group my address and adding that I'd have a platter of humus and pita waiting. Figuring it wouldn't be an issue if Mimi didn't know, I kept quiet.

During the following week, I sloshed through the puddled cobbles of Pioneer Square, bypassing the usual array of ousted citizens struggling with wilted cardboard, cigarette butts, and liquor bottles. After the bone tingling moisture of the waterfront, Elliot Bay's wood floors, alcoves, and nutty aromas lit me with the Hawaiian Island of all emotions: hope.

By then, I often met Dan during his break. We'd sit over tea and talk about books. Rumi, I told him, surprised me.

"Did you read the one with the penis shortening device?" he asked, folding his pale fingers into a ball next to his copy of Rumi. We sat on stools by a bookshelf of reference material, just behind the register as our tea steamed orange rind extract, so that I finally relaxed, despite wet shoes. "Because," he squinted against his eyeglasses, "somehow I never thought it possible that anyone, hundreds of years ago in the Middle East, no less, would mention the word **penis**, or even consider something like shortening it."

I agreed and he went on in his glinting, eyeglass way. "Some say he was gay." Dan sipped as steam clouded his lenses. "But I have my doubts. I mean, gay men don't want shorter penises. If anything—" He lowered his voice to a near whisper, "it's the opposite. Like with all men." Like a high school student, he kneaded his forehead, though it seemed odd that a grown man should be so nervous about the topic of sex. He placed his hand near mine. "I wanted to thank you," he said, thrusting out his nose.

"What for?"

"Your place—" He said, a twitch running over his cheek. "You have no idea how long we've had to sit in that disgusting kitchen. Months. It's hard to talk poetry when you're surrounded by fish bones, hot dogs, and the color of slaughter."

"I know. What is it with Charlie's kitchen?" I laughed, wanting to pass over the details of hosting in Mimi's living room. "An hour in that place and I smelled like innards." Dan coughed laughter, cupped the tea in his hands and thanked me again. "Did I ever tell you?" I said. "My mom thinks I should live in an Ashram, sleep in a pool of sandalwood oil, and give away my last pair of underwear. It's crazy, but I've given up everything. My apartment is so empty it smells like whatever's in it. I dare you to walk in with French fries and ketchup. I guarantee the place will smell like a burger joint for weeks afterwards."

"Oh my god! That's so cruel!" he said, placing his teacup on a shelf, adding that he'd rather dip himself in peanut butter than drizzle ketchup in a vegan's kitchen.

"By the way," I said. "Don't thank me until you've sat on my floor." Because, by then the red chair Mimi had "donated" was completely off limits, with a note stating, "If you can't keep me clean, don't sit!"

The Situation Gets Worse

Needless to say, Mimi and I weren't talking—and maybe that's why I spent so much time at Elliot Bay. True, I got news of Mimi through her mother, Cathy. Every Wednesday and Sunday afternoon, Cathy rang to ask pointed questions and abrasively dish out advice. If Mimi wasn't around— which was often—I was forced to take the call, frustrating preparations for dinner. The mere sound of Cathy's voice wilted my appetite. Her calls felt no kinder than an HR Executive's order to lay-off an entire department before Christmas.

One late afternoon, she broke into a meal of bagged lettuce with: "Hi there, Jane. Mimi's not happy about things."

"I see." I croaked. "Well. I kind of knew that."

There was a brief silence, followed by: "You so knew, didn't you?" Cathy had a habit of repeating phrases as a kind of power play. "And I so don't want to get into your business, so I'll just leave it at that." I asked if she wanted me to leave a message for her daughter. "Yes. Actually. Yes. She's always out, so yes." I told her Mimi was likely dining with Todd at some downtown Chinese restaurant. "That unbelievable child of mine!" Cathy chimed—her way of trying to be chummy. "She's always been crazy about Chinese—especially chow mein. Remember how she went through a whole carton when she was only three? Or maybe you don't. But it's always been noodles with her. Now that she's been promoted, she's probably out all the time."

"Promoted?" I asked. "I didn't know she got promoted."

"She didn't tell you?" Cathy's breeziness was like a joint she passed around a circle of strangers—euphoric for those who inhaled and choking to those who didn't. "That girl. That so over the top kid of mine!" I could hear Cathy shaking her head through the wisp of a laugh that trailed behind the word "mine."

"She hasn't said a word."

"You **two**—" Cathy said, still light-hearted. "You've known each other since you were in diapers. You two are like sisters. And you know sisters: so many ups and downs! But really—" That was the most Cathy had to say about our deteriorating living situation. "So, I'm so absolutely thrilled that she finally has a decent salary. The hotel just offered her a dream opportunity with full benefits. Just what she wanted! I'm so proud of her!" Through the earpiece, I could hear Cathy's pride rippling like streamers in a windstorm.

Mythic

Days later at Elliot Bay, I wandered the aisles, jobless, hungry, wet and exhausted while Dan organized, ordered and recommended books. Slinking into a corner, I glanced at an overpriced copy of the *Ramayana*, which I'd read years earlier as an Amar Chitra Katha comic book. While a senior in college, I wrote a short paper on a translation of the epic, discussing its literary merits as India's very own *Odyssey*. Two males warring over the kidnapped Queen Sita, as if she were Helen of Troy, a woman who represented earth, motherhood, and the supernatural but who really must've been a pawn, so that now the hours I'd spent on the essay seemed like a bunch of bloat and gas, especially as I slouched in one of the bookstore alcoves, skimming the section about Ravana stealing and probably raping Sita—

As if to confirm the pointlessness of all my previous points, I heard my name spewing out of the ancient Indian jungle like an eruption. "Jane? Jane—" the howl of a monkey, the roar of a tiger, followed by, "is that you?"

My name had rarely graced public spaces, and I'd never heard it as a pulse amid the dissidence of shuffling feet, flipped pages, whispered comments, or the crack of floorboards under pressure. Surprised, I looked up.

In front of me stood an Asian woman straight out of a myth. She wore black slacks and a brown suede jacket. She smiled teeth that needed braces, though her lips were glossed burgundy, making her flawless skin and shoulder length hair as luminous as an ocean under a full moon. It took a moment to shuffle through banked memories, but soon the past surged like a rogue wave into the present. I was overcome by a vision of sophomore year in high school—of so many hours lost to untangling who had a crush on who, which hair dye caused split ends, which eye shadow looked good with which outfit, and what nightclub played the best music. A "Cure" concert and hundreds of pizza lunches passed like a windstorm though my Psychedelic Furs brain, breaking through the patent leather gleam of my long lost Betsy Johnson boots. And like that, here was my long lost friend. How did the woman remember faces and so easily pick people out of a bookstore as if I were an old tube of lipstick in of a pile of new ones?

Unexpected meetings will shake even the darkest hearts out of depression and alienation. The *Ramayana* fanned shut, its back cover showing Sita in the midst of being swallowed by the earth, and just like that, as I stood up, everything began cartoon-like spinning—poor circulation. It had to be poor circulation that made me blurt, "Holy shit! Parvati?" I wobbled and she nodded, grasping my shoulders.

We'd stopped hanging out after sophomore year in high school, though we'd briefly bumped into each other at an art show in New York the summer between senior year and college. She'd been dating the artist—whose oversize Julian Schnabel-esque canvases rippled with a matrix of bones—while I arrived with a friend of a friend who wore black eyeliner like Adam Ant and spoke with a Russian accent. "Parvati!" I hugged her, shook my head in disbelief. "What are you doing in Seattle?" She looked like a thousand dollars flapping in the breeze on a sidewalk.

"No, I think the question is, what are **you** doing here?!" Parvati didn't laugh so much as continue nodding smiles, bracing me to the ground with her firm hands on my shoulders. And then she let go and stepped back to appraise my worn jeans, acne-riddled skin, and ruined hair. After more surprised words, she said with some concern, "You look like you could use something to drink." She squeezed my shoulder as if to force out the exhaustion. "How about we get something."

We linked arms, having begun to prod and grasp the way we did long ago, and we took ourselves downstairs to the café, where we divulged how we'd fled New York for Seattle within months of each other. She'd arrived three weeks into September, determined to focus on printmaking and multimedia at a local art school in order to "lose the corporate career path" and "get back to center." In fact, she admitted, while sipping a café latte, she'd really wanted to get as far away from her Ex as possible, because, well, he was sleeping around and had an opium habit.

"You married a drug addict?" I asked with a surge of despair.

"Everyone has an opium habit," she said. Was it possible that someone as promising as Parvati had also settled for a loser? It only made the sad fact of my unfettered state, my on-the-run mentality, more pathetic. How had we both managed to fall so far from where we'd been in our Betsy Johnson days?

"And no. We didn't marry!" She sang, stretching her arms and taking a deep, yogic breath. "Me? Married?" She seemed amused at the idea. "My goodness, Jane. I mean, you knew me when I was thirteen. You know I'm not the marriage type. Not even Greg. Remember him? I think you met him at that art show a few years ago?" When I made a sign of recognition, the shadows beneath her eyes grew darker. "**Him**," she said, emphasizing the word "him" as if saying "him" had become the sole purpose of sipping steam while holing up against the eternal rain. "He's the guy. We lived together for two years and that was it."

Like me, Parvati had arrived in Seattle jobless. Like me, she knew only one person—a woman named Nana who was getting a BFA at UW and had lived in Rome, New York, and Rio. It turned out Parvati and Nana shared a spacious International District two-bedroom. "Nana's an amazing artist. You'd really like her. She speaks fluent Italian and Portuguese. Didn't you speak French for a while?" as if language, like a pair of underwear or a lover, came and went. "You should meet her." We eventually finished our teas, exchanged phone numbers, and made plans for dinner and a hike. Little did I know what I was getting into.

Literary Salon

As the puzzle pieces of my Seattle world came together, life at Harvard and Republican got knocked up. Sunday finally arrived. Mist cloaked the streets. Clouds hung over the brick building. Soggy pedestrians accepted the approaching winter as inescapable, just as the once silver carpet in my living room inevitably turned ghostly lavender in the minimal daylight.

At 3 PM, as I placed overpriced pita around a tub of QFC hummus I couldn't afford, Dan rang my bell. In the doorway, he thrust a bottle of red wine into my hands. "I hate wine," he said. "But you said you don't have furniture so I thought we should celebrate."

"And I don't have glasses—" I said, carrying the bottle into the kitchen. "Just coffee mugs—oh, but wait." I said, remembering the single, loathsome party Mimi and I had hosted after moving in. "We might have some party cups—"

"Perfect—" He eyed my bare kitchen. "Worse case, we can swig from the bottle." He squinted at the kitchen cabinets. "By the way, nice place. Much nicer than Charlie's. But I see what you mean—no furniture. You're barely alive."

"Freudian slip?" I said, opening a cupboard.

"Oh my god, no!" he sputtered, widening his mouth to approximate a grin. Mimi's few edibles lay on an exposed bottom shelf: two cans of tomato paste, a jar of peanut butter, three plastic sheathes of spaghetti, a can of garbanzo beans and a jar of pickles. Above that, I spotted half a package of napkins and one small stack of red plastic party cups.

"Here we go—" I handed the cups to Dan, who bobbed behind me, clueless of Mimi as a rubber ducky in choppy waters.

"So, do you guys eat in here?" Dan asked. "Like where do you eat?"

"On the floor. Oh, and that chair over there—" I pointed to the red behemoth lazing just outside the threshold of the kitchen. "That thing is off limits. No one is allowed to sit there but Mimi and Todd." I tried not to wince as I said their names, not wanting to be asked to rehash my last encounter with them, the way they stared me down until I'd slunk back into my bedroom.

"Oh my god!" Dan burst into what could only be called hysterics. "You're joking!"

"Sorry, no jokes allowed either—" I said, faintly heartened by his response. I didn't intend to be manipulative, but I could no longer deny Dan the list of risks associated with hosting a "meeting" in the apartment.

"You realize that you're basically living with an abusive teenager twice the size—"

"Yeah, well…"

"Yeah, well. Right! I mean, if I were you—do you mind if I just wipe my nose on that thing?! Spill red wine all over it?!!!" He raised his fist in an act of fake aggression at the red chair. His hysterics continued whole-heartedly as he grabbed the bottle of wine from my hand and leaned over as if to dash the bottle against its armrests. "And how did you meet your so-called roommate?" He asked. I raised my eyebrows, once again preferring "mums the word" over vomiting up the past.

"Long story, but in a nutshell, we're old friends—" I hoped to leave it at that as I sank to the floor next to the chair. I had no intention of sharing further information, though back-story sometimes emerged through body language.

"More like old enemies," Dan said, encouraging me. "Oh my god— She sounds like a nightmare."

"Well—" I said. "That's what happens when you know someone too long." The doorbell rang, and a contingent of wet readers sloshed into the apartment, where the red chair became the focal point—besides Rumi, hummus, and a diminishing bottle of wine—of conversation. Fifteen minutes into the meeting, talk leapt from the red chair to the wine to Rumi to Baudelaire's intended meaning when he said, in *The Living Flame*, "They are my servants, and I am their slave, And all my soul obeys the living flame."

"He's talking about artists," Connor, the effeminate, goateed blond piped up. "The absoluteness of being one—artists who pass along their inspiration to other artists as if they're one being. Giving away their souls as a gift to the future while becoming muse and creator at the same time. It's like birthing. It's the artistic cycle!" These ruminations leaned on the exuberance of my previous statement about how no one should be an artist or a writer unless willing to die for art and the living word. Connor stared at me as we sat around a single lamp, its glow harshening lines around our mouths and on our foreheads.

"I don't know. I'm more literal." Dan said, blinking at his crossed legs while tracing the rim of his cup with a forefinger. "Sure, Baudelaire's talking about the nature of artistic existence, but I don't think he's exclusively referring to artists. I see it as a very simple kind of statement about how we serve each other because that's what it means to be alive."

The group pondered these two views, some responding that both came from the same fabric, but no one ventured more than that as the rain thickened and gusts riled the droplets that pelted windowsills. Darkness glowered in the corners of the room, and the wine bottle rested in the corner of my eye, its green glass blackened by wine residue. A sour, faintly metallic aftertaste filled me with warmth that weighed my empty cup with the poignancy of Baudelaire's attempt to reach those beyond his desk and time. My toes tingled, as if waking up to some hidden principle. And then, as I asked whether anyone would mind if I finished the wine, a grating sound came from the front door.

"Oh shit—" I groaned as Dan turned his clueless lenses on me, eyebrows already high on his forehead. And then we heard her in the entry, speaking fiercely through what must have been gritted teeth—something about Todd always spoiling afternoon plans because he had to catch the Seahawks, and why couldn't they just get naked together without turning on the damn TV.

For a long moment, the room lay beneath a hush as our circle transitioned from Baudelaire to fucking in front of a TV to blatant voyeurism. Worse, Mimi couldn't see us from the foyer, likely only aware of the pitter-patter of droplets against windowpanes. If I dared to smile, as I wanted to, I'd initiate a grand game of telephone and everyone would break into laughter. So, I did nothing.

"I really need to lie down," Mimi was saying. "So could you please not ask me to do anything for you!" We heard her throw down her wet umbrella, and then she stepped like a wet rag into view.

What she felt when she saw us, I can only guess. But based on her blank expression—the way she eyed our ruminating group as she whitened—fatigue rippling into the kind of outrage that distorted features, I would bet my rent money she felt as naked as a lizard lying on its back. Betrayal written on her features, she turned to a hidden Todd, probably prodding his shoulder with a finger.

"Oh god—" She said loud enough for everyone to hear. Todd, with his bright mouth and towering figure, came into full view beneath the archway, his forehead a freshly plowed field of irritation. Very likely he still needed to curse out his girlfriend for being a PMS fanatic, but he braced his hands on his hips as Mimi huffed, "Of all the days—" shaking her head at Todd's wet pant legs and red snowboarding jacket. He had become a Grecian pillar against her emotion and the words, "I so need,"—the rest whispered.

As she spilled demands into Todd's ear, our group peered up at Mimi's profile.

I should have walked over to her, placed a hand on her shoulder, and said, "Mimi. I'm sorry. I meant to mention—" Instead, I remained seated, and said, "Hey," as if nothing had happened. "I didn't know you were coming home so early."

"Yeah." She said, pulling away from Todd's ear to face the half-light. Her lips were thin and pale. "So, I kind of need to pull the bed out so I can lie down. I just threw out my back—" Her voice stung cold, direct as a blade on granite. "So, do you mind?" She nodded toward the group like an executive firing an employee.

We'd sat on the floor for only half an hour, but the wine, drained from our cups, was just beginning to loosen our tongues.

"So we just started." I began in a brave frame of mind, more defiant than compassionate. If need be, she could lie down in my room until the hour was up. "We literally just started our book discussion—"

"Book?" Mimi thinned her eyes, but she didn't allow her voice to grate beyond business tone. "When did you start a book group?"

"Um," Dan said, raising a finger and squinting at me, though speaking mainly to Mimi, who was at his back. "So, we can just head over to the mall down the street and find a café. We're fine."

"No. That's okay. It'll be too loud—" I said, "and we don't have much more to go." For Mimi I added, "Literally half an hour." But Dan, well trained by his foster home days, wasn't going to sit through Mimi's journey towards self-combustion. No surprise that he sputtered through life by choosing the path of non-confrontation.

"No. It's fine. Really," Dan insisted. "We can just—you know—head out." His eyeglasses flashed in the harsh lamplight, encouraging the group to gather itself. Connor's blond goatee, butt crack, and ripped shoulder bag struggled from the carpet while the scratchy sound of jackets rubbed the wrong way towards the door. Mimi stood sentry as the damp and stuffy room emptied out. And I was left to deal with Todd's Doric stare, his white lips sneering distaste, his pent-up fury prematurely ending my summit as hostess of literary salon.

Very Well

Months after moving in, the apartment's sparseness became a sign of what was to come. Though I finally purchased a half-price mattress from a warehouse in Renton and a table lamp from Ross, I still didn't have any place to put my underwear, socks, blue jeans, or sweaters, which spilled from my suitcase onto the closet floor.

Mimi's alcove was equally ill-equipped, its two entries inhibiting privacy. Less sanctuary than storage facility, her room resembled the recessed chamber of a Murphy bed plugged with a futon, a pile of bedding, and dirty laundry. The single clasp lamp aimed at her ceiling barely lightened the gloom. It didn't help that in the kitchen a crate served as a table while, unnervingly, the red chair remained a bloodstain on our friendship—no better than a scab on the carpet in front of the TV. Otherwise, the apartment lay like a Midwestern field: wistful, vacant, awaiting a storm.

After the failed literary salon, it came to me that living with Mimi meant limiting society and culture. All future book clubbers would have to park their studious asses elsewhere, and strangers, especially those I met off-job, would never be welcome.

After the incident, we didn't speak for a week. But then, Mimi appeared half-dressed and groggy, full of statements about how one should live with respect and good communication. "I am so, and I mean so definitely not warm and fuzzy about having people lounge around my room drinking wine from Todd's cups when I'm not here. Okay?" She blurted, tugging at her bathrobe, her hair awry. Had she always considered the living room an extension of her personal space? I questioned this assumption, and she could only stare at me.

True. Todd's snoring and early morning gas often interrupted my preferred routine. And true, Mimi's shoes lay jumbled against one living room wall. But could I allow her to take over the space when I paid more than she while making less? Not wanting to tangle with her razor-sharp voice, I asked a lot of questions, which only encouraged more ranting, beginning with (what else?) an HR lecture about positive communication practices and ending with an impersonation of a used car salesman who never gave in. She would win at all costs, while I wallowed in shame.

"You really want to play this game?" she sneered. "I so don't know who you are, Jane. You walk around like there's no one else in this world but you! Holing up in your room and then inviting the world over for an afternoon of drinking! And then you want your roommate to be thoughtful? Take some responsibility for your choices!" It was a lot of *pummel the victim* and *bleed the sick girl*. And it got worse when she called the book group a "futile attempt at gaining control," followed by a bone-chilling glare as she shouldered past me into the bathroom. Later, she stuffed a note under my bedroom door. It detailed how I should "take responsibility" for my karma and "be cool" while she hosted dinner the following evening, requesting that I lock myself in my room for the night. I caught a movie instead.

Days later, without warning, Mimi spread a picnic blanket in our living room, announcing a second round of revelry—this time involving Todd's entire household. It was Saturday evening, and she seemed all laughs, clapping at the deranged antics and rude jokes coming from guests who yelped, somersaulted, and hollered like circus clowns. When Jody—Pete's ever-annoying girlfriend—no doubt impersonating Marilyn Monroe by wagging her egg-shaped tits and bowling-ball butt (I saw this through my keyhole), cat-calls broke through my locked door and breached my earplugs, causing me to throw *Oliver Twist* across the room.

Possibly around midnight, Todd rapped on my door to ask if I'd like the gelatinous remains of spaghetti marinara—a gesture of **what** I could not tell—though I thought I heard stifled laughter from the living room. It hardly mattered, because I knew they knew I didn't eat meat. I shook my head and shut the door, punching my mouth with fistfuls of soggy leaves from a bag of "Spring Mix" I'd snuck into my closet.

By the time Jody had overdosed on butt thumping noises, our angelic apartment manager, Jack, broke up the party—but not before marinara sauce left war stains on the kitchen floors, with a single blood-colored smear sullying the prairie-vast living room carpet.

For days afterwards, a wooden spoon lay on the counter in a crusted-over globule of sauce.

Oh Shit, Just a Second

My own attempts to cook at Harvard and Republican were hindered by my lack of utensils. Unwashed dishes clogged the sink, leading me to believe that Mimi didn't intend to share culinary tools. Crockery, silverware, and water glasses languished in hazy water as several generations of flies feasted, died, and were reborn in the remnants of too much carousing. Inevitably, I ended up scrubbing while lonesome Saturday nights wheezed into blackness. As an award, I stuffed my face with lettuce and cardboard flavored cereal (a treat). I continued to favor cheap, tasteless, and precut greens over the more expensive locally grown heads of lettuce lying like wedding bouquets beneath QFC's garden lighting. Back to going through three and a half boxes of Shredded Wheat per week (enriched with iron), I often downed the dry squares at dinner, as well as breakfast.

Restaurants were unthinkable, especially as temp jobs proved to be less than steady. When I finally stumbled upon a temp gig that paid $8.50 an hour, I felt like I'd broken a glass ceiling, with $10.00 an hour tantamount to winning a lotto jackpot.

Around this time, I became obsessed with Barbara Erhenreich's *Nickel and Dimed*, realizing that my life had been torn from those pages. Every afternoon I clambered like a desperado to the University of Washington, hoping to snatch a weeklong job the way a seagull snatches a breadcrumb. I begged the receptionist to ask for a temp-to-perm situation—one that might actually come with the miracle of "benefits"—but she only stared at her screen with a blank expression.

It took two weeks to land my first one-day gig as a receptionist, where I made close to $50.00 after taxes. When I got my paycheck, I threw caution to the wind and bought a pound of chanterelles at Pike's Place Market. Ravenous, I raced back to the empty apartment to sauté the orange fungi in one of Mimi's forbidden pans. Gorging myself on the shriveled shrooms only invited bouts of gas. But I didn't regret the feast and promised myself another after I got the next job.

That I ate mainly fruits and vegetables should have caused me to pause. But no, I'd grown shaky and more than a bit winded, and still I didn't think. By then, I'd broken out of bagged iceberg, splurging to include romaine, Boston, red and green leaf lettuces. For two months, I indulged in Bugs Bunny carrots—until my fingertips turned orange. Eventually, I began drizzling my salads with oil and vinegar. By Halloween, I'd purchased a $2.00 paring knife whose blade twice slit through the padded region of my index finger. Disregarding personal injury, I indulged in slicing up several polished red delicious apples, their waxed bodies expressing juices that slickened the countertop.

Oddly, I began phoning my mother daily, leaving long, despairing messages on her answering machine, twice scoring a conversation that circulated over the vast mistake of leaving New York. "I can't continue like this, alone in this city," I said, repeating this mantra every time I left a message.

In response: "But you wanted to leave. And listen," Nora said, caught in her own reverb loop. "I never thought it was a good idea for you and Mimi to move out there together— You've always had a rocky friendship. I remember you two in preschool. You fought over everything. Just like sisters. But you wanted to leave. So, you're there now, and you need to do what you need to do."

Inevitably, Nora became distracted by the acts of washing dishes or applying makeup. There were occasions when she became flummoxed while removing a jacket or while searching for house keys. Inevitably, she broke off with: "Just remember— Oh shit. Just a second. This stupid—" as closet hangers scraped across a metal bar, followed by the ocean-sound of a hand on the mouthpiece, a muffled: "Yes, yes. I'll be off in a minute." And barring that, all I heard from her was an impatient sigh that led to, "What were you saying, Jane? Something about a job?"

Occasionally, she hammered a sore nerve by adding: "You've been miserable for years, Jane. Everyone can see it. And you haven't been shy about letting us know. As for coming back to New York—there's nothing here for you—though, if you want to come back, I'd be happy to see you."

Exasperated, she terminated our calls with: "Damn this... (zipper, jacket, washing machine, mop)!"

During multiple conversations, I sometimes heard Sue, Jill, Mandy, Jennifer or whoever circulated in the background, joking, clapping, or singing. Once the background laughter grew so loud that I barely heard Nora's voice. When I asked if I'd interrupted a party, she laughed: "Oh, no sweetie. It's just a couple of The Avatar's students. They stopped by on their way downtown and wanted to know if I could join them for dinner." Predictably, this fact brought me back to my original sad point, and the cycle of loneliness began again.

Calls About Philosophy

Again it was, "Mom, I'm not happy—" My mantra.

"Well that's something you can change." Her reverb loop. "And by the way, who in the world is happy? Now there's something to complain about!" She laughed, making light, as if she'd been released from prison and had tricked herself into feeling free as a child.

"Please, could we cut the philosophy?"

"But why? Isn't a change what you need, Jane?"

"Not really."

"Look, you can carry unhappiness all around the world, but that's not going to make it go away. So, don't delay the inner journey. Take responsibility and change." Again, the land of Werner Eirhardt.

If I asked, "Mom, do you think anything ever changes?" Her answer sounded like an instruction manual, its repetition so lacking in the particularity of my situation that it sounded like a pastiche of self-help jargon. I couldn't take any of it seriously.

"Look into yourself, Jane. Make the decision to be happy. That's it. It's a decision. You decided to leave New York—and I wasn't for that, if you remember—but you left all the people you knew. Now that you've done it, make sure you do what you went out there to do."

When I burst into tears, she said: "Come back then!" But thinking better—because she knew I'd never allow Mimi to push me back to that previous life of barred childhood bathrooms—she folded with, "Unfortunately, I don't have a place for you here." Good. I would never retreat, though I huddled with knees to chest, crying while clutching the earpiece in the overcast living room.

When the depression had turned into a never-ending flow of tears, runny nose, and clogged throat, Nora suggested a visit to a pill dispensary. "Try St. John's Wart. It's calming and will help you find center." I reminded her of my first meeting with The Avatar, when I'd spent hours each day practicing a form of meditation called the "mirror meditation," how I'd neglected to eat.

"Jane. It's up to you, but finding your inner light will do you some good—" And then she asked how I'd feel about The Avatar calling me.

Eastern Mysticism

Over the years there'd been other versions of The Avatar, beginning with Maharishi and culminating with Swami Namananda's successor, Devotananda. During my mother's joyride through Eastern mysticism, I'd become more cynical, particularly when a journalist discovered that one guru had stashed a few million in a Swiss bank account, while another had secretly bullied her brother out of his rightful position as co-guru. Nevertheless, part of me wanted to believe in the spiritual path. And so, I occasionally dallied with The Avatar, a newcomer in my mother's life who was far more radical than any of the others.

The first time I met him, he looked like a gangster with his bald pate and black suit. He glided over and extended his hand, showing the perfect teeth of his smile. I gave $100 to the blond woman from Hungary whose lipstick looked too red, and then I spent five minutes lying on a leather sofa in The Avatar's darkened session room. Cooing for me to close my eyes, I felt him spread hands over my forehead as he inhaled and exhaled fantastical, unbelievable bits of sunlight that swarmed like bees through the neural pathways of my brain. Sparks floated on The Avatar's breath like diamonds, diving into my forehead and leaving me giddy, surprised, disbelieving but as open as an African savannah.

Odd, because from the first mention of The Avatar's name, I'd doubted the exhaled light, which seemed too Biblical and fantastical to exist—something Dante or Milton or Shakespeare might've dreamed up. And not everyone saw the light—but the flashes and sparks sank like neutrinos through my skin, entering my skull and spinning through gray matter.

"Doubt—" Nora said that evening, toweling off after a shower as I sat on the toilet before bed— "is just the body's way of holding onto Maia." She pulled her silken bathrobe from the door hook and slipped into a pair of clogs. "But he's real, and he's been able to reverse time and make people disappear." This odd piece of information caused me to conclude that The Avatar's entire operation was nothing more than an H.G. Well-ian fantasy, which led me to further conclude that my mother Nora had lost her mind.

Nevertheless, if it was okay for her to lose her mind, so could I. After all, my grandparents had recently left me tens of thousands of dollars, and I'd worked throughout the summer between freshman and sophomore years, accruing a tidy sum—making The Avatar's $100 fee seem like a trip to the zoo. Therefore, I gave myself permission to sip at The Avatar's spiritual table. But, sip was not what I got.

One Small Favor

"I know how you feel about The Avatar," Nora said during one of our longer phone calls. Rain zigzagged across the living room windows and rattled the downspouts, leaving me to feel as though I'd been padlocked in a calendar-square in October, the red chair bleeding through the carpet. "I've never pushed you, Jane. Never."

"So why suggest that I talk to him?" Mimi's futon lay twisted like a wrestler in a dead end of shadows, a body in the gutter, though she hadn't slept there in days.

"Because, Jane. You don't like to hear it, but he's an important part of my life."

Later, I'd sit on the kitchen floor and press five peeled apples into my mouth. "What if," I said, "I walked into the mountains and never came back."

"Jane. Whether you believe it or not, The Avatar helps people. People don't come from all over the world for nothing. He helps people. When I was sick, he healed me. I couldn't eat anything. And then I met him and now I can eat everything."

"I thought your nutritionist was responsible for your recovery."

"Yes—But if it hadn't been for The Avatar, who knows if I'd have made it. I was really sick, Jane. The Avatar really did heal me."

"Right—So." I scissored through the conversation to the subject that most bothered me: What to do about my life.

"Do you want me to call Cathy, have a chat?" Nora asked, the only helpful offer in there.

Back then, Nora and Cathy still talked on the phone and even ate brunch at Sarah Beth's Kitchen or meditated on the rock outcrop at Sheep's Meadow. At least once a year, Nora took the train to Westchester for the annual "Goddesses Slumber Party" at Cathy's sky-lit condo where a bunch of women dressed up like Athena, Aphrodite, and Medusa, sharing beauty tips, vitamins, and the latest spirituality news.

"Maybe I should just get on a boat to Victoria," I said, lowering my voice, one ear expecting the front doorknob to bang into the wall. "Cathy won't understand, but whatever." If she needed to pick up a change of clothes, Mimi usually arrived between 4:00 and 8:00 PM. "Has Cathy said anything?"

"No. We don't talk about you kids. We have plenty of other things to talk about."

"What if I never called you—" I said. "You wouldn't call or know if I was alive or dead." Nora didn't answer, and then like a clown dragging a bad act off stage, a call beeped on her other line.

"I have to take it—" she said, an easy out. Nothing was so simultaneously beneficial and destructive to a relationship as call waiting, but then I'd finally snagged one small favor.

No Fair!

A day later, I dialed her, and she actually picked up. "She's concerned."

"What do you mean?" I said. "Who's concerned? And how do you know?" The rain wouldn't stop pounding the sills, the patter beginning to feel like pennies passing through my skull.

"Jane. There's a lot more going on than meets the eye. First of all, Cathy said Mimi doesn't know how to talk to you."

"What do you mean? How does she know? She never talks to Mimi, and is she serious? Mimi doesn't know how to talk to me? She just has to talk!"

"Well, she's concerned—very concerned about you. And I haven't wanted to say this, but a lot of us are."

"Concerned about me?" Had I landed in a middle school bathroom where the other girls spoke of their concerns that I not steal their boyfriends? "What does that mean? As if she's concerned."

"Oh, wait a min—hang on. Let me see who this is." Her voice clicked out of place, beyond atmosphere, and I hovered in space-time for endless moments before she clicked back. "I need to take this call." There was nothing to do but sink to the floor and lean my head against the red chair.

Later, as I shoveled peas into my mouth and read and re-read a paragraph written by a dead man, the phone rang. My first call of the day.

"Jane, I finally have a moment, and now it's getting late, so I have to make this short." Nora never knew how to rest in conversation.

"You never call. This is amazing. Did you remember my number or did you have to dig?"

"I don't have time for this. Now listen. I have to run out—so just let's move forward. Okay? I don't want to upset you."

"What? Upset me? How would you be able to do that?"

"Jane, I didn't get to tell you what Cathy said." Schadenfreude played like a violin in the back of her throat while I paced in front of the living room windows.

"So, you don't want to upset me?" My throat felt hoarse. "And wait a minute, when did I ask you to talk to Cathy?" For years she half-listened, made decisions, and got it wrong, while for years I complained, never asking why I couldn't get over my parents or excuse their faults. They were human, but I was too young to accept that excuse, and it was so easy for rage to usurp pedestrian patience.

"That's not fair—" Nora said, the phrase a five-year-old might use, but which I'd heard countless times, as far back as the first memory. "You asked for help!"

"Not this kind!" Every one of our confrontations disintegrated into tantrums.

"You wanted me to find out what was going on! So I did!"

"No—no, that's absolutely not true…I didn't—"

"You said—" It took five minutes to move past the misheard and unsaid, and then she almost hung up.

Worn out but stretching the cord into the kitchen to pull peas from the freezer, I said: "You and Cathy came up with a final solution of your own—" I found it comforting to invoke Hitler, Stalin, and Mao as I laid a pot, its rim lined with rust where the Teflon had chipped away, on the stovetop.

"Okay Jane, if you're going to be rude, I'll hang up—"

"No. No. Just say what you're going to say—"

But then she wouldn't divulge a single fragment. There were a lot of, "Why should I's" and "When will you grow up and learn to be more grateful?" and "If you're going to spend your life treating people this way, you'll never get anywhere." But then, after I apologized and promised to think before I spoke, she finally relented with: "Okay—But I'll say this, Jane. I'm not going to be disrespected—"

"That's right, disrespect. I know disrespect!" Thus began another tantrum with each minute growing more gnarled, until the water boiled and the peas bounced against each other in the pot, our voices colliding as she told me I had wrecked her.

"Why do you keep going on and on?" I moaned as I spooned peas into a bowl. "Why?" The call had turned into the longest production of *Long Days Journey Into Night* ever produced.

"I quit!" Her voice lay low, dull, and defeated. "I need to go!"

"You're quitting because of Atlantic City!" I always got her with Atlantic City. Later I'd regret bringing up Atlantic City. But at the time it felt good, like tearing off a hangnail. "You've never considered consequences, have you? You planned it! You went out of your way to keep me in the dark."

"This is so unfair," she said. "You call for help. I do what you want—and you play innocent before throwing everything back in my face.

You bait me, and then you blame me. It's your pattern. You and your father's. You both have the same stupid pattern—" Her voice skyrocketed, becoming brittle in the gravel pit of anger that lay several layers beneath the marble surface of her positive thinking reality. "This is so unfair!" A perpetual child, I stayed on the line, fearing that if I hung up I might be cut off forever. "Listen," her voice simmered. "If you want to push me away like all the other people in your life, you keep doing what you're doing! But you'll end up like your father! And don't ever, **ever** accuse me of—of, this ridiculous—" Her words galloped into me like a horse escaping fire—followed by the oblivion of the click and the endless copper bell of a dial tone.

Trapped in the unfurnished kitchen, I managed to stuff myself with peas, most of which had disintegrated in the pot. Half an hour later I whispered "Mom" into her answering machine, which picked up cordial, but unforgiving.

In the Arms of the Hermaphrodite

But I could never tell Nora about what happened after my second session with The Avatar. I told no one just as I told no one about the way his hands breezed over my breasts or how he whispered that I was a goddess. None of it seemed right in the context of the Branch Dravidians and Aum Shinrikyo, when there were so many gullibles who'd been swindled of their life savings, left to rot after decades of acne and incense and mornings that began at 4:30 AM.

Pundits said cult followers were lost, brainwashed, and easily depleted of resources by spiritual teachers who hung out at places like The Open Center—whose openness turned no wallet away. But I thought I was better than that. After all, I knew myself at nineteen, and wouldn't spend another dollar on a man who blew a few bright lights. But then, I lay down on his sofa for the second time.

There are few words to describe an experience that few people have had. All I have are metaphors and likenesses, because describing a ball of fire—shooting like a missile up my spine, the heat of a thousand, already-spoken-for suns rising and falling an infinite number of times and breaking apart the cortex of my being, cartilage, spinal fluid and nerve cells shattering as I lay paralyzed and melting in an atomic soup—simply isn't enough. Only later would I understand that my body had merged with my mattress and with all that lay beyond the floor beneath my mattress, and with the quantum miasma of a million dimensions. Only later would I understand how awed and stunned I was at the burning explosion in my tailbone that burst through the top of my head—what other gurus called the Sahasrara. It was as if I'd been removed like the iron core from the center of the earth and had finally been set free to swirl like a cloud somewhere beyond the edges of the room.

Did I know that when the episode ended around 3:00 AM—when I gathered my legs and somehow made it to the kitchen faucet where I gulped water and wiped the sweat from my forehead, later stumbling into the bathroom to piss—that I'd never understand or again experience such a feeling? No, I only fell exhausted and empty back into bed, where I found enough strength to scribble the experience in a notebook.

But it wouldn't end there. Swept into darkness again, I found myself in a hall so enormous it contained all of humanity—all those from now to all those who'd ever been to all those who would ever be. At the front of the hall, resting on a throne, sat the hermaphrodite—a woman with a beard, but also a man with breasts. This was the true Guru—and s/he waved, beckoning and gesturing for me to come forward. Walking up the aisle, I realized that s/he was pregnant, though her/his arms were thick as a weightlifter's. Without a word, s/he took me in arms like a daughter and held me as I held her/him, and as we embraced, the space between us no longer existed, because every bit of language and knowledge evaporated into a funnel that became billions of stars and a high-speed chase through the universe, blackness dotted with galaxies, a thousand dimensions into all that was and would be.

After that, nights exploded into dreams, and days merged with nights where people looked like generic, oblong insects with heads that wobbled atop stumps connected to elongated trunks. Bodies became laughable for the odd, disjointed way they got around. And my own reflection fascinated me in new ways. Who was I? And what other crazy experiences could I find behind my eyes?

Hungry for a repeat of the ball of fire, I stood for hours in front of a mirror, staring at myself through flashes of light and green and gold auras, putting off term papers and final exams while my floor mates cultivated relationships with professors who would later provide references and job leads. Immersed in my reflection, I was certain that these sparks of light came from The Avatar's faraway breath, which broke against the shore of my head and blew me away.

But how could anyone choose to emulate all those crumbling people within all those cults? I was certain that I'd never fall for it, always the first to avoid books by Deepak Chopra and articles torn from *Om Magazine*. Titles like "Finding the One in Us All" and "Dialing Up the Deep Unconscious," which lay like abandoned children next to cubbies at yoga studios. They rubbed me the wrong way, and made me think of fuzzy-eyed twenty-year-old girls opening their legs to frumpy, 70-year-old gurus like Sri Rajneesh who hadn't been the first to screw over a harem of devoted virgins in the name of universal love. I knew the story of "Krishny," the fourteen-year-old blond (they were always blond!) who'd attracted the attention of her aged guru. She'd been invited to sleep in the guru's private Ashram garden in Upstate New York, and had promptly gotten pregnant.

But this knowledge wouldn't stop me from spending another $100 for a five-minute session, because I'd fallen in love with the flash of light that pierced my forehead—because as much as I hated to admit it, I'd lost my spiritual virginity to my mother's teacher, guru, shaman, avatar—The Avatar.

The Pressed Rabbit

I knew Stan wanted to make an impression, even when he snorted coke. When he couldn't take "it" anymore, he retreated into a windowless back room, only emerging for the dinner table, where he sat like Henry VIII, eyeing the platter of lamb in its puddle of blood, greasy fingers prying apart turkey or chicken breasts, depositing muscle into his mouth, a slick of animal fat surrounding his lips and dripping down his chin, a wilderness of chest hair revealed after he'd unbuttoned his shirt in the heat he generated during the act of feasting. Every meal became a banquet at a prison, an endless trial where every exertion caused him to break into a sweat.

But I knew I wasn't like him, and I told Nora when we finally spoke a week after she'd hung up on me. This time I lay twisted in my sleeping bag. Only 4:00 in the afternoon, but already dark, I tugged at the phone wire, which stretched from the living room.

"I'm not like him," I said. "And she's not **concerned** about me. She's pretending."

"You've got to wake up, Jane," Nora said, repeating another Cathy-ism for my tired ears. "She told me that you lock your bedroom door."

"Well, so would you! They've taken over the apartment—" As usual, Nora's silence led me to believe she was rummaging through her closet. "Why don't you believe me? Mimi is full of shit. Did she tell you that at one of her parties, there was a fight? A women tried to punch a guy, and Mimi started screaming FIRE—"

Nora, of all people, should have known what it felt like. For years, she complained of feeling like a rabbit caught in my father Stan's bed— calling up the family story that she refused to hear now that I was in such a position. As he told it, my father had found the wild rabbit in his backyard. Small as a pinky, it smelled of humanity after he touched it, and so it couldn't be returned to its mother. Therefore it ended up in a cardboard jewelry box, which Stan took to bed.

One morning he woke to find the box gone. He searched and searched, crying but not finding the bunny. The following night, as he slipped beneath the sheets he felt a crumpled cardboard chill in a damp corner. Pushing back the covers, he discovered the broken box with the baby rabbit pressed flat, cold, and still.

During those dim days when I rarely sanded the hull of The Old Christy or asked JNB if he wanted to get coffee, when I spoke to no one all day but the checkout person at QFC, I too lived in a hutch. Mimi and I no longer knew how to communicate. We no longer had occasional thaws, like that one Sunday in August when we strolled Pike's Place Market to blow a week's worth of cash on produce, jams, and baked goods, intending to sauté eggplant and tomatoes for a pile of homemade linguine. No more moments like the time we lay on our bellies, twirling ribbon around our fingers as we talked about the connection between sexuality and spirituality. This was before a cemetery's hush reigned.

"You so think I'm going to go through your closet, don't you?" Mimi said, attacking on a rare evening when, without Todd, she languished on the red chair, inhaling a bowl of spaghetti. "I don't even wear your size!" Recapping how the lock automatically clicked when I shut my bedroom door and left the apartment, she slitted her eyes. But it was natural to shut doors when leaving. Everyone did it. "Natural! Oh **Please**. There's nothing natural about shutting yourself in!" Mimi retorted. "Meanwhile, I leave everything hanging out so your book friends can enjoy a little intellectual orgy on my futon!" Because I didn't want to appear petty, I neglected to mention that the book club met elsewhere or that a favorite Ricki Lee Jones CD had disappeared on a day when my door had been left open.

Once Mimi became so upset—had I sullied her red chair?—that she flung her 165-pound body against the wall between our rooms, causing the sheet rock to vibrate as several small paint flakes drizzled from the ceiling. No knowing what set her off—but the thud of her body remains with me like prescience. For this reason, I kept a low profile. With few alternatives, I vanished on weekends when she and Todd bedded down in the living room where they brunched on mimosas and eggs before inevitably leaving yolk encrusted dishes and sugar crystals in the kitchen sink.

Fortunately, the unusually mild winter offered me the outdoors. Whether El Nino or La Nina, the mountains and the water were dazzled by the holy event of slanted northern sun breaking through clouds, the kind of beauty that ignited elation in anyone with eyes. Heavy atmosphere over Bainbridge pine opened to a heaven-song of sun holes that reflected silver over water. Gray fields of moisture miraculously drifted south, blown towards the turmoil of Mt. Rainier rather than over the city. Like immovable steel furniture suddenly freed, high-pressure systems steered clear of the Puget Sound, giving Seattle hours and, once, a couple of days of eye-piercing blue.

I tried to commune when these events took place—often joining a loose collective of hikers in flannel, cable knit sweaters, and fleece. These were the Mountaineers, joined by Gortex and a monthly newsletter that listed dozens of treks. During August, I hiked more than twice a week, which meant waking before sunrise to make the carpool. Often, hikes were upwards of eight miles over winding, loamy trails, broken by picnics of nut mix, wedges of bread padded with peanut butter and jelly, baby carrots, and slivers of apple. On a downed log or behind the group, I avoided eating more than a few carrots. But when it rained, the hikes required more gear and planning—both of which didn't come easily, which meant I often caught a chill and came back wet.

Out of habit—especially if Mimi and/or Todd slept on the futon—I vacated the apartment, anxious to circumvent confrontations. Walking meant dodging rage, something I'd learned after so many years around my father. Here were my rules: Out the door early, rain or shine, before pre-caffeinated disaster struck—always better than ineffectual bribery, flattery, or pampering. Best to assume that my absence gave others the chance to release sexual tension—as I well knew because I occasionally woke to Todd's intoxicated sexual pants.

Lack of privacy was the least of my problems. By late autumn financial woes kept me awake at night, breathless, disturbed that the last of my inheritance had dwindled to less than a few thousand, my meager earnings falling short of my spending needs. I regularly sweated through sheets, turning on a lamp to drag out my checkbook and crunch numbers at 3:00 AM. Once again, I seriously considered returning to New York to live in a former colleague's hall closet. And then, UW temporary services called—

No Bunny's Hutch

I dove for the phone, "UW" on caller ID, ready as anyone to embrace the canned coffee, the cotton scent of central air, the endless supply of Excel spreadsheets that came with a temp position. I wanted nothing more than to be tethered to a desk—a perfect "first knot" of safety that transported me away from Mimi, Todd, and all the other "known unknowns."

"I have a fantastic gig for you—" Human Resources said. Like Mimi's mother Cathy, the woman on the other end accentuated keywords like "fantastic" and "enthusiastic" and "resourceful." How had we all become so enamored of keywords?

Turned out, a high-powered group of Epidemiologists at the Fred Hutchinson Cancer Research Center (a.k.a. "The Hutch," as in rabbit hutch) needed support during a one-week-long Native American Cancer Training

Workshop. It wasn't really a desk job. But I'd support intelligent people and might even meet the offspring of the Anasazi. It sounded almost interesting. Best of all, it paid more than $10 an hour—a bounty. "Oh yes," HR added towards the end of the call. "They need you right now. Like this morning."

Fifteen minutes later—in a white button down, polyester slacks, and loafers—I clipped back my bleached hair and sniffed my armpits. Mimi wasn't home, which made poking around her toiletries a breeze. I scanned her shelf of $80 perfumes and found a bottle. Its silver nozzle—cap long gone—and its urine-colored liquid begged to be spritzed. Lifting my shirt over a boob, I exposed an armpit. The deed done, I reeked of cut grass and vanilla bean.

As I walked the nearly two miles to the weird glass building full of Epidemiologists, I couldn't help thinking of Pedro De Serrano, the castaway I studied for a college project, after his rescue from a desert island. Hair down to his rump, body covered with ape fuzz, scabs, and scars, Pedro never fully reunited with civilization after so many years on a waterless, treeless island that offered only tortoise shells for cisterns. The man subsisted on the sundried flesh of turtles, sucking blood directly from their veins just as I subsisted on bagged salad and frozen peas. Like a yogi, he slept on bare rock pounded by sun, rain, and wind, the way I'd slept in a sleeping bag, first on the floor and then a mattress. For eight years he lived with no one but turtles, wiping out every civilized circuit in his brain, leaving him with diamond nerves that sparked at the smallest detail. *A dish lies in a sink smudged with tomato paste. A phone rings exactly eight times. A capless bottle of perfume is placed on a shelf where it accrues dust.* These details filled the deranged with more than loneliness—a feeling I knew well on the island of Harvard and Republican.

Though I wasn't yet a freak the way Pedro had been in the years after his rescue, I felt close to one. I clung to my routines the way Pedro had clung to his hair—which he kept as a dangling mass until his death. Like Pedro, I'd never expected to be weathered by storms, left to dry like turtle meat on the shore, an explorer of nothing—which was how I was beginning to feel on the streets of Seattle.

But somehow, I made it to the Hutch—its labs and offices looking more and more like a rescue ship for the fact that the woman in HR called it one of the top cancer research facilities in the country. At the entrance, a bald man held open the lobby door for me, but I didn't take the hint.

Perfume and the Epis

Alexis—the project coordinator of the Native American Cancer Workshop—met me at the elevator, holding out her hand.

"You found us!" she said through a grin that would never fully disappear during my two weeks at the Hutch. A twenty-something like me, Alexis's casual chic—all $200 yoga pants and Ecco slip-ons—made my button down shirt and brittle hair look like refugee-wear. No doubt, she spent vacations rock climbing in the Himalayas or building hay-bale homes for the poor in Peru.

She led me to a windowless office of blond wood surfaces dotted with the usual steel canisters of pens, paperclips, rubber bands, and Post-its—everything in its place, no flotsam of stray papers within sight—keyboard and monitor beneath shelves of binders that climbed to the ceiling. Limber and yogic, she leaned against the desk, her teeth brightening as she suggested I take the chair. Did offering the only chair equate pity, self-abnegation, or good manners? Either way, she had what I didn't have: relentless purpose and poise.

Sneezing, she pulled a red bandana from the bag lying beneath her desk. "Perfume. I'm allergic—" she mumbled as she blew hard into the cloth. I sat as a pool of heat flooded the vent that was my collar. How much easier it would have been to open a window and leap out.

"I completely agree—" I said, as if agreement eliminated Mimi's offensive scent from room and armpits. Alexis's relentless smile closed the topic.

In the coming weeks, I avoided deodorants and followed Alexis like a tagalong, wishing I could be more pleasant, agile, and focused. Errands included pouring—and on two occasions, spilling—coffee for seminar participants, photocopying hundreds of PowerPoint slides that ended in the trash, ensuring that projectors and bathrooms were in operation, and, at exactly 12:00 PM, rolling out a cart of plastic platters piled with ham and cheese sandwiches, chocolate chip cookies, and shiny red apples. If someone sneezed—which seemed to happen often—I darted forward with a box of tissues. If Ted Beck, the seminar leader, held his hand parallel to the floor and pressed it down through the air, I knew to turn out the lights.

Like Alexis, I acted fast when Ted needed something, because he'd spent half a lifetime as a semi-pro tennis player—and because, he laughed a lot but never seemed at ease. More athlete than "Epi," Ted couldn't sit still. When forced into chairs, legs jittered with the yips, as if he hankered for a thousand laps around Fermi Lab. Adrenals surging, his eyes bulged, neck taut with muscles and ready for a 180-degree spin towards the next viral outbreak. Everything about him belied the life of a number cruncher sitting at a computer. His torso and legs had the elongated appearance of a Claymation character, and his voice sounded dry and sun-stripped. Cheeks and forehead deeply lined, hair bleached white, anyone could see he'd spent years smashing a ball into his opponent.

Fascinated, I expended down time studying Ted's knuckles, which were red orbs after years of grasping rackets. In Dockers and a dark blue polo shirt, tennis shoes and a pair of eyeglasses that he propped on his forehead like a pair of shades, he considered disease an extension of "the game," something to be retrieved and then wiped out. As Ted told a small group during lunch on the second day of the seminar, he grew up a sun worshiper in Phoenix, flirting with his own death every time the sun rose. Sucked dry, he retreated to the moist north coast to: "replenish. I'm such a prune that it's taking me years to feel wet again."

During the many slide shows we yawned through, I learned that Ted converted to medicine at the late age of 26—thanks to one of his tennis companions, a surgeon, who asked if Ted wanted to learn more about a doctor's life. It turned out the surgeon worked for a teaching hospital, where opportunities for promising students could be arranged. As Ted saw it, he lucked out.

"If it weren't for that guy, I'd probably be waiting tables on bad knees, and fighting off a case of melanoma." As Ted put it, a mentor could never be underestimated. "This doctor's slamming balls over the net and saying, 'You can't play tennis for the rest of your life. You've got to make a living.' It's a good thing he planted me on my feet, because I never would have made it as a tennis teacher." It made sense that Ted welcomed the blanched interiors of medical facilities, though by week's end, he proposed to me with, "If you want, I could mentor you."

That was the nicest offer anyone had ever made, but before I could consider saving humanity and pulling off a smile like Alexis's, I'd have to reckon with several personal tragedies, including the fact that I hadn't planned on introducing Parvati to the docks.

Unintended Introductions

But on a mist-laden Saturday morning before Christmas, my old bud from high school unexpectedly sashayed towards me, carrying a latte. In the cold morning light, impressions easily shifted as the water turned from the kind of velvet blue that obscured details to a luminous silver that highlighted Parvati's flawless complexion. Five hours of sleep had left me feeling like a walking rash bandaged in limp hair, which only made the fact of her presence more unsettling.

I'd woken at 4:00AM in order to massage a fifth layer of wood-goo onto the deck of The Old Christy, because I'd lately decided that my weekends should revolve less around the Mountaineers and more around rubbing down wood and chatting about my days at The Hutch with the Native

Americans and the fight against lymphoma with the only man in Seattle—JNB—who'd actually become verbose about his grandfather's untimely death which, according to my online research, was under investigation.

"Yeah, the old man's head was hard to crack—" He continued, fondling the deck boards with a palm I longed to lie beneath. He looked up at something over my head, possibly a heart in the sky, surprising me when he added, "Hey, do you know her?" tipping his chin and raising his brows. I whipped my head around to find Parvati's paper cup at eye level, its plastic hood discharging steam.

"Hey!" I said, standing up. "What are you doing here?"

"I happened to see you—" Parvati said, as if nothing could be more natural than visiting Lake Union while the dawn sky squeezed out another round of moisture. Laughing, she negotiated the wave action of the walkway.

"When you could be home flipping pancakes or soaking in a tub," I said. Odd that she felt compelled to explore the docks at all. But then I'd told her about The Old Christy and JNB when we met up at a café a few days after our surprise meeting at Elliot Bay.

"I found a kiosk that looked more interesting than my bathtub," she said, trying to stabilize her latte as waves from a passing boat rolled beneath the deck.

During introductions, JNB didn't shake her hand but stared at her, suggesting a tour. Eyes fixed on her unbearable skin, he then pummeled her with questions. I followed them through the small vessel, forgotten. From the moment Parvati said his name to the instant she strolled away wagging her bottom—while he digested her—she laughed at everything he said.

Meanwhile, I held her cup—which she handed me as an offering I couldn't drink—wondering what made her so euphoric. They hardly noticed me shivering in the hold that was stuffed with boxes of gear and canned goods. JNB told stories about past expeditions—the one in which The Old Christy almost met its end when an orca mistook it for a walrus—reminding me of the Oliver Sacks book about *The Man Who Mistook His Wife For A Hat*, which might easily have been titled: *The Man Who Mistook The Love Of His Life For An Employee*. For this emotional torture, JNB barely paid me enough to buy tissues for my tearful eyes.

When I got back to the desolate living room at Harvard Avenue East, I finally cried for close to an hour in an under-heated corner. Eventually, all I could do was slump against the wall, staring as rain streaked the windows and rattled the downspouts.

In the doorway, Mimi shook her umbrella, hair wet, a storm in her eyes. I can't tell you what initiated it—maybe it was the note I'd left on the red chair the week before, in which I spelled out how Mimi should finally wash her own dishes—a note that had caused her to stay in Leschi five nights in a row. Or maybe it was the comment I slipped in a week earlier, after arriving home with two bags of produce: "Hey Mimi, could you do me a favor? Could you maybe clean the toilet?" Whatever it was, the tension between us had grown from your basic cube ice to calving blue ice.

In her down coat, her double chin—the result of too many lattes and platters of midnight spaghetti—appeared massive. Dropping her umbrella, purse, and keys onto the hall floor, she hefted her extra chins into the living room. Glaring at me, she said, "I got your note. And while we're at it, Jane," venom in her voice. "Just so we're clear. The bathroom's not just my mess. You haven't cleaned the hair out of the drain for weeks.... And please don't and I mean **don't** use my **perfume** or my **chair** as an excuse to tell me how to live in my own space." Without a word, I stood up, walked into my bedroom, and shut the door with as much grace as I could muster. The satisfying click of the lock sent relief through me—but then, I heard her knuckles, all that rage pounding the door.

What could she find so infuriating? Of all people, I was the weakest. And yet, she came at me until I had no choice but to say, "Yes?" my tone clearly stoking her fury.

I heard the words as she pushed them through her teeth "Would you **please** open the door!" The emphasis on "please" weakened my intent to scream, "fuck you." I said nothing.

"I am so completely," she raged, "and I mean **completely** not interested in you running away! This is not about you being so 'oh my god above it all' to deal with other people who only want to offer help because you so clearly need it!" I didn't answer, and she continued. "You completely don't get the importance of communication, do you? Do you?!" Her yell reached the top floor—where Jack, no doubt, smoothed fudge brownies over his boyfriend's rump—followed by an oblivious: "Oh my god. Whatever!" Mounting pressure caused my locked bedroom door to vibrate with the heat in my cheeks. I would never open the door that protected me, the door that barred me, the door that gave me freedom, the door that held me back.

A moment later, she was back like Jack in *The Shining*. "You are such a piece of work! A huge and I mean **huge** piece of work!" She didn't so much raise her voice as shimmer with fury, so that I almost saw her corpulent lips stumbling over the words. "I can't believe that you can just walk in here," as if she hadn't just walked in, "and start giving orders via notes, and once someone else has something to say in return just retreat into your locked room like a little princess. You are so inconsiderate, so self-absorbed, and so completely and I mean **completely** barren of heart! You are so not the person I used to know as a friend! A **friend**! Oh my god, this experience living with you has been so infuriating and so completely and utterly disappointing!" Inside, an emotional geyser welled up. I tried to stop myself, but I couldn't— It spilled out of me, the unthinkable. To shut her up, I invoked her dead father.

Heartless, Again

The exact words are wiped from my memory—though amnesia sometimes scatters crumbs of the before and after. Had I whispered that not even her dead father wanted to live under the same roof with her? Or had I simply stated, "And that's why your father left you before you were born!"

Either way, the words turned to bullets. I knew I'd knocked the wind out of her. Somewhere in the world two cars collided in an open meadow, igniting a fireball that meant Sati was dead, and Shiva was ripping out his hair. It was unforgivable. I had whipped below the belt.

I heard her zip the puffy coat and gather her keys and purse from the floor, followed by the front door slamming shut.

Enough

I'd had enough. I was done with the gray sands of my living room, but I couldn't leave, because it was too hard to breathe. Against the wall I sank, no one in my world but a smattering of acquaintances.

I didn't really want to be a smudge on Mimi's past, but then I could no longer moderate her moods—which had swung back and forth on the winds of each day. Todd could put up with her angst, which spilled like curdled milk over their sex and spaghetti, the sauce-splotched napkins falling like battle armor to the kitchen floor—clues to a universe hinged on passive aggressive behavior.

Part of me felt relief: No more Todd with his jocular catcalls, *"Mee Mee,* get your booty in here!" No more beer bottles crowding out my lettuce in the refrigerator. No more retreats into my bedroom during parties when Pete's giggling girlfriend felt it necessary to cross-examine me on how I could possibly get through life as a vegan. No more Pete knocking on the front door, asking for Todd before hinting that his girlfriend was a convenient interlude, that what he really needed was an intelligent fuck with someone like myself. Most of all, no need to emotionally rescue Mimi from clashes with Todd—the only time she found me useful, a five minute ego-booster— not that I'd been privy to a surplus of gratitude. Mimi's fickle kindnesses lay far and few between as short-lived sweet nothings. For years to come, I'd think of those months in the same apartment with her as a period dedicated to walking on hot coals, when every run-in left me singed.

The next morning, eyeing me as if I were a convicted murderer, Mimi insisted one of us move out. We had several months left on the lease, but I had no guarantee of stable income. Worse, going solo to find and secure a new apartment felt impossible, overwhelming. With her ongoing job at the hotel, and a boyfriend who had a history of lying for a lease, she had better prospects.

"I'm not moving out." I said, digging in for the first time. I couldn't look at her double chin, but I stood firm in the kitchen doorway while she held open the refrigerator door and stared at its mainly empty shelves. Pulling out an open carton of milk, she gulped from its cardboard lip. If a fight threatened, I wasn't going to stick around for its eruption. No regrets. None, whatsoever.

Goodbye, Hello

"Good riddance!"

<u>A Reliable One</u>

The day Mimi and Todd wrestled out their beached whale—the futon—and shunted the only chair (good riddance red chair!) from the apartment, I met Jessica. My ad for a roommate elicited several phone calls, many seekers immediately struck down. I wanted a woman in her mid-twenties, preferably a grad student or professional because the two most desirable traits in a cohabitant were responsibility and a packed calendar.

Struck down was the single, harried-sounding mother with two-year-old son who said, "I cook, I clean, my kid is quiet. And we like to sleep a lot." The gay man in his forties who regularly watched late night movies, smoked cigars ("but I lean out the window") and came with a wrap-around sofa, glass coffee table, "lacquered" dining set and a number of other "plush" furnishings—which made the whole mess seem overwhelming and demanding—wasn't an option. Driving home the point, I didn't answer his voicemail after he added: "Do you have a full-size kitchen? I bake a very addictive coffee cake!"

The woman who could clean the apartment once a week in exchange for a $50 discount never got a call back. A flush bank account and a lack of baggage won bonus points, so that when Jessica said she'd moved from the Bay Area, had a steady job, and wanted something for a year, I asked her over pronto. On the phone she sounded easygoing, almost wholesome when she asked what I liked to read, because she "really" loved a good novel and enjoyed sharing literature.

At first glance, Jessica, with a ponytail that smelled of Herbal Essences, a belted rain jacket, crisp jeans and quartz ear studs, fit the twenty-something-rising-in-the-world bill. Pursuing social work, she hoped to enter U.W's graduate program in Psychology. Furthermore, her resume said she'd studied at Stanford, spent a year at Oxford reading Thomas Hardy and George Elliot, and was fluent in French.

In the living room, she clasped her handbag and a black file folder. Eyeing the emptiness, she said: "This is really nice—I love the molding! It reminds me of a Hopper painting." I hadn't thought about my lack of furnishings as Hopperesque (that belonged to the blood-red apartment Mimi and I had rejected), but I let the reference go. Giggling, she segued to what she wanted in a living situation.

"First, I have to say, it's so cool that you've worked at UW? They have a really great Psych program? Right now? I'm working for this social welfare nonprofit downtown?" She ended most sentences with the upward intonation of a question. "A lot of the work is with mentally disabled people, but I'm getting great experience? I only get $8 an hour, but my mom helps out, so I don't have to worry about rent— I'm like always on time? Plus, I really like this kind of set up—just two people? You know what I mean? It makes for a really supportive living space? You know how it is when you have like three or four roommates?" She sounded positive, focused, and most importantly, funded. "You can do so much with this place," she continued, noting the kitchen's glass cabinets. "I'm like a really low maintenance person, but if you need design tips, I am into Décor and just love all that stuff—"

"You don't mind that your bedroom has two entrances?" I said, picking up on the upward intonation. "It's not very private, if you know what I mean?" She had other options after all, and I needed the $400 Mimi wasn't paying.

Jessica seemed to need giggling, which made her ponytail wag. "I so don't mind an open space—" She giggled. "I love that there's nothing here, you know what I mean? It's like an empty pallet. I've seen lots of places and this is like really nice for what you're asking. I mean look at this amazing kitchen—and the wood trim around the windows! And the carpets are amazingly clean! So much nicer than a place I saw yesterday with a dark blue rug that had like a layer of white dust on it and smelled like someone's sick dog?"

She'd be able to move in, "Right away! Like even tomorrow if you want—" I was surprised at the speed of her decision. She'd been in the apartment for no more than twenty minutes. But, relieved that I wouldn't have to call back the guy who wanted to pay $350, I took Jessica's check with its Golden Gate Bridge and overly elaborate signature, and sorted out the move-in date before settling the 50/50 split of utilities and phone bill—long distance calls paid separately. All squared away, she said: "So, is it okay if I just drop off a few things tomorrow night?" I gave her the go-ahead and returned to more pressing issues, like how to stop mourning JNB while I looked for another paying gig.

George and Bill

The mere mention of the Burk Gilman Trail—which sideswiped Lake Union where boats were moored—increased the speed of my wrongly-valved heart, because in my mind, JNB's hands caressed my thighs instead of The Old Christy. Socks soaked, I stumbled along the trail, stopping at UW's

HR office, where I found no jobs. Close to penniless, all I had left was the prospect of hitching a ride to a place known for quick bucks. When I placed the ad on UW's free-ride board, I told myself a change would be therapeutic, hoping that a graduate student might be reckless enough to drive 1,100 miles along I-84 E., singing folk songs with a stranger who rejected pork rinds and beef jerky in favor of string beans.

That evening, as I fisted pre-washed lettuce into my mouth, the phone rang yet again, likely "backwash" from my roommate listing—though each ring brought to mind JNB. Occasionally calls seemed to stem from pubescent boredom. Only that morning a guy with a Russian accent, claiming he'd gotten tired of Chicago's beef business and totally understood my vegan preferences, called to ask if I'd like to hear him play cello. Then there was the caller who claimed to be "George of the Jungle," in search of a room where he could treat me to a little lion licking. I'd immediately hung up.

Exhausted but addicted to picking up the phone, I had not choice but to confront the next caller—who sounded emotionally incontinent. This is how the conversation went:

"Hi," he said.

"Yes?"

"Hi— My name is Bill."

"Yes? Can I help you, Bill?" As always, I kept a professional tone, though I already knew I should hang up.

"Yeah." His throat sounded like it was plugged with peanut butter when he said, "You put an ad up for a ride to, was it Las Vegas?" His voice veering towards falsetto, he added, "The end of next month?" I knew he was wiping tears of laughter from his eyes.

"Yes. That's right. I'm interested in a ride."

"What kind? I mean, which part? Where?" He cleared his throat, deepening the timbre. "By way of Cali? Or through Nevada?" When he said Nevada another burp of hilarity broke loose.

"I don't have a preference, though the fastest way is best," I replied.

"I could maybe go there. But I can't say yet."

"Would you be driving that way then?"

"Me? No. Not me, no. No. I'm calling for another guy named Bill." Again, a faint itch of laughter lifted the edge of his voice. Why I continued after this, I don't know—but it may have been due to desperation.

"Bill. Okay. I see." I said, pulling a pen from the plastic cup I kept near the phone, thinking it ridiculous but following protocol as I scribbled the name on a fragment of paper. "When will Bill know his plans?"

"I'll have to get back to you about that," the man answered with a weird exhalation that sounded like a stifled guffaw.

"Okay. Well." I said. "When can you get back to me?"

"How about next week." Full-on laughter sprang through the earpiece.

"Okay," I said, knowing it was ridiculous, but continuing just to continue. "I'm not sure I'll be going there anyway. I might just fly—but if this is real, yeah. I'd like to know." In wild cascades of laughter, he hung up.

I crouched on the carpet as if peeing in the forest, phone to my chest, puzzled by who would play such a trick. Who hated me other than Mimi and Todd? Possibly Pete or his girlfriend, but definitely not JNB, Parvati, or the book club people. There was Ted and Alexis—but not them. Who knew I'd posted a ride request at UW? And why would whoever it was pretend not to know me? All night and the next day I wondered. First "George of the Jungle," and then this—both callers sounding suspiciously similar. What desperate character wanted to toy with my head?

For years I continued to wonder who or what was behind all this, especially as more strange phone calls piled up, followed by the first of many strange incidents—all ultimately leading me back to who else, but you.

Sudden Run-Ins

Funds daily shrinking, it became difficult to pay for heat, light, the occasional pack of gum—let alone shell out hundreds for plane fare and a hotel room. Struggling, I delayed the trip to Las Vegas that Nora had suggested in our last conversation before I told her that every flight was booked. During the sallow months of winter when darkness hauled me through the hours like a corpse tied to a truck, desperation clung to me like plastic wrap, covering my days in a way that spoiled even the heartiest of holidays—Christmas. Wreaths hung on doors. Lights twinkled on foliage. But I was valueless in a town vomiting money, little more than a shiver in my vacant room. And still, life knocked into me with its surprises.

Sometimes it got so bad that I dug into my pockets to find enough change to indulge in a doughy, butter-less shot of potato peppercorn folded into a crinkly brown sack. As hard as it was to watch others dunking their daily breakfast into froth and sugar at Noah's Bagels, it was harder still to face the truth.

One gray morning, as I tore into the soft bulge of a peppercorn bagel, Parvati caught me in the act. My mouth stuffed, I had no time to hide.

"You're eating!" She said, as if this rare act should be announced to the entire bagelry. I didn't know what to say, because our sudden run-in at dawn qualified as suspect—particularly because Capitol Hill waved its flag so far from the International District.

Like her namesake, Parvati looked her usual radiant, relaxed, and holistic self, a goddess in blue jeans, pink scarf, and beige coat. Fresh from the outdoors, she appeared almost virginal as joy discharged from her in sharp contrast to the bleakness of the morning. Most disturbing, she wasn't alone.

Patting my shoulder instead of offering a half-hug, she nodded towards the glass case of radioactive-looking bagels, where I found proof of what I suspected but never wanted to admit. He had his back to me. I knew by the way his coat fell over his shoulders, the way he ambled to the napkin dispenser where he stirred his coffee and shook the half n' half from a steel thermos. She didn't need to say anything. But she did.

"So when," I might have said. "Did this happen?" Or more falsely, I might have tried to cover up dismay with, "You go girl! You completely amazing lady! This is great. Why didn't you tell me?" While all I really wanted to say was, "you two-timing little fuck!"

But no. None of that came out of my mouth. Instead, I pretended not to understand, saying, "So has he got you volunteering?"

"Not yet—" She said, point blank, a friends-with-benefits smile beginning to transform her bedroom eyes into disco balls. She continued, a blush highlighting the sparks shooting out of her eyes. "Actually—it's kind of funny. It's not what you'd expect—"

"Don't tell me. You're going to Alaska with him and then you're going to get married?" I'd pried open the clam a little too quickly, with a bit too much elbow grease. In seconds, Parvati's bubbles and pinkness washed down the gutter. She understood, but pretended not to as she stared at me, the whole matter of my infatuation on the table.

That's when his wood-fondling hand grabbed hers. Like a husband, he gazed at her perfectly straight hair, her smooth cheek and barely perceptible nose—a mere bump on her bland face. And when he turned his magnetism on me, a black hole sucked me into his eyes.

"Nice to see you somewhere warm." His voice sounded like it could rumble the earth. He smiled over the tendrils of steam rising from his cup, which he gripped with his boat hands. Had he grown up in the Pacific Northwest, not in Boston, he still would have had nice hands.

At some point, maybe after I'd downed the rest of my obscene bagel, I asked how long they'd been together. As if I should know better, Parvati sang: "Oh just for a little while now. You know—" She spoke more to him than to me, becoming faux-shy as she gazed up at him—the relentless floozy. "JNB has so much to do. And," she began with a tease, "I'm his faithful adventure seeker."

Turned out, they'd gotten together the day I'd introduced them.

In the years to come they'd be forever thankful—or so their laced fingers suggested—as JNB circumnavigated the globe, guiding and fucking his thrill-seeker through the rugged, open waters of sexual exploration.

It didn't seem right that in this one life the two of them could have all that I wanted but would never have—the feeling of naked love and reassurance found only with each other. It didn't seem right that he got to "sail away," and be a death-seeker who never became a casualty, that he could lick the outlines of many lives without plunging in, that he could slurp up whoever the fuck he wanted, that his fortune had dubious origins because he'd almost lost the game when investigators suspected that he'd knocked a gun against his grandfather's head. So let her have him!

"Let me know," he was saying to me as he bit into the sesame seed, nova scotia bagel Parvati held to his lips, "if you can get down to the boat today." Like one person, one body, like Siamese twins, they danced through breakfast as a chill triangle of air—made colder by my feelings—swept through the bagel shop from the swinging door.

I had to remember that he'd soon head for the outskirts of the civilized world where the nose of a humpback would remind him of the woman—me—who'd sanded that deck until her hands had turned to bone. But this fact hardly helped. I'd already been diced into a thousand pieces.

Always a Sucker

Of course I wallowed in pain. To wallow is a pig's game. And mud is a protective salve for those of us who are suckers, which is why I spent a Friday evening slurping wine—votives flickering—as Parvati dangled a loop of clam linguine near her perfect lips, pretending—it seemed to me—that I had no feelings. Playing the same game, I asked the question every woman's magazine has asked: Was the sex good?

Ever the prude, she answered in that coy, false manner—chin dipped, eyes peering up from her plate. "He's really, really nice—I mean, his hands." She gazed at the votive that shouldn't have flashed between us. "They know exactly what to do. And my god, I've never felt so close to anyone." Pain rained down my throat, collecting as a pool in my abdomen.

"But," I said, wanting to remind her. "He's leaving—"

"I know, I know!" answered Parvati, chest aflutter—a pair of wings flapping beneath her sweater. A line of linguine fell from the tines to her tongue. As she chewed, every pore in her skin glowed, olive oil glossing her lips when she smiled. "But that doesn't mean we have to be all buttoned up—" I gulped my pinot, which left me feeling false, factory made, mass-produced. "We have a very nice arrangement. That's why he's here all winter! To be with people. Understand?!" She spoke as if everything about sex and love and the rest of life was obvious. And yet, I didn't and wouldn't understand.

Pit E

For days I rolled around "the pit" as a force of habit while Jessica settled into her 8 x 8 room. She unpacked two suitcases and filled our refrigerator with vegetables. It turned out she obsessed over plastic bags of lettuce and frozen peas as much as I did. To keep our edibles separate, I used a Sharpie, scribbling my initials on every culinary item I purchased. Often, when I got home from the store or from trekking the waterfront, Jessica would be seated in the living room, cross-legged like a Buddha on the carpet, clutching a bowl of warm peas, her ruby lipstick smeared at the corners as she scooped spoonfuls into her mouth, bemoaning her day with "clients" at the social welfare facility whose name and location I never learned.

During our first dinner together, Jessica waxed on about her family. Most impressively, the father played football for the Raiders. Her parents, like everyone else's, divorced by the time she crawled, and now her mother—a "beauty queen" who grew up in Pebble Beach—lived alone in a spectacular Belvedere stucco wedding cake that overlooked the SF Bay. From a thin black sleeve tucked in a corner beneath piles of clothes, Jessica pulled out a single photo of her mother, a prim-looking woman with shoulder-length hair who wore a wide-brimmed hat, half her face in shadow, her back to the ocean. Jessica gazed at the slender 50-something. My father Stan would have flushed a pound of marijuana down the toilet to lie naked for one night on the beach with Jessica's mother. "She's just like this amazing mom?" Jessica, the model daughter, was saying, "Really amazing! I mean oh my god, if I could be half of her?!"

But Jessica's mother's wealth didn't bring ease to daily life. One evening Jessica threw open the front door, hyperventilating over having to wipe shit from a client's ass, her cheeks red as her Betty Boop lipstick, eyes popping in the aftermath of the fetid brown dribble that had slipped down the man's leg where it sullied her shoes. "I can't take it. I can't!" She bellowed, throwing off the ruined shoes and shoving them in the trash. For the first time since she'd moved in, her expression looked like that of a cow's during slaughter. "These people. Oh my god! They aren't people?! They're lab animals in little trapped spaces?! They're not human!"

A few days later, she materialized in my bedroom doorway shaken—though less visibly—her chin quivering as she related how, at lunch time, she'd called for a straight jacket, this while a client performed self-mutilation, tearing the hair and skin from pubis while bashing head against a doorframe.

It sounded too unreal, like a documentary about sanitariums in the 1950s. This wasn't how psyche wards operated. But as Jessica described it, the woman scratched off her eyebrows with a fingernail, nearly puncturing an eyeball, blood gushing from the forehead and cascading like Niagara Falls over her jaw line. Part of me couldn't believe such gore. This had to be a story. It all seemed so un-medicated and Dickensian—even as signals of post-traumatic stress paled Jessica's lips and twitched her eyelids. Disbelieving and nonchalant, I told her to take a shower, watch cartoons, and chill with a bowl of frozen peas.

But the following Monday, she came home maimed.

"I mean," she began in monotone, her jaw trembling, strands of hair pasted by tears and cold sweat to her cheeks. Leaning against the wall beneath the living room archway, she spoke through dry, nearly white lips. "We had to wrap him up really tight, as tight as the jacket gets, and my boss Harvey had a needle six inches long and stuck it in the guy's butt three times to get him to sink? Like the guy almost died?" But not, she said, before the client managed to take a bite out of her right calf. In fact, this story seemed to make the least sense. After all, hadn't the patient been on meds? Everyone knew that psyche wards were full of people swimming in meds.

As if to remove my doubts, she tentatively rolled up her blue jeans, wincing as she revealed a layer of gauze and bloodied cotton balls beneath two strips of bandage tape. When I saw the swollen and mottled skin of the wound, her story seemed even more unbelievable for the puncture marks that looked as if produced by a hyena. Despite stitches and layers of bandages, her calf would eventually require laser soldering.

But at the time, I had no choice but to believe her when she whimpered, "I'm so glad I had that DTAP a month ago? But still? Now I have to take like all these antibiotics, even after they irrigated. It hurt like hell, oh my god!" She went on about sitting all afternoon in the ER while a nurse and a doctor reviewed the biter's medical chart and the program director disbursed advice. Jessica told me she "completely embraced" those few hours on Vicodin, zoning in and out as the borders of her day dissolved.

During this period, I tried to avoid painful topics, but Jessica listened too well—especially during that first month when I foolishly told her everything.

Everyone I knew in Seattle (except Mimi)—including JNB, and Parvati—thought I left New York for a fresh start. No one understood that I'd never really left, that in fact I couldn't move past my past. And still, the hospital, the car, the smoke-infested room I rented from the wannabe-Broadway-star-but-mere-mom who finally kicked me out, still existed as silk-screened images that layered my days, which had become more minimal with every passing minute. Only Mimi had understood some of this. After all, she loved mentioning the hospital when she meant to inflict pain.

Confession

First there was Rudy's point of view. Then there was the eighteen-wheeler's perspective as it swerved into the sedan. Eventually, I obsessed over the bug's point of view as it was flattened beneath the overturned vehicle, all those worms wiggling within mud gouged by spinning tires, the crumpled windshield, and finally the upside down man crushed inside. The only witness—matter and light—knew that everyday I drifted further away from my own point of view.

For some reason I shared this with Jessica as we lounged on the carpet beneath the Christmas lights strung around molding. As we ate our peas, stories of Ben burst like a flashbulb and filled the room. I'd pickled and jarred him in the left cupboard of my brain, noting a first kiss in a kindergarten stairwell, our parents joking about an impending marriage though his penis was no larger than his index finger. I mentioned the plywood house at the back of the playground where we stripped naked and giggled, how seventeen years later, we rediscovered each other in bed.

On our first date, he showed me footage of him dropping from an airplane. He spread his arms, the picture briefly erupting with static before his parachute sprang open, the static clearing to fabric unfurling like Isadora Duncan's last windblown scarf, an exclamation point descending ten thousand feet. I babbled about Ben's smuggled cigars, hand-carved humidors, illicit trips to Argentina, a master carpenter in Vermont who siphoned maple syrup directly from trees, about liking tweed jackets with patched elbows, about the smell of dry pine forests that wafted from the hair on his chest.

I didn't mention Wupatki or the time I discovered him eating fried clams with the stinky dancer who spread her legs too wide. I neglected to talk about how Ben fucked me while I spoke with Mimi over the phone.

"Hey," Mimi had said. "So, I have this friend, and I so think you'd completely like him—" She'd wanted to set me up on a blind date, and I said yes, while Ben leaned in and beautifully fucked me.

We loved sex but not being faithful. I neglected to tell Jessica that I abandoned Ben in the hospital, that three thousand miles east of Harvard and Republican he was either in recovery at a physical therapy facility or dead.

Sure, his friends were losers—especially the dancer, with her frizzy hair and naughty pout, hating the way she moaned on and on about Twyla Tharp and Martha Graham. For years since, I've wanted to forget the way she slipped an arm, redolent of B.O., over Ben's shoulder, the little "friend peck" on his cheek, the illicit nose-nuzzle to his neck when she peeped, "See you later." I knew they sucked opiates from a blue bong that flew like a witch through an endless Halloween night of futons in front of TVs showing Jackie Chan's foot meeting a rival's jaw.

It was all so sad. Rudy, the "Wuss," believed Ben loved him—Rudy, who couldn't see his son's missteps. Ben, the addict—was this why I ran from the hospital?

Confessing to Jessica, I claimed Ben needed me to go. Anyone with eyes—especially someone pursuing a sociology degree—could see Ben's plaster casts still twisted around my imagination, all those tubes stuck into him plugged into the apparatus that pumped emotion to the darker side of my spirit. Loss had a way of resurfacing like a skeleton uplifted from an ocean floor, its cold outline usually arriving at 3 AM.

Jessica looked sympathetic, her forehead pinched, her ears trained on every vocal tremor. Occasionally she interrupted to ask the obvious. Why hadn't I contacted Ben since moving? Why allow wounds to fester? Why, she wondered, did I still feel anything for a man who betrayed everyone close to him? I had no answers.

"So, call him?" she queried with raised brows. "You have his dad's number, right?"

"I can't do that—" I told her.

"No, I think you can, Jane," All behavioral therapist. "If you want to find closure—" And when had I explicitly said I needed closure? "Just call—"

But I couldn't get near the phone. I had pride. I owed no apologies. If anything, I owed myself applause for putting as much space between me and him as possible.

A Plan

The sitcom began Friday evening, when everything felt black as a vampire's cape. After we'd downed our peas and lettuce, Jessica slammed her palm against the carpet and yelled, "I have an idea." Five nights we'd huddled under Christmas lights like backpackers roasting ourselves over the fiery topic of Ben. Five nights Jessica lay belly-down on the carpet, picking through the white pellets of QFC rice cakes discharged on a bath towel. That night she panted, "Let's call him!" like we were in Jr. High.

"No way," I returned, my heart in my forehead. "It's not happening. It's too late!"

"But why," she persisted. "It's only 8:30 there." (This didn't mean anything. 8:30, for me, was bedtime.) But Jessica persisted— "You said he stayed up till 3:00."

"That was before the coma!" I went so far as to roll my eyes. "There won't be a call. Period. And what if he's not with Rudy; what if he's dead."

"All the more reason!"

Usually I could be plied like putty from arguments. But I dug in. Was it pride or fear of bad news? Was it the thought of Rudy, who hated me? A call would only underline that fact— "Tell his dad you're someone else. Actually, wait a minute. I know. I'll talk for you."

"**No**. No. No. No." I held up my hand, shaking my head, ready to fling something at her. "Pretending and harassing his almost or possibly dead son? NO!" And then a moment later: "What are you going to say anyway?"

"I'll say what you've been saying to me." Sartre's *No Exit. The Book of Revelations*. Krishna speaking to Arjuna.

"No. No. No—" Again, the upheld hand: The discussion needed to be terminated.

But like a bad miniseries the back and forth continued until Jessica finally drilled through me with, "I can be someone Ben met at a party ages ago. I'll be Jenn. Everyone knows a Jenn."

Teeth digging into my fist, I was no better than a sun-roasted rodent when Jessica added, "Trust me? This will be the best thing you ever did!"

Execution of Plan

When had anyone trusted the Cheshire Cat? Jessica smiled and pressed the phone between her ear and shoulder, patient, persuasive, all social worker. At first, I wouldn't give her the number, but she waited with that non-confrontational smile, as if offering tea to a table of people playing bridge.

Like so many in our self-help nation, Jessica glorified the simplistic, using aphorisms and one-liners rather than elongated, thought-out arguments. *It's best to get over him*, she said. *Face the music, fly into the storm, be committed to getting over the grand "it," whatever "it" might be. Take the bull by its horns. Ride the next wave.* Yes, she was giving me the pep talk to end all pep talks, and I would change my life, God damn it! Calling Ben, she said, was the only way to get over my pride and sew up wounds. Dialing his beeper number, would be "downright simple" and "easy-peasy."

Amazingly, my address book still provided information. Out of its faded pages fluttered the scrap Ben had penned with his number when we reconnected. There'd been a hundred occasions when I'd flipped through this directory, searching for this very scrap among skyscrapers of information— half as many times I hadn't found it. It had to be meaningful that this triangular sail of paper fell between my knees, the only evidence that Ben had traversed the ocean of my life.

I gazed at his handwriting, trying to figure out how the loops of his name and the upright 2s, 5s, and 8s of his number led back to his fingers. Beyond those numbers, I had little proof that he'd existed: no videos or emails, hardly any photos, just a few tree fibers speckled with ink.

At the time, the plan sounded fool proof—even elegant. In essence, the strategy only required a short exchange, with a tease of more to come. We'd beep, he'd call back, she'd pick up, and then she'd procure information.

Swimming in perspiration next to the phone, but staring up at the icy ceiling, I heard Jessica punch in the number. Pressing the * button, she hung up. I caressed the tooth marks I'd inflicted on my fists, releasing pregnant-woman exhalations through my circled lips. We listened while rain, lifted by gusts, nested against the living room windows. Still no ring. I rose to switch on the kitchen light, which slanted through the doorway and blanched a far wall.

Back East, it was 9 PM, the time for reading in bed, when his beeper could be in the kitchen next to a can of chicken noodle soup. If he held a remote and flipped from a National Geographic special to HBO, he might have the beeper in his pocket where it would buzz against his hip and ignite a faint sexual response. Or Rudy might be complaining about hospital bills— *those nurses, those what do you call them people who can't be trusted*—while the beeper vibrated in another room. After ten minutes, Jessica wanted to try again.

This time, she got a recording—the number had been disconnected. "No!" I cried, worst-case scenarios beginning to form into real possibilities: He'd collapsed during physical therapy, the beeper now packed away in Rudy's attic. Worse: Death from painkiller overdose, beeper buried with him in casket. More problematic: Ben and beeper lost in the Vermont wilderness, mauled and chewed by black bear—beeper swallowed and then upchucked into a remote stream— Or most likely, Ben simply comatose after crashing his car for the second time while driving back from Vermont—beeper left like road kill to pollute the loam.

"Are you sure you dialed right?" Back and forth, pacing the floor like an eraser over a page, I couldn't find the context. But no—she wasn't sure, and tried again. Again, the feminine voice intoned: "We're sorry. You have reached a disconnected number. Please check your number and dial again."

No choice but to revise the plan. It was all: "Shit! Now what?" Followed by Jessica's: "You said you had his dad's address. We could call information and get a number?"

"No. We can't. It's too late! Rudy's probably in bed."

First Connection

Answers lived in tangled cords and plastic earpieces—but they hadn't always. Nora liked to say that in the old days information required community relations and niceties like hand delivered letters, door knocking, bowing, and the occasional basket of edibles. Answers required knowing who to know and how to make an entrance.

Though I'd never learned the niceties of baking banana bread and writing my name in calligraphy, Jessica insisted I find Rudy's contact info. Breathless, expecting the worst, my body turned Catholic: hands clasped for prayer, my forehead downward as if awaiting a waterfall of darkness. I remained, unmoving, as she reached for the phone.

Was the Quantum universe delivering a punch when that very phone sang like a siren, so that in slow motion I yelled, "Get it! Oh my God! Get it!"? My words, thick as syrup, seeped through the walls and ceiling. Two beats later I whisper-yelled, "Jessica!!!!" whacking the carpet with an open palm. "Jessica!" A Lepton seemed to spring from her forehead as, attempting to shut me up, she flapped her hands and frowned.

Gripping the phone with one hand, cupping the mouthpiece with another, and then cradling it against her ear, she murmured, "Hello?" Instantaneously, she'd become a sex therapist. I inched closer to the earpiece, but found it difficult to hear more than a muffled vowel or fricative. In the moments that followed, Jessica's mouthing and gestures eventually expressed the gist of the conversation. Here's its reconstruction:

"Hello?" I knew his voice, the pauses, how he took a breath before saying, "You called?" These were the first words I'd heard from Ben since the night I ran from the cab. Jessica murmured something, staring at me and pressing a finger against my lips as a gush of air exploded from my nostrils. Next, he said, "Who's this?" Did I detect curiosity or paranoia?

"Don't you remember?" Jessica breathed. "We met at a party? Last summer? It's Jenn?"

"Jenn?" There were thousands of Jenns, but I shook my head and mouthed: "No, no—not last summer. This summer!" and pounded the carpet.

But Jessica ignored me, carrying on. "How are you?"

Whatever he said, was something like, "Okay. How are you?"

"Okay." Her voice pierced my ears, needles in each lobe—but I thought I heard him say:

"Where are you?"

He must have known our location. He'd dialed the number on his beeper. But he pretended not to be familiar with the area code.

"I moved out to Seattle last spring," she answered, blinking at me with a strange smile.

"Seattle?"

"Yeah. Ever been?"

"No."

"Where are you?"

"Home."

"Where's home these days?"

"New Jersey." It sounded banal, I gestured for her to speed up the give and take, find out more.

"Duh. Yeah. I knew that? But where in New Jersey? You never said." He probably hated the word "duh," because there was a pause followed by a response I heard loud and clear.

"So, why are you calling me now, Jenn?"

She barely blinked. "Because?" Jessica said, lingering over the word like a fashionista swabbing perfume beneath her earlobe. "Because, I met someone? Someone you know out here?" All questions—I'd forgotten how much Jessica liked to end her sentences as if they were questions.

Widening my eyes, I shook my head. No use. She turned away. I shoved my face in her line of vision, slicing a forefinger across my lips like my first grade teacher, meaning Jessica should shut up or lose her ass. She ignored me.

"Yeah," he said. "Who?" I yanked the phone cord in a game of tug of war. Delivering myself in mercy, I lay down on my belly and pounded my palms against the carpet, not quite stifling the hyena inside. I was at the circus, wearing polka dots and glitter and stumbling on one leg across the tightrope of shame. Would I always be a child witnessing the slaughter and skinning of my own future?

"Do you know a girl?" Jessica murmured, still eyeing me. "From New York? She moved out here? We were just talking? It's so funny? She said she knew you?" Like a beached humpback, I struggled to breathe, sucking air. I'd sent him off a road, down a hillside, into a coma. I'd abandoned him, screwed over his father. Now I was tricking him. What kind of person backstabbed and then showed up to explode the remains?

"Yeah?" Jessica whispered, her pupils steady. No smile, just eyes. "She's like one of the coolest people I know?" Silent laughter exploded from me, slammed into my ribs, with what no one would consider joy. My hands pressed to mouth, my eyes dripped tears.

"So, what's her name?" Yes, her name?

"Her name," Jessica smiled, pausing because she knew I needed that pause. And then, with those damn eyes that never moved, she delivered a bottle of cyanide. "Her name is Jane."

<u>The Conversation</u>

It began with endless, giddy, marmalade chatter, a lot of, "Yes, it's me," and "Holy smokes! Hi—" and "Wow, I can't believe this!" A lot of straight-talking, big-smiling, butter-rolling, taking on the tones of an auctioneer. "This is so funny. Really, so funny. What a coincidence. My god, it's great to hear your voice. It's been, what, two years? No, more— How funny—wow—" Always the "wow."

He couldn't get a word in as I siphoned a monologue from a sleepless night of planning. A steady flow of updates spilled from the slaughterhouse of emotion that I should have bled off long ago. As I packed the conversation with, "Isn't this funny," and "So amazing!" so that all mention of what had happened to him in the hospital stayed behind my verbal blockade. Medical complications and the topic of Rudy were off limits. I enforced an information blackout by pretending the severed ear and crushed limbs hadn't existed. Most importantly, I refused to say what I wanted to say, which was: "You careless, thoughtless, addicted, heartless son of a bitch. You thought of no one but yourself. No one! You didn't just almost kill yourself. You almost killed me—!!"

Instead it was all, "Me? Yeah. I'm fine. Perfect—I've been here about a year. Can't believe it. Yeah. A year. And yeah, it's been raining since before I was born. But I'm liking the hikes, the Cascades, the coffee, all that. So funny, you know, where we end up." Jessica had disappeared into her bedroom, leaving me with the odd sensation of having fallen through the floor.

He saw right through everything—I could hear it in his tone when he said, "Yeah. Sounds like you've found your place. Funny that you and Jenn both happened to meet out there."

"Yeah. We met at a party. So weird that we both knew you— She brought up Vermont and I asked her if she knew a Ben just because, you know, I remember you spent a lot of time up there before we met. Of course she knew you because Jenn knows everyone. Even George Lucas." The lies sounded more absurd by the minute. "She mentioned your cigars, something about one of your friends, Javier? Julian? I don't remember. But anyway—" Like the typical novice liar, the more I over-explained, the less credible I sounded. What was supposed to be an explanation of coincidence became an awkward, false silence that I spoke over while pinching the thin skin of my thighs.

"So, anyway, I knew it was you. And then I had to talk about our camping trip—" A mistake to open that door— "Enough about me though."

This landed between us like a confession of self-absorption. "How are you? Where are you? Tell me what you're doing. Are you better now?" Always hiding behind questions, I didn't really want to hear the answers. "You're better—I know that. But where do you live? What good things are happening in your life?" The question landed like a margarita on a Mediterranean beach strewn with unshaven humanoids scrounging for American cheese wrappers in a thousand-mile garbage dump.

Later, after hanging up, I'd gulp two glasses of water and look in the mirror, trying to understand what I'd heard.

"So." He'd begun, his breath coming through the wires. "That's a big line up of questions." He sounded wiser than me. "There's not much to report. Not much at all. I'm enjoying the summer at my dad's house, reading a lot and spending time with friends."

"Reading," I said, irresponsibly, like a ditz. What could be more difficult than talking to a man I'd once loved? "Wonderful. What? What are you reading?" It could be Proust or Melville or Dean Koontz—none of it mattered—and he knew.

"A hell of a lot, actually. Yeah. Just a lot." He settled like a grandfather into quiet. I could almost see his hands resting in his lap as he rocked in a chair, back and forth.

"Wow. How great... to read and not be distracted. Wish I could do that." Again, the lie that he saw through. At this point, it was clear I had a looming problem: The possibility that I'd cave, become mute, unable to launch new questions or pat him down with flattery, or continue with the "Oh wows!" and the "that's wonderfuls!" Everything would blow away like feathers in a gust.

"So, your friends," I said. "You've been seeing a lot of them?" I kept waiting for him to say something real.

"They come by," he said, "we talk." He missed the access-point. Strain lay around the edges of these one-liners.

In kindergarten he'd been a boy of few words, but had never been this spare. At first I thought these could be drug-induced pauses. But after a moment, I figured there was something more to the vacuum between his responses. Holding back, avoiding answers, he seemed to be waiting, playing chess against my frivolity, watching for moves, restraining himself while I spoke in circles without thinking, while I aimlessly wound from one pat statement or question to another, talking everywhere but saying nothing of significance, so that the real conversation was invisible, so that when I hung up, I felt bereft.

For days to come I longed for catharsis. I had chattered at him but hadn't alluded to our unfinished business. I wanted nothing more than to call him back. Our awkward reconnection simply framed an infinite number of conversations lacking maturity, confrontation, and depth. Finally, it was clear: I was less than empty.

Everything and Nothing

Of course I rejected Ben. Of course I chose protection. Of course I ran. Because it's always easier to sheathe the self in delusions.

It wasn't just the blood and bandages, or the loony dad pressuring me to get married to his comatose son. Like the syringe and the prostitute, self-protection enabled self-absorption. I fled into myself. It was easier to flee than to feel repulsive and depleted in the company of someone better, more beautiful, more alive than me—because Ben, despite addiction, had always been worth more. Deep down I knew I'd never be anything to him but a fuck-sack.

After hanging up and trying to find myself in the mirror, I discovered Jessica already asleep next to an empty salad bowl. At a loss, I dialed the International District and begged Parvati for intoxication. We found it down the street, at a table in front of a red and yellow expressionist canvas that encouraged babbling over sherry.

Ben, at age five, was invincible. He thwacked sticks against the tire swing, made *pachoo pachoo* sounds with his two-finger gun, sputtered bullet-spittle as he stumbled over black rubber tiles towards the silver chains that dangled from nearby jungle gyms.

"He was a risk taker," I droned at Parvati. I'd intended to avoid her. But she was the only person I could call. "I so wanted him the way an addict wants a drug." A gulp of sherry I couldn't afford, and I was back at it, talking about how medieval he was—something knight-in-shining-armor—a quality that followed him into his twenties, when he got into tournament fencing, martial arts, and the waves at Mavericks. He went to Japan to train with a Sensei. He read *The Art of War*. In first grade, he rescued a girl named Elizabeth, who'd been locked by a bully in a closet that looked like a cloisonné egg. Ben wrestled the bully to the floor and sent him crying to his punishment. Yes, Ben always saved other girls.

"What kind of kid does that for honor?" I said, blinking at Parvati's stare. Her finger traced the rim of her glass. She studied me. I'd revealed too much, more than she'd ever reveal to me. Who cared. I kept talking:

"How do good people turn?" Here, I made sure to stare back at Parvati, who looked down at her wine, took a sip. "I'm talking about betrayal. Backstabbing—" The words hovered in the rust-colored air beneath a disco ball, candles flickering on the tables behind us. "Great in bed, I have to say."

Parvati leaned forward and twirled her glass of burgundy, her eyes glazing into a suppressed yawn—as if boredom could hide guilt. "I won't bore you anymore—" I murmured. It had been a busy day, she explained. I said, "Right." Almost added: "And we both know who you'd rather be with."

I imagined Parvati lying beneath Ben's twin, JNB, wrapping her legs around his torso while a saxophone blew through the bar's sound system. Orgasms of chatter rose and fell. A man to my left clapped his hand on his woman, the two falling into each other with hilarity. I raised my voice. "What do you do when a man doesn't love you back? You're supposed to suck it up and focus on your career. **Right.**"

Girls, Ben once told me as he licked his finger. Girls should be treated with respect—but that didn't mean falling in love. Running the finger along my inner labia, slipping it into my vagina, sweeping it around and then pulling it out, he talked about Lillian, his mother.

She'd been a tall, blond mirage, an adolescent fashionista who'd walked the runway and lounged nude on the July page of a famous wall calendar. She ended her affair with clothing—or the lack of it—when she met Rudy in a parking garage across the street from a talent show. Fed up with a profession that focused only on the body, Lillian found the "real world" in Rudy. Why, I often wondered, did Ben find it so necessary to tell me about his mother while fingering me?

Consumed with performing well, he later explained how much he honored a woman's naked body, like mine, as if I were a piano played for sensations, the keys on my limbs caressed for repeated sexual peaks. Like every narcissist, Ben believed all women, from virgin to workingwoman to elder-dame, needed a composer (who else, but he) to organize her inner song. Sampling different bodies improved the world.

Penis next to labia, he whispered that if he'd been alive seven hundred years ago, he'd have lived at court, protecting and quietly fucking his way through every wife, daughter, and grandmother that happened to be in his company.

I needed no further explanation from my friend with benefits. I must ignore the other sexual partners and pretend to support his ice-climbing trips when he'd been "this far away" from plunging from a frozen waterfall near Middlebury. I must pretend delight when he described getting sucked out to sea on his surfboard during a visit to Maui. If I contemplated the question of why bad things happen to good people, he didn't because he didn't require that life make sense.

In kindergarten, when an art teacher named Barbara uttered the wrong word, setting him off—because she looked like a giraffe in espadrilles, because her button down shirts were tucked into calf-length blue jean skirts, because she often lingered over Ben's finger paintings—he plunged a pair of steel scissors into Barbara's ankle. I remember it clearly: shrieks, blood dribbling from the wound, several teachers converging on our classroom.

Afterwards, in the hallway, I watched Ben as he stood against a wall, eyes wide as gobstoppers, mouth frozen in a fixed "Oh" as if he still gripped the scissors. I was sure that he'd be taken away forever.

But at recess, I followed him. Beneath the play structure, I found him strategizing against an invisible opponent, and I asked if he had any Freshen Up gum—

"No," he yelled. "Go away," thrusting me into a thistle bush.

For the rest of that year I squatted by the playhouse as if pissing, lingered by the sandbox, useless and friendless except for Mimi, while Ben teased his new fascination in pigtails, Ruthie, who idled by his elbow wearing the same mini-skirt that Dorothy Hamill wore on the ice rink. While Ruthie got treated to Freshen Up, I stared her down. If I'd done anything wrong, anything to make him push me away, it remained a mystery until decades later—when sitting at the bar I finally understood. It had taken Jessica and a lot of pretending for me to get it.

"Oh my god. It's too funny!" Was I laughing or crying? "It all came down to playing house. I insisted he play my husband. We were five. What was I thinking?" I shook my head. He wanted nothing to do with my house, preferring to spend the rest of time dangling from monkey bars, because who wanted a lonely cardboard kitchen?

"You're too romantic," Parvati said. "You're the kind of person who wants to be special, the one they'll marry, all that ridiculous, fairy tale stuff." She rolled her eyes and shook her head. "You know what you need?" she continued. "A good fuck."

"Yeah—" I murmured, staring down into my glass, fatigue at its bottom.

"Oh"

Parvati was right. I obsessed over my crushes—stared across art rooms, science labs, lunch halls, schoolyards, the way my mother meditated while my father rode a motorcycle through landscapes of emotion, my father who rose like Everest but collapsed beneath constellations of sexual trysts and drug trips, so that when lucid, he avoided his family. His show of affection was minimal.

And my mother: In the kitchen, spinning a piece of string around the ankles of a stuffed chicken whose body, she said, resembled a small baby's. I tried conversation, but she only cleared her throat. Likewise, my mother's gaze fastened onto that nameless, faraway place in the air that was ungraspable. I came to think of this as her dreamscape-gaze, which haunted those who wanted out and which was the source of all want—and therefore all that I wanted.

In grade school, I stood next to Ben for a class photo, already uncomfortable on the chessboard that stretched into the future. Photography lamps pinned us in a blur as we said *cheese*, the flash causing my eyes to tear.

Had it been the lights or my proximity to Ben? Or had it been that during a friendless year, I'd become less than the shoelaces on Ben's sneakers. I was caught staring at the floor. But, he felt what I felt. In the photo, his eyes were wide, his tan sweatshirt, brown corduroys, and sand-colored hair falling over his eyebrows, lips looped around, "Oh!"—the same "Oh" that had rested on his lips after he'd stabbed our art teacher's leg with a pair of scissors.

Year later, in bed, as he dipped into me, we never revealed more than what simmered on the surface, but skimmed the waves of each other's bodies, never daring to lower ourselves into the depths where love's electric maneuvers could take us down.

"I hate this," I said to Parvati amid the mash-up of hair and coats, wet leather and alcohol confusing the exit.

"What do you mean?" she laughed. "Where's my umbrella—" We knudged past shoulders and hair.

"I'm so tired," I murmured to the many faces near my face. Then drizzle glanced my eyelashes and cheeks, chilling my core. "Who has everything?" I wrapped my cloth jacket close. "Having everything doesn't make everything work out. So why try?"

Parvati held her bag over her head and said, "Go home before you fall down."

"Fall down! Hah! Me fall? I never fall. He did, but not me—"

Something Is Not Right In the State of Denmark

Barely a month of Jessica, I opened the front door, threw down my keys, umbrella, and backpack only to find a lesion on our living room carpet. At first it looked like mud ground into the wool. I dashed to the kitchen, grabbing a rag, soap, water, thinking to scrub it away before it caked into permanence. But as I leaned down to pour soap onto the spot, I recognized the shadow—an indentation, a depression rather than a lump of misplaced manure. Our Midwestern plane had been desecrated, the gray wool pile trimmed back to almost zero, snipped down to the beige backing like a militiaman's skull. A meaningful chunk of the rug had been gouged out.

No simple fix, the carpet had been ruined. Replacing it would cost more than the rental deposit, which was no small sum. I sank to the floor, already broke, and remained motionless for more than an hour, waiting for Jessica to wander into the emotion that grew in me like toxic algae.

In she strolled with sitcom cheer, lugging a plastic sack of groceries that, I could see, contained frozen peas, two heads of iceberg lettuce, and a box of Shredded Wheat. It suddenly occurred to me that her habit of steaming vegetables was as repulsive as her black boots with their chunky heels—pumped up versions of my own, two sizes larger. Her worn jeans, black shirt and wool sweater, her rose-colored eye shadow, and smeared lipstick, suddenly coalesced to mimic me.

"Jessica." I said from my invisible corner in the living room, making no effort to soften the sharpness of my tone. "Could you tell me what happened to our carpet?" She halted by the kitchen door, spinning on her heels like a top, plastic grocery bag swinging on her wrist. Half-smiling, she stared.

"Oh my God!" she squalled two beats too late. "You completely startled me. I'm so sorry. Oh my God! I didn't see you!" Nervous laughter seized her upper body as she set down the groceries at the kitchen threshold, flicking on the light. "I am definitely not here."

"Well," I said, struggling up, my legs and head tingling after motionlessness. "I've been here a long time—" I sounded like my father before he lit a joint. "Wondering what happened to the damn carpet." I dunked my head at the excised area that was highlighted by the kitchen light.

"Carpet?" Jessica squinted at the spot, as if searching. She placed four fingers over her mouth in what at first looked like disbelief, but then seemed to be an attempt to cover the smirk of a five year old witnessing the bloody knee and tears of her best friend. "Oh-oh my God!" She sputtered. "That. Oh that. I was going to tell you before you saw it, but you got here before I had a chance—"

"Okay? So. What happened?" All schoolteacher about to break up a yard fight, the disapproval in my voice throwing her off guard and causing her to blink like a "don't walk" sign.

"Oh my God, I'm so sorry," she began. "I was chewing some gum and it accidentally fell out of my mouth while I was talking on the phone. I didn't know what to do so I just thought I should cut it out since I couldn't pull it out any other way."

Though this sounded reasonable, I told her to be more careful, adding, "You realize you're probably not going to get your deposit back—" She said she "totally" expected to lose her deposit, and would even pay for any additional charges if necessary, and was just glad I didn't throw her out right away!

"Oh, come on," I said, softening, more than gullible with head to one side. "I'm not asking you to leave—I just want to make sure we don't end up trashing this place." I reminded her that I didn't get a steady paycheck. She promised with "all my heart and even my mom's" not to make any more messes, letting me know she'd be **really** careful—even pay an extra hundred for the month. This settled the problem so that we could wordlessly consume our identical but separately purchased and prepared dinners of lettuce, boiled vegetables, and fiber-pumped starch.

The Natural World

"This too shall pass."

Trickster

Nature is a trickster—something I should have known as I layered on wool and fleece, shoved feet into a pair of hiking boots, and struggled with a plastic poncho I'd picked up as a freebie from a donation box outside a yoga studio. Blame the whole thing on Starbucks, its chai laced with whatever it was that made people susceptible to bad ideas. According to Parvati, it would be "fun" to brave the icy trails looping a popular ridge half an hour from the city.

"If you weren't," she began, pulling a twenty from her wallet, "so obsessive, I'd pull out Monopoly. But you obsess." I didn't get her logic, nor did I agree that I had a problem, but I thought following a fool up a 90-degree slope lashed with freezing rain might endow me with the same seductive edge that had attracted JNB to this "friend" of mine.

"I told you how I wasted all those years," she said after I ordered the overpriced drink from the pin-lipped and bullet-necked barista, "avoiding things. Depressing. Anyway. The elements never hurt anyone." I silently disagreed, unzipping my backpack and pulling out my depleted wallet. "Stop wimping out and trust." She added, throwing her twenty on the counter, and waving away my attempts to pay. "I'll get it. And I don't care about excuses. I'm picking you up tomorrow morning!"

Morning came too soon at 6:30 AM—still dark. It didn't feel right to be stuffing my backpack and my bulk into the bucket seat of Parvati's rented Honda. But within minutes, we'd hurled the Space Needle and Lake Washington into her rearview mirror, flying along a slim, pine-and-fern-framed stretch of road where our headlights became laser beams that burned the frost off tree limbs. Eventually, we reached the damp trailhead where only one other vehicle, a pickup, huddled next to its flashlight-bearing owner. This last person on earth hollered at two German shepherds poking in the mud until they leaped onto the back of the pickup just as the wheels spun out. When they were gone, the lot felt as empty as the fake bravado that kept me going during the drive over.

But all chatter met its end at nature's front door. No more talk of Jessica or the gouged carpet. No more, "Am I paranoid or is she lying?" No more, "But then, all my roommates have been a little off." A chilled cocktail of unease spilled into my belly as Parvati slipped out of the driver's seat, and slammed the door behind her. Still strapped in, I breathed the cold pinesap air blowing through my open window. "Shit. It's freezing— How are we going to do this?"

"You're paranoid," Parvati muttered, attempting to lighten my mood, but only succeeding in stretching her arms wide and inhaling. When, in lieu of humor, had she begun to insult people? "It's simple. You're neurotic and she's a crazy from San Francisco."

In response, I rolled up the window and stuffed my hands into my gloves. I would not move unless she forced me out.

"Oh, come on, Jane. You've always been so superstitious," she said through the glass. I would not be called superstitious. Nor would I be found frozen to death in a rented Honda.

I got out and shivered beneath branches of moss that sprinkled cold droplets onto my forehead. Daylight, no more than a purple rime around the edges of the trees, didn't promise much and quieted our voices. Had this been the miniature Siberian Taiga beneath an indigo carpet like the one I'd seen in an obscure thriller called *Iced Over*, I might have been prepared. But the headlights threw me, striking a nearby tree before giving way to the station wagon that skidded onto the gravel behind Parvati. I nearly screamed, "Shit! RUN!" as a cloud of exhaust and a spray of pebbles caused the branches to release several crows. But I didn't because I couldn't move my trembling knees as the driver—a dim outline—threw open his door, all Will Ferrell dipped in REI for a scene in *Christine*.

Walking around the hood to dominate the headlights, he leered at us in his high-tech snow goggles and orange parka, black hoodie patting down an abundance of hair that made his chin-stubble look like it had been drawn with pencil. Legs spread ninja style, he nodded at Parvati and yelled, "Nasty drive up here. Did you see the dead deer?" Parvati stared at the man as if the trailhead had been replaced by a ballpark. Bizarrely, she began laughing, as if the possibility of rape and murder in the forest were a mere comedy of errors.

"No, sorry," Parvati said through laughter, stepping forward and leaving me to my pounding heart. "Didn't see it!" She took another step towards the man so that her profile fell into the headlights. Waves of adrenaline magnified details. With clarity, I scanned the station wagon, noting an unmoving, dark figure in the passenger seat—a figure that looked like a stuffed version of the pill-popping psychiatrist from X— Medical Center who'd nearly driven me off the road as we carpooled to a Mountaineers hike.

"Is this hunting season?" Parvati asked, catching her breath. I scrambled towards her, slipping on the gravel.

"Come on," I whispered, nudging her with an elbow that did no more than cause her to double over in another fit of laughter. It was frightening to watch her lose it, her body shaking, her hands clasped to her thighs. And then the dude in the orange parka stepped forward.

"You okay?" He asked, though he clearly didn't care if she or anything was okay. She didn't respond, and he shrugged, turning to me. "I hate road kill." He winked through his weird goggles, his eyes looking like painted eggs. "Hate it! Rots to hell," He said, looking very Doctor Strangelove.

"I know," Parvati managed to say, straightening up and wiping a tear from her cheek. I placed a hand on her shoulder. We would face it together. "So who goes first?" Parvati asked. The flirt! Did she expect me to save us? Did she intend for me to drag her back to the Honda, where I'd tell her to shut up? But then it was all: "Your friend, who's that in the car?" The goggled, boogieman twisted around to get a good look at the mannequin in the front seat of his station wagon—a vehicle that screamed "gangsta." He seemed befuddled, his stubble trembling as if at a loss.

How easy it was to stumble into an experience no one wanted. How easy it was for an old friend to give away one's life as if it were no more than an Easter egg. What else could I expect from someone who'd stolen JNB? Of course I'd be knocked off in the wilderness. Of course I'd become silage for a psycho who'd rape and strangle with his goggles before rolling the remains in mud to be left as an afterthought. That's what I got for enabling a fool by agreeing to hike Hades!

But like my father Stan used to say, what we see is not always what we get.

"Hey Luke," the killer yelled. "Come on, man, get your butt out here!" The mannequin in the wagon swiveled his head to stare out the passenger window. Horrifying when it pried open the door, pressing itself through what looked like a crack—as if it couldn't be bothered to open the door fully.

Turned out the mannequin called Luke had a fleshy British chin and miniscule, colorless eyes beneath a brow-less forehead that made his stained, Bugs Bunny teeth look like they could bite through a pair of steel pliers. Wearing a navy blue parka and combat boots, he epitomized "bloodcurdling" as he strutted past dripping moss hanging from branches. None of this made it any easier to imagine fighting off the killers by kicking them in the nuts and poking their eyes while fleeing through ferns as cold and wet as an icicle-bog.

"Jane," Parvati said. "Remember that party on Lake Union I told you about?" Now she spoke of parties, as if I could think of parties. She'd lost it, had flung all mind over the cliff that would soon be my end. Had she succumbed to brain fry? Had Starbucks fed the child one-too-many flip-out lattes? As Stan used to say, "Permit a native New Yorker to rent a car, and never see a road sign again."

But then, *what we see is not always what we get.*

In a matter of seconds, Parvati and the boogiemen became chummy, virtually reclining against pillows and passing around a bong as if everyone had turned into teddy bears. It was all, "Yeah. I know. The eye patch is sweet,"—on some pirate they called D—. And then it was all, "Yeah, killer swimming pool," and "I'm way into the driveway of broken glass," and a little of, "Remember that $100,000 vase I accidentally smashed after diving in?"

Soon, Luke the mannequin began moaning about night classes at UW, something about Java script giving him migraines. And then the stubble-dude in space goggles, who Parvati now called Bob, mentioned Boise, Idaho and the Owyhee Mountains, seasoning his talk with "masters program" and "anthropology" and that "school in Boston."

It took a while, but then it dawned on me. Parvati kind of knew these rapists. We had run into acquaintances in this haunted forest. I stood speechless, shivering, spent as I tried to get my head around this new truth while Luke eased up to me, silent, eyeing my rain poncho as if ready to binge on a bag of candy corn, which unfortunately compounded the trait of appearing dumbfounded.

Of course Luke subsisted on glances, lost in a state of incomprehension among women. Of course he felt intimidated by Bob's achievements, the way I felt furious about Parvati's—and Mimi's—self-mastery and ease around men. Of course Luke's lack of self-worth would become more apparent when he inexplicably descended into chuckles every time Bob spoke. And of course Luke glommed onto me.

It turned out, Bob met Parvati over Monday night whiskey binges that had taken place next to one of the famous glassblower's many ovens. (Perhaps that explained the broken glass in the driveway.)

Later it would become apparent that our "friends" had not come to the trailhead accidentally. Parvati had invited Bob to join us for the hike because she thought I'd enjoy a little "company." Luke had merely tagged along.

Once it became clear that I'd be hiking through dense wood with these characters, I succumbed to mud. While Luke inhaled the freezing rain, and dug his bunny teeth into his lower lip, Parvati bounded ahead, laughing. I didn't get the joke, but tried to understand, even when, at one point, Luke stretched his arms out to whack my chest, accompanied by a stunted, "oh, sorry." Chin wobbling, he continued to add insult to injury with a stiff-as-fake-leather, "It always surprises me to realize how much I miss the fresh air when I'm in the city. There are too many coffee grinders in that town!"

Only minutes into our introduction, my hands and feet felt like peeling birch bark, stripped of all sensation—despite long johns, two turtlenecks, a wool sweater, fleece jacket, knitted cap, plastic poncho, and two pairs of wool socks within water resistant hiking boots—all garage sale finds. Meanwhile, Parvati seemed not to notice the flurries that settled on her eyebrows. And Bob—all goggles and head of bronze curls beneath orange hood—appeared oblivious. Wagging a gloveless thumb towards the trailhead, Bob paused to trample on what he dubbed a poisonous scourge, adding, "I'm eliminating a terrorist of the natural world!" This, if Parvati had her way, was to be my Virgil through the wilderness of my late twenties.

It didn't take long for Bob to transmute from eco-terrorist-obliterator to Sierra Club game show host. He began by pointing out obscure trailside specimen and lecturing on a range of survivalist techniques—which he said was his favorite pastime. While we hiked up the grade, he elaborated on historical trivia that blew through one ear and out the other, Luke stumbling behind him with a flabbergasted expression. Often, Bob countermanded Luke's stiff praise with, "Come on. Everyone knows that—" Inevitably, Luke caved into what appeared to be self loathing: a downward stare with a miffed shudder of his shoulders.

While I deflected the barrage of facts that spilled over Bob's thistled chin, as I failed to diffuse the competitive gymnastics between these two non-rapists, Parvati abandoned me. She wandered far enough ahead to become a black smudge against the whitening slope, which made me furious—until it dawned on me. Halfway up the trail I understood. Bob's love affair with trivia and Luke's stumbling articulations had been motivated by orders. These two men had been given a task. As Bob's hips shifted beneath his backpack, as he leaped over mud puddles and leaned into each stride with concentration, as arms of dangling moss brushed my shoulders and mist slanted into my eyes, I got it, I understood why we were there. It all came down to sex.

Did I Need Some?

We walked and we walked as I'd always walked: Like deadbeats craving repetition. The trail stuck to the soles of my boots and squished with a loam of slug debris and cedar tailings that gave off a nose-stinging odor. Like four crazies, we ascended through Hemlocks, calling up visions of Socrates at his death, flurries whipping the landscape into a pale batter that frosted my exposed fingers, lips, and nose. A whiteout faded the outline of the Cascades. No one but us four dared the trail—no joggers, no rock climbers, no dog walkers, no mountain lions or bears, no Tin Man or Scarecrow.

Worn down by Bob and Luke's verbal jousting, I excused myself and plodded towards a head-spinning ridge where I crouched, bared my shivering rump, and peed beside a patch of frosted-over alpine grass—pondering the fact that for tens of thousands of years people peed in the grass almost as often as they screwed in the grass. Peeing, I listed towards hypothermia, watching the dark contour of a hawk perched on a nearby branch. I felt so cold he could have pecked my brains out and I wouldn't have noticed.

It couldn't have been more than a minute that I crouched alone. But it seemed longer than a battle with intestinal parasites, because nothing spreads time's legs more than fear. Because at that moment I spotted another smudge, black as Ingmar Bergman's death, approaching and growing larger. Whatever it was, it came as fast as the shot of adrenaline that bolted up my spine. Panting towards me, huffing frost clouds, the smudge sharpened against the bleached landscape. It would be upon me in seconds, despite the sleet-cold grasses freezing my butt cheeks, the ground and my boots jaundiced by pee, my flapping poncho catching on a nearby branch. Yes, I finally understood: It could happen that fast. You could be caught butt naked in a deep freeze. Yet, no one imagines themselves being ripped to shreds, claws tearing through gear or puncturing spinal column, belly, or chest. No one expects to be a *Darwin Awards* headline, to be buried by an epilogue that describes a preventable mauling. I wouldn't allow myself to die there.

It took me a few beats to respond. But then, thanks to that shot of adrenaline, I bolted up, pubic hair on display as I struggled with my long johns and blue jeans. Summoning my inner dominatrix, I whipped my backpack in front of me like a shield. The black-death-thing halted paces away, its mane gargantuan and smoking, it torso as wide as a tree trunk. Gusts of freezing rain needled my cheeks, and I couldn't see more than outlines, everything blurring into tears as I gurgled out, "GET AWAY!"

Waving my pack with one hand, zipping my fly with the other, I managed to scream louder: "GO, GO ON, GIT!" Knees shaking, I lashed out at the blackness with my backpack, swinging into gusts. "FUCK!!!!!" I knew the others couldn't hear me through the wall of wind, but I couldn't quite resign myself to the choice I'd have to make: Succumb to predation or leap from the mountainside. It would be so easy to choose the white space behind me that offered endless flight. But something stopped me from turning to the cliff's edge as I yelled and swung, yelled and swung like anyone who wanted to live—a damn good thing too.

And then, I was in the quiet pearl that was the sky, completely isolated by the elements. It was as if I lived between two planks of plexiglass where particles of ice stuck to my hairline, and gripped my brain in a kind of mania—like brain freeze after a thousand, addictive licks of Italian ice. Eyebrows became snowdrifts; nostrils released glaciers of snot. I floated over the woman with bleached hair. She looked like me, and she was waving her backpack at a smudge no one could understand, because warmth had become a memory. And why didn't the woman break for the ridge? Because she spotted the metal cone dangling from the black smudge's neck and realized it was a cowbell clanging softly against fur.

Surprise!

At first there was no telling whether the dog's muzzle was friendly. I saw no owner, which meant I had to play it cool. Shaking but pulling myself together, I struck out towards the others, ignoring the animal's whimpers as best I could as it plodded behind me and probed my bottom with its nose.

I'd left the others by a Hemlock where the trail became steep. But everything had become snow, and they were nowhere—not beneath the branches or behind the boulder paces up the trail where I'd last seen Luke dipping his fingers into a bag of potato chips. I listened, actually wishing Bob would flip his hood with, "Found a furry admirer?" or even, "Looks like you're a magnet for all kinds of petting—" But nothing.

A rustling and I spun around, expecting to see Luke's enormous teeth chomping wise cracks at the dog. A whiff of his onion breath would have felt like finding a cup of hot tea next to an ice cube. But no—instead I smelled Parvati's floral shampoo, followed by the sound of the wind that seemed to say, *"Leave it to Jane, the mad woman sniffed by fur!"*

"Let the poor boy sniff you," Luke would advise if he were there. His chin would wobble in pre-laughter, and I would back up to a trunk and be flattened by a blast of wind howling up the cliff side.

Woozy, not sure of what was in front of me, I kneeled. Cold poured through me and spread, churning like a milkshake in a blender. *"He'll get tired of you and he'll be gone—"* Bob in the rear would say, thrusting his gloved hand before the dog's nose. *"I know you,"* he'd sputter as the dog began licking the black leather. *"As the world's oldest breed,"* Bob would continue, his goggles impressing no one but the guidebook in his head. *"The chow chow—isn't that what we have here—is a guard dog initially meant to ward off enemies of China's greatest emperors. Chows probably originated in Siberia, that land of mosquitoes and untimely deaths, but have come to represent the dynastic lines of the Han."* He'd nod like Wikipedia into an electric wind.

I looked up from where I crouched by the trunk and watched the dog shake excess moisture from its coat. A windshield of ice dropped from a branch and shattered at my feet. *"She's not going to attack unless she's provoked,"* Bob would have added, speaking the obvious.

"I need to go back," I said. Bob's imaginary stubble spread like egg-soaked breadcrumbs over his cheeks, forming a smile. The landscape had begun to dissolve into the dim quiet produced by low blood pressure. I stuffed my head between legs, my poncho billowing. When I finally looked up, I discovered that I still crouched alone with the dog. Its soft head probed my fingers, and cold wetness from its nose imprinted itself on my skin. I waited, beyond shivering, as a high whistle sliced through the nonstop wind, followed by, "Moo! Come here Moo! Come on girl!"

Tall, because they're always tall, and wearing some serious looking gear, because gear equated virility and financial success, the man's gloved hands gripped expensive walking poles, because walking poles signaled gravitas. From far away, his form looked super human among the pines. Eventually, I'd notice his boots—which laced in criss-crossed steel hooks that reminded me of cantilevered bridges—as well as the NASA under-jacket that irredesced with the color of white opals—probably an REI-find that cost upwards of $300. A daypack served as the cherry on his outfit, its ten netted pockets bursting from bungee cords that x-ed up the pack and held foil packets that glimmered like a metal spine. But I saw none of this until later, when my mind came out of fuzz. I did, however, notice that he swaggered towards the cliff side, prompting the dog that kept me alive, this Moo, to get moving.

She loped towards her master, whose upper face lay concealed by a flying saucer rain hat. Skidding over patches of ice but stabilizing himself with his hiking poles, the man called, "Sorry. Don't worry about her—Moo sometimes gets distracted." Nearer, he leaned down to pat his dog's ears and to extend a hand to me with, "Never short on intros when she's around." His voice was now familiar, but where had I heard it?

Staring at this vision of opal and bungee cords, I wasn't sure what was real. I held my breath, thinking that Ben had flown out to help. He'd arrived in Seattle and found me.

"You okay?" The man said, reaching for my elbow. Stiff and shivering, I nodded as the light shifted and his features became someone else's: More rustic—snow-brows over blue eyes I knew from somewhere but couldn't place in the slow motion of the cold. "Didn't know you'd be here." His pupils plodded the terrain of my face, hiking towards his next thought. Stubble—what was it about Seattle and stubble? Strong frontier bones. A steady voice. A sense of purpose. Later I'd wonder why I hadn't made the connection immediately. But bandaged by layers of fleece and cold, I had no need for connections—because whales dove into and fed off of the past.

"Come on," he nodded and grabbed my elbows. "Looks like you're really cold." I slipped, struggling to stand, allowed him to grab beneath my armpits and stabilize me.

"Thanks." I said, finally on my feet. "I'm lost."

<u>Nothing and Everything Is Real</u>

Everyone but Parvati knew, like the back of their hands, the signs of hypothermia. Even Luke—who pulled animal crackers, trail mix, and a chemical blanket from his pack—even he understood that if you began shivering and then stopped shivering but were still in the cold, you needed to get warm fast. From afar, Luke looked perverse ripping open the chemical blanket and sticking it into the space between his belly and his pant-fly—an act of madness because everyone knew the chemicals irritated anything near it.

"Granola," I heard Bob say as I approached, "is an oat snack made for survivalists—and survivalists are an oat snack for creatures of the night! Night is a shooting range for carrot eaters, and carrot eaters invite night shot to the range." He seemed to be enjoying himself as he swiped an animal cracker from Luke's baggy and bit its head off. "What the hey, man. There's nothing but bears in this-here, these parts, these days. Whatever happened to all the mastodons of yore?" He was laughing at something in the trees. And when he spotted me, and then the man next to me, and then the dog, he nodded as if sizing up potent rivals. "And who, may I ask, have we here?" Bob aimed and pitched the line like a snowball.

My rescuer smiled down at Moo and tapped a walking pole against a boulder, not yet realizing that Parvati had invited these nutcases into nature. My anger at Bob and Luke for abandoning me was growing, but I felt too cold to say anything. Instead, I let everyone else figure it out.

Moo was introduced as a dog who loved winter hikes—and loved rescuing people. Bob added that Moo's coat looked waterproof. "And nice bark on that beast, too, I bet," Bob burped, moving into dominant posture, gloved hands on hips while I numbly removed a baggy of icy carrots from my pack—the only food I'd brought along. "And," Bob added. "I'm also referring to you."

Before my rescuer could respond, Parvati called out from an alcove of pine branches a short distance away. "There you are!" She slipped down the trail like a gold digger drawn to promising rock. It had to be the opalescent jacket and iron-man walking sticks. "You found us!" And what did she think? That it would be my responsibility to find them when they'd deserted and forgotten me? But then, she wasn't referring to me. "I'm so glad you left early. I thought you'd be at the dock all morning—" So, it wasn't fortune that had thrown JNB across my path.

Beyond Parvati's alcove of trees, the view had disappeared and become a white soup, the kind that lures the hungry to their deaths. Suddenly, we all understood the cliché I'd been thinking of before settling into Parvati's

Honda: Death shows up like a friend, quickly, when you least expect it.

Adjusting his coat around his neck and pounding the mud from his boot soles, JNB said, "Looks bad. Let's get off this mountain—" Larger flakes had begun swirling around us, whitening Moo's coat as she whimpered. It didn't take long for the others to motivate for an early departure.

For the next hour, liked dazed fools, our group struggled after Moo, stumbling down two miles of iced-over mud that had once been a trail but had turned into a chute to hell. Several times I slipped, cursing, and nearly breaking an ankle. My body felt like sandblasted silk as I stumbled, regardless of others, across a hundredth boulder and shredded my plastic rain poncho until it looked like a pompom. Many more times I scraped my elbows and shins, twice bruising my gluteus maximus—loudly and sarcastically thanking Parvati—once sliding three paces down a section that broke against a boulder that nearly cracked my coccyx—a calamity that would be repeated more successfully later that winter.

I stumbled after JNB and Moo, praying for a duplicate of me to show up and wave me through. I envisioned the Honda as a fallout shelter in the vacant lot, the drenched collar of my wool sweater pickling my skin where droplets shimmied, hypothermically, down to my belt buckle. Lips purple, skin bloodless, fingers, toes, and mind numb as a catatonic's, I finally shut my eyes in the passenger seat.

It was a miracle when Parvati blasted the heat and steered us back to Capital Hill, the Cascades rippling behind us in a gray, timeless repose where nothing in my life touched me as it used to—not wind, ice, or chance meetings with men who looked like Ben. Not a single thing ignited me against the friction of life, as dead tissue and dead mind settled in. Nothing in the mountain range evoked prehistory as it used to; nothing about the earth awed me with its slow picking and choosing of traits; nothing about these particular events in this particular time meant anything to me anymore. Not my mother, not the mountains, not the memory of meaning. At last, nothing was everywhere. And yet, Parvati drove right through this inner nowhere, saying, "You're eating at my place tonight."

Too Many Adventures

While the Honda idled like a strung-out roach on Harvard Avenue East, I wanted to yell, "Thanks a lot for nearly killing me!" But Parvati leaned her elbows against the wheel, turning to appraise my cheek, the one covered with acne, saying, "Bob and JNB are coming over." Had I detected Schadenfreude in her tone? If so, it struck me with the force of a bullet blasting through silk. But I couldn't help tearing up when she said, "I'll have wine, vegetables, and heat. Bring bread. Come at six." Once again, I couldn't find it in me to decline her invitation.

In the shower, as hot darts steamed against my shoulders I couldn't forget the sensation of JNB heaving me up from the mud, his grip beneath my armpits. And when I paid for bread at the QFC, and then waited for the bus, as I rang Parvati's bell, I couldn't get his muddy grip out of my mind. Weak and exhausted, baguette pressed to breast, I wanted only to stumble into JNB's bed.

Instead, Bob appeared at Parvati's door, his goggles gone but his stubble still there, corkscrew curls echoing the corkscrew wine opener he fondled next to a bottle of Merlot. "You're wanted in the kitchen, now, in the kitchen," he intoned, nodding from the singed yarn that was my hair to the hallway. "The lady of the house is mashing garbanzos and black beans into some kind of experiment and would be grateful for your assistance." I entered the compact foyer and instantly spotted JNB like a glowing Eastern Orthodox icon lounging on a brown sofa with beer in hand, looking very much like Ben. Elbows on knees, he flipped through a book dedicated to what I'd later discover showed early 20th century nudity.

"Here," Parvati said when I discovered the beige kitchen where she leaned into a mortar and pestle. "Take that to Bob," she huffed, raising her chin to indicate a nearby midnight-blue bowl already overflowing with bean paste. "Apparently, he likes hummus. And don't put it in front of JNB or he'll eat the whole thing—I mean literally dip his hand in." She dropped the pestle, causing it to cackle on the countertop, and thrust the bowl and a plate covered with triangles of pita into my hands. "Get Bob to stop hording wine in return. Glasses are on the second shelf to the right—" Again her chin drew an invisible arrow to an upper cabinet where I found several old jam jars that had been converted into cups.

Two hours later, after we'd filled up on pre-cut carrots, salad greens floating in Italian dressing, and pita wedges dipped into what amounted to crushed garlic that caused lipstick to smudge and bowels to inflate, Bob suggested we play Trivial Pursuit, a game I loathed. I declined, wanting to leave but also wanting to delay JNB's bedding of Parvati, which was bound to happen later that night.

After all, the evening had been laced with whale talk—a conversational aphrodisiac for JNB. Rather than flirting with the "Master of Trivial Pursuit" (a.k.a Bob), I asked about the barnacled male Humpbacks who'd appeared the previous summer and had circled one of the females in Chatham Bay. According to JNB, two males in a single pod had actually hung out—an especially strange phenomenon—one that warranted a full television crew financed by National Geographic.

"They've never been seen doing this before. Whales," JNB said while nibbling the last pita wedge, "are otherworldly. Incredibly sensitive. And though they have a following, they're completely under appreciated, mysterious animals. I'll be at on deck tomorrow. Come by and we'll grab coffee."

Before I had the chance to digest this loaded invitation, Parvati literally shouldered in, the sleeve of her droopy shirt falling to reveal an upper arm: "Hey. I thought you were coming with me to that thing. Remember?" She eyed JNB from across the coffee table, intensity washing over the empty plates. "Don't you remember? I have that art show? And then the trip to Victoria?"

"Whoa, that's right!" Bob shot in, always the left fielder, slamming his palm against the coffee table as if he'd always been the focus of feminine want. "I got it. I am there—But," he turned to me. "If you're into dinner, I'm right there too. Let me know when and I'll carve out some time—"

It was all too much. I stood up—all child before the candy man, overwhelmed by the idea of a bus ride home—and pretended exhaustion, grabbing my damp coat, which lay across a ruined arm of Parvati's sofa. "Lovely evening—" I said, pushing myself into the damp sleeves, the headache of cheap wine pulling down my jaw and cheeks while I zipped the chilled coat to my neck.

"Are you going already?" Parvati nudged her bare shoulder against Bob, who swayed like a bobble-head about to topple. "Don't worry, Bob," she wagged a hand at his noodle hair. "I'll give you her number—"

"And when haven't I wanted a woman's number?" Bob babbled, twisting around to wink at me like a lover-in-demand. We all stared at the puffball of Bob's head. "Not that I've requested the numbers of other ladies. Except," Bob prattled on, drumming the coffee table with his forefingers, "for maybe, oh, I don't know—Sarah, Jessica, Lisa, Penelope." He burst into laughter, once again slamming the tabletop with his palm, his rumpled and damp army fatigues looking more and more like clown-wear. "Not to worry," he called as I turned away from the brown sofa. "I'm just pulling your leg."

And Still More

I'd had enough pulled legs to kill a starfish. Back at my apartment, wiped by Parvati's shoulder nudging—not to mention the gas-inducing garlic paste—I saw a sliver of light coming from beneath Jessica's door. Past midnight, it was unlikely that she'd want to talk, because weekdays she usually got up at 6 AM. But I needed someone, so I whispered, "Hey Jessica," assuming she was lounging with the bathroom copy of *Delta of Venus*.

Rapping the wood lightly, I added, "You up?" I heard her exhale. "Guess what—I just spent the evening with JNB—" I heard the muffled sound of her turning over beneath her sheets, followed by heavy sighs and groans.

I gently turned the knob and crept through the crack into the tight space next to her bedding. The room felt unusually cold, a draft flowing in through the wide-open window, which yawned above where she lay naked, her freckled back to me. On the bed sheets, next to her hair, rested a kitchen bowl whose white rim was marred with what looked like dark sediment. It could have been anything from mud to brownie crumbs to crushed burnt toast soggy with tea. Next to the bowl I spotted a balled up napkin smudged with her burgundy lipstick and what looked like mascara. Thinking she slept, I turned off her lamp.

After washing up, I lay down to think of JNB in his androidescent opal jacket, and that's when I heard the floor creak outside my door followed by the shy sound of her knock.

"When did you get home?" she muttered through the door. Opening it, I found her rubbing eyes with the backs of her hands. She appeared to be recovering from a disturbance, her face all red and puffy, eyes bloodshot.

"What's up, Jessica?" She doubled over in the doorway, suddenly heaving. "Oh god! What is it? Hey, what's wrong—" I rushed to her, but she shook her head, and pushed my hand aside, allowing the dry heaves to pulse more blood up her neck to her cheeks. Eventually, on her knees, after catching her breath, she looked up at me.

"Oh my god," she said, hand to chest, face blanched. "I'm just really sorry. It's nothing. Really. I'm just really really sorry. That's all. I'm like so sorry. I hope you'll forgive me." She straightened up. I noticed that the whites of her eyes were so bloodshot that I worried they might start bleeding. "I just want you to know," she continued. "I know I make all kinds of mistakes, but I really want you to know that I appreciate everything about you—I really do!" She hiccupped and shook her head, her face crumpling into itself.

"It's okay—it's okay. But you look bad. Are you okay? Should I call an ambulance?" (Hospitals would always be in the background.) She shook her head as I placed a hand on her shoulder and pressed her to me, inhaling something stringent in her hair. Tears overflowed her eyes and dripped from her nose onto my shoulder. Hugging and patting her back, I said, "Don't worry. I'm not upset with you. A rug is just a rug." She trembled and sniffed, pressing her cheek to my shoulder, the stink of something not right—alcohol, rot, and ash—increasing by the minute.

"Thank you, thank you, thank you so much!" she whimpered.

"No problem." I pulled away to evade the snot that inevitably spread over my shoulder. I appraised her eyes and lips, the streams coming from her nostrils. "You need a tissue. Go get some toilet paper and wipe your nose, okay?" She nodded, groggy and half-lidded, and stumbled towards the bathroom. When she returned, I asked, "Have you been crying all night?" She shook her head, looked down at the floor, her nose an inflamed bulb—a reminder of the many evenings spent bawling over what she'd dubbed "the factory of mental abuse" where she worked downtown.

"How long have you been home?" I asked after retrieving an additional wad of toilet paper.

She thanked me, honked into it, and then said, "I came home from work early—" She laid a hand as white as a scarf against her forehead. "I lost my key and had to ask the manager, what's his name, to let me in. He said it's okay. He said the key could be replaced. I'm so sorry! I'm so so sorry. I promise I'll pay for it."

I said nothing, only patted her shoulder the way someone tired of kitchen melodrama pats a counter. Then, as if there'd never been any tears, she clapped her hands together and cried, "Oh my god! I almost completely forgot! Your guy called!"

"What do you mean my guy?" I hadn't told her about Bob wanting to get coffee. Had he already gotten my number?

"You know. Ben. In New Jersey. He called." The outside blew in through her open window.

What Happened?

He'd called no more than half an hour after Jack the apartment manager left to order a new key. Actually—Jessica told me—she'd been resting in bed wearing only a t-shirt—no underwear—when the phone rang. Or had she just finished showering, begun nibbling on a carrot while dressing? It didn't matter, because she couldn't remember, because her day had been so unnerving, all her clients breaking down—one peeing on a sofa, another throwing fists at her until he was sedated with double doses of meds. It was unbelievable. But what mattered was that at exactly 9:30 on the East Coast, Ben had dialed and she'd picked up. Jessica, that is. Jessica had picked up, though he'd asked for me. For Jane.

Right away the subject of his whereabouts became topical. He'd been soaking in a friend's hot tub, thinking of me. Had I been contemplating him at that moment? Yes, I had in a remote way. I'd been sitting in front of a bowl of mashed garlic, talking to the only man on earth who looked like Ben.

At 6:30 Seattle time—right when Ben called—JNB had been staring at my straw hair from his position on Parvati's sofa, his fingers laced over his chest. On the floor, I'd curled into a ball with knees to chest, occasionally sipping wine or dipping carrots into that unforgivable bowl of hummus, my totaled ex-boyfriend still alive beneath the chalky tang of Merlot. In that New Jersey corner of my mind, in the netherworld of conversation that dwelled on two male Humpbacks vying for a single female, there'd been allusions to Ben.

A double helix of emotions sprang from sex but was tainted by death. Out of the blue, I'd remember Ben in bed, spurring energy that would rise through me like magma through a tube, waves of heat bursting into my chest before settling into my swollen navel. But then it all ended as I remembered that final whiff of hospital—an antiseptic odor like rat poison that would flush the whole sensory experience down the toilet.

Facts were facts. He'd been soaking in a tub, and she'd answered in the near nude. If she hadn't been wearing underwear when he called, where had their conversation gone? Had they entered into a hide-and-seek game of relating what they were wearing and what they were doing, slowly seeking out intimate places as they described themselves? Had it gone like this:

"So where's Jane?"

"She's out. But I'm here. It's Jenn." Or had she said Jessica? "What are you doing?"

"I'm in my hot tub, just wondering how she's doing—just wanted to talk."

"Oh. Yeah. Well she's out. But I'm lying in bed." Or, more likely: "I'm just out of the shower. I can talk. I'm feeling really relaxed. I forgot to put on my underwear."

"That's funny, I'm not wearing mine either—" Or had he said: "I like a woman who knows how to lie down without underwear after a long day at work." Had he called to say this to me? "Do you like lying in bed naked?" The whole exchange fast—I couldn't help imagining the possibilities.

"Yeah—" She might have cradled the phone against her cheek as she continued. "What about you?"

"I'm ready all the time," the heavy breathing beginning about this point, with the obligatory: "Jenn, tell me what you look like."

Had she adopted a phone avatar, in prescience of the web? Had she self-described as tall, slender, blond (always blond), and thin of thigh but with profuse bust? Or, had she lied about olive or tan skin she'd never have, about kinky and dark pubic hair, her belly button a lickable insy while her butt begged for probing like two separated cantaloupes—smooth and rich in the middle as a bar of nougat and melted chocolate?

Maybe she'd spoken the truth and mentioned her vermin-like coloring—the fact that hair and skin and eyes seemed to blend together, not a single feature outstanding. Maybe she described her plump, shapeless legs, and her swollen ankles—which ended in bunioned feet—while the moles that speckled her back and overblown arms appeared graceless. Or maybe she alluded to the fact that sometimes her breath smelled of dead fish or that her deodorant didn't last through the day. Had she mentioned how easy it was to see the dandruff sprinkled over her shoulders when she wore black? What about the fact that more than once her clients threw shit in her face? Had she disclosed the fact that she'd destroyed our carpet and lost the keys to our apartment?

"I like the sound of you," he probably said once she'd described her avatar. "Do you like having your thighs licked?" Perhaps she murmured that she did, licking her own finger and allowing it to ride up the inside of her thigh like an Idaho bullet. I imagined her bulk shifting beneath bed sheets. Did he continue with, "I like licking—beginning at the toes, all the way up—"? And where had this taken them? How far had they gone?

As Jessica and I stood in my bedroom, I studied the rims of her eyes, more red than the red of bawling, with her apology for numerous spoken and unspoken mistakes hanging like stalactites from the ceiling. Worse than the possibility that Jessica might have engaged in phone sex with my ex-boyfriend, was the possibility of a different conversation, which began with her saying:

"Did you know, Jane is totally in love with you—obsessed with you—did you know that?" Long, never ending pause—

"No, I didn't. She never let on—"

"Well, it's true. She's completely obsessed with you. She can't stop talking about you. She made me call you and say I met you at a party—" This would have confirmed three things. 1: The rightness of Rudy's premonition that I'd regret not sticking it out with his son. 2: The fact that my sense of guilt would forever botch any chance I had with love. And finally, 3: The confirmed truth of Ben's last few words to me about blindly making non-decisions at the detriment of those around me. I could hear him say, "Yeah, that's Jane. She's always been a little fucked up."

Tripling the torture of Ben's call was the fact that all my suffering had begun as a result of Mimi, who had introduced me to Ben at one of her New York parties. That was it: Every relationship began as it ended.

Sucker Again

Like my mother, I'd always been a sucker. And like Mimi, Jessica was incapable of comprehending what Ben meant to me—and for this reason I could never trust her. Compounding this fact in days to come, I'd discover her climbing in and out of her bedroom window—presumably because she again forgot her keys. On her fifth catwalk, I caught her leaping to the first floor's exterior brick ledge and confronted her.

"Jessica! What are you doing?" Once I'd lured her through the lobby and into our apartment with the promise of a solution, I began to sound like a parent. "Listen, would you please lock your window when no one is home. What if someone sees you and thinks you're trying to break in? Or maybe decides that climbing through our windows isn't such a bad idea?"

To this she threw hands up to her lips and cried, "Oh my god, you're right! I didn't think of that. Oh my god!" And grabbing my arm, with pleas and wetness in her eyes, added, "Please don't ask me to leave—I promise to make sure I remember my key next time. Just give me one more chance, please."

By the middle of February, the rims of her eyes always appeared red, her fingers twisting around each other to keep hands from jittering. She kept saying, "You're so completely right—I just can't believe I was so stupid to leave without my keys again...." For a short time, maybe a week and a half, she stopped using the window, replacing that habit by coming home late in the company of questionable figures who left her on the corner where she hung out long after their hushed goodbye. I erroneously assumed everything would be okay—because one evening I came back to the apartment to hear a ringing phone. I picked up and heard, "Hey, bitch. I got it."

"I'm sorry?" I returned, his words sounding fast and caffeinated while the answering machine blinked with twelve messages.

"You Jessica?"

"No, this isn't Jessica. Who are you?"

"That's kay. Just tell me when I can git Jessica."

"She's not home till later—I don't know when."

"Kay, that's cool. That's cool." And he hung up.

There were other calls, most of them hang ups. But by then I'd become very focused on my fifth, long-term temporary position at an onsite vaccination clinic for employees at UW Medical Center. I didn't have time to care what Jessica did, so I never questioned the calls. And then, one drizzly evening in late February, while I lay on my sleeping bag re-reading the scene in Oliver Twist when the Artful Dodger snatches the old gentleman's snuff box, I noticed something acrid and sharp coming through my bedroom wall.

"Jessica?" I called, throwing down Oliver Twist and bouncing off my bed. "Hey, Jessica? Do you smell smoke?" I wandered out into a fogged hallway where the odor sharpened and seared my eyes to wetness.

Turning the corner into the living room, I stumbled into a thickening cloud of charcoal-colored smoke that churned in front of her bedroom door. A cold gust swirled through the apartment from what must have been her bedroom window. Through the haze, I saw a stooped form: Jessica backing into the living room, coughing and flapping her hands in front of her face, an arm of orange brightness reaching for her from the black cloud that obscured her bedding. Lung clogging vapors billowed. "Oh my god!!!" She coughed as I poured round after round of water captured in my salad bowl. "Oh my god!!!!" She cried as I ran back and forth between the kitchen sink and her bed where, eventually, we could see the blackened oval in the middle of her comforter—the epicenter of the extinguished fire.

Again, her reddened eyes flowed with tears, palms grabbing her cheeks, her head shaking back and forth as she swallowed, gulped, and hiccupped air. "Oh my god!!!" she crumpled to the floor. "I can't believe this happened!!!"

It turned out this little excursion down the road of destruction had begun with a smoke-able item of unknown origin, followed by a catatonic compulsion to press head to pillow. If I hadn't called out to her, the whole apartment building might have gone up like doomsday.

Again, she pleaded with me to let her stay. "Oh my god! I promise I won't smoke in here anymore— It was just a single cigarette—I promise. Please!" Again, I found it hard to be anything but delusional.

"I didn't know you smoked," I said, eyeing her singed comforter. She flung herself into my arms, and I found myself once again acting the mother, patting her back and letting her know that it would be okay as long as she promised never to smoke in the apartment again. To myself, I reasoned that it was easier to ignore her new habit of smoking than to risk losing a steady rent check.

Another Call

The next evening, I came home to an empty kitchen. Relieved, thinking she'd gone out to indulge in a hamburger, I slipped into bed to read *Oliver Twist*, falling asleep at 8:30. The next morning, I didn't find her scurrying from shower with wet hair and towel, as usual. Nor, that evening, did I find her tossing a salad of chickpeas and corn. Two nights had slipped by without a single "Oh my god!" or "Please don't ask me to leave!" There were no water glasses smudged with burgundy lipstick, no smoke or air freshener or cheap perfume, no sudden outbursts.

At first, I didn't think much of her absence, because, well, Jessica was an adult and could manage her own affairs. It wasn't my responsibility to catalog her every move. But, as I told myself that I wasn't her babysitter, and that I wasn't responsible for her whereabouts, I also understood that if I didn't notice her absence, no one would.

One rainy morning later that week, as I slathered on too much hair gel, I got a phone call.

"Jay Jay?" came a woman's voice. "Is that you?" The voice sounded highly stylized, like that of a Polo enthusiast.

"Jay Jay?" I repeated the name, no longer surprised by wrong numbers—though for a moment I wondered if the woman meant "Mimi."

"Is that you, honey?" The woman cried with expectation.

"Um." I said. "Sorry. No one named Jay Jay here." But wasn't this 206-XXX-YYYY? Yes. It was. Well then, there should be a Jay Jay Hochkiss living there. "Jay Jay?" I asked again, paying attention now that I'd wiped the sticky stay-in conditioner from my fingers. "Are you talking about Jessica? There's a Jessica Hoch here."

"Oh. Thank goodness! I've finally reached you!" The woman sounded relieved, calling herself Tilly Taylor—a ridiculous designation that reminded me of a childhood friend's Labrador retriever. "I'm Jay Jay's mother," came a resonant, San Francisco Bay murmur. With the affability of the pampered, she filled me in: "You don't know how often I've tried this number—I've been trying to reach Jay Jay all week, but the machine picks up, and I know she'll never listen to my messages. I'm just so glad you answered. I knew if I called early, I'd get someone—this is Jane, isn't it?" I answered in the affirmative and explained that I hadn't seen her daughter for a few nights. "How many nights? Are you sure?" She sounded uneasy, though still affable. "Did she say where she was going?" Trying too hard to sound at ease.

"No," I said, longing for a breakfast of apples and boiled corn. "She doesn't tell me her plans." I explained that Jessica often arrived home before me, but definitely wasn't consistent in her hours. "Have you called her work?" I asked. A pause.

The refrigerator hummed a note of hunger.

"You know, I hadn't thought of that," Tilly said, inhaling deeply, taking her time. "I'm not sure why. Maybe you could help me, actually. Believe it or not, I don't have her work number. Would you happen to have it?" At this point, Tilly's voice risked a shake, as if she'd opened a closet door to a hidden reservoir.

"Sorry," I said, stretching the newly shortened phone cord in an effort to reach the fridge. "I don't even know the name of the organization, though I know it's downtown."

Her mother released a sound halfway between a sigh and a groan, followed by a pause. Finally, she exhaled, "I can't believe this," followed by a louder, "Look, I'm so sorry to involve you in this crap, Jane. But I need your help." I'd made it over the threshold, was even able to brush my fingertips against the refrigerator handle, stretching to grip and pull. "Jay Jay," Tilly prattled, "has always been reserved about sharing information," the phone crackling against the overstretched cord. "I just need a few pointers from you." Caving to the cord, I backed into the living room where the questions began.

A Mother's Questions

- Was it a state agency or a nonprofit?
- Where, generally speaking, in downtown Seattle was it located?
- Had Jessica mention the names of her coworkers?
- Did Jessica indicate, in any way, the type of client attending?
- Did she pay rent on time?

When I came up with few answers, other than violent stories, I could almost hear the woman pressing the bridge of her nose, shutting her eyes, and shaking her head. After several ancillary questions, the whole of it culminated in the dreaded request. "Jane, if you could do me the favor of looking in the phone directory for a short list of possible employers, I'd much appreciate it—" What choice did I have?

"Give me a minute," I said, placing the receiver on the carpet, stumbling into the kitchen, throwing open the freezer door, grabbing frozen corn, ripping open the bag, spilling its contents into a bowl and slamming the freezer shut. I rummaged through kitchen cabinets, lugged out the phone tomes and charged back to Tilly to say, "All I know is that sometimes clients wear straight jackets." I flipped through the directory between fistfuls of frozen kernels, finding the social services section and pressing corn into my mouth.

"Well," Tilly exhaled in that way of a reformed smoker. "Jay Jay never calls. Not even a couple times a week." Like a storm over Antarctica, the corn froze my brain making Tilly's brisk and business-like tone painful. "The last time we talked was Tuesday morning— You say you didn't see her Tuesday night?" I confirmed this fact, glancing at my watch. Had time sped up when I wasn't looking?

A sweater lounged on the sleeping bag in my bedroom, waiting for me as I contemplated my dilemma. Time required that I be in two places at once. Cradling the phone against my chest, I carried it to my bedroom door till the cord stretched to its limits. Spatially frustrated, I was forced to lie belly down on the floor as I reached towards bedding, scissoring fingers to pinch the sweater's sleeve whose threads lay within an inch of my fingernails. Why I didn't sign off, I don't know. But as minutes passed, resentment towards Tilly and Jessica grew into a mushroom cloud.

"Could you do me another favor," Tilly continued. I grunted, again glancing at my watch. Who had time for this? "I'm so sorry to ask this of you. I know you must be busy—" What kind of person apologized just to sound well behaved? Didn't she realize my job was at stake? No work, no paycheck, no home.

"You should know," Tilly kept going, more firm. "That Jay Jay has a problem."

Here she slowed even more, though I needed to relate that my car-less ass would be fried if I didn't make a break pronto. But the woman probably paid for Jessica's room, so I uttered a long, "mhmmm," followed by a tentative, "so, I kind of need to go."

But, carrying on, she seemed to be sipping a daiquiri by the bay: "She hasn't told you about her problem, has she, because it's always been hard for her to admit." The problem wasn't whether I knew about Jessica's problem or not; It was that if Jessica was in trouble, I could be guilty of not doing my part to find her. "Jay Jay should be on medication but sometimes—" and here Jessica's mother broke off before blurting, "Ever since she was a teenager, she's gone off her meds. When this happens, she turns to recreational drugs—not prescription, but street drugs."

I had always been slow to grasp the truth. But now things made sense, fragments coalescing like the dots of a Seurat painting, everything glomming together: the blitz of crying, the fearful pleading, the forgotten keys, the strange phone calls, the bedroom fire.

"At fifteen," Tilly slurred, breathless, "she was diagnosed with bipolar disorder. I've worried so much about this over the years. But she insisted. And now she's twenty-three—" Jessica had told me she was twenty-six. "All I can do is pay her rent—give her the support she needs to keep her off the streets. And now, it hasn't worked!" I cleared my throat, concerned the conversation would degenerate into bawling. "But thank goodness you're willing to help—" And when had I stated that I'd help? "I live a thousand miles south and can't, at the drop of the hat," (and did she know how to drop hats!) "fly to Seattle!" Two more minutes and I'd have to call in late. But then she said, "I'll pay you."

Paid Attention

"Ah," I began, remembering that Jessica's mom lived in Marin, that county north of San Francisco comprised of Star Wars fans pretending to crush grapes while "managing" ranches. "I see," I said, sure that a long line of patients wrapped around my reception desk, three nurse practitioners scrambling the database in my absence. How much was the time worth? "Tell me," I said, "what to do."

What To Do

An hour later, after flaking on work and ruining any opportunity for reassignment, I stood next to Officer Sarah Tundleson—Badge number 80ZootSuit—describing Jessica's physique, providing details that might illuminate Jessica's work and opaque social life. I squinted at the carpet, unable to offer the names of which corner cafés or parks she might have haunted, though I did remember what she'd donned that Tuesday (a duplicate of my Tuesday outfit). I also mentioned she sometimes went to happy hour and came home smelling of alcohol. Like most do-gooders, I had a terrible memory. And Tundleson, whose short, permed hair and thin lips left me feeling more focused than I had in days, refused to make light of Jessica's disappearance.

A uniformed wine barrel on two logs, chest sheathed in blue, Tundleson's thighs formed an alpha female's "A"—rather than an inferior's "K." For some reason this struck me as a reminder of how quickly shit happened.

Tundelson nodded and cleared her throat as I answered her questions about Jessica, her hands furiously scribbling shorthand on her leather-encased pad. Our dialogue ran something like this:

Tundelson: "What's the age of the person in question?"

My one-liner ("23 to 26 years"), followed by the clearing of Tundelson's throat and stiffening of her back.

Tundelson: "What's the height and weight of the person in question?"

My answer ("about my height, maybe a little taller?"), followed by her cough.

"How long has the person in question been out of contact?" My answer, (Hadn't I already mentioned this?) followed by a sigh.

The interrogation, with a lot of so on and so forths, ended when Tundleson bowed her head and stared at the patch of carpet Jessica had so expertly snipped. Then she spun around to absorb the apartment's lack of comforts, gazing at the empty corners and the vacant hall leading to my sleeping bag, open suitcase, and the hair-and-tissue infested bathroom.

"So," Tundelson said to my worried forehead. "I see you have no furniture in the living room. Is that her bedroom there?" She nodded at the door that revealed Jessica's fire-blackened bedding. She scribbled and said, "How long have you been living at this location?" I gave my answer, which was followed by the clearing of Tundelson's throat, a quick notation, and the realigning of the spread of her legs. "She been living with you that long too?" Out with my answer, followed by her nods while taking more notes. "Okay. Have you got a pen and paper for your case number?" Followed by: "We'll be in touch with further information once we have more to provide." She eyed the ceiling and walls, once again settling on the carpet's disfigurement before stiffly stepping towards the door.

"Officer," I called as she opened the door, concerned that I might be suspect. "Is there anything more I can do to help find Jessica?"

"Right now," Tundleson coughed, shooting me a look that made me feel like a murderer. "The best you can do is wait. You can also phone area hospitals to find out if anyone with her name has shown up. We'll be in touch." I nodded, already a convict.

Convicted

After Tundelson left, imagining Jessica stabbed, burned, soaked in semen, I dialed every ER in the area: The University of Washington Medical Center, Swedish Hospital, Harborview. Oddly, the switch operators directed me to various reception desks that claimed no knowledge of a Jessica Hoch or a Jay Jay Hochkiss. At X hospital, my inquiry accidentally got funneled to the voicemail of a Dr. Sherwood, the recording simply requesting that the caller, "Please leave a first and last name, I repeat, first and last name, as well as the time of the call. I'll also need the exact telephone number, including area code. Without that I will not be able to give a call back. Leave a brief message with the concern, and I will return your call as soon as possible. Thank you." I left a brief message, losing faith but willing to try every option. Two minutes later my phone rang.

When I picked up, a breathless man blurted, "You called?"

"Is this X hospital—" I asked, noting the caller ID. "Are you calling back about Jessica?"

"Right—" the man said.

"She's not here—"

"Yes, I gathered that from your voice message." Something about Dr. Sherwood's breathlessness sounded familiar.

"Am I talking to Dr. Sherwood?"

"Yes. Didn't I just say so?" When had I entered a Eugene Ionesco play? "This is Dr. Sherwood. You just called, and now I'm calling you back."

"Yes. I called. I'm just confused. Sorry. I'm not sure if you're the right person."

"Well, I'm the right person, and I'm waiting. I don't have much time. So, what can I do for you?"

"Yes," I said, anxiety growing on anxiety. "I'm looking for a Jessica Hoch, sometimes called Jay Jay Hochkiss, who might have showed up at the ER. She has bipolar disorder and a drug problem. For some reason, an operator forwarded me to your office."

"Jessica, Jessica. Hmmm. I don't remember that name coming through— But. What was that last name? Hushkie?"

"Hoch or Hochkiss." I spelled the last name for him, with him interrupting.

"Hold on—Wait. I need a pen. Okay, spell it for me." I did, and he said. "You'd think this shithole would have the budget to buy good pens. Piece of shit!" the sound of something thrown at the phone. "All day my computer's been crashing. What medical center doesn't have on-call IT? I'm a doctor, not a computer wizard! In a computer savvy town! Egregious! And can I find a patient? Not for a thousand fucks, I can't. Is this person in our system? That's the ten billion dollar question. This country is sinking in its own shit. A town with billions, with more sick people than Medieval England! And I mean sickos—every last one of them is certifiably insane. All of them!"

I had trouble following the anger crashing against me, clustering around pops and something that sounded like the word "brrrrrr," as if he were a dog shaking the cold from his ears. Or maybe I didn't want to follow—not because I couldn't, but because it was so unbelievable. Who was this guy? A patient?

To extract myself from the call, I played the accommodating customer service rep, ("You're so right!") and hung up.

Hours later, as I soaped my arms in the shower, it came to me. Carpooling to a Mountaineers hike in the fall, I'd been victim of a harrowing drive in which the pill-popping, misanthropic driver—doctor from X hospital—yelled, "Damn it! They're going to leave without us!" as he wrestled an orange vial from his pocket, pressing the gas pedal and plugging the exhaust pipe with road mud and flying pebbles, the mileage arrow swinging from 35 to 65 mph. I'd almost died on the way to that hike, and it had to be this same Dr. Sherwood who, before hanging up, had the nerve to add, "I tell you what I can do for you about this Jessica." He chewed on these words. "I'm here till six tonight. I'll keep my eyes and ears open! And I'll get back to you— I mean that. I'll get back to you. And if I do, then you'll know that doctors, not IT staff and office managers, mean business!"

After four hours of tossing in my sleeping bag, nose as stuffed as an olive, legs itchy with scorpions and spiders, I couldn't get Dr. Sherwood off my mind. When I imagined him slamming his head into his computer screen, I decided to call my mother. It was 2 AM back East, and of course, no one answered.

So I paced, shivered, and worried Sherwood had also made the Mountaineers connection and would track me down with his, "I'll get back to you." Thinking of this, I slid into my sleeping bag and covered my head.

Raging, he would bust through my bedroom door with Officer Sarah Tundleson in tow, grab my arms and pull me from the sleeping bag, pry open my clenched jaws and pour a thousand doses of Xanax into my mouth. He'd pitch pills at my forehead, with the Officer and Jessica crawling on the carpet at my feet as they gathered fistfuls of the little pellets. Together, they'd rise up and beat me with a baseball bat and slit—

But midway through this nightmare, I heard a thump against the front door—a kind of muffled bang like that of a distant garbage dumpster dropping to the sidewalk.

I curled deeper into my sleeping bag, whispering, *"om, om, om,"* straining to hear as the front door latch clicked. Motionless, my lungs stalled at a bank of icicles in my ribcage. Dr. Sherwood had come for me with his freckled and exposed legs, pants around ankles, bouncer-sized cock throbbing in the dark.

Had he found Jessica at the hospital, swiped her address and keychain? Had he driven to our Capital Hill outpost, intending to pilfer her collection of carbon-encrusted salad bowls, but instead finding it more satisfying to rape me? Was it all going to end as it did in the recent article about a woman who'd been tortured for two days—her eyelids slit with razors, her arms and legs tethered to bedposts, her blankets set on fire in some kind of horror-movie re-creation that stemmed from a roommate's lost set of keys?

Beyond my bedroom door, floorboards snapped despite heavy but practiced steps. My bedroom door shimmered like a thin piece of brown silk, and I hated myself for not locking it.

The Safety of Closets

Slowly, gently, I slipped out of my sleeping bag and shoved a stray plastic water bottle beneath my arm. Could I halt the rape by regaling Sherwood with a 1001 stories of Brahma, Vishnu, and Shiva? Could I wash his brain with chants (*OM OM OM*) while cycling through a yogic sun salutation? Was I so naïve as to think it was possible to talk down a rapist as if we saw eye-to-eye?

Tentatively, I inched through the dark towards the ajar bedroom door, brushing the soles of my feet against the carpet, super-aware of the sloshing water in the bottle, everything magnified by the silence. I stood by the door like a panel of sheetrock, and peeked through the crack.

There, a thickset and stooping silhouette stood beneath the archway that opened to the kitchen. If I planned it right, I could yell "OM," kickboxing and slashing my hands like a lunatic, and dash through the kitchen door to pull our only paring knife from one of the drawers. My advantage: I knew where kitchen utensils slept.

But what if the intruder already gripped a knife—or worse—a gun?

What if the intruder sold drugs to Jessica? He could be trigger-happy, might be carrying several handguns, like a load of excrement, in the sagging crotch of his pants. More disturbing was the thought of dealing with Dr. Sherwood, a guy who'd probably dug many graves beneath lines of coke.

With this thought cycling through my blood, I stood prepared to fight, knowing that I was no better than a collection of bones. Behind me lay the cavern of my closet. If I were five, I might have believed in the safety of closets, just as I might have believed that the dinosaur eggs encased at the American Museum of Natural History might one day crack open. I backed towards the closet's mothballs, hoping cry of hinges would be masked by a car alarm. Doubting everything, I stood too long on a creaky floorboard and it clapped.

Three beats, and then a voice: "Hey?" An uncertain whisper. This was not the jittery, snort-happy language I expected. "Are you up?" No, this was the feathery whisper of a woman. "Jane?"

Every cubic puff of carbon dioxide in my lungs discharged in an elongated whoosh. I flicked on my overhead, blinking relief as unconscious tears glazed my cheeks. I stumbled into the living room, where a lamp already clicked color into the world.

"Jessica?" I cried. "Where the hell!" I shivered in t-shirt and underwear, not sure I wanted to hug or hit her. "Where have you been? We were so worried—do you have any idea? Your mother—She was a basket case!"

A Land Without Trust

"I share your pain."

Mother

"My mother?" Jessica winced, the cluelessness of her lips and blinking eyes, the wrinkles on her forehead. She stank of alcohol mixed with something sour like dry vomit, still wearing Tuesday's now rumpled clothes: a pair of muddy jeans, a long sleeve shirt stained with what looked like sauce and grease, and an unzipped U.W. sweatshirt whose logo had been smeared with an indeterminate black crust. "What are you talking about?" She stood blinking as if I'd uttered the unthinkable.

"She called asking for you. I told her you hadn't been back since Tuesday, and she freaked out. So I called the police and filed a missing person report— Where were you?" Her hair hung over her face like melted string cheese, the oil almost dripping. Every last bit of peach had vanished from her cheeks, leaving her pale as a parsnip.

"My mother?" She shook her head. "What are you talking about? My mother? Jane!" She winced at the wasteland of the carpet. "My mother's dead. She's dead, okay? You didn't talk to my mother, okay? Okay? Oh my god!" Her voice high, her bloated hands rubbing her eyes, unexceptional tears spilling over unexceptional cheeks while my heartbeat skipped rocks over the imaginary surface of Lake Namananda, where long ago my own mother had meditated on a Pashmina prayer mat, wasting away all the summers of my childhood. Nothing made sense.

Only that morning, I'd spoken to Tilly, who "reasonably" suggested I call every social services facility in the phonebook. But only a few hours later, it all seemed a sham. Jessica cried and laced her fingers, pacing the carpet and telling me the story of her mother's battle with metastatic breast cancer. "She died two years ago. I know I lied to you about her paying rent, but I swear. I was there, at UCSF Medical Center—so was my brother. It's true. I didn't want to tell you. She's dead. Okay?"

"So who's Tilly?"

"I don't know! A fake!" She cried.

Later, after we'd shaken our heads and said, "I can't believe this!" for the umpteenth time, well past 3:00 AM, she picked up the phone to call her forty-something half-brother—more news to me—who lived back East in Jersey City.

Their conversation, which I overheard in bits and pieces through my now locked bedroom door, amounted to little more than that Jessica—who kept repeating "Oh my god!"—was in trouble. "Jake," I heard her say, "you can't do this! You totally can't let me crash—You can't!"

After Jessica hung up, but before I dropped into the dark, amorphous liquid where Nora and The Avatar wagged fingers at me, she gently knocked. "Yaaah," I groaned.

"Can I come in?"

"I'm tired—" I croaked, pulling my sleeping bag above my shoulder. "Time for bed—"

"Please Jane," she begged. "Just one more thing? I really need to tell you something. It can't wait." Though my eyelids weighed a thousand pounds, though cracking them open caused the whites to sting, I managed to get up and pull at the knob. The door swung open, and I squinted at the living room lamp and the dark circles beneath her eyes.

I fell back into my sleeping bag and repositioned the pillow, squinting at her swollen nose and lips.

"I haven't done anything," she said, lacing her fingers. "But I'm totally sorry I didn't tell you where I was going. And I'm really totally sorry that I set my bed on fire—it was completely an accident. And I'm so glad the apartment is okay. I'm back and I'm fine. Just believe me. I won't do this again."

"Rightokay." I slurred, "Fine." I turned onto my back, shutting eyes to black desperation. "No one sleeps anymore," I moaned, "Why the fuck not?"

She murmured something under her breath and then placed an icy hand on my exposed wrist, and said, "It won't happen again." I opened an eye. How was it possible that she couldn't take a hint? How could anyone be so dense? Was she taking advantage of my exhaustion to suit her purposes? "I promise," she continued. "I won't do this again!" She stared at me, all open wound. "So, can I stay?"

"I'm sleeping," I whispered, wanting to drop off more than I'd ever wanted a bowl of frozen peas. She didn't leave the room but stared at me until I rolled over. But her eyes bothered me. Her stare was enough to keep me suspended between alpha and zeta. "Wait. This doesn't make sense," I croaked. "Didn't you tell me your mother was alive?"

"I never said that!" Her yell hit me like plate glass, breaking open and exposing the other Jessica.

"You did," I said, struggling up, certain I remembered correctly. "You showed me her photo—the one of her in the hat. You told me I should meet her some time." My head was fracturing into an ache.

"I told you that was my mother. I didn't say she was alive—"

"Yes you did, Jessica. You said I should meet her."

"No. No I didn't—" We had reached an impasse, mirror meeting mirror where the truth didn't lie in between, but lay within a lie.

I fell back, wordless, no better than a split pea rehydrating in a pot of boiling water while Jessica began a lengthy story about her mother's old business associate.

What little I gathered, amounted to a mashup of questions. Apparently, the business associate oversaw the Trust that provided Jessica's rent. But now, according to her half-brother Jake, the associate was threatening to discontinue funds "if things didn't change." I didn't ask Jessica what "things" needed to change, hoping that she'd leave me in peace.

"So now do you understand?" she whined. I turned towards the wall. "You have to believe me!"

"Jessica," My throat felt sore, forehead pulsing. "I'm done."

"But please—"

"No Jessica." A piano rested on my chest. The music sounded off color, too bright.

"Just believe me—"

"Okay," I groaned. "Whatever. Goodnight." She stood a blurred outline over me. She must've stared through me, her stringy hair stuck to her cheeks. Soon there would be a new storm of tears running down her sand cheeks. But I yawned, drifting off into plasma while Jessica dimmed like a dying bulb.

Eternal Now

I rinsed Noxema from my cheeks while the same "fuck yous" that crashed my dreams at 6 AM kept crashing. There'd been a lot of, "This is total bullshit!" and, "No fucking way! She's such a bitch!" which led me to conclude Jessica hadn't understood the first principle of good communication: The more you riddle a person with verbal ammo, the less effective it is.

I turned off the tap and tiptoed back to my room. On the way, I avoided a view of her spitting at the mouthpiece.

"What the fuck does she want from me?!" Jessica sputtered. "To like stop altogether?!! Cold turkey? She totally knows that's impossible! And you do too! And then she like calls my roommate and totally tells her a bunch of bullshit lies about my being sick in the head? God! Jake? She's like a nightmare!!" Her voice fell to a harsh whisper, lost to me as I shut my bedroom door.

Morning rain pulsed my head. At some point, in the kitchen sipping tea while Jessica cried in her bedroom, my hands began shaking. Here were the facts:

1. I depended on rent (and thus shelter) from a woman who might or might not be bipolar, depending on whether I believed the invisible mother or the arsonist daughter.

2. I was isolated in a city whose inhabitants could be seen as either reserved—and thus hard to read—or blitzed out on various recreational antidepressants.

3. I'd become estranged from those who once might have been able to help. For instance: no Mimi, Parvati, or, most importantly, my mother.

4. And speaking of my mother: I'd left several messages with her new roommate(s), a massage therapist named Elaina, who said "yeah," instead of "hello," and who sometimes became interchangeable with an executive assistant named Lori-Anne. Or was it the other way around?

And then I had to contend with the macro: While the rest of the country got high on Wall Street, hard times slammed all hopes of anyone like me maintaining a middle class existence, let alone any existence. No more summer weekends in the mountains, my future of gutters and peeling plaster and shouting matches seemed set in stone.

How did Nora stay sane while gathering roommates from The Avatar's brood of transients, barely cobbling together enough cash for her pre-war apartment? I worried about her as much as I worried about my own situation. Without that apartment, she'd be turned out, and because, at fifty-plus, she couldn't get a job, there was the very real possibility of the street.

Compounding these worries was the issue of my recently released father. Post-slammer, his existence in a former-colleague's attic had diminished him to a kind of Captain Haddock who brandished a black flask—stashed in the glove compartment of his 20-year-old Ford—while eyeing local police stations. The only thing I could do to help my parents was to hope—and occasionally call.

Actually, it wasn't Jessica's business that I dialed Nora twice a day. After all, I'd designated Nora's number as one of three that got unlimited long distance. Often, I hung up instead of leaving a voicemail. I hated to be cloying, but it was important to verify that Nora hadn't been evicted. When we did speak, she insisted that everything was fine, despite the clicking and popping sounds that dappled our calls, which could only mean one thing: The landlord had bugged the line.

Facts were facts: After losing her job as the "Guru of Publications" at a nonprofit called "The Art Of Giving," Nora's income was slashed to $1,322 a month. Meanwhile, her savings had dwindled to an amount she refused to disclose until I wrestled it from her by refusing to admit what was in my account. $320 was all she had, which meant she relied on The Avatar for rice cakes, canned beans, toilet paper, and trips to Atlantic City—where she dropped miscellaneous credit cards into the many ATMs surrounding the slot machines.

Further, Nora's solvent but old world parents had lost faith in her, calling her an "innocent" who took "exorbitant" trips to "uninhabitable places" with a "hoodwinker," who offended their modesty and frugality—traits that had allowed them to retire to a planned community located in the hills above Laguna Beach.

Nevertheless, Nora continued to live in an eternal **nnnnnoooooooowwwwwww**, hosting The Avatar's banquets. I'd attended one of those brain-numbing feasts. That one featured chicken bathed in cayenne pepper, wedges of mantra-graced cantaloupe amid fireballs The Avatar had mastered with the help of a half-nude dancer ringing bells. It didn't help that I no longer trusted Nora's accounting abilities. I'd been burned when she withdrew eight hundred dollars from a linked savings account. Apparently, in Atlantic City for a quick gambling excursion, she'd practiced "chancing it" by dishing out my savings in exchange for a losing streak. (Eventually, Nora repaid me—but not until I closed the account and accused her of stealing.) Was this why some people said we lived in a land without trust?

"Jessica—" I called from the kitchen. Steam from my tea rose to my nostrils, a reminder of the hibiscus my mother sipped when, as a tot, I sat in her lap. I walked into the living room to find Jessica slumped over, post-phone call, speechless, red-eyed. At that moment, nothing about her seemed false. She'd cried. She'd yelled. She'd claimed not to know. It was possible she'd spoken honestly. Maybe Tilly was the pretender. "Jessica," I said again, because what was a lie but the choice to see things differently? "I know what you're going through." Was it dangerous to make kind statements to someone who'd possibly lost her mind and probably had phone sex with my half-dead, ex-boyfriend?

She sniffled and glanced up, but seemed not to see.

"I know, it seems like no one gets it—" I tried to sound less the counselor and more the big sister. She turned her back to me, because I was full of shit. But I continued: "Oh come on! I believe you. Your mom's dead. You're not alone. You know me. You and I have similar problems—" She looked at my feet as if my ghost had arrived to blow her away.

Far away, outside the house where I spent my earliest years, lightning struck an elm, rattling dishware on a dining room table. Did anyone know how much that tree meant to me? Or about how, when I turned five at what I called "St. Patrick's" instead of "Cleopatra's" Needle, my father punched my mother so hard she fell to the sidewalk and scraped her chin? Had Jessica or Mimi or Parvati ever sat on a deck and watched their mother spoon sliced strawberries from an engraved bowl to her split lips and bruised tongue, the wrought iron dinette returned to its upright position after it spent a night inverted? Yes they probably had. It was an old story that everyone knew. But three casserole dishes had been destroyed at the summer rental near Shandelee. And everyone knew that no one in America in the decades between my birth, in the 1970s, and the day I would die lived in a whipped cream and apple-pie world, because in the end, everything, including the headache that pulsed in my temples, got flushed down history's toilet.

"Let's forget everything—" I said as rain slashed the kitchen window, washing away the elm and the inverted table.

Born In America

But memories can't be forced from overwhelmed minds. She didn't come home that evening—or the next. And by then, I knew I couldn't be held responsible for another person's troubles. A week later, I still hadn't articulated how, beyond lipstick and bagged salad, Jessica and I had become one person. Since my contact with her purported "mother," conversations with Jessica became one-liners. I spoke platitudes and she stopped smearing our water glasses with burgundy lipstick.

For a week, I struggled through nights broken up by visions of my parents floating over my third eye. I wrestled with Nora's toner cartridges, flinging peas and corn at them. In his bacon-colored kitchen, I told Stan to stop pretending. I watched my mother turn into Jessica as she embraced my father while the fat on a leg of lamb liquefied and dripped onto the oven rack. One minute: a battle. The next: sublime fields of childhood stretching towards a horizon of snipped carpets. At midnight, lying in bed like Scrooge awaiting the ghosts of Christmas, I heard slammed doors and suicide threats. Love and pain curdled in my belly like the childhood dinners of rice and bacon that ended as vomit.

So, the past was the past. Live in the moment, where Nora planted a thousand affirmations like those in the gift bag of vitamins she'd pressed into my hands before my flight to Seattle.

"These weren't cheap," she'd said, handing me the bag of clicking bottles. "I got you Herbalife." I thanked her, but as soon as we parted, I trashed the vitamins and all her hand-written affirmations in the nearest can, feeling that if I didn't my mother's desperation would mushroom into my life. I couldn't allow Nora and Stan's medieval battles to catapult me from my first yellow bedroom into future relationships, where I'd forever drink the poison of their marriage, all their madness slithering into my bed— Because

I knew my father had fucked a sixteen-year-old student the day Nora gave birth to me.

Like other American children, I grew up spiritually celibate until someone threw a Hindu god at my head, as if I'd learn to understand love or something like it by staring at Shiva in his frozen dance. And still, my family could be counted as lucky—or so Nora insisted. Our table offered waxed apples, hormone-laced chickens, and genetically modified brocco-flour. We lived in buildings—albeit without much heat—and we still talked to each other.

"In Africa—" Nora liked to say, because Africa was the last resort. "There's nothing but rice. How lucky," she kept saying, "to be in America."

Another One Bites The Dust

Three and a half months after she moved in, barely a week after I learned of her half-brother, Jessica left Seattle—and possibly the West Coast. She never told me why. Something had terrified her to the point of no return, because, last minute, she'd purchased an airline ticket to a destination she insisted on keeping to herself, packing quickly and leaving everything—including a keepsake of frozen vegetables—but a suitcase of t-shirts and blue jeans. Her departure was so swift that I had trouble downing bagged salad. To this day, I don't know where she hid herself during the second half of 1998—though some months later, I got a letter from her, thanking me for putting up with her—no return address.

Again, I panicked, in need of a roommate. Thankfully, I had help. During a last meal of lettuce together, Jessica had sympathetically thrown me a lead. Though she'd previously hypnotized me with apologies, she now "acknowledged" her "responsibility" to me, and felt it was her "duty" to help me figure out my "new life."

"I think," she said, spearing a carrot round, "what you totally need is a cool, artsy type to keep things sane," as if she hadn't lost it, as if there was every reason to feel at ease with a recommendation from her. "But," she added, "I can't see you living in a loft with tons of people banging heads and being loud?" I wasn't sure whether Jessica meant this in seriousness, but the day a cab drove her off to the airport, she told me about this "amazing artsy type" looking for "a cute little room," preferably in Capital Hill. "Oh my god? I almost forgot? I told her to call," Jessica said when she handed over her umpteenth pair of lost but found keys. "Hope you don't mind."

Enter my next renter, Zelda, an Estonian transplant who worked in a Belltown clothing boutique when she wasn't studying the love life of Serge Gainsbourg and sustainable urban design at UW. A virtual basketball player,

Zelda towered over anyone under 5'10". Her big-boned face and knee-high suede boots were buffered by broad-collared shirts belted over long skirts like those worn by Midwestern moms when I was an infant. Did it surprise me that she found Leonard Cohen "bewitching"? Or that she ate bread and cheese with almost every meal?

In fact, Zelda was anything but vegan. Daily, she shunted sacks of sausage, brie, brined fish, eggs, and heavy cream through the front door, stuffing the refrigerator as if it were a turkey. At dinnertime, after cluttering the kitchen with her olive-colored ceramics and deltoid-building marble cutting board, she prepared aromatic casseroles of pork, morels, and wild rice. Or she pulled out a skillet to sauté chicken in heavy cream that spattered onto the stovetop and left the apartment reeking of lactic "fatcid" for days afterwards. And though she said little, she sipped two-buck chuck from green and red Moroccan vials etched with painted gold—which made everything look exotic.

When Zelda ducked through the front door for our first meeting, I worried that she'd find the ceiling too low. With only a week left before the rent check was due, I couldn't afford to lose her. I worried more when Zelda's questions became probing, as when she asked, "How much time do you spend in the bathroom?" followed by, "and what about the kitchen?" As stomach acid flooded my throat she lingered in Jessica's old bedroom, gazing at the walls for close to fifteen minutes, pacing back and forth, repeatedly opening each door, caressing the ceiling with her up-stretched hands, and stomping on the floor as if to test the neighbor's patience. I waited in the living room, concerned. But I refused to offer sales pitches, sitting cross-legged on the floor, trying to appear the yoga instructor.

Eventually, she circled towards me and announced that she'd move in—but only if we could pull up the mottled carpet, which had acquired a "Cat In The Hat" appearance with its many penny-sized, charcoal-colored spots—not to mention Jessica's creative cut-out work. Overjoyed, I shot up from yoga posture and told Zelda, "no problem!"—little realizing the devastation to come.

Her last request, before signing her check: The carpet had to go **before** she moved in, because she owned a truckload of handcrafted Estonian furniture. In essence, I needed to prepare for a household of antiques her father had shipped from Siberia by way of Alaska—items such as a massive ebony chest draped with navy blue calico speckled with yellow flowers like the meadows around Lake Peipsi (over which the phone and answering machine would collide), or the mahogany sofa whose moth-eaten cushions rotted beneath orange brocade, the whole scene lit by a filigreed lamp whose switch appeared lethal, especially when its wobbling bulb flickered to life.

A Never Ending Flurry

Would it be too harsh to say that domestic demands were taking a toll? Zelda and I spent our first weeks together sanding the living room floor. Instead of returning from UW Medical Center to share stories about old boyfriends, or read a biography of Serge Gainsbourg, we stuck surgical masks over our noses, got down on hands and knees, and leaned into the hand-sander on loan from the ever-patient apartment manager, Jack. Speechless, we created flurries of sawdust that infiltrated sinuses and splintered lungs. Minutes into the project, the sneezing began, followed by sensations of a meat tenderizer hammering the lower back. At night, I lay like a bruised banana, aching and stuffed up, unable to turn over.

Matters didn't improve outside the apartment. The gray skies of March refused to exhaust themselves of the Puget Sound's piss, making the Space Needle appear sickly, if not a doomed spacecraft.

Unexpectedly, my old "friend" Parvati swung by one drizzly Saturday morning to ask if I wanted to take a walk. Remembering our excursion in the woods, I hesitated long enough for her to express an opinion. Glancing at the unfinished floor, she shook water from her umbrella, making meal worms out of the sawdust. She assured me I was getting myself into trouble—that a project like this would "never end" and leave me with more than a headache. She suggested that I hire a professional—like Bob for instance.

"And, where's the money to pay for Bob?" I asked, as we stepped outside into a cloudburst that soaked my shoes. "Nice day," I added. "For a walk—" Parvati, who never seemed to mind, frowned.

"This," she said, wrestling with her umbrella like a Mary Poppins wannabe, "is nothing. The floors, however, are definitely going to be somebody's headache. And thank goodness, not mine." Shrugging, she began laughing. The joke that had transformed this once quiet, Asian goddess into a mean-spirited hussy eluded me.

Later, at the Starbucks, when I asked Parvati about JNB, she merely said, "Never mind. He hates sawdust." Something had shifted in Parvati. She no longer seemed interested in acting like she meant to help. Sarcasm riddled her speech as much as it riddled my thoughts. Something had caused her to become prickly—even outright mean.

We hadn't gotten together since the garlicky night of hummus, but I knew she didn't miss my company because she hadn't been in touch. To make peace, I invited her to join my reading group, which "intrigued" her enough that we sipped our hot drinks without spilling any more sarcasm.

After Mimi left Harvard Avenue East, I'd invited the book group back into my living room. Every other Sunday afternoon we shivered over bad wine, deconstructing Rumi or Plath. To freeze things further, once the sawdust entered my world, Dan—an asthmatic—and our dwindling assemblage of readers, insisted that I convert the apartment into an air tunnel, even when temperatures lingered at 40 degrees.

"This is lethal," Dan whined at the living room. "I vote for every window open. And maybe we can sit in your bedroom?" My bedroom was the only remaining room that contained a carpet. Finally, instead of bonding on wood floors, the reading group again met at cafes, highlighting the fact that my life had become a tangle of meaningless interactions, people pouring into and out of my days.

There was the couple, Franz and Letty—two Floridians who'd landed in a cottage near 23rd Avenue East that ruled over lake views and a plethora of parties that included a traditional Sukkot tent dappled with garden blossoms and homemade sushi. At Franz and Letty's I met the slender, pale and plum-colored Ceci whose circuitous journey from Chicago had left a few too many acne scars on her chin. Ceci elbowed me into joining her at a depressing single's event where double-chinned men in their 50s bragged about their kids dropping out of college so they could emulate Bill Gates and "get techie." While circulating through singles hell, I met Lucy, a budding writer whose teeth were crooked and thus never properly brushed, and whose day job as a social worker left her looking startled, unblinking, and seared around the ears.

Men, too, finally—and cynically (inevitably)—pushed in and out of my world. As I waited to hear from Ben/JNB, I instead got Peter—an avid skier, ex-New Yorker, lover of Latin music and pelvic twists. He came to me by way of Franz and Letty, of course. They'd mingled at some media-related ball partially funded by Microsoft's video production department. Peter, whose left cheek was disrupted by a large mole, was otherwise quite handsome and reminded me of Sean Penn during his Madonna days. Unfortunately, he spent too much time talking about burning through his stock options while failing at hip gyrations.

Meanwhile, Ted, no longer mentor material or my boss at the Hutch, drove up to Capital Hill to whisk me off to a "reunion" that involved a performance of flamenco, followed by tapas, and an awkward glass of wine that culminated in some tepid pawing in the front seat of his Subaru station wagon. After Ted, I embarked on an easterly journey with a thirty-something UW medical intern known to some as Jeffrey and to others as Dr. Jay. Jeffrey was an athletic oncology specialist from Connecticut whose small eyes, thin lips, heavy jaw and untouched complexion described entitlement and a potential secondary-career as a health pundit on Oprah. Jeffrey invited me to several power-yoga dates, the two of us championing sweatpants and t-shirts, twisting until our faces reddened with pain, upending ourselves in contraptions meant for Roman torture. Then, unexpectedly during one date, the limber yoga instructor who ended her sessions with hypnotic neck massages mesmerized Jeffrey. After that, the man never phoned me again.

Next, I met Eitan, an Israeli with a waif-like build who hiked like a feather on a breeze and ended his dates with delicate hugs accompanied by repressed moans. His many patents in cell phone hardware were accomplishments he touted regularly over our meetings at cafes, which never amounted to anything more than caffeine-induced hand games. Had I become callous? Perhaps.

And then I met my emotional match. No one knew how to pretend better than the man with the most common name I'd ever heard. Only he could make a deep impression where no impression seemed to take. Only John Jones—not to be confused with other Johns—could force entry.

John Jones, two syllables that blandly drooled from lips, was a name so common it dominated countless pages in countless phonebooks across America. There had to be more than 13,000 John Jones nationwide, but my John Jones had a physique and livelihood that couldn't have been more exotic. Despite his name, John Jones insisted on being memorable—though not likeable.

John Jones

When I wanted nothing to do with Johns, I met John Jones. Parvati had dragged me to a glass-blown coral reef—a space of ethereal capsules located on the north side of Lake Union, east of Queen Anne, where she'd landed a job as a video archivist.

That drizzling April afternoon, I left the clinical halls of UW Medical Center and hiked along the Burke-Gilman Trail towards the studio. Eventually, like finding a secret cave, I discovered the driveway of multicolored pebbles of blown glass. Like everything else associated with Parvati, the door opened too easily.

Inside the barn-like warehouse, everything was dark except for blitzes of fuchsia, lemon, and ochre octopuses arcing over me. I'd entered Carl Sagan's spaceship in *Cosmos*. One could almost hear ocean waves and synthesized harmonies coming from each spot-lit piece of glass.

Deeper inside, lit from all directions like a Faberge egg, lay the famous pool of turquoise, indigo, copper, cadmium, amber, saffron—the coral-like glass a hyper-chromatic section of the Great Barrier Reef. Parvati had already described how the glass blowers dove in to retrieve golden swans or unraveling magenta tendrils—gifts for visiting billionaires. And beyond the pool, the dining room chandeliers shimmered like extraterrestrial amoebas, overriding the floor-to-ceiling windows that hovered above the silver lake. The studio's boss—all iconic eye-patch and rotund build—made no appearance the day I met John. But then, everyone said the famous artist rarely showed his face.

When Parvati guided me into "the pit," where silica stretched like ribbons of caramel, I stood in awe. Four glass blowers danced around, bracing long metal wands—ending with what looked like gobs of jelly—against their pelvises. The blowers began spinning their wands, thrusting them into flaming holes in the wall, pulling them out again to form imperfect spheres that collided with other imperfect spheres to create pieces for what Parvati told me would be the grand chandelier of the Bellagio Hotel in Las Vegas. Entranced, I watched this X-rated show of glass blowers pressing lips to wands—kissing, twirling, and blowing lumps of glass that spread like orgasms and birthed enormous amoebas.

The ovens glowed like those in Auschwitz, but who couldn't love the syrup dripping into so many new forms? I didn't know what to say when Parvati whispered that she had a crush on one of the blowers—Sergei—who happened to be a glass-star in his own right.

"He sells in Pioneer Square," she whispered. "Bill Gates bought one of his vases." It didn't occur to me to ask about what happened with JNB, because this thin dude in black—Sergei—didn't seem muscular enough to heft a tornado of ruby glass, which he kept spinning until the glowing globe flattened into a disk.

Sometime during this hypnotic experience, I felt warmth at my back, as if the ovens flamed behind me. The heat brushed uncomfortably close, and I whipped around to find a man, about my height with hands on hips, hair buzzed brown, eyes fire-worn but emotionally childlike. I absorbed his stare, which eventually broke when he glanced and nodded at Parvati, who nudged me with her elbow—a clear, "Oh no...not that guy"—though she pretended to smile.

"Hey, Parv," he drawled, though he dove back into my eyes to taste what I wouldn't offer, confirming that, yes indeed, he was an authentic hick. My admirer's uneven teeth doubled his hick upbringing, as did the slap on Parvati's shoulder, the whole mess of his sweat-stained undershirt, tarnished jeans, and mud-crusted hiking boots applauding the fact that every day was a work n' beer day.

"I seen you showing the wares to ya friend here," he said in a way I couldn't duplicate. "Like the pool—" When he smiled, the skin beneath his brown eyes and along the bridge of his nose became eroded with gullies.

"Yeah," Parvati stepped back. "So you're back."

"Yep, they called me last minute. So's your friend like it here?" He tore into me with another eye-drilling stare.

"Yep," Parvati said, grabbing my elbow.

"Does she have a name?" Who wouldn't feel mocked by the third person?

Parvati lifted her chin, eyes downcast. "Right," Parvati began, stepping closer to me, both protective and backstabbing. "Jane, meet John." She appeared confused, stiff and reserved as the blockade of her laced fingers hit her pelvic bone. The shy fog that usually enveloped her during introductions didn't float in. Instead there was this brisk Parvati. "We're only here a few minutes. We were just on our way to get coffee." To me, she lowered her voice, "We should go," and glanced at her watch.

"Where to?" John said, ignoring the hint, fists shoved into pockets while checking out my exposed collarbones. "Some of us might be breaking soon—" He raised his voice, for the benefit of others. "Talking of beer." One of the blowers responded with a taut-lipped whistle.

"That's okay." Parvati picked up the shoulder bag tucked like a paperweight between her feet. "We're going."

"Gotcha." All smiles. "But hey, Parv, I been meaning to invite you to my studio."

"Oh, thanks." A slammed door in his face. Turning to me, she leaned into my ear and whispered, "Coffee time." I zipped my coat to my chin and began walking away from the constant explosion of orange issuing from the clamshell openings that centered this man cave. "Don't ask about John," Parvati began in a low voice, our subject paces behind, though I could feel his stare.

Remembering JNB and the many incidences when Parvati somehow didn't quite get it, I thought a beer sounded good after all. "All I'm going to say," Parvati went on as I slowed, "is he used to blow here, but was told to leave. Oh, and he once told me he wanted to throw me on a bed of melted glass—" She threw eyes at me, adding, "So—" Her point landed like a vulture on a dead gazelle.

But I wasn't dead, so I stalled, and John got the idea. "Hey, Parv!" he called, jogging after us. "Been meaning to say. I'm selling," his hand on her shoulder, us stopping. "Just finished my first big chandelier. Studio's pumping out wares!"

Parvati clapped her hands and with a tense laugh, said, "That's great, John! Yay!" Again, making for the door we would never reach, because men with simple names never backed down.

"Once I get it in my head," he said, walking alongside us, "it's done." He seemed to be alluding to that bed of liquid glass. "I'm all up. Done and ready to fire-up—" He rubbed his sandpaper palms together with double meaning. "Lots of space to create magic. I been meaning to invite the crew over for bourbon and cheese."

Despite Parvati's efforts, we ended up knocking pints with the glass blowers—except for Sergei, who insisted on perfecting a chartreuse amoeba, thus avoiding the humid hole-in-the-wall just blocks from the glass palace. This disappointed Parvati, who, despite her plan, pressed into a sticky pleather bench beneath depressing lighting that made even the peppiest glass blower yawn. She glared at the table, while I sat across from an unimpeded Mr. Jones, whose contradictions lived on his buckskin face. I found everything but mildness around his eyes.

Out bolted lightning stares that magnified his slow, boyish smile— the kind that emitted a 1950s afterglow. He'd physically aged before his time, leaving the impression of a boy-man whose hormones and inner clock had somehow sped up like a poorly timed turntable whose LP shot off wrong notes. Dissidence became mystery.

Turned out, John taught at Pilchuck and didn't apologize for skewering famous artists. "Where's the boss all day anyway?" he yelled over his pint, opinions and gossip flowing like piss. I sipped my pilsner through a straw, which made him crack up. He reminded me that people who sipped through straws got drunker faster. "But go on. I'll take you home," he said, pressing his knee against mine.

As I sucked foam, John stared with his x-ray vision, leaving me feeling lost. After a second round, Parvati pushed me into the lady's room, where a single sticky orange toilet seat reeked of urine and industrial cleaner. I felt sick and leaned against greasy, cold ceramic tiles.

"You're in trouble," Parvati said. "Remember what I said? Remember the glass bed?!" I wagged my hand at her "bewares" and floated along, hardly caring that my tolerance for alcohol amounted to that of a three year old's.

Back at the table, John regaled me with tales of initiation into the world of glass, sprinkling compliments that included, "you got movie star looks…." He admired my lips and liked the way my purple eyeliner enlarged my eyes. Hardly embarrassed, I laced my fingers beneath my chin and listened as he decried a city full of "crunchies" dressed in nothing but flaxseed, Birkenstocks, and fleece. I was, he said, a moonlit revelation not unlike Veronica Lake amid the masses—or, better, a freshly blown glass vase surrounded by dead fish.

As John poured flattery over my naked drunkenness, Parvati wouldn't lighten up—even when he chanted the chorus of, "Betty Davis Eyes." I liked that she had to watch me get the attention. For once, I was central while she (or Mimi—or whoever else vying to challenge me) sat in the corner.

"Marlene Dietrich lips," he murmured, another lightning strike at my lipstick. "Grace Kelly hair." I rolled my eyes and drawled, yeah, right. "Yeah, right!" He mimicked, smiling crazy teeth, "You betcha, right," slapping a palm on the sticky tabletop. Again, Parvati elbowed my rib, but I enjoyed ignoring her pained stares and the tug on my wrist. "So," I said, "we're going to your place to make dinner, right?"

Rain cut into the fogged windows behind him, where a dark blue glow meant night. But he liked that I read books, and insisted on getting my list of favorite writers. I began with Dickens, hit some contemporaries, but settled on Tolstoy, Stendhal, and Flaubert. All men. He didn't ask why. If he read, it was usually nonfiction, and mostly, "stuff about glass," but sometimes, "I seen articles on travel, you know, and it's like, now there's a place I got to see." He hadn't flown anywhere substantial in two years. Not since he'd started building the studio, every dollar burned by the ovens.

Again, Parvati nudged me with, "Okay. Time to go." But then he mentioned the Himalayas.

Borderless Borders

Two weeks later, after I'd sworn to Parvati that I'd never give him my number, I sat at his dinner table—a second date—and watched his old skin move over his younger bones. "I trekked through Nepal. This was maybe, oh heck, I don't know, ten years ago? I made it to Tibet on complete accident— didn't know it. I seen these hikers and figured out after talking to them that I was in another country. Back then, that was the border. What got me onto glass was, I seen an old sadhu blowing outside Kathmandu, at some kind of sandpit with one of those sand *mandalas*, and that's when I knew what I needed to do. I had to blow like my brothers up there at the top of the world."

It turned out John was less hick than hippy. At fifteen, he'd left home for Spokane to visit an Aunt, and then moved on to Seattle. He got into glass casting, molded tchotchkes like salt shakers and baby shower spoons, graduated to tea sets, dishes, sconces, and finally to sink basins, all the while taking courses at Pilchuck. Two years into his new life in the Pacific Northwest, he started blowing for "the boss," and finally began selling his own vases and bowls at a downtown gallery. That's when a dark owl flew into his corner.

On impulse, he married, but soon all the fighting punted him down a black hole. He became a coke addict with every vein in his body shot like my dad's, his heartbeat and brain stranded on the whirligig that surpassed all senses. Six months after divorcing "the sponge"—his wife—he'd emptied his bank account and his house had drifted into foreclosure. To finish him off, "the boss" fired him. The story sounded familiar.

But he held my hand as we sampled tumblers of Walla Walla Voignier. I nodded and listened. "What saved me?" John said to my question. "Don't know."

This hardly seemed adequate in the face of the vegan dinner of fungal specimens he'd selected with fellow mycologists from a fern-dotted trail, the baby pumpkin stuffed with wild rice and garnished with root vegetables from his garden, the basted pear with comfit that I couldn't eat because it swam in sugar syrup.

No one needed to know what saved him, because two bottles of local wine—both completely drained—deposited us on his wall-to-wall carpet where our limbs twisted and vibrated like fire-breathing dragons, his only vocalization between caresses and salivation: "give me your lips!"

Passed Over

I ended up regularly stripping for John, a man who spent every Saturday morning like *Candide*, tending his garden. He treated downtime with me—if there was any—as an excuse to indulge in trail maintenance, which began when we parked his blue pickup in overgrown thickets, and devolved into hours of weed whacking and roving that ended with body-throbbing tumbles at an obscure mountain lake or, worse, an untouched clearing spiked with nettles. With this kind of man, I was in a constant state of exhaustion— and, for some reason, I couldn't fall in love. So I kept going.

Then came that notorious holiday of death, Passover, when John stayed in his garden and I should have sniffed out the warning signs. Though I had little patience for prayers, I'd been orphaned one too many times during one too many holidays, so I accepted the invitation from my ex-Hutch boss, Alexis.

The potluck, she said, would feature vegan "gefilte fish" and "dairy-free macaroons" (weren't they already dairy-free?). With relief, I learned that Ted would be slamming tennis balls in Arizona, leaving me free to mingle with four other Passover foundlings.

Bearing a plastic tray of kosher carrots, celery, mini-tomatoes, and broccoli florets, I braved the bus to Green Lake, where Alexis and a housemate shared a cottage. Low clouds weighed on the damp pine needles beneath the lofty conifers overwhelming the neighborhood, reminding me that none of the aromas seeping from so many kitchens would make me feel at home. But Alexis's house, a single story white construction with a diminutive lawn surrounded by a chain link fence, looked warm, despite being mired in an army of trees.

Balancing the vegetable platter, I should have retraced my steps, because the odor of Bragg's liquid amino acids drifted through a window. But I didn't listen to instinct and cut towards the front door, where I smacked up against a second warning.

An ear-splitting roar spanked the air. In seconds—lightning branching through my forehead—I became a piece of meat, mere inches from a gaping jaw. The creature, both pit-bull and Great Dane, strained its neck and scratched the pavement, its teeth gnashing between snarls. The animal yanked, horny and relentless, at its chain, gaining power as it dodged back and forth in the neighbor's penned yard, at one point, nearly bounding over the fence.

Heart in mouth, I scrambled up to Alexis's door step, the dog flashing its teeth, attempting to swipe a chunk from my arm. In the commotion, my platter of crudités toppled, carrots and mini-tomatoes rolling down the bowling alley of Alexis's walkway. This, and only this, caused the dog to simmer down to a mere bark and finally a growl as it sniffed and pawed a runaway carrot.

Only then did a figure appear behind Alexis's Venetian blind. There's no knowing why I pressed the doorbell instead of running. But the door clicked open, and I heard a cheery: "You're here!"

Alexis grabbed my shoulder and pulled me inside as if her front yard were a battlefield. Immediately, I encountered a sultry blast of living room air, everything redolent with what I'd discover was indeed vegan Gefilte fish. Wearing slacks, a black turtleneck, and tasteful silver earrings, Alexis looked ready to run the CDC, enhancing the frumpiness of my hiking boots and fleece.

"Oh great," she cried, ever-smiling, grabbing the now depleted platter of crudités. "More vegetables!" It wasn't clear if this was a joke. Steering me to a brown chair beneath standard Christmas lights hugging the molding, she pressured me to set down my backpack, which, for some reason, I didn't feel comfortable doing.

"That dog didn't scare you, I hope," she said, smiling. "I forgot to mention—his bark is worse than his bite—" I lied and said he was a pup. "So, hey," Alexis went on. "Ted told me you guys went out! Wow." Her spreading smile reminded me of why I felt infantile after being in her presence for more than five minutes. "Here, come meet everybody—" She settled my paltry potluck offering on a side table, and squeezed my shoulder as if to say, "no worries about the paltry offering."

Soon, I was introduced to the man who'd eyed me through the blinds. As he scooted to one side of the sofa, he looked confused by his beer bottle, as if it were a baby's rattle—though he had to be between thirty-one and fifty-five. Massive amounts of facial hair and a football fan's paunch expanded him into what I mistook for a gregarious temperament.

"So," Alexis said. "This is Thomas, a friend from way back." Thomas peered around the room and gently tugged his beard, smiling.

"Nice to meet you," I gurgled to Thomas's nod.

"Thomas and I went to school together in Boston," Alexis continued, because everyone went to school in Boston. She picked up one of the platter's remaining carrots, cigaretting it between two fingers. "He's now one of the lucky ones, working for Amazon. You and your stock options! Mr. Millionaire over here. And it's only been how long? A year?"

"No, more like two—" His voice, too faint, hardly explained the paunch. "You're losing track of time, Lexi! That doesn't bode well." He reveled in the pretense of being middle aged, while his massive belly rose and fell like a bouncing yogi beneath his flannel shirt. "Actually, she and I," Thomas giggled, speaking to me but really to her, "can't seem to get the timing right." This confirmed my suspicion that unexpressed eroticism lay behind Alexis's smile. But the smile remained as Alexis blinked, frozen by the sour note of Thomas's statement.

Swallowing, and peering at the Christmas lights, Thomas's grin disappeared. He shifted forward on the sofa and fingered the discarded metal cap of his beer. It was almost embarrassing a moment later when he succumbed to a session of neck kneading with his free hand, while thankfully Alexis figured out how to move on.

"So, it's a smaller evening than I originally planned," she informed. "Two of our guests couldn't make it—So how about coming into the kitchen." She led us through a dinette into a 1930s kitchen of metal cabinets and black and white linoleum tiles. By a counter, a woman tore lettuce into a wooden bowl. Nearby, a lanky guy of indeterminate age spoke in the low tones.

"Guys," Alexis cried, as we crowded between the refrigerator and a slender oven. Thomas stood behind me, breathing heavily against my neck. "This is Julian." Alexis gestured to the ageless man whose blond hair and extremely thick white eyelashes almost passed for albino, except for his hazel eyes. "And this is my housemate, Carly."

Here, I encountered a mass of curls framing black-rimmed eyewear. Turned out, Carly epitomized an intellectual chatterbox who made everyone feel small by mastering the "look" every wannabe Ph.D. emulated. Clearly, she knew how to accessorize and gesture to her benefit, eroticizing statements with fluttering shoulders, and shaking out her hair when shaking hands. Unlike everyone else, Carly smiled only for Alexis, which accentuated the problem that was Alexis: the obligatory smile that prefaced other obligations.

As we collided with each other and the narcotic music seeping through speakers dangling from the ceiling, I had the odd sensation of landing on a Caribbean island I'd never enjoy. It's no surprise that the sensation was magnified when Carly mentioned working for a private library funded by a Seattle billionaire—which set off a discussion about class.

Names and places got thrown around the kitchen. Someone had seen Bill Gates in a Madison Park cafe. Someone else knew someone who belonged to Howard Schultz's Temple. Jeff Bezos sneaked around bookstores. Paul Allen and Steve Ballmer shot the breeze at the stadium. Someone even mentioned Paul Allen's mother, sister, and dog (did he have a dog?), and then the others blew fifteen minutes talking dog sleds, yoga, and skiing.

It turned out Carly and Julian lived for yoga, while Alexis believed in wearing ski goggles on the slopes. Thomas, balancing on a stool, admitted that the best he could do physically was duck tree limbs on a downhill stretch, so long as he could grab a beer at the end of the ski run.

"I won't bore you with my first and last day on a hill," he groaned, a warning that he didn't mean it. "Let's just say, I don't have finely honed ski antennae. But somehow I end up on slopes. It's a masochistic habit—"

Thankfully, Alexis cut in with, "Oh, hey guys. Let's head into the dining room!" as she grabbed two bowls of vegan gefilte fish from the refrigerator. The pale, beige cakes floated in gelatinous fluid, making the glass bowls look like they belonged in a lab. For laughs, Julian compared the hors d'oeuvres to lamb's brains, emitting a "blah" that he quickly retracted when Alexis glared at him—which reminded me of Nora's guru, The Avatar, who often said, "There is nothing to proo!" as in, there's nothing to prove. What a nice, passive thought—the kind that left the listener dumbstruck and faultless as an upside down giraffe. Apparently, I didn't have to do anything to be okay, even as the world expected the exceptional.

"Julian's still an adolescent," Carly said. The poor man's near-white brows arced in pain over his eyes. "Well it's true. You are." She shook her hair, turning to me. "Ugly as it sounds, he's never cooked for me. And we've been together two years in May." She gave her boyfriend another look and swiveled to open the silverware drawer.

I hated this kind of public flogging, like Stalin exposing non-existent flaws in political relationships that would end in the gulag, the parading of flaws almost a status symbol—as if publicizing "drama" endorsed one person's superiority and strength over another—a dynamic that seemed to infect every group setting I'd been in since moving to Seattle. As if celebrating flaws, Carly wouldn't let up: "I can only assume Julian doesn't have the skill to compete with Alexis's cooking."

Pushed to the margins, Julian and Thomas carried their bowls of mock gefilte fish to the dinette, glancing empathetically at each other while a dinner of obtuse prayers ensued. We sipped a thousand sips of kosher cabernet that tasted worse as the strain between Carly and Julian increased.

Clearing plates, Carly growled at Julian, who'd remained non-verbal throughout dinner. Alexis excused herself for the bathroom, while Thomas, the Big Green Giant, settled on the sofa next to me, not wanting to disturb the frozen peas in his gut.

Looking uncomfortable, upper arms pressed close to his pectorals, he said, "So yeah," inauspiciously allowing his fingers to play with his beard. "I grew up on a pig farm in Ohio."

I would never marry a man who grew up on a pig farm.

"Really?" I said, remembering a farm in Pennsylvania where the lung-stinging stench of pig shit ruined a summer. I said: "That must have been different—"

"Yeah," he nodded with his fingers still jammed into his beard. "It was definitely different—in a weird way. When I was thirteen we moved to Columbus— What about you?" He dared to glance at me through the corners of his eyes.

"A product of the Upper East Side gone wrong." I still felt proud to be an ex-New Yorker—similar to the way the less than one percent felt proud that they'd gone to that school in Boston—because I knew others thought of the "City" as central to everything. As I expected, he widened his eyes and kept nodding.

"Why'd you leave?"

"Too busy—no outdoor space." Thomas's width beside me felt overheated and stank of matzo ball soup. "It's a tough place—"

That's when it happened: another thunderclap—*ice water gushing over a naked breast; a 747 dropping 10,000 feet.* Glass shattered, followed by a cry. **"OH MY GOD!!!!NO!!!!"**

Thomas shot up as if he'd been waiting—expecting—trouble, while Alexis pounded down the hall, calling out, "Hey, what's wrong?"

More cries, indistinguishable from hiccups or coughing, the words: "No!!! Oh no!!!! Lexi—Oh my god!!!! Please—Someone. Please. Lex—"

Thomas bounded through the dinette and into the kitchen. I followed seconds later to find a bizarre scene.

At first everything looked confused: the kitchen bulb flickering, sizzling, reluctant to shine over an unfolding tragedy—a body down where it should have been up, a body rumpled, white, stark against the linoleum, skin glossy like plastic wrap. Thomas leaned on one knee to study the face, shadowing the figure.

Carly shrunken and shivering, leaned against the kitchen sink, arms wrapped around waist, eyes wet and startled. "I don't know what happened— We were talking. Is he okay?" I stepped back as she whimpered like the neighbor's dog. Alexis, the medical practitioner, peered at Julian's prone body, which was surrounded by diamond-like shards—a broken glass bowl. "He was changing the bulb—just holding one of those bowls, about to put it down—" Carly shook her head. "One of the cheap bowls. He'd just dried it. My god—Is he okay?" Carly, confused but not confused, shivered.

"Jane—" Alexis said without her smile. "Call 911. The phone is in my bedroom. Down the hall, to the right. Carly. Get the broom behind the back door—and the dustpan—" I ran down the hall looking for the bedroom on the right, not realizing I was laughing. Shock and awe lived on my crazy face.

There would be an investigation. But I flicked on the overhead to piles of textbooks, papers, and clothing. It took a few moments to find the Betty Boop phone nestled beneath a pile of underwear next to a mattress. I dialed 911 for the second time since I'd moved to Seattle.

When I returned to the kitchen, Thomas still leaned over Julian, puffing into lungs while pushing fists into the thinner man's chest. It could happen this fast. What once felt normal could become abnormal and life wrecking.

As If Nothing Had Happened

"We were interrupted, I think—" Thomas said later, as if nothing had happened. We drove back to Capital Hill, trying to forget the ambulance that had taken Julian to the hospital while the police had asked questions. I sat unblinking in the bucket seat of Thomas's Subaru. A dry prune clogged my throat. My forehead felt numb, and a balloon in my abdomen was about to pop into nausea. It was past 2 AM, and the Subaru stank of sweat and mildew.

We'd felt sick well before the seizure of yellow and red lights whirred Julian away. Eventually, we'd followed in two sedans. Carly, hadn't really cried, but pressed wads of tissue to her nose, her eyeglasses riding on her forehead as if wistful for summer. "I don't know what happened—" she kept saying as Alexis shut the car door.

"You were talking about New York—" Thomas now blurted. I couldn't think of anything but Julian's snow-white features—the way his lips parted to wine-stained teeth, a pale tongue, paramedics shuttling him through the gray ER archway. Why would Thomas talk about New York when no one had been passed over that evening?

"I was in New York last year," he persisted. "On business." Nothing about Thomas could ever be confused with businesslike. His eyes were too mild, beard too folksy. He wore flannel. "Our clients took me to this place on the Upper West Side called Carmine's. It's all big platters, Italian style.

My grandmother was Italian. She used to spend all day cooking. I ate more pasta, scampi, and zuppa di muscles than anyone should eat in a lifetime." Thomas, the long-winded, definitely fit the role of corporate anomaly. No bullet points for him. He couldn't stop talking about nothing while my head ached over Ben.

"In Ohio there are no good restaurants, no places that leave you feeling like you could still eat even though you don't think you'll ever eat again." At a stoplight, Thomas finally stopped talking. He contemplated my profile, and I worried that he wanted to feed me meatballs while I sat naked on his lap.

"So," He finally said as I struggled to keep my eyes open. "Two things. Why's your hair bleached? And where's Harvard and Republican?" The motor hummed a lullaby. Somehow, I laughed off the hair comment and directed him towards my building. "Okay," he said, the turn signal ticking like a metronome. We turned off Broadway where the night jaundiced around night lamps surrounded by floating drizzle. A ragged couple stumbled towards the QFC. I could almost smell their hair, which hung like tree moss as they leaned into each other.

Thomas said, "I'd like to see you again," as the Subaru glided into a spot next to my apartment building. I slipped out and stood on the curbside, blinking at the drizzle. Thomas leaned forward and extended his arm to prop open the door. "I have tickets for a performance of whirling Dervishes. I saw them perform when I was in Turkey. They're coming next week. Interested?" Because of Rumi, I knew about Dervishes. "Good. I'll see you next week." He was about to shut the door when he hesitated. "Oh, hey. Do you like artisanal bread?" I must have nodded, still sinking in the pool of gelatin that surrounded the vegan gefilte fish I hadn't eaten. "Good. I'll bake you some loaves. And oh—" Rain spattered the passenger seat and cold drops fell down my collar. It was time to slam the door and bury my head in thoughts of Ben. But unwilling to see me as anything but drenched, Thomas threw out a final question that outdid all the other inappropriate questions: Incidentally, did I like skiing?

Breaking Down

"Perception is reality."

<u>Artisanal Date</u>

He'd already admitted to being a masochist, and so why not spin snow on the slopes instead of dally with Dervishes, because, as he claimed, "It's the last of the season."

Gray swallowed the Space Needle that Saturday morning, but Thomas sheared the curb with his sweaty Subaru. We'd discussed the plan over the phone—my last chance to bail, but then he'd mentioned that Julian had miraculously regained consciousness in fits and starts—though he still couldn't speak.

"Electrocution followed by stroke." He mused. "No one knows for sure. Makes you think twice. Hey, you sure you don't do downhill?" Gone was the subject of Julian, already ski-lifted out of our minds. "Okay, let's plan on flat ground."

Envious of the pajama-clad Zelda, who'd nearly dissolved in the arms of her snoring boyfriend while listening to Stereolab, I hefted snow gear, borrowed from Parvati, to the curbside.

I didn't have a choice. I either skied with Thomas or ditched my chances of getting a permanent job. All night, I'd lain awake, sorting out the logic: Alexis needed me to sidetrack Thomas. Ted, king of the Hutch, adored Alexis, and the Hutch was beloved to UW. UW's HR department bent over backwards to appease its most prestigious partners. Thus, Thomas equated UW job.

That morning, reviewing this logic, I'd downed several apples with my bowl of Shredded Wheat. Already, the tight elastic band of Parvati's ski pants cut into my abdomen. Making matters worse, after I'd settled my distended midsection into Thomas's overheated vehicle, he grinned and presented me with a package of layered newspaper, surrendering its slipshod bulk with a nod that caused his beard to abrade his flannel collar.

"What's this?" I asked, disturbed by the perspiring car.

"Open it," he urged, waiting for a Dervish to whirl out of newsprint. A soft swishing sound of anticipation issued from his nostrils. The newsprint crackled as I discarded multiple layers. Nestled within was a bulging plastic bag, wilted—like a blanched placenta—around something warm. Unfurling the bag, I confronted the thing that I knew would make me sick: a tepid foccaccia, its crust pearled with oil and condensation.

Thomas smiled as if the loaf were his son, and with Biblical gravity said: "Ground the meal, captured the yeast, pressed the olives and baked it this morning. It's herb and garlic." Already, I despised the plant that had birthed the garlic bulb he'd mashed into the loaf, even as he described waking well before dawn to knead the starter into fresh dough. A heavy yeast and garlic current wafted through the car, whose fogged-over windows seemed to put on weight as they registered the doughy intruder.

"Thomas!" I overdid the enthusiasm, my voice cracking. This lie and the discomfort of Parvati's waistband caused reflux to burn my esophagus. "Thank you! Wow. It must've taken you hours."

"Yep," he nodded, gazing at the loaf like the lovelorn. "Took about five hours—I was up at three getting it prepped."

"Wow." I feigned awe. "You must have kneaded your arms off."

"I feel like I'm about three years old, actually." He grinned. I didn't catch his meaning, but smiled back. "I've been baking a lot this winter. This one took the most out of me. One of my baking buddies told me the best breads get the right muscle—just like the best starters need the most time. And guess what?" I stared at his beard. "I'm still not sure if I gave it enough time. But this loaf took a lot of time. And it's for you." He squinted the edges of his eyes in a show of false modesty and fondled his beard.

It was all very sweet, but I turned from his ape face to gape at the obese loaf—which looked like it could sponge up the condensation pearling on the windshield. I considered asking whether this mass of gluten was vegan. But I put that aside, choosing instead to praise Thomas's handiwork and thoughtfulness. I tucked the stinky lump back into its sack, not wanting to show appreciation by sampling the boule. I couldn't. I loathed the idea, because the pressure of the elastic band caused the scarfed apples and dry Shredded Wheat to circulate like a python through my innards.

"So," Thomas said. "You think this is a good day for skiing?" On cue, he jerked the Subaru in gear, kicking off our journey towards Crystal Mountain.

Crystal

Why Crystal Mountain, I'll never know. But the name "Crystal" has always left me anxious. We could have gone to Steven's Pass or Snoqualmie, but no. We had to shatter ourselves against the slopes like crystal glasses. The reason: Thomas had slalomed Crystal dozens of times, both downhill and cross-country. And what argument could I use against a name? I didn't know ski snow from a moraine coated with sleet.

Twice in my life I'd latched skis to my unsteady legs—and on both occasions I'd fought gravity like a chin-fisted Mohammed Ali. To me, skiing belonged to self-mutilators—hapless suckers who'd been lured into a death cult. I'd seen the aftermath of too many Christmas vacations misspent at overpriced ski resorts—the smashed noses and jawbones, the casted femurs, the pinned wrists. Long ago I'd pledged never to encounter a snow-shrouded lodge. Yet I was allowing Thomas, a man who didn't believe in deodorant, to launch me, like a missile, into ski country.

"We've got a slew of choices. I've explored only two," Thomas said as we sped on 1-5 towards the mountains, making good time—no traffic to delay the inevitable. We hit 405 and Renton like we'd been beamed-up by Scotty. With stomach acid, up rose a vision of arm, leg, and rib casts like those on a fourth-grade friend who'd spent a month lugging a plastered calf of penned well wishes. As far as I knew, she never again jumped rope. But Mount Rainier—predictably invisible—mocked my all-encompassing fear, which threatened to erupt while I faked ease as Thomas described the trail beyond the ski lift.

Passing through Renton, conversation swerved towards the, by now, renowned pig named Herman. As Thomas dissected why pig dung stank, my stomach heaved again—the contents not quite making it to my lips. His lecture dashed past a trucker-sister, and three-point-turned towards (what else?) bread. I was going to be flayed on the mountain, and because of this, I found it difficult to appear interested. Already exhaustion tugged at my legs. It didn't help that a rush of flurries killed speech as wipers swished across the glass, never quite chasing away the flakes. I didn't care; let the car skid off the road.

I stared out at passing branches, Thomas focusing on asphalt. Occasionally a curse farted from his lips. And then, like that, the flurries disappeared, prompting more nauseating instructions on how to knead dough. Proud of cataloging types of flour and yeast, Thomas clearly wanted to impress that one, special girl—not me—who cared more for domestic skills than big wallets.

Upon arrival, the Crystal Resort parking area was clogged with cars, forcing us to the regrettable outer lot. Exchanging the Subaru's tropical atmosphere for a blast of Arctic air only blurred my vision, fingers and toes turning to tingling marble. The end of my scarf flapped over my eyes, until I stuffed it into Parvati's tight-fitting parka. With the wind, my gut grew more distended, a twisted balloon pressed by a waistband that cut off circulation to my thighs.

Meanwhile, Thomas's cheeks filled with color, his eyes sparkling. He seemed downright zesty in his corduroy coat and fleece hat, donning gloves as his nose hairs bristled with expectation.

"Strong wind!" Thomas bellowed into a gust that lifted snowflakes off our tire tracks. He held up King Kong fists, pounding them in parody against his chest. "Good for the slopes!"

"Yeah. So. Where's the lodge—" I returned, pivoting to get my back to the wind. We bent across the outer lot, eyes on our boots, lodge-bound and bombarded by ice crystals.

"Ayne!" A high voice called out, "Ayne!!!!"

Scarf slapping cheeks, more ice crystals darting at eyes, I squinted at three approaching figures. Snot ran towards my upper lip as they yelled, "Ayne!!! Old up!" They couldn't be calling me, yet they walked towards me, balancing skis and poles on their shoulders. Odd that these bundles recognized me in a bundle of borrowed clothes. But Thomas stalled, curious.

"You know them?" he asked, amused but also concerned.

Moments later, they came into focus: Franz and Letty—the hosts of a hosomaki and sashimi Sukkot I'd attended—each looking like they'd arrived from the Weimer Republic. Next to them, Peter, the salsa-dancer who'd apologized for kissing me, sported a snow-spanked cheek that made his mole look like an unboxed truffle, his plaid scarf less practical than noose.

"I love this!" Letty sang, all flapper girl. "*Hello hello hello!* My newfound friend! Fancy meeting you here! I knew we'd run into someone today—I told you!" she nudged Peter's chest with her shoulder.

"Piece of advice, my friend. Always defer, always defer—" Franz murmured, ducking head and winking at Peter, as if playing parlor games in the great outdoors.

"You flatter!" Letty laughed, all Daisy Buchanan to the wind slapping our faces. "No one listen to anything this man says. He's lost his mind. Which is good. Let's keep it that way." She patted Franz's shoulder, her long, pale features—initially off-putting for their thinness—more fascinating with every turn of her chin. Her watchful, walnut-size cat's eyes and dark hair in tight bun—scarf perfectly wrapped over her hairline like a swim cap—made her look like a 1920's starlet. A taut, synthetic jacket highlighted her black ski leggings and gave her the look of a vampire setting out for a swim.

Feeling sorry for the corduroy coat, which hung like a soaked blanket over his shoulders, I introduced Thomas, who nodded his snow-sprinkled beard, everything about him slovenly. Peter, assessed the situation with a theatrical once over—as if he and Thomas were roosters on a dance floor, their spines tense, jaws thrust out and pulsing, noses high for a sniff of the other man's pheromones. But soon Peter dismissed Thomas with his profile—which emphasized the bulb of his nose. He turned to me, pressing a horny arm against mine.

"You told me when we had dinner," Peter said. "That you didn't know how to ski." An awkward silence, Letty playing with the fingers of her gloves. He continued undermining me by asking what I'd been doing since we'd slow danced to Mercedes Sosa at a downtown lounge—as if our kiss had been a beginning rather than an end.

He then cupped my elbow in his gloved hand and, taking charge, gently pushed me towards the lodge, Thomas trailing us with what I imagined was a lined forehead. I reminded Peter that after our evening out he'd never called. This got a laugh and a, "What are you talking about. I called you five times." A lie, I was sure.

But I didn't have time to say, "Right!" because Thomas pushed between us with, "We're headed to explore the trails down here." In a tense cluster, we moved towards the ski rental counter, where circulation temporarily revived beneath heat lamps as Thomas pulled out his credit card.

"So you're going cross country?" Letty said, pulling off her gloves by a pile of equipment that stank of toe jam. "How perfect. Which trail?" She perched on a bench crowded with over-excited adolescents, and effortlessly latched on her skis.

"Not exactly sure yet—" Thomas began, once again alpha rooster as he leaned our rented equipment against a chaotic wall. His face looked pinched but puffy beneath his brow-hugging ski hat.

"Have you been to the upper trails?" Franz interrupted with a whiff of Breathsavers. "They're amazing. You can't beat the views. The entire valley, and there's some serious wildlife up there. We found this crazy trail two years ago—"

Thomas humphed and nodded, flicking his nostrils with thumb and forefinger. "You guys want to join us?" Franz persisted. "We're packing in some serious victuals." He patted a massive backpack, which rested on the ground next to him—a thing I hadn't noticed earlier. "A little red, some fine cheese from Pike's Place, prosciutto—"

"I don't know—" I said, eyeing the pack and then Thomas, who fiddled with his beard and stared off into the arduous but boring distance. "I haven't skied in years." It took some courage to admit this, but I worried more about a broken femur than about Franz's opinion.

"No worries. You'll pick up where you left off—" Letty said, waving her hand. She yanked out her elbow, the invitation of a smiling showgirl. "It's like driving. You never forget your ski legs. And you have to see it up there. Despite what you think, Franz never lies. Plus, I personally packed the to-die-for picnic, including the red." This hardly raised my confidence that we'd have a good time. Everything in my body yelled *NO! Don't do it!!!* Parvati would have walked away. Mimi would have laughed. But not I—not the chanting, yogini-relativist that wanted to be one with all. Was it so obvious that I couldn't withstand the pressure of a bent elbow?

<u>Against Better Judgment</u>

Not that I should be so hard on myself. Letty had a talent for wrapping persuasion around people's necks, while Franz stared at the mountainside like a rapist planning his attack. Peter was no better. He blinked at my legs as if I'd pulled down my pants, leaving me to feel exposed. I wilted and turned to Thomas who wagged his head in half-agreement with the others. Yes, we should go and why not? There was wine and cheese in it for us.

"I'm not sure—" I said in a last-ditch effort as everyone else pulled on skis. "You sure it's okay?" I had no backbone. Already this group of acquaintances owned me. They'd hang me as easily as feed me.

"Let's go," Thomas said, settling next to me on the bench like a pile of wet mud, his face rife with cluelessness, his lame coat lamer by the minute. He considered me—the night's potential fuck, the possible future wife—and added, "But it's up to you. You're the one getting back to it."

"You only live once!" Letty yelped in complete control of her admirers. I knew leadership tactics, knew preachers of "new paradigms," I understood group manipulation. After all, Letty was an HR exec.—which meant she lived for The Forum and all the psychobabble that crumbled the homemade breakfast, lunch, and dinner of every corporate worker in America. Her very pores reeked of Jonestown sweat, something I hadn't quite noticed at her memorable Sukkot party. But in retrospect, it was clear. She'd lectured employees on moving past fear to see the positive in every deadly-situation—as in "let's swallow this pint-sized tumbler of arsenic and pretend that instead of killing us, it will give us life-everlasting."

"Wait—" I wavered—my last gasp, my wimpy, up-thrust hand voting for the lower trail.

"You'll regret it—" Franz pressed, leaning forward beneath his obese backpack. It didn't surprise me that adults, like kids, reveled in raising the pressure. Each one vied for a top-of-the-world position, especially Fidel Castro-fascinated Peter, who folded his arms and beamed a comrade smile.

I succumbed.

We glided towards the chairlift, its cables wobbling—flimsy wicker baskets dangling over hair-raising dead ends of snow-covered boulders. Peter thrust forward, slipping beside me and Thomas to showcase his Latin hips.

"You guys know each other long?" Peter began, his incisors like yellow corn against endless veils of white. Snow highlighted the age of teeth. Time decayed everything, making the primordial muck of plaque and dehydrated bone a disturbing revelation.

"Not long," Thomas shot in, as I struggled to keep skis straight beneath me. The tips kept criss-crossing, making an X shape near the up-curved toes of the skis. The last time I'd gone cross-country skiing at Sheep's Meadow, Central Park, I'd tumbled into several snow mounds.

"You also work at UW?" Peter said, changing the subject and turning his mole to Thomas, who ski-stumbled in his heavy-set corduroy way, never quite skimming the surface of the powder.

"Nope. I'm a programmer." Thomas's facial hair had collected ice droplets near his nostrils, glass beads he brushed off with a gloved hand. When he thrust against his poles, shoulders rising and falling with the movement of his arms and legs, he huffed clouds of exhaust that condensed and froze on any nearby solid.

"Nice!" Peter said, swiveling towards me as my legs stuttered to an awkward stop. He slid around to my other side, sandwiching me like a pile of roast beef between two famished males. "I kind of program too, but mainly do marketing stuff at Microsoft. So where are you?" As if "where" could explain why I had chosen this schlump over a swivel-hipper like Peter.

"A start-up in the warehouse district called Amazon," Thomas answered, looking straight ahead to the line of waiting skiers. We'd filed towards the circulating chairs, stalling as a kid and his mother hopped on a swinging bench. Thomas pulled off his gloves to tug his hat down to his snow-dappled brows. "It'll be brisk on the lift," he said, turning to me. I had become less aware of the cold as the swaying chairs, devoid of passengers, dropped on their tenuous hairline towards the spot where I'd become airborne. Each bench carried two people, but for some reason Peter lined up next to Thomas and me, refusing to wait for the next bench.

"I don't think we can get three on the lift—" I blurted, trying to calculate our collective poundage. Thomas easily weighed over 200 pounds, while Peter wasn't too far behind—never mind my own 110 pounds. "So, you realize," I added, my voice kind of shaking, kind of high. "I've never been on one of these—"

"You haven't?" Peter asked, genuinely surprised, though he knew I'd never done downhill. "Virgin territory. You'll be back." He looked ahead with a smile, ignoring my concerns. It was hard to watch Franz and Letty in front of us, nuzzling each other's necks, careless of the benches floating in to whisk them away.

A moment before "lift off," Letty turned to me with the kind of smile that knew how to get its own way—a smile that accentuated the walnut hardness of her eyes, her black ski cap tight as the Red Baron's headgear. "See you guys up there!" She winked an exaggerated farewell. And off Franz and Letty flew, like two black-browed albatrosses flying the coast of Antarctica, their ink-like skis swinging over dead still snow. Receding into the distance in a time warp of endless clock strikes, the universe ever-expanding, I watched the white open up before them, as if they and only they kept going.

<u>Pure Flight</u>

"Okay," Thomas said, lifting his poles, "Hop on." The bench swung up behind us to grab our asses in a perversion of dangling skis. Three helpless fools, the metal bar slid over our laps. Once in its grip, everything gently swayed. I had no choice but to say, "Not bad." Squeezed between the two men and their heavy breathing, I profited from the primordial fire pit of their metabolisms.

Peter eyed Thomas, and then leaned towards my cheek, murmuring, "Look what you've been missing," as if I'd missed more than views. This gave him an excuse to wax-on about trips to Aspen, the long johns, earmuffs, and down jackets of his youth, his first slope at age four, the cultivation of technique that led him to master the "passion-dance of life." In contrast, Thomas said nothing, gazing ahead as if he'd been bred a couch potato. Best not to pay attention to either man.

Below, and all around our swing, evergreens dotted the white, the whole mess bound for a distant, gray-to-gold sky. The wind rustled rather than slapped. Ice particles no longer felt like sandpaper against the skin, so that eventually I played with my dangling skis, despite earlier concerns that they might unclasp and tumble into oblivion.

"So," I turned to Thomas. We were halfway through the twenty-minute ride. "How do I get off?" Thomas's eyes crinkled in a half-grunt, half-laugh that didn't bode well next to Peter's Disney cartoon smile.

Peter readjusted his poles. The bench wobbled back and forth, causing me to grab the lap-bar over my thighs. Sadists played such games. They invited girls who couldn't swim onto boats, rowed them to the middle of lakes, and then rocked back and forth until they gave up their virginity. "Don't think too much," Peter said, patting my knee. "You got on; you can get off."

I'd never gotten off of anything very well. It felt wrong when Thomas leaned against my shoulder, tickling my cheek with his beard and said, "Just make sure your skis are straight. Keep your poles up at your sides. It'll be fine." Hardly comforting. I saw how easily someone could miss the mark and get smacked in the head with the bench.

Peter, a natural pundit, began describing the slight dip in the snow at the jumping-off point, using his gloved hand to mimic the downward angle of the slope. "Nothing you can't handle," he said, nodding at the snow. "Piece of cake. The whole thing is designed to be navigatable by novices." Always falling for experts, I nodded, mouth dry, hardly noticing what sounded like bird chirps.

As we approached the drop off—that is, the plateau where Franz and Letty were just then diving like two penguins off their swaying bench—I noticed the dip Peter had indicated. From afar it appeared a speed bump. But as we closed-in, it grew to become no mere snow-wrinkle or tot-slide, but a looming chasm, deep as a crevasse, shimmering and glacial with packed snow—or was it ice? Somehow people seemed to be skittering downhill on their elongated, fiberglass feet, as if negotiating an obstacle course of pits and dips and boulders that led to a meeting area some 50 to 100 feet away.

"You sure," I said, breathless in the squeeze, "that cross-country skis work up here?" And then, before Thomas or Peter could reply, the drop became destiny.

Down Hill

We fell. Or was it that we pushed off like swimmers in a race? Abandoning the warmth of a bed, we plunged into a pool of ice water. The result: Everything, including common sense, slipped out from beneath us. Our contented squeeze became a threesome of suspended animation that involved splayed skis and billowing hair and tipsy poles over a metallic white surface that shimmered under a bright spot that had broken through the clouds.

There came the rush of other skis, followed by my own sounds of scraping—fiberglass hitting white where everything divided, feet this way and that. Yes, I realized in a flash, the slick surface was ice that funneled the innocent to a frigid end. Managing to almost stand, I didn't twist an ankle or burst my bowels. Yes, I'd found my knees and feet, thinking that maybe this wasn't so bad.

But then, disturbingly, heinously, and predictably, my skis crossed. My poles jabbed the air, poking at oblivion. There was no place to go but down. It was either head first or "smack down." Rather, bottoms down, where my boney, vegan-withered rear slammed the earth in a way that shuddered a line of falling Dominoes up my spine. Pain zigzagged through me and, once again, Superman was thrown from his horse, Ben thrown from his car, waifs thrown off ski lifts where, eventually, everyone must face the best and the worst of themselves.

At 110 pounds, I considered myself small, but this was the kind of butt thump one survived only in grade school—when one was no heavier than a rag doll. In my twenties, however, I had lost all resilience. Nerves strummed and shot and reverberated from my coccyx to the top of my head, pain an explosion that broke the air with a scream.

Or was it a grunt?

While Thomas and Peter slid down the slope to end in perfect pirouettes that I didn't see, I was robbed of my legs, unable to stand up, coordination blown out. On hands and knees, my rear-end high as a hot-air balloon, I tried crawling but the skis wouldn't cooperate, followed by a new worry: a man yelling that there were others ready to jump from the swaying lift, about to land on the very spot where I flapped like a beached salmon.

It must have looked perverse as, in a single bound, two masked ski men in superhero outfits, sped like spiders to tether my broken body in a death cocoon that became a toboggan. They hauled me, head first and bullet fast, down the jagged slope of my life, an eternal expedition that left me feeling simultaneously a missile and a fetus.

Broken Up

Thomas, the conflicted good Samaritan, hunkered by an infirmary window, hands stuffed into pockets as he studied the white profile of a slope not far from where my toboggan was parked beneath heating coils. A bald guy in a brown sweat suit and snow boots leaned over me, caressing my arm and asking if I could feel anything. His eyes were large and watery—like a Loris—almost kind if it hadn't been for the blood vessels, which looked like pink pinworms swimming in the whites of his eyes.

My head ached, and I felt tired, but I could move—just not much. He took a deep breath and delicately unzipped my coat. He rolled up my pants and stuck a thumbnail into my shin. I squealed. "Good," He murmured.

Then he asked where it hurt the most. Pain was a crab in a cave. It burst out in a surprise attack. I indicated the area around my sacrum, the upper reaches of my butt. Placing his hands beneath my armpits as if I were a stuffed doll, he maneuvered me on the cot. Nerves exploded as my bottom grazed the mat, causing me to moan until he resettled me on my side. With some awkwardness, he removed my coat and fondled a spot on my back.

"This hurt? Okay. How about this?" There was something erotic about being attended to, though his breath stank like the handlebars of a New York subway car cooked with gloves.

Later, he tapped my knee, his bare head glistening and nodding. "Good," he said, turning to Thomas, who stood philosophically stroking his beard and staring through my chest as if I weren't there. "She's only broken a tailbone. Maybe a concussion—but more shock than anything else. Could've been worse. Not much you can do about a tailbone. It'll heal on its own." To me he added, "Take your Ibuprofen, Tylenol according to dosage, and in a few weeks it'll feel like it never happened." I'd dodged, he said, a bullet.

I barely made it to the car, a hammer nailing a Crucifix to my bottom.

Thomas had to twine my arms around his neck and heft me with my cheek pressed against his coat. Amid car exhaust, I slid sideways into the back seat, riding shockwaves. Eventually, 1000 mg of Ibuprofen tempered my nerves, pain subsiding to a dull throb.

At my apartment, Thomas rummaged through my backpack seeking his home baked foccacia. The misshapen slab materialized from the depths like a meteor, its surface puckered with oil and sweat that gave it a beyond-unappetizing appearance. But he turned on my oven to, "crisp it up." He filled a pot with water, and then found the T.V., playing with its rabbit ears—shameful technology pushed behind two spider plants.

While we stared at Star Trek, Thomas munched on his loaf and pushed dough balls into my hand. I slumped against two bed pillows, trying to avoid splinters from the newly sanded floor, which Zelda and I had never varnished.

During a commercial break, Thomas leaned towards me, his crumb-flecked beard inches from my lips. "May I kiss you?" he asked, expelling yeast breath and staring into my eyes with the fireball signals that usually inhabit romance novels or X-rated comic books. My tailbone again throbbed. But along with dough kneading, he'd learned to seize the moment before the moment seized those around him. On hands and knees, in crawl-mode like a toddler, he grabbed my arm. Stunned by this primitive, sexual position, I stared at his dangling paunch and then into his face, speechless, woozy from all the drama, my body too absorbed by aches to recognize anything about the day as romantic.

"Wow," I said, turning to face the blinds. "This is kind of—" I wanted to say "unexpected" but couldn't finish my sentence because he'd nearly crawled on top of me. His lips loitered near mine as a blur. His eyes boiled with primordial mud, pent-up geysers ready to shoot into the vacuum of my own. All I heard was the breath swishing through his nostrils.

"This isn't the moment, I know," he panted, his breath stale dinner rolls smothered in eggs. He lowered his eyes to his hands, which rested on the splintery floorboards. The TV blared a synthesized giggle. "But I feel," he whispered, "overwhelmed by what happened today." He sat back on his stock-optioned heels—giving me a chance to inhale—gazing at me over his flannel torso while he pressed my hand and rubbed it between his oddly smaller, hotter and smoother paws.

"Seeing you there at the drop off—and then down in the infirmary. I felt—I don't know." Releasing my hand, he scratched his temple. "I felt so helpless. I wanted—I really WANTED," this word filled the room, "to help you! To get you from there," he pointed to a spot on the floor, "to over here," another spot. Here was an admission, a life-endangering mistake shrouded in suffocating breath. I turned away.

"Tell me what to do. I'll do whatever you want. I'll rub your back. Sweep your floors, clean your bathroom. I just want—" Such formal oratory felt alien in my bare living room, like green slime on a countertop. And all I wanted was to heal my ass. "I just want," he paused and searched my face, "to kiss you."

Absurd timing: Here was an example of the bad taste certain men thought certain women found sexy—the kind of advice one excavated from a porn magazine. The guy was an Asura stealing the nectar of immortality from Amar Chitra Katha's comic books. Did Thomas actually think he could "churn the ocean of love" to get "Amrita"? There would be no marriage vows between us.

But as his beard grazed my jaw-line, he looked desperate, inhaling and exhaling like a hard-run horse. Urgently, inappropriately, he pressed his cold, wet lips to my chin, where they smeared towards my bottom lip. My own lips must have felt unappealing with dry lipstick. Like two flints smacking but not striking, our mouths emitted no sparks. As his facial hair frayed my skin and his lips writhed over mine, all I could do was watch the blur of his eyebrows.

The kiss never should have been, though Thomas seemed to want to linger, forcing it, pretending to wrench his mouth away. Eyes shut as he withdrew, he convulsed: "Thank you!" I wiped my lips with the back of my hand. When he opened his eyes, my belly turned over.

"Excuse me," I said, swallowing nausea, uncertain of exactly where I needed to go—only knowing that I needed to get away from the odors of yeast and sawdust.

"What's wrong?" He said, looking concerned. He'd settled into a hunched position of rounded shoulders and paunch, no longer prepared to pounce.

"I need a moment—" I grunted, struggling up despite the machete hacking my lower back. I wobbled towards the bathroom, managing, "back soon."

I flicked on the bathroom light, shut the door, my eyes like worn out circuits in the mirror. "Shit!" I whispered.

When I emerged, I found Thomas resting on his side and caressing his yogic belly, one of Zelda's couch pillows propped under his armpit while he gazed at a tearful Julia Roberts. He twisted around to look at me. "I hate this crap!" he said, thumping his fingers on the floor.

"Yeah—" I said.

"You okay?"

"Yeah—just needed a moment." Pause. "So—" I wanted him to

leave but didn't have the bad manners to ask him. "What should we do?"

"Relax. Enjoy more bread." He smiled. "Drink some wine—" He glanced at his backpack and nodded. "I've got a bottle in my pack." So, he would settle for splinters, lie there till midnight—or until someone sang him a sexy lullaby. I wouldn't have it. Minutes later, I saw him to the door—where, thank goodness, he didn't hand out another loaf of bread or ask for another kiss.

Once Again

Skiing, like moving to another state, had been a bad idea. But in the end, I'd been lucky. Not so for the people I left behind. When I finally heard the story, I felt like a bank robber who'd gotten away with millions. Who'd have guessed that two tragedies could occur in a single day? How could I have known that Peter's wooing me would actually leave me with more than a broken tailbone? The symphony of life rarely breaks its tempo, except when trios dance.

Because of my tailbone, it didn't seem odd to get a call from Thomas later that week.

"There's been a snow event," he said when I picked up.

"A snow event? What do you mean?" I said, thinking it a joke about spinning Dervishes on an ice field.

"Your friends. The people we skied with. There's been some kind of problem."

"Problem? What are you talking about?" He'd heard it first on the news. And then, because we'd just been to the resort, and because he favored news about wilderness survival and natural disasters, he looked into it.

All afternoon at Crystal, while Thomas drove me back to Seattle, the ground had shimmered like sugar on vanilla ice cream, white beneath snowless skies—what snowboarders called "awesome." The desire to rise to the heavens, someone later speculated, might have been too strong. Everyone on the mountain took advantage of the sudden break in weather. No one stopped for hot chocolate. No one gave up a lift ticket for a dip in the Jacuzzi. In fact, the lift rarely saw such brisk business. Even the cross-country trails swelled with skiers. Under such exceptional conditions, how could it not be spiritual suicide to depart the slopes?

Perhaps the crowds explained why no one remembered seeing Franz, Letty, or Peter. There'd been plenty of cross-country skiers at the resort, but most stayed below. Only the stray car in the outer lot, with two days worth of snow on the windshield, alerted resort staff that something was amiss. And then, it took searchers another full day to gather that not one but three were missing.

Too scary to believe, I kept saying. Nothing was 100 percent accurate or right or real until all the proof could be laid out. But Thomas said it looked pretty bad. We wouldn't know for sure for days.

Death by ice, someone wisely said, felt like endlessly slipping across an infinite field.

Lost In Nowhere

With all this bad news, something other than location had to change. But in the days, weeks, and months that followed Thomas's call, I couldn't figure out what. I only knew there'd been too many tragedies in the few short years since Rudy's phone call. It didn't matter whether I lived in New York or Seattle—a disaster, death, or cruel twist of fate would find me. And yet, all I could think of were platitudes: *"The more things change the more things stay the same,"* and *"No matter where you are, there you are."*

Not yet in midlife, it already seemed that most people I knew had wilted or disappeared or flat-out rotted away. Like Linus in *Charlie Brown*, death's cloud forever blanketed me. While the car, with its caked-over windshield, ossified in the outer lot by the mountain, Franz, Letty, and Peter's family members searched with recovery teams, desperate for answers. Ten days after the disappearance, no bodies had been found, and the worried faces simply floated away into oceans of grief that I knew too well.

Under the circumstances, how could my phone calls to my mother be anything but desperate? As any psychologist will say, the more I beckoned, the less available the recipient. I'd dial and wait six rings before realizing no one would pick up. It got so bad that I couldn't leave my apartment without reaching my mother's answering machine. I spoke more to that machine than I did to all the humans surrounding me in that alien city.

Oddly, when the ache in my lower back began to lessen my phone betrayed me, turning the tables with a parade of hang-up calls whose caller ID stated, "Private Number." The calls began innocuously, one here and there. Quickly, however, they became aggressive, ringing three or four times in an evening, the bell jangling until something or someone picked up. When I did pick up, I found breathless stillness, as if a mask had been thrown over the other end of the line.

At first, I considered these sales calls gone awry—some obsessive-compulsive database screwed over by a virus. But I never heard the marketing call's botched recording or click. Instead, the line buzzed with far away cicadas, as if someone's lips had frozen around a convoluted, persistent code for something I didn't understand.

Eventually, I compiled a list of potential callers. Ben got knocked off the list right away, because he didn't need to play games. I ruled out

John Jones, because melting glass thrilled him more than melting women. JNB only went overboard for humpbacks, Alaska, and Parvati. It couldn't be Thomas either, because he revolved around baking bread, Amazon code, Dervishes, and email updates about "the three lost skiers." I ruled out every last man I knew—including Peter who had disappeared into the wilderness. I thought of Mimi, but she'd never waste a "precious as pie" moment on pranking an ex-friend.

But what about my ex-roommate, Jessica?

The Experiment

At midnight, she entered wearing a trench coat, dark lipstick smudged upwards towards her eyes. Behind her, several faceless and naked men climbed through my bedroom window. They held Molotov cocktails, threw them at the floor, which turned into orange snakes that swallowed my still-intact, but seriously soiled bedroom carpet.

I sat up, breathing hard at my own stupidity. Of course—how had I not seen it? Clearly, Jessica had never been a social worker trying to land an MSW at UW. Of course. It all made sense at 3:00 AM: Her "mother" who wasn't her mother had been the first clue. And her lost keys, her erratic schedules hinted at foul play. And that resume she insisted on sharing at our first meeting—all of it was fraudulent. I should have known, but had confused her collegiate "vulnerability and cheer" with honesty.

I had no choice but to conduct an experiment.

First, picking up, I chanted, "hello" to the static of deep space, and then hung up and wrote down the time of the call. This cycle repeated twice, and each time I logged the hour, number of rings, and what happened. First six and then twelve minutes elapsed between the calls. Like clockwork, the phone rang twenty-four minutes later. I collected my data, finding the pattern, always picking up to the hum of faraway cicadas.

Forty-four minutes later, when the phone rang, I said, "Hello, whoever you are, please stop calling or I'll call the police." That tactic backfired. For close to an hour, a carillon of rings drilled the apartment, with barely a minute separating each round. If I picked up and hung up, the phone shot off another round seconds later. Freaked by these war cries, I tried everything from burying the "plastic banana" headset to thrusting it out the window. But it rang and rang, leaving anyone in its wake a *Clockwork Orange* prisoner whose eyes had been pried open to a landscape of flayed humanity. This torture cycle rouletted around three more times as I logged each pulse, until I succumbed to destruction and yanked the phone cord from the wall.

After a sleepless night, I initiated a new strategy. I picked up, deepened my voice and growled like Stan, "Who the hell is this?!" Nothing. When it rang again, I tittered like Nora, "I'm here. I'm listening." Still nothing.

My experiment produced two outcomes. The first: exhaustion followed by flu-like symptoms, which caused me to miss three days of temping at UW Medical Center's cancer ward. I was let go, leaving only a single month's rent between the street and me.

The second: Zelda conveniently spilled the news that she and her boyfriend couldn't take the constant telephone racket. They'd decided to move in together on May Day—a day that couldn't have arrived at a worse time, because UW students would be embarking on summer break, thereby flooding the rental market with cheap housing. The only remaining renters would be transients and summer vacationers who claimed they wanted yearlong leases but would bail after Bumpershoot.

Zelda's news and the loss of my paycheck threw me into panic. I dashed to the Apartment Store and to the University of Washington listing board, scrambling for a visiting graduate student or researcher flush with cash. My own reserves could take me, foodless, through the month. And because I'd never been on Welfare—let alone food stamps—I had no idea how to apply or whether I, as someone not only qualified for employment but also endowed with a college degree, could receive help from the Feds.

When April 25th arrived with morning drizzle, I still hadn't found Zelda's replacement—though there'd been one call (between the hang-ups) from a record store clerk with two Rottweiler's and a pregnant girlfriend whose baby was due any day. I almost invited him to visit the room, but got real when Parvati—by then the only person who picked up her phone—pointed out the reality of the situation. "Tell me you are not going to hide two Rottweilers, a pregnant woman, and her boyfriend in that little apartment?! Please!"

True, living with five other "breathers" was better than a slab of pavement outside the QFC. But in a building with flea detectors in every mailbox, somehow this option added up to something far worse than complete ruin. I'd be kicked out and left without a rental reference. It wasn't worth contemplating what would become of me under those circumstances.

Walk It Off

Not a single person came to my rescue. And why would anyone? John had driven off with his bowls and platters, to exhibit his "I been to Tibet" story at a glass show in San Miguel de Allende. JNB milked The Old Christie with the help of the chow named Moo. Thomas packed his sweating Subaru with several loaves of well-oiled foccacia, off to visit a cousin in

Portland, while Parvati fled Seattle's exploding pollen count for the relative relief of wedding air inside a New York Cathedral. Even Jack, the "apartment manager demigod" on floor three, had disappeared with a message shoved beneath my door, which stated that he'd be "out of commission" at a friend's cabin near the Hoh Rainforest.

But spring didn't stop me. I continued to walk in mildewed clothes, taking side streets to the choppy waterfront of docks and jetties, braving Sunday mornings when the crows pecked at road kill. Rain dripped through my aging umbrella, which looked like a bat's wing as I dueled gusts. Boxing the wind, I leaned into the one-two punch from north and west, my canvas shoes sloshing with gutter water, my jeans drenched, hair whipping my cheeks until split ends became a single sopping snarl.

You couldn't call it self-torture, because at 5:30 AM I needed the vacant path and the Cargill grain elevator at the end of Myrtle Edwards Park. I needed to walk into the salt air. Sleep and flipping pancakes to Patsy Kline in a warm kitchen were for others, not me. I squinted at the "COSCO" and "HANJIN" cargo ships. Wheat, corn, and soy pellets blew from funnels, disbursing grain meant for the world's bottomless stomach, leaving so much dust in my nostrils.

Across the train tracks, street lamps glowed around vacant office buildings. An infinite number of mirrored days hung from the sky, while everyone else in the western world copulated on creaking bed frames. I wondered how long this sameness could go on, because I knew the world would be different in ten years. But I wouldn't be different with it.

The Bottom Before The Bottom

On the morning of my twenty-seventh birthday the shelves of my fridge were empty except for a shriveled potato, a mostly empty carton of Zelda's leftover milk, and half a Hershey bar I knew not to eat though hunger drummed my belly. The QFC and Starbucks hadn't yet opened. But down Broadway, between Noah's and a shuttered bar, a sign blinked on and off in a gated window. I had no choice but to forage this fluorescent cave, where I discovered an enervated man hunched over and murmuring into his cell phone, eyelids drooping next to a black and white screen of soccer players kicking a ball.

At the freezer, my fingers shook over packs of Bird's Eye corn, Green Giant peas. Carrots and bananas didn't cost as much as the frozen items. But, shivering, I snatched the usual peas and corn. Next to the gum rack, a shelf offered a single head of iceberg lettuce and a five-pound sack of Idaho potatoes. My birthday breakfast would be simple: boiled peas au corn with potatoes on a bed of wilted leaves, the whole thing doused with Zelda's left-behind, take-out soy sauce—which might or might not still be in the cupboard. Cost of said feast: $4.67, a budget conscious celebration of yet another turn around the planet.

Back in my bedroom, I pulled on dry clothes, so hungry I didn't flinch when the phone rang, its "unknown caller" icon flashing me like an exhibitionist. This time, I didn't pick up, thankful to be guarded by an answering machine.

During another round of ringing, I scarfed my birthday feast, not stopping to taste, and then stood naked as running water drowned out the ringing. I soaked, got out, stared at the mirror, studying the two-foot talons of my bleached hair.

My style had remained static for years. In middle school, I'd gone blond to look like Christie Brinkley. But after so many years of bleach, follicles had shriveled. Hair dropped out at the faintest tug. Wherever I walked, a disturbing trail of keratin fibers—like a trail of misery—fluttered in my wake. All too often I discovered dander and hair like failed endeavors on other people's clothing—including the sweaters of strangers who happened to brush up against me. And yet, I was at a loss as to what to do with my festering scalp. Was it too crazy to become a Swami?

It was my hair that kept me from picking up the phone—a thing I'd later regret. While I manhandled a tube of lipstick and scattered tissue over the countertop and coerced a damp jacket from my closet, I missed my last chance.

Rain jangled the downspouts. But by then, nothing could stop me from exiting into wind where pedestrians bent over sidewalks, some tugging leashes, others scurrying in rumpled jackets towards doorways cluttered with mashed cardboard boxes. I dashed down Broadway towards Seattle Central, searching for that special treat that would top off my birthday like a squirt of whipped cream. Then, through the spray, I spotted the red neon sign, blinking on and off like a bedroom straight from the Pigalle.

Fury

An hour later, I paced the living room, sawdust sticking to my soles, yelling "Fuck Fuck Fuck!" until I soaked my buzzed hair in the sink. I pulled at the roots as if to pull out every last follicle. Cursing, I fought the impulse to murder the fey lavender frill who pretended to be a hair stylist—the demon who'd done this.

In bed, I gripped handfuls of pixie knots, tugging at the weeds of anger growing over the Boy-George creature that had danced around my head with his scissors as if he couldn't decide whether he had a libido or a disco ball down his pants. An imposter, he'd convinced me to snip off my keratinized shield. I should have known: The "Hair Connection" signage looked like it pointed to a sex dungeon, its blinking arrow like a boner for an upper story.

Had I—as the stylist suggested—dropped in like Typhoon Sadie for a whirl with Virgil through hell? Yuckiness nattered in my gut, because I knew this bad haircut resulted from childhood trauma, rotten karma, the Asian subcontinent, and the impending dissolution of western civilization.

For days, I paced, livid at my near baldness, unwilling to relinquish rage even when Parvati reminded me that hair continued growing in the grave. It infuriated me that the stylist's lip-stud twinkled when he said, "Well this is a surprise! Did we have an appointment?" And when I explained that I was a drop in, it was all: "And why not? It's only half a century before I officially open!" He pretended to be disgruntled, but then pursed his lips in concern. "Look at you. Of course you're a drop in." Could it get any worse than a wannabe who wore black leather pants, snakeskin cowboy boots, and a lavender blouse studded with the kind of gold buttons that made Donald Trump's signature architecture look paltry in comparison?

But besides bad taste, hell, and near baldness, two additional things bothered me. First, I couldn't stand the mildew weaving itself into every corner of my being, including my crotch. Second, my new roommate Evie nearly bolted when she discovered that the phone rang from 6 AM to near midnight. Two days into her stay, the phone disappeared, leaving the apartment ring-free, creating endless hours for reading and sleeping, prompting me to wonder why I hadn't thought to permanently put the plastic banana out of its misery.

For days, nothing felled the forest of contentment that came over me once that ring had disappeared. But by week two, the quiet began to grate. Holed up in my sleeping bag with Turgenev, my journal, and a bowl of Shredded Wheat, I no longer felt as if afloat on a luxury liner. By week three, I began pacing the apartment as if I'd lost my bookmark in time. Agitated, I was hungry for something I couldn't remember tasting. By the end of the month, I'd been rendered invisible. I longed to be summoned, for someone to recall me, dial me, and dump me with a click.

Stranded on my silent island, I couldn't focus or think. Days slipped by when I spoke to no one but my own reflection, locked in my bedroom where I masturbated to the image of Ben and only Ben, concerned I'd never hear his voice again. I had no choice. I dug up the phone and plugged it back in.

It was Memorial Day, and all that was left was karma's laugh track.

Memorials

That morning I dithered, sweeping, folding underwear between readings of the *Tibetan Book of the Dead*. As I hefted laundry to my closet, the phone miraculously came to life, its cord again stuck into the wall. Oddly excited, but hesitant, I fought the urge to pick up, wandering into the kitchen to fill my kettle.

When the answering machine beeped, I heard, "Hello. I'm trying to reach Jane." The familiar male voice rose above waves of static. "Is this Jane's number? I've had the damndest time, been calling for days. Where've you been?"

I dumped the kettle beneath the faucet and rushed (with teabag in hand) to pick up. My fingers trembled as I hugged the earpiece to my ear.

"Yes—Hello!!" I said, emotions rolling through me. He hadn't forgotten. He'd called. Ben was trying to reach me! My knees trembled as I paced the copper area rug that Eve had thrown down on the bare wood. "How are you? What's going on? Really good to hear you! It's been ages." As on every other occasion, it was hard to tamp down mania and shut up.

"I know; it's out-of-the-blue," he said with a tone that suggested a head cold. "I told myself, she's not going to be there. But I wanted you to know." He broke off, stumbling to find words through the wires. "So," he hedged, with a lack of confidence that belied my memory of him. "It's kind of unexpected, I know. But I needed to call. So, I dug around, got your number. You okay?" This confused me. Didn't he have my number? And what was this: "Was I okay"? This was different. Did he finally care?

But I kept pretending. "Thanks for asking," I said. "I'm fine. What about you? Still reading and thinking about new possibilities."

"What are you saying," he said, not pretending.

A massive ship turned in the turbulent waters of my mind, everything reorienting. "Who is this?" I said to the buzzing line.

"Have a seat," the man who was Ben and not Ben said. "I'm okay here. I'm getting through this, handling all of it just fine—the logistics and what not. The hospital guy who covers all the psychiatry over there, he's been making good like you can't believe. The whole thing's a mess, but something I can get through. Actually, it was him suggested I call you—" He stopped and exhaled a heaviness that could have sunk a thousand Jupiters. "You know, right?" His voice branched into three painful points, one high, one medium, one low. I didn't understand. He sounded like Ben.

"Actually," I said. "I'm not following. Who is this?"

"You don't know who this is?"

"Not a clue—" Though, again I was fooling myself. I knew exactly who it was—but the man never answered questions. "This is Ben, right? What's going on? I'm confused. Go on. Tell me." Water spilled into the sink, but I couldn't turn it off. I plucked at my teabag, its string dangling the way my hair once dangled to the middle of my back. I began looping the string like a random thought around my ring finger, and then I remembered the end of the last conversation, when Ben had mentioned the possibility of a visit. Everything depended on improved physical health, but he might be interested in moving out west for a Masters program at UW, yes he might, especially as he'd always wanted to visit the Northwest.

"Do I really need to say it?" Came Ben's voice. "Because you know, and it would be easier if we could just get through this without—" Rudy's words dragged him into hyperventilation. I didn't know how to respond. It wasn't my job to save people.

But then, he told me.

Ben had tried to reach me. "He got a fever, had this idea that you could help him," Rudy said, clearing his throat, which sounded like two tectonic plates scraping against each other. "This was maybe two, three weeks ago," I remembered the phone ringing before it stopped ringing, and I now wondered which calls had been his. I kept breathing. "And then, last Tuesday—It was my fault—"

"Who thinks of sepsis? He was doing well," Rudy said. I didn't want to probe, preferring the blurry sound of a thousand violins to the harsh trumpets of truth. "You know now—" Rudy said. "And thank you for talking to Ben before he passed." What was it with Rudy and euphemisms, platitudes, and Hallmark card niceties?

His voice dropped to a whisper. "He probably never told you, but he told me he loved you—" I didn't want to hear it. The sink overflowed with water. My kettle floated like the motorboat my father Stan once steered towards an inlet of crabs that washed a summer in Cape Cod into the Atlantic. Rudy should have been Ben. He should have been saying, "I'm coming! I'm flying out next week!"

You'll love it here, Ben. The water, the air, the wildlife, Mt. Rainier.

Bad Joke

I remembered that October walk to the UW Admissions Office. It was an afterthought, but the wet and cold made my hand tremble as I scribbled down his address on an information packet's envelope, which was so delayed in arrival that it might have been flown cross-country by a carrier pigeon.

"He appreciated getting something from you," Rudy told me during our call, when I stopped believing that I could repair a mistake. "It helped. He read the brochure, front to back."

"Good—" I'd blurted, mucus running down from my nose to my lips, hardly aware that I was crying. On the windowsill stray raindrops spattered my copy of the *Ramayana,* where it would stay for days, because he'd bought it for me at the Strand. And I knew that he knew that I knew what it was like to be Sita, falling through the earth's crust.

"A lot of people kept him going. He said you most of all." This sounded like a lie that Rudy had told everyone else.

"But no. He told me," I blurted with the vague sense that Ben might be sending me messages through the wet tea leaves I mashed between my fingers. "He was getting better." He'd been to Wupatki, had lit match after match at our San Juan mountain campsite, the flame never more than a line of blue.

Details fell through the earpiece like candies in a dream. He'd been alone his last year, reading Tolstoy, Dickens, Lermontov, Goethe, and his last days had been filled with enormous doses of antibiotics, I-Vs that left his fingers cold, his eyelids weak, lips bluing, microbes swimming through blood vessels and shutting down his liver, kidneys, pancreas, heart. An anomaly— No!—a miracle that Ben had lived as long as he had!

"But Rudy, I don't understand. How did this happen? When did this happen? I don't understand." No one would ever understand.

"I don't know. It took two weeks," he was saying. "Not even, and pssshhh."

"Why didn't you call? Why didn't you?"

"He tried and now I tried."

"I don't get it. You sound so okay. He can't be gone. This is a joke! Put him on!"

"I'm sorry," he said. "I know."

After hanging up, I went into the kitchen to turn off the water. The linoleum was covered with a thin sheen of wet, but I did nothing to dry it.

<u>No</u>

Nothing could be believed as the room tipped sideways in a way that caused me to ask questions, as if questions stabilized situations. To undo what couldn't be undone, I asked the tea leaves about something Rudy had said: "You should know, before he died, he and I were looking at Las Vegas." Was there something I could do that would remove the fact of this loss?

It had been a surprise to me that during those last months Ben thought of moving to Las Vegas, so close to the western landscape where

I'd spent the summer of my most beautiful year. Turned out he'd wanted to study Chinese medicine, hadn't really wanted to join me in Seattle. As if emphasizing this point, the mashed leaves spilled into the cup like flakes in a snow globe, staying afloat, unsettled.

It was true: Randomness guided our lives. Choices were random, and no one could predict their outcome. The world was a giant meditation hall full of lives that wanted to sound like music blown in from the south, accompanied by visions of mass-produced canvases showing mauve mountain ranges ascending into an infinite sunset, humanity awaiting the close encounter that time would bring.

The leaves finally settled, looking like a woman resting her elbows against a coffee table. I thought of my mother.

I asked: "Where is this Chinese place in Las Vegas? Where were you thinking of going, Ben?" But I knew nothing, only that all the world's weight rested against my forehead and in my throat. Would I ever hear from Rudy again? He might live past the year's end. Or he might not. I'd heard it in his voice. He'd already left the earth.

<u>Reincarnation</u>

I fell into bed, drifting on veils of rain lifted by solstice light, with The Avatar and my mother flying to Las Vegas. Dinosaurs and water and steam shovels woke me to a lonesome tangle of sweaty sheets near 3 AM, tears everywhere.

After my 5 AM run, the doorbell rang. I opened the door, and Mimi stood like a surprise party, her figure and face changed. She'd grown puffy, more than a double chin framing the lower half of her face where a faint beard left its shadow, her fake fur jacket tight as a hotdog casing around her torso, her thighs jammed together beneath blossoming hips, her blue jeans shoved into combat boots whose boxy heels inflated rather than minimized her belly. Anti-fashion had finally caught up with Mimi in Seattle. Like the gum-chewing Violet in *Charlie and The Chocolate Factory*, Mimi had swollen beyond her frame's capacity. It had to be all those triple chocolate lattes—not to mention the pies.

"I'm looking for a piece of mail," she huffed, garlic breath filling the foyer, a cold eye to my shorn skull. "I was wondering if it accidentally ended up here—" There was no *"And would you look at you! How the hell are you!!!"* or sing-song, *"Sugar, you are just too amazing—look at you with your super-cute dream-cut!!!"*

Against better judgment, I asked her in, and she stumbled through the remnants of sawdust, nearly knocking over my one remaining spider plant. Adding to misery, she said, "So, that was brave. You cut your hair and pulled up the rug. Does the manager know?" I mentioned Zelda's obsession with bare wood and her refusal to take (and leave) the room unless the rug disappeared.

"Okay," Mimi coughed, squinting at the iridescent threads of Evie's Kashmiri throw rug. "I so wouldn't say it's perfect, but it's habitable." This, I took to mean one thing. She was sort of pissed at me, and might stay pissed for a year or two, but wouldn't remain pissed for the rest of our lives. "You do know that Todd and I moved into our own place a few months ago." This was a statement, though it should have been a question. "A two bedroom. A few blocks away. On the third floor. Floor-to-ceiling windows in the living room. Our own terrace. Only $750." She glanced around and bit the side of her lip, adding, "Oh and two bathrooms." She'd always wanted a terrace and two bathrooms. For some reason, I felt relieved that she'd settled only blocks away, though the possibility of running into Todd at the QFC filled me with dread.

All easy-going, Mimi couldn't help highlighting our lack of seating with, "We're furnishing the apartment with antiques. Todd got this amazing sofa from the 20s."

"That's nice," I responded, reserved, lounging in the cool corner of my emotional wine cellar.

"His parents are so amazing. They're giving us a lot of free stuff, getting rid of this absolutely incredible and unique dinette that's maybe not even two years old." She folded hefty arms, slightly out of breath as if she'd climbed a flight of stairs. "So, any mail come for me in the last week or so?" I told her there was nothing, but if I found an envelope with her name on it, I'd make sure it landed in her mailbox.

"Okay, well then—" she rummaged in her faux Prada shoulder bag and pulled out her organizer, her face bloated and tired. "My new address." She braced a pen between her front teeth as she unzipped the booklet. "Is—" she murmured, drawing out the word with pen still between her teeth. She leaned the booklet against a wall, took the pen in hand, and scrawled down her address, stopping twice to shake ink into the pen's ballpoint. "You can call this number—" She scribbled a 206 number and tore off the sheet. "So. If something comes in, I would so appreciate it if you could get it to me as soon as you can. **Please**. Here—" She thrust the paper at me, impatient to leave. "And if you can't do that, I'm still working downtown at the hotel. Just call them there and ask for me." I nodded, slightly offended by her tone, but speechless in the face of it.

I glanced at the paper and folded it in half. She didn't know about Ben. And I wouldn't have cared if Mimi sobbed over his death or regaled me with platitudes. I wouldn't tell her, especially in the face of all this Schadenfreude. I said nothing as she curtly said goodbye. I simply shut the door.

Soy Chai

Since revitalizing the phone, I again began to call my mother twice a day. When she picked up, she inevitably sighed at my hello, pretending to listen, inserting various "mhmmms" and "ohs" while tidal waves of desperation flowed out of me. Blooms of acne—not sugar generated—arced across my forehead as I rambled about my last boss at UW, who discovered an irreversible mistake in my data entry. Apparently, I'd accidentally replicated a database, creating fifty plus versions, a tangle that would cost the department thousands of dollars to correct. I'd been written up, fired, and permanently barred from the University. I told Nora about the last hundred bucks in my bank account, the fact that cafés, splurges on baguettes, the two-dollar rack at Urban Outfitters—even weekend jaunts to Goodwill—had long ago disappeared. What would become of me? Would I end up in a cardboard box?

But Nora continued her "mhmmms" and "ohs," as I talked suicide. I pictured her seated next to her computer above Lexington Avenue with its storefront awnings, her dining room crowded with papers. I knew she didn't have the energy to care. Her own troubles—including a disgruntled housemate who threatened to inform the landlord of the toxic toner cartridges riding up the walls—required that she ignore everything but that which kept her solvent.

Apparently, The Avatar was sending her to Las Vegas, where he'd begun to build a following. "Interesting—" I said. "I was just talking to someone about Las Vegas."

"You must be tuned in."

I considered Rudy and Nora. Maybe they'd take the same flight from Newark airport and end up living together in the gambling capital of the world. Why not head for the money? The idea was more interesting than walking past cafés whose interiors sweated body odors, causing windows to pearl with droplets. I whiled away afternoons, envious of café-goers more flush with cash than I. Cut loose from corporate healthcare, I hated their infected nose rings. I loathed the books they read, the journals they scribbled in, the chatter they spewed into cups of espresso that induced heartburn. I despised the June drizzle falling on the skylights. Yet, I still longed for friends. And Parvati, like her namesake—mother of the universe—was the only one left. She hadn't yet deserted me, because she had an agenda.

She stopped by one morning, offering to treat me to chai, the first in months. At the cafe on E. Pike—cathedral ceilings, long windows facing downtown—she asked how I was doing. A sun hole had opened over the skyline of buildings that looked like silver Zippos. Why say I'd spent hours crying into 3,000 miles of phone wire as the trees along Republican revived their Irish hue and all of Capitol Hill got giddy for the solstice? All I offered was, "I'm fine."

"Good, so we're going out tonight—" she began, lifting a latte to her lips. Flush from salsa class, Parvati looked more superhero than Copacabana in her blue Spandex, a black sweatband highlighting the sheen above her upper lip. "A little wine, jazz, good **eats**!" Pressing my arm, she gazed at my face. "You look tired!" I nodded and told her I hadn't slept well. "Take a nap!" Because, she told me, we were going to Wild Ginger. She and Nana were celebrating—and that included me.

I'd dress up, because why not? And Nana would drive me home in her converted mail carrier truck. "But you look so depressed. And don't wear that t-shirt!" She sounded like Madam Fashion. "It's on me!" Parvati added, the guilt at having stolen JNB dripping over her features like blood in a horror flick.

"So, I look that bad—" I said, interested in the bagel and cream cheese that slumped on a plate in front of her. I could've eaten ten of them, despite being vegan, but glanced away.

"Really, Jane—" The words came in bite-size pieces. "It's not that I'm **saying** you're," pause, chew. "You know," another chew. "Looking **bad**," sip of latte. "Not at all! I just mean," bite, chew. "You can **tell**." Another sip. "You look really, I don't know. **Sad**." Finger to lip to wipe away dollop of cream cheese. "Like you're kind of **sleeping**." Licking finger. "And I know why. But it's **summer** now." She peered at my spiked hair—never having critiqued the haircut—before taking another sip. As a waterfall of chai fell into her—leaving a cloud of whipped cream to mingle with sweat on her upper lip—my stomach turned.

Only Parvati absorbed large doses of whipped cream without showing it, because her Asian frame metabolized sweeteners and fats better than mine. I lived in awe of her, knowing that in the past months, despite a diet of leaf matter, I'd gained almost five pounds—which I discovered when I couldn't squeeze into an old pair of jeans. During the transition from Zelda to Evie, I'd succumbed, falling off the carrot-and-peas wagon in favor of white rice and those ever-present boxes of Shredded Wheat. With a starved metabolism, my belly and thighs captured the excess calories with gusto, crazed by the surge of glucose in my blood stream.

Maybe that's why I pleaded with Parvati. Huddling over my chai, as if ill. I claimed a headache and lower back pain, because everything about a night at Wild Ginger sounded exhausting—like arriving at Burning Man without water, like spending a night in a Port-o-San, like frying in a Tesla coil. 8 PM bedtimes were nice. So what if I liked staying in?

"Jane. Jane. Jane." Parvati murmured. "**Listen**. You're going **out tonight**!" Wonder Woman had pulled out her lasso. "Nana and I are not going unless you're there. So you're coming—!" Relentless.

I surrendered by lifting my mug and steaming my eyes— "Right. I'll go. But," I insisted, "only if I walk."

Re-Inventing Time

"Time heals all wounds."

And Now, For You

Crazy, all that reluctance, because it became the night that changed the rest of my life. But like most life-changing events, I never saw you coming. In fact, everything was mundane randomness—except for how energetic I felt. But anyone would attribute that to the chai. Still, I remember arriving home too keyed-up to nap. I took a shower, and then pulled on jeans, a pine-green sweater, and a faux diamond choker Ben nabbed for a dollar at a flea market we'd found on our way back from Bear Mountain.

After leaving the apartment, I had an hour to spare. As I walked towards the waterfront, the light flared—too spectacular to be random—like a flag of woven gold draped over Capitol Hill. I wasn't alone: Everyone on the street seemed stunned to the point of tears as three sun holes merged to form a blazing blue mouth. Hawks soared around glass towers. Golden shafts hit the pavement, and shadows came alive on the sidewalk for the first time in weeks.

I had the time, so I slipped inside Elliot Bay, searching the bookshelves, stalling at the poetry section. Hungry for something, possibly an explanation for this elation, I found a stanza that described a drop of light after a thousand hours of darkness. It was 5:30—nearly the end of Happy Hour—and I was getting wasted on poetry.

But then I spotted Dan near a table in a back corner. He was organizing newly arrived volumes, looking thinner than when we last ruminated over Rumi. The book club, with all its stinky and ill-kempt attendees, had inexplicably dissolved after Dan fell for an Akita named Shirley. If I hadn't felt buoyant as I leaned over a pile of books to sniff their wildflower pages, I might have noticed his face. Instead, I rattled whatever I touched.

"Hey!" He jolted backwards, stepping on my toes, his glasses teetering down his nose with a glint that made his eyes appear small and sharp.

"*Hey*" I echoed, smiling and still not getting it as I elbowed an unstable stack of hardbacks. They trembled, but did not tumble.

"Jesus," he moaned, placing a palm atop the stack, before redistributing the books into smaller piles. With annoyance, he added, "Just look interested in the books. I have to keep stacking. Politics." He stared at the back cover of a David Guterson novel and flipped it over. His jaw looked tight, and his voice sounded parched when, after taking a deep breath, he added, "Why are you here?" It was a sentence loaded with meaning. "Not, I imagine, to purchase more poetic wisdom—" I emitted an obligatory half-laugh, trying to remain light as I told him about Wild Ginger and the impending evening of jazz.

"So you're joining me to kill time—my familiar, unending role in life—especially these days. The guy to come to for senseless time killing." He pulled off his glasses and wiped a smear with the bottom of his shirt. "Nice to know that I'm so useful— Even books ask me to kill time in the useless pursuit of organization by alphabetization—"

Though Dan and I rarely spoke of intimate things, especially since the Mimi episode (keeping conversations focused on books), I understood that a childhood in the foster care system—which began in Topeka, Kansas and ended with a household in Nebraska—had thrown him off his horse one too many times. Somehow, I knew he'd been a runaway subsisting on little sleep, bouts of retail, and a disparate collection of community college classes—like the one in LA where he relaxed into his sexual calling. These few details I gathered from specks of conversation that had leaked from between the pages.

"What's wrong?" I brushed his shoulder with my fingers, but he stepped back. "Is this self-pity for my benefit or yours?" This statement— copped from HR Department manuals, thanks to growing up around Mimi's mother—required a smile, which wasn't my usual approach.

"What are you talking about?" Maintaining an even tone, he slammed down one of the softbound volumes, causing the stack to tremble again. "I'm not on a pity trip. I'm on a trip whose destination is truth—" He didn't seem angry so much as pained when he wagged his head towards a dark alcove where he meant for us to continue our conversation. "Just follow me, please—" All manager-helping-patron, we wended through the maze of political commentary and historical sociology, past the less threatening cookbook and gardening sections, finally circling towards the shadows of the occult.

"Okay," I said when we settled into a cave of astrology and Tarot. "What's up?" He stood next to me, flannel garb emitting the odor of ash and beer, his jeans crisp but dirt-encrusted, his fists stuffed deep into pockets.

"I'm done," he whispered as if he'd murdered a customer. "I'm moving. To Chicago. Next month. That's what's up. And these dumb **fucks**—" his voice cracked through the whisper, "who run this shop, not to mention my ex-, can go to **hell**—" Face reddening around the edges, he appeared ready to punch a bookshelf.

Struck by this news—not to mention the surge of anger, especially from a guy who never seemed fazed—I stepped back, now my turn to feel the spines of books graze my bottom. In a hoarse whisper, he rattled off his complaints, spit flecking the air to amp-up the rant.

"The thing is, they're putting someone else—someone completely clueless and new—in the managerial position and, even though they won't fire me because they know they need my expertise, they're cutting me down to floor staff…. And don't get me started on my ex-, because I'll just go off—" He pressed a fist against his forehead and stared at me with bull's eyes. "He's been playing around with guys I know, while saying I'm the only one because I pay his god damn bills—but we know what that means. He's a non-fucking-committed fag with a stick up his ass—" His lips—white—trembled, and I stared, nodding into the caustic whisper. "What nobody **gets** is that I'm not going to **fucking** put up with this **shit**—I'm out of here. Next bus. I've got an offer to join a bookstore in Chicago with connections to some publishers who could eat this **hellhole** city in one bite. Why should I stick around? I'm sick of the rain anyway!" He stared at me, eyebrows raised, shoulders pushed against earlobes, palms spread and thrown to his sides, flannel collar grazing his stubble. "I'm done! With or without **Shirley**!" The dog.

Awash in this cascade of inappropriate exclamations, I couldn't begin to ask an innocuous question about whether poetry had the power to heal the mental state of an orphan. His problems seemed miniscule to me. So his boyfriend was unworthy of love. So what! And so what if Dan hadn't made manager. He still got a paycheck. I almost told him to give me his job. But then I remembered all the volumes of Dante, Rimbaud, and Baudelaire that Dan seemed to adore and thought it best to say nothing because the boy hadn't ever lived in a real home and only needed a little time away from the morbid monologues of the ousted and distraught.

I stood by him, nodding at his complaints, which poured out until he stopped cold and sighed. I'd seen this sigh before in Rudy. Anger had finally settled into exhaustion. Shoulders slumped, belly protruded, fists rolled back into pockets. Finally, an opening.

"So—" I said. "When did this happen?"

"Saturday. I made the decision and that's it. I'm done. I can't be here anymore." His jaw slackened. His eyes pouched. A customer ambled into our nook, but finding the remnants of a verbal inferno, detoured to another alcove.

Like every other foundling who'd retreated to the Northwest, Dan had reached his limit. A casualty of rootlessness, he'd recoiled to this high corner of the country and could go no further. Immersed in an angst that was fueled by the never ending gray, he'd finally have to confront himself and make some very real decisions about how to let others into his life. I alluded to this, oddly so wise about others, but Dan's ears shut down, as mine had. It was so easy to see another's missteps, so hard to see and pick one's way out of one's own.

He slipped out of our corner of the occult—no longer enraged by shadows—only to encounter fluorescence, where several costumers descended upon the only staff member wearing glasses. Dan, the bulls eye of all questions, blasted off for Interior Design, where more customers—as if Velcro-ed to his flannel shirt—erupted with questions. The orphan of Seattle finally disappeared. Poof: a sea creature swept away from a riverbank of shelves.

I left the store just in time, walking towards my *No Exit* moment, unaware that I'd make my second life-changing mistake—an outcome no one could have foreseen, because before moving to Seattle, I'd stumbled upon someone else's terrible mistake during a warm summer morning at the East 79th street entrance to Central Park, the road overflowing with joggers, dog walkers, and mothers with strollers—I'm talking about the woman.

At first, no one, not even me, noticed her resting on a park bench, her hands laced over her belly. She was barefoot in Indian cotton pants and a t-shirt. Bright orange curls surrounded her face, but time stilled to zero, making the fuzz on her forearm appear painted, the arch of her eyebrows as perfect as they'd ever be. Against that stillness, I walked into the quiet of her smile, which was slight but steady, as if she dreamed of something she hadn't seen in years. It made her skin glisten.

Beneath her raised head there'd once been a large sack—what I imagined contained the remnants of a rooted life—possibly photos of a baby, a mother surrounded by laughing children, a first dog or birthday party. Perhaps there'd been a ring handed down from a grandmother or a card from a lost love, or a diary describing a picnic at Bear Mountain—or a description of how she'd tripped over a doorjamb, scraping her knees on the sidewalk that was also her bed. None of these things would ever again prop her up.

She leaned against that invisible backpack, as if her lost life depended upon it—skin already plastic-decay turning to leather. And still, a smile remained as muscles stiffened and blood congealed. She'd been dreaming of something, maybe a place not so far from her mother's arms.

Like Dan and the woman who ended up on the park bench, my foot rested on a last doorjamb. I could see the canal that carried people from the world of rooftops and grocery stores and banks to the turbulence of the open sidewalk. I saw the ATM where I'd withdraw my last atom of power to purchase survival, and because of this I told myself in the moments before I met you that I'd never stop walking.

The Man At The Satay Bar

Salt and ferry fuel mingled with seaweed as evening light broke against South Seattle and Bainbridge Island. I was early—though I felt late as I stepped inside a curry, garlic, and lemongrass confusion that only made Billie Holiday sound more provocative. Candlelight already flickered like an old film projector against a wall of windows.

At first, I felt relieved. I didn't have to think too much, could be molded by the atmosphere, because any restaurant that chose fusion and design over flavor and comfort encouraged a person to be impressionable. (Later, I'd determine that it was design that deterred me from taking action, making the choice for me.)

Still, after Dan's news anything would feel like a Caribbean vacation. The votives soothed, as did the bar, which stretched beneath rows of dangling, stemmed glasses, making wine the boring but sensible choice. Of course I ordered the cheapest white on the list, hoping that Parvati would cover the rest. "A sharp little baby from Chile," the bartender called it. I pulled out one of my last twenties, pretending not to care about the price as I lifted my glass by the stem. It was unforgivable to spend so much on wine— but what could I do? After stuffing the change into my wallet, I wandered to a raised table without stools.

Already, people hovered over small plates. Only a few empty tables with "reserved" placards remained. Placing my glass on the table, I pulled off my messenger bag and glanced at my watch like a student waiting for class. At the door, four Aveda blonds with pink lips and high cheekbones crossed arms over couture blazers and negotiated with the hostess. Like the women, a high percentage of diners wore expensive forms of khaki—likely purchased at Barney's or Neiman Marcus, costing half a month's rent.

Embarrassed by my lack of polish, I pulled off my frayed jacket and balled it into my bag. Sweat broke around the then darkening roots of my bleached but chopped rat's nest, my sweater suddenly bathed in mildew. I leaned forward to obscure the torn flap of my messenger bag—whose broken zipper had been jerry-rigged with a safety pin. Like Dan, I wanted to leave. Like Dan, I had nowhere to go. Like Dan, I couldn't convince anyone that I was qualified.

But then, the air changed. Behind the blonds at the hostess desk, the light brightened around the broad shoulders and strong features of a man whose eyes searched the interior as if surveying a battlefield. At first, his perfectly combed salt and pepper hair and closely snipped beard yelled school administrator. But then, his eyes denied anything having to do with government salaries or tedious paperwork. Anyone could see his brilliance, because next to him, the restaurant appeared to dim. I'd seen this before—in great works of art or in movies when a certain actor's face gave dimension to a flat screen. But I'd never seen anything like this within twenty feet of me.

Fascinated, I tried not to stare at his slate gray shirt, which echoed the coloring of his beard. But I couldn't help myself as he scoped out the interior, clearly combing through options, his hands on hips, exuding intention and strategy. That's when his eyes fell on me, when a rubber band smacked me in the chest, producing vibrations and colors, as if the air between us had been enhanced with CGI, up-shifting the peach in his skin, the blood in his lips, his eyes driving into fields of curiosity, turning him into "you."

But how do I describe what we both experienced? On the outside, your shoulders stiffened, and then you withdrew, as if wanting to hide. Had you lost your purpose for the evening, disgusted by a woman in rags? It wasn't that I had a Cinderella complex. Everyone could see it: You filled the room, the way you likely filled every city you explored—while I didn't.

Later, when men picked me up for drinks and the director's cut of Airplane II, I'd see your expression revived on their faces as a blur of disappointment through my tipped-back glass. You looked like a movie star, while I might have been a kitchen rat. It didn't help that you stood next to yet another blond in a beige pantsuit. How could I not feel awkward as I glanced at the ceiling, picking up and putting down my glass as pretence for being there?

You watched me for a few moments, and then you whispered into the blond woman's ear. At the time I thought she was your wife. But then, I looked up and the two of you had vanished. Had you backed out? Had you ducked behind the hostess's desk? Had you dodged the gawkers by scrambling into the kitchen?

I searched the votives. You were gone—had forgotten your wallet— or maybe your wife's car keys. Or maybe you hated the menu or the bickering women now pestering the front desk with shakes of their beautiful hair, while everywhere outside gray caused the gulls to drop shellfish dinners against the docks.

Hoping you'd return, I never took my eyes off the entrance. Would Parvati and Nana bump into you on their way into the restaurant? Would you say, "pardon—" or "so sorry—" or nothing at all?

Then, in the doorway, you reappeared alone, staring, your lips parted. A veil of light floated around you and spread over the entire space. Years later, I'd ask myself whether this was an optical illusion or whether my eyes were adjusting to the changing light in the windows— But at the time, I considered it a wave of electricity that blazed through the air and bound me to you.

You wandered into the restaurant, no blond in your wake. Like a turtle, I ducked and turned my back as you approached. I felt you pause mere feet away before you moved to the satay bar, which curved towards the rear like a nude sunbather.

My wine glass, its stem between my fingers, felt as cool as a waterfall spilling over stones. Garlic and meat roasting in an amber glow warmed my forehead and made the floorboards both smooth and insurmountable. I forgot what I'd come to do, who I'd meet, what the next morning would bring, because I felt your stare coming from the satay bar. I'd known you my whole life, though I'd never seen you in all the days of my life. You'd once crossed the Himalayas, carrying the Vedas. You'd once flown around the earth like Superman in a rage over the loss of Lois. You flickered somewhere in my pelvis, where every life I'd ever lived left a shadow, and I knew your future, because like a platitude or my shorn head or a thousand stories told by a thousand lost people, I'd heal you. And you'd heal me.

Problem #1

All night—even after Parvati and Nana arrived—I felt you watching me from the back of the restaurant. Throughout a dinnerless dinner of small talk, I performed for you while downing my Chilean white, trying to sparkle more by readjusting my fake diamond choker with a forefinger. Nana had parked her mail-carrier truck across the street, and when she dashed out for a jacket, Parvati teased me about toying with the necklace. But why care for phony diamonds when, after sundown, Wild Ginger became a cavern a flicker with firelight?

Looking back, the problem that evening was more Nana than Parvati. A psychologically well-adjusted femme fatale—if such a thing exists—Nana was daunting for her equestrian skills and Jacklyn Smith black hair. She diminished every other female in the restaurant. Men virtually inhaled her, even while dipping their forks into their wives' meals. It didn't help that Nana wore skin-tight black jeans and Lycra tops that showed her belly ring, or that her bone structure reminded me of Lynda Carter during her Wonder Woman years, or that she carried herself like Angelina Jolie in Tomb Raider. After all, at thirty-two, Nana—a.k.a the man lasso—still loved partying. She'd lived in New York, West Hollywood, and Rome, and therefore had mastered the body language of the sexual invitation. Most of all, she didn't reek of mildew—despite living with Parvati in a pit in the International District.

Unfortunately, it was hard to hate Nana. Jovial but vulnerable, she had the Northwesterner's earthiness—a drinker's approachability. Avoiding the morbid, disdainful outlook of the habitually philosophical, she'd been spared the "mental" diseases that afflicted so many urban dwellers from the east, who simply lacked the medicine of greenery and space. She saddled horses. She appreciated rural communities. She regularly hung out with extended family and therefore rarely drowned in despair.

It isn't surprising that I cowered next to her, picking at a hangnail or tugging at the remains of my hair. Next to Nana, I was no match. Lowering my eyes and ignoring the satay bar, I settled into listening-mode as she described a nameless man she alternately wanted to marry and string up in hell. He'd left town to "see the country," out of contact for two months without a single call or postcard. This after the man insisted they motorcycle to Vegas, get married, and visit the Liberace Museum. But of course, last minute, Nana discovered he'd been fucking a cousin. And of course, well-adjusted Nana laughed it off, lifting her pink lady, wagging the triangular glass so it sloshed amusement. She shrugged and shook out her hair, while I passed my hand over a new pimple and heard more stories of the ex's infidelity—hilarious to Nana.

"And here's the fucked up thing," Nana said, all smiles. "I'd take him back." Parvati and I advised against this, after which Nana shook her head, ardent. "No. You don't understand—I'm never giving this guy up. He has an incredible dick—" She laughed into her drink. Parvati glanced at me—I glanced back. We'd heard and lived this before. We disapproved. But because Nana laughed through life and we didn't, in ten years she'd marry an investment banker, birth two children, and move to Beijing—while we would not.

"You ever smell the shit before it arrives?" Nana continued when sizzling platters hovered with the hiss of rattlesnakes over our table. Parvati seemed overwhelmed by her garlic green beans. Nana leaned over yellow squares of chicken skewered on three steel tongs, while I called for a final and wallet-devastating glass of Chilean white to ward off suggestions that I order a meal or share their food.

"You never eat!" Parvati said as she pitched her fork into the greens. "And this is so good. It's **vegan!**" But I refused a taste, because of the man at the satay bar—you. I wouldn't fill myself, because, as far as I could tell, we were in private conversation somewhere above the tables, in the ether outside the spectrum of visible light.

Problem #2

In fact, the problem that evening wasn't garlic string beans or Nana. In retrospect, it had to be me. Deserting the dinner table, us girls crowded around the bar, angling for a good spot as the jazz singer—a tall, dark woman wearing pearls, beige slacks and a dangling silk shirt—took the mic to her maroon lips and, with a low voice, murmured, "And now it's time, ladies and gentlemen, for a little coooollllll jazzzzz." She smiled, the gloss of her lipstick shimmering as people adjusted in their seats, chatter settling down to a quiet buzz.

At first, there were languid songs, lullabies that relaxed eaters into post-binging dreaminess—songs of love and loss and sadness that trilled on crests and sank below the surface. But by the fourth song, the singer had gained courage, and with her shoulders flung back, her face raised to the spotlights on the ceiling, her eyes squeezed shut, she released a gut-wrenching belt that caused her lips to gyrate, poor acoustics magnifying the peel until it nearly exploded eardrums. Covering blown-out ears and mouthing apologies, Parvati and Nana dashed to the lady's room, leaving me alone with my broken bag, which contained a plastic pouch of Parvati's garlic beans.

Self-absorbed, embarrassed, I gulped a last drop of wine, looking, no doubt, like a dumpling stuck with a toothpick between my eyes. And then you stood beside me in gray shirt, jeans over cowboy boots, the entire ensemble bolted down by a rodeo-champ's belt buckle. It was as if a country of blue hills with a villa on a cliff rested somewhere in your chest, Homer in your brow, and Hamlet in your liver. A Triceratops grazed on the starship exploring your neck. Your lips knew the Mariana trench as you blinked at the singer's pearl-encased throat. Close up, I began to understand the fact that your features were printed on a deck of cards for a game I'd never win.

During a break, as the singer lay down the mic to adjust her shirt, you said, "Your first time here?" Or was it, "first time?" as if we'd just pulled apart after an hour between the sheets. I nodded, yes, a furnace in my chest. Heat rose up my neck to my jaw.

I'd always had trouble hiding feelings. People saw through me. Emotion tumbled like a rider from the back of a horse, flooring me. An old teacher once compared me to Sarah Bernhardt whose face turned crimson when playing "shy" on stage—except I was for real. Everything showed— shame, anger, attraction. Blood gave it away.

"Nice style, but that last piece—" you began, half smiling. My brain felt as brittle as the hair that sprang like hay from my scalp. I knew the blush and my jeans, too tight, accentuated the pimple forming at the base of my nose. But somehow I responded when you asked my name. You repeated, "Jane," as if you'd expected its consonants. Sweating, I asked for yours.

"I'm," you paused and blinked the blink that exposed a lie. "I'm Bill." The name didn't fit—too common, informal, abbreviated. Your name was not Bill, because you seemed uneasy, as if protecting a wound or a gold nugget. You blinked the blink of diffidence, but no one would cross you. Did your real name lie beneath clouds of learned behavior? Yes. Aloofness tightened your gestures, caging you until everything important became an understatement.

"Bill," I said. You blinked. "Nice to meet you—" We'd already met, but how and where? You asked if I'd like a drink, but we were interrupted.

Fresh from the lady's room, Parvati pressed my shoulder with her hand. "It's too crowded—" she barked into my ear. Next to her, Nana smiled, eyeing you and waiting to be introduced. Names followed, and you offered to buy us a round. Stepping towards the bar, you turned first to Nana, asking for her order, your gaze lingering over her exposed and pierced belly button. The fact that you asked her first, that you seemed fascinated by that belly button, is very important—because it determined how I'd view the rest of my life.

She chose a frilly concoction dominated by a nameless soda and laced with liquor—the whole production propped up by a paper umbrella. Next, you took Parvati's order. She stuck with the obvious: A glass of red. "And last, but not least," those words bore into me like a reamer. I don't know why I chose Irish whiskey—no ice—but you seemed interested in my choice, asking, "Are you Irish?"

While you handed around the drinks, I tried to figure out your intention. It should've been obvious, but I saw two versions of you: the first, well mannered and kind; the second, stopping at nothing to feed endless hunger.

You had more questions for me, but leaned towards Nana as you asked them. "Where do you come from?" Was this the question of an innocent, or the question of one too awkward to know what to say?

Of all the people to ask, I was the worst. I'd lived as if not belonging—because hadn't everyone been taught to melt into the American pot—a worldview Ben and I had articulated at Wupatki? I, like everyone else, was a derivative of every ancient tribe that had wandered the earth. Hadn't Nora always said, "We children belong to and come from everywhere," making it senseless to query one's homeland? But I answered, "I'm from many places," my tone imparting, "Dumb question. Why ask?" Which really meant that I wouldn't be purchased for a drink—especially by the kind of man who stared at Nana's belly.

You—the man who called himself Bill—blinked, and then turned to appraise the singer, who once again moaned into her mic. You sipped your Jack Daniels.

Did you step back and turn to Nana, already fed up with me? Possibly. At some point you asked her, "and you? Where are you from?" as if this were a competition to determine who'd be yours that evening. Nana laughed and pushed her beautiful hair behind her ear.

Did you see her as exuding:

1. sexual confidence
2. natural beauty
3. a happy-go-lucky attitude
4. a chipperness that made her armpits sweat pheromones
5. a belly dancer's willingness to roll?

Did these qualities add up to equal perfect one-night stand material? If so, she'd already won. Everything about the way your eyes traveled up her thighs spoke of sex. Your gaze virtually tacked her to an imaginary corkboard bed.

Already, I knew the outcome. We'd never stroll the waterfront of rippling light as the foghorn changed our moods. I'd never hear about the World's Fair. You'd drive off in your Fiat/Saab/BMW, the seat next to you cold, your legs never warming mine, because Nana showed her perfect teeth and flipped her perfect hair, saying, "I'm half Italian, half German," all kid skating an ice pond.

Everything about her yelled, "take me," while I mixed my whiskey with a plastic straw, knowing that nothing about me was subtle or soft—not hair or blush or all those knife-sharp responses I lanced in your direction.

Nana asked, "What about you? Where're you from?"

"My family's half Spanish, half German." That should have clinched it—the common German ancestry like Wagner gluing his never-ending operas to your common ears. The outcome was sealed.

But not entirely, because this was no ordinary meeting, and I still stood inches from your shoulders, sniffing the bourbon on your breath. Somehow, conversation turned to Rio, where you'd hosted Carnivale, said I looked like an attendee. Had I been to Rio? Swirling your drink, this time you leaned closer to hear me. But Nana's belly button pulsed up and down as she laughed at the idea of Rio—a crime trap. Venice was better for costume parties. You sipped booze, stared at her midsection.

That's when I turned to Parvati to ramble about the proposed demolition of the Cinerama. *Why*, I sputtered, *was this institution going to be destroyed?* Which led to the proposed demise of the football stadium. *Why*, I grew flush, *was everything being turned to dust? Seattle*, I couldn't stop myself, *kept destroying itself when it could be a great city*. And then: *If it were me, I'd convert the old stadium into a museum for computer history*. Parvati stared, bored but nodding as Nana reveled under your gaze, divulging the mysteries of art instruction.

But then something happened. It caught me by surprise, like the tenor in Mahler's 8th. You held your tumbler of JD, and I held my Irish whiskey, and your knuckles grazed mine. Skin touched skin, maple syrup melting into sensations that shot through my vagus nerve. Call it orgasm. Call it endless time. Call it the oldest story ever told. Words are pointless. Our breath rose and fell, beginning and ending and finally connecting us beneath a single skin.

But you still stared at Nana's belly. So, I pulled back my hand.

After that, the evening fell apart. Talk liquefied into alcohol, the room twanging like a banjo, a rush of reverse-words bursting like feathers from a pillow the size of the world.

Later, somehow, I landed on the lumpy backseat of Nana's mail truck, whose sliding front door wouldn't shut. Cold air blasted tears down my cheeks. Some part of me knew that my life would never again be the same, because hadn't The Avatar predicted this when Nora gave the phone to him the night before? Hadn't he blown light through the phone, chanting "Sadhu, sadhu, sadhu," finishing up with the prediction that in a few days my life would never be the same?

You didn't follow us out to the street, but stayed at the bar, having accepted my thanks for the drinks with, "You're very welcome." Your eyes stuck to mine a second too long, but I turned away, embarrassed by the stench of garlic string beans coming from my bag. You asked about the doggie bag as I handed it to Parvati. I explained that hospital workers never waste "good food." This seemed a novelty to you, the idea of bagging up restaurant food. It made you smile, even as I wrestled my decrepit, crest-fallen messenger bag over my shoulder.

The mail truck's engine turned over with pops and sputters. I wiped the wet from my face and stared through the windshield with glass eyes. Irish whiskey and Wild Ginger sounded so exotic. *Why had I left?* **Why**—the question got tangled in my brain—**left had I, and you gone where?** Why and where left had I? How go did I?

I'd gone because Parvati had caught Nana's signal: the shake of hair followed by widening sidelong eyes. But I knew nothing about the truth.

The Truth

"Oh my god, that guy—" Nana, overcome, screeched like an alarm clock in the driver's seat. "What a perv—" She hit the gas pedal and the truck jerked forward. Her laughter was pure self-indulgence as she unveiled the information that would pinball through me for years to come. "He actually asked me if he could lick my belly button!"

When I heard this little piece of news, the fact that you'd slipped your email address into her hand, all my notions of "Bill" evaporated. You shrank to the size of a pea. How disappointing. You hadn't turned out to be incredible.

Yet, as we drove away, the sputtering engine in my lungs and night tugging my eyelids, I still felt the pull of you, still felt your knuckles against mine.

"Are you going to email him?" I asked. It was a stupid question.

"Damn girl!" Laughter that never ceased, "Are you serious—" I gazed at the passing, dark storefronts, at a couple holding hands—clearly anticipating sex—at a figure walking alone with face down, hands in pockets. Blinking at that lone walker, I thought of your face, wondering if you might seek me out with a blurb in the *"Missed Connections"* section of *The Stranger*. Because where else did strangers meet, but in print? Or, maybe we'd bump into each other at Pike's Place or on the Burke Gilman Trail. *But why Nana? Why did she have your email address?* Why hadn't you charged after me, grabbed my hand and ordered me to stay. You could have used one of many excuses: "You forgot something—" or "Have another drink," or "Take a walk with me." But that would have required the kind of foresight only found in books.

The Beginning of Nowhere

The next morning, as with weeks to come, I awoke thinking of Bill, anxious to pick up *The Stranger* and browse the *"Missed Connections"* section, hoping to stumble upon "Jane" or "Bill" or, at minimum, "Wild Ginger." For two months I collected the freebie, my fingertips darkened by its ink. Nothing. It was as if I'd never met "Bill."

Again, everyone else had "each other." Again, it was May. Nana and Parvati booked seats on Amtrak for a week of sushi and marijuana bars in Vancouver. My housemate, Evie, who, I realized one morning, perpetually emitted the quasi-lavender/lemon scent of 409, no longer slinked around the spare decor, but stomped in and out of the apartment at odd hours, occasionally leaving postcards from the Lesbian dance clubs she enjoyed between tutoring gigs in the Renton school district. Her chipper goodbyes left me feeling so depleted that I settled onto our single kitchen stool to graze on food I couldn't afford: Shredded Wheat, Melba Rounds, and wedges of highly waxed, slightly mealy Washington State apples.

Finally, sun broiled the sidewalks of the bipolar city, which had begun to slip into its manic phase. Café drinkers traded cappuccinos for frappuccinos and stayed out late for moonbeam hikes through the forests. My weekdays continued to be filled with anxiety as I struggled through two temporary, part-time gigs at downtown firms—both of which only paid minimum wage. By month's end, I had cobbled together enough cash for rent and only rent—which meant a continued, steady diet of cheap food purchased on my only credit card. Most mornings, I downed four to seven oversized irradiated apples, priced at only $2.99 per sack. Occasionally, and only on Friday nights, my bagged salad and Shredded Wheat evolved into a feast of rice, lettuce and frozen vegetables in soy sauce drained from Evie's leftover take-out packets.

I attributed this culinary progress to Evie's matronly presence. When she wasn't darting off to meetings or night clubs, she wiped down countertops, scrubbed the toilet, and prepped square meals—which usually involved two slices of rye, a pile of cold cuts slathered with mustard, and half a jar of sweet pickles. These meals evoked memories of kindergarten, the way Nora used to slice my bologna sandwiches into triangles and sheath them in saran wrap, tucking the wedges into my Wonder Woman lunchbox— whose plastic thermos was always filled with juice. Somehow, I connected Evie's sandwiches to my mother's eventual obsession with nutrition.

Scarfing rice, I pretended not to be lonely or lacking. I plunged into books whose living, dead, and forgotten authors had never reassured me. But distraction had become a salve for monotony and need. If I was aware that my twenties were speeding by, no one could have known. Like every other young woman I knew, I didn't seem to care whether all those eggs spurting from their ovular lairs were fertilized. At my ripest moment, I became my least fruitful, having grown barren—a feeling I couldn't shake, even after my emotional equal, Dan, split town for a friend's sofa in New Orleans, which had usurped Chicago, because the publishing job had fallen through.

A day before his departure, by some miracle, Dan had bumped into me on the way to a used bookshop on 15th Ave, where he planned to sell off his library. Loaded down with bags, he dug out a used copy of Octavio Paz's "The Double Flame: Love and Eroticism" and thrust it in my face. He'd planned to turn it into cash, but thought I could make better use of it.

It turned out that Paz, who'd just died that April, spoke to me. After reading *The Prehistory of Love*, I wandered the city as if I'd scraped my match-like head against the sidewalk. Enflamed, I flickered. The very name "Bill" infused me, as if those four letters ignited all my memories. Everything in my life flickered like an old movie flickering on its reel, because again and again I saw and felt you in the votive light of Wild Ginger, swirling your drink, leaving me on a constant playback loop in which your knuckles continually skimmed mine.

Lost Pioneer

Mid-June, on a Thursday between part-time gigs, I wandered into Pioneer Square. Baskets of flowers hung from lampposts surrounding the Alaskan totem, tourists streaming from ferries, gripping sunhats, digging into backpacks for sunscreen. I envied them. They believed in something as they marched towards storefronts, a toddler crying, hands high stumbling behind his father.

"Nice weather today." This jaded pick-up came from a man a few paces away, his grin almost genuine, though his teeth were too white. "You into music?" he asked, but didn't wait for an answer. "I'm looking for a marketing person for my online music company." He added that it looked like I knew marketing.

Odd that he should choose me out of the crowd. Was I so obviously unemployed? It had to be a pick-up, because I was as far from professional looking as a whale—especially because the cut offs I wore made my unshaven legs look like rotting parsnips. Not that he presented success. His dreadlocks and nose ring didn't jive with his blue button down shirt and khakis, reminding me of a high school student trying to crash a tech conference. During his five-minute interrogation, which focused on what kind of music I liked ("Everything"), how much education I'd had ("BA"), whether I could bang out a press release ("Sorry, haven't done that") and what I did for a living at the moment ("Temping. Part-time"), I felt like I'd been stripped naked. Somehow the resume I happened to be carrying landed in his hands. Pulling out a pair of geek eyeglasses, he perused it, nodding.

Had I always been so hopeless? Could he see the desperation pooling at my hairline? Could he tell that the latest in a line of temp agencies had failed to call me for a third week in a row? Did he know that there was only one part-time job between me and the street, or that I needed an infusion of cash to buy a week's worth of peas to keep me alive? These were boom times and yet, not even the lowly temp circuit wanted me.

So I said "yes" when he offered to buy me a Starbucks frappuccino. We settled on a velveteen sofa and talked about the job and compensation. Eventually, he introduced himself, as if it were an afterthought. "Oh, yeah, so my name's Bill."

What could I think? The name discharged like a rocket launcher in my ears. It couldn't be. If he was a Bill, then I was a flapping hundred-dollar bill lying on a sidewalk overrun with panhandlers. The man looked more like a Rufus or a Ricky than a butchered version of the Norse-derived "William." Even in tech-wear, he had sabotaged the name Bill. But, like I said, I was desperate. So, I stuck around and asked him about funding.

Apparently, someone with deep pockets—a guy who lived for music—was backing the start up—which meant Bill could pay me $11 an hour, plus stock options, but I'd have to start tomorrow. Oh, and I could work from home. All reservations, the very few that I had, flew the coop. What did I need to do to get this job? Bill said, "write some stuff for my website." So I shook his hand and jammed his business card into my pocket.

Doubt didn't crash the party until I got back to Harvard Avenue East, where my headspace settled down to reality next to a box of Shredded Wheat. I sat on the living room floor and wondered, popping buttons of cereal into my mouth, what brilliant nerve cell had fired and made me hand over my resume—the one with my address. I met the guy in Pioneer Square, home to tourists and transients alike. And where was his office? Starbucks? Sure, I had a business card, but anyone could cop a square of cardboard, stagger the name Bill (sans last name) across a black background and materialize a phone number.

Survival instinct kicked in. After a restless night of dreaming of sleeping in a Pioneer Square doorway, I awoke to sweat. Where was this posited hourly rate of $11 plus stock options going to take me? Would I actually write "content" for an online music start-up? Or would I undress for Mr. dreadlocks (dubbed "Bill")? Could I really afford to find out? I picked up the phone and dialed the number on Bill's black business card. I didn't wait for the answering machine to beep, but began blathering about another gig, so sorry, maybe we'd work together in the future, but good luck.

That week I begged for work from a receptionist at the temp firm, but she stammered, "S-sorry. We're shutting down the temp pool for summer. New policy. No new spots 'til October." I freaked.

"What do you mean, shutting down?"

"We're closing for summer vacation—"

"That's ridiculous—" I said. "People don't close for the summer. What kind of firm is this?"

"I don't know. But I know I'm done here at the end of the week." No further explanation.

At this point, the begging began. "Couldn't you tell someone I'm willing to work for minimum wage?"

"I'm sorry," and then, "I have to take another call—"

"But—" She cut me off. I called back. Halfway through her *Hello, this is*— I said, "Look, I really need work. Could you pass me on to—" I gave a name.

She said, "Sorry, — is out," and hung up. This cycled through three more rounds before I threw the phone across the room. With no place to turn, I panicked, running out onto Broadway with flecks of Shredded Wheat clinging to my shirt, thinking to search for a retail position. All I had in the bank was $173.84, and with my mother broke and my father basically dead, what could I do? Float through the month ingesting nothing but water and Evie's packets of soy sauce? Leap off a rooftop overlooking Lake Washington?

<u>Anything But That</u>

In fact, sometime that summer my father was no longer a parolee. After spending much of 1995, all of 1996/97 and half of 1998 in a minimum-security prison feeding victims of Hansen's disease toast and jam, he got through parole and booked a flight for the sunset. I suspected he still had some serious funds socked away in a bank account in the Cayman Islands. But because he never reached out to me after Nora divorced him, I could do nothing more than make phone appointments for conversations that disintegrated into the usual argument about *who* betrayed *who*.

It was better to take anything over begging and conceding failure to a failed man. So, I was overjoyed when I was offered a receptionist position at a HIV/Aids clinic not far from Capital Hill. A week later, I covered phones and did data entry in the miniscule clinic as I tried not to notice nurses drawing blood from sausage-mottled arms. I typed in the names Ben and Bill several times a week.

Every time I typed "Ben," my windowless corner of the windowless room turned into a movie of the taxicab where Ben's face closed in on mine as I ate grapes in a tent to the sound of Rudy's panic. When I tapped the name "Bill," I smelled Irish whiskey and saw a slate gray shirt in a flicker of light that expanded, over time, into a sun. Eventually, Ben and Bill became one unattainable entity—one dead, the other seated on an enormous throne that rose into the ether, higher and faster than the fastest spaceship. How could I ever get over those two names?

By week's end, I knew which Bens and Bills had died (because everyone seemed to be dying around me). After hours of inhaling the remnants of emotion and exhaustion and flatulence, I rushed into the street of fuchsia light blending into the blackness of space. All I could do was walk. In Volunteer Park, I traced the Olmsted reservoir and the Conservatory of Flowers. Then I moved on to Eastlake Avenue North, across Portage Bay until I landed on UW's quads. By July, I'd made this journey a practice, treading the same route evening after evening into the weekend, somehow tracing the same sidewalks as if trying to hold everything in place.

All this time, Mimi remained invisible—though she lived only two blocks away. In mid-summer that changed. I received news of her through an out-of-the-blue call from Mimi's mother, Cathy. "I have so been meaning to call you," Cathy murmured into my ear. "You girls. I'm soooo concerned—" It turned out—no surprise—that Mimi and Todd had fallen, literally and figuratively, into choppy waters.

The trouble began when Todd's business took a dive due to a leaky boat, which had provoked fights—always present but now more violent and prone to leaving scars. When, in late May, Todd retreated to a friend's houseboat on Lake Union, Mimi's apartment, according to Cathy—who'd visited—devolved into ruin, unwashed underwear staggering across the carpet, the stink of days-old salsa and dry pee mingling in the stuffy interior.

"I can't tell you how bad it was when I was there. I'm soooo concerned," Cathy was saying. "She soooo needs to leave Seattle. But no, she's waiting until the fall because of the hotel. She really needs a friend. So if you two could please make up and check in with each other—"

Twice I spotted Mimi on the street, but each time she turned towards a storefront, while I suddenly became engrossed in the flap of my messenger bag. But anyone could see her bangs fell greasy over her once flawless forehead—which now revealed patches of acne that couldn't be ignored from afar, leaving a bad impression. Most disturbing, her expression—downturned lips beneath tired eyes—was that of a zombie. Though her weight had stabilized, all the glumness of the world caved her shoulders beneath the attire of concierge extraordinaire.

Oddly, Mimi's impending departure terrified me. The evening after finding out, I sat in my room, unable to read or think or do anything but gorge on apples.

Within days of Cathy's news, I bumped into Parvati in Pioneer Square. "I'm packing. A friend offered a ride across country!" How convenient, now that JNB had departed for the icebergs of Glacier Bay—or wherever the humpbacks plunged—she, too, was abandoning Seattle. She eyed my messenger bag as if it indicated everything there was to say about defeat. "I started packing last week. I'm shipping stuff to my mom's place. All the furniture is for sale. Do you need a practically new futon?"

"Wow. This is big." I could barely get the words out.

"Yeah. We're leaving as soon as my friend figures out plans." She knew I wanted to know whether JNB had given up on the humpbacks to drive her across country—but I refused to ask.

"Is Nana driving?"

"No. She's staying," she said. "But she's moving into her own place. Oh," she focused on my bag again. "I have a nice desk with 1972-style drawer handles." I declined the 1972-drawer handles, but congratulated her on the decision to leave.

The evenings darkened earlier, and I longed to be far away, someplace where I could sip from coconut shells and lie on palm-shaded verandas backed by aquamarine shores.

"Why are you leaving?" I asked a few days later when we sat on a bench by Olmsted's reservoir, looking out at the Puget Sound, the Olympics as ragged as an old man's profile half covered by a beard of clouds. She shrugged, said, "There's not enough for me here. I need more."

"So, it's back to New York," I said, not wanting to admit the threat of losing another old "friend" to transience.

That evening, I walked straight back to Harvard Avenue East rather than taking the marathon detour to Birk Gilman and UW, desperate enough to phone John-the-glass-blower. But hadn't he left for yet another weekend on Orcas Island to search for wild-grown edibles? Hadn't my lips been usurped by the lips of his most recent starlet, a nameless college student who was taking classes at Pilchuck? Because of the other woman, lately John and I had curtailed interactions to "smash-ins" at the QFC, where he found me next to the apples.

The last time we collided over the Granny Smiths, he went on and on about his success as a businessman. It seemed he'd nabbed an account with Neiman Marcus and now blew high-end Christmas ornaments, sinks, and chandeliers for established techies who slapped him with their checkbooks, adding the un-laughable pun, "blow me away with the unexpected."

After learning of Parvati's plans to leave, however, I had no choice but to coerce John into showing up at the produce section, where he stared at a roll of plastic bags dangling above the lettuce. He seemed more than disinterested—downright bored. After all, he'd moved on to another Greta Garbo. But he still had physical needs, and I knew he'd never reject a blatant fuck. Why else was he there?

There'd been many loneliest of lonely evenings when I'd dialed and he'd picked up, usually with something like, "I got these baubles. Want to see—"

With me saying something like, "Area baubles like boobies?"

And him responding with, "You want to suck one to find out?" followed by, "Give me your lips—" followed by the sound of his truck burning rubber as it parked in front of my building.

No longer feasting on autumn vegetables from his kitchen garden, he usually arrived fully sated and burping. "Give me that ass," he'd say as I fell to the bed, where he squeezed my breasts and butt until everything in between hurt. He'd massage my face, pushing my cheeks and forehead upwards until my mouth stretched to become a sneer of gums. Harshly, he'd rub the glass cinders, tarnish, and scum off his palms and onto my skin until my body felt like a decomposing rag. Each time, the sex became rougher, dirtier—more rape than pleasure.

But that evening, as he dunked in and out of me, never gazing into my eyes but peering at the wall, it hurt so much that I cried for him to stop and pushed him from me. Furious, he grabbed my arm, twisted it behind my back, and shoved me, tangled in blankets, off the bed and onto the floor. Without a word, he stumbled into his clothes and slammed out of the apartment, leaving me stunned and bruised on the carpet, no tears forming—just the knowledge that I felt utterly alone, lost, wasted, banished, desolate, demolished, sunken, and forgotten.

After that, all I could do was call my mother, though I knew she didn't have ears. I cried for what felt like hours, threatening to end it all, ranting like the winds of a blizzard that I couldn't "deal, not for one more second." My mother sighed, not really listening, enduring rather than engaging. In her opinion, I wallowed in melodrama rather than in the creativity of transformation. I, too, she said, using the self-helper's tired metaphor, could sprout wings like a butterfly and flap off to become a better self. I could, *Wake up, pull out of the dark and burst into the light.* But I didn't agree with the idea that the victim must take responsibility and stabilize a world that another had spun out of control.

So, I refused to accept the platitudes, each one dropped into the phone like coins into a slot machine. "Take it one step at a time," my mother kept saying. "Baby steps. It'll all work out...." She followed this up with another self-help diddly culled from The Avatar, who'd moved into an apartment directly above hers. "Bring light back into your life. Look within, not without—" Could she say anything more hurtful?

But then, as if she knew I'd hit bottom, she dug up the right words. She said exactly what I'd been waiting to hear for years, ever since my parents' divorce when I'd been barred from my childhood home. A new line of conversation suddenly lifted me from my spot on the floor, so that I began pacing with flutters in my belly. "One of my roommates," she was saying, "is leaving this fall. Your old bedroom will be available in mid-September."

"Really?" I sang, no longer trying to prove anything. "Are you sure? I mean, is she really moving? That would be amazing—Oh my god. Yes—"

But as I grew more enthusiastic, Nora grew more businesslike. "Rent runs $500. Utilities included. Toilet paper and food are separate. You get a shelf in the refrigerator and a place for non-perishables in the kitchen cupboard." I'd never heard her speak so succinctly.

When I asked if the rent could come down to match what I was paying for the room on Harvard Ave. East, she said: "$500 isn't bad for the City. Isn't that less than you paid before you left?" Explaining that I had exactly $458 in the bank, she interrupted with, "I'm not worried about that. You'll find a job—And, of course everything is furnished."

I hadn't seen my old bedroom in years—which meant I had no idea what to expect. In childhood, the room had been painted canary yellow, a color I'd grown to hate so much that I plastered the floor, walls, and ceiling with artwork and record album covers. But since then, I'd been told the apartment had been overhauled, re-invented with the help of free boxes and thrift shops, spiritually uplifted by southwestern furniture, sisal carpets, and earth tones—which meant that I wouldn't have recognized it had it been featured on the cover of *House Beautiful.*

"Let me know by August 15th," Nora said before hanging up, "or the place goes to someone else."

At first it was all ecstasy over the very real possibility of returning "home." But then, in the following weeks, doubts began to invade—especially on my last hike with the Mountaineers when we took in an alpine lake with its meadow of bluegrass, fescue, Indian paintbrush, and buttercup. The air stirred and the outline of a mountain rested against the sky as if time had just settled down for a long rest. It seemed that the smell of those plants and the touch of wind over the lake would never leave me, so that I mourned their loss. And by the month's end, as clouds passed over the Sound and I thought of leaving, I grew more and more agitated. Because by then, like the alpine plants that kept growing in my memory, I couldn't forget your name.

United
States of Being

The Avatar and The Unfound

"Home is where the heart is."

The Key

 As any traveler knows, a return to one's childhood home is never straightforward. Returns never provide simple solutions. Loose ends rarely get resolved, and expectations always undermine reality. So it was that September afternoon when Jane walked into her childhood bedroom where the framed poster over bleached bedspread, and bamboo desk drawers covered with grains of dust weighed on her more than all the mildew in all the living rooms on and off of Harvard Avenue East.

She'd packed up the Seattle apartment only two days earlier, dumping bedroll, towels, lamps, metal pot, plates, and silverware into a storage facility she couldn't afford. She'd flown six hours, taken the subway, walked her bags up Lexington Avenue, stored them in the earth-toned hallway before testing the rickety futon. She'd used the toilet, washed her face before her smiling mother gave a hug. And then, The Avatar knocked on the door.

Lexington Avenue roared up the stairwell from the lobby below. The Avatar, amid a rush of laughter and high fives, stood in the doorway, insisting with all his baldness that Jane join him for a dinner that overlooked Manhattan and the many bridges of traffic tying together the boroughs.

"Yessssss," he exhaled over city noise. "Tonigh' is special!" After more than twenty years in North America, The Avatar still couldn't handle his "ts," speaking with a thick, indeterminate accent. "You and Nora and a few more. We celebra' at Windows on da Worl'! Da place to fine a new worl'!"

At $100 a plate, The Avatar suggested, the postcard views of the Empire State Building would be perfect. Windows, he added, transformed *everything into everything plus plus plus!* Cash would flow, debt would rise, and the price of a piece of sushi would push the envelope. A single hosomaki roll costing as much as ten grocery bags from the Food Emporium made each grain of rice heavy as an apple, and therefore a thousand times more delicious. This was capitalism's greatest trick.

But Jane thought only tourists draped Windows-on-the-World napkins over their laps. This hardly fazed The Avatar. He waved his hands back and forth with, "Come to dinner. It will be fine! We are all travelers!" Patting her shoulder, he added, "In two hours, we will ligh' the worl'."

He shut the front door only to fling it open a second later. "No, I see someting," he said, looking into her eyes. "Give me your keys and bring me

Nora! I will unlock your heart firs'." Fatigued by the flight and return home, Jane didn't think. She handed over her newly acquired keys, and Nora, who'd been down the hall within earshot, scrambled into shoes, ready to dash after The Avatar, who'd already headed downstairs to join a group of followers in the lobby.

On the way to the Battery, by the 86th street subway, Jane lost the group. She'd bumped into an old friend who couldn't stop talking about her new apartment on Madison. For five minutes, the friend rambled before saying, "Let's get coffee. My treat!" Then it was: "We're traveling to Indonesia next February," and, "My fiancé is buying a second home—" and, "I'm so grateful it'll be in the Catskills instead of the Hamptons!" Jane felt depleted. Sweat trickled down her chest, and her breath stank of the underworld due to the rooibos and ginger tea. Therefore she arrived at the Twin Towers an hour late, concerned Nora would be disappointed as The Avatar and the others stabbed at shrimp cocktails.

In the lobby, far below the floating restaurant, she felt what she'd later consider a premonition. Others would say the same thing after the 911 attacks. But she was certain of her own premonition, because in 1977 she'd visited the towers with Nora, Stan, Mimi, and Cathy. In the plaza, by the black marble fountain, she and Mimi had gaped up at the two dizzying towers, disturbed by the illusion that the buildings were toppling, tumbling upon them. It wasn't just the 1993 bombing that devastated the building's garage, but other premonitions—not only having to do with the Twin Towers, but also with New York, and the man named Bill at Wild Ginger, and her mother, and The Avatar.

Whatever pushed her to approach the elevator, tell the guard that she had reservations at Windows on the World, didn't have the power to push her upwards. The elevator doors opened, but she turned around and walked away, despite a rumble in her belly and the keys The Avatar still had in his possession. The premonition caused her to flee a sushi dinner worth ten bags of groceries. She dashed to the subway, inhaling ionized dust as newspapers and debris blew through the Fulton Street station. She got off the train several miles from her destination, choosing to walk, invisible among college students clacking towards parties, everything blanketed with the odor of rotten eggs, exhaust, and baking bread, so that she stopped only to buy water and crackers near NYU.

At 1:15 AM, she stood outside her old and new home. The second story windows appeared dark, almost laughing at the fact that The Avatar had her keys. She wondered whether Nora would wake to the buzzer. So tired, Jane thought if no one let her in, she'd lie down on the stoop.

The limestone brick building of fire escapes and entablature—

cornices, friezes, columns—had too many gargoyles for happy dreams. They'd frightened away the ground floor flower and stationary shops of the 1970s, and even the gourmet deli of the 1980s, leaving only an espresso and crumpet shop that had the white-linen cleanliness of a spa.

Permanent shadows collected beneath the gargoyles: A childhood of skinned knees from roller-skating into the stoop, a jogger raped blocks away, amid Central Park's cherry blossoms. There'd been midnight fistfights between the panhandler James and another flayed piece of humanity whose face seemed to be peeling. Near those gargoyles Vladimir Horowitz refused to tell Jane the time, and Woody Allen once walked by, arms linked with Soon Yi. Never mind that Paul Newman, looking exactly like the graphic on Newman's Own's salad dressing, once bumped into Stan.

Her parents had moved in during the Carter administration, when no one wanted a three-bedroom, 1.5 bath prewar apartment with parquet floors, because high rises (pleasure gardens of a Jetsons' future) offered balconies, rooftop recreation centers, and no fewer than two hundred neighbors.

But then, the Reagan era arrived. Nostalgia overran the country, making prewar buildings quaint. Rent soared, and the landlord attempted to oust anyone paying less than market price. Harassment ensued. Elevator service, hot water, and heat petered out. "Renovation" became a keyword. Only theirs and one other apartment remained occupied as the lobby and upper floors got sheet rock overhauls and morning drilling spewed suffocating clouds of plaster, inciting lawsuits that led to all-out war between landlord and tenant.

For several winters, Stan and Nora fumed as they huddled in parkas around the oven. In bed, they wore earplugs, never fully able to minimize the headache of midnight jackhammers. For days, rust-tinged fluid drooled from their faucets leading them to bottled water. They boiled baths because the furnace was on the blink. Before doing homework, as her parents bickered and slammed doors, Jane warmed her fingers over the kitchen stove. Nora— somehow Nora persisted, playing the martyr, giving up to appease others, living through the landlord's harassment campaign while trying to ignore her sexually-slippery husband's behavior.

Therefore, it was no surprise that when Jane buzzed Nora's apartment and waited for the chirp of a voice, she heard only static. What else could she do but loiter beneath gargoyles? But she buzzed again and again, punching in a number that gave no response.

Gargoyles All Over Again

Then she remembered that more than one high school chump scaled the gargoyles to rap on her window. Twice the climbing had ended with sirens that drove the gallant climbers into plaster casts for three-months of recovery from broken bones. But because she'd had the longest travel day of her life, she peered up and down the block like a thief.

No bus, no taxi, no delivery truck rumbled by. No one but the desperate wandered the sleepy Upper East Side. The only indication of wakefulness came from a storefront a block away. She'd never known the city to be so quiet. An alarm sounded in the distance, perhaps across the East River or twenty blocks downtown, but mainly all lay still as a noon desert, because the gods ruling night had placed their bets.

She tried the buzzer one last time, determined that if no one answered, she'd take off her shoes. She listened. She took a deep breath, and then leaned down to remove her sandals. At first she considered leaving her socks on to protect her toes. But then she remembered the chumps who'd broken their ankles. Climbing with bare feet would allow her to grip the cool stone more easily.

She'd never scaled sheer rock before, had never sampled the climbing wall at REI. She had no idea how to negotiate a building's facade. But she boosted herself up to a smooth, marble nodule beneath a concrete flower blooming next to a light fixture. If she did it right, she could struggle up to one of the winged gargoyles, and then to the concrete ornament just beneath the window ledge of her bedroom. Had she left the window slightly open? If not, could she somehow edge over to a roommate's window and knock? All this would require good planning and keen concentration, which seemed to be limited. But she had no choice, even as she wavered, dizzy.

She reached for a second concrete bulge, tugging herself up, reaching for something slick and ovular, her skirt hooking onto a hidden protuberance. She wouldn't look down. She wouldn't look sideways. Just up—as at the Twin Towers—to the far off ledge with her mother's air conditioner. That's when a grating noise, like fingernails scratching a chalkboard, burst from the intercom.

Surprise seared her brain, and she slipped. Sliding from the second foothold, she dangled over the metal railing that edged the stoop, everything going blurry with sweat and adrenaline. Fingers aching, her hands slid along the cool stone, and in a flitter of terror, she dropped several feet, nearly breaking a leg against the sharp marble corner of the platform supporting the railing. Mercifully, her foot caught the brass banister rather than the platform. But in the process, she whacked her knee and the back of her hand on something profoundly hard.

Pain hollowed her out, clipping sight, sound, and breath. Eyes shut, she was paralyzed by sensations traveling through her, forgetting the crackling intercom that sounded like a microwave full of popcorn.

She collapsed over her knee, her hand hot against her chest. More squawking that must have been talking came from the intercom, but she didn't respond because blood oozed from her knee, which she could barely bend. And then, when she thought she'd pass out, she squinted at her mother, wrapped in a blue bathrobe, waddling towards the lobby's glass doors.

Nora Lovins had arrived to open the lobby door.

Hinges squealed and a breeze of lemongrass and lavender—the familiar scent of expensive skin creams—lifted Jane's hair. "Come in! Quickly!" Nora said, a hand shielding her gleaming face, hair rollers, and the darkness beneath her eyes—ever aware of appearances, even past 2 AM. If she'd been naked and Lexington Avenue had been full of men, she couldn't have appeared more distraught as she adjusted her robe.

"It's the middle of the night! The buzzer's broken—you have to call first—" Nora seethed, turning her back to Jane's wounds. "Come in," Nora continued in a harsh whisper, more conscious of sleeping neighbors than her daughter. "Where are your keys?" She pressed the elevator button. "I don't have any spares, so don't tell me you lost them." Jane limped into the elevator behind her mother—though the apartment was only one story up.

"The Avatar has them—"

"Oh," Nora said, a hand still fluttering over her face. "Where were you?"

It would take several years for Jane to forgive Nora's lack of concern that night, though physical wounds eventually healed, just as Jane got used to the redecorated rectangle of her childhood bedroom, its single window opening to the same red brick building across the street. But where there'd once been warmth, there now was wheat-hued coolness that changed the light over the lumpy futon and antique wardrobe.

Mornings, she woke up sweating under the sand-colored bedspread, feeling as if she'd dropped like a bunch of smoking sage onto cracked stone. Often she felt as though she'd never really opened her eyes. It was all a mistake—right down to the borrowed slippers she placed on her feet.

An enthusiast of reflexology, Nora loaned her renters special slippers whose insoles sprouted dozens of rubber nodules that were supposed to stimulate various nerve endings in the heel, arch, and toes. After five minutes in the slippers, Jane's nerves exploded as needles attacked her innards, leading her to surmise that foot torture amounted to a kind of control. And yet, for no known reason, she continued to wear the slippers and to sample Nora's collection of befuddling massage tools, also available to renters as a reward for being so easily controlled.

Further, after waking, Jane scurried down the hall in underwear, her bowels backed up, toiletries jangling in her traveling case, only to discover the bathroom occupied by one of the four other renters already waiting in line. Once inside the lavatory of antique floral tiles and tin ceiling, she locked the door and ran the shower until she could relax enough to use the toilet. Days after perfecting this routine, oval patches of acne hatched like fish eggs on her cheeks and chin. Days later, the fish eggs developed into boils that bubbled beneath the skin. In despair, she dabbed the lesions with benzoil peroxide and began avoiding the many mirrors in the apartment's main rooms.

Change was inevitable, but did it need to be so bleak? Where once there'd been an upright piano in the dining room, plywood office furniture proliferated, the surfaces overrun with supplies. In fact, every corner of the dining room hosted office junk: three rickety desks, two rolling chairs that squawked when pushed, a bookshelf absent of books, a fax machine that spat out illegible messages, two gray filing cabinets bleeding paper and file folders, and two outdated phones. Furthermore, throughout the apartment, toner cartridges lived wherever they could: in piles next to doorways, hovering near the ceiling on top of shelves, stuffed in closets where shoes used to be.

The only remaining piece of furniture from Jane's childhood was the mahogany dining table—one that had witnessed too many arguments— where Stan used to ladle out chicken soup packed with peppercorns that made him yell, "Whooh!" until his nose dripped. It prevailed in front of the nonworking fireplace whose mantle still held a pair of tall Chinese candlesticks her parents had acquired at marriage. Such remnants only encouraged stasis and regret.

The morning after Windows On The World, while Jane sat at the dining table, Nora emerged from the pantry wearing her tortoise shell eyeglasses and ill-fitting jeans whose back pockets glittered hearts, the whole look more repulsive for its western-style belt, saying, "You never told me about last night—" Hitching up her breasts was a peach halter top that revealed the bulge of her mid-section and the freckled padding of her upper arms, making the strand of Swarovski crystals clasped to her eyeglasses a ludicrous choice.

Never before had Jane seen her fifty-seven-year-old mother—always prudish in frilly collars—wear an outfit more appropriate to Dolly Parton. Shuffling towards her in this fashion blunder, Nora carried a heaping plate of scrambled eggs and toast, her napkin threatening to float into the oblivion of office supplies.

"Did you eat?" When Jane answered that she hadn't, Nora pursed her lips. "Take some eggs and wheat-free toast from my shelf in the refrigerator."

"That's okay," Jane said. "I'm a vegan, remember?" By now the soles of her feet, confined to the therapeutic slippers, were on fire, causing her to remove each slipper and shove them under the table.

"How do you like those?" Nora asked, nodding at the slippers. Jane shrugged her teen-angst shrug and shut her eyes. "Sorry you didn't make it last night," Nora added, as if an afterthought. "You missed something special—" Nora eyed the discarded slippers and settled onto a squawking chair. "So, the slippers?" She smiled, showing the stained enamel of her front teeth. Again, Jane didn't answer, only massaged her foot, because Nora had a way of persisting when all signs indicated that she shouldn't.

"Next time," Nora said, "I hope you'll come. The Avatar opened a new space last night that was extremely powerful!" She maneuvered fork and knife, catching a lump of egg. "What about some toast? Or an orange? There's one on the kitchen counter. I also have some tea—" Guilt, Jane assumed, had finally prodded Nora to act mother-like.

Biting into toast that left beads of berry jam between her teeth, Nora chewed and leaned forward to press the start button on her computer. Its bell rang like a reproach against the broad hips and ample belly anyone could see Nora hated, because every curve and pucker of her midsection tested the durability of her jeans.

"Shoot," Nora exhaled. "This always happen—" She put down her toast, straightened her back and sucked in her belly. "We ate so much last night! The food was magnificent—but I over did it and now my back." Hands moved from belly to the spot above her tailbone. Kneading the area, she explained that lately everything was giving her trouble. "But," Nora said between grunts, face crumpling in pain. "You really missed something."

"You okay?"

"It's just a spasm. Where's your breakfast?" The chair moaned as Nora adjusted herself, and Jane wandered into the kitchen of brick walls and bookshelves converted to accommodate packaged food, pots and pans, and rolls of paper towels—everything listing to the right where an archeological dig replaced the floor. Layers of chipped linoleum brought back memories of stubbed toes, roach motels, and mouse droppings.

"Hot water's in the pot," Nora called from the dining room. On a shelf, Jane found several boxes of tea. She dropped a bag of mint into a chipped mug of painted roses that reminded her of old women wilting on sofas.

Back in the dining room, her mother tapped the keyboard between nibbles, becoming more and more absorbed in work. This eating in front of computers was a new habit. Nora had always been a meticulous, civilized eater—queen of respectability to Stan's boorishness. Where Stan downed two onion-slathered burgers in five minutes, Nora twirled her fork and knife as if the two were Fred Astaire and Ginger Rogers, every last morsel caught by her tines. And when she finished each meal, there was a profusion of napkin dabbing—first her lips, then her chin—with everything tied up by a session of tooth picking that had become so important to Nora that she once requested a gold toothpick for her birthday.

"Something stopped me," Jane said out of nowhere. She watched Nora's freckled shoulders as they bobbed up and down at typing speed. "I couldn't go up." Her mother hummed in place of reply, tapping the keyboard's letters, which grew into a tangleweed of words that blew across the screen. "So," Jane continued. "What happened?"

Nora's chair screeched as she took up her fork and leaned over her eggs. "Well," Nora began. A flash of pain moved across her face. "Oh no—" She squinted and shook her head, dropping her fork. Jane thought it was her lower back and stepped forward to help. But then Nora grabbed the mouse and slashed through a large section of text. The screen redistributed words, and Nora stared, murmuring, "Who invented this?!"

Like every other morning since her return, Jane left the dining room feeling as if she'd spoken to the air.

Unfinished Conversations Exacerbated by Roommates

There were a lot of people with a lot of problems crammed into that apartment, which didn't help matters. Besides Nora and Jane, there was Juanita, Blaire, and Helena. Blaire was Nora's age, had lived in India for too many years, having left the States distraught after the death of a son from cancer and the loss of her husband to a younger woman. She subsisted on disability payments and therefore chose to sleep on a rollout yoga mat in the living room.

Juanita, in contrast, had arrived from Juarez, Mexico and worked as a nanny. Because she paid less rent than Jane, she was given Stan's old study, a room that compounded depression for its cave-like qualities. Barely a nook, its faded brown carpet was slashed and duck-taped in two spots, its dusted-over windows permanently shut to the alleyway beyond.

Because Helena, the youngest of the bunch (besides Jane), worked as a physical therapist at an Upper East Side gym and made three times as much as anyone else she got the best room in the apartment, and therefore was the happiest. Once a guest suite, her room overlooked Lexington Avenue, its oversized window in its molded alcove ablaze with morning light, the golden walls and walk-in closet with built-in chest of drawers truly enviable.

One evening, when the roomies were out and Jane was stuffing herself with salad and crackers in the dining room, Nora paused over the plate of pasta on her desk, her eyewear refracting the computer's light. "I want to discuss something with you," she began. Disconcertingly her hair, no longer in curling irons, fell to her shoulders in auburn tendrils that rubbed Jane the wrong way for its ditzy, 1977 I'm-a-playboy-bunny aura. This seemed at odds with the Nora of old, who'd been a worshiper of museums, bookstores, and universities, the humanist who'd gravitated towards indigenous jewelry, patchwork jackets, homespun fabrics, and long skirts. "I know," Nora said, looking across the space/time continuum to Jane, "what you think of all this—" She wagged her head at the room.

"All what?" Jane asked, putting down her fork, the mounds of toner cartridges as painful to her as the painful reflexology slippers that dug into her heels.

"Everything," Nora said. "This apartment, the toner business, The Avatar—" Like the apartment, Nora's cartridge recycling business hadn't yet produced a high standard of living, its deficits more pronounced around The Avatar, who ingested everything. But as Nora often said, it was only a matter of time, magnitude, and increasing awareness before the earth and its citizens would shift away from darkness towards the light. Likewise, the more cartridges she recycled, the more solvent the business would become, thus healing the world.

In the face of this saintliness, Jane could only be confused. Sainthood in Jane's America had always seemed akin to martyrdom. Yet the belittling of one's self in the face of others couldn't be praiseworthy. And hadn't Nora belittled herself for too many years?

Slipping back into the reflexology slippers she'd kicked off earlier, Jane loathed the idea of being critical of a woman who'd given up so much for others. But Nora left her no choice.

"Okay. Yes," Jane said. "I hate this."

Nora seemed not to hear, dabbing her lips with a napkin before saying, "We don't have to talk unless you want to. But I just need to say—" She glanced at Jane's feet within the slippers, bringing all attention to the ligaments fanning towards Jane's toes. "You look so thin."

Like every unfinished conversation, missed connection, and unnerving memory, this and only this would stand out. "All you eat is salad. You won't even touch oatmeal. Not a slice of bread or a little peanut butter—" Nora stared at her daughter, chin quivering. Then she swiveled back to her computer and returned to typing.

Could Have, But Didn't

During that period in New York, when she could have been building a career, getting married, and starting a family, Jane squandered a hundred afternoons by circling Central Park's reservoir with a relentless sameness altered only by the seasons, always ending her private walkathon at "St. Patrick's" (or Cleopatra's) Needle in "the self-centered heart" of her day. Once in a while, she detoured to the paths of Shakespeare's Garden—where Ben had once gotten down on a knee and waved his arms wildly to broadcast cheesy lyricism. Less often, she endured a nostalgic trip to the "Meadow," where in high school she'd blown away another hundred afternoons on crappy marijuana, while not fucking a particular boy whose family had lived next door to her mother's apartment for two years in the early 1990's, evidence that she'd trashed her teens and was still mentally trashing them.

But for Jane, time had become a migraine in which the un-fucked neighbor, Ben, JNB, and Bill bled together as one big ball of regret that turned to panic, which shook her awake at night, leaving her little energy to "pull herself together" and thus appear "put-together." Once again, she failed to get a temporary job. No one wanted her rosecea or her stained teeth. No one could stand the odor of dry soap emanating from her hands—or the singed remains of her hair, or the bruised colors of her outdated wardrobe. When they saw her resume, they assumed she couldn't stick with anything— not a job, not a city, not a friendship, not a lover. To everyone she seemed as flimsy as an invertebrate without its shell—a pink blob minus a backbone and therefore the epitome of a glass-half-empty personality.

Evenings she slumped in bed, catatonic after gorging on a bucket of steamed vegetables. She never sought company, because her walks along 5th Avenue continually plunged her, like a water-boarding victim, into memories.

It didn't help when, one February morning, Jane entered the dining room to find The Avatar, seated and murmuring in Nora Lovins's ear. The computer flickered in the background as his finger traced one of Nora's bare shoulders. He seemed riled up but secretive, his expression jazzed as he leaned forward in a swivel chair, eyes wide as cartoon cyclones, his bright teeth scintillating against his bald pate. Showing little surprise, he turned to Jane with, "Gooooo' to see yoouuuu, JJJaannne—" elongating the words in his habitual way.

When she first met him, Jane found it difficult to understand his extended vowels and dropped d's and t's, as if "goo" for "good" were a baby's language, the "donn" for "don't" pushing certain vowels into his sinuses and leaving her flummoxed. But she finally understood The Avatar as well as she understood her father—which wasn't saying much—though she surmised that much of what The Avatar said hovered in the realm of metaphor, as when he held up a finger and announced, "You moo through a door and fine the opening!"

He wore belted jeans, black sneakers and an expensive button down shirt—mango—with the sleeves rolled up to his elbows. The only sign of a health problem was the appearance of pregnancy at his midsection, shortness of breath during excess activity and, under certain lights, intense pastiness. But such qualities only added to his "guru" mystique.

"You look sooo niiiiccce!" The Avatar sang as he rocked back to make the chair squawk, raising a hand to receive a slap. "This woman," he said, nodding at Nora's curling-iron curls. "She have save me soooo many tines! She does everythin' for me." Nora, whose glasses had slipped down her nose to unmask the dark circles beneath her eyes, smiled.

"I don't know about that—" she said. "I just do what I can." In February, the tank top she wore was unsightly over her drooping shoulders, which resembled melted putty.

"Nooorrrraaaaa. Baaabyyyy!" He smiled, "This is hoooww she plays, like she have no future or passs'. A real bbbaaaaabbbbyyyyy!" The Avatar's nasal tones fired into the room, laughter terminating in a groaned, "Baaabbbyyyy!"

In charge, he nodded at Nora, speaking in the third person. "You cann' belie' how much this Nora does—Noooo-bbboooodddyyyyy!" He jabbed two Yoda-like fingers into Nora's ribs, causing her to hiccup, pain crumpling her forehead. "Without Nooorraaa bbbaabbbyyyy, noooo-bboooodddyyyy this wouldn't be!" Nora's eyes glittered with tears. She set down her pen, the backs of her hands causeways of blood vessels that braided up her forearms until they became embedded in thicker tissue.

"So kind of you," Nora said, bowing to The Avatar, always believing in the unbelievable. "It's so good to have you here."

Fuming, feet on fire, Jane flicked off the reflexology slippers she'd stepped into at the door. "Mom. You've said that a thousand times—"

"It's just so great!" Nora said, gazing at The Avatar, who smiled, nodded, and slapped his armrest with an open palm.

"Nora is my little baaabbyyyyeee!!" He said. "Noraaaa!" He lifted himself, catching his breath as he leaned against a pile of cartridges. "Jane. Tonight you haaww to come to dinner—I tol' Nora to bring you. A feast tonight! All my students will be there. And goo' wine!" His too bright smile disappeared as he chewed the inside of his cheek. "Come!! There will beee many." The Avatar's habit of repetition grated on Jane as much as the way he clapped Nora's shoulder. "We will haawww soup. It will be soooo niiiiiccce— the little Nora and the big Nora!" He raised a hand for another high five, coercing Jane into slapping it—though she only wanted to eat alone.

<u>Dinner</u>

And why hadn't she stayed home to watch *Contact* instead of join the others upstairs? Did the reluctant journey to The Avatar's sofas surpass Jodie Foster's contact with aliens on Nora's ten-year-old TV? Did SETI's search of deep space have anything to do with the fact that The Avatar's feng shui apartment was a futuristic version of Nora's rent-stabilized husk downstairs?

All she could absorb upon arrival was Vangelis's *Blade Runner* theme music that later turned the open kitchen into a dystopian spaceship of granite countertops and bowls of plastic grapes, pineapples, and passion fruits, every glass and piece of silverware shimmering like jewels under recessed lighting. Night siphoned streetlight glow into corners, airlifting the deprived to a spiritual plateau that resonated with the clean and deathless abodes of the ultra rich.

Chatter crashed into the sound of knives whacking cutting boards as several people avoided collision in a kitchen ruled by "red tongue" chicken, "chili speckled" pork loin, and The Avatar's own "dirty soup" made with ginger, red pepper, and a "secret ingredient" that caused lips to boil and noses to run. As guests chopped, shouting jokes that turned laughter into hysteria, the red pepper became airborne, sparking something in Jane's throat and causing her to double over, coughing while Nora, transported to the land of the "selfless Self," pulled metal folding chairs out of a closet.

The Avatar's voice rang as he emerged from his bedroom, stumbling into the kitchen, breathless and holding up his palm for slaps with that, "I know who you are," gaze of an established guru. "Heyyyyeee!" He chanted, chewing the side of his cheek as he appraised a blond. "Marriaaaaa!" he murmured. The blond giggled and slapped his raised hand. "I see. You are here! Here you ARE! And who is here is here to hear the best!!!" Laughter, giggles, more high fives all around.

The Avatar joined the crowds in the kitchen, and everyone began chopping and gazing, gazing and chopping.

"Buuurrlll!" The Avatar shouted, slapping the shoulder of a broad man whose shaved head echoed The Avatar's, though his seemed only marginally larger than his nose. Burl bowed with hands pressed together, whispering a prayer. "You have met Nora Baaabyyyy here," The Avatar said. "She know how much I li'e to chop!!!" The Avatar grabbed Nora's knife mid-chop in order to take up slashing carrots.

"Yes," Burl said, still bowing, as everyone stood silent, watching, enamored. "We met just minutes ago. We talked about your new video!" Bits of carrot from The Avatar's chop-chop flecked the air, one hitting Burl's chest.

"Youuu haaww' never seen anyting like this!" The Avatar said, flicking carrot rings from the cutting board into a bowl. Then he pulled a yellow onion from a basket and held it up so that the students crowded closer. A concentrated hush overcame the apartment as The Avatar took a chisel-ground blade from the knife block, gripping its black handle as if to behead. Expertly, he flayed the onion with a single flick of his wrist, revealing its pale body. With lightning speed, he slashed its flesh, hara-kiri-style, the apartment echoing with steel striking wood, fingers receding as the vegetable shrank to slivers and released an invisible spray that induced tears in anyone standing within ten feet. Pale ball a shredded pile, The Avatar released a last bit of onion, his knife leaping into the air. "This is wha' we dooo here!!!" he cried as Burl bowed again. "You are the onion. I am the knife!"

Food demonstration over, The Avatar made his rounds, dipping an index finger into pots whose concoctions bubbled like lava, licking and sometimes double-dipping before shaking in more cayenne pepper.

The Avatar, as spice evangelist, was relentless. Addicted to "zing," he despised blandness, insisting that enlightenment depended upon a hot tongue. During meals, he lectured on the importance of conflagration. No reason was given as to why students should subject taste buds and gut to fire. Instead, all were told that an understanding would come in time.

When The Avatar ladled curried chicken onto a pile of rice, Jane began to feel ill. When he stabbed a piece of pork loin, prodding it into center position like a pregnant woman on a doctor's table, she nearly doubled over. Taking a bite, he nodded and looked around the table. The others hadn't yet filled their plates, and the seats were empty. Soon one, then another, settled down with food, Jane swooning but building a hill of rice she didn't intend to eat. She ladled out some "dirty soup" only when The Avatar glared at her plate, nodding and pinching a slice of pork with two greasy fingertips before stuffing it between his slippery lips. But throughout the meal she could only pick at salad and nibble bread.

In the aftermath, Nora burped into her fist, regarding the mustard-hued slurry on her plate, and murmured, "I ate too much!" But one of the students was coming around with a platter of cookies, and The Avatar had pushed back his chair, saying he must go to his room, that he'd be back.

"Would you like some?" The student asked, presenting the tray of cookies. "The Avatar has requested that we each take one and enjoy!" Overeating at The Avatar's bidding equated embracing abundance. *You live in abundance!* The Avatar often said. *And you live in joy! Neber let yourself live less than you are!*

"I hate to waste food—" Nora said, smiling at the platter. Jane watched as her mother took two cookies and nodded thanks.

"Everyone should take one—" The student said, offering the platter, cookies resembling miniature, dried cow pies. Reluctant but wanting to avoid a scene, Jane pawed a brown paddy and slipped it into her pocket. Nora chewed the cookies as if belts didn't exist, her lips reddening. Simultaneously, it seemed, everyone realized that the cookies had been laced with The Avatar's favorite secret ingredient. But no one gulped water or coughed or got up from the table to find a bathroom. All simply kept munching, some even cramming entire cookies into their mouths as if they'd never tasted anything better.

"Eat rice to squelch the fire—" blurted the man named Burl. He sat grinning in the chair across from Nora, absorbing the struggle of others with his small eyes. He leaned forward and said, "water doesn't work." Nora, eyes tearing, blinked at him wordlessly, spice exploding the connection between tongue and brain. Bowing baldness, Burl advised, "Remember," tapping his fork against his plate. "This too will pass—"

A pause settled in the room like a threat, but Burl extended his hand across the table, gripping Nora's. "You can do it!" And then he reached for Jane's. "I know what this is—" he said.

Thereafter, Burl, like a gorilla, took up where The Avatar left off, lecturing on the origin of spices, their healing properties, how heat aided circulation, how cumin killed parasites, how turmeric healed wounds, how this last supper of spices spawned the dawn of perspiration. "It's working. You're sweating out toxins," Burl proclaimed, though time had stopped for Jane, who hovered at the edge of a black hole where people were stretched beyond the proportions of their actual selves, and Burl's neck and chest reminded her of Bill—though Burl's face lacked definition and didn't inspire gravitas. On the other hand, Burl's CIA man quality was fascinating, despite the fact that it seemed his pituitary gland had dealt him a bad deal. He had to be a secret agent, because somehow he'd gotten the others to clear his plate, which took a certain mastery of dynamics.

She settled next to him on a sofa, guessing he was in his late forties/ early fifties—hard to tell, noting that he avoided elbow nudging and shoulder grazing.

"Rice is an opiate," he murmured. She smelled the curry on his breath. "Starch is better than water for putting out fires! And forget about Coke. Don't you agree, Sir?" The Avatar stood over them, leaning on the sofa back, and staring down at Burl's head. "Serious, dude—" Burl gibbered with an airy laugh. "When I was in Indonesia, it was the rice that saved me from total destruction!"

"Yah, yah—" The Avatar nodded faint disapproval, chewing the inside of his cheek, distracted as his hand caressed his pregnant belly.

Then, as if waking, erratic as a toddler, he threw himself down on a nearby chair, animated and snorting semi-laughter. "NO, BURL!" All chatter in the apartment stopped. "You should haaww' eaten TWICE as much spice— It would have giwen you an unbeelieeevable experience—" It was as if The Avatar had entered a monastery and unveiled a sex toy. "The spice of life!" The Avatar roared, taking back the center of the universe. "This is wha' you wan'—but when it arrives you canno' take it!!!!"

For the next hour, as The Avatar spoke, the students became as still as the painted figures in the Sistine Chapel. The apartment swooned as everyone, except The Avatar, discreetly fought overblown guts. Again the sofa was a squeeze, chairs scraping the floor as The Avatar garnished his speech with dramatic gestures and demonstrations, turning to the blond named "Maaarrriaaa" sitting at his knee and telling her to shut her eyes. He rubbed his palms together. She shivered. He blew on her forehead. She gasped. He flicked fingers over her eyes. Her head fell back. He clapped his hands. She giggled. He held a carnation to her heart. She gazed ahead like a mute.

Revelations, tears, lights danced before eyes until The Avatar barked, "RISE." Jane, aware that a gaseous snake circulated through her, could barely stand. But somehow she managed, tense as more chairs scraped against sighs, heavy limbs made heavier by retained water. The rumpled group acted as one, backs dripping perspiration when The Avatar murmured, "Close your eye and hum *mmmmmmm*."

Eyes shut, Jane began humming, but stopped when a paralyzing pain lurched through her bowels, gaseous snake so coiled it might rip her open. But she would not move, struggling to focus, wanting nothing more than to crawl into the bathroom, roll into a fetal position, and submit to wind. She concentrated on Burl's *mmmmm*, which resonated against her own, and Nora's lavender hand lotion, which wafted by on a draft of sweat.

The sermon finally ended when the blond woman named "Maarriaa" bawled in a corner, others pressing their hands together and gazing at The Avatar. At last, Jane snuck into the bathroom, thinking no one would notice. When she returned to the sofa to slide in next to Burl, everyone in a circle around The Avatar's black armchair, she was reminded of *Duck Duck Goose* in preschool. "You have released energy—" he announced, staring at Jane. "You are in fear and unworthiness—" She blinked. Had he spoken of her gut? Did *he know*?

The lights dimmed. Darkness fell. The sound of "*mmmmmm*" reemerged from invisible throats. On the sofa, Jane watched the outline of The Avatar flicking his fingers at the room as if dispersing handfuls of fairy dust. This went on for some time, the *mmmmmm* reverberating off walls, everything swaying. But then a loud clap shuddered through the darkness and The Avatar shouted, "OPEN YOUR EYES!"

The lights shot up, and the startled group ceased to moan. He stood in the center of the circle, beaming teeth, shaking his finger at one person and then another. Slowly he said, "Da… Spice…. Of…. Life…Is… Now…. All…. Yours!" With that, he stepped forward, bending down to whisper into Nora's ear, and then into "Maaarrriaaaa's," before leaving the circle. Wordlessly, he took Maria's hand and led her down the hall to his bedroom.

Nora remained on the floor, swaying in the aftermath. Next to her, a man stood with head bowed, hands high in prayer position. Others wandered, silent, into the kitchen to wash dishes. On the sofa, Burl stared at Jane, his small pupils like acupuncture needles. She rose, still embarrassed. "Well," he said, bringing his fingers together over his balls. "Thank you for initiating an amazing evening!"

"Initiating?" Jane asked, half aware of the elderly woman sitting on a nearby stool, dabbing her eyes. "What do you mean?" She'd done nothing. She'd merely needed to release air.

"If you hadn't spiced things up," Burl winked, "we wouldn't have gotten that amazing experience. That guy is like, shit—" shaking his head. "Scuse my French—he leaves me vibrating. And I didn't even get your name."

"Name?" Jane asked, the idea of a name as absurd as the idea that stomach trouble could initiate the sublime.

"Yeah. What do people call you?" He was laughing, thrilled by his own ability to gab. "Man, what a dinner—" He hiccupped, fist to chest, and then stretched out his legs, patting the cushion next to him. "Sit. You're making me nervous. And don't think I'm not noticing that you STILL haven't told me your name." She didn't sit, but placed a knee on the sofa's armrest furthest from him.

"What's a name?" She said, looking down at his broadness, imagining what Bill would look like if he rested on the same sofa.

"Man," he said, shaking his head and scratching the shorn scalp above his ear. "More puzzles—" He allowed his arm to fall against the sofa back. "You're going to make me guess—"

"Names don't matter," she said, and he raised eyebrows so blond they were almost invisible.

"Yeah, well, that's a matter of opinion. So, what's your mom call you?" They were in a movie. They were talking about nothing because there was nothing to talk about.

"It's rains in Spain," she said. "Guess."

"So now I have to sing?"

"Right. So, my name is…"

"Jane," He said. "Where's it raining in Spain?" She was surprised he'd figured it out. "Good to meet you. Can we find out more?" She got up, walked over to the dining table. She fingered a bowl of rubber bands, beads, and dimes lying next to some eyeglasses. She grinned at the students mutely washing dishes, aware, even with her back to him, that he'd followed her holding a stray tumbler.

"Ever been to—" He began, his voice near her ear. He leaned against her, reeking of metal and sweat, and laid the tumbler on the kitchen counter where several students wiped down dishes. "Indonesia?"

"No." Only idiots or two year olds answered men who breathed down their necks. But she intended the word to mean more, because he seemed to like challenges.

"Well, you don't know spice until you've been there—"

"I've eaten plenty of Asian cuisine—" She stepped away, half turning. If she didn't look up she could fool herself into thinking that she stood next to Bill at Wild Ginger. "What is it with exoticism?"

"You won't know till you've been."

Expecting the Unexpected

Because Jane "dodged the slumber party" at The Avatar's apartment, preferring to slip downstairs where the heater pipes knocked until 4:00 a.m., garbage trucks jerking up the street as they digested the city's trash, Nora was pissed.

"Do you realize," Nora seethed, "what an honor it is to stay? Do you know how many people would give their right foot? He wanted to show you a special light!" Jane's stomach hurt, though she lay in bed. "How many times does an incarnation of Vishnu offer a trip to Mars?"

She didn't want a trip to Mars. She wanted none of it—couldn't stand the constant struggle against the vacuum cleaner of falsehoods that sucked up the last bits of her will. So what if The Avatar had offered a night of light? She'd heard too much drivel from that fool, Burl (who turned out to be "building a city out of sand," whatever that meant). Worse, turned out that Burl would be stopping by.

Already mid-morning, Nora leaned against the doorframe, looking ridiculous in her spotted bathrobe, her hair in knots after a night in a sleeping bag.

"Why did you say he could come?" Jane asked, curling into fetal position.

"I don't have time for this, Jane." Nora's face exuded exhaustion and fury. "He's coming over." She adjusted her robe. "That's all I know. I'm just bearing the message. He'll be here in half an hour." Wasting no time, she slipped down the hall towards the bathroom.

"Oh. I see." Jane called, propping up against her pillows. "Run along and avoid taking responsibility." Throwing herself into pin-needle slippers, Jane stumbled towards the locked bathroom door, knocking. "Can I at least wash up?"

"Just a minute—" came Nora's voice, Jane's feet numbing in the horrible slippers. Moments later, Nora opened the door with, "You can shower while I shave."

"So couldn't he come by later?"

"He almost came down with me, but I told him to wait." Nora's voice sounded pinched, her neck and shoulders taut with rage. "Don't involve me." Standing at the sink, Nora flicked hair from her face, appraising herself through an ancient pair of glasses—the ones that glared at Jane that time Mimi insisted a Barbi Doll had ransack the "pharmacy"—a.k.a. the toiletry cabinet.

Five days of gray skies lay ahead, clouds circulating over the mess of Lexington Avenue, panty hose and heels and job listings, placement agencies ignoring Jane's resume, the week already no better than a brick wall. Jane had no time for visitors with self-help talk. But what choice did she have when Nora looked livid?

Avoiding eye contact, lips pinched beneath deliberate blinks, as if foulness had entered the room, Nora pulled out a pink tube and drew a line over her lips. Wordlessly, she brushed rose onto her cheeks while Jane brushed her teeth, and tried to disregard the cold shoulder by focusing on the acne running across her chin—made worse by Nora's haughtiness coming through the mirror.

The enormity of feeling between them—the Quantum spookiness that linked them—no longer seemed interesting. Instead, there was only sorrow and a list of aphorisms they might repeat every time they thought of each other. Nora had never hidden the fact that she was jealous of friends with grown daughters who owned businesses or headed departments. When conversations turned to those daughters—one at the pinnacle of a prestigious law firm, another chief executive of a major advertising company—Nora squinted, nodding, as if struggling to force down a tasteless meal. *How nice to have a daughter with accomplishments beyond schooling.* But this lost soul, Jane, had always been lost. And there was nothing Nora could do, except appraise and then avoid the thin frame and bleached hair of her daughter—that universe of disappointment.

Rubbing cream on her veined hands, Nora didn't ask why, but could already perceive the bleak outline of her daughter's future. In the bathroom, Nora suspected her daughter of wasting countless opportunities—flirting with men like Burl instead of finding more promising bedrooms, like The Avatar's. But whatever Nora saw in her daughter that morning sank into fatigue.

Exhausted, the mother put down her comb and said, "That man. He's overwhelming." It wasn't a joke. The faucet ran and her eyeglasses glinted. Anyone could see that Jane had undermined Nora, who'd given up everything for her daughter. It was hard to understand how a post-feminist era woman living in one of the wealthiest cities in the world, holding a decent degree, was devoid of career and husband. Here was a daughter who faulted others but who buckled in the face of self-appraisal. Here was a daughter who pretended to be concerned but hurt others. "I really don't understand," Nora spat, "why anyone with a head on straight would talk to that man—"

"What don't you understand?" Jane asked, pulling a towel from her shoulder. "I talked. He talked. We joked." Secretly, she agreed with Nora. *Shockwave* was the word Jane had woken to in the middle of the night. It was true. Burl bulldozed over conversations with his loud hee-haw laugh. He blistered everything he rubbed up against. You could see it in his sun-reddened skin, smell it in the hot air coming off his chunky forearms, and sense it in his weird, hairless gorilla build. The man created shockwaves everywhere he went, like when he barreled into The Avatar's bedroom, enthused by some joke he wanted to share, where anyone could have told him he'd find the blond named "Maaarrrriiiaaaa" kneeling, topless in a thong.

"Jane. You're a grown woman. Do what you want—" Nora said, turning heavy thoughts towards the medicine cabinet. She hadn't wanted to over protect her child, but Jane had always been a sylph, a constant source of worry. And now, too many things required attention—including The Avatar. Because Burl's little joke and habit of barging into bedrooms had caused a public relations mess that could only be smoothed over by an expert. And who might that expert be? Who wore a nun's face and spoke like a librarian? *Burl needed to shut his mouth.* Because who was expert enough to convince him of this fat fact? Who cooled down heated situations? Who else, but Nora who had already instigated her plan.

Without a word, Nora left the bathroom.

Later

But she had no choice. She had to play the gracious mother and say, "Well, it's so nice of you," because Jane loitered in the bathroom like a spy sweating over the poor decisions of the previous evening. "Jane?" Nora called down the hall. "Burl's brought you something! Come out!"

"Just a minute—" The girl still wore only a t-shirt—no bra, how could she be so flagrant—a floozy dashing to her bedroom.

"Nice space here for a Manhattan apartment," Burl was saying. He had the stringent breath of the self-absorbed. "Not dinky like most. The Avatar's looks smaller. And they took out his walls, which is saying something. It's the long hallway." He peered around, and Nora could tell he ached for a tour. But she motioned towards the car-wreck-of-a-sofa, and he fell onto its torn cushions.

"I do my own floor plans, so I know space," he barreled on, oblivious to the lump of his crotch that drew Nora's eyes. "And I'm talking for each and every project I oversee. Never took a class, never paid a dime, just got in there and learned on the job." Nora chirped *how nice for you.* He laughed false modesty, waving a hand, and then jerking his head around the room. "So, she coming? I got to get a move on. The Avatar wants me, and I think you, to go to some kind of pastry dig downtown—and then he wants to do something solo with me and Maria." Nora could feel the barb of Maria's name digging into her side, but would avoid speaking of the thong incident until Jane was out of earshot.

To the hallway, Nora called, "Jane!" then, "She should be coming—" Again, "Jane! We're waiting!" Down the hall, behind Burl's head, Jane stood in the shadows with raccoon eyes. "Jane. Either come out or tell him you don't want to see him. He's leaving and wants to give you something."

A war cry in her eyes, Jane tripped like Raggedy Anne into the living room, shouldering past Nora. Acne climbed her cheeks, but Burl shot up from the sofa and laced fingers in front of that bulging fly.

"Here's the woman. Out of hiding!" Burl boomed. "Rise and shine, young yogini!" He grinned, dipping his small head in a bow. "So I was saying to your mom how much I want to give you something. Last night we talked Indonesia. So, I've got this item." Burl dug into his pocket like a man at a peepshow. "Something I've carried since back in the day— I've got a few of them, so don't make a fuss. I knew when I saw you," Burl grunted. "This had to be yours." In a flutter, he yanked out a bulb of white tissue paper. "Middle of the night, I woke thinking, what the fuck did I do that for? I should of given this to her after dinner—but all that stuff was going on—" His neck was enormous, like Mr. Clean's under his smile. "So!" He thrust the wad into Jane's hand, and she unwrapped it without a word.

Beneath the paper stood a miniature red and gold statuette of a winged creature. "That's Garuda— Vishnu's buddy." Burl said, nodding at the details while Jane eyed the object, barely interested. "This bird aids the guy who sustains me, so I think of this one as a must-have item. My good luck charm for you." He stared at Jane as the painted bird wobbled in her hand like Jerzy Kosinski's horror.

"Thanks—" Jane said, thankless as always.

Still Later

Later, Jane struggled over whether to keep the charm or trash it. She asked herself how she could have spent more than three minutes with the man. From the start, she'd wanted nothing to do with his Garuda. She didn't care about Indonesia. She distrusted his motives when he said, "yogini." Yet, she allowed him to stick around, wanting Nora to admit that as a paying renter and adult Jane had the right to make her own choices. And yes, she was comforted by the simplicity of Burl's mind and the gregariousness she didn't need to supply, because she had nothing else to do, half-believing all his swill about travel, money, fine living—despite the fact that his fingers were too large.

Lady Tattoo In Central Park

All week, Burl barged in, got comfortable on the ripped sofa, spreading arms, displaying hip-handles and nipples in his newly acquired black spandex T-shirt tattooed with a silver pirate's skull. He jiggled tumblers of ice, "edu-macating the gals" about Vegas, and most definitely lapping up the yogini, Jane. And thank Vishnu, the "madre" excused herself, slinking into the dining room to sniff her cartridges, leaving Burl to bare his soul to yogini—as he did on a walk through Central Park.

He'd invited Jane to tango down the paths beneath bare branches because he wanted to, "kiss a bombshell in the world's most romantic park!" And because he'd been to the city only twice, once on a class trip and once with his satanic **Ex**.

"Young chumps don't know hard." They stood by the reservoir, the water as silver as the sky. "Then they get married," he said, nauseated by the thought of Suzie, how she'd nearly scratched out his eyes at the Central Park Zoo. "No way I was going to let a woman make or break my reality!"

Who knew what set Suzie off—maybe an over-salted pretzel, or the coins Burl dropped into some clown's hat. Whatever it was, she turned loony on him with, "What the FUCK do you think I want? Your open ASSHOLE?" and, "Don't FUCKIN' tell ME what to do, you SONUVABITCH!" while the sea lions barked and parents slipped by covering kid's ears. At some point, Suzie had launched herself at Burl, jabbing her dart-like nose and twig-like fingers, cursing his sorry ass, her pale face contorted in a flurry of black hair, fierce but thin voice causing the animals to howl, chirrup, and rush back and forth in their pens.

The torrent of spit—eventually broken-up by a cop—left Burl defeated, head in his hands while satanic Suzie continued to abuse him, slashing her sharp nail across his cheek, causing a line of blood to pearl during the solo cab ride back to the hotel. Remembering, he gripped Jane's hand, aware that the girl shivered—despite the 60-degree temperature— under swaying branches, wind blowing up their nostrils, making boogers run. He wanted the tissue in his pocket, but no, he would have a kiss and it would be better than Satan. "It's all real," he said, ending the story. "Actually, I hate New York."

Burl found Manhattan confusing, polluted, and stuffed with shirts who thought too much of themselves. "Only four things worth visiting. You, The Avatar," he ticked off on his fingers. "The park, and—" that one other thing on the island of trouble—"Trump Tower. Pure gold parked on a corner," as if Fort Knox wasn't wasting away.

Next day, he revealed Lady Tattoo. This time, by the reservoir, they stared through chain link fencing at the Upper West Side skyline. "Love of my life. Right here, over my heart," he said, pounding his chest. Wind rushed at them, but he lifted his shirt where his nude blond lived next to a freckle on his left pectoral. "It's you—" he said, grinding a smile. "Fucking crazy! My tattoo is you!" Joggers flitted by, a few glaring, but he kept the shirt up.

Before it was needled into him, he doodled for hours, imagining the woman he wanted. "I finally got something together, took it to the artist." And ended up with a figure that never failed him. Who needed Viagra with a woman like that? Tits the size of balloons, waist small as a waif's. But it was the hair, the short, perky, blond wisps that he liked best. "It's you," he kept saying, though he hadn't yet stripped yogini. "Weird," he said, shaking his head, staring as if he could see through the padding of her jacket. Fucked up, because he imagined her as a girl, too, walking among the honeysuckle, chewing milkweed.

"When we get somewhere, I'm going to rip off your clothes," he breathed, closing in on her lips. She stepped back, but he tapped his chest. "Right over my heart!"

He'd always be tough, paunchy, crass, bald, old enough to be her daddy talking too much about satanic Suzie getting screwed in her grave. But he knew how to fuck, and he knew money. And that's what women wanted.

"You're coming to Vegas. I'm flying you out— You won't want to leave." She'd done nothing but listen, and that was enough for him.

Jane and the Garuda Man

When the plane touched down, she slowly gathered her bags,

welcoming delays, exhausted from more than the flight. Passengers shuffled forward while all she could do was contemplate stowing away in the airplane's engine. Desperation drove people to extremes. She'd read about a guy who'd made it home after three and a half hours chained to landing gear where, at 30,000 feet, he'd shivered, blacked out, but then revived to semi-consciousness after the plane taxied to the gate. How hard was it to become a refugee?

But in the end, she walked the aisle.

Barely a month after meeting the "Garuda Man," there she was in glitter, light, and slot-machine hell, slipping onto an air tram, hating but fascinated by the beam of light shooting star-ward from the Luxor, the "Big Apple" skyline, the Eiffel Tower whose height reached less than one third of the real tower in Paris. Would she gawk at The Bellagio's famous chandelier—especially because its glass had introduced her to John Jones? Strange that Burl timed the trip to coincide with the grand opening of the "world's most spectacular casino!"

Like a pinball, she slammed into the aircraft-hangar sized baggage claim where electronic billboards burst the capillaries in her brain, causing her eyes to tear. She had trouble breathing, rattled by ads for spas promising deep-tissue torture and plates of lobster tail, the eerie glow of liquor bottles morphing into dancers kicking legs that killed.

Breathless, she stared as Blue Man Group's toilet paper engulfed an audience, Cirque de Soleil's humanoids contorting into donuts that rolled across a stage, lions and tigers leaping through rings of fire uplifted by Siegfried or Roy. More eye-candy rose to the stomach-curdling lullaby of never-ending pops, twangs, and bells. Almost beautiful, almost ethereal, the spinning sound of winning and losing was hypnotic and addictive. Coins dropped or did not, but the electronic chant kept asking the same question: Why work when you can amass, deplete, amass, deplete wealth with the flick of a wand?

Weighed down by luggage, no place to go, she idled at a bench, watching the back of a man about Burl's height. He loitered at a carrousel, bald, same broad neck and deliberate gate. But then, he turned, all black eyebrows, mole, and puffy cheeks—right out of The Godfather, leaving her to wonder, "what if Burl never shows?" She had only $56 on her—barely enough for a taxi, never mind a hotel. It was stupid—reckless—to accept tickets from strangers.

Twenty minutes slipped by. She didn't own a cell phone. And where were the payphones of yore? As she contemplated this, a flutter of red, the color of dry blood, grazed her cheek, filling her nostrils with rose.

"Angel babe! You made it!" Bare, apish arms grabbed her from behind, squeezing her till her ribs nearly cracked. Struggling for breath, she stared at his freckled hands covered with coils of hair. He nuzzled a sandpaper chin against her neck, plowing his nose into the glands beneath her jawbone, so that she got a whiff of ketchup and musk cologne.

"I sat there watching," he rasped, releasing her. "Twenty holy mother-fucking minutes. You didn't see me!" He crushed her fingers, twirled her—backpack and all—like a pirouetting ballerina until she faced him. She found his grin: a revelation of teeth straight from a horror movie. If he'd worn clown makeup, he couldn't have been more disturbing. Add to that the Spandex t-shirt that gripped his hip handles. "Girl! You made it!" He was hyped, grabbing her carry-on bags though she clung to her backpack like it was a lifeline. "Come on! Baby!!!! Get excited!!!" Was it possible that he clenched his teeth as he gyrated his hips in a little dance, before steering her through an obstacle course of people churning towards various forms of desert transport? Would she make it out alive?

The Real Deal

"Look on the bright side."

Burl's Idea of a Good Time

If New York was a bitch lying on a chaise lounge with its skyscraper-ass naked and waiting for a fuck from one very hot dick of a suburb, then his town—his McMansion-strewn desert plateau—was the stud. To him, Las Vegas, land of construction deals, private jets, Steve Wynn, MGM Grand, and a thousand millionaires beat out all the rest, because Vegas was the Lamborghini of all cities. Not twenty years ago a mafia-roasting horse-town, it now dominated the graphs of Wall Street. If he had to ramble on to yogini—with her crazy-beautiful bleached bobb and skinny little calves he'd like to tongue-fuck up to her scented panties—about how Vegas was the g-spot of the universe, then hell, he'd buy her a thousand tickets, glitterize her with his gi-normous TV, and spangle her heart with plans for a waterfall made from real desert rock he was building into his living room wall. Because it wouldn't be long before he'd be pulling out his French ticklers for a bang in the bedroom.

A millennium ago, when he left his sinkhole of a ranch house, exchanging his carport in Phoenix for a real garage, he couldn't have known that his daily affirmations of "I am a millionaire," "Everyone wants me to pave their rambling paths," "I am in demand AND in command," "My bank account keeps growing and overflowing!" would kinda, sorta come true. No one in the early 80's had any idea—couldn't have known that Wayne Dyer would figuratively splash around in Hugh Hefner's pool, charging up the Playboy bunnies with positive thinking. Because damn him if he hadn't positive-thought his way out of his marriage with Ms. Satan.

Yeah, he'd been ahead of the curve with positive thinking. He'd nearly redefined the land of beautiful sidewalks. Back then, no one but black suits with ties to the mob and maybe a few desperate showgirls in diamond tiaras moved to the southwest corner of Nevada. Here was a valley, hitched to Hoover Dam, which counted its stars lucky to be a Hollywood-bound stopover for blackjack and a lap dance. The town had always been a Liberace-meets-Sinatra-on-flickering-billboards-kinda-destination. Just the idea of all-you-can-eat buffets, the regulars binging on slot bells—of the cash-run music ricocheting off the smoky insides of windowless caverns—paled every New York nightclub.

Most of all, he felt at home in the desert. He loved its dry, feathers-to-prickles-in-your-throat heat that left the hairs on his arms like shafts of fiberglass, his skin the peeling bark of an aspen tree. He loved the sun baking his shaved head, wouldn't give up his bottled water if all of Lake Mead flooded his home.

Why had he moved to Vegas from its lesser-desert cousin Phoenix? Lots of reasons: the first being that casino dough had more yeast in it. Money in Vegas meant more, grew larger in the head. Once his wallet got a syringe of black jack, the lowbrow walkways he smoothed along strip malls in Scottsdale failed to appear profitable.

It helped that when he drove Ms. Satan to Vegas she was two months pregnant. He was sick of his nosy in-laws getting mixed up in his family life, parking their beaten sedan beneath his Phoenix carport, insisting they reopen every wound inflicted during his years with the "Mrs." Everyone knew Ms. Satan belonged in a strait jacket—and so did his in-laws. It took real discipline to thrust them from his mind. Because don't get him started on Ms. Satan, who wouldn't sniff at fake tits though she could've made a killing at dancing instead of serving cards. Her jet black hair—like a Japanese Geisha's (damn her)—and her pale brown eyes (double damn her) would go disarmingly erotic around his ex-buddy Carl (triple damn her), because of course he hired an overpriced jerk who called himself a private eye to follow and photograph them.

What once made him cum several times a night soon made his stomach turn. The only good that came of their five-year trial was their daughter, Brianna. At sixteen, the gal aspired to be the dancer her failed mother had never been. And, of course, his gal looked like a dancer with her long legs and crazy-beautiful golden hair, with her pink lipgloss that smelled like strawberries—which he insisted she wear only when they ate dinner out, because a gal in high school needed to be au-naturale or she'd become a party favor for bachelors.

Though, actually, he didn't mind dropping a few thousand on dance classes, tap shoes, the shiny tops Brianna wore everywhere. Now these were tops to disarm the male. All metallic flecks sewed on satin, mermaid tops flowing over every contour—little slits in the sleeves allowing shoulders to peek out, a neckline school-girl appropriate but low enough to show collarbone. Because everyone knew Brianna would never be a bookworm.

His gal spent most days with Ms. Satan, though Burl often got the call to take Brianna for the evening while Ms. Satan entertained. What kind of mom couldn't throw together a pot of noodles, or spread peanut butter and jelly on two slices of bread? What mother skipped paying rent, and dialed her ex-husband for a last-minute handout so their kid could keep posters on the wall and sleep in her own bed rather than out on the street? What mother had the thankless heart never to pay back her benefactor—**not one penny**—not, even, a thanks? The woman didn't deserve two minutes of his time, even after she finally scored fake boobs.

Fact was, Burl was a giver, a *positive* animal who enjoyed sharing good vibes, especially when he took Brianna to the mall or down to the strip to eat serious doses of sushi at his favorite casino, Mandalay Bay.

True. Despite the weird mom, Jane, the yogini, reminded Burl of Brianna. He couldn't help notice similarities. Sure, yogini was shorter than his gal, with brittle instead of smooth hair. (He picked the stuff from his clothes. But that didn't bother him. Though maybe the woman had too much hair, because at the end of an evening no one wanted fuzz on a golf shirt—or worse—caught in the throat during a kiss at cocktail hour.)

Hair aside, Burl knew. The moment she sidled up to The Avatar's dinner table—with all that bantering, those eye-rolls and blushes flowering up her neck to flood cheeks and forehead—he began to sizzle. By the end of the evening, after several solid stares that melted her like a butter sculpture next to flame, he knew she'd be naked with legs spread by the next evening. It helped that The Avatar—his *Never-land* Guru—encouraged flirtation, egging it on with jokes like, "Buuuurrrllll, you shoul' take curry and cayenne to bed!!!"

Anyone could see the yogini hungered for a good fuck, because mainly she ate nothing—just rabbit food. All through dinner, she picked at lettuce and carrots while ignoring the curried chicken over basmati. She turned away from kabobs of cubed beef, mushrooms, onions, and peppers whose aromas drifted down the table. The girl was undersexed, miserable, and wasting her life on marmish-ness. Plus, he could tell she'd never loosen up unless someone like him—a master of empowerment and affirmation—showed her the way.

It took only two nights.

At first she vacillated over Vegas, couldn't have looked more beautiful, with that post-coital bush, her arms and legs giving way on the sprawl of The Avatar's king-size bed, burgundy sheets twisting around Burl's thighs and grazing his penis, the blond goddess tattoo next to his left nipple a mirror of his fuck-mate.

Beyond The Avatar's shut bedroom door came nasal utterances occasionally interrupted by the laughter of an entourage of aging beauties in pashmina shawls, long skirts, and dark red lipstick.

Using old strategies, those that nabbed Ms. Satan, he intermittently talked, caressed, and sucked. *Things*, he'd started to say, *were heating up in the desert—more than hell's kitchen's thermometer.* The cash graph was climbing. The real estate boom looked like a field of poppies where once there'd been string beans—because everybody in the hammer and nail business understood this to be the boom of all booms.

Next to Burl, the chick looked small and believing, like a child about to laugh, her mouth open, her eyes roaming the ceiling—a gazelle about to be sacrificed. But then, she shut those eyes and whispered, "I don't gamble."

What the fuck was that?

"Then you'll never make any real money—" he said, turning her slightly to press his palm against her buttock.

Vegas had gone giddy. Lake Mead had begun to steam. Housing starts were eating up mountainsides. Stucco and clay tiles were the stampeding hooves of the bull market taking over tracts once windswept with sand, the outer reaches of the shimmering valley going for all cash— If you didn't get into the mosh pit, you'd miss the cash craze.

"Everything's money," Jane murmured, her eyes still shut. He wanted to bite her cheek, but he licked her neck and said *yes*, grabbing both tits. She had pale, nicely shaped tits with small, pink nipples he could perk to hardness and crush like cherry buds between his thumb and forefinger.

"Last month I put down all cash on acreage outside the bowl. You should've seen. I flipped it a week later. Made enough to buy a whole other lot. Me and my guy Warren, we've got several developments like this going at once." She turned to him, finally opening those eyes with the eyebrows finally rising with interest.

"So why isn't everyone rich?" She asked, her body putty under his hands.

"Don't ask. I just know I got what everyone else doesn't—"

"Then nothing matters—" She said.

"None of it." He said, smiling because he knew that wads of cash would turn this babe, like every other babe he'd womped, into hot tapioca. "A few mill at auction is nothing. We always turn a profit."

Finally, she fingered his collarbone, thick as cattle bone, flushed from years of sun. She flung a leg over his freckled paunch, where the humidity of her pubic hair released a fruity blast of pheromones.

Fact was, he had it all planned. Once his bid got taken, he'd throw up the tract housing Warren and he devised on notebook paper in a Starbucks at the edge of civilization. He'd subcontract to the guys from Zacatecas and Michoacán, because they knew concrete, travertine, sandstone, and granite like no one else, and in the not-to-distant future, he'd find his name sneaking onto the Forbes list of billionaires.

"Put it this way," he said, pulling the actualization of his tattoo lady firmly onto his hardening, condom-less dick so that everything in the room became hot and moist and engorged. Breathing hard and directing Jane's hips up and down so that her sweat-damp bob fell forward over her blemishes, her tits going up and down, he grunted: "A lot of us are making more on land deals than poker—a shitload more."

More Fun With Burl

After a thousand years in ranch style, cookie-cutter hell, Burl had finally found style. Emulating his wealthier business buddy, Warren—a developer and serious off-road biker who wore leather jackets over neckties, and was originally from the Big Island, Hawaii—Burl pulled together enough capital to start building an indoor waterfall of faux dolomite boulders and river rock, fussed up with little islands of fern, a luxury he'd dreamed of having when he was a kid playing in his parents' Silver Stream, where five crammed together until his dad landed the Chevy dealership job in Phoenix.

"It's like this," Burl told yogini that time they strolled by the dank Hudson. If his arm crushed her waist he didn't notice, because they boogied a solo act along the sidewalk, trailing several of The Avatar's followers. Unlike those less couth accompanying the spiritual teacher, Burl avoided burping up the $500, mediocre steak and fingerling potatoes that had been served to eleven unconscionable eaters earlier that evening. Against his will, he'd charged the entire fiasco to his Visa, having meditated through the overpriced, under-ambianced, pink lighting of the grill called "Curlycue."

A humid breeze, rife with algae and sewage, flowed up from the river as he began a well-rehearsed list, ticking on his fingers. "First, we got five star chefs." He bolded the statement with a shot of laughter, followed by a new finger. "Every designer from heaven to hell—you name it." Shot of laughter and new finger. "Sunshine, year round," laughter and finger, "brand new properties—not like the crumbling bull you guys got here. Good schools. Great hospitals. Golf. Nightlife like you can't EVEN begin to imagine. Shows. Shows. And more shows. A damn good university. World-class visitors from all over the world flying in every, and I'm talking every, **single** weekend. I mean, how could you NOT want to **cum**." His eyes bulged as he lifted and wiggled all his fingers at her pussycat profile.

She was a stubborn little bitch, nearly making him beg to buy her a ticket. The Madre had to be at the bottom of it. He knew it. That woman, Nora Lovins, he could tell she had it in for him from the start. All her faux uppity-ness and spirituality, all those over-protective glances—the kind that left him wondering how a twenty-seven-year-old put up with a mother who treated her like a two-year-old. But he left those thoughts behind, focusing on the positive. He would entice yogini by wrapping his arms around her and whispering, "Money flying off the walls. I kid you not."

She pulled away so that her upper body—cotton-coddled breasts and all—fanned from him. She turned her head towards the screwed-up lights shimmering on the river. But he pressed her more tightly to his pelvis. "Woman! What do I have to do? I mean, the BEST parties. You've never seen so many jets flying in—from Hong Kong, Singapore, Saudi Arabia, Bahrain, Europe. They all come." Tightening his arms around her waist, the breathlessness of it.

They'd fallen a full block behind The Avatar and his eight overfed, wishy-washy students, including the yogini's buttoned-up and totally unappealing madre. "You need to see what you're missing!" he continued, "I mean what is this?" motioning at the rotting brick fiascos called housing along Riverside Drive. "A hundred years old and people are spending what? While the best fucking time you'll ever have's in the desert. Shit. You need a good time. Anyone can see that."

Nearly three blocks ahead, The Avatar began flinging arms towards maple branches, doing some kind of dance with his fairy-dusted hands, causing his groupies to cheer and wave their arms too. Burl ignored the fuss, saying, "It's all about being real." He grinned, following up with the kind of searing stare that melted the insides of every woman between the ages of 14 and 90. "Your momma has you in a vice grip at the throat. Ever notice the way she hovers over you?" The yogini's eyes flamed him, all wide as if he were some ginormous steam shovel digging too deeply.

"Excuse me?" She sounded like the fembot of his Visa card after he breached his limit. "Excuse me—" She pulled away, but he grabbed her hand.

"You ever catch how she looks at me?" Burl barked. "Like I'm termite shit. The other day—"

This got the yogini to shoot off her wad in a way he'd never stand if HIS daughter were doing the same. A whole lot of: "What are you talking about—" and "My mom could care less who I'm with," and "I've never seen her look at anyone like they were 'termite shit,'" and "If anything, she's love-thy-neighbor-before-thy-daughter—"

"Well that's not what I see, babe. No sirree BOB. You guys are like an old married couple." He'd aimed to hit a nerve. **Bingo!** She cut loose from his grasp, clacking the cobbles towards one of the putrid green benches the homeless used as cots. She surveyed the shit-smeared ground next to the bazillion year old stonewall that some Olmsted disciple designed. She turned and absorbed him like a sponge, yelling, "You're certifiable!" And he knew it was love.

Gravitas

All Wayne Dyer, he breathed, "Let's get real and not hide behind suppositions. I'm buying you a ticket." Hadn't Burl shaved his head to look first and foremost like good ol' Wayne, his true teacher and stylist? Hadn't Wayne's comely gaze exuded purpose, a gravitas not achieved by most garden-variety chumps? Finally, in maturity, Burl had that *what-do-you-call-it-thing* that made women glance twice when he walked through a door, his shoulders slightly swaying over steady, know-it-all hips, because his hairless mazard had finally given rise to a certain seriousness that his auburn-fro-of-youth had belied.

There he was, like a shot of single malt scotch, watching Jane melt beneath the charge emitted from his eyes. Because he'd thrown a football to the 50-yard line.

She held two palms against the goose bumps fringing her cheeks, fluttering like a butterfly, "I don't know Burl." The woman was a piece of work: one minute Godzilla, the next New York's sylph. "I've never been to Las Vegas—"

And yet, he could tell she teetered, because she blinked too much and her gaze kept veering towards the ground. He cupped his hands around the chill flesh of her hands. He could tell she wanted to be wrapped up, like a tamale, inside his corn husk warmth, wanted to emerge from the soon-to-be waterfall in his living room and go shopping on the strip, wanted to dangle Mandalay Bay yellowtail and raw clam over his gaping maw, to exchange shirts with Brianna—his amazing and fucking beautiful Brianna—to become aroused on his massive, satin-encased bed with the feeling of his cock rubbing against the heat of desert scrub—because there was nothing scrubby about her pink, fleshy cunt. They both knew. This chick wanted all that he could give, and hell if he couldn't give her everything she wanted.

And then she saw the light. And then he made plans, deep and involved plans. And then she came.

Burl's Real Deal

But the problem, he had to admit, was he never tanned. Born the color of chalk, growing up with the complexion of a Neanderthal, he lived for sunscreen and vitamin C ointments. Caked the stuff on every morning in an unsuccessful attempt to protect what was cursed as jicama flesh. Since before he could remember, he'd acquired a permanent ruddiness, probably due to a genetic propensity for Vitiligo, leaving him to appear as if every pore had sucked up and digested the rays of a sunset. No matter how much cream he slathered over his face, the capillaries in his cheeks became engorged. There was no hiding awe or addiction: It all showed up, especially around The Avatar.

"I gotta tell you," He told The Avatar during that first session at Warren's adobe mansion set on a Biblical thrust of desert near Red Rock. "You're the real deal." *The real, fuckin' deal.* Looking back, he'd always searched for the "real deal," and finally it stared right through him with those sand-to-sage eyes.

Like Wayne Dyer, the Avatar was bald, with those same impeccable teeth, except that he blew snickers through his nose, singing, "Buuurrrrl, I am here for a reason. You are here for a reason. We are fin'ing the reason behin' all reason." That first meeting (and could you call it a meeting? Or was it actually an encounter, a collision, a melding of spirit?), The Avatar had given Burl a secret phrase to whisper in the shower every morning, to be chanted three times with his eyes closed and his hands laced before his substantial groin: *"Here is possibility!"*

Since then, Burl intoned, *"Here is possibility,"* three times every morning, lacing fingers, adding a round of *"mmmmms"* that sounded like he'd reached orgasm and was in the process of melting down the drain—this, right after a daily affirmation, like the one he repeated in his shower the morning of the yogini's arrival: *"Avoid low energy substances."*

And finally it was Thursday—no weekend rush of drunks and money-grubbers. The yogini was due at 2:30 p.m., which meant he had to get his sorry ass out of the shower, down some coffee and a Pop Tart (cause who had time for Eggos drizzled with Aunt Jamima?) and get the sprinklers going. And that was the least of it. Before swinging by McCarran, he had to get his sorry butt to Warren's to check over their bid, maybe sign some papers if costs came down ten percent. Then he had to head over to Ms. Satan's, pay her off with $1,500 (the bitch!), and pick up some flowers at Smith's—preferably red roses—so he could start yogini's visit right by drizzling rose petals over her needy pubes.

He loved that she was so thirsty with need that she could suck a casino dry. Anyone could see the yogini was wilting in the bloom of life. Just thinking about mending her turned him into a heated, throbbing needle.

The valley already an oven on the drive to the airport, he didn't care because by sunset he'd be bracing her tiny, flawless, and completely inebriated, sushi-stuffed body between his legs, delivering the first of his gravitas thrusts. Because it was the only way he could help. He knew she needed him to feed her, needed him to devour the pain that he could hear beneath every one of her words.

And when he watched her squirm in the baggage claim, when his rose slid against her cheek, he could tell she liked it.

"Money's waiting to be plucked, just like this rose," He said, and later while gliding along the black pill-bug conveyer belt somewhere between baggage claim and his car, where he'd slammed down a quick bite, he added, "Baby, I fuckin' love it here." He propped her gray duffle bag, or whatever it was—backpack?—against his shoulder while panoramic images showed acrobats dangling by the teeth from tinseled welcome banners that became the burgundy lips of Donna Summers, which broadened to emit lyrics no one heard before zooming down her throat.

"You got to admit, this is like nothing you've seen! Tell me this airport isn't the fucking coolest—" Carrying the rose he'd handed her with the deepest, breath-sucking kiss, the yogini looked like a split yam oozing awe.

Turned out the only reason yogini came was because The Madre planned to accompany The Avatar on a gambling spree. Turned out The Madre, with an ugliness that caused him to question whether Jane's firm skin would last the decade, had bent schedules to fly in. The good news: He'd convinced Jane to stay at his pad.

It helped that six old biddies accompanied The Avatar everywhere, making Lorie's cottage in Henderson a tad too small for yet another air mattress and shower hog. Unfortunately, right there in the airport, with slot machines ringing and Spandex hobbling over spiked heels (followed by the Dockers and sweatshirts of parents pushing strollers), the yogini insisted on forfeiting their first romantic afternoon. It was only 3:30 p.m., so how could he refuse when she pleaded to visit Lori's 2,500 sq. ft. hovel on an already deteriorating plot of scrub and gravel overlooking the lesser side of the Strip? He had no choice but to let yogini "check in" with Nora and The Avatar, and "get acclimated" to his valley.

"Woman," he brayed, dropping her bags (what did she have in them, sand?) in the back of his Explorer. Like a gentleman, he walked around to her side and opened the door, because what did these chicks want? Red carpets and roses. He paused to pin her against the tinted window, planting another hottie on her lips. "You sure you don't want to dump this stuff at my place?" Her breath hung between them—the stale edge of a five-hour flight partially masked by the piece of Trident gum he'd thrust at her in the baggage claim.

"If there's one thing," he murmured, "We got to do before we do anything else." And he allowed his whisper to linger near her lips in a miasma of warm exhalations. She turned her head to the side, giggling. Light caught a pearl of saliva that glinted over the remnants of her pink lipstick. And then she gazed up with those fucking crazy-beautiful eyes, moist and melting as a trusting animal. He wanted to push her through the door right then, unzip his pants, and bury himself in her flesh—right there in the garage surrounded by all those hollering kids amid squeaking luggage wheels and blasting horns and carbon monoxide farts.

<u>Ladies</u>

An hour later, sweating, burping, feeling the airport-grilled-and-scarfed polish sausage jostling in an acidic stew in his stomach, still wanting to disassemble the yogini's non-descript outfit, Burl accompanied his reluctant fuck-mate to his new/old friend's, Lori's, bon-fired living room. But Lori, a lank baby boomer whose magenta curls matched her décor, bathed him with salutations that involved dipping in a head-to-the-tiles bow. Her dottiness was fueled by airy smiles that suggested the corporeal was secondary to the spiritual.

Anyone with a brain cell could see Lori had been airlifted from reality. Even her house hovered at the outer reaches of the ionosphere with its gauzy curtains and sun-saturated furnishings. Everything, down to the picture frames, was magenta and orange, including the shawls of the five followers crammed onto the velveteen sofa. Two other simpletons lounged, ankles crossed, on air-conditioned floor tiles. And still another individual of confused gender prostrated him/herself, head down, distended and veined legs springing motionless from a pair of Bermudas. The whole scene begged to be swallowed by Lori's gaping, magenta carpet.

Floating in scarves through the living room, a box of tissues in hand, Lori breezed by with, "The Avatar is in the back giving sessions—" Her curly hair was fussed up with a beaded comb, garnet hoops plugged like talismans into wilted earlobes. As she gazed at the followers, her eyelids fluttering like the iridescent wings of blue butterflies, Burl wondered if Lori had developed a thyroid condition. Her attention glazed in and out, wandering the room.

With jitters, she spoke as if the sound of her voice had unpleasantly awoken her from a dream. "Oh, it's so—Tissues anyone—" Lori peeped as if giving to the homeless. As she placed the box on the coffee table, a lavender-scented breeze surged up Burl's nostrils. *What was it with these ladies and their scents?*

As if on cue, he fell into a sneezing fit, bringing on more sweat until his armpits and hairline became an irrigation system that refused to turn off. Dripping, Burl's fingers b-lined for a tissue. But they got there a beat too late.

Turned out, the only other man in the room, squeezed between women on the couch, had the same idea. Turned out he was a short dude—shorter than most women, in fact—the kind of dude who enjoyed beating **real** men, like Burl, to it. As if on cue, "little man" snatched up the last wad of tissues in the entire house, crumpling it into a ball and tucking it into his pocket.

"Allergies," little man blinked through his heavy accent. Noticing Burl, he pulled out a single tissue and deigned to drop it into Burl's hand.

286

The prick had to be celibate, had to be in his mid-forties, had to blink like it was his native right. All this while pretending he meant well, because little man thrust out a hand. "Alain—" he sneered with his slam-dunk, euro-snob accent.

As Burl and yogini settled on the floor, the little man named Alain exhaled pedantry to the group, getting so excited by his own voice that he nearly ejected himself from the sofa. Before long it came out that he'd flown in from Paris, believed in multiple sexual partners, had studied with two Rimpoches, and religiously ate garlic—which surprised no one within a twenty-foot radius of his little mouth.

Little man (a.k.a. Alain) explained that he was a nutritionist who'd written a screed about the French fry epidemic, and was on a research trip to the U.S.—probably disparaging teenagers for eating breakfast—when he met The Avatar. Turned out, little man's seminal paper—about sedentary fifth graders sweating adipose into their desks when the thermostat barely grazed 65 degrees—gave him the right to squawk on NPR. Alas, little man stank up the room.

Little man blustered on about his Berber heritage and his mom's determination to spur growth by raising him on regimen of groats, split peas, turnips, and freshly killed game. As everyone learned, Alain advocated "a caveman diet" that required grazing upon home-cooked lentils, sunflower seeds, dulse, and organic lamb shanks. "No spice!" The mere idea left Burl's libido in the sink.

Did The Avatar know? Not a chance. But little man spoke ardently through his salt and pepper beard and thin, highly-charged mouth, a tangle of troubles creasing his forehead, causing him to appear vitriolic, probably because his shalwars and jacket—bound by braided waist-straps—was stultifying.

But next to this ninny sat the only human cocktail worth the sofa: a buxom heifer with some seriously toned arms, the whole package gussied-up with makeup, all salon-blond wisps flowing like silk around honey-hued eyes. Every strand on the woman's head swayed like seaweed, making those high cheekbones and pink lips into a box of candy. Eventually, when little man paused, this femme fatale riding the sofa introduced herself as Grace—as in Grace Kelly. But not really, Burl soon learned—because the chick turned out to be Alain's sidekick.

Who knew Alain and Grace were lovers? Burl figured they were at the end of their relationship, because they avoided eye contact, turning heads away when one was forced to pat the other's thigh or hand.

Later it would be difficult to remember how the conversation turned to Vegas. But somehow Burl found himself shitting on the verbal "can."

Alain, no longer coveting approval from fellow couch-potatoes, launched himself from his velveteen thrown and charged down the road of cultural criticism. Soon little man slashed the air with his hands, cutting down every newly paved driveway, every roof tile and doorframe that "damaged" the valley. He stopped mid-sentence only when Grace, with lowered voice, placating but haughty, said, "Calm down, Alain! You'll give yourself a heart attack." Anyone could tell she'd seen this too many times. But no. Little man would not back off. Let him have a heart attack as he spat out one fiery statement after another with karate chops, one almost walloping Burl's head.

"And how is it," little man bleated, "that humans live in this hell with no water?!" Again, Grace's drizzled French into little man's ear, augmenting intonations with a half-assed pat. But no—all attempts to cut down the Napoleon-wannabe failed.

"It's disgusting," little man spouted, "Even the children are fat. So much waste everywhere! It is, how do you say? Unconscionable? Fat children! This is freedom? No. This is shame! Why spend holidays gambling? This is paradise? No! An oven of death where the water comes from recycled shit!" Alain's hair-clogged nostrils seethed, his rasps reminding Burl of pigpens beneath a freeway.

After that, no one could do anything but dwell on stomach acid and the stink of garlic, ketchup, and sweat sullying the room. Truth be told, Burl didn't want to cause trouble. Especially at The Avatar's gathering, with the yogini drowsing next to him under the shadow of her Madre, who sat in a chair flipping through a rolodex. Besides, hadn't he turned over a Wayne Dyer leaf? And who had time for pedantic, new-age-vitamin-popping, lentil-chugging, know-it-alls wearing a Rimpoche's drawstring underwear?

But Burl mixed concrete and hired the guys who paved the roads and sidewalks this French fry drove and walked on, sidewalks his crazy-beautiful kid roller skated when she was ten, the very tar-tops Burl would drive to get yogini back to his manse—if possible—*pronto*! But little man was getting in Burl's way.

Burl tried to be Wayne Dyer, smiling into thin air, blinking back anger. But he couldn't help it. Even-toned, he shot back: "Have you heard of Hoover Dam?" He wanted no more Champs Elysee speeches from a guy who slipped stinky B-complexes between his teeth. So, why wasn't little man, "shoveling algae—or better, organic chicken shit—in the hull of a ship?"

Alain "pffed" with a shake of his beard. **Spineless.**

Burl pulled Jane's hand into his lap, trying to hold back, looking for the effect of a horizon line. Alas, no: He had to say it loud and clear, "Don't listen to this moron— Let's go—" But yogini's jetlagged legs had turned to beanbags.

Ignoring her complaint of headache, he propped her pale, heavy-lidded, drooping self against his shoulder, saying, "Come on, baby!" But the Vegas climate and popcorn-farted airline air had turned her into a twice-infused teabag. Getting her out of there would be a hassle, because if he knew Lori and Nora, he knew the evening was already gone.

And then came the nail in the coffin: "Let's," yogini murmured, "sleep here tonight—" leaving him no option.

Staying would require expertise in steering clear of curried chicken and basmati rice cooked up in the fuscha kitchen. He'd have to deflect the invitation to cash in with The Avatar at an Excalibur black jack table surrounded by old biddies *ooohing* and *ahhhing*, slurping daiquiris, and gossiping about "chance encounters." And sure as sunrise, he'd have to excuse himself from covering the tab for The Avatar's entourage's desserts and cocktails.

At this point, it didn't matter whether he scored a business deal in the waiting area, because most people already pretended to be meditating. All Burl wanted was a slice of corps-de-amore with the lady tattooed on his chest. Anyone with a brain cell had to see that's what The Avatar wanted too—a nice piece of pie, preferably slathered with butter. But even The Avatar, with all his spiritual wand-waving, was stuck with a cluster of half-stale crumpets—led by the fustiest crumpet of all, Madre Nora—none of whom had been buttered in half a century.

Endless

Because of Lori's dazed and confused hospitality, and the disturbing image of her dangly earrings ripping through her long-gone lobes, because she swayed in an approximation of bliss and anguish, with her soft spoken but awkward, "ahem, hi there. Can I offer anyone—" when confronting her guests, because her tacky clash of wind chimes spun on a draft in the kitchen window, he couldn't get away. Yogini's headache—that death knell for any man dreaming of pie—didn't help.

Burl's un-fucked fuck-mate kept leaning into him, rubbing her temples, muttering that she had to lie down— When he suggested they drive to his manse, she sagged and moaned, "No—Let's stay here—"

He argued there was no place to lie down—especially next to the androgynous body attached to the varicose-veins busting from a pair of Bermudas that smelled like sweating goat cheese. But no, the yogini moaned until Lori used a brain cell and poured the chick a glass of Gatorade.

They'd been in Lori's house an hour when Burl's stomach committed sabotage. The first rumbles erupted when Lori pulled out the peanuts. What could he do but give in? Because, well, if he couldn't have pie then he'd have to succumb to the promise of t-bone steaks and spaghetti drizzled with marinara sauce, maybe a helping of mashed potatoes on the side because, well, there was nothing like mashed anything with butter to get his sensual nerves refocused. He'd almost forgotten about the little man from Champs Elysees when things got dicey.

"What's that smell?" yogini rasped in his ear before turning away to encase her nose in a cotton sleeve.

A beat later, The Madre began staring at Burl's beading forehead like it was committing a crime. The old biddy looked like Justice Ginsburg— cloaked as she was in black and a lace neckerchief—encased in a leatherette chair whose wire armrests and legs begged to be an S & M contraption—a Knoll knock-off.

The living room—now saturated with methane, CO_2, garlic, and B.O.—had turned a corner to become a highly charged olfactory annihilator that threatened to explode. Someone, other than Burl, had compounded the stench with his stinking feet.

And that's when little man spoke up again—as if his lips were sewed to his nose: "Disgusting!" The man had real nerve when he held a palm to his nostrils and extracted himself from the sofa to prey on the bathroom. Making a fist, Burl held back—because beating up a little man made anyone with half a brain cell into a knucklehead.

With every minute the room ripened, The Avatar's students coughing, squirming, and covering their noses. Clearly, everyone considered Burl the bowel out of which muck erupted—which infuriated him, because the culprit came from France.

And it hurt that The Madre clearly wished Burl would fly away on his Garuda when all he wanted was to care for her daughter. Couldn't she see that he—with his bon-ami, big-ass frame, and freckled lower arms—could change atmospheres? But The Madre, kept squinting at him, as if every cell in her body rebelled against him. Did she still hold a grudge over that business with The Avatar and Mariaaaaa?

Where was The Avatar anyway?

Burl spoke up. "Ladies, Paris stinks too." Never one to waste time, he got down to business. The sooner he cleared the air, figuratively and actually, the better his chances of running off with yogini. "Someone please open the windows—Lori?" He pulled himself up from the sunset carpet, his butt burning with stalled circulation, left leg numb, a head rush making him lurch. He caught the arm of the sofa, adding, "I know the AC's on, but what about fresh air!" This was the problem with old biddies. They never opened windows!

Feeling like a terrorist holding an oozy, Burl faced The Avatar's followers. They peered up at him, awed and startled, like mashed couch potatoes. He could have batted the hell out of a Wuhan wind gong and still no one would have moved for the windows. Only Lori's eyes bulged with something approaching awareness (or was it her thyroid condition?), both glazed and alarmed. She darted up from an S & M dining throne, trembling as if a bomb had gone off.

"Of course, of course!" She sputtered. "Yes. Let's open a sliding door. Why not? Just, let me—" She tripped over M. Varicose Veins, who still lay on the floor like an oversized Voodoo doll, causing a domino effect that ended with Lori slam-dunking into an indoor cactus. Squeals of pain, hiccupped apologies, tortoise-like movements as M. Varicose Veins actually crawled into the kitchen to procure a Band-Aid.

In the aftermath, Burl finally cracked the sliding door, and a draft of sage-scented air spun through the living room, a welcome tornado that lifted the miasma of endless time, leaving everyone to inhale cosmic dust until little man's strained lips appeared at the periphery, his little fingers spritzing lavender deodorizer around the room—leaving Burl with the conviction that someone had better pave over France.

No Exit

"So where's The Avatar?" Burl managed, half breathing again. Lori shivered despite the heat and wagged her folded arms—a kind of message to the invisible. They were living through that overrated play Ms. Satan dragged him to before Brianna was born. *No Exit.*

That's when little man began yammering about spiritual journeys: "What is real when everything is Maia?" and, "Where do we go after The Avatar?" and, "Does the light go too?"

This was enough to launch The Madre into a lecture. "These are great questions, Alain." The pundit always began by complimenting the ignoramus. "Very good questions." The more the expert, the more one stalled. "It's very simple. For instance—" And good pundits always digressed with a comparison. "What happens when you eat something very good? How does your body feel afterwards?" Adding questions onto questions only added suspense.

"It depends—" little man—the argumentative shit—thinned his lips, lacing fingers over drawstrings. "I see what you say, but it's a wrong parallel."

"Metaphor," Madre said, primping hair—trying for chanteuse though she looked like a pilgrim. "When I'm around The Avatar—" She paused, her eyes on yogini, who rested on a stool, noggin against knees. "Time disappears." True. Madre—and let's not beat around the burning bush—looked like she'd been forgotten by time, right down to the ironed fold of her pant leg, and those pumps belonging to World War 1, and the lace scarf tethered like a boat-mooring to her neck, which belonged to a 19th century gold prospector. And what the hell was she doing? Turning into The Avatar's marketing guru?

"When we move through time without mind—" The woman couldn't stop twitching smiles at Lori and little man. "We move effortlessly. This is what The Avatar gives. Effortless movement beyond time. A lifetime of good meals!" If she were a grade-school student she'd sit at the front of the class, pass around handouts, and line up first. Because Madre Nora was the eraser girl. The honest pilgrim. The true devotee.

And what, Burl wondered, had happened to the halter-tops and culottes she'd worn on her own, New York turf?

Sick of noise, Burl gave Grace a twice over, contemplating what he'd do to her in his bedroom. Leaning against the kitchen counter—yogini was too slammed to notice—he tried talking up little man's bitch.

A painful hour later—during which few budged from Lori's living room except to leave droplets of piss on bathroom tiles—light fizzled from the sky, leaving Burl aching like an over-extended rubberband. His entire body and brain wobbled as if stuck in afterbirth. The Avatar—usually the first to stir a party—hadn't appeared, having ensconced himself in some back room, likely fondling another blond "Maaarrrriaaa."

Pity

Dinner sounded less interesting than a PB & J, because every matron in Vegas had barged in on his date with yogini. Old biddies commandeered the prepping of a puritan meal of baby carrots, celery, broccoli crowns, and lentils churned with ballpark mustard. He despised the gratuitous basmati rice with its orange dots of fake saffron. He wanted to flush away the sorry chicken chunks drizzled in a coterie of dysfunctional spices. Most of all, he wanted to swing a tennis racket at the dinner rolls pulled from a supermarket-brand plastic bag.

Meanwhile, yogini stumbled around the kitchen pumped up on two Ibuprofens and a thimble-size glass of wine. (At least The Madre hadn't raised her gavel to that!) Under the track lighting, yogini looked liked a shorter version of the blond android played by Daryl Hannah in *Blade Runner*, making Burl want to lick her neck and shoulders before sucking a tit. The girl had to stop wallowing in self-pity and get on with the fun. Because everything awaited his fingers, tongue, and hardening male bees' nest.

He became hard, and didn't care who saw. Let Nora cough up her bib. Let Lori roll her eyeballs across the North Sea. How could he do anything but admire this babe? There she was, deftly handling a Pyrex dish of lentil salad while kicking shut the refrigerator door, showing off her little toes and those long arms smooth as candle wax in that little tight t-shirt.

Yeah, yogini definitely deserved that plane ticket, even if he had to admit his daughter was more beautiful. And, really, the fact of yogini's lesser beauty had something to do with a serious skin condition that peppered her otherwise flawless cheeks (and sometimes forehead). But what the fuck. They'd already had some good tumbles, and what did hair or skin mean in the end?

Obliterated

He stared her down till she covered her eyes, because it might be hours before she'd see his waterfall. She cowered next to the counter, as if the boogieman had brought home a carcass for dinner. Impossible that he was the cause, because he'd kissed her in the airport, flung a rose at her feet, had chauffeured and sat on his ass till the sun literally fell off the horizon. What scared her? The aging hippies practicing head rolls and arm stretches as they splashed vinegar and mustard on the salad?

He sidled up to yogini, wrapped his arms around her, and murmured, "Wanna get out of here?" She stood with her back to him, and he pressed his hard cock against her spine. She quivered but pulled away, wandering down the length of counter towards the head-rolling hippies.

Nearby, Grace sat on a barstool, elbows like icicles against the countertop. His eyes absorbed her thin wrists, studying the concavities of her anorexic but somehow exciting collarbone. He'd like to tickle and melt the blips that were her breasts. He imagined flicking his tongue over her small nipples. If it weren't for yogini, he'd lick Ms. Grace from big toe—stopping at that belly—all the way up to her impeccable cheekbones.

"Been to New York yet? Damn garbage trucks," he began, settling on a stool by Grace. "The city's a sewage plant seconds away from the apocalypse. Stuff flying up in your face when five buses go by, one right after another after nothing but taxis and the assholes driving to million dollar closets people call apartments. Don't start me on the damn bistros. Ever walk into one of those joints? Jane can tell you—" He swiveled eyes towards yogini, attempting to rope-in Ms. Stand-offish-because-I-have-a-headache, to no avail. "That place on Broadway, remember? That rotten piece of flesh they plated?" Huffing half in jest, half in pain as he remembered the credit card bills on his desk. "Couldn't down a single piece of that leather. You couldn't either," he said, eyeballing yogini.

First her wrinkled forehead; then her "ohed" mouth. Not confusion.

It wasn't surprise that smeared her face, but some kind of ape-shit whatever. Fury. He winked—but too late.

"What?" he cried. "What? I'm right, right?" Yogini's mouth thinned, making her skin look like blanched plastic, like an uncooked sausage.

"I don't eat meat, Burl—" She sneered, her face pinched—a female version of little man. What could he do but babble about "Curlycue"?

"Yep, we hated it. Who eats mashed turnips?" Kneading forehead, fingers hot, he turned up the corners of his mouth, a kind of "just joking, and now aren't I your loving-blunderer" expression that imitated a begging dog. This usually softened women—but not yogini, the frozen cunt. "Oh dang," he murmured. "Scuse me, hon, I know about your vegetables." His wrinkled forehead hurt about as much as his chest. Because, what had happened to him? Had he become a filthy old man no one liked? An insensitive bastard people wanted to park in dog piss by a hydrant? He folded into himself, staring down at hands that meant well in his lap, hands that could make things happen. Heaviness settled in his throat.

Jane turned her back to him, her bleached hair worse than Nora's gavel-glare. Wordless, she strutted out, leaving him to feel repulsive.

Minutes later, the kitchen bustled with activity, dinner almost ready. Still Burl remained silent. He could feel The Madre frowning at his slumped posture from her station by the refrigerator. Grace stroked her hands and stared into the living room. "Enlightenment—" Burl muttered, his usually buoyant face a deflated balloon. He'd had enough of women seeking enlightenment. Then he remembered his mother, a good woman who worked too hard sweeping sand from their trailer home. She'd died too young, misshapen by sadness, which he forgot every day until he remembered somewhere in the back of his chest.

He patted the kitchen counter with his palm. "Smells good," he said, miming a drumbeat. "Scuse me, sweetie—" He nodded to Grace, avoiding a view of The Madre. Hating that yogini had skedaddled, he wondered where the fuck she thought she'd sleep that night. In The Madre's sleeping bag?

He circled the counter and darted down the hall towards the bathroom, suspecting that yogini was hiding in the tub. She had it in for him, but he wasn't going to take any more shit. He'd flown her out, and now where the hell had his well-planned evening gone? The roses, the satin on his bed, the partial waterfall splashing over his expensive (that was an understatement) interior stones, the cinematic flat screen that cost him a thousand nights at the MGM Grand, waiting to be flicked on during post-coital exhaustion. Where had all that possibility gone? It had been sucked into The Avatar's whirlwind of recklessness—pureed into one of his stifling dinners—because no one had to tell Burl that spiritual robes caused trouble.

Since setting eyes on The Avatar at Mandalay Bay's roulette table, nothing had gone right for Burl. One glance at the credit card bills waiting on Burl's desk confirmed this fact. More than $10,000 racked up on five Visa cards in just three weeks—and how was he going to pay it back if he bidded on the vacant lots Warren had tagged as "not to be passed up?"

Burl rapped gently at first, glaring at Lori's bathroom door, which reeked of lavender oil. "Woman, open up—" he began. Above the door was a blue plaque that read "*Joy To The World*" next to a painted sun.

When the door didn't open, Burl pressed his ear to its hollowness, picking up the whirr of the ceiling fan. Mumbling a curse and knocking again, he couldn't stop himself. He yelled, "Come on, Jane! Open up!" When no one answered, he lowered his voice, saying, "This kind of thing happens all the time—how many times do you forget I live in the old development near the strip?" Over the phone, she'd forgotten more than once, certain that he lived near The Avatar's center in Henderson. "Come on! Let it go. I'm starving. Let's get the hell out of here and grab some real food— No one will miss us. You like Japanese, right?" But for all he knew, she could be wallpaper.

What the girl needed was a good spanking!

Gritting teeth, he yanked the doorknob and twisted the locked little piece of shit with the fury of hell. Still nothing. Raising his knee—and this was where he erred, because later he'd dream of his mother reminding him to watch his bones—he pressed all his weight against the hollow barrier. Two, maybe three seconds of this, and a loud—no make that a thunderous—blast of disintegrating wood shimmied the interior. His kneecap burst through, splintering the wood and opening a gaping hole not unlike a tunnel to Neverland.

A thousand milliseconds of pain later, a tsunami of motion—a clamor both inside the restroom and down the hall. He heard the gasps, the swallowed horror, the shockwaves moving across magenta carpets and ending in frantic voices. Then followed the first stages of a lawsuit: Lori shrieking, "What happened? Oh my god—Oh my god!"

His mother once said he didn't know his own strength, because his bones were too big. He'd nearly ripped his poor mom in two during birth. He'd had a thousand head whacks from running into things— Hell, he'd once survived after colliding with the fender of a parked school bus. He and his dad were the same in this. They survived because they'd calcified. And because of the strength of their bones, he'd promised never to beat a woman—except maybe Ms. Suzie that once. Other than that, true to his word, he hadn't. But that didn't mean he couldn't beat up buildings instead.

Knee still a piece of the door, his numb face found The Madre's. Always the first to arrive at any disaster, she stared, grabbing Lori's arm to bring about order. "What's going on!" Madre hissed, the tied neckerchief enlarging her words. "What have you done?" That's when the pins started to slink up his leg from where splinters stuck into him. No one stepped forward to lend a hand. Wobbly on his feet—he might fall and crack open his skull for all they cared—he managed with tears springing to his eyes, shame all over him, to pull his leg from the hole.

He heard only a whisper of feet coming from within the bathroom before the door fell off its hinges.

A Truly Dark Place

It was dark inside, but he could see that her lips were bare of lipstick, her eyes wide as red-rimmed flower petals. The head-rolling hippies surrounded Burl, so close he smelled the sweat coming from their bodies.

"It was an accident," Burl said. He'd meant no harm, and hoped to show this in his face. But no one seemed to notice, because they stared into the bathroom, where the darkness whirred with something other than Jane. "I thought she was stuck in there—" he muttered. But only The Madre's eyes pivoted from the bathroom to bore into him.

"Jane. Come out—" The Madre said, still staring at Burl, still holding up arms as if working to control crowds for the police. Jane emerged, a bright hickey on her neck, her clothes and hair disheveled. All Burl could think of was the damn Parisian, with his oversized diapers and his pompous nostrils, couldn't help envisioning little man stuffing his groats and lentils down her throat.

But before Burl had a chance to make fists, The Avatar sauntered out from behind the shower curtain. He stood near Jane, all teeth and laughter through lips smeared with lipstick, sputtering: "What is dis? Dis is crazy, Buuurrrlllll! You haven' learn to knock?"

And then Burl was digging in his pocket for his goddamn credit card to shove at Lori and tell her to charge it, go ahead, take it! And, no, he'd do better than that. He'd fix the goddamn door himself, which bought him a moment, but not the right moment, because The Avatar patted Burl's back, placing an arm around his shoulder, saying: "Is okay, Buuurrrlllll. You and she can still stay for dinner." But Burl would rather dine in hell than sit at Lori's table.

Dinner Talk

Mountains of cash couldn't have pried Burl from his anger. He'd never forgive The Madre for her meanness. And though she'd laid out mounds of gut-curdling *vegetablese*, like the lentil salad that listed next to string beans drowned in amino acid sauce, looking like "toad food" drunks foraged for in alleyways, Burl wasn't budging. Like a punishment, he'd refused the brown sauces, hating the curry that made his mouth water and his stomach grumble. Everyone except Burl sat inside on an S & M apparatus—while Burl idled in his SUV, drumming the wheel and occasionally nodding off. Already, it had been half an hour of exile, no end of waiting in sight. But he'd promised yogini she could sleep in his bed, and he'd stand by his word, hell or high water.

Ravenous and furious at once, he imagined mangling Lori's wannabe-Knoll-but-really-Goodwill chairs, wondering how anyone could sit for so long and not bust a knee through a bathroom door. Still, he wouldn't bust his car keys through his dashboard—because he wasn't in the business of abandoning people.

Worn down, he finally muttered, "fuck it," and got out of his vehicle. He rummaged in his trunk for that slim black item meant to scare off thieves and strained to smile. Like a shadow, he entered the residence—watching from the doorway before eventually pulling up a chair. Still smiling and holding up the gun, he gazed around The Avatar's table, unwilling to show other emotions.

Napkin-less, he devoured the lentils, but avoided the string beans. Furious—he could feel the blood pumping in his temples—he began talking real estate, striking up with Lori. She sat at his elbow, delighted, tittering, eyebrows raised, wind-chime earrings tugging at lobes, already forgiving his knee and the incident that occurred at the front door.

"Surprise!" He'd cried, laughing manically. She'd whimpered, shaking, her eyes blown up in her face like balloons. He'd fallen back laughing as The Avatar approached, knowing it was only a joke. The Glock handgun he pressed against Lori's temple kept him laughing through The Avatar's invitation to chow down, all gurus ever-forgiving and giving way.

Thus Lori sat next to Burl at table, nodding, inserting "mhmms" between sips of water. Only after The Avatar cleared his throat and insinuated that they were having a breakthrough did Lori stop nodding.

"Something," The Avatar said, "very big is happening!" The room hushed, because between dusk and midnight, a great spiritual eclipse would break open their hearts.

"Hallelujah!" Burl hurled the word at The Avatar's forehead, though he wanted to throw mustard sauce at The Madre's face. But he kept one hand on his Glock, the other on his fork. "Good for us! So you think this is news? Here's some news." He'd piss the news on these people, because they didn't know anything about open hearts. "You can't build hearts the way you build a city—unless your name is Donald! But in Vegas, the skies the limit. Because

I build paths— Hell, I build civilization!" A cactus of cayenne pepper and curry grew in Burl's nasal passages. Sneezing, he talked right through, didn't even wipe his nose, because who cared if his snot killed the atmosphere?

The dining room stared. The Avatar kept smiling, nodding, smiling.

"You've got the big Wynn, and you've got the little wins. You've got guys in between—guys like me—who slice off a hunk of American pie, eat it and spit it right back out. Munch a few acres of sand, throw up condos. Opportunity, **baby**, one hundred percent opportunity! Right here. **Right God Damn Here!**" He thumped his forefinger on the table, and grabbed the rice bowl, filling his plate for the second time.

Ever the somnambulist waking from a Sisyphean nightmare, Lori nodded again, as if Burl was a newly discovered planet. But The Avatar's smile had disappeared, yanked away by a frown as Burl continued, despite the surround-sound of pale faces. "If you want answers, folks—"

"Wipe your nose," The Avatar barked, thrusting out a napkin. "You are a big baby—" As if this could eviscerate Vegas.

Ignoring the napkin, Burl kept yammering, waving around his mock Glock, nasal fluid dripping onto lentils—because who gave a shit whether The Avatar toasted the midnight sun. At 9 PM, after hours of spoonfuls of lentils and basmati, Burl wasn't going to stop until he'd had his fill. Eating, like breathing, like speaking, was Burl's right, which meant he'd hold table for as long or as short as he wanted.

Shoving his fork around his plate, plunging fistfuls of food into his maw, Burl pattered on, maddening The Madre by dipping his tines into serving bowls, never stopping until his belt buckle gave way.

But then little man, sitting two chairs down, decided to go Paris-on-steroids. He cut in with, "This is crazy—" When would the little man learn not to tangle with Burl? "Anyone can see," little man spat, "this is a, how do you say, tantrum. This city is nothing. A mirage— What will happen when all the building ends? What do people do? Dig in the sand for water?" Everyone in the room stared at little man's cold lips, while celluloidal Grace tipped her head—all agreement—her pupils as chilly as her chest was flat. *Plywood.* She was empty as plywood, the furthest thing from grace—the kind of woman always disgusted with everything in front of her. And all Burl wanted to do was hammer her slack mouth into the wall.

Not that Burl cared what these effetes thought! But he wasn't going to play the nodding, accommodating American. *No sir.* He held up the Glock, pointed it at little man, blurting, "Hate to disappoint you, **DUDE**." An intake of breath, a hush, all eyeballs on him. "Building's just the beginning! We're done with the Bellagio. Project over! Finis! Mr. Wynn's got it wrapped— It's opening in days. Switzerland to Dubai are flying in. Which probably means you're leaving. A little less of you will be a lot more for us." Burl smiled and pulled the trigger. A squirt of water projected across the table and soused little man's eye. France doubled over, yapping like a lap dog.

The Avatar held up his hand, but peace would not be had. "This is way more crazy than the Louvre," Burl continued, blood in his earlobes. "We're talking new construction. One biggest-ass chandelier, that's 40,000 pounds of glass suspended from the ceiling. 14,000 square feet of interior conservatory flowers—cut by **my paths**. And I'll be there, in with the Milkens, the Doles, the Saudis. In a few days, this town will be the sweetest spot on earth— And after it's over, I'll be getting in on another casino, another development, another cash-in. Because baby, there's always another. That's how it works out here. So, go shove that up King Louis' ass!" Burl threw down the squirt gun, but kept smiling while Lori's eyes roved over his face.

But then, he felt yogini's soggy hand on his upper arm. He shoved it off, pissed, stood up to make for the front door, but was stopped by The Avatar's laughter.

Laughing Stock

"Where's Buuurrrrlllll? Where's da man who laughs?" The Avatar said, belching into his fist, before whispering into The Madre's ear. The old biddy was always handy. She pulled back The Avatar's S & M chair, allowing The Avatar to totter over, patting his belly. "Tine to finish all dis!" he said, jabbing a finger into Burl's chest. The Avatar stood four inches shorter than Burl, but reached up with his other hand to press down Burl's pate. Burl flinched as fingernails dug into his scalp, nerves zapping along his temples. It was as if The Avatar were training a mad-dog to sit.

At 11:00 p.m., when Burl should've been bagging the yogini, the group slumped on Lori's goddamn sofa, fresh waves of gas percolating in colons.

"Well," The Madre sighed, the idea of dessert a crime against humanity. As always, The Madre sat in for The Avatar, while only The Avatar moved about freely. The others waited like marionettes, swaying back and forth, pandering and devoted. While yogini's sweet ass dozed on a barstool, The Madre became more pedantic by the second, her eyes swooping from face to face with a soft, hazy expression of compassion—a mannerism pilfered from various gurus.

"The Avatar has several students beginning an intensive tonight," she was saying. "He's preparing to open the space so that we can have a clearer experience of ourselves in the coming weeks. This is a process that involves patience and understanding." Turning to Grace, she said, "Speaking of understanding...I understand many of you are familiar with other teachers.

The Avatar is not like any other. For those of you who want a completely new experience of life, here is a genuine way to connect." On it went until, "I'm happy to answer any questions—"

Burl—yawning, eyes red—managed to raise his hand. He stared at The Madre until she couldn't ignore him. After all, she'd dared to moderate what he hoped would be a revolution. At $1,000 per student, this little evening of vegetable grazing wasn't cheap. Moods were quickly plummeting—quiet rage egged-on by digestive discomfort. One look at little man's squinted eyes and any doubt of hell's existence was annihilated. The Parisian might know sense after all.

"Burl," The Madre said, distaste soured the holy vowels of his name, as if he sat naked, rubbing up against the yogini's child-mind. And what would The Madre think of the lady tattoo on his pig-pink chest? "You're lucky we haven't asked you to leave." Was this a gesture? Was The Madre acknowledging him?

Normally, Burl would've countered with, "Actually—I'm not done—" But he needed the yogini's naked body against his groin.

Past midnight, the hours ejaculated into the dark. Lori tripped into the confines of her befouled bathroom, plywood door in tethers. The Madre droned on: "We are kuje buildings or landscapes in various stages of construction— Or, as with me, in various stages of renovation!" In the half-light, The Madre's teeth appeared bruised, devastated by menopause. "The Avatar is a great source of understanding and help. He's refreshed my experience of life."

"My experience," Burl groaned at the five followers lying in fetal balls, snoring on Lori's floor, "tells me 'damn right.' Right here, there's a new frontier with new paradigms—So where's The Avatar?" Little man, in his drawstring underwear, rested on an S & M chair with head flung back, eyes shut, howling lines of saliva.

"As The Avatar says," Nora incanted, "look beyond the surface to see the openings." To see the openings Burl shut his eyes, imagining only one.

At two in the morning, Burl awoke gasping. Shaken, he dug into his pockets for car keys. Yogini rested her head against the kitchen counter where everything smelled like death. He'd leave with or without her. He listed in the dimness, stumbled forward, spotting Lori's slumped shoulders over the sink, where she rinsed the last water glasses for the dishwasher.

Obviously, The Avatar had entrenched himself with Grace. She'd disappeared minutes after he had. They were probably sampling pheromones at that very moment. But Burl wanted to believe in The Avatar's "Hhheeeeeeyyyyyyeeeee!" and the flashes of insight coming from his mouth, waking everyone up. He needed the patter of the group the way dry ground needed rain. He ached to feel The Avatar's fingernails breaking through his scalp again, because his life had become a series of senseless interactions—smiles and deaths that meant nothing, entrances and exits from deals, and escapes from people he didn't understand. He needed this guru because he was in deep—stuck in the goddamn, fucking web.

Rebel Without a Cause

Deep down, he knew yogini was a rebel. She'd surprised him. She wasn't her mother's marionette, after all—because the next day he got what he wanted the way he always got what he wanted. He licked yogini all over Vegas until maple syrup dripped from her underwear. Which made him think she'd never leave. And she wouldn't leave until they'd seriously celebrated at the Bellagio, maybe talk nuptials if things worked out.

Burl had it planned. He'd "rev up" with a jaunt to Prada, where yogini would get fitted in a leather sheath. Next, he'd speed the Strip in his Miata, sideswiping the frumpy. Finally, the night of the Bellagio's grand opening, he'd valet park at the casino's entrance, seek out and chat up Mr. Wynn (a nice guy who understood the importance of pavers) and corner Sumner Redstone, John Malone, Ted Turner—or whoever else arrived by private jet—reams of cash splashing black jack tables. Less importantly, he'd click heels with yogini on certain tiled areas—his babies—located kitty corner to the Conservatory of Flowers, and within sniffing-distance of carnations and Scottish moss maybe slow dance and smooch under the lobby's massive new chandelier.

"Art, baby," Burl grinned, kneading yogini's forearm, because two-plus days into the visit they still hadn't found a moment to properly fuck. "Mr. Wynn's got one very fine art gallery—Van Goghs and Monets." His coffee mug lay cold. But none of it mattered, because yogini's muffin-breath flooded him with ideas. "We're getting you a dress." This wasn't a sugar daddy week for nothing! He knew where to go. He could have sung the names—Prada, Dior, Chanel, Armani, Bottega Veneta, Gucci, Fendi—as he slouched on a Starbucks sofa, high on corporeal real estate. "Baby, there's nothing in the world like you being here!! Dreams are real. Want a mansion? Here's a mansion. Want fame, goddamn, turn the corner and find it. We're in the Pharaoh's chambers, the pirates' wake, the—" He searched for more comparisons, stumbled over names—that palace in the French countryside that wasn't the Louvre, that building some Indian guy built for his dead wife—and no, he wasn't going senile. No one in his family had ever died of dementia. But yes, at post-fifty, he'd begun to forget names just like everyone else.

Better to move on to stargazing—and not the kind viewed from campers. Billionaire stargazing. He wanted to share temples for the rich with her, where they could be surrounded by moats of beautiful devotees— because every Siddhartha, like himself, made Vegas home. And in that way, he took his yogini to the million dollar tables.

Departures

"The impossible is possible."

<u>40 Days and 40 Nights In The Desert</u>

Late in her second day on the planet they called Vegas, the sky turned into a pink flamingo that dipped cirrus-cloud legs into a boiling cauldron. The air spat heat, drying her armpits and making her sprout pimples.

Her journey from the sleeping bag on Lori's rug—where she'd collapsed near morning—to Burl's parked SUV, had sapped her of energy. But Burl was jamming to go, all pent-up coyote vibrating in the 90-degree heat, inhaling dryness like it powered his core. He ran through a must-do list—first Starbucks, ("because everyone's into coffee"), followed by dinner at the Venetian ("cause it's almost night all over again!"), and most definitely midnight (or maybe morning) at Red Rock. "Yeah, that's tomorrow. But tonight—" He had surprises, one involving whipped cream and *hot spots*.

"Yogini, it's so damn hot we're going to **The Beach**. We're ab-so-**fucking**-lutely going—" On the curbside, while pointing his keys and unlocking his sweltering SUV, he ran and danced in place like he'd done at the airport. So, why was she sliding in? Because she felt guilty? Because he'd paid her way? Why when things didn't look so good? Earlier, in front of Nora, he'd pinched her butt, causing a stone to drop into her gut. Didn't that make it clear that she should vamoose?

He kept saying, "Baby," bouncing into his seat behind the wheel. "This is great!" Strapped in, she could barely catch her breath, the motor rumbling exhaust that overwhelmed the cul-de-sac. "Finally! I got you to myself! With The Avatar's blessing." She felt dizzy, inhaling fumes as he leaned towards her and nearly bit off her lips, pushing his tongue between her teeth. "Mmmmm," he pulled back, leering, grabbing her hand and licking the salt from her forefinger, succeeding in sending chills of fear up her spine. She tried to smile, play happy, not wanting to gag. It helped to stare at herself in the side-view mirror. "Oh Man! You're one hellava cupcake."

For some reason Burl insisted on exploring the libretto-swamped canals of the Venetian, because they must "make up for lost time" by swilling wine, twirling forks, and "savoring the romance." She hadn't eaten since the night before, but she couldn't imagine dining at a casino, because since getting off the plane, she'd needed a bathroom because everyone started lining up at Lori's— And when she finally got her turn, The Avatar cornered her—slinked in behind her—claiming that he could "unlock her heart" with the toilet mere inches away. That's when Burl smashed the door, and then there'd been no chance.

But somehow they now stood beneath the fake sky overlooking a chasm of gondolas, overhearing a lot of, "Awesome!" and "Totally a thousand times better than the real thing," as cigarette smoke circulated through the ventilation system.

"You got to love it!" Burl was saying. He grabbed her elbow, and steered past the doublewide couple waddling towards an ATM. More than a few desperate figures sucked up obese platters of fettuccini, kids bawling, a gold-to-purple sunset fading around them like the end of time, leaving Jane to waves of nausea. Tailgating a waitress tending tables by the Grande Canal, Burl boomed, "You'll love this place. They've got veggies." He gestured to the entrance. Jane stumbled into an interior of gold foil and red tiles, where Burl pushed her into a chair.

"Forget the prices. Get the expensive stuff, the extra large lettuce head or the grilled tree bark." He laughed, slapping his palm against the table and rattling the silverware. "Go on, yogini. Check out that menu. Everything's on me." Gripping the rhinestone-studded menu, he eyed the neighboring tables like a famished dog, eventually calming down enough to peruse the list of overpriced pizzas, which, on the tables of nearby customers, looked like pancakes dotted with turds.

Ready to order, Burl grabbed her hand, squeezing it. "Nothing like dinner to get us in the mood—" he murmured. "You look beautiful!" Against her better judgment, she smiled, bowing her head behind her menu. Not that she wanted to dangle her fork over a bowl of $30 frisee—not with her stomach in knots. Every delay was welcome.

"Let's get some red—" he said, picking up the "Bevande" menu. "Great pairing with spaghetti and veal-whatever-the-fuck." He threw down the wine list, leaned forward, and gazed into her eyes as if she were a newborn. Raising his finger, but never taking his eyes off her, he barked at a random server: "Two reds. Your house brand—"

Staring at Jane's face, not a word passed between them, until, like a miracle, a bottle appeared—something highly recommended by a lithe but well-endowed blond in lingerie. She carried two twanging glasses in one boney hand, poured and thrust one sloshing goblet in Burl's direction. He stuck his nose in the rim, swirled the wine, and swished it over his teeth as the waitress kept watch like a dominatrix.

Winking at the blond's chest, Burl nodded, giving the go ahead, so that she poured a long red leg of liquid into each glass before swaying towards the next table, Burl's eyes lingering on her backside. "Mhmmm—" he moaned, off in some fantasy. But then, he sat straight, held up his glass, and cleared his throat. "A toast!" He said, nodding for Jane to lift a glass.

As if quoting a sage, he began, "I'm so glad you decided to be with me on this occasion, yogini. You have filled the hours so far," in the few they'd been together, she thought, "with more than I can say. Love ya, Baby!" He smiled anthocyanins and gulped the rest in his glass.

It was an endless meal of fondling hands, falsely intense looks, and broad statements: "This is so great—oh man, oh baby, I've waited so long." Yeah, only three weeks, she thought. "You need to lighten up, yogini—enjoy yourself now that you're out of that hellhole New York, away from The Madre! No more hovering over you! No more," in falsetto, "'honey, don't do that!'"

The evening hit a low point when he suggested Jane sample his veal. She reminded him, for the second time in two days, that she was vegan. But this didn't faze him, even as meat sobbed, apologetic, in a strange gray sauce. "Sure you're not interested?" he tempted, thrusting out a triangle of gray flesh. It dangled from tines, dangerously close to her nose. She inhaled a pungent whiff that reminded her of a clogged toilet, further unsettling her stomach. The only thing she could do was press a napkin to her lips.

"No, Burl," she managed, pushing back her chair. This was possibly the tenth, "no" she'd offered since her arrival. In fact, very few words had passed out of her since touch down at McCarran Airport. She'd remained wordless at Lori's. And now, in the casino, he mainly steered as if she were a drifting boat—except when it came to gray meat.

"Okay, woman. If you want to miss a good thing, that's your choice. All I know is I try to live in the moment, with as much positive energy as I can. It's all attitude." He shoved the meat between his lips, his cheeks aglow with wine. Chewing, he pointed his finger at Jane's third eye. "That Garuda I gave you? Let me tell you," he tugged a nugget of gristle from between his teeth. "You want to fly with the Lord, you won't waste time on carrot sticks and Beano."

More meat, more chewing, more distended cheeks, followed by a fuel spill of self-help statements. Like raw sewage, the repetition of hackneyed phrases stank up all possibility of real conversation. Acting the savior, he spewed the same affirmations he obviously repeated in front of every mirror he passed. "Daily practice is everything. I'm telling you. It's amazing. I highly recommend it. It's about believing and living **NOW**! Speak and act **from** your intention, **for** your intention, and **by** your intention! Find peace of mind and you'll find peace everywhere! Call up your wisest self and face adversity with your best face."

He gulped wine, poured more, and loaded the table with one-liners, his words pocking the red placemats and dinner platters with spittle. And then, he paused, confusion all over his face.

"Shit. That reminds me. That's the thing about The Avatar— He knows the secret of getting down. He knows it starts with **you** and ends with **you** and no one else! It's all about **you**! All about your choices. Take responsibility. Hell is your own damn fault. Because no matter what happens to you, you always have you." From the start, Jane couldn't swallow this kind of packaged wisdom, especially when considering prisoners of war, which proved that "creating your own reality" was a lot of bullshit.

In truth, Jane had reservations about everyone—especially The Avatar—who regularly gambled and sometimes cornered young women in bathrooms moments before their sugar daddies shoved their knees through doors—who'd become a cliché. But for some reason there were still a lot of Maharishis and Sri Rajneeshes in Rolls Royces paving their way across America, because any sadhu who understood geomagnetism and could manipulate mother earth's iron core—could ignite kundalini and exhale ribbons of insight through his nostrils, could warp gravity, shift the earthbound to the light-bound with a flick of a pinky—had to enjoy a few perks. Because, after all, anyone who had that kind of power was welcome to screw his way through life. And why not? Everyone else was doing it. Why not hump like Playboy bunnies and enjoy the moment, because who, in this age of the future, really believed that sex without boundaries was damaging?

Burl's Manse

In the early, halcyon days of fatherhood, when he'd held his baby Brianna, he didn't give hell about casinos or paving stones. All he cared about was his little blond fuzz in candy-cane outfits. Burl's loser-brother Jack—who lived in a shit trailer by the same shitwater canal in Phoenix—once said he'd give away every car in his lot to buy a baby as beautiful as Brianna—which made Burl proud. But now Brianna mainly flicked insults at Burl's face.

Still, being a dad made him more of a man. When he first got into the yogini's pants, when The Madre still acted like Burl was a gentleman, he kept saying, "You women!" pausing to let this sink in. "It's fucking crazy! Two peas in a pod." But when yogini asked him to explain, he couldn't think of anything Brianna and yogini had in common, other than coloring.

When they fucked, Burl liked that yogini's eyes stuck to his tattoo as it rose and fell. It made him feel like a true Garuda flying high with love. In New York, he started thinking of the infinite possibilities that could materialize from a union. They'd make a good team. He liked that The Avatar winked after Burl emerged from the guestroom—with its rattling radiator— wearing only a towel, liked being seen scratching his bare chest, stinking of morning breath. He liked muttering, "She'll be out soon. Got any coffee?" And it was telepathic when, more than once, at the breakfast table The Avatar sang: "Hhhheeeeeyyyyyyyyeeeeee! Two lovebirds— meant to beeeee! Sooooo nice—! I see many many tings in your future!"

When Burl first nailed her in New York, yogini had squirmed beneath him as if he were King Kong fisting Fay Wray showing novice eyes—just like Brianna's.

Actually, Burl knew where they'd tie the knot, knew which ring he'd slip on yogini's finger—the gold band with three pinprick diamonds he'd spotted at the Zales outlet on Las Vegas Boulevard South. He couldn't wait to show her his beefed up, re-stuccoed ranch house. Next to that hellhole on Lexington Avenue, his slate flooring, glass dinette with leather chairs, wall-to-wall carpeting in the bedrooms, would look like a dream. She'd gape at the almost-finished interior waterfall with its babbling-brook sound more babbly than any real brook. He couldn't wait till she got hooked on switching the brook on and off, frothing it up or down by sliding the dimmer switch next to his refrigerator. As the water flowed, they'd lick each other's armpits and sink into his prized Temperapedic draped with furs, where he'd get tantric, pluck her nipples as if she were a Fender Stratocaster and he a vibrating Jimi Hendrix sinking into her with smooth, driving glides that left her vulva quivering and red as raw meat, leaving her heifer's hole dry and prickly with sappy pine needles glued to her labia! *Who said a little S&M didn't wake up the soul?*

If anyone knew how to woo a teetotaler with exotic drinks, it was SlyMaster Burl who'd overcome the pain—or was it loss?—that settled in every cortex of every creature roaming the earth by filling his days with endless distraction and speed. With the help of Viagra, he knew French ticklers, dildos, water vibrators, and anal products—the kind that made massages, luxury cars, and vacations to Maui seem like appetizers. So what if nuzzling her neck already felt like an old habit he carried from one woman to another, because he'd build this relationship into Wayne Dyer's idea of heaven.

From the start, this was his mission to remake her world. He'd drilled Dyer into her ears like fancy gold earrings, because he aimed to reconstruct a new, happier Jane if they were getting married. Because who else could fix her soul, change her mind and eyes?

As his buddy Warren once said, "you leave the continent and your eyes are never the same." Now there was a man—Warren. He'd visited Africa to explore and invest in Big Oil, and returned home with intestinal parasites and a bitter view of humanity.

Bitterness aside, Burl couldn't do anything but promise the world.

Okay, call it what it was. He **enticed** her, a snake charmer making music from a hike up Mt. Charleston, or a spin around Red Rock with its 13-mile loop of trailheads nestled in mesquite. He'd teach her about desert plants like yucca, desert candle and larkspur. He'd celebrate the wilderness with his feet, because wild horses, like Burl, still existed.

At the Starbucks he nuzzled her cheek and pressed his nose into her sweet butter skin. Later he sniffed her sweat where it dried on her neck. For this he promised a thousand chess pieces of love and formation. He promised communion and used the word commune when he sang: "I want to commune with you," strumming air guitar in his living room. "Like a creature," he sang, "I'd fly to you, all the way to the end of the horizon." Wayne Dyer would've been proud.

He promised the dress. He already knew what it would look like— the same as in that reality TV show about three western women gussying up their torn dresses, because they'd been through cattle branding, motorcycle rides, and a lot of sex. He could see yogini wearing a torn dress in Red Rock, climbing on the ancient Keystone Thrust Fault—a name he liked because thrusting anything, even a fault, bode well, because only he could change the world.

Blown Away by the Great Dust Storm

Her first encounter with The Avatar took place after Nora hyped him as the new Namananda, who, legend told, walked through walls and could be in two places at once. The Avatar wasn't just an ordinary enlightened being, but was Vishnu himself, ushering in a new Yuga.

That first visit, the room was dark. Jane lay on the sofa and shut her eyes. The Avatar caressed her cheek and blew a stream of white, red, and yellow sparks that melted into her forehead like sugar snowflakes dropped into a pan of sizzling butter. As lights descended into her, an eerie glow embedded itself in her brain like alien creatures from the Andromeda Strain. The sparks made her giggle, and The Avatar, in turn, kissed her cheeks, caressed her breasts, and told her she was beautiful.

She exited the chamber feeling giddy, light-hearted, somehow immune to worry, as if she'd drunk five forevers.

That evening, after dreaming of the hermaphrodite, she gulped from the bathroom faucet, wrote words in her diary and lay back down to begin a strange new life. The next morning, she couldn't be still, feeling detached but confused, as if something was pushing her further away from everyone and everything she knew. She was living someone else's story—in the world but also outside of the world, wanting but not wanting, no longer connecting to experience in the same way, so that it seemed nothing could break her down any further, because she'd already crumbled to dust.

Her sense of self had been blown for nearly a decade when Burl took her to the Venetian. Yes, The Avatar was amoral—but she still believed in him, something she'd never be able to explain to Burl.

Somehow sensing this, Burl said, "You think too much," and burped into his napkin, his plate a mess of meat scraps. She'd said nothing since the arrival of the Caesar salad and Tiramisu he'd ordered and pushed in her direction. Egg dressing plus cream pastry did not equal vegan and therefore slowly congealed beneath the vent blowing cool air over their table.

"Ready?" He finally said, whacking the table with his palm. Her gut and head hurt. Her eyes felt heavy. She didn't care, but dreaded the drive to his house. Despite instincts, she drained the red wine from her glass and nodded. Her ears buzzed, and her head twirled when she stood up. The ground swerved, and the Venetian sky warped and darkened as it tried to mimic night. She heard a song, with lyrics, like a jingle:

What's real isn't real.

"Hoh!" She gripped the table as the floor slid out from beneath her. "Oh. Whoa—" She slipped or tumbled, and he laughed and grabbed her around the waist, because instead of dinner, she'd downed an endless helping of crapola wine.

"This is just the beginning baby. Don't get bombed yet!"

After a few drinks, words didn't come any easier to someone who'd never much talked, but she managed to groan, "I'm really tired—"

In college, guys urged girl-friends-with-benefits to drink until they vomited. But not her. A careful drinker, she'd never vomited.

"Easy does it. Let's go—you're tipsy. That's all. We'll get something to wake you up."

"No, no, no—" she moaned, shaking her head. "No more—" There was the problem of allergies and acne. "Please—" Her face lolled against his shoulder as they stumbled between tables. He liked pouring—that was the problem—and she liked drinking. Yet it didn't matter as they moved through people and indigo eternity, and a perfect night-settled over the canal, approximating the darkness of the garbage-strewn waterways of Venice. "The wine," Jane kept moaning as Burl propped her up, at some point, on a bench near lots of legs and noise at the entrance or exit.

"Take a sip," he said. "Baby, you got to see my place." His voice came with a paper cup that became a series of disconnected flash cards of bitterness and heat. And why hadn't they stayed in the restaurant where coffee drinking was easier, quieter, and darker? This fluorescent bitterness was too bright. Where was she? She sputtered, blinked, coughed black liquid. Her stomach burned, the acid rising towards a blank window that reflected her worn expression, where she saw eyes and questions, her own lower lip soft and drooping, her hair singed to a bleached crisp. She could feel the discharge of air-conditioned frigidity all over her skin. Most disturbing of all, she saw skin lesions across her cheeks and chin. And then, everything inside broke loose. She'd blown it—everything.

The Big Kahuna

The sky transformed the linen curtains into bars of light, and Burl jabbed her shoulder. Despite the Tempurpedic, Jane lay on her side, a cardboard doll battling gas, shit, and the remains of nausea and headache. In bed, she'd sprung sweats, pushing back covers only to shiver and pull them back over her shoulder. By morning, the bed felt like flu. She blamed sleeplessness on both the air-conditioner's on/off hum, and on Burl's lack of hospitality. There'd been no time for the bathroom.

Five hours earlier, Burl had unlocked the cheap door of his 1962 ranch house and presented the working-class luxury of a laminated entertainment center. Ignoring Jane's request for a bathroom (hadn't she gone in her pants?), waving off the fact of her jittery heartbeat as coffee masking drunkenness, Burl half-carried/half-pushed her inside.

In the foyer, she stared at black tiles, a tan sofa wrapping the living room around a ginormous screen that spilled wires hooked up to concert-hall-sized speakers. Miniscule windows enhanced the prison-like mood, generating sensations of claustrophobia exacerbated by the only photo in the entire space: a black and white close up of Burl's tattoo.

She blinked as details descended into the gas tank that was her digestive system. "Do you have a bathroom?" she asked again, as if she hadn't asked a thousand times before while the pain in her bowels became a pang for death.

But Burl knew nothing of death, because he grabbed her hand and steered her towards the shadows to celebrate a sore in the floor: a gouged-out blight, like an eye that had been removed. While he discussed the blight with great pride, calling it a "canal," Jane noted that it looked like an elongated commode stretching the length of the living room and into the dining area. The wall-mounted cobblestones, and the spillway, Burl was saying, hadn't been completed. In great detail, he described the waterfall that would gush through the front door, where it would gurgle and purr through the entire house and possibly wash through Jane. And just like that, the thought of all that water pushed opened the doors of her body. She couldn't stop the pent-up deluge, because warmth and wetness melted her inner thighs.

He didn't notice the darkening of her pants, but kept talking. By fall, he was saying as pee soaked through her jeans, waves would fill his inner canal, and he'd have his very own Venetian. Oblivious to everything but the sound of his voice echoing in the near-empty house, he described how the small, interior stream would connect to another waterfall that would flow from the front lawn, and circulate through a slit next to the front door. Water would glide all the way to the bedroom, where he hoped to install a chaise lounge cushioned by more water.

"I'm thinking of putting the sofa," he said, gesturing to the gargantuan piece of furniture enfolding the living room, "on an island that you could get to from a little bridge. A little platform that could slowly spin, like the restaurant in the Stratosphere. My buddy Warren did that in his house, except he's got the stream hooked up to his waterbed. I'm too attached to my Tempurpedic to install a waterbed. But a chaise. Yeah." As the pee cooled, Jane didn't ask what would happen if water flowing into Warren's waterbed got polluted by lighter fluid or acid, because all she really wanted was a toilet and a bed.

But no. She would see more, beginning with the home's "Big Kahuna."

"And the Big Kahuna is—" Burl said, drumming forefingers on the back of the sofa. "My babies." These "babies" were two alarm systems, *because in Las Vegas you could never be too safe*, especially with a house only blocks from the Strip. A known company covered the basics, but the other alarm system was of his own creation. "My Big Kahuna."

This "personally created" alarm system had been inspired by Looney Toons and involved a series of strung mechanisms. If the wrong person opened a window the wrong way, he or she could trigger the stereo system—which also fed into the "GINORMOUS" TV speakers—causing a blast of Black Sabbath to decimate the neighborhood. Accidental triggering of "THE BLACK KAHUNA," as Burl called it, had only occurred once as a result of vermin.

"But baby, what a scene!" It had alerted neighbors up to twelve blocks away, and had so alarmed the old lady next door when her house nearly shook off its foundation that she needed to be hospitalized. Needless to say, when police arrived, Burl barely skirted a $500 fine. But to this he only laughed. "It proves," he said, "I've rigged this place to survive every intrusion!"

His other traps were far more Bugs Bunny-ish, causing Burl to caution Jane against checking out the closets: "Do not, I repeat, **do not** explore under **any and all** circumstances." Much less problematic to the neighbors—though hugely tricky for those within Burl's dwelling—these traps involved nets that swooped down from trapdoors and hidden shelves.

"And don't open the kitchen drawers!" he added.

Her knees trembled as the pee chilled to air-conditioned temperatures. But soon she worried about how he might have rigged the toilet—especially as she hadn't yet recovered from the nasty episode of vomiting at what turned out to be a 7-Eleven two blocks from his house.

"Don't ever," he said, finger wagging her face. "**Not ever**, for any reason other than fire, **open a window in this house**!" She nodded, murmuring assent. "**Don't**, and I mean **DON'T**, and I mean **never ever** open a closet without using a master key. I've got those here on my master keychain." He opened a drawer in the coffee table and pulled out a colossal circular of keys—enough keys to open every door of a university—and began jingling it like a janitor.

"Basically, don't get near a closet unless you want to end up in one of my nets. And if you do, don't expect me to cut you down." He said this with a leer that, even through her malaise, caused chills, a feeling she should've felt when she first met him. "Like I said, stay away from the kitchen. I've got the cabinets bugged—one of them with steak knives. So, what I'm saying is, you need to be careful about what you do in my house. **Follow instructions**."

Where had her sense of self-preservation been all these years? When had she cared? She should have stayed away from this man, but she'd flown right into his trap. She had to get out of there, but her legs could barely move.

He grabbed her hand, and moments later she swayed in the doorway of his bedroom, floating above the beige wall-to-wall carpet, the neat queen mattress that looked like a slab of concrete on a raised platform. Black satin pillows and an onyx comforter with reverse tiger-strips reminded her of oil slicks. With headache, she could still feel repulsed by Burl's bed.

"I need the bathroom" Jane managed. He hadn't yet noticed the pee, hadn't minded that her shirt and the edges of her mouth were speckled with dry vomit.

"Go ahead—" he laughed. "This isn't jail. Go on. But make sure you get sugarcoated for a little mmmmm aaa hhhmmmm...." He began his stationary rumba, and she slipped inside a white-tiled nook that reeked of cheap cologne, Ivory soap, and disinfectant. She shut the plywood door and tried to tune out the sound of Burl's humming. But flipping on the ventilation fan to ominous white noise, she sensed he was waiting with ear pressed to door. And then she searched the walls for cameras.

Perhaps it was the slight creaking sound or the two dark bands at the doorjamb, where a shadow staunched the bedroom's amber light that made her queasy. Or maybe it was the way the cardboard walls and doors made everything transparent. Whatever it was, she felt paranoid.

On the toilet, she focused on the Formica cabinets with their chipped edges, worrying that he'd rigged them with sarin gas. All she needed was a window and five minutes. But then she remembered Burl's warnings and lost that idea.

No dignity, her sphincter discharged air. Backed up, she gazed at the ceiling where she spotted a post-it with the words: "I AM IT," so that she gave up and turned herself out of the lavatory, still clogged like a poorly maintained sewage line. As she suspected, he was right there.

"How about fresh panties—" He held up her pink underwear, waving it like a flag. He'd opened and rummaged through her luggage, which gaped up at her, disheveled, from the foot of the bed. "Or maybe," he licked his lips, undoing his belt where his belly relaxed at the buckle's release. "We should just see what happens if I change you myself—" She ached as he approached. He unzipped his jeans—still wearing the black t-shirt with its disturbing silver pirate's skull.

Inches away, he paused, surprised or terrified, and sniffed the wet-dog air surrounding her. His face contorting around his nose, he growled, "Holy shit. What the hell is that smell? Go take a shower woman!" He stumbled back and collapsed on the bed, squeezing his nose between thumb and forefinger.

Beneath the spray, soaping her belly and breasts, she puzzled over why he hadn't noticed the stench earlier. Had he set up that moment to make her feel more ashamed? Or had he genuinely been too excited by the house tour to notice odors? Either way, she was overcome. And though she found Burl repulsive in multiple ways, she doubled over with the disgrace of her body's foulness, its subterfuge, its self-absorption, spiraling down an interior drain that led to her own spineless nature.

Red Rock

That morning, as she struggled, exhausted and ashamed, he announced that Red Rock awaited, that they needed to set off by 7:00 a.m. if they wanted to beat the heat. It was urgent that they get going, because he had a list of things to do before the Bellagio opened later that week.

He'd already brewed coffee in the kitchen, expecting she'd gulp the black liquid after all that vomiting. No breakfast though— It would slow them down and heat them up. They'd eat later, after the hike. She was still absorbing the night's misfortunes: her constipation, and Burl's violent, unprotected fucking—which had taken place after the shower while she lay helpless and unmoving on his sponge-like bed.

Still, hunger and thirst had returned. Oddly, she hankered for cream of wheat, a treat she hadn't eaten since childhood when Nora had stirred the white grains into hot milk. Back then, Jane watched, hypnotized by its bubbling and thickening into bowls that Nora sprinkled with brown sugar and chunks of melting butter—gold bracelets melting on snow—believing everything melted into sweetness and beauty.

"Here's the plan," Burl said. She sat on his bed of black satin, her nudity grotesque with goose bumps, her bristle hair knotted near her scalp, the corners of her lips caked with sand, her half-shut eyes filled with grit. "Figure we make the park before opening, so we get the best parking. You got to love that place, but man. The crowds. You got to see it when no one's there."

"But," she croaked, her throat rough as a twice-baked crouton, "What are we going to do—" Already sun slanted through windows.

"Damn, woman," he whacked the mattress. "What else? We already talked about it— You really were out of it." He shook his head like all he wanted was for her to get real, wake up, and stay on subject. "I told you. We're meeting infinity. I'm taking you to the horizon—"

"Oh." She looked at her hands. They seemed too small for infinity. "I didn't realize it would be this morning."

"Yeah well, that's okay. Get up so we can get out of here. Otherwise, we won't be able to go till next week. I've got a shitload booked!" He said this as if he'd waited long enough only to find out the sex was subpar.

She had no choice, pushing forward against a room full of mud, stumbling to the toilet. Afraid to shut the door, she sat on the can, still constipated, her breasts resting against her abdomen. She was thankful when Burl pounded out of the bedroom for more coffee.

"Here—" He thrust a mug into her hand as soon as she walked into the kitchen. Hungry for anything, she sipped. Sugar and caffeine bored holes in her stomach, but she no longer cared. Finishing her cup, she placed it on the counter, careful not to jostle the kitchen drawers.

"Which ones are rigged?" she asked, each drawer a window into his mind.

"All of them—" he said.

She asked for water, and he took an unwashed glass from the sink, sloshing it with tap, and handed it to her. "Taste Lake Mead. It's a hell of lot better than drinking the Hudson." Avoiding conflict, she didn't mention that New York didn't get its water from rivers.

He filled two army-navy canteens with Gatorade that sloshed against screw-off caps and slung them over his shoulder. She asked that her's be filled with water instead, but he said, "Baby. Gatorade is what we'll need when it gets to be triple digits. I know. I took these on a lot of trips— They saved my life I can't tell you how many times!" He patted her shoulder as if she were nine, the way she asked such questions. "Let's get out of here—"

Moments later, they sat in his SUV, air conditioning blasting dust. They drove past endless shopping centers, the luster of the Strip pale as Jane felt in the bright morning. She stared as the Stratosphere, the Luxor, New York New York and all the others shrinking against the russet mountains. They drove along W. Sahara Avenue towards Summerlin, into an endless sameness of stucco and clay roof tiles, bland incarnations of Spanish colonial.

"This is what we do," Burl said, nodding at golf greens veined with cart paths. "We're talking the hottest neighborhoods in Vegas— It's this or Henderson. It's the green belt— You got to love the lawns up here. And the views. I get loads of work from the retirees. Lots of money in these cul-de-sacs. Ex-doctors, lawyers, Hollywood types."

It seemed anathema that anyone would choose to live in this alternate earth of *The Martian Chronicles* meets *The Twilight Zone*. She hadn't been prepared for this newest-of-new suburb-escapes, where hearth and home rested dry and bored and brain-drained. Vaguely, she sensed that each house, with its few distinct markings, blushed the same peach uniformity. There were no red, yellow, blue or purple doors above the Strip. It seemed this bland homescape of colorless entries led to insanity, each construction differing only slightly in its mental reordering, because without color there were no choices. In this controlled setting, where the aged withered into the sand, monochrome equated death.

Furthermore, it was too easy to get lost in the mazelike, no-return streets. It seemed to Jane that once you entered the gates of Hell, the spiraling cul-de-sacs branded you a castaway, adrift among the "elderly" who drifted through their "golden years" in relentless, sun-tiled discomfort.

Again, she wanted to flee, but she couldn't have opened the passenger door if she wanted to. In the airless confines, her lungs became hot air balloons as new construction blazed past—billions of dollars of wood, drywall, concrete, and China-hewn hardware—the whole experience clipped from a 1950s sci-fi horror flick. But Burl was chuckling. "These half-brains come out here from hell knows and think they know everything." He shook his head in disbelief.

Scrub for the Hippy Chick

Yes, Burl was petty, self-aggrandizing, aggressive, and controlling. And yes, he didn't know the meaning of a social cue. But he knew good material, and he understood what it took to construct a home. And though she didn't understand why, she wanted something from him.

They drove towards an ethereal bowl of fire—what Burl called the "epicenter" of Red Rock—into fire-colored outcrops of craggy, castle-like formations that jutted into the sky. Jane gripped her armrest as they jounced over the road and her innards reeled.

"You got to love it!" Burl sputtered, but she couldn't imagine exploring the geologic drops and heights of time, though she'd done so before—in many past incarnations. Not long ago, she and Ben hiked Zion, through similar chasms. But next to Burl's metallic breath, barely cloaked in musk cologne, she felt very far from awe. Instead, the mere sight of outcrops chapped her lips. A pit latrine would have been more appealing than speeding past junked space rocks.

The air conditioner barely kept the air tepid, making the prospect of abandoning the SUV's relative cool an act of insanity. But Burl parked in the already baking lot, asphalt already sizzling blurry air. Nearby, a dented red Honda hunkered beneath a week's worth of dust, windows nearly opaque so that the vehicle seemed to beg for a square of shade as if begging for another life.

"WooWee!" Burl hooted, heaving around to the backseat, causing the SUV to tremble. "Canteens!" He grabbed their straps and swung the jostling canisters onto Jane's lap. "Sunscreen!" He pawed a yellow tube and pitched it at her head. "Hats!" He shoved a red UNLV baseball cap onto his hairless pate. "You got one?" he barked, turning with raised brows. She stared at him, exhausted. "Oh shit, you're gonna fry. Damn. What the hell were you thinking? Shit." He scowled at her lap. "Well. Too late now. All right. Listen, here's what we do when we forget hats. We make one. Come here—" He snapped his fingers, and then gripped her shoulders. "Come on. Get close." He pressed down and yanked, leaving what would become an oval bruise near her collarbone.

"Ow!" She yelled, but he ignored everything but the itch on his cheek, which he pawed.

"You got an extra shirt or something?" She shook her head, massaging her shoulder. "Damn, you're unprepared. Okay, so here's what we do—" He opened his car door to a wall of heat. "Shit, already an inferno—" He hopped out, and shambled to the back of the vehicle and opened the back. "Always drive with rags—" He rummaged and pulled out an old t-shirt slashed with a charcoal bolt of grease. "Doesn't matter what we use— Desert like this would make Dolly Parton into a hippy chick."

At first Jane refused to tie the nostril-searing fabric around her forehead. But Burl insisted, keen on "hippy-chicking" her even if they had to stay in the "damn" SUV until sunset. "Serious—you're not hiking without protection, and we're not leaving till you see this place—"

Worn down, Jane tethered the soiled rag to her forehead, inhaling heady fumes. Twenty minutes later towering convolutions of burnt sandstone shifted around them, Burl's boots crunching ahead, while Jane's feet already felt like sweat-soaked oven mitts. The motionless air dried and pricked her throat, her eyelids like cotton stuck with thistles. Burl's neck already looked like a boiled lobster tail broken only by two white stripes of zinc oxide, the same he'd smeared on her cheeks.

Sun struck, they pushed through the heat, sweat instantly fizzling away. If she licked her lips, the moisture vanished, leaving her more seared than before. Her tongue soon turned into sawdust against the velvet of her inner cheeks. Periodically, she drank orange-flavored fluid from her canteen, trying to keep pace with Burl's "scratch-rush, scratch-rush " footfall as his wordless back directed them beyond the boundary visited by tourists. They took a narrow trail, a pencil line that scrawled across the ruddy formations and twisted up towards a spire where sun intensified with elevation gain. Against comprehension, the temperature dangled from the triple digits like a trapeze artist.

Burl stopped at a bend, squinting through shades at the brightness. "We'll take this up to where I had my first revelation." He fumbled with the cap of his canteen, his fingers puffed and spotted like grilled sausages. He gulped Gatorade, gripping the cap. When he was done, he grinned. "Nothing like the desert to give a man revelations— Holy places you'll rarely see—" His distended fingers slipped as he re-capped the canteen. He shook it to hear the slosh of what was left.

Little of his narrative about the Paiute got through to Jane. Her ears, like her brain, half worked like rusted equipment. And her vocal chords felt inoperable as dryness seemed to peel away all strength. Occasionally she sipped, but the Gatorade evaporated from her tongue in seconds. Ice and dripping melon and juicy peaches sliced with an ice-cold knife floated through her mind. With every step, everything swelled with heat, with nausea—especially when they slacked or when she shut her eyes and the sun turned into orange and gold swirls, the caustic stench of grease seeping into her as the rag tightened around her forehead.

Eventually, she rasped that she wondered why they needed to go so far? Couldn't they have revelations below? His answer came as laughter. Eventually he added, "What's that saying? No pain, no gain. A spiritual teacher once said you get perspective taking strides—"

He turned to her, eyes bloodshot, cheeks flushed with the warning of heart attack. She considered his build: hefty around the middle, thinner in the legs, with those telltale vertical lines in his earlobes that her father used to call "death lines." If Burl dropped, she'd have to scramble more than three miles down slippery scree—all crushed sand and pebbles—to seek a random person in the empty lot. Of course, there had to be a ranger somewhere, but where? She might not find anyone. And then she'd have to drive the long road back to the retirement community and call for an ambulance. Why did she seem to always get herself into these situations?

"Burl." She laid a hand on his shoulder. Her pine needle throat fluttered feathers and glue, words crashing into each other. "Let's turn back."

"Hell no! What are you saying, girl!" He whipped off his baseball cap, exposing shining scalp. He fanned his cheeks. "I've been up here a thousand times. In all weather. We're not turning back."

They pressed on with distended legs, through the throb of caffeinated blood in her temples. Thirst, fatigue, heat combined to prepare a feast of death.

"Come on—" He groaned, the rapture in his eyes frightening. The view had opened up more, but to Jane it all seemed flat in its beige and rust and bright expansiveness though a breeze softened the blow of so much nothingness. It caught the singed strands of her hair, whipping them back—lifting away the noxious stench of motor fuel emanating from her head rag until the rush in her ears dropped to zero, leaving a stifling and ringing stillness.

Tumbleweed and oak brush shrub scratched at a sky of broadening contrails she'd never reach. If only she could be pulled up and away and taken into the cabin where the flight attendant served crisp, cold fluid with scooped ice in a plastic cup. She stared at the ghost of the plane as Burl grabbed her arm, still panting with revelations. He pushed her against pebbles that pocked and scraped her hips and buttocks.

"Good," he croaked, eyes darting at an enemy platoon that wasn't around the bend. "We're here." He tugged at her t-shirt with ragged, senseless gestures. "Too tied up in thoughts. All the time, thoughts—" Eyes from sky to the oval of his baldness, to the cheek smudged with clay. He pulled off his sweat-soaked golf shirt, bringing it over his head to show his mottled and flaccid belly.

"Yogini!" He thumped his tattoo. "You're it!" As he moved, the tattoo shimmied. She focused on the white cream of thirst rimming the corners of his lips, couldn't take her eyes off this sign of dehydration. It played around his speech and reminded her of a chemistry teacher she'd once had in high school, all that white glue of thirst turning into strands of desperation and shame between spoken words. "Stay there—" His breath dropped onto her like horse manure, and he grimaced as he unbuckled his belt.

She'd always remember that hardest, most scraped spot of earth. But she made it easier by lying still, knowing she'd been tired since childhood, since before Ben died in the hospital just days after the accident, because that's what really happened and that's why she left Rudy in the cafeteria, tired since she stopped making choices, because choices meant nothing to her, tired since Nora's gift of a cinnamon teddy bear, since the story of Namananda—before all of it. Because she knew she had no place in the land of the willful. Yet someone once said, "it's a choice not to choose." And if she could choose not to choose then she could choose to choose. Catching at this thought, she watched the sky divide and undivide over Burl's up and down motion as all the sand in the world blew over her.

Sand

"Tomorrow's another day."

<u>Silicon – 2000</u>

Things change, whether we like it or not. But still, nobody needed to know that number 14 on the periodic table—Silicon—was the second most abundant element on earth, the foundation of quartz, sand, opal, clay, and mica, that it transmitted infrared light, and siphoned photons into lasers, computers, cell phones, and every gadget Jane's cousin Neil dropped onto his dining room table because quartz had taken over the world.

Somehow she'd made it through Red Rock and Burl's kitchen cleavers, escaping by bus and air, eventually landing in Nora's inkjet-cartridge hovel where she took solace in the chipped paint and roaches of her childhood, bawling when she inhaled the scent of rose hand cream wafting through the apartment. Like a torn umbrella, she collapsed beneath the soulless months ending the 20th century.

Months later, she again pinged cross-country, arriving sleep-deprived and acne prone. Without questions, she shared toilet paper and accepted a room in Neil's Sunnyvale ranch house. After two weeks, she got used to the 409 cleaner, metal folding chairs, and industrial lighting of his living areas.

Everything about her new silicon life fitted—like a perfect digit—into each unit of time. Again, she embraced routine, beginning days with a jog and shower, organizing time around food and a job search. The walk from Ranch 99 on Wolfe Road to Noah's Bagels on El Camino Real broke up the hours of web surfing in Neil's study. She pretended to want a job, but spent more time on the personal ads and the black websites of UFO enthusiasts. The world, after all, would soon enter the end-time of Y2K.

She knew this because, daily, after sweeping kitchen tiles and raking the yard—but before leaving to work as a chip engineer—Neil wallowed in Y2K. "No one gets it. Civilization is a goner. People who work with code know it. Economic collapse. Mass starvation. Nuclear war. No one in this lifetime has lived through anything like what's coming."

Panic invaded these lectures, eventually descending into the netherworld of Neil's obsession. "In all practical terms, you have a whole species that now relies entirely on maybe two natural resources: dead dinosaurs and silicon, which means that if you didn't have the Jurassic Age and, more importantly, the ability to purify sand and glass down to their most basic element—silicon—humanity would be lost."

If her mind wandered during Neil's lectures, it wasn't her fault. Silicon Valley and people like Neil had neglected to consider the world of the pot-smoking aliens who attended the dancing saptas of her youth. Where did they live (or die) in the Y2K dystopia?

Two weeks of Neil, and her head bubbled with textbook facts. But relocating was imperative to figuring herself out. She needed Neil's Y2K rants because without them she'd rove the littered field of recent history and lose herself to the desert of the past.

Grateful, she listened to tech-trivia, slurping it with her breakfast tea, digesting it with dinner, and dreaming it all night. Eventually, she too conceded that all life depended on the refinement of sand. Because, hadn't she been whittled down to nothing in the desert? Hadn't her life simply been a process of crumbling? Hadn't her will—disintegrating as a result of earthly tragedy—turned into cosmic dust? And though she had no desire to be buried in sand-talk, she thanked Neil for all the edification.

To Neil, all other subjects were irrelevant. If she asked him whether his kitchen held a metal fork—she hoped to stir boiling udon without melting a plastic Spork—he spoke of cleanliness and the upside of disposability. Further, because of his generosity, she felt some guilt about not paying rent. (After all, he'd taken her in when there'd been no place left, because somehow, somewhere within his buttoned down shirt and belted dungarees, Neil had a heart.) Inevitably, practicalities caused disagreement—in the case of flatware, the ecological nightmare of a billion used Sporks.

"That's why I reuse them," he qualified before leaving the room. She was left to consider that silicon chips, ("unlike potato chips," he'd joked), had to be handled in a dust-free environment. Metal forks carried dust. Sporks sealed in plastic didn't. "Everyone knows dust kills your mother board."

Countless times Neil spoke of donning a bunny suit for the dust-free zone of the clean room. At CIT—where he tried completing a Masters despite having to take intermediate Spanish—he'd handled silicon wafers on a near-daily basis. "Most people don't know wafers look like UFOs."

Smitten with wafers, he took up cell phone hardware just when the wafer business exploded. "Who needs Moffett Field when you've got wafers and a real salary?" Because the few friends from CIT who still tuned into the Star Trek-track had ended up in the economic vacuum of a grant-driven universe. You had to feel sorry for them, because paychecks, unlike dust, didn't descend from outer space. "Dust bunnies are way uncool—especially when you figure they won't feed, clothe, and house you." He neglected to mention that a Masters in "Humanities" made the fruits of a Star Trek grant sound cushy.

Beyond Neil, there were Sunnyvale's broad streets, each plowed with fresh pavement. Perfectly sculpted juniper bushes exhaled nouveau wealth, making Burl's casinos and strip malls look passé. An outsider, Jane power walked through Brady Bunch blandness, puzzling at the draw of half-million dollar (that would soon become million dollar) ranch homes sandwiched between office parks. Fortune 500 companies like Apple, Oracle, and HP compounded the blandness with campuses of empty lawns and faux ponds—everyone stuck indoors.

But she was thankful Burl hadn't slit her throat like a sacrificial lamb, that she'd avoided becoming a toner cartridge in her mother's dining room. Somehow the ranch homes seemed like salvation. Sure they needed environmental upgrades—some hiding lead paint and asbestos—but the driveways offered a sense of purpose. And the numerous BMWs and Expeditions made her hopeful.

Like everyone else in Silicon Valley, Neil boasted that his property was worth $600,000, despite laminated countertops, olive-hued linoleum, and a wreck room that opened onto a backyard with a stunted orange tree. The value of things seemed absurd. When she shopped for ramen noodles and bok choy at Ranch 99, for instance, she couldn't help but gasp at prices. Worse, when she arrived at Neil's door with four suitcases and $300 to her name, the snot-hued sofa in his wreck room looked so like the furnishings in Seattle's YMCA she briefly considered returning to Nora's.

Eighteen years younger than Neil, she read novels while he skimmed Scientific American and the Wall Street Journal. His social life depended upon games like EverQuest and Ultima Online, while she couldn't get through a full round of Monopoly. She worshiped books, dyed her hair and, like many her age who'd studied the humanities, hadn't gotten past high school trig. Meanwhile, Neil went on mental joyrides through black holes, spouting String Theory, leaving her dizzy at the notion of other dimensions with crazy "flavors." And yes, she balked at living with a man, even if he was her cousin—particularly because she didn't understand how she could pay him back for his generosity—because it hadn't been her idea to explore the foreign country of his Silicon Valley guest room.

It had all been Nora's idea. Half a year after Red Rock, Nora finally made a phone call. Early February—a month whose heart was filled with despair—Jane stopped temping because she worried that the Bellagio's chandelier might instantaneously shatter and maim those beneath. After all, glass was technically a fluid, not a solid, and gravity could pull molecules downward, causing panes to bulge and pool at the bottom. "How crazy," she kept whispering, "is that!" Which led to the no-return topic of forces in nature that caused people to cave-in—all of which Nora ignored. At first.

Things took a darker turn when Jane began spending hours on the computer drawing anorexic Barbie dolls and opium poppies that turned into intricate, abstract line work meant to showcase the way glass moved over time in the Bellagio chandelier, but which amounted to nothing more than ornate doodles—such as the ones children scrawled in the margins of their notebooks. That's when Nora took action.

"Disturbing" and "unsettling" were words Nora used when she spoke on the phone to her sister Susan, a research scientist of Lawrence Berkeley Labs. Susan had been sanded down by two divorces and had raised two boys while teaching and getting a Ph.D. Plus, she liked fixing problems and making plans. Plans worked.

So, that's how—a day later—Neil offered his place.

Bottom Line, Ranch 99

But that didn't mean Jane couldn't have a bank overdraft, which hit the day after her last purchase of prepared salad. It hurt that the bank disputed her math, further demeaning her. They'd proven, with a printout, that she'd dipped into negative territory—her checkbook a collection of flubbed calculations. All this, despite the fact that she'd cut meal portions in half.

With only $37.29 in her wallet, she had no choice.

Pangs issuing from her own gurgling stomach woke her, but she couldn't summon the courage to phone Nora and ask for a loan. Famished night and day, she didn't tell Neil—who suggested that she take an HTML class to boost credentials. She avoided mentioning that the fees to attend a class at DeAnza Community College would wipe out the last of her food money because the whole thing pissed her off.

After all, she'd spent the same four years at university as the recent graduates who seemed to be making millions running dotcoms, but who now insisted she take unpaid, three-hour tests to "prove" she could spell. It pissed her off that kids who'd read Cliffsnotes instead of Dickens could breeze into six-figure positions while she, with an equal but different education, could barely fill a piggy bank with pennies. How much education—how many classes and degrees—did she need before someone paid her a living wage in exchange for tapping her life away on a computer in a building as bleak as a prison? Three months of half-day interviews, of scribbling down "free" ideas and she still couldn't get paid. It seemed everyone but she was driving a shiny car and paying all cash for property.

And why did she keep missing the financial boat? Why did everyone else have an "Angel Investor" —which assumed that only the heaven-bound achieved financial success—that threw money at peach fuzz chins as if the dotcom dedicated to dreaming up gift ideas could be the next Coca Cola? She'd always done the "right thing," had always dogmatically followed the rules, had "paid her dues" (that ugly phrase thrown at all who lived outside the industry's "box") year after year working as a temp, serving society as an upstanding citizen (she paid taxes, didn't do drugs or steal) who, alas, didn't possess a strong enough constitution to hold a useful college degree.

One evening, towards the end of summer, Aunt Susan stopped by Neil's to say, "It's so nice to see you settled in. Neil's been living alone too long." She handed Neil an enormous bowl of julienned carrots, yellow peppers, and zucchini. Susan's insistence on eating meant that after days of deprivation Jane could finally dine on a meal that didn't revolve around bok choy. "There's no meat in this. It's all vegetarian," Susan said, moving towards Neil's dinette.

They settled on the metal folding chairs that surrounded the nondescript table that was parked within view of the sliding glass doors that opened to the scrawny orange tree. Susan devoured Neil's takeout steak and potatoes loaded with gravy while a platter of chicken nuggets twirled in the microwave. "I don't know what he did all these years living alone—" Susan said, sawing her steak. Alone was what they all were, but no one spoke of this.

Instead, Neil left the table for the nuggets. When he returned, he gripped his Spork, wordless, and gazed at his plate with a blank expression. Jane tried not to imagine him rattling around in the house during one of those many evenings before her arrival, but she couldn't help seeing him in the empty bedrooms, patting the bedspreads and staring at the walls as the light sank around him.

Susan pressed her hands together, preparing to speak about the importance of family and building a life rich in relationships. But Neil cut in, suggesting they take their dinner into the backyard. "What an idea!" Susan said, breathless at the idea of eating next to the orangeless orange tree. She patted her chest while the hinges of her metal chair cackled.

Later, when it became clear that this was Neil's last dinner with his mother, Jane would never forgive herself. But at the time, while she chomped on chopped vegetables, she couldn't help it. She loathed the subject of enriched uranium festering in Russia's nuclear facilities, detested the prediction that someday, somewhere a dirty bomb would explode a dense urban area—probably New York—taking out a ten-block radius and leaving a square mile forever a wasteland. "Yeah," Neil said biting into a chicken nugget, "it'll all be because of Y2K!"

With Y2K Jane lost it.

She lanced into him, jabbing a Spork of speared carrot, forcing her counter argument in his face—building the case that people, **plain old people**, would always be more important than computers, that humanity had always outsmarted the apocalypse. But Neil liked arguments as much as games. Dinner hijacked, memories of the meal would forever be a battle between math and literature, with Neil throwing statistics and Jane countering with quotes by Milton and Shakespeare.

<u>Who Are You?</u>

Like the urge to argue, life inside a computer—because wasn't that Neil's life?—was contagious. His two PCs functioned differently: one was dedicated to 3-D mapping the solar system while the other was meant for gaming and the web. It was on this computer that Jane began seriously surfing.

To be considered for a near minimum-wage admin job, she needed to spend hours compiling an online personality. If lucky, she might interview for a job with stock options, which meant undergoing a three-hour test that was basically free work for some dotcom.

Dozens of resumes into the search, Jane quickly realized that giving away "free" things (not to be confused with "freedom") meant giving up eating and sleeping. It also meant walking in shoes that were falling apart. It occurred to her that she might be experiencing a new kind of slavery in which everything was free except for food and housing. There was "free love," "free surf," "free samples," but not free Ranch 99 at Cupertino Village Shopping Center.

Far from cheap, the store never offered free packages of udon, though it was within walking distance of Neil's computer room. But the store became a place to daydream about feasting, more holiday than headache. Far more interesting than craigslist's blue fonts, the supermarket's aisles became beaches of brightly wrapped Asian foods—with shoppers culled from HP's Office Park across the street—making it a manageable trip to China.

On one particular afternoon, after wandering the aisles amid fish guts and tanks of squid, crab, lobster, and sea urchin, Jane snatched a packet of udon from a shelf, leaving the land of the free and entering the land of the eternally invisible. For what felt like hours, she studied the dollar and change in her hand, weighing it against the udon's candy-colored packaging, its crinkly plastic and red lettering pulling on her stomach.

At Neil's, she had become addicted to Asian noodles, gorging on udon, later favoring buckwheat—enjoying the individualized portions tied with a thin strip of paper that mimicked the fortunes inside fortune cookies. When she still had money, she boiled entire packs, all twelve servings, often absurdly early at 4:30 p.m., and sat alone in Neil's wreck room, slurping and flipping channels.

Not once did Neil return home to find her in the throes of noodle binging. She hid the act well, knowing that he never returned before 8:00 p.m.—the very hour she lay down on a Spartan bed pushed against the wall. Many nights he worked on replicating the solar system on his 3-D PC, never knowing that her last dollar had long ago slipped into Ranch 99's cash register.

PC

Susan would never see Neil's finished solar system. Nor would she fully grasp the all-encompassing shift in reality taking place because of the computers she helped to code. Nor would she learn the outcome of Jane's web surfing. She certainly wouldn't have believed the stories about a billionaire, would have considered them the result of a psychotic episode. But as a computer scientist with a long buried interest in gossip and drama, Susan would have been interested in a lost piece of history, a misstep, a poor choice that could only be understood in retrospect.

Four months after Jane moved into Neil's, Susan died. No one understood why Nora couldn't make her sister's Memorial, despite the claim that: "We're leaving for New Delhi in three days. We already have tickets." At the Memorial, as Neil read from a card Nora sent with flowers, ("Susan was a light in a dark world. She was the best sister anyone could ever have—") his hands twitched against the podium.

Days after that, Jane sat in Neil's computer room, trying to send out job applications. But she couldn't focus, found herself surfing the web, staring but barely absorbing. One page after another slipped by without leaving a mark. By then, Nora had left for India—though not before a brief call from the airport. "You know, Jane," Nora said, "I was so sorry not to be there—"

"So, India."

"Yes. The Avatar always promised to take us beyond the horizon. And now he really is!" She sounded excited, as if finally, on the brink of old age, she'd seen a rainbow for the first time. Giddy, she talked about the open-ended itinerary, about how her roommates would know how to reach her from day-to-day. "I'll still be running the business. Cartridges don't walk into recycling plants on their own—" Before signing off, she said, "Jane, you know I love you. When I'm back I'll visit and see Sue's memorial stone."

Later, it'd be emotionally difficult to separate that conversation from the discovery made immediately afterwards. While Jane tapped the keyboard, sorrow rose and curled like an ocean wave slapping the screensaver's sand dunes. She clicked the mouse, initiating yet another web search. Thinking of something Neil had said about chips, she typed a random term that pulled up a history of Silicon Valley and stumbled upon the names of Bill Hewlett and Dave Packard. It was mystifying—how they'd emerged like saplings amid the Valley's fruit groves surrounding Xerox Park and Stanford, mere miles from where she sat.

One link after another found her drifting like a sand grain across continents of history, site after site, until she landed at the Computer History Museum's timeline, which included many names connected to many photos:

Douglas Engelbart—responsible for the computer mouse and windows technology.

Faggin, Hoff, and Mazor—responsible for the first computer microprocessor.

Lee Felsenstein—designer of the visual display module.

Moving right along she stumbled on more famous entities: Steve Jobs, Bill Gates—names everyone knew—Michael Dell amid a lengthening list of computer pioneers. Here were the men—all men—who built the computer industry: dozens of pale foreheads lined with calculations; dozens of black, rectangular eyeglasses above dozens of beards grazing dozens of shirt collars. She scrolled down to the blurbs—the "famous" quotes—not reading but taking in various photos. And then she stalled, catching her breath.

The photo, it made her blink—and then squint. It wrapped her up into a ball of disbelief, made her double-click to enlarge the pale face hovering over its folded fist like a massive sun over a timeless rock formation.

Half the screen was lost to the man's slate shirt. The other half showed skin supercharged by gold-rimmed eyeglasses that circled obsessive irises. Beneath, lips held back a smile, a tended beard resting against that fist like a natural wonder. Around his eyes she spotted passion, as if the photographer had cracked an x-rated joke right before clicking. Like someone cryogenically preserved and then thawed for new life, she gazed at the screen in disbelief—disbelieving that any screen could provide a window on reality. But she knew the face. There was no mistake. Right brained, every face embedded itself in her memory. No mistake; it had to be him—the Wild Ginger man who'd called himself "Bill," who'd continued to wrestle with Ben in her mind among a thousand other memories, despite the fact that she'd met him only once, nearly two years earlier.

As "Bill" stared back at her, she read his name beneath the photo—and it wasn't "Bill." It seemed the photo knew this, was in on the joke. He'd tricked her. And why hadn't she known? Hadn't he hesitated in speaking his name? Or had that pause been imagined? She tried to reconstruct that long gone evening at Wild Ginger, but found herself questioning everything and whispering: "No! This can't be real..."

In fact, since that meeting at Wild Ginger, "Bill" had been reformatted in her mind as a Superman/Shiva, appearing in daydreams as an emperor of love, especially after the countless hours of Burl's rabid pelvic thrusts, which she'd escaped—breasts and vagina barely intact—mainly because of Bill.

She closed her eyes and he quietly swirled his Jack Daniel's. Yes. In some ways, escaping Burl had depended upon Bill, who made the difficult easy, because the morning after the opening of the Bellagio, after Burl had whipped her with his belt because she'd vomited three martinis and two ejaculations into his bathroom sink, she'd pushed back the tiger stripe comforter and tiptoed around while Burl was showering. She swiftly pulled together and stuffed a pile of clothing into a carry-on bag, avoiding closets and drawers laden with nets and knives before she clicked out the front door—which emitted a high squeal. But she knew he'd be naked, awash in lather, and so she sprinted towards a 7-Eleven, where she pretended to be intensely interested in packaged sandwiches, before breaking for the bus stop.

Though her breath was sour from half a night of sucking cock, her hair uncombed around a tempest of acne, she aimed for the airport, certain she could pay back Nora for the changed the ticket.

On the plane, she closed her eyes and thought not of Burl or the fact that he probably had been wearing red Speedos when he dashed outside with kitchen cleavers, roaring like Megadeth. No she thought of Bill, which was fine, because Burl never phoned Nora's apartment to ask why the tattoo-woman on his chest had left without swilling coffee or grabbing the shriveled rose whose petals bruised his kitchen counter.

Thanks to the memory of Bill, she simply walked out of that situation and thereby changed the course of her life. She no longer needed to buy anyone else's vision. She wasn't a tattoo. She wasn't "destined" for anything, didn't need to find her future in any other soul but her own. All she had to do was leave, reshape the story the way the desert had been reshaped into golf courses, strip malls, casinos, and McMansions. She walked out of Burl's week the same way she regrettably walked out of Wild Ginger and Ben's hospital—except that she didn't feel guilt or shame or pathos after leaving Burl's vomit spattered pillowcases—especially after that long night searching for Bellagio's high-rollers.

For her, there'd never been anything to harvest in those fields, because Steve Wynn, the Bellagio's billionaire developer, had been seated near the million dollar black jack parlor surrounded by beautiful people too comfortable with their bone structure, hair, and fabrics—which molded too perfectly to their perfect bodies as they eased into celebration with tumblers of amber liquid. Wynn celebrated with a complacent slouch, while Burl idled nearby, devouring views of the tycoon like a dog in a vat of ground beef.

He pushed Jane onto a bench, pinched her arm and pointed to the ex-con billionaire Michael Milken, who sauntered in sneakers and jeans up to Wynn. "Now there's one hell of a guy," Burl gurgled, awed by Milken's "genius." "The Avatar. He's nice for your basic lost soul, but he's not going to buy your dreams."

As the evening progressed and Jane's eyes stung from a combo of cigarette smoke and Burl's statements, couples limped across the marble floors towards the ringing wind-chime-and-music-box tunes of the slot machines that, aided by liquor, sent Jane to bottom. 2:00 AM and a fourth martini, sipped while wandering circles under the light cascading from the Bellagio chandelier, pollen drifting from the conservatory of flowers, found Jane once again vomiting. She swayed towards a bathroom to clean up, crying over the irony of the chandelier.

In Seattle, she'd watched its creation, knew that its makers were anything but simple, unknown men, with their Billy goat legs—which sprang up mountains and pushed their fuck-mates off beds—which transformed the chandelier from an object of beauty into an example of hypocrisy, which in turn made it incredibly dangerous. What, she thought in dizziness, would happen if the pieces fell like supernal life forms, spilling down like a waterfall to shatter over her and bring on a glitzy death few would contemplate beyond headlines?

Steve Wynn would never care about a lone woman lying in a pool of shattered glass and blood. He would think only of insurance, of his lost chandelier, of his business's reputation, of his gently tanned, middle-aged life. And swaying into Burl's arms, she had wondered why certain people accrued material wealth while others with equal or more potential did not. This was an economic question having to do with capitalism, irreversible choices, lost opportunities, and survival of the fittest, all of which would forever ping-pong through her mind. And so, she considered this as she studied Bill's photo on Neil's computer, understanding that she would look at this photo again and again on that and on many other computers as the months ahead became years.

The Unreal Real Bill

The more she clicked and the more she learned about Bill, the less she believed. The first fact, that he was twenty years older than her, made some sense. But the second, third, and forth facts left her stunned. Her heart palpitated when she found out he was wealthier than Steve Wynn and lived on Forbes List of Billionaires—which meant that he owned at least one Boeing 747, yachts the size of cruise ships, a couple of islands, and countless properties in resort towns and large cities around the world. His permanent residence, which turned out to be a few towns over—Atherton—filled several acres and was essentially a compound of mansions and guesthouses. Most intriguing was the fact that he'd briefly been married twice but was now single.

Disturbed yet titillated, Jane clicked Yahoo's search field and typed the words "gossip" and "girlfriend" after Bill's real name. She would never be able to rest until she knew everything there was to know about him, because she must meet him again. But he traveled in high circles, and she had no contacts and even less money. How would she bump into him? These thoughts percolated with feelings she couldn't name. She loathed the idea of being a gold digger—though at the time, she had to admit that his wealth increased her attraction to him. And she wasn't ashamed to admit that the knowledge of his worth fulfilled a long discarded childhood wish: to be Cinderella. But considering her financial desperation and her many romantic traumas, it felt safer to sit at the computer than to seek him out in person. So, she surfed after him every day by waking in the morning and igniting the computer like a joint and inhaling a deep whiff of "Bill" news. And she wasn't ashamed to admit her web addiction, because suddenly the World Wide Web was the doorway to this very important person she'd lost. And she'd lost so many. But there, on the screen, she'd found the only one that seemed to matter:

Bill, who might have forgotten her, but would never disappear.

Bill, who would lose his hair, but never his mind.

Bill, who would fill her days, but remain unchanged by time.

Bill, who was the man who would never admit to being Bill.

Search and More Search

It wasn't difficult to sit at the computer now. Where she'd once been reluctant, she now clicked through the last hours of summer, searching, more than ever devoted to the screen. September and then October, the air more crisp, leaves dropping—but she didn't notice. Instead, she dragged and dropped photos: one showing him clean shaven next to a woman, another of him in a black tux; still others exposing a varied collection of eyeglasses— some square with dark brown rims, others oval with metal or invisible frames. She had her favorites, becoming familiar with his dress code—which centered on button down shirts, gray or white, though rarely blue or dark green. His salt and pepper hair, rarely scruffy around the ears, seemed heavily treated for a conservative appearance. This, and his tendency to avoid emotional abandon, enhanced his square features—branding she attributed to the fact that every tycoon must project determination, resolve, and fatherly wellbeing—traits she found in his photos, but not in her memory of him at Wild Ginger.

Marketing wealth was like marketing beauty. It required airbrushing and attention to detail. Perhaps that was why Bill's website avoided any reference to the many years he'd spent as a hippy. But history would not be so easily dismissed. She discovered "retro-Bill" deep in the electronic stacks where his 1972, long hair titillated her inner thighs. Doubly erotic, his ponytail and low-belted corduroys screamed techno-rebellion, as if his hips and ideas shoved their middle fingers up Nixon's nostrils.

And then, there were the computers hanging out like lovers, each with a different style and attitude. These various incarnations of silicon became works of art next to his contemplative gaze. There was the wall of spinning magnetic reels that might have taken over a wall of illuminated texts. There was the boxy gray matter with keyboards and dot matrix printers that lacked design but buzzed with hope. There was the mid-90s, beige-head resting on a thin, beige neck as if developmentally comparable to the person seated at a desk. And every time the cold screen light bounced off Bill's eyeglasses, the same cold screen light bounded through Jane's nervous system, ensnaring her with a squirt of serotonin.

Two months of searching for Bill online left her desperate. She couldn't take it. She sent him an email through his personal website. It was a two-line note asking about the environmentally focused philanthropic arm of his venture. She thought of Nora's insolvent recycling business, all those toner cartridges piled to the ceiling, overflowing the dining room, printer junk claiming the only real home Jane might ever know. Vaguely, she hoped that Bill would throw cash at a warehouse so that Nora's cartridges could leak carcinogens onto something other than her mother's dinner.

She wrote carefully, and then read over the two sentences eight times. The official part of the email ending without a "Thanks" or "Best" or "Sincerely," but simply with "—Jane." But below came the clincher, a PS: **"Just wondering. Have you ever listened to Monday night jazz at Wild Ginger?"**

It was more than a hint. It was an invitation. He had to remember—though it occurred to her that he might not recognize her name. Jane—so easily lost in history, so ordinary that it melted like bland crumbs in the mouth of any speaker who had the option to say something else. And yet, the email with her name pinged through fiberglass threads, flying at the speed of light, somehow finding its place rather than getting lost in everywhere.

For the next two weeks, each morning before walking the empty but perfect pavement to Noah's Bagels, she checked her inbox, hoping for a response that never came. *He'd missed the message. Her email had gone into the void. The address had been defective.* But miscommunication had never deterred the obsessed. She would find another way to him.

The computer, like a black jack table, made its promises. Every day there was new gossip, new images of Bill, new discussions of his possessions, new views of his outsized and moneyed life. Every day she discovered more, as if trekking across an unexplored frontier.

He'd had an affair with the actress named G.D., followed by a tryst with the rock diva M.R. Linda Carter appeared next to him like a startled possum with her heavily glossed lips and vampishly made-up eyes. Surrounding Bill were coteries of Botox women or girls too anorexic and tall for anything but the runway. Yet occasionally he held the hand of a plain-faced woman whose dress never fell quite right, which gave Jane the hope she needed to keep clicking.

Only To Find

There were parties. Two hundred and fifty celebrities gyrated as he hosted a cruise of the Straits of Gibraltar. There was the $8 million horseracing event in Mongolia, followed a year later by a ten-day excursion to the Galapagos with a hundred close friends. There was the costume party in Tuscany where Phoebe Cates, or whoever-it-was, dressed like a Borgia, playing queen to his king. He served caviar-strewn crackers no one ate when he might have served ten thousand rice-balls to starving children. It seemed odd that a well read, thoughtful, and educated man immersed himself in expensive but hollow partying for those who'd reached the top. Never once did he invite someone working three jobs for five kids and living in a house the size of a closet. It seemed that the rest of the world was no more than a pile of Yurtle-less Turtles for his throne.

Again, she faced the persistent question: Why did wealth choose the self-serving over the deserving? Not that Bill was un-deserving. Actually, he seemed quite kind-hearted in his own way. But, why hadn't he surrounded himself with more interesting people, like Jane for instance, who couldn't tear herself away, especially when hunger overwhelmed her so much that her stomach hurt?

As months slipped by, the clicking became a strange, symbiotic communication that only encouraged obsession. Part of her knew she was a web stalker. But in her mind, Bill became one also. Everything she read about him had been edited, vetted, and given the okay. She knew he gathered cookies and I.P. addresses. She knew he insisted on privacy, that those in his company—guests, visitors, employees—sign nondisclosure agreements, meaning that legally no one could write, talk, or whisper about him or his property without consent. All had to be kept under wraps, secret. And this only made everything about him more interesting.

<u>Hunger</u>

Six months at Neil's, and she still didn't have a job—this during the boom. Her cash resources, given a brief reprieve from Aunt Susan's estate by way of a check for $500, still induced misery. But Neil hardly noticed the hopscotch lines furrowing her brow, which only increased her isolation, guilt, and self-loathing. He'd set aside a shelf in the fridge meant for her food, and as her reserves dwindled to an apple and a carton of rice milk, he never asked why or whether she was getting enough to eat.

By October, less than $300 of Susan's money remained, which meant impending death for the already malnourished. Lately, she'd combined breakfast, lunch, and dinner into one monster meal of carbs, stuffing herself like Thanksgiving turkey with shrink-wrapped bread from Ranch 99.

But eventually, even bread would go. If no money came in, she'd be forced to subsist on remnants left in trash receptacles. Freebies and samples, as plentiful as they were during the boom, weren't enough, despite what she discovered one Saturday afternoon walking along El Camino Real.

From blocks away, she spotted several tents crowding a parking lot outside the CalTrain station. Colorful fruits brightened tables where she wedged herself between shoulders and shopping bags, grabbing samples with tongs. There, she gormandized on slices of apple, pear, orange, pinches of almond, walnut, pecan, bits of cracker, bread, and muffin.

Thus, Saturdays became "free meal days," when she headed for the Farmer's Market as if her life depended upon it, walking a full hour to gobble handfuls of granola, followed by a visit to Whole Foods.

One afternoon, as she slinked back towards Neil's house with a chin full of acne, she noticed a blue SUV leisurely rolling along the asphalt. As the vehicle slipped past in what seemed slow motion, she peered through the window to find a man in a slate gray button down shirt wearing tinted FBI sunglasses. Staring—no digging into her with eyes she could feel rather than see—he seemed ill-at-ease, raising a palm to unsuccessfully cover his beard— as if he were ashamed or confused or uncertain of how much to reveal. But this gesture only made him more noticeable.

Later, she debated whether the man behind the wheel was who she thought he was, but she knew the side part of his hair, knew his shirt, his hands, the marshmallow quality of his complexion and the tapered fingers. One instant of eyes meeting through sunglasses and the click of connection was too strong. She was certain; it had been him.

Bill had come, by himself, to find her—rolling along El Camino Real, mere blocks from Neil's house, slowly, alone, staring at her.

But why? Between them there'd only been a drink and a mystery email—that was all. She couldn't believe he'd come to Sunnyvale to see her. No, he had to be researching a start-up, was likely startled by the sight of a ragged backpack and fried hair wandering the suburban cleanliness of El Camino Real.

All afternoon into night he drove through her mind, scanning the horizon with his tinted shades, his blue car, his gray button down shirt to impart the message that he'd come to begin a quiet—secret—relationship.

Of course it had to be a secret. Of course he'd come to find out who'd so fiercely dined on his name, using so many search engines. Of course Neil's desktop had overflowed with cookies—the name "Bill" typed a thousand times in a month. Everyday, she clicked for Bill. More than 500 hours of clicking, one search for every minute.

In all, she found only fifteen standard photos of the man. The rest were pixilated rogues. But she had downloaded them all onto Neil's computer, had dredged up every last photo—each a downed ship wasting away on an ocean floor composed of digital data; photos hidden beneath stacks of information, each 2-D rendition lost in the web's archives, embedded in articles, cloistered in histories, and thrown away with gossip.

Before getting into bed, she paced her room, wondering if Bill knew where she lived. Did he know how she'd gotten from Wild Ginger to Sunnyvale? Did he know her bank account had dropped to within dollars of zero? Did he know about her night sweats and panic? Did he know that startups expected her to work without pay, that she'd written five unpaid articles, seven free marketing blurbs, and two restaurant reviews that enabled her to scarf half a dozen avocado rolls in half a minute—everything published online and read by no one but her now dead Aunt Susan? Did he know that Jane had suffered through twelve writing tests for and interviews with companies that offered only stock options—like the one where three blond guys in jeans to her business suit had knocked Coke bottles while she kneaded her forehead? Did he know she felt like a girl in a boy's tree house when the three blonds asked her to slip into a cubicle—a stripper in a black box—where she brainstormed ideas to get consumers to click a bundle of useless but free cyber-samples? Countless hours wasted, precious dollars lost to Caltrain—the many rides to Palo Alto, Mountain View, Redwood City, Menlo Park, and San Francisco ending in failure as she trudged back to Neil's, all those office parks and interviews ending in the same way: free samples but no job. Did he know?

Her black interview dress and pantyhose—purchased at Filene's Basement on the Upper West Side before she lost her savings—seemed too fancy and old fashioned for Silicon Valley. In interviews her suit and hose met a twenty-year-old exec in a t-shirt, leaving her to feel over-the-hill, already crashing the ceiling in her twenties—a GenX loser—when the VC-backed techie in the interview chair rocked back and forth and frat-boy laughed at her name.

Bill had to know that he kept her going, that his gray shirts, eyeglasses and grander-than-thou lifestyle kept hunger from eating her up. Thus she surfed after him, discovering the genius of placing quotation marks around his name. Where once there'd been only headshots, now there were wide-angle views.

At first she was shocked by what she found, as if a window had been thrown open to reveal a swamp rather than a tropical paradise. Had he always been so wide? Had his legs been so like a troll's? Firmly rotund, his belly draped over his belt buckle like a sagging pillow. And then, what had seemed a healthy complexion at Wild Ginger appeared doughy in bright sunlight or in the shock of a flashbulb.

And yet, she liked his lack of gloss. There wasn't anything about him that tried to be winsome. He couldn't care less about his physical appearance. So, she kept daydreaming about getting a job in his company, lying naked on his desk, and taking his penis into her mouth, because everything about him grew more delicious.

One Friday, she read that he'd donated ten million to the World Wildlife Fund. Next, she devoured a gossip column about a party with supermodels and film directors he hosted with the actress, C.D., that lasted a full week in the Greek Isles. Then, she discovered an article about how he'd seduced a married T.V. producer. The lucky lady had worked for his media group, but hadn't approved of his behavior, and now he was embroiled in a lawsuit over sexual harassment. A week later, as if legal battles could be swatted away with good deeds, he promoted literacy education in the western states. There were dozens of photos of him surrounded by children as he cut the ribbon at an inner-city school. The next day, he sailed a $50 million carbon fiber water slasher in the America's Cup. The press touted the boat as the fastest piece of nautical engineering ever constructed. For weeks she closely followed the race, but felt overwhelmed with sorrow when she read that the boat came in 2nd due to human error.

By December, once again her last ten dollars slipped into a Ranch 99 cash register. With less than a week's worth of bread to go, she made a last-ditch effort and begged a temp agency. They offered her a week-to-possible hire administrative gig at a medical center's development office. In the end, she hardly blinked at giving up web content, stock options, and flexible schedules (which meant sleeping in an office to make up for long lunches and limitless soda), gladly taking a seat in a windowless room next to a roadway riddled with ambulance sirens. She was back in her element—

again able to afford bagged salad.

Yama In Paradise

As she walked the sandy paths beneath the swaying fronds of Stanford's Palm Drive, it became painfully clear that her life had been torn from the comic about Princess Savitri. As a kid she'd been obsessed with the story of the princess who'd chosen to marry a landless and powerless prince destined to die within a year. For an entire year, Savitri lived in dread of her husband's death, and when the day arrived, she refused to leave his side. When he fell, his soul was seized by the god of death, Yama. But Savitri wouldn't let her husband go. She stalked Yama, called out to him, praising him, begging until the god couldn't take it anymore. To get the woman off his ass, Yama offered Savitri anything she wished—except the return of her husband.

"Please," Savitri pleaded. "Give me one hundred children." And when Yama complied she added, "I can't have kids without my hubby." Yama, blown away, realized that she'd outwitted him. And so, the prince returned to life, forever instilling in Jane the belief that love could outlive and undo death.

Like Savitri, Jane had almost—but not really—married a man with a death sentence. In the end, she hadn't had enough love or the wit to undo death. She'd left Ben to rot, choosing not to stalk death but instead ended up stalking a billionaire whose footprint she could only find online. Some nights, as she clicked through photos, this online path seemed futile. But she'd become addicted and couldn't tear herself away.

That evening, after spending half a day surfing for Bill, she found herself walking by the Stanford Shopping Center in the awkward office gear Nora had long ago dubbed, "artistically professional," which Jane now realized was synonymous with "clown-like." Vaguely, she despaired over a new trail of cystic acne along her chin, wishing she could dress like the students, in blue jeans, rather than a pillow skirt and cardigan. Despair and insecurity covered the ground with live oak leaves and kept her eyes lowered. But the heaviness in her limbs could not keep her from looking up at the white Lexus slowly driving by.

Through the windshield, she saw his profile: salt and pepper hair gelled to the side, black rim glasses he wore on casual occasions. A slant of sun lit his white button down, highlighting his beard and the way his hands settled loosely on the wheel. As she stared, he turned his head away—towards a woman across the street—as if not wanting to be seen. He kept turning away, no longer watching the road, turning until she saw the back of him—such obvious concealment.

He'd come to see her again, providing certainty. The other time had left her in doubt about whether the passenger in the teal Jaguar had been Bill. There'd been the beard, the gaze, the expensive eyeglasses. But the Jaguar had been a full block away and it sped by too quickly. But now, this sighting clinched it. He was real, and it made sense. Bill was Silicon Valley, had endowed Stanford, had funded start-ups in Mountain View. Bill, an Angel to the world's computer Mecca, had to drive through Stanford in white button down shirts. But why had he turned away? Why not stop to say hello?

She spent two sleepless nights pondering these questions and several hours surfing for articles alluding to his presence at Stanford. Nothing turned up. Exhausted, unsuccessful in her search, she could do nothing but allow Bill's name to move through her like a secret code.

Berkeley

It took a month to find a place, but when she did, she packed in an hour, cramming bags into the trunk of a Ford Escort clunker called "Little Red"—willed to Neil by Aunt Susan, who ultimately dumped it on Jane with, "You could use it more than I." He tried to smile. "You need mobility." Jane didn't know how to thank him—especially after Nora's absence from Susan's Memorial. Instead, she pressed the gas pedal, causing the metal husk to rattle at 60 mph until the exit ramp at Berkeley's Ashby Avenue, where the brakes squealed.

She was anxious to cosign the lease on a live/work space originally built as a deli but reconfigured for the residential rental market, which had "blown through the roof." In such a market, no sane landlord thought twice about violating codes. But, a room of her own was a room of her own, even if Jane's new housemate, Beth, didn't mind having to walk through Jane's bedroom to reach the kitchen and shower.

Beth was a project from up north, recently released from art school and therefore paraded all black outfits with the wide-eyed expression of the sleep deprived. Because Beth owned a Mac G3, knew Flash, and could bring in $25 an hour to Jane's piddly $10, Beth got the larger bedroom. The palatial ceilings throughout softened this fact during a tour of the apartment, and it helped that Beth's zaftig build indicated a sedentary, late-morning lifestyle—implying that the two women would have opposing schedules. Further, Beth indicated that because she needed to build up her graphic design portfolio, she'd rarely have time for a cup of tea or glass of wine. This suited Jane very well, as there was only one counter in the cramped kitchen, forcing extra bodies to stand at the window when eating.

As Beth raked in the big bucks by transforming a fish's fin into a waving appendage, Jane wondered how she'd pull together her half of the rent: $600. Though she found a job, she struggled to feel secure within the cracked stucco housing along San Pablo. It didn't help that the building appeared ready for demolition—the battered front door an ideal spot for a midnight piss, the listing of a rotting deck, the misalignment of window frames. The backyard was overgrown with vines and plum trees that produced golf ball-sized fruits the landlord, Rafi, pressed whole into his mouth. Rafi, wiping auto-grease on his t-shirt, owned a garage full of pipes and wire a few blocks down, which meant that every week he made the rounds, checking in and collecting rent checks from his five Berkeley buildings, once boasting about the purchase of a 3,000 square foot house near 4th street, which he intended to renovate for his family.

But there was something special about the place. After all, it was beneath Rafi's cracked roof, in late afternoon light, amid the sharp odor of dog urine, that Jane took the plunge and quietly wedded herself to Bill—but not before Mimi had a word to say.

It had been years since Mimi flew into Jane's radar. After Seattle, she'd moved to New Jersey to be close to her mother Cathy who'd always claimed that Eastern winters had more character than the wet darkness of the Pacific Northwest.

One evening, not long after moving to Berkeley, Jane picked up the phone to hear Mimi's voice, sharp and bright as the old days. "Hello you crazy old piece of work!" she laughed. "Where the hell are you? I got your number from your mom's roommate—and I have no idea, absolutely **no clear idea** where 510 is." Soon it was, yes, she'd put on almost sixty pounds, out-weighing the puffiest months on Capitol Hill, but she felt happy as a peanut butter and jelly sandwich, and plus, she reveled in being single with her "newfound sense of self." Hearing her voice again felt like a softball toss back to another era—but stranger and harder, like a cold glass of water after a march through the desert, both painful and welcoming.

Closing her eyes, Jane tried to imagine Mimi in her obesity, tried to toggle the image of a once beautiful woman with one of expansive cheeks, chin, and butt. "You would not believe how cool it is not to care—" Mimi said. "I'm so free, and it's like WOW!" Confiding that she'd made a huge mistake and was *oh so sorry* that things had worked out the way they did—Mimi admitted to low self-esteem.

But she had found peace after struggling with a cigarette addiction. Hell, she'd fought hard to restrain herself from midnight binging on Wheat Thins and ice cream. She'd faced the rampant horniness that had pushed her into the arms of undesirable man dragged home from bars, because things had gotten so bad she'd almost taken another lethal dose of pills. But then, like a miracle, she'd summoned the courage to "break habits and rein habit" to become her true self. She'd come around.

"If you really want to know, I got help. And thank god, because going it alone is so completely and unbelievably scary. You so have to come clean to truly live!" she brayed, segueing from personal pain to Jane's lack of fortitude. "You need to get clear to change your life, Jane! There's no time to waste! Do it now!" She hammered her points, challenging Jane to "GET" what she was saying about "living in honesty" and "opening up" to others. Mimi, queen of all dinners, had vanished behind a scrim of "committed" language ready to "get" itself into the heads of others with....

Why hadn't they gotten with the program when they lived under the same roof? Sure, their friendship had rotted behind many rows of daily concerns, and sure her "EX" (she vowed never again to repeat Todd's name) had been a train wreck— "I hope I never see **him** again!"—But anyone could see that Jane was drowning in jealousy and clearly wanted a relationship of her own. "And clearly," Mimi had taken the brunt of the jealousy. "You so know," Mimi murmured into the phone, her voice placative. "I completely and I mean **completely** never got it until I got with my own program! You just know, deep down, how much there is to change."

It didn't help, she went on, that Jane was a clean freak—no, a control freak—to a fault. What was all the B.S. fuss over a few dashes of tomato sauce on the kitchen counter? "Let's face it, Jane, you have so got to laugh. Spaghetti sauce is **not** worth losing friendship over." And if the cleanliness issue baffled Mimi, tarnished trust could be improved with a little shoe shining. But both parties needed to **commit** to shining things up. "And I am so completely committed!" Especially now that she'd left her "EX" (his very existence nauseated her).

She could finally think again. She was finally able to see how lost she'd been in "that boy's" company. Like when she came down with pneumonia and needed him—"And oh my god, I so needed him!" But he'd gone off with "those completely filthy losers! And that's not the worst—it get's worse." The boys had left for a long weekend. "Camping and fishing in the Cascades—" leaving her to die alone on the damp sofa, barely enough food in the fridge to feed the cat.

Add to this, he'd begun to yell about small things, like the used tissues she accidentally left on the coffee table. And he berated her after work for holing up in the bedroom with a book instead of dragging out a beer the way they used to. She'd returned the favor by ignoring him when he wanted to have sex until the miserable night when he pushed her into the "skanky" backseat of his car, dragged off her panties amid flailing legs and fucked her for the final time.

That was it. She kicked him out, called her mom, and sold everything but a suitcase full of clothes. A week later she caught a flight to Newark. It wasn't so bad living with her mother. "It's a boatload better than with the EX."

The only drawback of the return: During the flight home she'd pecked at a tasteless slice of breaded cutlet wedged between two pieces of dry rye that left her with a painful case of colitis. Oh, and she felt no remorse over the bribe of $1,000 that let the "EX" off the hook for rape. "He tore me, Jane. And I don't care if that psycho ends up at the bottom of a lake. I'm so completely lucky I made it out alive." Because though it happened years ago, it felt like yesterday.

To Jane this final testimony seemed melodramatic. For one who'd been raped many times, a single backseat episode hardly qualified as a story. But then, Jane had to admit at least Mimi still cared enough about herself to do something about it.

Reconnection

Their reconnection deepened as the days passed. Each time the phone rang, Jane felt a surge of joy, as if she were inching closer to some lost piece of herself.

"Hey," Mimi said during a fifth call. "I feel really bad about something I never told you."

"Never told me?" For some reason Jane felt loss, though she hardly cared about untold things because she only worried about cobbling together rent and money for a single, daily meal. But anything Mimi thought, felt, or said—except when she'd lived with Todd—still carried significance and weight.

"Oh my god!" Mimi groaned. "I feel so funny about it," She squeaked out a laugh, as if unable to restrain a windstorm in her belly. "Promise not to get freaked out—"

"How can I promise before I know?" They were now nearly thirty. They could avoid promises.

"Girl. You so have to. I have got to and I mean GOT to have a laugh with you. Not a freak out!"

"Just tell me. What is it?"

"Okay okay. It's only that I'm so completely ashamed that it's funny. But no, it's really funny."

"So?"

"So, I met one of your," and here the sound of her voice burst into a puff of air.

"Yes?"

"One of your guy flings!" A bark of laughter. "And he was—" Mimi laughed so hard wind exploded, by way of earpiece, Jane's eardrum.

"What?"

"I know, it's not funny yet—but wait!"

"One of my guy flings? Who?" Mimi kept laughing, snorting, barking until eventually she let out a sigh.

"Okay. Wow. I'm crying here."

"Yeah?"

"Yeah. That guy, John, down on Lake Union." Jane's mind numbed around an image of Parvati, JNB, and the Old Christy. But then, Mimi said, "You know, the glass guy," and here Mimi belted out another laugh. "The blower. You know. That glass guy." And everything became a vast field of mismatched associations: the Bellagio, a dinner of stuffed squash, a boat bobbing in an imaginary bay of icebergs. "I met him through that nameless dick, my EX."

Mimi described a party, how "the blower" (John) approached her, thinking her single, winked and slurped his scotch and soda. He'd commented that she reminded him of a film star. "When I told him I was from New York, he asked if I knew you. You were definitely—make no mistake—on his mind. But he was a complete freak! And I mean a **complete** freak!" She laughed so hard Jane could hear the snot blowing out of her nose.

"Yeah—" Jane managed, remembering the night John threw her off the bed and dashed from her apartment. "So—you met him and he tried to pick you up?"

"Mhmmm. I'm telling you, it's hilarious—"

For the first time since they'd reconnected, Jane felt like hanging up. But before Jane could sign off, Mimi spilled the unexpected.

"I heard about how you guys ended it. He told me."

"He told you?" It seemed impossible that he'd admit to fucking and beating a woman, especially while he was trying to get Mimi in bed.

"You can't and I mean **can't** allow fuck ups into your life, woman," Mimi said as the stench of urine wafted through the crack beneath the apartment's front door. It was near midnight on the West Coast, close to 3:00 a.m. back East—the hour of the urinators. "He talked about tying you up and slathering you with caramel, and I so couldn't see you doing that—I mean, it's so not you, Jane." This disgusted Jane, these lies, and she couldn't tell whether they'd been generated by John or Mimi.

"I have to go—" She couldn't talk anymore, her eyes pricked by needles or the radioactive particles flying from her computer screen. "Time for bed," Jane said, head pain growing profound, not-to-be cured by a bottle of Ibuprofen.

"Anyway, I needed to tell you or I knew I wouldn't be able to get back to sleep in the middle of the night—past 3:00 here." It was selfish of Mimi to disturb midnight with her confessions. "I'm in the mood for getting real," Mimi sang to the tune of, "I'm in the mood for love—" as if reality were an improvement on love. "And speaking of getting real. Are you seeing anyone?" This was the first time Mimi had asked.

It turned out she only wanted to talk about herself, the fact that she'd embraced being single—though she admitted to hating anyone who might've given in to eroticism instead of soul searching. "Actually," she said at 1:00 AM Cali time, "I confess. I've been wondering about this one guy from your past. I so know you have thought about similar things." Mimi wouldn't say his name, but Jane understood. The screw had tightened in the middle of her forehead: Ben, another pockmark of pain. No doubt, Mimi had heard of his death though Cathy, who'd heard it from Nora. "Honey. Forgive me. Forget I said anything. Forget it. Forget it." Mimi, had a way of endearing herself by wiping away reckless questions with a tonal shift. Yet, how could someone so thoughtlessly tease out memory until it bled from the chest like a horror movie? And why didn't Jane hang up?

They talked past 2:00 AM and it was expensive, but Jane couldn't stop. "He died not knowing that I cared, so no. I don't have anyone."

But

Mimi would never know about the web searches, the slow moving cars, the fact of Bill, because who could believe what Jane had seen while jogging on Hearst, a street of quaint and manicured homes, wood smoke mingling with morning fog? She saw it below the dog run: a red convertible BMW or Miata with black leather seats where a man with salt and pepper hair parted on the side gripped the wheel. It was the parted hair, plus the gray button down shirt, that made her look twice—and the fact that he slammed the brakes mid-street, staring at her through his rearview, scrutinizing her shorts while shielding his eyes with a palm as sun topped the Berkeley hills. That's when she caught a flash of silver and orange on his finger. But after he revved the engine and sped up the street she doubted herself because the ring may have been a trick of light.

Later, her mind wouldn't let go. For days she descended into the pool of him, swimming towards the red convertible and his rearview—leaving her to the dial-up connection's *zing-zong-zang* screech as she gorged on white rice.

First there was Yahoo! Then there was Google. Then there was the morning she found news of him in Berkeley. He'd gifted millions of dollars to a research facility focused on genetically modifying the immune systems of rats. In a videotaped speech, he stood at a lectern, occasionally looking up through eyeglasses at a crowd of serious expressions. She watched a dozen times, memorizing every turn of his head and clearing of his throat. According to an accompanying article, Bill practically lived in Berkeley, as he needed to check in during the three phases of the project: construction, design of research programs, and staffing of the facility.

After reading the article, Jane's phone began ringing. Picking up, she said hello and heard only silence, the vacuum of outer space. She hung up, and moments later the phone rang again, thus introducing a new pattern to her down time. Over the next few months, she picked up to silence again and again, sometimes cradling the earpiece long enough to hear a click, other times slamming the phone down in frustration just as she had in Seattle.

The calls came like clockwork, every evening, with only occasional midday bursts on weekends. At first, Jane thought the calls were solicitations from Nigeria or Mississippi, as all nuisance calls were the brainchild of spammers and fraudsters pick-pocketing the fiberglass strands that circled the planet. But after the fifth evening, when one of the calls contained a singularly revealing element, she knew.

A True Revelation

Beth, having extracted herself from Photoshop, had wandered off with a gaunt newcomer named Claude, who'd hovered in Jane's doorway with an elongated, spectral "hi there, nice to meet your domicile," before backing out through the kitchen door. Then the phone rang.

No longer rushing for the phone, she eventually picked up and heard the muffled cadences of a tenor, then the chime of an alto followed by an intermittently clapping audience that eventually roared with laughter. She listened, dumbfounded, to this distant reality, no longer wondering which bored telemarketer had dialed her corner of Berkeley. She listened for a full minute, the audience clapping. "Hello," she said again, too chicken-shit to say something meaningful, like, "Can we talk?" Stuck in the land of prepared speech, of platitudes and clichés, she couldn't dig into her heart and break free. But then it didn't matter. She heard the click, and the caller was gone.

Later Beth returned with a boule of bread and no Claude, and invited Jane for a rare glass of Peruvian merlot, which pooled in plastic cups in front of the flickering, five-inch TV that rested on a shelf above the counter. Normally neither watched, but for some reason Beth found Billy Crystal in a Tux, rolling around on stage before a pan of laughing and clapping celebrities. Thus began the revelation.

A delayed airing of The Academy Awards—the lie of calling it "Live" somehow insulting Jane. Gulping wine, bored with the "same old, same old," but accepting a second pour of wine, she stared at the screen, and within minutes she heard an audio snippet that could have rattled Hoover Dam.

Billy Crystal's voice deepened to introduce a "must-pause-moment," that rose to Bjork's piercing cry, (tenor to alto to applause) the show swerving from cornball one-liners to something ethereal and unknowable. That moment rang in the truth—Billy, the neighborhood kid who knew too much, swindling the crowd into thinking he was charming for exaggerating the mundane, as if he didn't aim for humor as he paused with slightly raised eyebrows during an obvious moment and murmured to the audience that he knew they picked their noses.

At first, it seemed impossible that an audience member would call during the Academy Awards—impossible that anyone would surreptitiously dialed her number in his lap. Imagination, it had to be imagination taking over. More likely that Burl worked as a bouncer at the Academy Awards. More likely it was Mimi playing a practical joke, wanting to apologize for making life "oh so incredibly, undeniably tough!" for her friend. But Jane knew better. She knew so well that all night she tossed in bed, imagining Bill with his date, how afterwards he undressed that date while wanting to undress Jane.

In the morning, she woke to surf the web, digging up a new photo of him—this one showing his arm looped around a blond. The blond wore all red to match her lipstick, reminding Jane of the stale rose Burl had dashed along her cheek when she arrived in Las Vegas. She dragged the photo into her "Research" folder, and hid it beneath other unremarkably named folders. It was only the beginning.

Coincidentally

Though she'd landed a temp job in the city, finances remained bleak. Years of money worries had finally frayed not only her wardrobe, but also her viscera. She barely managed the case of colitis or IBS—she didn't know which—that had afflicted her since Seattle. Nervous sweats, too, seemed a never-ending deluge. When she swiped her BART card at the Downtown Berkeley station and dashed for the swill-colored platform that chanted arrival and departure times, she worried about the draft of body odor that followed her. Yes, there was relief when the silver phallus flashed into the station, creating a wind that whipped up both stink and a ticker-tape day of trash. But relief didn't last. On the train, as passengers pressed into cars, pulling books to their faces, shame collected in her armpits, the spicy stench a revelation that she neared the gutter. And yet, expressionless, she stood by the exit doors where anyone and everyone could inhale a whiff as they passed, because she hoped that she might one day be able to stall the door as Bill jogged onto the train.

Sweat and her colon affected her forehead. She tried to relax, eyeing the Berkeley hills as if they were Bill's bed covered in sheets of fog. When the train dove into underground muck—tracks slicing into West Oakland, along the derricks that pulled ships through the Golden Gate—she thought of Bill's yacht, which was the size of a freighter.

As the train screeched through the tunnel, and when she cut across lawns towards Pine Street, she searched for his car. She entered a building, took the elevator to the fifth floor of beige cubicles—a maze for real estate agents avoiding their boss who redesigned his office every year because he had so much money he didn't know what to do with it but brood and rock at his glassed-in desk, a flipped-out monkey in his leather chair.

One morning, as she emerged from BART and headed to work with a pimple developing between her cheek and nose, she felt someone watching her. She turned to the curbside see an oversized Faberge egg, a Caribbean ocean on a hot day, an enormous gemstone embedded in gold asphalt. In a city bleeding wealth, the auto was meant to pull eyes. A man looked out though its windshield, his gelled hair and beard focused on her. Most noticeably, the ring flashed on his right hand like an orange lighthouse beam. He watched as she held up her hand to cover the pimple. She didn't know what she feared more: him or the exposure.

Later, when her boss dictated a lease agreement, she wondered how he'd tracked her down. No one had followed her, but had he used a mechanical mosquito or a laser eye to find her? Still, her boss yelled, "I'm three lines ahead! Let's go. Wake up!!!!"

And still, Bill wandered into her mind, especially after she left early that evening, anxious to get home to check the web and confirm that he'd been in San Francisco.

In retrospect, she couldn't pinpoint the moment when her life became all about Bill, but almost every day that month she thought she saw him. When she got off at 12th Street in downtown Oakland and walked back to Berkeley, he steered a green minivan around the corner of the Grand Lake Theater wearing aviator glasses and the orange ring. Another time, in Berkeley, she spotted a parked Lincoln Continental. He sat inside, watching her while he spoke into his cell. As she passed, she looked directly at him, and then he broke into laughter, turning on the ignition and revving the engine. For days, she wondered if he shared her with others, his private joke among other billionaires, as if she were a pet, an experiment, or a circus act.

That's when she began to wear visors with large rims that wobbled up and down as she walked. It was a way to obscure her face. Soon, she added a scarf that could be twisted around her neck several times and bundled against her chin.

Online she discovered that Bill regularly drove from Atherton to the East Bay. She found an article about how he parked his Boeing 757 at the Oakland Airport. This led her to wonder if he used the airport helicopter or car rental facilities. Soon, every helicopter and rental car became suspect. Viciously, she studied them. There were the red fire department helicopters that swooped low, the black police helicopters that circled apartment towers, the white and blue ambulance helicopters that b-lined for hospitals, and the TV station helicopters that hovered over freeways with cameras dangling from their noses. The small white helicopters seemed most likely to be his. They appeared when she hiked in the hills, stalling overhead as if a researcher with dart gun were tracking an animal.

It became very important to cut and paste every article that mentioned his name, particularly those describing his visits to U.C. Berkeley. She dragged countless photos of him standing with interest next to a computer, hands seeming to jingle waterfalls of change in the pockets of his slacks. Every image gave her another reason to find him endearing. In many he appeared purposeful. In others he seemed elderly, like a lost soul who'd wandered into the newspaper store of her childhood. Occasionally, he smiled broadly as if knowing more than she. And his half-sleeve engineer's shirts—a remnant of the Kennedy era—left her sorry she hadn't been around during his childhood. Had he worn those shirts since grade school?

She became envious when she found photos of him patting the shoulders of fellow techies in Las Vegas. During her working life, there'd been nothing more than a series of low-wage positions that entailed providing assistance, but when would she ever be among the crowds at COMDEX?

She could tell from the photos that people became giddy in Bill's company, laughing extra loudly, lighting up, sometimes trembling. Many simply stared in amazement, as if the owner of yachts and 747s were a god. If she could just carve a path to him, she'd be his and he'd be hers—even if it meant countless Friday nights appraising kimonos while reading yacht-racing stats.

At Cannes that spring, a photographer snapped a photo of Bill gripping the elbow of a blond whose cheeks glowed at the close proximity of money. Jealously, Jane studied the photo. Bill held a tumbler of amber liquid—a Jack Daniels probably. Maddening that the man chose such predictable beauty. Where was his taste? Who did he think he was, fucking a new girl every week?

Jane couldn't help herself. She cropped out the blond—he was always going for those damn blonds—and slipped a photo of herself into the vacancy next to him. All this she did alone in her walk-through bedroom, careful that no one saw. If Beth saw, she'd want to know more and then it wouldn't be a secret, and it would be clear that Jane was a screwball.

She couldn't be crazy, because week after week she spotted Bill in dozens of different vehicles, including a Z6 that idled next to a temple on Grand Avenue. How could she not pause at the air-conditioned entrance of the Ace Hardware across the street on that humid morning when her armpits dripped beneath her black turtleneck? And when she did, he lowered his sunglasses to the bridge of his nose and stared back. Absolutely, it was Bill—but how could she prove it? She couldn't respond with anything other than walking, though she hoped that he'd either call her name or vanish.

Next, he rode a moped, wearing a black leather jacket over his gray button down. A woman with blond hair, wearing a miniskirt that revealed acres of thigh, gripped his hip handles, the bike zigzagging through traffic. What was this approximation of a love affair, the moped carving a sex-crazed path towards a bedroom somewhere beyond shit?

How could she not study the jpegs in her "Research" folder? The women next to him were usually small, Caucasian, with big boobs, wearing gowns that made them look like daughters wanting permission to date someone else.

Jane's own body had changed during her three years in California. Her hips had widened, despite avoiding carbs after dark. Nothing she tried worked. She'd long given up breakfast and lunch due to the time and cost, subsisting on a single, 5:00 PM meal of lettuce and boiled veggies. No more Ranch 99 noodles or Acme bread or white rice. Even Shredded Wheat became a casualty. She had completely reverted to eating like the Ashramites who meditated on Namananda, maintaining a steady flow of bagged salads.

Years of eating this way had whittled her down to the smallest size she'd ever been, and still, it wasn't good enough. On the scale in Beth's room, she weighed 106 lbs. At 5' 7" she knew this wasn't healthy. But she'd have to do better. Skinny was what Bill liked.

And then she reminded herself that he knew more about her than any of his girlfriends realized. He knew which online articles she read, which photos she downloaded, even which keystrokes flew from her fingertips. He'd broken into her computer—she could feel it. The mouse swerved around the screen more slowly than before. He'd seen her bedroom, had paid to break-in, had watched her routines. He could have anything he wanted. He wasn't Big Brother, but was her secret Big Lover. And no other woman, not a single one of the many women who'd held his hand before the cameras, would ever be so visible. He watched her and only her—her dwindling body. He'd turned the camera's eye around to focus on her quiet, isolated, unremarkable life. But no one would ever know, just as no one knew what had happened to Jane's mother, who'd come back to the miraculously retained apartment on Lexington only to pack up the cartridges for good, because Nora and The Avatar, with a small group, had fled the continent.

Love Ins

"You gotta do what you gotta do."

<u>Words, They Can't Describe</u>

Nora had no idea where they were going that morning, but she rushed through tooth brushing, not bothering to pour water from the bottle, instead applying toothpaste to the dry bristles. For the sake of time, she skipped makeup and hurried directly downstairs, worried about missing breakfast—not that she felt hungry, not after excreting a tapeworm. But for some crazy reason, all night she lay awake thinking of her sad little girl, her confused only baby who would never know the spiritual light beyond herself. What could be sadder than a grown woman retaining the narcissism of an infant, stuck in self-absorption and fear? How had such promise been twisted into so limited and lost a creature? At thirty, Jane talked only about her problems, rehashing the story of why she'd never married or couldn't keep a job, bemoaning that she was always alone, because who'd sit across from a skeleton stuffing itself with frozen corn and iceberg lettuce? Whose fault was that? Not Nora's! She wouldn't accept the blame. No, Jane couldn't pin life's problems on a mother who'd only sought her daughter's happiness—whatever that meant.

When Jane finally got the position at the University—after so many years of complaints—she still couldn't find it in her heart to say, "Hey mom, how are you?" or even, "Hi mom. Hope you're feeling well."

The phone conversation that still kept Nora up at night took place almost a year before the move to India. Nora should have known not to pick up. But she did, and it began with, "You really blew it, mom. **You**. Not me." As if Nora were to blame. "You slept with him and didn't think that was disgusting?" The yelling radiated and tightened around Nora's forehead. She would be sixty that summer, and all she could do was hold the earpiece far from her cheek.

At some point Nora heard, "I was a good daughter. I listened to you. I tried. But you blew it!" As if The Avatar's light had exploded their lives the way he'd exploded Nora's body with a love so infinite no one could ever touch it. As if no amount of kindness or warmth could open a sun hole and shine through the clouds that pressed against Jane's rain-drenched mind. Of course she'd lived in Seattle. Of course she'd allowed a small physical act like sex to pulverize her spirit. Couldn't Jane see that The Avatar's body carried God's light? But, "You fucked him!" Jane kept yelling.

Often, especially back in New York, Nora rehashed that call at the rude hour of 1:30 AM, struggling with sheets and trying to distract herself with, "Where do paperclips go?" and "How much is in the business account?" and "Is the computer still on?" Could she pay for her single administrative employee this week? Would the repair guy arrive the next day to stop the dripping water on the top shelf of the fridge? Would the soymilk and sprouts survive?

Such thoughts invaded that night in India. And when morning arrived, she woke to hiccups—gastric strain—before realizing Little Squirrel had already left the room for the main floor cafeteria, where adventures always began with, "Nooooorrrraaaaa!!!!" followed by clapping, and later— after a light session on the lawn—with, "Come with me!" as they stood by a line of green and yellow motorized rickshaws trembling with expectation.

That morning, with The Avatar and Nora, Little Squirrel squeezed into the rickshaw, saying, "That was amazing— I never felt the light like that!" while sweat, curry, and sandalwood wafted up from the cab's seating.

Nora was almost twice Little Squirrel's age, more mother to Little Squirrel than friend. Long ago, they'd ceased speaking of family. "I'm always amazed. You know?" Little Squirrel said. The Avatar, steadily nodding, gazed at the waif and then turned to Nora.

"Noooorrrraaaaa," he said. "You felt it too?" Lately, he rarely asked Nora questions, and for this reason her day would be extra important.

"Words," Nora said as they jounced toward the carpet shop. "They can't describe." As soon as she said it, she heard Stan saying, *Bullshit. Another fucking platitude. Come on, Nora!* Heat welled up in her belly so that she said, "It felt like lightning. It blew me away."

Again, Stan, the lost soul, told her to get real: *Nora, you were always a follower.*

"Dear one," she found herself saying, "Your work. It's so profound, so true. I no longer have words." The truth had wiped away language. Where language had once been sharp, a knife to twist through the heart, now reality blazed and vibrated and created magnitudes of space in her brain. All the doubt connected to speech had been blown clear by the brightness of The Avatar's face leaving her to the highest state of being. Words had disappeared, leaving her mind completely blank. And yet, she still remembered her daughter who rested like brocade over the diaphanous light of Nora's new life.

The rutted road jounced the landscape, and Nora barely noticed the poverty that marred the fields of bug-infested crops. She never saw the squatting forms with upturned faces wrangling with the brush as they picked the harvest and excreted, picked the harvest and excreted.

Closer to the Hamandir Sahib, by a small and cluttered street barely wide enough for a car, The Avatar pushed her and Little Squirrel out of the idling rickshaw, marching ahead to a cluster of carpet shops. He would unroll ten fine carpets in the apartment in Bangalore. Nora would set up and maintain The Avatar's first Ashram, which would host several month-long seminars.

"Beyond survival!" The Avatar said in the days before Nora boxed up her life at the miraculously retained, rent stabilized apartment on Lexington Avenue. No one could know how long she'd be gone, but every last item had to be packed away. Her roommates would make sure the landlord didn't learn of the sublet.

"This is a journey for great adventurers and explorers!" The Avatar said when he talked of moving to a country with more than one billion people. "For the fearless! For the free!" They'd leave no trace. "Thinking thoughts make fear. No thinking, no fear—just *go go go*." And hadn't she worked on "no thought"?

Now all was quiet and nothing-mind, where no carpet the world over could be as beautiful or comfortable as this quiet mind. No earthly element could touch the surface of this choiceless quiet. Not even a waveless ocean like the one the Gods stirred to form the nectar of immortality, Amrit—the centerpiece of Amritsar—rivaled the placid surface that was Nora.

Before and After Placid

Her mind hadn't always been so placid. There'd been a time when she needed busy things and busy bodies. When Nora first met Stan at a friend's apartment two blocks from NYU, she thought his puffy cheeks, long hair, and blood-colored lips signaled mania. His talkiness dominated the room. His heavy Brooklyn accent posed political arguments that made him sound dumber than Howdy Doody on crack. But he stood over six feet tall and wore black slacks that gave his legs a kind of elegance. His out of style Linden Johnson black shoes and burgundy sweater brought out the strength of his chin. And the color in his cheeks deepened when he peppered the apartment with the view that America was made of beanbags that couldn't care less about civil rights.

After yelling, "To hell with the honkies running Washington!" he turned to Nora and asked her to dine with him the following night. All her friends stared. She hesitated. She fingered the mother-of-pearl buttons on her cardigan—too modest for public words. But then Matty nudged Nora and whispered, "What are you waiting for? He's hot. If you don't go, I'll go."

The next night, Stan arrived at Nora's front door carrying a package. He handed her the brown oval, which she unwrapped while he gazed at her. Inside the butcher paper was a package of Oscar Meyer bologna. On their second date, he brought her a loaf of Wonder Bread, its polka dot bag reminding Nora of the circus. On their third date, he handed over a pack of Doublemint gum. She liked the bologna best and told him so. Thereafter, he never arrived without sliced meat, saying, "cold cuts here," as if knowing the future. "If you picnic with me, I'll get you gum afterwards."

When he moved to New Jersey, he introduced her to apple cider, making her sentimental and willing to believe he could take care of her. By then, they regularly necked at the movie house down the street and joked about buying her turtlenecks. She'd already begun to ignore his bathroom humor, though she still pretended to laugh. "Get this, get this!" He often said, signaling another clueless, off-colored joke. "Dr. Saunders carries a load for John! That's right. That's where he belongs—in the John!" For some reason, merely whispering "John" cracked up Stan, despite the fact that Dr. Saunders, an academic advisor, probably didn't know what "John" meant.

Their wedding involved a professional photographer, a temple on 12th Street, and an aisle lined with white lilies whose scent overturned Nora's stomach as she gripped her father's forearm. She'd never forget the rose-colored carpet, the white taffeta sheen of her wedding dress as they blurred into each other. But it hardly occurred to Nora that Stan's jokiness signaled mental illness.

After the ceremony, Stan took Nora to his apartment, wrapped her in bed sheets and ejaculated their first and only daughter into her womb. Jane arrived small, barely six pounds, but she cried every hour, spitting-up most of her formula. She punched her fists against the crib bumper, didn't look at anyone directly, and learned to walk and talk late.

If only Nora had known, she'd have sought help from the start. But she didn't know better, and thought the newborn bluster was normal.

When Jane turned five and Nora discovered TM meditation, around the time Stan discovered drugs, the first signs of distortion emerged. It started with clinginess and evolved into an overactive imagination. Jane's imagination didn't just blossom; it exploded, taking over the entire household. She spent hours dressing for a play she never performed, donning blankets as if they were brocaded gowns from another era. Several times Nora found Jane bowing to an invisible "audience."

At first Nora thought it was cute: imaginary friends, a dramatic flare. But when Jane confessed that an audience the size of the whole world wanted to kidnap her, cut her up, and throw her into a washing machine, Nora grew concerned. That's when she reached out to her own remote and superstitious mother.

"Careful," Nora's mother advised. "Precious ones shouldn't be so precious. Wash her mouth out with soap. Make her sleep on the floor. Give her cod liver oil. It's good for the system."

After feeding Jane cod liver oil and brown sugar, Nora sought no further advice from her mother. The stomach trouble lasted only a day, but Jane continued to clutch Nora's legs, too frightened to be left alone. "No mommy. Don't leave me!!!!" The clutching took place everywhere, with delicate arms that couldn't be pried loose.

"Such a sensitive child," Nora's mother said during a rare visit. "Watch the sensitive ones. They never grow up right." As foretold, Jane never had.

If there was anything to be grateful for, it was the discovery of Namananda and his Ashram. Thanks to the Guru, Nora treated temperament with the best medicine: meditation. Excessive imagination simply pointed to an over-stimulated mind. Sensitivity could be dulled with repetition and with practices focusing on finding balance from day to day. Maia, the dance of life, had somehow disrupted Jane's mental equanimity. The only remedy was reprogramming. With reprogramming, one could appreciate the here and now—get the perspective to participate in life.

Yes, Namananda had been in two places at once—but he knew what was in front of him. He felt empathy for walls the way he felt empathy for his own mother, stomach, and head. If one knew how to see it, the eternal NOW (like the sound of OM) could be opened like a clamshell to reveal many universes within a single universe.

"Mom!" Jane cried that Saturday long ago after a night of chanting Namananda's name in the meditation hall. "I see little blue lights around your head—" Nora had driven them to the Ashram to get away from Stan and the summer rental—a farmhouse on one hundred acres located by a winding road near Shandelee.

"You go for that bullshit," Stan seethed, "don't come back till morning. I don't want to see you—" According to Stan, Nora had no right to take their daughter to some reinvented corner of the Borscht Circuit to sing Sanskrit verses about a Brahmin born in the Himalayas. "Sing Hebrew for God's sake. Tell Bible stories. But don't fill her with a bunch of Indian children's stories that teach people they're not worth a pig's knuckle!" Horror!

Nora drove the thirty miles to the Ashram every day that summer, coasting the foothills and inhaling cow manure, hoping that her little girl's mind would become symptom-free through proper practice. This and only this would free Jane of a world threatening to collapse.

<u>No Words, Again</u>

By the time Nora grew disenchanted with Namananda's Ashram and the Guru's living successors, it was too late for Jane. She'd completely disengaged with reality, drifting from place to place, believing Brahma, Vishnu, and Shiva would rescue her from the pain of the world. But by then Nora had found The Avatar, who was an anti-programmer, the polar opposite of Namananda.

The Avatar was mystical, not mythical, and couldn't be idolized. He wasn't hung up on clearing away excess thoughts, and he wasn't dead. Instead, The Avatar taught a small group of disciples—thirty at most—who cooked and ate with him, traveled and gambled with him, levitated and disappeared with him. He was the *Carpe Diem* shaman she'd always longed for.

For this, Stan, barely restraining himself, sneered, "The Avatar should go blow himself with a John in a John!" Followed by, "And go blow yourself too!" when Nora slammed the bathroom door. She'd explained it a dozen times, but still he couldn't bring himself to "hand her over to that charlatan." Couldn't she see how she was being swindled?

He went too far when she asked for two summer weeks. "To do what?" He whined. "Become his concubine?" And then it was, "Shit," He stood by the bathroom door, using the reasonable tone of apology. But no he wasn't apologizing. If anything, he told her, she needed to apologize to him. Seconds later, he yelled, "You're not going to spend half my IRA on blowing that charlatan, Nora!" Later, when she opened the door, spit flew from his lips. "It's the same bullshit! The same shit!" Stan punched the doorframe, inflaming his fist, red in the face, jittery from a fresh snort of coke. "You're so fucking gullible. These guys take you for a ride into a sinkhole you'll never get out of. What kind of bubblehead did I marry—" His voice broke, though he continued cursing and staring at the carpet, wetness in his eyes.

He was an old, balding, sagging, jowled wreck. He looked like a boxer dog about to fart himself to death. Even Stan's sweaters were on the brink of death: thinning, pearling, shabby at the sleeves, because all his extra earnings disappeared into a trail of coke that circled around The Avatar's gambling coffers.

Four times a month, Stan bought Ziplocs of white dust but told Nora she was a thief for handing over their savings to The Avatar, who, Stan claimed, floated her on orgasms by short-circuiting a flashbulb that pretended to be God. Of course Stan wasted his evenings on Dan Rather and dim blonds.

True, Jane took courses at CCNY, while the apartment became a war zone. Yes, Jane tried, though she rarely came home, avoiding both parents. That's when she claimed that her kundalini shot like a comet up her spinal column, revealing universal secrets and bringing mental gifts, such as instantaneous answers to the biggest questions. At night, she apparently awoke to find a miniature sun hovering over her bed. When she reached up to touch it, the golden orb zoomed out her window as if aware the sleeper was awake. Other times, Jane claimed, when she ate rice cakes for breakfast, a flash of lightning blazed across her forehead—as if The Avatar had sent God's last breath.

When Nora heard these things, she said, "Well, Avatars unveil the invisible and make the visible unseen. But be careful. You can't always trust visions." Maybe Jane thought it cruel that the validity of the visions was in question, but Nora had reason to worry that the visions might be symptoms of a chemical imbalance.

After Jane rented a room in the Village, Nora legally separated from Stan, who'd begun lacing his coke with dope and call girls, engaging in what Nora suspected was money laundering at an underground political organization. At that point, it didn't take much to get rid of Stan. He handed over his keys with, "Good riddance, you cold fuck!"

It wasn't so much the separation, or Stan's arrest for selling coke near a school, or the legal battle with the landlord, or the fact that Stan, from his jail cell, told Jane the one thing he shouldn't have ever told. It was the fact that drove Jane to move out of state where cups of tea couldn't be had, where Nora couldn't figure out what was going through her daughter's head.

Over the phone, Jane grew unpredictable. She'd always been quiet, the kind of girl who did what people asked. But that quality degenerated into self-absorption, so that during their last call, a different person spoke.

There was no place to go from there but into the dirt beneath God's fingernails. There was no end except to end. Such yelling, cursing, and accusing—there was nothing left that Nora could see but an outline of a daughter she'd never known. It was impossible to listen, because a fire raced through Nora's bowels, especially when it was: "You fucked The Avatar! He fucked us both!" That was not the daughter who sat crossed-legged and listened with a smile that everyone called sweet.

There were no words. No words, at first. But then, fury rose like Kali pounding her feet against North America, her necklace of skulls swinging into the Continental Divide. Nora had been wrongly accused!

"Thankless Jezebel!" Nora had roared. There would never be another word. "You two-faced, thankless, thoughtless, corrupted, flawed creature who dares to call me a mother—Don't you dare make me choose between The Avatar and you!" Because, as far as Nora was concerned, Jane would never hold a candle—not the tiniest slice of atomic spin—to the light that blazed within The Avatar. The truth had nowhere to go but to the heart, where no more words could be born.

Before slamming down the phone, Nora uttered a controlled monotone, "You really want to know—Well then, here goes. I will always, ALWAYS, choose The Avatar over you!" It almost felt good to say it, almost, but for the overlap of Jane's throat shredding the phrase, "Go fuck yourself, NORA LOVINS!"

No Home, No More

She promised herself she wouldn't talk to Jane ever again. Of course, Nora had many other things to think about, money being the foremost issue. The death of a once plush savings—which the divorce had devoured—had been a great loss, leaving her to shunt toner cartridges around the city. There was the landlord who wanted Nora shipped out in a cardboard box. She worried that one day—in order to survive—she'd be forced to sift through the sandwich wrappers and containers of a midtown lunch crowd.

But it hardly bothered Nora that no one—not her parents or her so-called other family members—but The Avatar and his closest followers knew about the radiation treatments for the thread-like cluster of cancer cells discovered during a routine mammogram. That alone would have been enough to worry over. So why spend two minutes thinking of a daughter who cursed her out? But Nora did, though it had been months since the radiation. She felt ready to let that Jezebel know. It would be good for Jane to realize the world was impermanent, that death would soon come for mothers and daughters alike.

It would be easy to pick up the phone, so long as Nora didn't give it much thought. So, one Sunday morning at the end of many years and a summer, before her final trip to India with The Avatar, she opened the directory on her desktop and found the last phone number she had for Jane. It was in California. After ruining his life with a spate in Franklin Correctional Facility, Stan refused to be kind to those who had meant him no harm. Perhaps that's why Nora felt impulsive. She reached out to him because she could, and eventually she received his call. "I told you, I can't give you any information—" Stan said.

"Why not?"

"Because I hate you—" They didn't get much further, before, oddly, Stan u-turned, saying, "Shit, Nora, why did you do it?" She sat back, the squawk of her office chair triggering a sharp nerve in her forehead. Hadn't she woken that morning from a dream that framed the window lying across from her bedspread? Hiding in the curtains like wisps of remorse was the five-year-old Jane wearing the black patent leather shoes and navy blue pinafore that made her spindly arms and legs look so vulnerable. Looking back, Nora had to admit that at five her daughter had been the most lovable she'd ever be. At five, the girl kept busy drawing princesses, her pigtails springing from her head like two brown rabbit ears.

But memories now caused Nora anxiety. Had she misunderstood her daughter the way she'd misunderstood Stan all those years? Had she been wrong about Jane's mental state? Had she been wrong about everything? Had Jane simply been a normal child in an abnormal world? Occasionally Nora considered this possibility. But then she brushed it aside. Regret for something she might have done wasn't worth her time. The present promised so much more. After all, The Avatar didn't believe in contemplating the past. There was the important work of "being engaged" in the moment, of organizing accounts, developing workshops, intensives, brochures, pamphlets, and Web sites that would make her new life so much more meaningful.

And yet, she scribbled the digits that Stan told and then those that AT&T's fembot recited into her ear. And then she dialed the 510 area code number, letting it ring and ring. She was about to hang up when a generic recording asked her to leave a message—and though she worried about who might eventually hear the message, Nora began.

At first she spoke formally, but loosening up midway, she blurted the truth. She had been through cancer and now she had to leave again, possibly forever, but what did it matter if two related people had nothing to do with each other—because clearly Jane didn't care if her mother existed. It was a foul way to reach out to the estranged. "But, just in case you might want to know," she yielded, thickness building in her throat, because she suspected they might never speak to each other again. "I'm leaving for a very special place. And maybe I'll reach out to you from the other side. Possibly. We'll see."

Jane II

Time Immeasurable

"There's no time."

<u>Nothing But You</u>

During those post-millennial years, my mother went back and forth between India and New York several times until I lost track. No messages, nothing—which was fine since we hadn't talked in real time in an age—only left occasional blips on answering machines. But that hardly mattered, because by then I knew everything there was to know about you, Bill. I knew which of your mega yachts cruised the Caribbean, the South Pacific, and the Mediterranean. I knew which shirts you liked to wear to which baseball games. I knew that you spent time on the Big Island, Hawaii, that your extended family and a slew of tagalongs joined you at a villa in northern Italy. I learned that you liked silent films—not just Chaplin and Keaton, but folks like Mal St. Clair and Mauritz Stiller—and that you played chess with Anthony Hopkins. I knew which orchestras and startups you funded, which astronomical innovations and gadgets you believed in, and how many cups of coffee you drank per day. Yes, I knew which women were privileged enough to receive a token BMW when you decided it was "over."

No surprise, you loved women almost as much as you loved cars and yachts. These women had cellophane hair, strong jaws, cheery smiles, monster tits, and Twiggy thighs. At almost every social occasion—stadium, gala, barbecue—you leaned into a different version of a similar woman. I saw the pictures. I had the proof. I memorized their blue eyes and the expressions of awe that most men found erotic—as if the women were already on their knees. These babes usually crossed their legs, hiding shame or protecting themselves against the hordes of less beautiful women (and let's not forget the less-moneyed men) who also wanted to wear expensive panties. Your feminine changelings—to me, one massive woman who was also a multitude of "hers"—I called Kali, destroyer goddess wearing a wreath of skulls. Somehow, every one of them ended up wearing a death necklace, each of their names buried deep in the gossip columns that refused to decompose in that trashy corner of the web-verse.

But I loved that you searched for me as much as I searched for you. It was titillating to watch you drive by in your arsenal of vehicles—like the pine green minivan I spotted on almost every corner. I had to feel sorry for all those women. They had no idea.

But I did. I knew you enjoyed regaling me with your collection of highly waxed and detailed sports cars, many of them a sexy silver or black, though the one I liked best was painted a particular shade of robin's egg blue.

As years passed, your vehicles became more practical, almost fatherly, though they were sometimes comical— Once, you drove by in a white VW Bus that sputtered dust at a stop sign and caused my eyes to water. Squinting out at me through the square side window, you held up a hand to cover the lower half of your face, as if to hide or protect from close scrutiny—further proof of your guilt.

By the end of 2005, I no longer worked in the city. I'd moved to a one-bedroom in the "Gold Coast" of downtown Oakland. The apartment— stuck in an unretrofitted building thrown up in 1960s when it should have been knocked down—bordered the rougher side of Lake Merritt. Scary that the ground floor garage of beanpole columns would one day snap in a 4.0 earthquake, that the walls were so thin you could see through them with surveillance equipment. But the amber carpet that released clouds of dust even after several passes with the industrial vacuum cleaner that I rented from Home Depot, and the aluminum window frames that added a flavor of dejection to the urine-stained, vinyl curtains hanging in my living room were all mine. I didn't care that it was difficult to close the shades on their aging tracks—often I didn't—because at last I didn't have to think about anyone but you.

Despite the name Gold Coast, the neigborhood was dotted with similar flimsy edifices, probably the brainchild of some real estate tycoon whose intention must've been to call up visions of Hollywood. But I had the lake—which was really an estuary off the Bay—whose ducks, coots, egrets, and pelicans almost made me happy. Thanks to the 1950's, when GM decided that 580 and 880 should cut Oakland to pieces, the once highly attractive lake fell to ruin, becoming more decrepit with each decade, giving me the opportunity to live amid parkland overwhelmed with goose shit and bedraggled pedestrians.

And then another tech boom birthed nostalgia. And then Mayor Jerry Brown jogged around the lake, inhaling the stench of muck that permeated the shoreline. Lake Merritt wasn't the Pacific, and I might not have been Marlene Dietrich lounging in her mansion, but suddenly it wasn't just the birds that drew binoculars.

After years of roommates, living alone felt like finding love. No more explaining a vegan diet. No more drug pushers or angry boyfriends or ignored questions. No more wisdom about the dangers of bleaching hair—a thing I couldn't seem to stop doing. Most important, no more roommates cuddling up to their man-friends.

Cuddling didn't exist in my universe. But that hardly bothered me.

I liked sitting in the kitchen alone, downing my bowls of greens. I liked wandering the streets of my own city as if a tourist. I got through weekends by planning airtight expeditions that avoided playgrounds with families or bucolic vistas where couples congregated. This meant avoiding the Farmer's Market and certain restaurants featuring votive candles, the kind that called up visions of Wild Ginger.

When I first moved to the Bay Area, there'd been some men. I'd dated my cousin Neil's buddy, Fuoad, who—despite double chin—had a nice laugh, good earning potential as the CEO of a startup, and an interest in foreign films. I knew nothing about him except that he ate meat, which didn't bother me at the time—that is, until I heard his story.

What blew it on that final date was the alcohol, not the flickering votives. There he was, sitting across from me, all hands folded around the base of his wineglass, talking about a childhood in Beirut. His parents had been killed by a sniper. His brother joined a militia. His sister had been raped. And him? He'd been forced at gunpoint to run laps around a high school track field while biting a dead dog gravied with a previous runner's vomit.

I tried imagining this childhood, the taste and smell of that limp dog, its soggy fur spotted with flecks of undigested food, the barrel of a gun pointing at Fuoad's fourteen-year-old forehead. I wanted to feel something for this man who was buying my dinner, who'd struggled to get over his parents' deaths, his sister's rape, his brother's certain demise. He'd come so far and worked so hard to chew something other than that dead dog. I wanted to understand his predicament, the horror his too-young body had gone through. I wanted to listen, to see through his glazed over eyes, and nod and reach out to take his hand, to kiss it, to press it to my cheek. But nothing in me responded. All I felt was disgust, horror, an incredible sadness, and that closing gate in the chest that comes after too many stories of pain. The only door left opened in a cavern full of shame over the feeling of disgust. Had I permanently closed down to humanity? I searched for something in myself that signaled compassion, but all I found was emptiness. I knew this was not how a human should feel. I knew there was something wrong. But all I could do was move on.

After Fuoad, I befriended Penn, another Ranch 99 devotee. I met him only days after Aunt Susan died. Penn hadn't lived through a war, was a horticulturalist almost twice my age, owned a ranch house in Cupertino, ran marathons, paid for dinner, movies, and plays without expectation, and joked, laughing at everything I said. Promising.

One day, while we trekked across the Golden Gate Bridge, he admitted to a foible. "I've always had this horror streak in me." He was gazing at the Bay and then at the San Francisco skyline, as if it were one of earth's bruises. "It should all burn! And I was thinking that one day, to protest it, I might jump—"

Thereafter, nothing Penn said seemed funny. I could only wonder how horrible it would be to travel future years beside him. I kept hearing his complaint about humanity, and it sounded worse than a childhood of war.

In the end, I felt justified in believing that the only man for me was you, Bill. Clicking your name became routine. And anyway, my schedule left no time for a real man with days beginning at 5:00 AM and ending at 8:30 PM. Daily duties were as follows:

1. Brush teeth, wash face
2. Tend acne by dotting sores with a Q-tip of benzoil peroxide
3. Pull on jogging outfit for 25-minute jog
4. Encounter mold-encrusted bathtub
5. Take shower, careful not to touch the black growths between tiles
6. Dress and prepare breakfast of white rice, millet, or bulgur wheat (purchased in bulk at a health food store)
7. Trek at 7:00 AM to an admin job at a lab

Campus was five miles away and meant passing The Grand Lake Theater, Piedmont Avenue, and the Safeway at 51st while keeping an eye on traffic in case you sped by in your green minivan. Sometimes you swerved around a corner, flashing your orange ring and making my heart leap. After a sighting, replaying it in my mind for weeks, I verified your location by searching the Web. Often I compared the way you swerved or glanced at me with video footage or jpegs I collected in my "Research" folder. Sometimes I searched for new jpegs showing, for instance, just your hands, wanting to study your finger and the orange ring. Hours of rehashing events; hours of searching for images of body parts or gestures; hours remembering that you'd driven by to see me and only me.

At the lab, pretending to be imperative to those of higher rank— hoping they'd never realize that I sucked at organizing people and unnecessary paperwork in my windowless nook—I switched on my computer, only to find the ubiquitous blond crossing her legs as you chatted up players in the baseball dugout or dined with Hollywood's best. As always, I downloaded everything to a flash drive, wishing you'd appear at the door.

Then, on an unusually warm January day there was an incident. The eucalyptus grove outside Life Sciences Addition was flush with students eating sandwiches and reading because it was too beautiful not to inhale the balm of climate change that made crows startle squirrels. I sat in my cubby amid drosophila as sour air circulated from a recently emptied lecture hall and an instrument was knocked against a bench. The elevator doddered up and down, too unhinged to carry anyone. I focused on a to-do list of reimbursements, reservations to Dublin, scheduling of postdocs and a visiting researcher.

That morning, I found a pile of journals on my chair: *Nature, Science, PLOS*—my boss's way of saying, "I'm gone today, but get to work pronto!" I tended to the postdoc named Lara who complained that there were no lab markers. Like most ambitious people, Lara had a talent for making underlings feel as if they belonged at the guillotine. Pure disapproval, she rarely smiled and relished diagnosing problems by listing all that had gone awry—the type who, when outwitted, merely said, "Good you remembered—Right!" Lab markers in hand, she returned to her bench to hammer. That's when the siren shot through the white noise of the centrifuges.

Occasionally, sirens stirred the lab, but mainly as drills. This time, the siren persisted with flashing lights, its cyclical screech as panic inducing as toxic waste spills or metastatic cancer. I sprang from my desk to find another postdoc, Jorge, tweeting at his bench and not raising a brow. Another postdoc wandered in from the microscope room, balancing a tray of tubes in her gloved hands while I envisioned exploding hoods and mutant antigens leaking from the pathology labs downstairs. Mere years after 9/11 and people already blew off alarms. No one in the lab made a run for it. Instead everyone stood around pondering whether they heard the whine of fire trucks, contented to nest with their Petri dishes. Under the circumstances, one couldn't ponder. I leaped into action, taking charge of the lab techs, agro-botanists, and neurobiologists who so clearly believed bodies were lesser than minds.

"Hey," I yelled, my bag already in hand. "Come on!" Jorge, with hazy smile, put down his iPhone. He'd always struck me as the epitome of an inert gas wanting to be a free radical.

"Yeah. Maybe we should vacate—" Jorge began, looking at the door.

"There wasn't an email—" Lara said from the far end of the lab, still living for lab markers. It was her death, not mine.

"So," an undergrad said. "What should I do with these—" She held up three plastic vials, and that's when I pushed into the blurry hall of sirens whirring over researchers reeking of B.O. garlic, and spearmint gum.

At the stairwell, I almost broke my ankle, but Jorge grabbed my elbow in time. "You okay?" He said. I nodded but kept going. I filed out of the building, reasonable, despite the temptation to trample. This was not a raucous crowd, though everyone aimed to be sensible but superior.

Postdocs spread like spilled milk over the lawn, curdling into clusters under the sun. Jorge edged towards me, tall, inert but faintly attractive. At twenty-something, his smile was all surfer dude with that Bob Marley meets Bob Dylan appeal. Everyone knew about his upcoming trip to Borneo, where

he'd research a rare arthropod and, "most definitely do some scuba diving."
It was easy to like and dislike Jorge for the same reasons. He was either
in a haze or grossly inappropriate, lurching like a drunk towards forbidden
subjects: nudists wandering beaches in search of shrunken heads; opium
infested wildernesses where children cooked the flowers. Somehow, topics
like sex and child abuse hadn't yet canned him—possibly because he spoke
as if every "trip" was launched by cannabis.

Smiling and massaging my shoulder with a far too familiar "Comere,"
Jorge pulled me into his circle. Loose jeans belted low beneath his grunge
undershirt and plaid button down, he eased into an inappropriate stare that
involved long consideration of my breasts. I folded my arms, searching for
someone else, but this only encouraged him. As he rolled up his sleeves and
revealed a tattoo of a crouching tiger (why was there always a tattoo?), his
skin a drum's hide over muscles, he seemed about to ask me to undress.
Everything Jorge did was a performance for some feminine entity standing
to the left of his gaze, so that when he offered me a piece of mint gum that
I didn't take, or when he complimented me on the way my hair framed my
forehead, I sensed he meant those words for a woman standing behind me.

"So," he twanged, a seasoned player. "You think this was handled
right?" He nodded, winking as if speaking about two very different things.
"Drills. Man. They suck, except it's a nice day. Days like this, I say, who **gives**
about drosophila—where's my Frisbee." He leaned forward to launch an
air Frisbee and made an "oh" with his lips as the invisible disk slid from
his fingertips. "I'm always saying, people gotta dump their dungeons and
get some fun—" Again he winked—a reference to my cubby-office—again
settling eyes on my unamazing chest. Though he kept the small talk going—
weekend trip to Tahoe and the "very chill" weather—I'd grown into someone
who didn't trust small talk.

"Jorge, what are you trying to say?" I said to his lazy smile.

"Trying to say?" He asked.

"Yeah, what are you really thinking? And why are you talking to
me?" He looked at me as if I'd slapped him across the face.

"Just thought I'd check in, you know—whatever—"

"Yeah, well. It seems like there's something else on your mind." My
burgeoning courage didn't miss the mark; something had jostled Jorge's brain.
Anyone could see that my spiked words had entered his forehead where the
skin bunched up around my remarks.

"So," he said. "Maybe I do. Maybe Borneo calls—or maybe someone
needs a head shrink." He turned away, and trotted towards a cluster of guys
from the M. Lab. "Dude!" I heard Jorge say, relentless, possibly speaking shit
about me. He swayed with that torpid nod, clueless of the running joke about

how his "fish line" hooked the wrong "ladies," who were reeled back to his one bedroom in Rockridge, unaware that women like me rolled their eyes every time he said something like, "Want to see my killer Blue? She's extreme! A procambarus clarkii."

As I stood alone in a patch of sun, cleansing myself of Jorge, something urged me to turn towards West Circle where FEDEX trucks usually parked. Instead I saw what looked like a sculpture: an aquamarine convertible—possibly an Italian make—with top down to reveal a black leather interior and a pale, bearded driver in sunglasses, salt and pepper hair gelled into curls around his forehead, hands resting on wheel. From my vantage point, I couldn't see "the ring."

Sun lit the silver bits of his hair into an aura, everything uplifted by breeze and the smell of cut grass. Somehow, I heard what I saw as an enormous bass throbbing the floorboards that supported the reasonable and real. Behind those sunglasses I knew his eyes, which were magnets pulling on the organs in my body and turning me inside out. My ears buzzed with the sound of a tampoura, and I knew that you were just as amazed by the vacuum between us, which filled with feeling. We'd been plugged like those long lost modems into a serious connection, one that simultaneously caused palpitations and paralysis.

You didn't move, didn't open the car door or look, but kept eyes on me, probably thinking, digesting, studying, absorbing as everything slowed down and the leaves stopped moving, as the clouds became Rorschach tests, and conversations faded into the buzz of particles drifting south, while the two of us hovered above the scene, groping at the magnitude between us because we'd uncovered the endless gaze of time.

And then the wind ripped through a thousand leaves, rearranging sound into the whirring of sirens, whirling white and red lights cycling up Shattuck and onto Centre Street.

If I wasn't mistaken, you smiled.

Erotic Confocal

Of course I spent hours re-enacting the entire episode. Charlie Chaplin twirled a silent cane and tumbled across the high wire inside me as I puzzled over why a man I'd met years ago tried to clip me down like a specimen in a Zeiss Confocal where every one of my flaws could be scrutinized, my spirit cupped in his palms.

Of course I imagined opening the passenger door of your Maserati/Bugatti/Lamborghini/whatever, picturing a bodice-ripping adventure through the Berkeley hills, in which I leaned into you, car swerving around sharp turns of dry pine needles, fog funneling through the Golden Gate as, in my mind, we parked only before a very big, clean bedroom, where you undressed me and drizzled massage oil onto your palms for a slow dance of nakedness, where the love-making never ended. Of course I blew my erotic mind with fantasies, knowing that I sneaked a peek of the physical joys others knew.

Serotonin

True, every time I saw your face I got a rush. By then, I couldn't live through an hour without clicking your photo. It got so bad that I endangered myself. My boss needed a flight to Tokyo, but I paused too long over a patchwork of "Bill" photos before minimizing the window.

"What's that?" my boss asked, staring at my monitor. Panicking, I mumbled forgotten words that left me feeling ashamed.

After that, I opened multiple windows at once to appear as if I were researching the cost of lab markers and colored tape. But it was hard to tear myself away from your features, and sometimes I became so desperate to be done with the obsession that I imagined impulsive acts like flinging myself into scary countries like Saudi Arabia, Yemen, and Afghanistan. I imagined living in purdah just to forget you and lose myself in the far away, turn distance into a maze so complex that you'd never find me and I'd never find you.

Vaguely wishing for my mother, I clicked images of Hyderabad's Rajiv Gandhi National Airport, which was listed on Wikipedia as an attraction. This led me to photos of temples shrouded in the exhaust of cremation. I knew nothing of the soot that clogged distant lungs or the dysentery that loosened bowels or the funeral pyre Yama burned in front of Savitri's house. But there had to be a way to dedicate my life to something other than you.

Occasionally, I understood that I couldn't live the rest of my days in a dungeon whose only window on the world was a computer focused on you. But then, it occurred to me that the grass is always greener, that the closer I got to Hyderabad—or anywhere else, for that matter—the more putrid and detestable it would become. I'd be repulsed, nauseated. Conversely, the farther away I got from Hyderabad, or "Bill," or anything else I might find alluring, the more appealing and desirable it would be.

But so many evenings alone had worn down my spirit. I found myself swimming in questions as I binged on broccoli and Brussels sprouts, my head unsettled. Had I mistaken your identity for some look-alike, a visiting researcher perhaps? Worse, I sometimes contemplated the horrifying notion that you'd never existed at all, that whatever I'd seen of you had been a bubble of desire on the lips of an invisible whisperer—meaning that maybe I needed a serious dose of Lithium. What were the chances "Bill" had donned FBI sunglasses and parked on Campus to watch me? What billionaire would find a woman like me so fascinating that he'd stare his much-in-demand-afternoon away? Inconceivable—and yet you weren't an accident.

Yes, a lot of people would have said, "Get help, right away!" But for some reason "help" seemed absurd, because I couldn't believe that you were a mere hallucination, especially because I'd never dropped LSD, and because the day the sirens went off and Jorge surveyed my breasts, two students tripped the building's alarm system by "accident" while carting lab equipment through the halls. Had you rigged this accident? Had you paid starving students to kick-start the alarm and drain the building while you innocently sat in your chariot waiting for the rabbit—me—to emerge from its hole? It had to be a game. You were talking to me through the wires—except you weren't talking. You were acting on and manipulating my environment as a perverse form of courtship.

Or worse, you were orchestrating an enormous practical joke, laughing at my pain with your cronies. This made sense. It was conceivable that billionaires required forms of entertainment more profound than reality TV, that billionaires eventually found orgies and 747s dull because even billionaires—especially billionaires—needed squirts of serotonin.

That evening, after the surprise drill at the lab, as I downed steamed vegetables seasoned only with salt, I knew that "Bill" aimed to consume me like a last meal. It made sense. Why else was he everywhere?

Unhinged?

Countless run-ins in the years that came and went like binges and purges, with maybe a hundred missed but not missed near misses, each one collected in the inbox that organized my memory—millisecond of indubitable sightings that spawned hope but left me feeling invaded. Most of the time, you stared through a windshield or side view mirror. Occasionally, I spotted the sadhu lightning of your ring—which I began to think of as a ringing bell on your steering wheel.

You had the financial power to be everywhere at once, even when fog drifted over the city like sprayed perfume at the end of 2006. A rare date with a computer programmer named Norris found me at the Filmore, where we prefaced a brand of "uber-cool" music—electric guitars beneath nasal vocals—with tepid Thai dishes that quickly turned into gas. The romantic light of an autumn evening was not romantic, mainly because Norris kept going on about "Buggie," a 1970's funk comeback.

Later, in the dark hall, Norris's admiration of Buggie, who stumbled onto stage wearing a ruffled shirt and a fro, seemed absurd, especially as Buggie slurred lyrics and scattered notes with drunken shiftiness. This kind of shoddiness might have been okay during the decade of divorce and self-help, but it wasn't so popular in post-9/11 San Francisco. The performance fizzled, with one critic later generously calling it, "underwhelming" and "less than unimpressive."

As Buggie murmured, thumbing his guitar with downward motions (resentment over his delayed comeback?), Norris remained enthralled, swirling a second martini in his boney hands. I was bored and in pain—not just because of the poor performance or the troublesome Thai food, but because Norris was too nice. His high-wasted jeans—cinched by a thick belt whose buckle made the bulge of his penis obscene—and his concave chest only doubled the insult of the bad music. I could do nothing but wish for "Bill" as I struggled not to quickly down a third scotch. I needed a bathroom and a bed, but I stayed, because earlier, in the rose light I'd seen a leather jacket, black jeans, and white helmet turning a corner on a moped. At first I had my doubts. This was not your usual garb—but inside the Filmore I found the black hole.

On later reflection, it was clear. I'd been telepathically beckoned.

Outer Space

I saw the Rockport shoes and the braided belt, the twitch of your ring finger, the unbuttoned collar. I could have drawn a picture for the police. You nodded, but kept watching me. I had so little iron left inside me by then, yet I was still drawn. I almost walked over and kissed you as Norris bobbed his pelvis to the crappy music. It would have been easy to flutter my fingers against the back of your hand, but I couldn't move. Was it fear that kept me from you or the idea that "Bill" might be a fabrication of my mind?

Freedom or Proof

From that night until this morning, several years later, it's been impossible to delete the man leaning against that wall watching me as Buggie's drunkenness undressed the night.

For years, I've reimagined that dark corner, putting myself to sleep with images of your face. Sometimes I visualize the parking lot outside my first apartment, or the curbside by West Gate, or the Peet's that Sunday when, stunned, I stared at the back of your salt and pepper head with its growing bald spot. You were ordering an espresso I knew you'd never drink, because you'd come to watch me sip tea and read a book beneath an oval of light.

Once, while I gnawed a wedge of sourdough by the entrance of La Farine, your eyes burned holes through the side window of your minivan across the street. At the laundromat on Grand Avenue, as dryers whipped me into new understanding, you could have ripped off my clothes. That was the time I "felt" you stare through my back—because I knew you were sipping bourbon two restaurants down.

On the way out, I peaked into the restaurant that looked like Wild Ginger. Inside couples leaned into conversation, but two men loitered by the kitchen door along the side of the building. The one wearing a white apron— the dishwasher—nudged his buddy and lifted his chin in my direction, mumbling something, eyeing me as I hustled to my car. Before I pushed the keys into ignition, they'd dashed into the restaurant, where I knew they alerted you. This was proof.

So, you stalked me while I stalked you online. It was true: Our relationship contained all the complexity of a traditional love affair. Yes, it was built on alienation and was carried out over long distances—certified by stares and sometimes glares—but our feelings only deepened with time. I knew this because you often showed up in the minivan, parking near my apartment, and watched me with tenderness, occasionally smiling. I looked down at you, wishing you'd call out. Other times, you ignored me, driving by with a beautiful woman, as if to say, "I can have whatever I want. I don't need you."

Once, I got so close to the minivan that I smelled its interior of leather and coconut oil. Your pale fingers with manicured nails and the orange ring rested on the wheel. You smiled, because you wanted to drag me up the hill to bury me in a Grimm's tale castle. I kept walking.

Year after year of this made me more prudish. I crossed my arms, pressed my lips, hunched around my breasts. An article in the Mercury News announced you were funding an East Bay start-up: a software firm in Emeryville that produced "kickass" wireless tablets. A piece in The New York Times talked about your interest in Nanobots and a contract with the CIA to provide high-level surveillance equipment. This news generated enough heat in my pelvis to shut down a fuse box.

By then I couldn't stop. I was addicted to the computer. I tried pulling away, taking long walks as I always had, but my mind kept recycling news and photos. I needed help. For months I'd holed up, only leaving my apartment for work, walks, and errands like laundry or food shopping. But I admitted my obsession to no one—not even during the summer solstice, when I accepted an invitation to join Chica, a lab technician who claimed to be a widow—though I didn't 100 percent believe it—who was a mid-twenties transplant from Monterrey with a two year old that often landed in the care of a neighbor.

Still driving Aunt Susan's decrepit Ford Escort—a piece of junk that trembled at 55 mph—with hand on the wheel, elbow on the driver's sill, blasts of bay air gushing through hair, I watched silver light spark the fog. Moisture sifted through the spires of the Bay Bridge. Chica and I gossiped about Jorge. He'd asked her out.

I hadn't talked so freely in years—not since before Ben—making it a revelation to speed up Geary, past Japan Town, towards the Aves. Around 30th Ave. —as we sped along Golden Gate Park, cedars bowing around the windmills cycling bits of evaporated ocean—the view uplifted me, a loved dessert I hadn't eaten in a thousand years—too long since I'd felt this lightweight, nothing mattering.

We parked off the Great Highway, beneath a modern glass box reflecting the Pacific, The Cliffhouse. All awestruck-Cali, Chica yelled, "Shit! Yeah!!" She threw up her hands with the endless time that came with being free of kid and lab. "Our peeps should be down there, that way." She motioned to a cluster of people gathering at the rockier side of the beach, by the cliffs.

Shoes off and thrown in the backseat, I followed Chica over the sand, every grain sifting through my toes, giving in to babbling. Chica said I should never stop bleaching my hair, but trash the makeup and black jeans. Black, she claimed, indicated depression.

But who cared about black, because wind lifted Frisbees and dropped them like tortillas onto glass waves while wet dogs mangled balls, kicking up sand as they dashed towards their owners, toddlers stumbling and clapping at the foam tracing their toes, surfers in wetsuits ducking towards their cars as silver-to-gold light curved around them.

I bent over and rolled up my pants. I'd wasted too many years at a computer. I'd missed what every human should never miss: meals with friends, pottery classes, songs around campfires, popcorn in movie theaters, beef jerky, Scrabble, peanut butter and jelly sandwiches eaten in the middle of a hike, men with beards who listed their favorite Woody Allen movies, phones calls with my mother. I'd once been the kind of person who stroked the sand with my fingertips and believed I could build an entire life out of small grains. What had happened? How had I wandered so far from the immediacy of this beach?

But at the peak of euphoria, I made a mistake. I remembered. Yes, I looked up from the sand. Leashed to habit and tethered to ticks, it was a chronic disease, this remembering, so predictable, because I was an addict who couldn't get over anything.

I scanned the beach, searching its population, once more seeking eyeglasses, gray cotton, the beard, that sadhu-flavored ring, so that when Chica yelled, "Guys!!" clapping, and jumping, tripping over her feet as she ran into the aura of what looked like fluttering bright fingers, I couldn't rejoin her in freedom.

The Fire Dancers

From afar they were beetles with iridescent wings. But up close, as the air cooled, wet sand caking feet, the forms circling the bonfire became men and women dipping driftwood into flames. "Nunez!" Chica yelled, and to me, "What a freak! One day he's going to turn into a fried squid!"

Soon we merged with the fire people, Chica calling, "Pierce, my man—" and to me, "He loves Cocolita," —Chica's daughter.

Pierce and Nunez, twins but for their coloring—one blond, the other brunette—wore surfer shorts that showed off buff bodies beneath delicate faces, leaving me to realize I was almost twice their age.

"Chica!!" Chanted the male choir. "Como estas Mujer?" The brunette threw a torched piece of driftwood back into the fire and stumbled into a threesome hug with Chica and the blond dude. I watched, an invisible, aging marm who'd donate a kidney in exchange for their physicality.

"Hey, Pierce," Chica said, tugging the blond's arm. "Meet my friend, Jane. She's the lab secretary—" The title felt like graffiti sprayed over my face. The word secretary left me demeaned and embarrassed, as if a stranger had diagnosed me with halitosis.

"Cool," Pierce nodded as all my potential coolness faded. In agreement, the fire popped.

"Yeah," the brunette (Nunez) mumbled. "Glad you could make it—"

Pierce, it turned out, was more reserved, standing back and allowing his darker twin to take the stage with a handstand and a grunt. "Welcome to summer!" Nunez exalted after turning upright. Once again, these weren't my people. I didn't belong. I searched for gray but didn't see it, only found Chica glowing in firelight, all amazement while nothing amazed me. Nunez dashed more driftwood into the flames, where it exploded with a spray of sparks before flickering a message that I couldn't read because the ocean was too old and loud.

A circle of friends formed around Nunez as he propped the cold butt of the upright torch against his chin, his chest heaving but steady with concentration as his dark curls fluttered against the back of his neck. The crowd began to clap, *one, two, three, one, two, three*, with the hypnotic rhythms of call and response, a kind of Jugalbandi that rose in strength as Nunez "handed off" the flaming driftwood to a lithe woman wearing two long braids and no top. She took the torch on her forehead, regardless of her bobbing nipples, staring up at the supercharged flames against the purple sky.

"Go Hedda!" Nunez yelled amid the howling of a tribe calling the stars. More fire dancers took the stage, centering the clapping circle, passing the flame as if passing love or life force on to the next generation, until a ripple of excitement entered the ring. It was the kind of excitement that came with news of a death, but it also felt like the excitement that came with proof of a groundbreaking theory.

A tall man with dreads emerged from the cluster. He held a long stick with a blackened wad of fabric at its end. The crowd rearranged itself. On one side there were the fire-balancers. On the other, this man dipping his stick into the flames. *To master fire,* the man said, *you have to eat it.* He held up the stick. "This isn't a trick," and his mouth became teeth and tongue—an image of pain.

It was around this time that I felt the presence. It wasn't the oncoming stars or the great spirit of the earth, and it wasn't the primordial of *homo erectus* or a remnant of a past life. It wasn't even the idea of Namananda or of Ben or my mother. No. I felt as if my skin was being scanned—every inch recorded by a hidden camera. Somewhere near the edge of the crowd, in the darkness but definitely to my right, was a magnet. Two, in fact, and they were digesting me, these two eyes that made me self-conscious and alive, more worthwhile and alert. I was drifting into Octavio Paz's double flame, which only wanted to be wanted.

"Holy smokes!" Chica said next to me. "That guy. He's insane. He was here last time, pumping himself up with something, then cutting or burning himself. I don't know. But he's more shot with holes than a dart board!" She nodded at the fire-eater's dreads, his cut-offs—which made me sad for some reason. He looked like a child, his knees skinned, his legs too thin, and I wondered where his mother was, if she still had a photo of him as a baby, if she called him everyday or had died. This concern was an old feeling that felt new to me. But then, the boy with dreads downed a second bite of heat, sucking up the last light at the end, and the feeling disappeared.

"I wouldn't want to be busted up and shit," Chica said, "Thirty years from now, he's not going to look so good. Know what I mean? I probably would've stopped with that first butt tattoo. And maybe that nose pierce—definitely wouldn't have done the lip job. It's like he's been through the Inquisition. Look at him!" Chica's straight talk struck me as odd. I couldn't agree with her. She was from Oakland. Didn't everyone in Oakland appreciate the tribal aesthetic, because body art was a kind of war cry against the white-collar, high-tech conformity spreading through business parks and gated communities? Wasn't tribal revival a retreat from silicon, a direct assault against commerce and the developed world, just as Burning Man—

spawned at Ocean Beach in the 1970s—and barter in general—was meant to tear down the stock market and uplift the proletariat, as the barter loving sometimes contended? The pierced, the pained, the freaks of the world who dared to step out—even within the safety of a group—gave me (the freak of all freaks, *the secretary*) hope.

For that reason, I allowed myself to feel you, Bill. I wondered whether I, a mere lab animal that you'd caged in a technological spotlight, meant anything more to you than that fire-eater or the go-go dancer in her crystal-studded bikini that took over after the last flame was devoured. Like the fire-eater and go-go dancer, I performed—the only difference was that I never took a break, or put down the torch, or receded into darkness, because you'd always sit at the wheel, or speak to me through the news—an invisible but powerful entity.

I looked around the fire circle, at the varied faces as they chanted, hands clapping, and I still felt you.

Excusing myself, I began walking the circle's rim like a space station, gliding past people's backs and rear ends, noting the way firelight framed each person's hair—planets backed by sun. The sound of crashing waves and clapping hands reminded me of the sound of all those childhood dancing saptas where I danced circles, propelling myself with others, leaping and twirling and bounding, clapping concentric circles around an inner sanctum of harmonium, tampoura, and drum, chanting *Jaya Jaya Guru, Jaya Jaya Guru* for every mother and Guru in every Ashram around the globe.

No one, not even a billionaire, could have guessed what would become of us.

Reenactments

For weeks after the bonfire, you spun around my mind with the many arms of a fireside galaxy. I'd caught you watching me, and saw your paunch between the flaps of an unbuttoned engineer's shirt. You wore checkered boxer shorts that revealed startling pallor and, of course, bare feet. I turned to find a mixture of pain and elation on your face, a leer meddling with the sweat on your forehead. I never doubted that you appeared partially naked, delirious and agitated, as if howling simultaneously from your anus and your third eye. You darted into the darkness, and I took off after you, pursuing your flapping shirt, boxer shorts, bare feet, adrift in darkness. I couldn't find your trail as I shoved past a toddler sucking her thumb, her mother saying, "Simone, thumb out of mouth! Now!"

Blasting through the gateway of a couple holding hands, I had no time for detours. Their arms felt like ribbon, and I lamely excused myself from their curses. I lost you. If you were naked next to me, I never knew. I fell to my knees, guessing what it felt like to be lost in the Sahara. You'd blinked out of existence like a Lepton, quick as a lizard and final as a computer shutting down.

When I asked her, Chica claimed there'd been a "flasher."

"Who was that guy?" Chica asked when I returned. "You took off like you knew him—" I lied and said I'd mistaken you for someone else. In the car back to Berkeley, she said, "So many weirdoes tonight. That flasher. He cut into the dunes. Who'd you think he was?"

Hidden but Not Hidden, Lost but Not Lost

This wasn't the only time my billionaire scrambled out of his minivan only to evaporate before my eyes. Leaving work one evening, famished after an afternoon of digesting articles about your private jet, I felt you like a tongue licking my neck. Exhausted and hungry, my mind drifted to steamed spinach, sweet potatoes, carrots, zucchini, and the fetid shelves of my local market, when out of the corner of my eye, a cream-colored sedan.

It was parked across the green along the road through Campus. Next to the driver's door, you stood in black slacks, your beard nearly silver, your face pale beneath a receding hairline. From that short distance, you stared through square glasses. Clearly flustered but focused, a hand rushed up to your lips, running along your cheek, where it hovered to obscure the lower half of your face. There was recognition, always that timelessness. And then you opened the car door as if it were an invitation.

All my plans for dinner were disrupted by adrenaline. I almost took off running. Something about the way you looked at me frightened me. At first, I couldn't put my finger on it. But later, after I'd eaten, I understood. Nine years in the lab cave with those Safari search windows showing dozens of photos of your face had done me in. You were getting older, and so was I. Together, we were aging, lines running over our foreheads, loose skin pouching beneath our eyes.

I was so old I'd lost track of my mother's last address. Before she moved to New Delhi, she left a message on my machine. Later, there were mass emails to her blind ccs, photos of temples or views of the Himilayas. Eventually, those too became spotty. I once wrote her back, but received no response.

One evening, walking home, wondering how to reach Nora in India, I felt you across the street. A sedan, its windows tinted, sat in shadows, making it hard to see in. I squinted, and there was movement through the windshield—a white flash, followed by a blaze of forehead as you ducked for cover. I saw everything: your hands gripping the steering wheel, your now shaved but prominent chin, white curls falling over your forehead, everything cloistered in your car. Had you been waiting for me? Did you know my routine? Why were you sitting in a parked car on College Avenue? Yet, hadn't I read about your latest deal in San Antonio—an oil refinery on the chopping block?

Still, I doubted nothing, searching for your fingers and the proof of an orange ring. But before I could determine anything, you dropped your right hand from the steering column. You slinked lower, cocooning, but still, a smudge of hair grazing the window. It all happened in less than five-seconds.

You'd been hiding for a long time—that I knew. But I had so many questions amid confused surges of hope and loss. Instead of stopping, I walked, not wanting to increase your humiliation, your fumbling, my own bewilderment. Walking kept me safe but uncertain. If I'd stayed put, years of uncertainty would have been put to rest. But for years, I repeated the mistake—leaving before I should have, always left guessing whether you had been there, whether you existed at all or were a figment of my imagination— which I had no way to confirm. And I wanted to believe that you were there for me, but a spiral of uncertainty kept chanting: *"Might be him, might not be."*

So many hours were wasted scanning the Research folder stuffed with "Bill's" photos; hours wandering the streets with my eyes on every passing windshield; hours of logging the time and length of hang-up calls, knowing that I spent far less time studying the yellow photos a stranger had snapped of Nora Lovins standing in front of the Taj Mahal—an envelope of three photos, dated 2005, the last communication I had from her.

Besides Nora, there was Stan. I rarely thought of my father in his small Miami apartment, hardly imagined him slumped bald and tired on a white couch, cradling a beer, nothing hanging on the wall behind him. Somehow I knew he didn't touch coke anymore. Maybe he told me so, but I knew that after the demise of his final marriage, he liked prostitutes who didn't smile. If I stopped to consider this, I imagined him with head thrown back, watery eyes, and a languid spread of legs. Yes, he had to wear bathing trunks and golf shirts all day. I could almost hear him whistling at waitresses swinging drink trays, his chest hair riding up from his loins to enflame his neck. I didn't have time to imagine the flirtatious expression that spread over what normally was a face drowned in loss.

My father aside, I could admit to the semi-oedipal cycle that had spun out of control during my childhood. Of course I liked you, Bill. Anyone could see you reminded me of my father. You were the man in the Maserati, the guy in boxer shorts, the pale form at the Fillmore. Bill, the billionaire. The questions kept repeating themselves: Did you love me or were you simply stalking me for kicks—a lab experiment, a form of entertainment for buddies who joked about me over Jack Daniels? That's what I was, a good laugh for a man who set dominoes into motion, and then observed the path they took. You got a thrill as each chip slammed into another—addicted to toying with minds.

I knew you bugged my phone, and maybe even my house. After Chica asked if I wanted to go to the Christina Aguilera concert, a week later I read a press release announcing that the singer would be honoring "Bill" at an awards ceremony. Still more strange was the over-the-top-coincidental announcement of a scientific research institute that almost, word for word, picked up phrases I used talking to Chica.

Here's what happened:

Mimi's addiction to Xanax had been an ongoing problem since her days in Seattle. I knew this because she eventually admitted to downing two doses a day. Somehow, during a phone call, I told Chica about Mimi's depression, weight gain, loss of libido, insomnia, and pill popping. I circulated back to the fact that Mimi had once been buoyant, and now what? Sure, she spoke like Eckhart Tolle lived in her left ear, but what had happened to all that spunk? From there, we moved on to Chica's specialty—pharmaceuticals, and brain chemicals like dopamine and serotonin. Eventually, the conversation swiveled towards the import of figuring out the causes of neuronal atrophy.

"We know so little—but what if we could quantify compassion as a whole body experience beyond the chemical boundaries of the brain!" Nothing could stop me as this ideological bowling ball spun down a medical alley in my imagination. A first strike. Flush with mania, I held my own as if a master in a hall of specialists. I'd never been all that focused on neurology, but I'd overheard enough lab chatter—Jorge's in particular—to get a general feel for how chemicals in the brain worked. I hit the golden concept while sitting in an old chair from Aunt Susan's estate. I slammed a palm down on the desk I'd hauled in from a street corner.

"No, no! Wait!," I yelled, unveiling my genius plan with more slaps of my palm on the desk. I could have broken down a door. "Yes! That's it! Of course!" A wave of euphoria overcame me, as I knew that what I had in mind would transform humanity for many years to come. Nothing, I knew, just as everyone knew, would get done in a lab that relied on a patchwork of grants from the NIH or NSF. Funding was too scattered for laser beam projects. Grants didn't fund ambitious projects like those in science fiction. People, powerful people did! "Only," I said, very slowly and deliberately as you listened on the sly, having tapped my phone, "a very powerful, very wealthy person could take something like this and run with it." And yes, I knew I was speaking to you. "But of course," I slowed. "Of course, he'd have to give it away free. All of it. Free—yes, free!" My genius idea would forever implant itself in history.

Words like this, I know, will make you think me insane. But of course you would think that—after all that I've said. You might think I've inhaled too many reagents, solvents, peptides; that I've mingled too long in a party of lab air; that I've spawned a wild imagination after too many hours of bone-dry, mental paralysis; that my boss's Asperger silences had left me open to an explosion of interior chatter—the fatal type that ricochets off an object and punches through one's skull. Not so. Not so. All that chitchat about the finer points of a crustacean's patterning and sexual behavior—so engrossing to Jorge, Cara, and Ms. North Carolina as they manned centrifuges—did nothing more than ignite my mind.

So there I was, lecturing into the pinholes of the phone's mouthpiece. I thought myself brilliant, that voice of mine siphoned into a reverb. Or was it a faint echo? And how you listened, you, the only person to take on the challenge of building this project! I was sure of that, if nothing else.

Signing off with Chica, I felt satisfied that something important had been initiated. Now all I needed to do was wait.

A Thirty-Seven Year Old's Reunion

For years I'd waited for others, and no one had come to my door. By the time I turned thirty seven with a celebration that involved shots of vodka with Chica and only Chica, I knew my mother would never show up, call, or write. I knew I'd never tent with an alternate Ben—and forget walking across Wild Ginger's threshold. The years ahead looked hopeless. So, what did I have to lose? My hair? The elasticity of my skin? A child's dream? Another year? Another idea? Another evening of shoving lettuce down my throat?

Two weeks after my birthday, almost a month after that manic phone chat with Chica, all those years of waiting paid off. As usual, I ate my dinner in front of the computer, surfing after you, Bill. First there were the usual headlines about tech start-ups, Hollywood parties, but then, when I sorted the articles by date, something amazing happened. It took my breath away. I scanned the article, stared at its headline. It couldn't be. These things didn't happen to small people who sat alone in month-to-month rentals, scarfing lettuce and shivering because it cost too much to blast the heat. But I found your name in the first paragraph. There it was, **Bill**, right next to a figure so extraordinary I could barely pass my eyes over it. An astronomical amount of money—hundreds of millions of dollars—had been pledged to a new kind of lab research that would revolutionize human psychology. It sounded extraordinary, impossible. When had you ever given so much?

But I'd stopped believing in you during the weeks between my conversation with Chica and that article. After all, there'd been the issue of Mimi, which had started with a weird call that left me feeling lost, but also faintly thrilled.

She rang on a Friday evening—unusual—to tell me about a visit to Oakland. Could we, she wondered, meet up for a few hours? This alone surprised me. When had she last traveled? Ages ago. And we would meet for only a few hours after how many years? Where, I wondered, was she going, and why so fast? And why simply pass through without taking in the Bay Area?

"I know, it's sudden," she said. She would be flying with her three-year-old, Perry. "But please don't ask questions, kay Sugar?" A last minute flight for two must've cost thousands. I was too ashamed to have her over to my cramped pocket of Oakland, so we made arrangements to meet at the airport and then drive to the Zoo.

"Oh my god," she cried, lifting palms to cheeks larger than I remembered, baggage claim making her hands and legs shaky. We always seemed to meet near luggage. "What's happened to you?" *That's a long story,* I said, half hugging, more squeezing her shoulder. We stood staring at each other, ignoring three-year-old Perry, who lingered by our legs with the same bewildered expression I often found in my mirror.

"Could you really, actually, and so completely be the same person?" Never one for white lies, she kept going. "I mean, wow! Jane, your cells have definitely shed over the last, what, seven years? And how long have we known each other?" Perry pushed into Mimi's leg, molding her into a lesser known personality. "What is it, my little cucumber?" As we walked towards parking, she murmured, "I so need to talk to you."

On the drive to the Zoo, she revealed that her visit was one-third pleasure /one-third apology/one-third act of desperation. "I'll be honest." She sounded winded, as if she'd been hyperventilating for a year. "I'm so losing it! **Losing it!** I mean it's so not me to go off like this—to come all this way, **here**, to see you and then book another ticket to some place I've never been." Her face flushed, she whipped around to face the backseat, the rims of her eyes red as she pressed Perry's knee. Her voice rising to falsetto, she stammered, "And-and it's so not and I mean **not** because of my little sugar plum! He's so completely and absolutely the sweetest and bestest-ever kid!"

Listening to Mimi, I knew she was on automatic, hardly aware of what she was saying, her core trembling behind all that motherly glee, that in a matter of minutes she might collapse. And after so many years of living alone, the ramblings of her excessive language baffled me. What did she mean? And did meaning really exist? Why did she blast the world with adverbs? Was it simply unimpeded emotion? Did Perry, a miniature and more vivid version of Mimi, understand something about his mother that I didn't as his eyes glittered with more grief than joy?

"I know this is crazy," Mimi said when I rolled into the Oakland Zoo's parking lot.

"No. I wouldn't say that—"

"Yes, you so would! When have I ever visited you? We haven't seen each other in like I don't know how many years. And we almost never speak on the phone—and then, here I come, calling you out of the blue to mention a little breeze-through while I bare my soul, with all, 'hi there, coming to visit for a few hours.' And then I'm here, like, I don't know where the F-ing H- I'm going—" I stared at her reddening cheeks, listened to the suck of air, watched the tears spilling as she shook her head, placed a forefinger beneath her nose, and inhaled. "Oh damn!" Perry began squirming in the backseat, his moans, his, "mommy, mommy!" as I shut off the motor. I'd been no older than Perry when Mimi and I first met. And yet, I felt nothing as I watched her cry, because I couldn't get you out of my mind.

Of course, I remembered my conversation with Chica. Of course, that morning, the New York Times headline struck me like a Martian windstorm. Who else would fund a major research initiative, donating $500 million to kick-start what would become one of the most ambitious, focused medical projects ever funded by a living individual—one that would delve into the inner workings of the human body and illuminate the effects of chemical signatures within the body, ultimately providing a "banquet hall of chemicals" out of which all life blossomed? They were calling this initiative a "The Great Chemical Signature Flowering"—my phrase, mine, leaving me with proof you'd been listening!

I couldn't get the thought that I'd reached you out of my head. A complicated set of emotions surged through me, even as I sat in the car with Mimi and Perry: paranoia, flattery, desire. There was nothing to do but give in to obsession. I couldn't wait to sneak Google into the crevasses of my evening, and beyond that, at the lab as I typed spreadsheets. Yes, I'd lost sleep trying to remember the details of that very important conversation with Chica, realizing that as I spoke into the phone and typed emails and texts, I lay naked before the fiberglass wires, monitors, and pin-dot cameras, which meant that every web search was suspect.

You could watch my keystrokes as I typed. I knew this because one afternoon I became consumed by an article detailing your investment in a software surveillance company that tracked people's shadows. It dawned on me that I'd been thrown open to you longer than I'd realized. For years, you'd secretly but psychologically stripped, raped, and flayed me. Everything I did lay exposed to you. And this exposure didn't stop at the electronic horizon—

it kept going, rupturing the barrier of the silicon chip, bleeding beyond an electronic heart into the real world where your examination of me found no limits.

The Zoo Story

No, the real problem for Mimi was—who else?—Mike, her husband-cum-self-absorbed-affair-stricken-and-dismissive interrogator. The man spent his weekends scarfing Lexapro and Paxil as if they were Goobers. Never mind that during the week he stayed out with his harem till past midnight, reliably screwing women named Farrah or Fergie or Felicia. He met these ethically numb entities on, where else, the Hoboken ferry—and sometimes craigslist. Mimi ignored the infidelities until the rare evening when Mike "graced the house" with his presence and gulped tumblers of Scotch while cursing Mimi's dinner and the evening news—all this while Perry played Legos at his feet.

"So completely crude and inappropriate!" Mimi shuddered. Could I take pleasure in an old friend's pain the way you took pleasure in mine? Perhaps, and why not? After all, I'd been through more than my share of heartache, had destroyed Ben, had been cast off by my family, leaving me to fumble through life for years. Wasn't it about time others experienced difficulty as well?

We still sat in the stuffiness of the car, and Perry had begun kicking his feet against the back of my seat, his hands over his eyes. "Sweetie," Mimi turned to face him, "Mommy is okay. You don't have to be upset. Really, everything is going to be so okay, Sugar." She pressed his leg again and turned to me. "Okay, so when do we get to see this Zoo?"

When we got out of the car and walked with Perry between us, holding his hands, I felt better about myself than I'd felt in years, because Mimi couldn't explain it—the reasons for Mike's demise. But she theorized that it had something to do with not knowing how to love—let alone communicate that love. Because, ultimately, she said, "when someone like Mike doesn't have the ability to heal whatever wound is festering inside, everything is a closed door. Someone like that is never going to be able to say, hey, I know what you're feeling and I so understand and love you." She looked at me as if this same message were for me.

Before I could say anything, Mimi admitted she wanted to leave the marriage the moment Perry was born, but then realized that, like most would-be single moms, she doubted she could support herself, especially after Cathy's business had taken a dive during the dotcom plunge. "After Seattle, I couldn't keep working hotels. And true, if it weren't for mom and human resources, I so completely wouldn't be here." She looked tired. "I love mom, but she's so never gotten behind what I'm all about. Especially financially. She's open, but only to a point. So, like everything else, life's tortures come down to money."

Mimi hadn't planned to leave Mike, thought she'd bide time till Perry got to college. But then came Cathy's birthday, and the "no god damn it," he wouldn't drive up to Cathy's Northern New Jersey condo. And no, Mimi couldn't take the car either, because yes, he needed the car through the weekend. *Really Mike? Really?* She'd yelled. *Yeah, really!* He'd responded. *And why the hell don't you believe anything I say?!*

It didn't take long before she spat in his face and shrieked, "Okay. Then fuck you! Go figure out your life on your own!" She'd grabbed her wallet and Perry's hand, dragged some clothes out of the closet, and flung everything into a bag while Mike whined about the law and desertion and how Mimi would regret this for the rest of her life! He'd make sure of it. "But the SHIT was too CHICKEN" Mimi said, "to bar the door."

Perry—the plump kid holding my hand and wearing Superman pajamas beneath a windbreaker—didn't seem to be listening as he toyed with his fingers, though I knew he was. Mimi was crumbling in front of him and the small line waiting to enter the Zoo. She pressed a tissue to her nose and shook her head. All I could do was stare through the entrance at the manmade pond filled with flamingos. Why had she come to me? Of all people, she chose to dump her life in my lap, all the while knowing how diminished I'd become. Meanwhile, her life had bloomed where mine hadn't, and now she was destroying everything.

Since the wedding I couldn't attend five years earlier, Mimi had continued her shocking transformation, which involved an additional twenty pounds on top of the twenty or more she'd gained in Seattle but temporarily lost for the ceremony. Her zigzagging weight had initiated a downgrade in fashion. After only minutes with her, I knew she'd permanently settled into a malaise of baggy t-shirts with company logos across the chest, black leggings that barely hid puckering cellulite, and knee-length sweaters that reminded me of old women holed up with cats and body odor. Much of the extra weight had collected in Mimi's bobbing butt and cheeks—causing the bottom half of her face—like her body—to appear burdened, as if a baseball had hit home plate beneath her chin.

"I so completely refuse to be bitter about back pain!" she mumbled as she eased onto a bench to tie Perry's shoelaces.

In the end, Mimi ended up staying for a week, as if she wanted to prove a point. It felt like a kind of revenge, that yes, she too had fallen hard. Doubling the point, after dinner that first evening in my cramped one-bedroom, she confessed to having grown flatulent—something she blamed on lack of sex, cheeseburgers, and white rice—which caused constipation. Pale, with poor circulation, she'd allowed facial hair to sprout over her once flawless chin, claiming she didn't care what the fuck people thought of her, and she upped the point by refusing to wear deodorant. I was left feeling poignant, at a loss, as if I were drowning beneath a dirge.

After a sleepless night on my living room floor, I could tell Mimi struggled to stay awake the next morning. After all, we'd both succumbed to Perry's 5:00 AM whimpering.

Over coffee (she now detested chai for its wimpiness), Mimi cursed the unforgivable fiasco of temporarily lost luggage. And then she sat on my sofa and cried while I stood over her, patting her shoulder, watching Perry fling himself into her lap.

Still, that afternoon we took Perry to the Zoo for a second time. A bright autumn Saturday when half the families in the East Bay wove their way through the exhibits. Perry begged to see the chimpanzees, tugging us uphill while Mimi kept stopping every few steps to catch her breath. Perry wanted to ride the merry-go-round and Zoo train. And Perry wanted a corndog. "And ice cream!" he cried. Yawning, Mimi gave him everything, and finished eating what he couldn't.

Scrambling around the other kids, Perry pursued his interests and yanked his mom's arm. He insisted they ride the Zoo Train with, "No monkeys, no monkeys," Mimi laughing for the first time.

"Let's so get to the real action! Let's so completely drag mommy to yet another line," she said, miming Perry's gestures. But I felt Mimi's pain as we wandered towards Africa. I felt the drag in my thighs as I stared at the faux veldt that served the double horned eland very well. "I'll take him—" Mimi said. "You go do something more exciting than a train," Mimi said, excusing me from a second train ride I didn't want to take.

Walking towards the elephant exhibit, I wondered why Mimi and I had ended up so tortured? In certain ways, I'd landed better than my childhood friend, who'd always shown more promise. How had she "so completely" fallen? What had broken her? Not Mike.

I stalled at the reticulated giraffes and watched their delicate eyes as they chewed from high yellow buckets tethered to fencing. A male giraffe sniffed the tail of a nearby female, his elongated penis slipping out of its fir sheath only to be rebuffed. He retreated, leaving me to consider why life felt like one big rejection.

At the aviary, the exotic birds left me still sadder, their plumage beautiful but broken, sexless, joyless, and lost like Mimi and me. At last, like me, Mimi was finally running from her life.

<u>The Zoo Story II</u>

But a strange thing happened that Saturday while I watched an elephant sort piles of thistle weed and eucalyptus with his trunk. He coiled the mass and lifted it towards his gaping mouth, this animal so much like Mimi, broken. I watched its thick, slow-moving legs and brooding eyes, the thud of its feet dragging up dust clouds. This lumbering creature, its curved back covered with dirt and fine hairs, doubled my fatigue until I slumped on a sun-warmed bench, gazing at the enclosure and the hill of million dollar homes beyond—a hill everyone knew would eventually quake despite the fact that everyone kept building homes the way elephants kept defecating and wild turkeys kept pecking dung.

It was an enormous circle, that stillness, those macaw cries that settled into stillness again. I closed my eyes. I'd been wasted by the years. There'd been too many hours in front of computer screens, too many BART rides, too many rotating roommates, too many solitary dinners. Somehow, I couldn't open the door in myself because the world was running out of time, because kids yelled and parents reprimanded as if no one was really headed for the endless quiet.

As always, I rested alone, chill air over my arms. Many minutes this way, and then I became aware, waking to the truth. At first, I felt it the way I felt the black car and the man pointing at me two weeks earlier. Someone was watching the back of my head. It felt like a gun. And it was a "him" who watched me—the "him" who stripped me naked, a razor slicing through my skull and releasing my brain. I was being watched.

Slowly I gathered myself, rising and turning to see a man with tar-black hair and a blanched—no, bloodless—complexion. Opaque sunglasses dozed like two snails over a conch shell nose, while his black gear reminded me of a Necromancer movie trailer I'd never forgotten, the zoom lens of his camera like a shiny missile, flicking sun into my eyes. Deliberately, he turned to an exhibit of flittering birds behind netting and pointed his camera at their yellow feathers, clicking millisecond shots.

I stumbled, quickly, towards the African Village, thankful to hear, "Jane! Over here!"

For the first time since she arrived, she looked almost happy, almost confident in her t-shirt and black leggings, waving with the old bravado alive in her fingertips—which made her look like she was cheering at a game. Pulling Perry close as he jumped and squirmed, she leaned down to whisper in his ear. The two jostled towards me, Perry far from calm as he left the shade of the African hut. "Straw roof!" Perry cried, excited, turning and pointing to the hut behind him, finally free to run circles, as if picking up on my urge to flee the zoo. Where I felt anxious, he giggled at the newness that saturated his over-stimulated body.

"Blame it on zoo crack," Mimi said when in spitting distance. "And the fact that we're getting hungry! Too bad he wants one of those horrible little corndogs— Do we have a choice when Jane takes us to zoos with lousy food? No!" Her deep-throated pant, the roll of her eyes. The insinuation that I was responsible for bad eating habits struck me as bipolar. Her mood had flip-flopped in an instant, her eyes all dread.

Tamping down anxiety, I ignored the long line that had formed at the Island Café in Flamingo Plaza and got pissed at the smell of simmering meat, French fries, and cotton candy bursting from the vents the way random emotion seemed to burst from Mimi's every gesture. "Since you won't be indulging," she was saying, "why don't you grab a table." She stared at the menu board above the registers, ignorant of my feelings and the fact that there'd always been hidden rage in her, a certain disdain for others I'd tried to side step during our entire friendship.

I wanted to b-line for the car, but before I could dart away, Perry grabbed my hand and smiled baby teeth. Irritatingly, he pulled me towards the hyena puppets dangling outside the gift shop while paranoia pushed me to search for the man with the camera.

"Perry!" Mimi yelled from the concession. "We are so having lunch! **Now!**" Hands on hips, Mimi looked brutal enough to scatter weirdoes with her bionic voice. "Perry!" Mimi yelled again, "Get Aunt Jane a table so we can sit!" Disturbing that this order seemed directed at both of us.

Perry shot off in Superman pajamas. I followed him to tables barely shaded by ineffective umbrellas that hardly seemed inviting next to a gurgling water pump and two curved beaks that got Perry riled up. He aimed index finger, spitting, "pachoo, pachoo, pachoo." The kid already pushed buttons, sitting through lunch, mouth gaping, tongue dangling, distracting Mimi from stuffing herself, and making sure I didn't scope out the area for the bird-voyeur with camera. No doubt the voyeur would be nicely paid, hired as he was to track me down.

Perry in my face, I repeated the same knock-knock jokes I'd hauled out at breakfast. Overcome, he drooled and giggled over his sandwich, his bangs tangling over his lashes, Mimi grumbling that he needed to finish his sandwich and get a haircut, finally giving me a chance to look around.

I saw him immediately, now that we were in the open. No more doubts that his eyewear came from a surveillance shop, because of the serious backpack he hefted—the thing had to hold 80 lbs of equipment—despite the shiny black jacket over gray jeans that made him look sickly. Most odd were the orange sneakers.

This was no crackpot scouting for an upcoming film or terrorist shoot. Pacing the plaza, he blatantly snapped photos as if I were Lady Di up from the grave, aiming hi-def-video-camera sunglasses at our table, recording our lame conversation by the Flamingo pool. Sweat coated his features like liquid Saran wrap, but he held the camera lens at chest-level, occasionally swiveling its glass eye in my direction. Later, back at headquarters, he'd probably get a laugh at my "claw and snarl" posture. I couldn't resist.

Meanwhile, Mimi devoured the remains of Perry's peanut butter and jelly pocket, tipping back a carton of chocolate flavored hormones (milk), and releasing a cluster of flyaway napkins: my cue. I excused myself for the restroom, shoving sunhat over my brows and heading straight for the paparazzo's camera. I thrust out my chest in a complicated message that, at the time, I thought looked like anger. But later, as I re-thought the moment, I realized I wanted the viewer to lick my nipples. It was as if I were ordering Bill to get his eyes off my sorry face and put them where they'd make a difference.

Be True

I crept towards my computer after Mimi and Perry were asleep, fumbling around for information, caught in my illuminated prison, computer screen a magnet that wouldn't let go. Every time the hard drive chimed open fifths, purred and whirred like a cat, my body despised its celibacy.

No one—not even Mimi—knew that I hadn't had sex, or any physical love, in nearly ten years. She would leave my cramped apartment and rush back to Jersey City without any clue. Not even she could withstand a week of aimless walking, kids museums, salad dinners, and Mike's threats to call in a John Doe. I hated her when she stood in my doorway, spilling tears, Perry tugging her jacket and begging for gum. Pressing up against me, she whispered, "I really came here to say something I so shouldn't have ever waited to tell you. Besides getting as far away from Mike as possible, I've been keeping a secret that I'm so sorry—so so sorry to have kept. I did the unforgiveable. And I so never told you." She pulled away, and stared at me with wet eyes. "I am so about to end our friendship, which I know kind of ended long ago, but I have to so be true now." After days together without a single mention of the time we lived together in Seattle, this last, single, lonely sentence somehow made sense.

Stalker

A revelation doesn't always feel like a Buddha ray shining wisdom through the mind. Occasionally, the revealed takes time to sink in—days, sometimes weeks—and it might not be comforting, especially during periods rife with drama. In my case, the truth drifted like a feather until it became a steel arrowhead that sliced through my chest. And then it felt like a thousand capsules of pepper spray had been poured into my heart.

And so, everything blew up the Saturday after Mimi and Perry left. For no apparent reason, I felt the urge to do something different, and instead of going to Safeway to pick up lettuce, celery, and squash, I walked the extra hour towards Berkeley Bowl. Autumn found me wearing Aunt Susan's sweater, a green/blue mélange of yarn that moths had pocked with gusto. College Avenue, engorged with students studying for midterms, distracted me from Mimi's final words. For days I avoided revisiting her secret. It was easier to get lost in cafes packed with sweatshirts and yoga pants, laptops glaring at the dark circles beneath students' eyes, hair—haphazard in clips—speaking of sleepless nights. Coffee steamed windows, and I only felt lost against them.

On Shattuck, I longed to see someone familiar. Maybe that's why I didn't feel disoriented when I spotted your hand resting on the wheel of a black Honda. And when you pointed at my sweater—signaling to the white van behind the Honda's bumper—I wasn't surprised. *Take notice*, the gesture said. Note was taken. Most definitely.

I knew those eyeglasses and those pale cheeks. It took seconds for you to wag your finger and confirm the fact of my existence to the white van before you turned off the street and left me alone again.

Later, with grocery bags, I stumbled through the front door of my apartment and the phone rang. I dropped the bags, picked up, sputtered, "Hello," only to hear nothing. "Yes?" I said to the quiet flutter in my ribs, another "hello," followed by the click that initiated three additional calls—each like lye on my dinner—so that when the phone rang for the fourth time I threw it across the room.

I knew who called. No call would ever again be accidental. Every disturbance and improbability had to be digested, considered, and re-considered. For instance, while strolling with Chica through the Eucalyptus grove outside LSA, a man with a Nikon aimed his zoom lens at me. Chica, ready for anything, huffed, "What are we? Victoria Secret angels?"

Days later, I was on guard, though I noticed nothing out of the ordinary: no hang up calls, no cars with tinted windows, no gesturing fingers, no sniper photographers, until I began to think about Mimi. Like her, I would do nothing about it. Let her go back to her husband and get beaten. Why should I care? She hadn't cared about me, so why bother with anyone but you, Bill? Why act on anything, even if doing nothing endangered my livelihood?

By then, my boss, Dennis, had dropped at least a dozen unsubtle hints, like, "What are you staring at all day?" and, "We have to get you away from the computer," and, "Reorganize the butterfly cabinets," culminating in, "Don't do anything else until that new set of Gynandromorphs is pinned and labeled."

Since joining the lab, I'd avoided the mess of the Lepidoptera cabinets, hating the idea of sticking a metal phallus through the many crumbling bodies that reminded me of what we'd all become: dry collections of cells breaking down into particles.

I avoided everything having to do with the butterflies, from printing labels to ordering pins. But Dennis rarely made demands, so that when he did, it indicated a situation of gravity. I couldn't afford to lose my job. I had to work for **The Man**. And this man couldn't be bothered with my phobias and obsessions. Tall, balding, freckled, nervous despite extensive social engagements and international travel, Dennis exuded an air of Walmart drab and fast-food regularity. The first time I met him, he wore the same cheap and scratchy shirts Ben's father Rudy wore, a familiarity that felt uncomfortable.

So, I had no choice but to stab thousands of dollars of dried Nymphalidae and Papilionidae—a few dermestid beetles thrown in—with pins that sometimes nicked my fingers. But I made good time archiving the specimen while my boss worried over undergrads thieving the most valuable wings. The carcasses served as an interlude, enabling Dennis to dream up more projects, like updating the lab's I.T. map.

He doth spake one morning: "Start with my computer. Catalog all software, I.P. addresses, and Ethernet connections. Then do every computer. And don't forget to tag the outside jacks and cords with appropriate I.P. addresses." What else could this be but punishment for being so enamored of you?

During that period, I occasionally got the chance to update Dennis's c.v. and website, which felt like a vacation. I almost enjoyed organizing his travel engagements, but most of the time I toiled over repetitious projects that numbed my brain, welcoming the mentally and emotionally dead end of the day. That's when I stopped reading and watching movies, preferring to wander the streets instead.

Truth was, the many years I'd spent as a pale and sweat-sensitive cave-creature had turned me into a moth in a lab that somehow survived while Dennis somehow continued to limp along the lecture circuit due to a single, early success, somehow convincing those with deep pockets to support his research. But nothing lasted forever.

A week after Mimi's brief visit, Dennis's unwillingness to publish new articles until all the research was checked over a dozen times had finally burned a hole in his once stellar reputation. He had neglected his budget, and all hell broke loose. To stay solvent, he had to giddy up and submit multiple

NSF and NIH applications—which meant I had to drop the butterfly drawers and I.T. cataloguing, scrambling back to the desk, where I could once again search.

Another Mistake

Dramas usually begin behind a curtain as a musical note falls through the air, with light rising to make a dark form into a person. But not a single, dramatic element lit up in the backdrop of my life to warn me, because summer was high on itself.

It began by a dead employee's bench, on a day when the lab was enmeshed in a two-day seminar organized for crustacean enthusiasts seeking exo-skeletal gene patterning in parhyale. Administrators never attended seminars, which meant that if I chose I could become intimate with centrifuges and lab benches, as the lab was vacant that day, leaving me to dust journal racks and surf the web. Even Chica had disappeared to hear the presentations. Exhausted by the chemical-laden air, I took a break from my computer to wander Telegraph Avenue, stumbling into Moe's Bookstore for the first time in ages. Upstairs, I found Rebecca Solnit's *A Field Guide To Getting Lost*, and was floored by how completely she seemed to understand my life.

After buying the book—the first in years—I wandered back through Sproul Plaza and headed for my favorite bench by Giannini Hall and settled on the wood slats, thinking I'd read for half an hour. Skimming chapter after chapter about deliberately getting lost, I could stop thinking about you, Bill, and became airborne in the skyscape of another person's point of view. No more images of your hands gripping steering wheels, of your stare, or your gray shirts and dark sunglasses. It was so freeing to once again read, to lose myself in Solnit's thoughts, suddenly free to think about something different.

As I got lost in the book, a twinge—a kind of worry—made me look up from pages I'd never return to. Someone was staring at me like the lion staring through Henri Rousseaus' famous foliage in "The Dream." I squinted, peering deeper into the cluster of tangled bramble dangling over Strawberry Creek, at first blowing off the sensation as a sensitivity to the squirrels dashing around as they were harassed by crows. But this twinge felt more acute than a flirtation with survival of the fittest. I was being visually eaten alive as a thrill rose in my abdomen. Partially obscured by the thickest foliage was the outline of a head, which seemed to be examining me from where it sat across the creek on the shaded bench that was carved from a redwood log. Damp and coolness floated up from the stream as I felt the man with his large cranium pondering whether or not he should eat me.

I saw his white tank top, the bulge of his paunch, his forward slump accentuated by arms that seemed to melt into the bulk of his upper body. He was beautiful and disturbing as he stared with the stillness of a lion about to pounce. In return, I watched him, the two of us staring like chess players bewildered by a stalemate. I couldn't see his features, but something about his "wife beater" and the shape of his upper body looked more than familiar.

Standing up, stretching, I held up Solnit's book as if waving a peace flag. "Why are we lost?" I wanted to say. "Come here." But instead of staying to see what might happen, I walked slowly down the path, back towards the lab.

Later, at my computer, I cursed myself for walking away. He'd been *you*, sitting, waiting for me, sending out an invitation to join you on the redwood bench. So what if you wore only an undershirt? It was a 1968 hippy bench made for hippy love.

Despairing over this botched second chance the way I despaired over that first chance at Wild Ginger, I slid straight into your Facebook page. And then I drafted a message.

Keep Trying

I was typing very fast and without thought, knowing that I had to hold back, say as little as possible, because you might pretend not to know me. So, I wrote something innocuous:

"Hi. I'm a big fan and would love to know your thoughts on where technology is going today. Thanks."

Heart beating, fingers trembling, all I could do was type this opener—reckless of me to type anything at all. But someone had cracked open my head, and everything inside was dribbling out. Like a skater swerving off course, I kept going, wanting to draft a communiqué about passion, regret, missteps and the loss of hope. I admitted to no longer believing in an afterlife or reincarnation. *All that exists is all that will exist. Only those who believe in everlasting life can claim to experience hope.* Somehow, with everything else, I'd given up hope. And so, I'd turned my back on you the way I'd turned my back on everything else.

I didn't believe my simple message would raise flags with security, because my real message was cloaked in aphorisms, words Wayne Dyer might have said before turning them inside out for Burl to repeat. But I knew you would uncover the meaning or shake out my true message. You would understand.

Before I could think too much, I clicked SEND. And then, like everything else I did, I immediately regretted it. Minutes later, I dashed from my lab/cave and headed for the emergency exit. Hands skimming railing,

I charged down the stairs for the fire door, pushing through to inhale the dandelion pollen rising as mist from the lawn, midday rays on my cheeks, sweat breaking over my forehead, the sky radiating real light—not the Jurassic light emitted from my monitor. Charging forth, disoriented, I circled the main path several times and then stumbled towards a slab of marble that served as a bench. Stalling, I patted my face—always failing to be at ease. My ugliness expressed in straw hair and acne-covered skin, my blinking eyes unable to appreciate the marvel of conversation all around me. I shaded my face with hands, always caught off guard, even as I saw the thing that might have fixed everything.

What did I see? What promised to smooth things over but only bothered me more? What, but a hat! Specifically, an African safari hat, the kind that had evolved from the bushwhacking Colonialism of previous centuries, and had been marketed so well by Banana Republic in 1983. I'd seen that hat hanging next to bamboo and fake palms in the store's Madison and 85ᵗʰ street location. Imagine the neighborhood: Isabella Rossellini pushing a stroller past that store. Imagine me being drawn into Banana Republic hysteria. Imagine hats dangling like booty from Baobab wood wall pegs. Imagine those hats hailing from a mother continent whose financial future relied upon pilfering precious stones, oil, and animals from people who fought over scraps. In a pile of bright cotton, I found my first safari hat, one that outshone all the hats in Manhattan. The hat was a puzzle of side-mesh, tough nylon, adjustable bands, and pale rims; Reagan-era hats worth more than a week's pay—hats that looked like they'd been worn by archeologists digging up the shores of Lake Haiqe. Imagine that I couldn't buy that hat, but had fallen in love with that hat the way I fell in love with the man wearing its reincarnation at West Circle. For the second time in my life, that hat came towards me, ferried down an asphalt path instead of an African river, its beige rim an artifact of the Serengeti at sunrise. Content and acknowledged—even famous—the hat rested on your pate, an expression less of entitlement than genuine joy. Not surprisingly, you walked towards me, seeming to say, "I've been there. But here you are."

Your smile was so kind, and yet it was also the smile of someone who had tasted the sweat on my skin, had felt my exhalations when I was aroused. For only a moment, I digested your bright smile. I made and unmade a choice as you sallied towards me. Sweating and embarrassed, a surge of pheromones and piss between my legs, I spun, not towards you as I'd dreamed so many times, but away.

Once again—a third time!—away I went in an explosion of emotional shrapnel. In Bollywood, Rama pursued Sita the way I wanted to be pursued, because if you pursued it meant you'd given-in and given up self-interest in favor of sacrifice, because no man after the 60's ever wooed a woman, and I wanted to be wooed and pursued.

At VLSB's stairway, I had a view of the quad, but there was only a green patch of bramble and lawn where you'd been. I searched for your hat, but instead saw surfer shorts and a brown t-shirt hurtling past on a skateboard, followed by two middle-aged blonds jogging in pink and black spandex. No echoes of Africa. No amazed grin. No you. Time, which had expanded, now shriveled, giving off a final whirl of spray like a sprinkler system shutting down. Had you dashed into LSA, or spun back to Giannini Hall? Had my vision merely been a safari hat on the head of a stranger who'd mistook me for a friend but realized the error and disappeared?

Closed Door

Days later, still no message in my Facebook account. In fact, I'd been blocked by you and could no longer dig up your profile. I searched Google news but only found that old photo showing you sitting pensively with chin on fist, a cloud over your eyes. How could I not feel remorse?

But I had other pains to concern me. My micro-managing boss, Dennis, had finally deduced that I was a drag on productivity. Everyone knew, and I quickly became the lab scapegoat. A usually easy-going postdoc threw a tantrum over the misplacement of certain important tax-related forms— their precise location overwritten by daydreams of you. *So I zoned-out! So I forgot to shut the file cabinet drawer! So Chica handed me two yellow sheets of lab labels, and I lost them, forgetting about their existence!* Right.

And then, while compiling a lab email list, a new grad student challenged me to a thumb-wrestling contest, won, and then blamed me for not including him on the lab email list. My ectomorph boss shook his head, bit his lip, and said, "Don't let this happen again."

Doubly upsetting, lately Chica had begun to wave her hands in front of my eyes with, "wake up, girl," and had taken to interrogating me. "What are you sniffing?" and "Where's your noodle been soaking?"

"Tired, I'm just tired, that's all—" I said when she asked if I was okay, though who would believe? Anyone who knew me understood that I still got my nine hours. But since Mimi's visit, I'd been dragging my feet like one infected with Epstein Barr. I didn't feel hungry. And I also didn't feel angry or bitter. I simply talked little, and heard even less.

After work one day, Chica crossed her arms, curled her lower lip, and raised her chin, diagnosing depression.

"You're in the pit," She said.

"What are you talking about?"

"You. You're lying to everyone including the walls."

"Oh come on—" I refused to get into it with her, waving her away like a gnat before dashing for BART. But later on the Fremont train, her words felt like spit in my eyes, clogging up my throat. One endless, tar-heavy tear eventually rolled out of me. It could have steamed the streets. But I kept the deluge back, and got home in time to binge on salad.

The next day it was all, "My friend, don't get so off-in-your-own-head." Chica's laughter felt less like a fit of the funnies and more like a slap. "You know Dennis. He says *nothing* until he makes a decision." How many times had she insinuated that micro-managers made a lot of waves, but rarely moved ships? And now she was all, "With him, that's it. There's no coming back once he's made up his mind. *I'm just saying.* And you and I both know you need to be here in the lab, not collecting bottles in shopping carts."

Throughout the day, sadness smeared my focus, making it hard to pin down a new round of Hesperiidae, Pieridae, Lycaenidae: husks once beautiful, but now brittle as seedpods on beds of foam. Each body was labeled with yellow paper crammed with indecipherable script detailing nothing of true importance—names, locations, death dates—except that I was constantly reminded of my own impending date with the morgue.

Pretending to matter, I huddled at my desk, inhaling your rancid, stock photos. Your image gave me life. Your two dimensional eyes and candid "I-want-to-rip-off-your-bra," smile leached into my retina. I hated that each headshot likely cost you more than my weekly wage. Still, I clicked and squinted at your finely angled glasses, your impeccably gelled hair, minimizing the window—almost caught by Dennis—but refusing to let you go.

Eventually, after so many years, convinced that my web searches and single-mindedness were the inevitable results of your covert directives—not OCD—I was determined to collect evidence. It was clear: We were cycling through a game of chase, tag, and capture. It was you, not I, who initiated the cycle. You—not I—had begun the stalking. After all your appearances in my world, how could anyone with two eyes doubt this fact, especially when you began showing up on the quad in front of the lab?

True, most mornings I arrived half an hour early and killed time by writing in my journal before heading into my life sciences cave. And true, whenever possible I sat on the damp grass wearing a floppy sunhat that reminded me of the one Nora had worn when I was a little girl. *Nora, my mother.* Mimi had told me that I could find her, but I chose to re-read my journal entries instead, and then scrawled lengthy new ones concerning your various appearances.

I had every reason to believe you watched me, because it wasn't often that one mistook a gray beard, or an overweight man in glasses. Occasionally

I'd been fooled like with the "regular" at the Berkeley Roma—an elderly guy who read his paper during lunch and exhibited the same square eyewear, beard, and blooming mid-section. For weeks I spent lunchtime drifting past the Roma's garden-tables, half obscured by a row of purple salvia. He was always bent over a newspaper, downing coffee. Pretending to eye the salvia, I tried to determine whether the nose had the same downward curve as the much-photographed protuberance that rested in my research folder. For days—no weeks—I questioned whether I had it right. The hair looked the same salt and pepper, but unlike you his complexion glowed with hell-bent circulation, leaving me to wonder whether the man I called Bill was simply a composite, a figment of the web?

It was so easy to believe the man in the cafe was the same one I saw online. Patch in a photo that fit the same contours. Match eyebrows and foreheads. Believe he's the same Bill standing in front of a lectern and presenting a grant, his profile frozen and ripped from an NBC interview. At home, I closed my eyes and tried to remember the café man, and then I scrutinized the screen.

Those first weeks, the man reading his paper was oblivious of my attention. I grew discouraged, uncertain of whether I could trust my eyes, because if this were you, Bill, you'd have looked up. You'd have felt me, recognized me, reached-out to me. Because this man didn't, it couldn't be you. Only a facial tick that quivered his left cheek, as if a bird lived beneath, riffled his steady reading. So, I convinced myself that his square glasses were not yours. He was merely an old man stuffing his face with muffins—not so different from Rudy in the hospital all those years ago. Wanting to "get real," I stayed away for an entire day. But unable to sleep that night, I returned the next afternoon to find him still sipping coffee, still pressing a muffin into his mouth, and still reading his paper.

Eventually, I concluded that the fingers of his page-turning left hand were too thick, too knobby, too calloused. Exhausted and deflated, I finally understood that the café-man couldn't be you, fully convinced when three articles that week claimed you were traveling in South East Asia. But by the time I had the courage to admit my mistake, the old man was on to me. Straightening up and leering as I passed, he dunked me with his muffin in a pool of shame. I couldn't have felt worse than if I'd run naked through the streets, pursued by winking old men wearing sordid smiles. Burning, I ran to the corner, crossed the street and made sure never again to slip past the Roma during lunch hour. And ever since, I've preferred taking the parallel blocks of Benvenue or Hillegass when walking towards Rockridge.

The 21ˢᵗ Century

Still, you kept tabs on me. I knew because of the cameras. Each one rifled my face at the least expected moment. It was brutal the way these hired investigators probed my chin hairs with their lenses. On at least eight countable occasions, I found myself pursued by the black Nikons. Again, Princess Di in her black car—I knew what she felt during those last moments as she tunneled into doom.

On at least three occasions, you appeared no more than an hour after the cameras. Who could mistake that combo of slacks and shirt and gelled hair, beard thick, baseball cap shoved down over eyeglasses? You appeared exactly the same as in the photographs inside my computer.

In photos you chatted with other billionaires, each wearing the understated garb of the 21ˢᵗ century—everyone mirroring everyone else's blandness. All those cookie-cutter expressions: the palm-to-palm slapping after games, the clustered hands on hips at Davos and Sun Valley, the satiated bellies burping decisions over everyone else's decisions. All of it infuriated and titillated me in a way that nothing else did, because no one could convince me that I was wrong about your pursuit of my footprints, even though I dragged myself around in Aerosols clogs rather than a diva's diamond studded heels.

By the time I turned thirty-eight, we were a sweating tag-team, your beard and black jacket a regular presence on Campus. My thoughts got tangled in the jacket's elastic wristbands, its plush, over-loved but slightly worn fabric like a bright flag on the quad. Every time I saw it, explosions like hope filled my abdomen. When your Louis Vuitton eyewear, your wide shoulders and curly hair snipped perfectly at the nape, flashed in my peripheral vision, or if your belly sheathed in engineering gear grazed my optic nerve, my brain swam.

Hope, mimicking perversion, had swelled and deflated in me for years. But during my final visit to the Human Resources department, it turned from the half-baked hope one feels in a church to—I admit—the high-flying mania of a mental hospital patient. In the end, my life's hope turned on a dime.

The Goodbye Girl

To make me feel crappy about my lowly position, the chair kept squeaking. Mentally I dismissed the woman reviewing my file folder and evaluation because her straight black hair and rectangular glasses were far from impressive, and her silk blouse and cardigan didn't intimidate my blue jeans or hair. When she sighed, turning a page in my folder, and when she clicked into her computer to delete my status, I almost smiled.

Behind her, a window opened on the white stairway I'd climbed to get to her office, trees surrounding the lawn beyond, where my favorite bench—donated by a dead employee's relatives—basked in a lace of sun and shade. The overhead lighting in the HR office flickered, but I stared at that bench like it was my only way out until my attention settled on a man's backside.

He lay in the grass not fifty feet from the window, wearing the familiar gray shirt and suit pants that ballooned over an equally familiar rump, a ruddy elbow resting on his hip. Like an elephant wagging its trunk, he opened and closed his hand, almost waving at the HR office's window so that I couldn't concentrate when the HR woman cleared her throat and began to detail a list of complaints. But he—that is, you—lay there, which meant we were the only people on earth.

It disturbed and excited me that you faced the memorial bench where I often wrote in my journal before work, where I'd seen you watching me like Rousseau's lion. Deaf to the HR woman, I swayed and placed two fingers against each temple. Blinking rapidly, I waited for your image to fade.

"Are you okay?" The HR woman said, refusing to use my name. To name me would be too personal. "Can I get you some water?" She glanced up at my shoulder, avoiding eye contact, shuffling papers into and out of my take-home folder. This offer to provide water was supposed to be an act of kindness.

But outside you still enjoyed the grass, an amorous ball in sunlight while students, nearby, nibbled lunch, their books part of the pastoral, pages and dry leaves flittering. "I'm okay—" I said, as the HR woman repeated her offer.

More troubling than your rear or your close proximity was the fact that you knew that they didn't want me anymore. And for some reason, because I finally had evidence that you'd followed me, it all seemed hilarious. I had to laugh. It was clear. You'd been tracking my whereabouts. It all made sense. Besides searching for photos of you, I had also researched the use of cell phones as tracking devices. My phone had given me away. You'd hunted me down, and overwritten my territory with your body by using the technology I carried in my handbag. Inconceivable that you lay in that secluded patch—my very own journal writing spot—by mere coincidence. Yet there you were, like a character ripped from the pages of my notebook.

How many hours had I rested on that dead employee's bench with my head propped against my shoulder bag, eyes occasionally slipping shut to imagine you next to me, redwood branches swaying as their shade fell over Strawberry Creek? How long had I been lulled by the scent of wet grass as the crows and wasps fought over cans of half-drunk cola in the seclusion behind Giannini Hall? If I lived to die in that spot, then you and I were kaleidoscopes colliding in moments composed of web searches, surprise spottings, and uncertain certainties.

Later, released from nearly a decade of duties, as I walked towards Rockridge BART, I stared you down through the windshield of a parked Toyota off College on Woolsey. As if you finally understood that you'd been caught, your gaze twisted from desire to wide-eyed shock—the shock I should have felt at being fired, but didn't because I had nothing to lose. Half-covering your face, half-doubling over, you tried but didn't succeed in hiding your panic. You accidentally knocked your forehead on the wheel, which caused the horn to blast in a way that embarrassed me. Maybe that's why I didn't approach. The idea of deepening someone else's shame was too close to what I knew every day. I kept walking.

Mimi called that night, but I didn't pick up. She'd gotten my email, and told me that if she could help she would. But by 2010, everyone dangled by a thread. Thousands of jobs fell off the tree of life each day. As night by the lake became a throat-tightening stench of algae and Canadian goose poop, I chose not to call her. Instead, I walked beneath the strand of lights that shimmered on the water, finally making it to the blinking marquee of the Grand Lake Theater. For no reason, I had my first surge of fear mixed with desire, but that hardly counted as a warning, because I stood in line to escape into the darkness of other peoples' lives, trying not to think of you. My emotions were overpowering, but I forced myself to stay there, intending to merge with the movie screen.

Then, while I waited behind laughing strangers, something made me turn to look at the street. Maybe it was the woman running the crosswalk, calling to her boyfriend about buying an extra ticket or a box of bonbons. Whatever it was, the red BMW convertible bore down on me, its motor idling at a red light—the same red light I'd seen in the cab when Ben walked away before his crash so many years ago.

At first, it was hard to confirm who was staring. But then, a magnetic field stretched between us, and time expanded once more. The few seconds it took for the light to change became an extended frame that would repeat again and again in the quiet moments between rest stops and changing lights in the years to come.

Your features familiar, were always distant and unattainable. While our stare pulverized clock-time, and turned us both over to the infinite like the pieces of a once perfect but now broken vase, I knew what we'd be to each other: a couple of runaways who'd been tossed from life—one by poor circumstances, the other by gifts too great to absorb. We'd never say a word about this to each other or to anyone. But we'd know each other better than any other person who passed through our separate circles in time. Knowing this was monumental. And as the light changed and the convertible sped away, I grew weak, shivering but also sweating—so that later, I couldn't focus on the film, and had to leave the theater early.

In bed that night, my thoughts broke like storm waves against the hours as I kept re-imagining the scene, because you—Bill—knew me, because while the BMW paused at the red light you'd shielded the lower half of your face but not your eyes, holding up your hand to show me the orange ring, because that ring bound us together and encircled us, reflecting us back to each other. There was no confusing anything anymore. There was only you.

Here and There and

An Immense Place

"I am the dream."

1

On the chipped linoleum floor of her twenty-second kitchen rests a stained wood stool whose legs wobble. This is the only piece of furniture she actually purchased for her tiny cooking space, which is a mere pocket in her studio apartment. No bigger than an oversized closet fitted with a two-burner stovetop, its two-foot long counter and half refrigerator is palatial compared to the last apartment with its hotplate. Her landlord, the congenial but neglectful sixtyish construction worker-cum-property owner won't rent for more than three months at a time. And that suits Jane fine, because most of the other renters are from Mexico or Central America, and she doesn't speak Spanish.

But it feels right to live in a pit located two blocks from the Fruitvale entrance to 580. In a place like that, it doesn't matter what Mimi said about Nora, because life never resists transience at freeway entrances. You live 3,000 miles away from someone who once counted as family—it makes sense to be as free as possible. And what had Mimi quoted Nora as saying? That living in cardboard suited her better than knowing a daughter who abandoned her family? Not for a minute does Jane buy it. No one from an Upper East Side apartment building likes living in a cardboard box!

"I know, that's what I've so been trying to and I mean trying to understand—" Mimi had whispered into Jane's ear. Perry had been at her hips, and no one wanted to make a scene. "I'm so sorry I didn't tell you sooner. But you so knew she lost her mind, right?" Going to India with a guru hadn't exactly been the same as losing a mind—though it was pretty close. But, yes, Mimi could delude herself into thinking it was okay to keep a secret until it wasn't okay. Who wants to inform an old friend that her aging mother has willingly chosen to be raped, slashed, burned, and pissed upon while living off trash cans on the margins of Manhattan? As far as Jane knows, her mother never ventured into India.

So why is it so "weird" to Jane's landlord that a nice, educated white lady like herself still lives on her own? Backstory is everything—but who has the patience or interest in exchanging backstory? All that matters is her capacity to pay rent on time. And it helps that she doesn't complain about gunshots or the drug dealers who regularly congregate on nearby corners and occasionally call out to her from across the street. "Das some skinny bitch" and "Shit!" as they laugh and add, "that shit is fucked!" while doing odd things with their hands and fists.

If she cooks in this kitchen at all, it's usually when Chicka deigns to swing by—which hasn't been more than twice, though plans have been discussed. Not even Jane's father has visited since moving to Kentucky with his umpteenth wife five years earlier. If his daughter isn't successful like his marketing guru stepdaughter-in-law, then she isn't worth a flight.

But other flights exist, like the one beneath the 580 underpass where a mural spells out "Informnation." As far as Jane can tell, no one in the nation is informed, despite all the information available on the web—a world she conflictedly dumped after the final words she'd typed in her secret blog to Bill ("There was only you."). Like that, she'd finally run out of money, had been forced to sell the last asset she owned—her computer.

But she can still buy a cup of tea at the Dimond Café. And occasionally she schedules an hour on a PC at the Dimond library. She still checks in on Bill, though with less urgency now that her blog is complete. Something happened to curb her "research" and writing—and it wasn't just the lack of a computer. It was the book tour.

Yes, she'd attended the reading at Zellerbach Hall. The tickets cost more than a week's worth of food, but she couldn't pass it up. And so, in the wake of dwindling resources—unemployment benefits almost exhausted—she purchased a seat in the orchestra.

On stage, his features looked gaunt, and his eyes seemed too small and spaced differently than in the photos. When he read from the book or answered the interviewer's questions, spit flew out from between his lips, and he had a tick of scratching his armpit with a forefinger. Saddest of all, the air in the hall smelled of coconut oil, and for some reason this sickened her. She slowly walked out of the auditorium, one of the last to leave. For days afterwards, she looked at the few print outs she'd retained, puzzling over Bill's features. Had she been mistaken all this time? Had her silly little blog—dedicated to him—been created for naught? No one had read the blog anyway and no one ever would. It would linger on Blogger for as long as fossil fuels could be sucked from the earth, and then it would vanish, unseen, as all things do.

But since then, she has managed to carry her cloth bags of groceries—lettuce, carrots, collards, and potatoes—up the stairs to her apartment. The sack handles always cut into her fingers, making it difficult to pull out keys.

For a month, Jane has been planning. She's got the spray bottle, bought the clippers, has set up an old bed sheet—which lies ready and waiting beneath the white kitchen stool. Tentatively she's prepared each salad, careful not to tear the old bed sheet with her clogs. She hasn't wanted to disrupt the stool, or the clippers, or the bottle next to them—which she looks upon as a kind of shrine, even though the sheet has become soiled with food debris.

Bill. Whatever happened to him?

Initially, she'd missed the news segment. But after an entire month slipped by and she hadn't spotted his likeness driving along MacArthur Blvd., she grew concerned. Online, in the library, there'd been a news blackout. Nothing about him turned up —not a single mention of his book or tech interests or the new movie he'd financed. At the end of the month, on a Saturday, it came to her that something was wrong. She spent $7.35 to BART into the city, wandering the Mission District in search of graffiti on murals, hoping a street artist would provide a clue to his whereabouts. And though the afternoon abounded with color, mariachi, whistles, and men rolling ice cream carts with bells on their handles, none of the murals hinted at where she might find Bill.

She ended up in a café on Dolores, where she flipped through a Learning Annex leaflet someone had left on her table. She'd never owned an iPad or Kindle. She'd stopped reading novels—or most book for that matter—years ago. Books—who had the patience for them?

Yet she'd returned to her small apartment and gulped a bowl of lettuce, three tomatoes, and a baguette from La Farine. Lying down, she stared at the ceiling. She couldn't stand it, but she'd have to wait until the morning.

At the downtown Oakland library, she typed in his name and shut her eyes. When she opened them, she clicked and read and then started to shiver. She'd been right. Something terrible had happened. Not long after the reading at Zellerbach Hall, there'd been a test. The test had happened to him, but it had also happened to her.

There'd been no one to call, to share this news with—and what did that mean? It meant that she was as good as a ghost, except that the men across the street kept calling her "fucked up shit." Under the circumstances, there was nothing to do but walk—even though every molecule in her body felt as heavy as a herd of elephants. Still, on the day she discovered the news, out she went, troubled by the image of him hairless and dwindling in a chemo-induced pall. What would Bill look like without his hair? Would his eyebrows disappear with his eyelashes?

It was on that day that she drafted her plan. Every day, for three weeks, she approached the stool—her altar—ready to pick up the clippers and shear off every last cilium length erupting from her scalp, brow, and eyelids. But as soon as she touched the clippers, a shot of cold undermined her decision.

It had been too long since she'd spoken to her mother. Only a mother could tell her why she'd been stalled for so long. But the India that was a street corner in Manhattan was farther away than the India across the Pacific. And how could she go back to New York with only $163? And how would she ever forgive, not to mention ever find, the impenetrable Nora Lovins?

2

Whether she likes it or not, this will be her last month in an apartment—her last morning listening to NPR on the jerry-rigged radio she found in a free-box outside a Rockridge thrift shop. No more breakfasts of Shredded Wheat or dinners of bagged lettuce. Soon she'll subsist on what the good people of America have decided to throw away. She thinks about the wisdom of shearing off the weight of her life—the copious and tangled strands of bleached filaments fighting to break free from her scalp.

During her twenties, hair had defined her as almost pretty but not pretty enough. Now four decades in (she prefers not the think in exact years), the drab weight of it labels her nostalgic for communes. Her relationship to hair is illogical—purely emotional. Since learning of Nora's lot, she's abandoned the practice of bleaching. Since finding Bill online, she's avoided haircuts as she did in her twenties, except for that one time in Seattle. Something about being unemployed has drawn her back in time. She's at once rigid and carefree. Despite the constant insecurity, nothing changes day after day. Like an experiment, waiting to die, she hovers on the cusp of life and death, in stasis.

She sometimes wonders whether people will notice her more when she is bald. Will the men across the street still call her "fucked"? She realizes they always will/never, because they don't notice her—they only notice the outline of her against the street. If she shrank to the size of a parhyale embryo, no one—not even her ex-boss Dennis—would recognize her as a living organism. And that might be a lovely state to be in. Still, she needs to feel right about cutting everything off the way she felt right all those years ago about cutting off her mother, Mimi, and Ben—because every day Bill's cancer cuts him off a little more from the rest of the world.

At the library, she occasionally finds new photos of him. He sits hairless in a suit, unselfconsciously talking to someone the paparazzi haven't captured. The sheen of his hairless pate glows in the light. There might be a blond woman sitting next to him, or an uncomfortable looking man who is trying to mimic Bill's posture. But none of it bothers Jane, because she has finally understood the nature of their private conversation. Their love might be clandestine, and it might be that no one else knows except the two of them, but they have reached a state of connection beyond death. And now that she has the courage to shave her head, to become a swami like Namananda, he will understand how much she loves him—the same as he loves her.

Soon it will be Christmas. She stands in her miniscule kitchen tossing romaine, chopped carrots, and sliced tomatoes. Everyone else has left for vacation or is inviting visitors into their homes. Her ex-boss Dennis is probably in Colorado with his family. Chica has sent word via a postcard that she's flown on credit cards to Cancun with her little girl and new boyfriend. They plan to para-sail.

It hasn't yet started to rain, but the gray spreads from the Bay to the hills and the sky deepens at 4 PM. Dampness settles into her skin, joints, and muscles, seeping directly into her blood vessels, though there's been no drizzle from the stratosphere all year. On the radio M— hands a microphone to C—, who begins discussing the problem of a girl in India. At first Jane doesn't pay attention. She spears lettuce and tomato with her tines, but after some moments she puts down her fork and turns up the volume.

"Here are two neighbors with an ancient history, M—. As Pakistan and India struggle to build diplomatic ties, with America seen as an unwelcome presence along the Afghanistan/Pakistan border, extremists, particularly along the border regions around Kashmir, have fomented the kind of violence that victimizes the youngest among them. Police haven't been able to determine the name of the girl, or the names and ages of the victims at the Lahore American School, but investigators have set the child bomber's age at around nine or ten—though very little else is known at this point."

"C—, can you tell us anything more about the group claiming responsibility for the explosion at the school?"

"What we know so far, M—, is that the extremist group calls itself an un-named ally of a group called Al Badr and has been around since late 2003. They've been critical of more moderate groups based in Kashmir, such as the Jammu and Kashmir Liberation Front or JKLF."

"Do we know whether the girl was at all affiliated with the group before the bombing? In other words, do investigators believe she may have been coerced?"

"Unfortunately, investigators have said they do not have any evidence either way. There's no telling, at this point, whether she was aware of her role in this tragic act of terrorism. We do know that before the explosion, it appears her head was shaved and that she was dressed to look like a boy." As Jane listens, befuddled, it becomes difficult for her to lift her fork, chew, or swallow. It's as if a rope has been wound around and around her jaw, neck and torso, causing her breath to still in her throat.

"Apparently, the girl managed to evade the Lahore American School's security staff." An enormous hand presses Jane onto the stool. She crumples against the counter, no longer listening, dazed by the strangeness of all the crossroads and interconnecting paths that sometimes come together but just as often don't. Investigators will never know that a middle-aged spinster in an Oakland apartment is about to shave her head. They will never know that her mother has claimed to live in India— They will never understand the importance of a hairless head.

Below, in the apartment downstairs, Jane hears a neighbor curse the fuck out of his wall. And then she thinks he is laughing. M— doesn't ask the final question. A simple question, really—one that every child asks of every parent. NPR and all the news gatherers of the world couldn't possibly understand the importance of this question. It begins something like this:

"Do you know," Jane asks the room as the radio voices rise and fall. The refrigerator shudders. "Does anyone know," she continues, the tightness in her chest and throat loosening up like an unclasped chain. "Do you know what happened to the girl with bleached hair from New York?" It's almost time to let it 'all go. "Tell me, M— and C—, where the hell is she?"

3

On her last day in the apartment, she walks down Grand Avenue, past Vo's Vietnamese restaurant and a cluster of Kaiser Permanente buildings. One of her old apartments is nearby. A toddler picks a flower from courtyard hedges. The girl is no more than two years old but looks big for her age, and wears pink and yellow like a doll. She spots a squirrel and her caretaker shakes her head, *no*. Mesmerized, though, the girl stumbles after the squirrel, only to watch with awe as the animal leaps onto a tree branch to skitter away. Reaching up, the child waves and cries and screams at the branches as if she's never seen anything so elusive. Her caretaker ambles over. "Time to go." The child shakes her head. "No! No! Here! Here!" Flapping her hands in that odd, autistic way, she stares at the tree limbs, her face crumpling, reddening, her fingers lashing the air, her legs running in place. She wants to catch the squirrel but can never catch it. And if she can't catch it, she'll never go home.

Eventually, Jane walks towards Berkeley. It takes a couple of hours, but she makes it to the bench outside Giannini Hall. A large crow—and she's certain it isn't a raven—caws at a squirrel, driving it away. But the squirrel refuses to leave the area, keeps dashing and stopping to stand on its hind legs as the crow hops towards it. It will not be driven away—stubborn or stupid. Still, the crow won't let up. It thrusts its beak at the squirrel's white belly, until the animal has no choice but to flee.

Finally, chilled and hungry, she leaves the bench and walks through an arm of fog that reaches towards the Berkeley hills. She doesn't know if she can return to the apartment. She only knows that she has no reason to return to its kitchen, because she has finally shaved her head. She has shaved for the man she loves, for the dead girl in India, for Namananda, and for the mother who is nowhere to be found.

Everyone else is taking their time this afternoon: the frat boys are out on their front lawns throwing footballs to miserable top 40. The scholars at I-House have settled down on benches to discuss geopolitics, the economy, beheadings, and climate change. Traffic slows along Bancroft, where a mass of protesters chant against the rising cost of tuition and the misappropriation of Native American artifacts and the country's growing hatred of people who come from other places. This is her last day here. Newly shaven, spun free, thrown into the wilderness, she ignores the fact that once again, as always, she's out of money, no safety net to prop her up. And she walks on, leaving the hotbed of Campus until she comes to the end of College Avenue where Broadway begins and the dipping light drenches the view of downtown Oakland.

And still she walks, not hungry or tired or even lonely. She walks because her passage through the many stucco vaults that have served her as temporary homes now lie in the accounting departments of ransacked banks only to be resold for millions. She walks because the human animal walks when it has lost all reason to stay. She walks because her legs are designed to carry her elsewhere. On like a nomad, a waif, a beetle, a timeless form, she continues, aware that she must walk like the mythic Savitri who trailed Yama in order to save a beloved, Bill, who does not really exist as she imagines, believing that she must marry him to keep him from dying, as he may in less than a year—no longer wondering whether she'll redeem herself for the behavior she displayed to Rudy and to Ben so many years ago at the hospital. She doesn't doubt whether she'll make it across the continent to find her mother in the cardboard box Mimi spoke of—though others might. Nor does she consider whether her father will ever understand how he so easily made wrong choices, each bad turn flowing from the first bad turn.

And still, she hasn't reached the end of all streets, which is what she searches for—because over the hills, away from the asphalt and the storefronts, she'll rest her head against her folded arms and close her eyes to listen as the coyotes rally for the coming night. Walking, she becomes her footsteps falling against the pavement, the rhythm of a chant, the *om, step, om, step, om, step* of a private pilgrimage, each foot falling against the spinning earth where too many wanderers have already made footfall, never having found what it was they were looking for.

Around Lake Merritt she walks—east along International Blvd. where Ms. Stein figured (rightly) that *there is no there there*, into the numbered avenues, where the taco trucks vibrate on corners to sell carnitas and ceviche, where the boom-boom cars rock on their oversized wheels while girls in less-than-miniskirts and silver stilettos stand on corners and flap their arms, where plump mothers sing and slap the shoulders of their sons who grip tightly to the strollers where siblings sleep through the ear-spanking whirl of fire truck and police sirens. Walking, she is invisible and immutable, split in two—a little like Namananda, but also a little like a smashed particle—never changing, though always shifting, as she watches like a ghost this life pass her by.

But she is everywhere.

ACKNOWLEDGMENTS

It's hard to know where to begin when thanking the people who have stood by during the twenty-plus years as I struggled to write something worthwhile—and during the more than seven years as this book developed into itself. All I can do is begin at the beginning.

Without my father, the poet James Reiss, these words never would have reached paper. He alone encouraged me when I had lost courage. His death, in 2016, has made this book's publication even more important.

Thanks, also, to the poet and editor Barbara Eve, who stayed on the phone and listened when I needed her advice most. Without the thoughtful and wise critique of musician and artist, Trixie Saporta, this book might have collapsed under its own weight. A thousand and one thanks to my husband, Ken Lupoff, who believed in me when I didn't and who still does every day. Thank you, Hilary Zaid, for sharing your desk and for the many walks and talks about our novels. Without Oakland's Rockridge Public Library's upstairs writing room and Berkeley's Elmwood Public Library's many desks much of this book would not exist. I am ever grateful to Cybele Zufolo and Todd Siegel for giving me a chance to read chapters from this book at "Word Performances." The novelist Jean Kwok deserves many thanks for advising me on the publication process. Susan Shapiro, thank you for inviting me to your Tuesday evening writing workshops and for all your ongoing support of writers. And thanks to The Squaw Valley Writer's Conference for giving me a chance, many years ago, to workshop the first chapter of this book with the then fiction editor of Little, Brown, Michael Pietsch, who also deserves my thanks. My gratitude goes out to The Edward Albee Foundation and Dorland Mountain Arts Colony where I spent a formative summer writing on two coasts. Thanks to all the good professors, writers, and editors at Columbia University—including Magda Bogin, Sylvia Foley, Ken Foster, Amanda Gersh, Joanna Greenfield, Janet Harvey, Laura Josephs, Devi Laskar, Mike McGregor, Julie Otsuka, and Elizabeth Stark—who sat through many drafts of earlier works and gave so much support. I am grateful to you all, and to all the other artists and writers I haven't been able to name here who cared enough to share drafts.

∾

And thank you, dear reader, for opening your eyes to these pages.

ABOUT THE AUTHOR

It's been a while since Crystal Jo Reiss published her first poem, *The Girl Who Pricked Her Finger*, in a Louisville Review anthology of children's poetry. She had to grow up, but she eventually received an MFA in Creative Writing from Columbia University, where she wrestled with narrative and penned her first novel. Between assisting a renowned physical anthropologist, serving as a transcription editor for a law firm that represented members of the Cosa Nostra, teaching college-level composition, and working on spreadsheets for nurse practitioners, she wrote for a variety of publications, including a trade magazine focused on post-production houses in the advertising industry. She has since cofounded an editorial and design business. She lives with her husband and son in Oakland, California.

•••

To contact Crystal Jo Reiss directly, visit www.janeiseverywhere.com.

CPSIA information can be obtained
at www.ICGtesting.com
Printed in the USA
FSOW01n0508190218
44744FS

9 780692 964453